ARTIE AND THE WOLF MOON

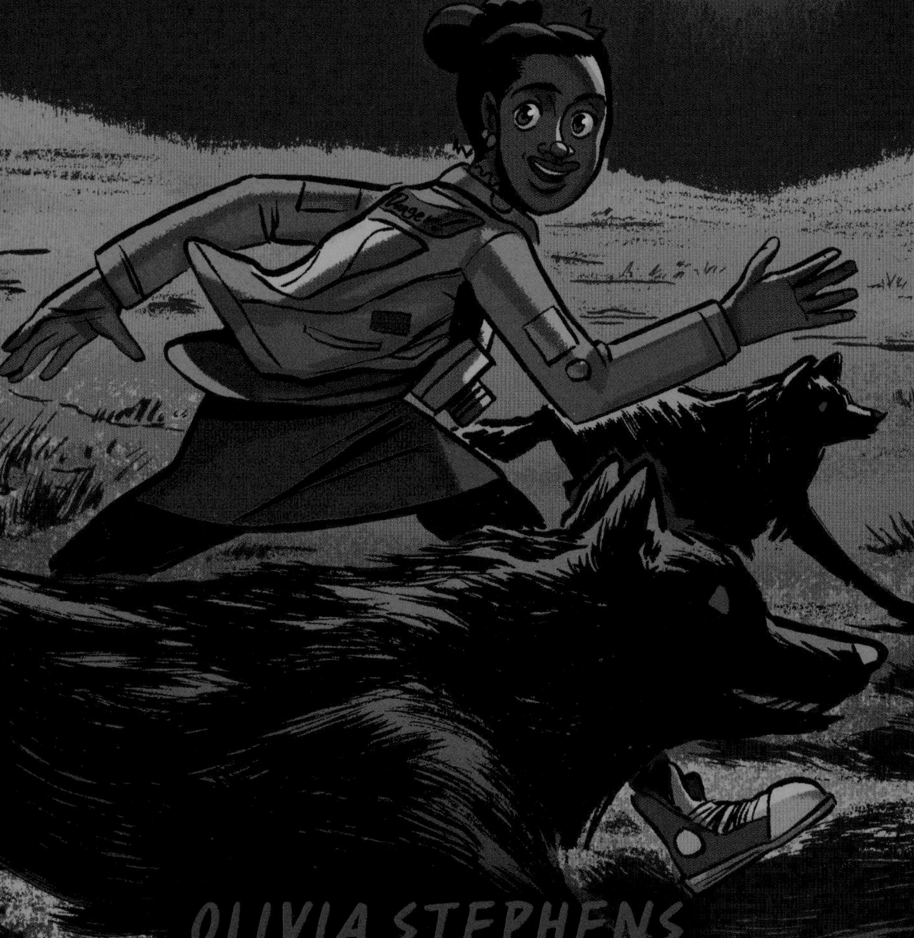

OLIVIA STEPHENS

Graphic Universe™ • Minneapolis

Graphic Universe™
An imprint of Lerner Publishing Group, Inc.
241 First Avenue North
Minneapolis, MN 55401 USA

For reading levels and more information, look up this title at www.lernerbooks.com.

Designed by Kimberly Morales.
Main body text is set in CCDaveGibbonsLower.
Typeface provided by Comicraft.

Library of Congress Cataloging-in-Publication Data

Names: Stephens, Olivia, author, illustrator.
Title: Artie and the wolf moon / Olivia Stephens.
Description: Minneapolis : Graphic Universe, [2021] | Audience: Ages 9–14 |
    Audience: Grades 7–9 | Summary: "Artie Irvin is thrilled to discover she
    comes from a line of werewolves, but as she dives into her family history
    and figures out her new abilities, vampires wait in the shadows." –Provided
    by publisher.
Identifiers: LCCN 2020006443 (print) | LCCN 2020006444 (ebook) |
    ISBN 9781541542488 (library binding) | ISBN 9781728417516 (ebook)
Subjects: LCSH: Graphic novels. | CYAC: Graphic novels. | Werewolves–
    Fiction. | Vampires–Fiction.
Classification: LCC PZ7.7.S7424 Ar 2021 (print) | LCC PZ7.7.S7424 (ebook) |
    DDC 741.5/973–dc23

LC record available at https://lccn.loc.gov/2020006443
LC ebook record available at https://lccn.loc.gov/2020006444

Manufactured in the United States of America
3-52796-39526-2/25/2022

CHAPTER ONE

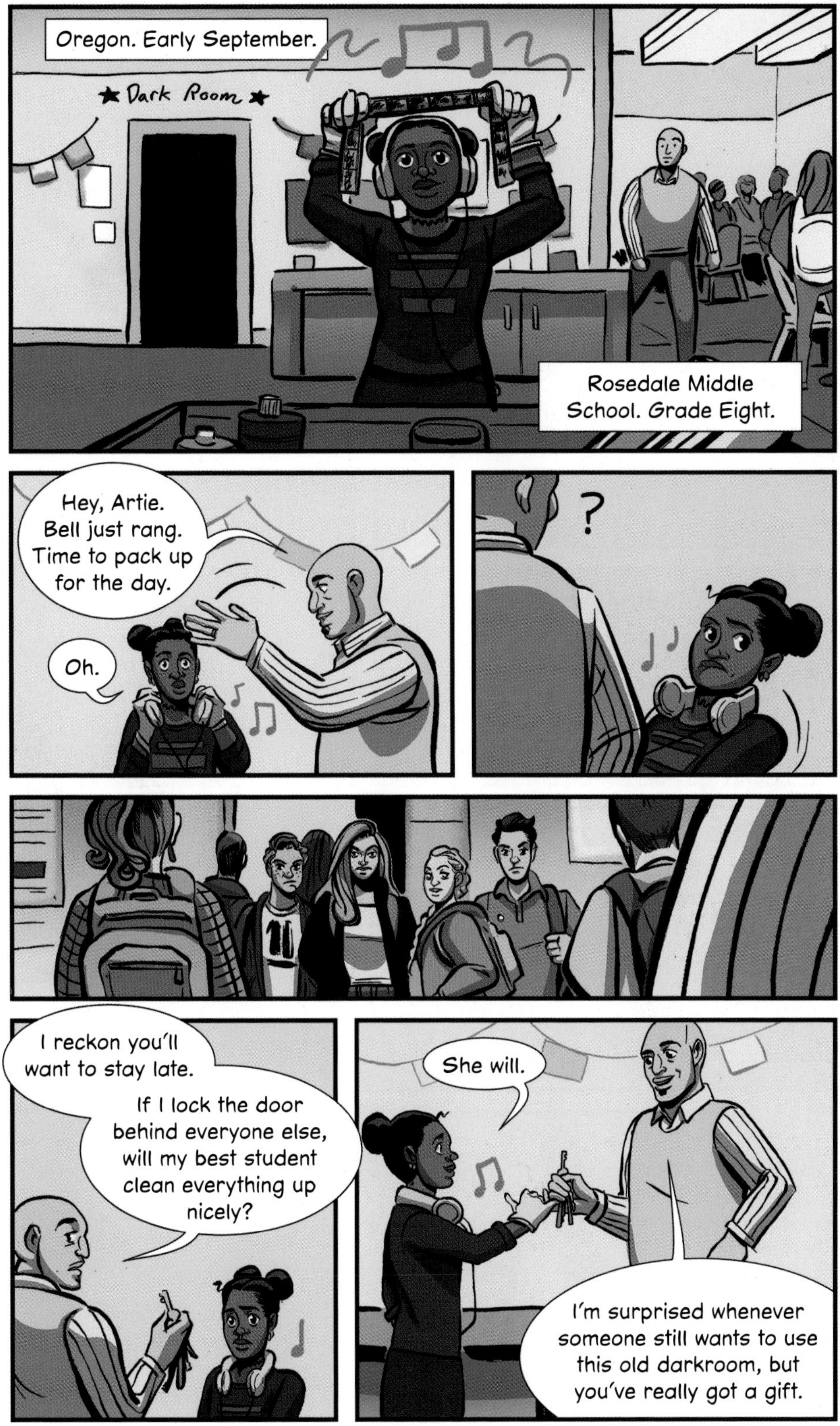
Oregon. Early September.
★ Dark Room ★
Rosedale Middle School. Grade Eight.
Hey, Artie. Bell just rang. Time to pack up for the day.
Oh.
?
I reckon you'll want to stay late.
If I lock the door behind everyone else, will my best student clean everything up nicely?
She will.
I'm surprised whenever someone still wants to use this old darkroom, but you've really got a gift.

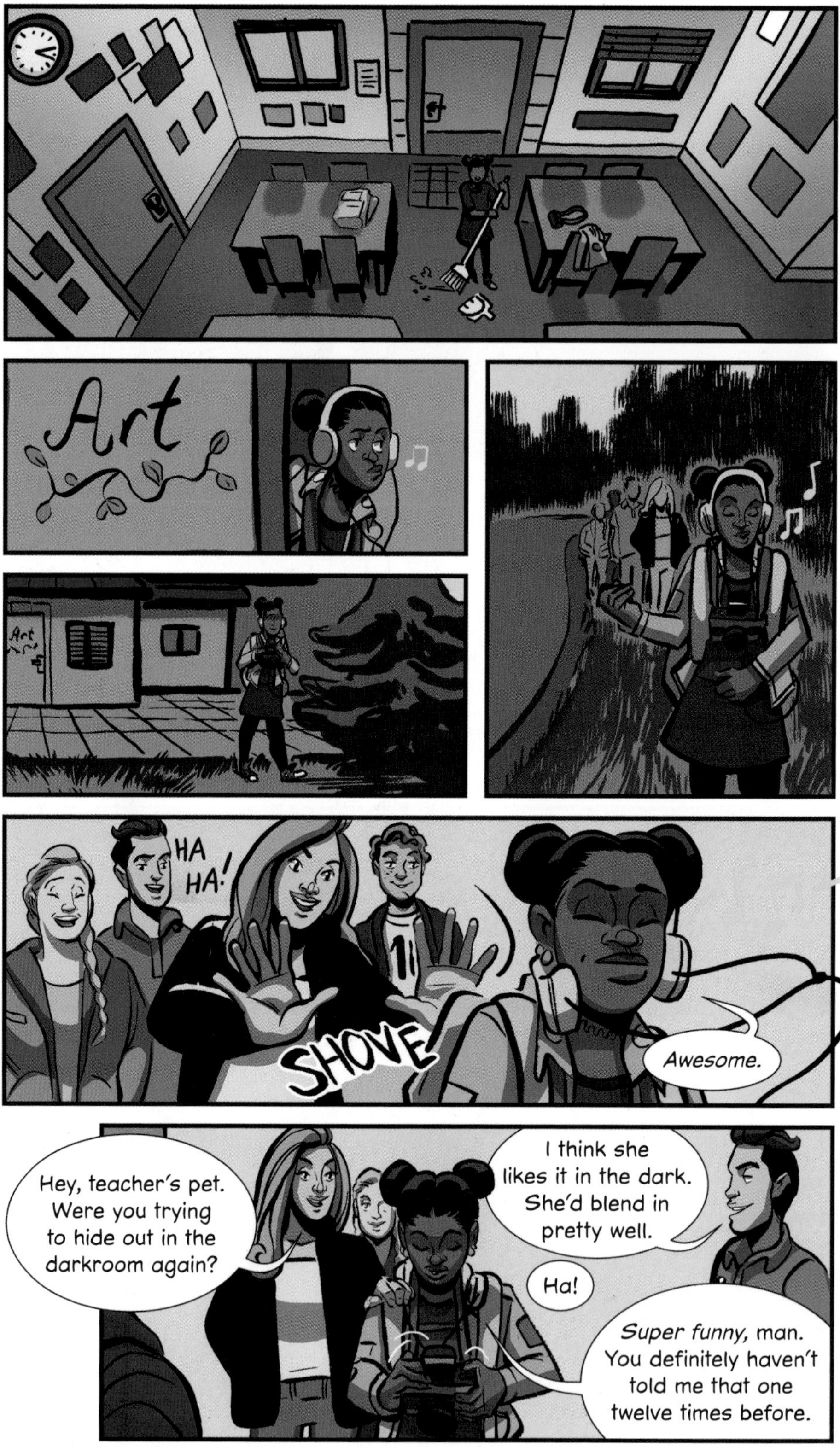

Art
Art
HA HA!
SHOVE
Awesome.
Hey, teacher's pet. Were you trying to hide out in the darkroom again?
I think she likes it in the dark. She'd blend in pretty well.
Ha!
Super funny, man. You definitely haven't told me that one twelve times before.

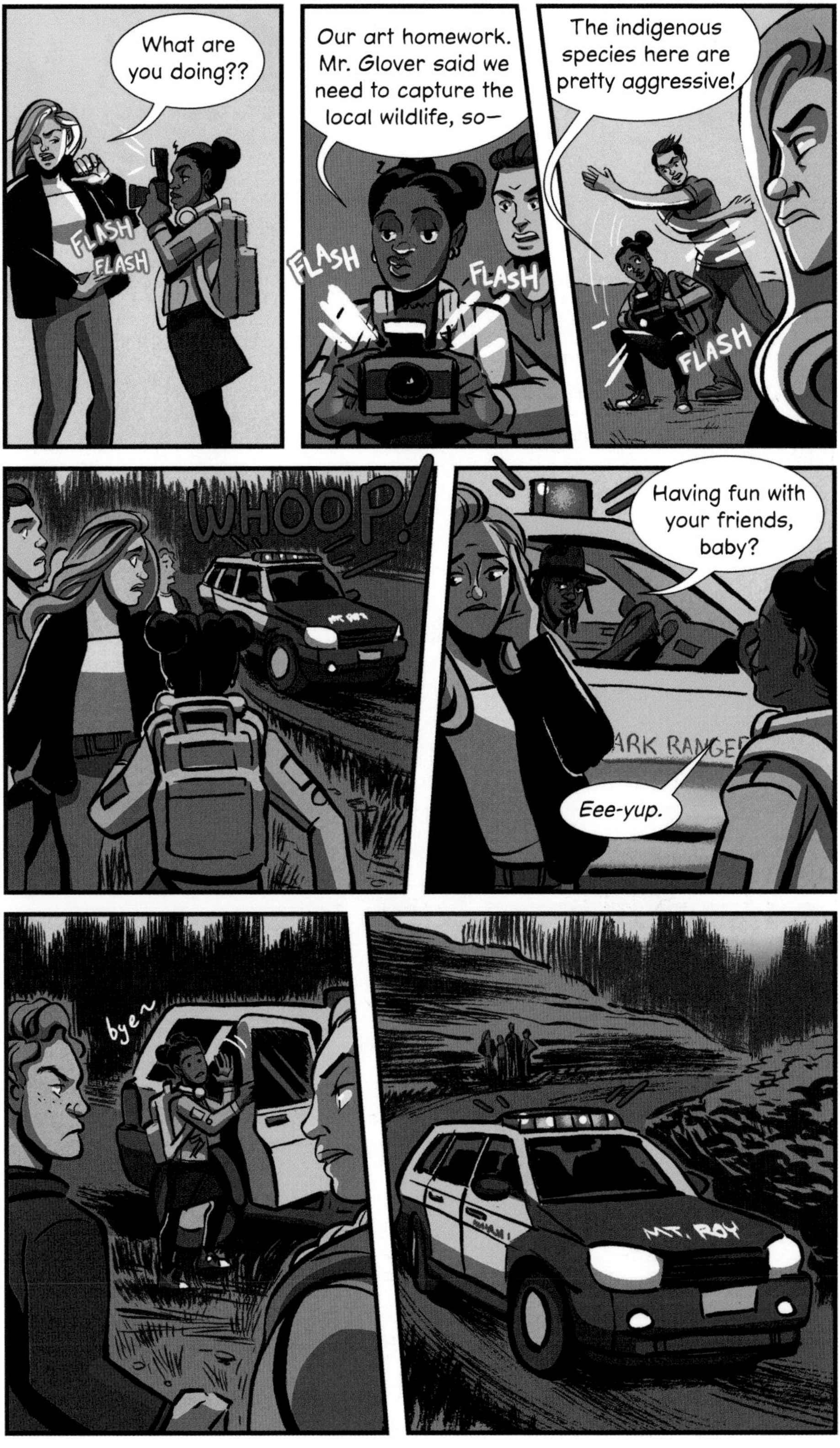
What are you doing??
FLASH
FLASH
Our art homework. Mr. Glover said we need to capture the local wildlife, so—
FLASH
FLASH
The indigenous species here are pretty aggressive!
FLASH
WHOOP!
Having fun with your friends, baby?
ARK RANGER
Eee-yup.
bye~
MT. ROY

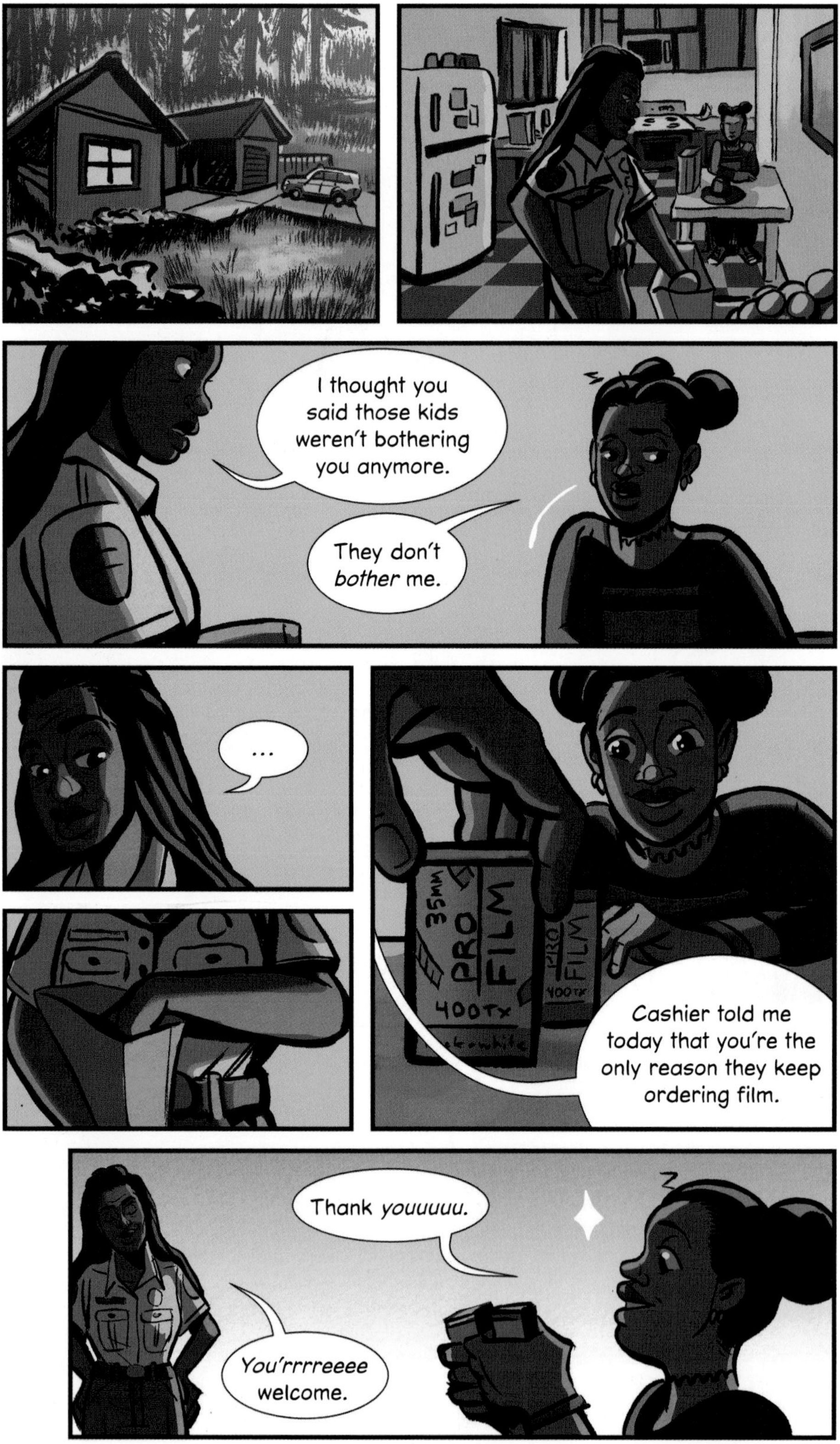
I thought you said those kids weren't bothering you anymore.
They don't *bother* me.
...
35MM PRO FILM 400TX
PRO FILM 400TX
Cashier told me today that you're the only reason they keep ordering film.
Thank *youuuuu.*
You'rrrreeee welcome.

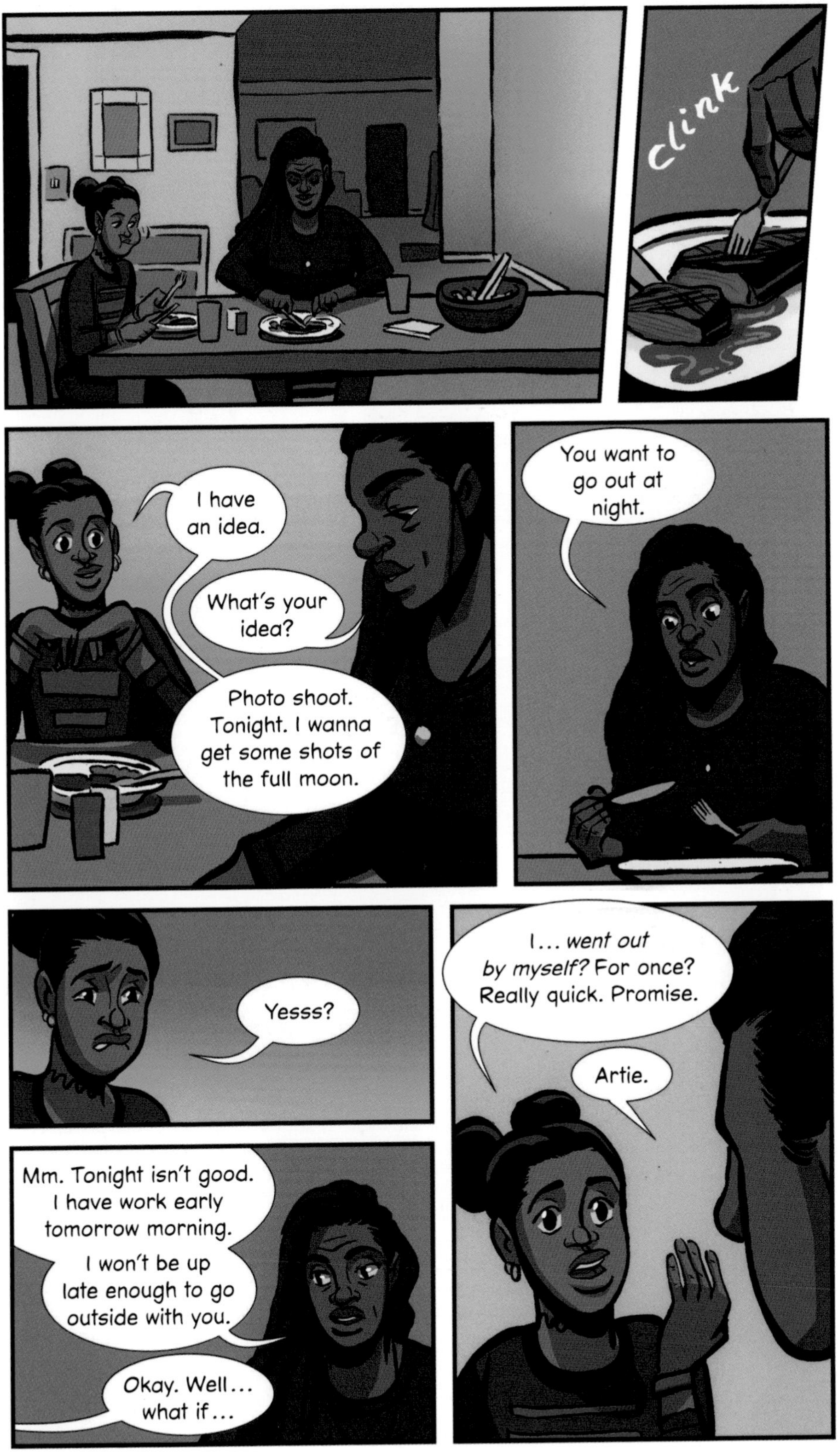
clink
I have an idea.
What's your idea?
Photo shoot. Tonight. I wanna get some shots of the full moon.
You want to go out at night.
Yesss?
I... *went out by myself?* For once? Really quick. Promise.
Artie.
Mm. Tonight isn't good. I have work early tomorrow morning.
I won't be up late enough to go outside with you.
Okay. Well... what if...

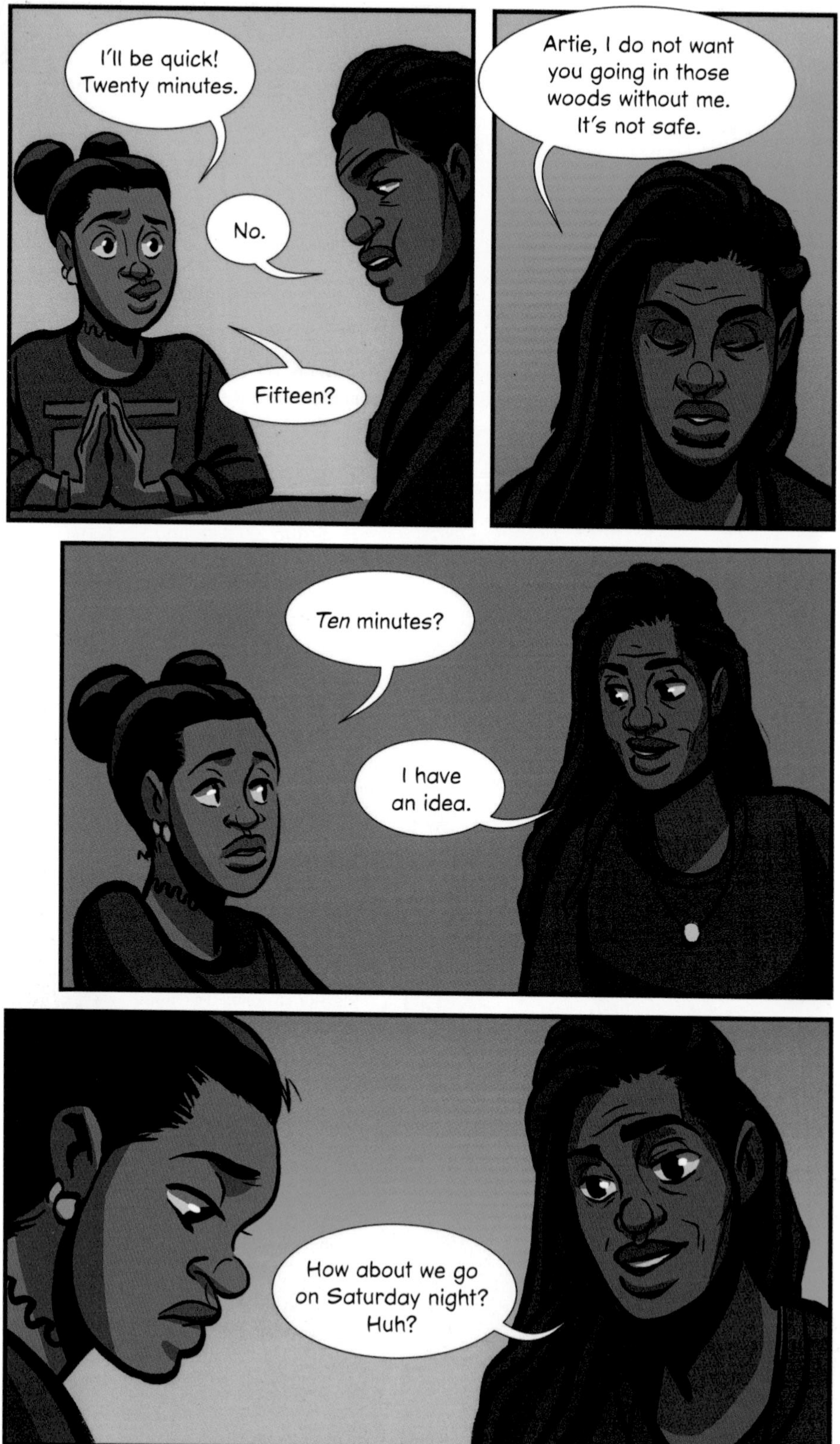
I'll be quick! Twenty minutes.
No.
Fifteen?
Artie, I do not want you going in those woods without me. It's not safe.
Ten minutes?
I have an idea.
How about we go on Saturday night? Huh?

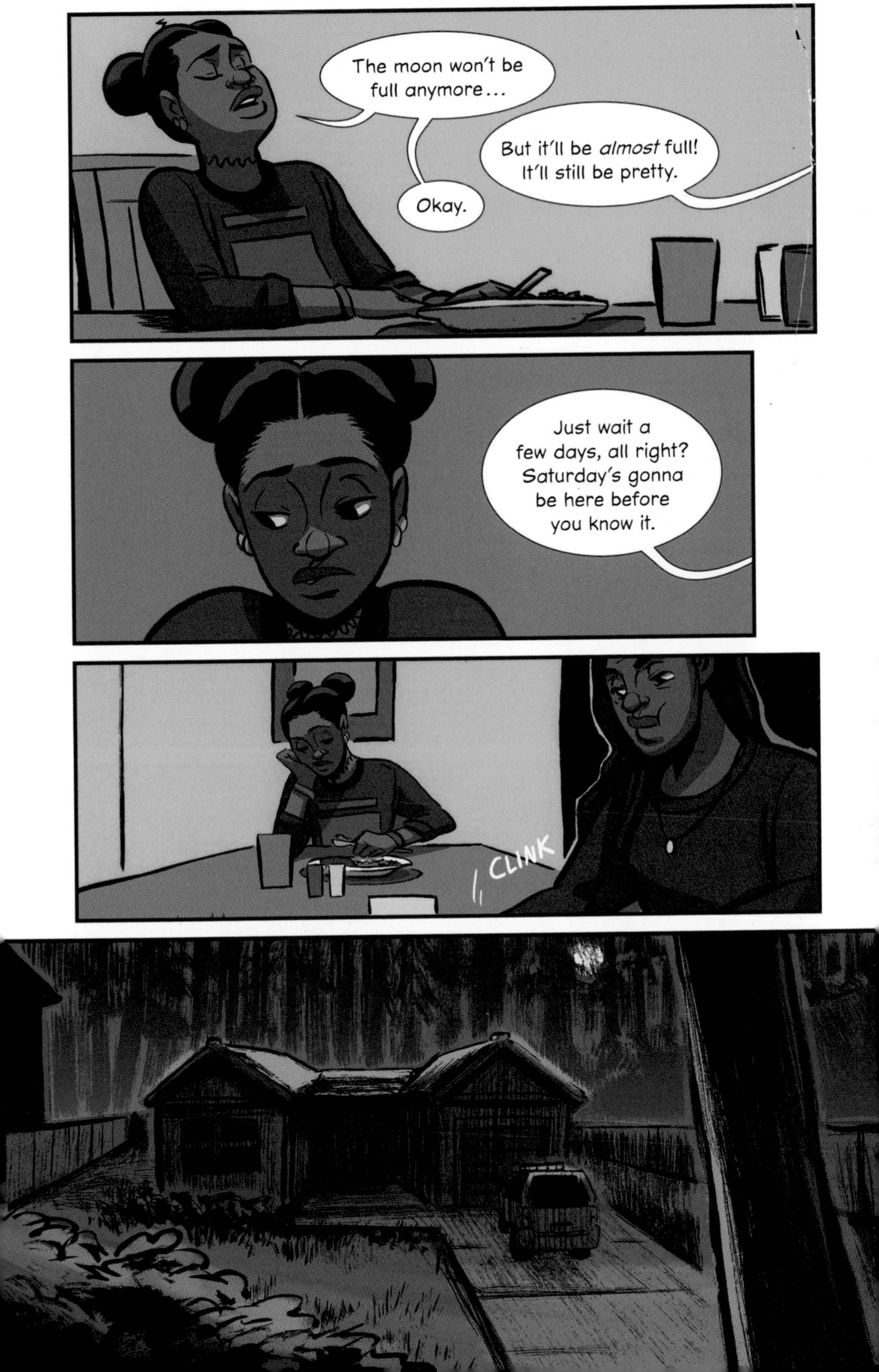
The moon won't be full anymore...
Okay.
But it'll be *almost* full! It'll still be pretty.
Just wait a few days, all right? Saturday's gonna be here before you know it.
CLINK

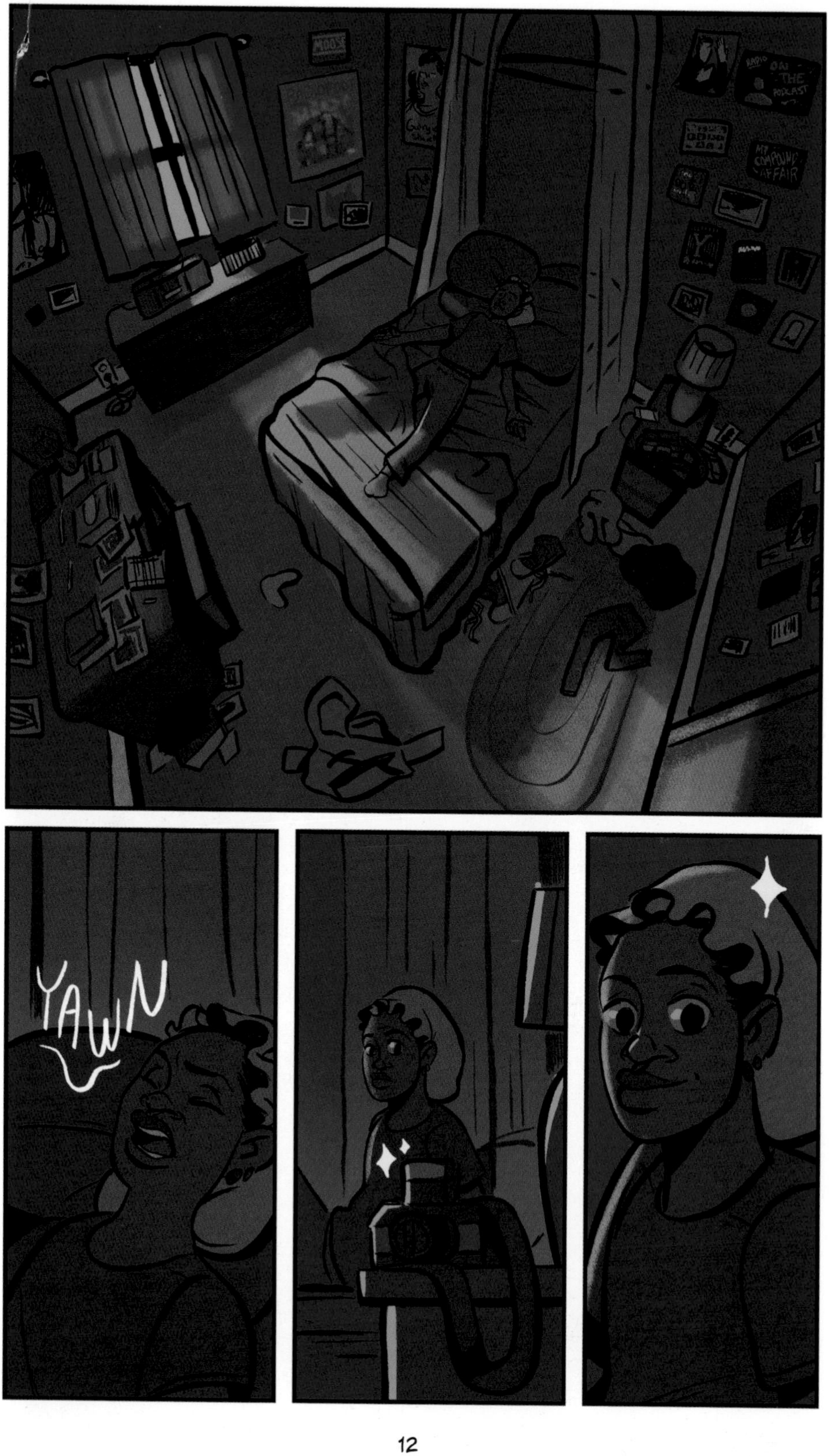
MOOSE
RADIO
ON THE PODCAST
MY COMPOUND AFFAIR
YAWN

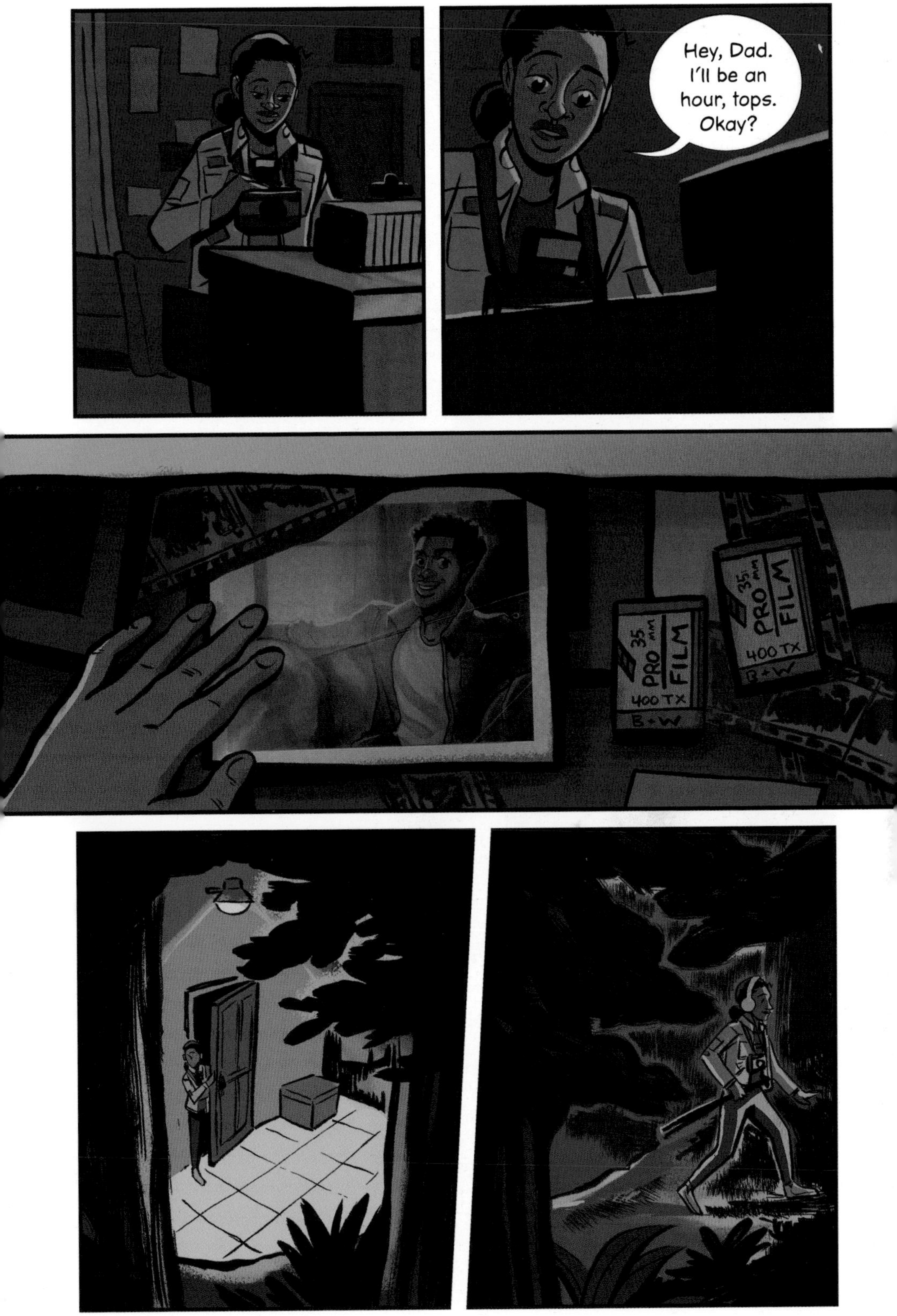
Hey, Dad. I'll be an hour, tops. Okay?
35 mm PRO FILM 400 TX B+W
35 mm PRO FILM 400 TX B+W

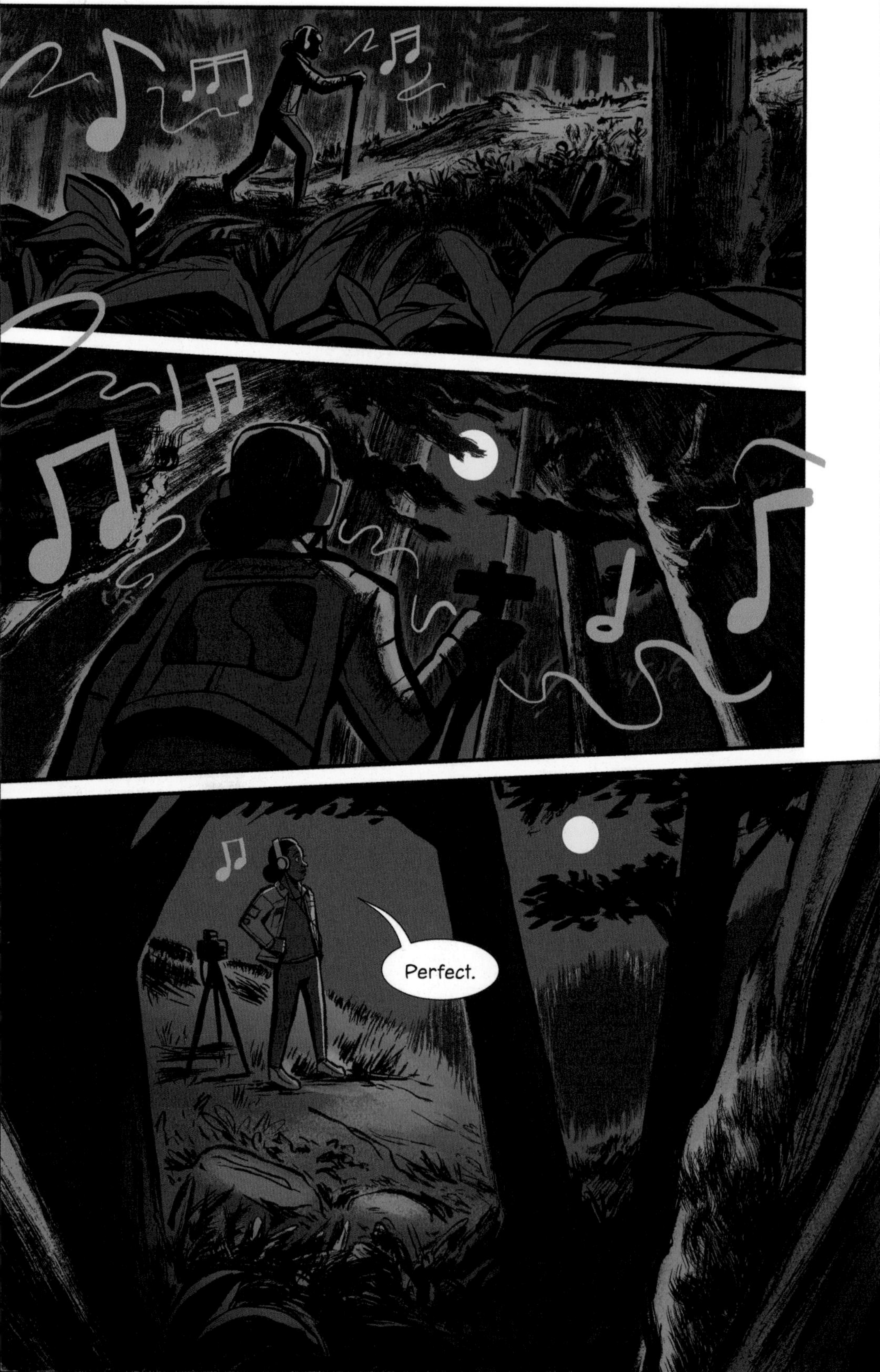
Perfect.

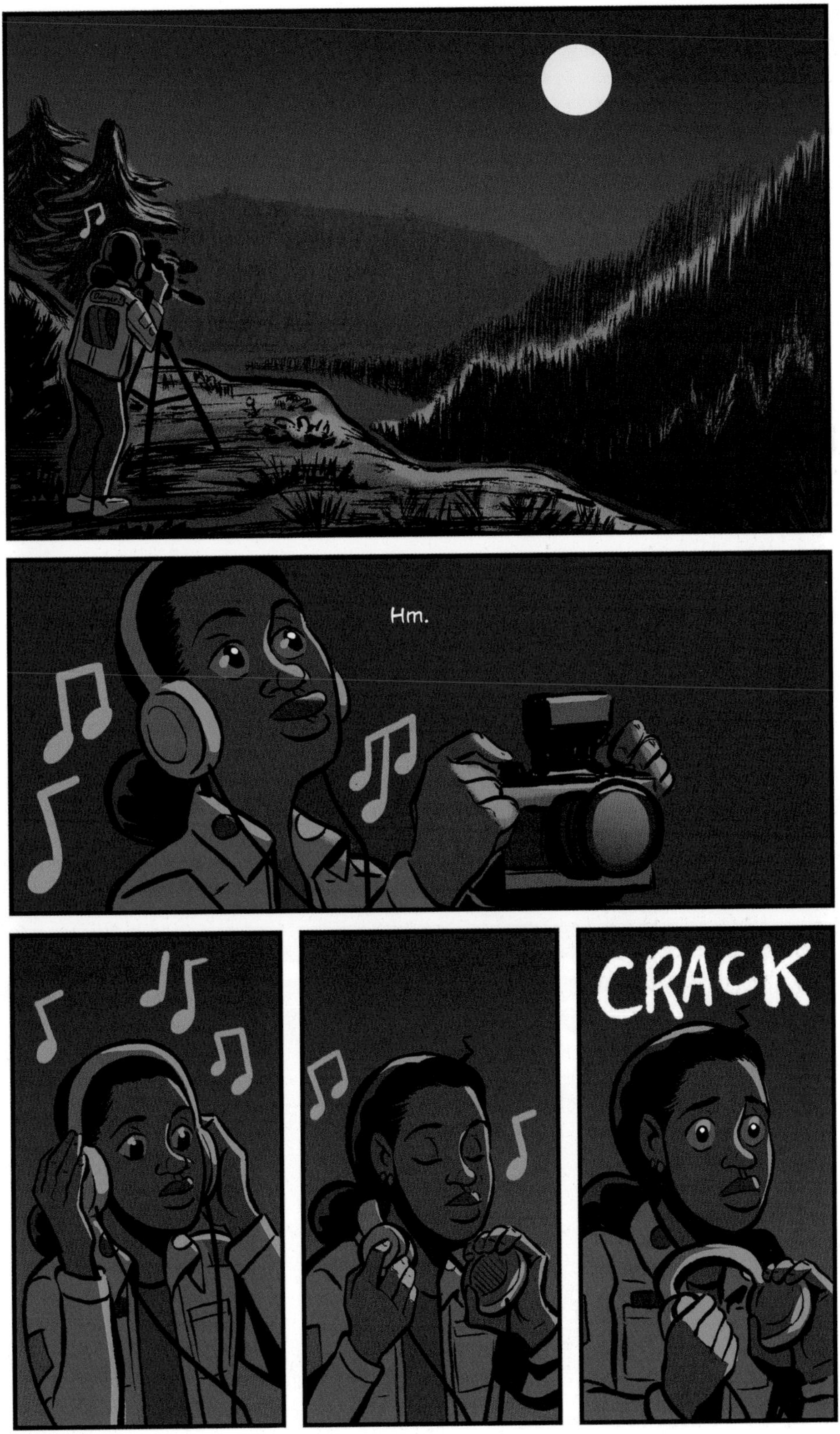
Hm.
CRACK

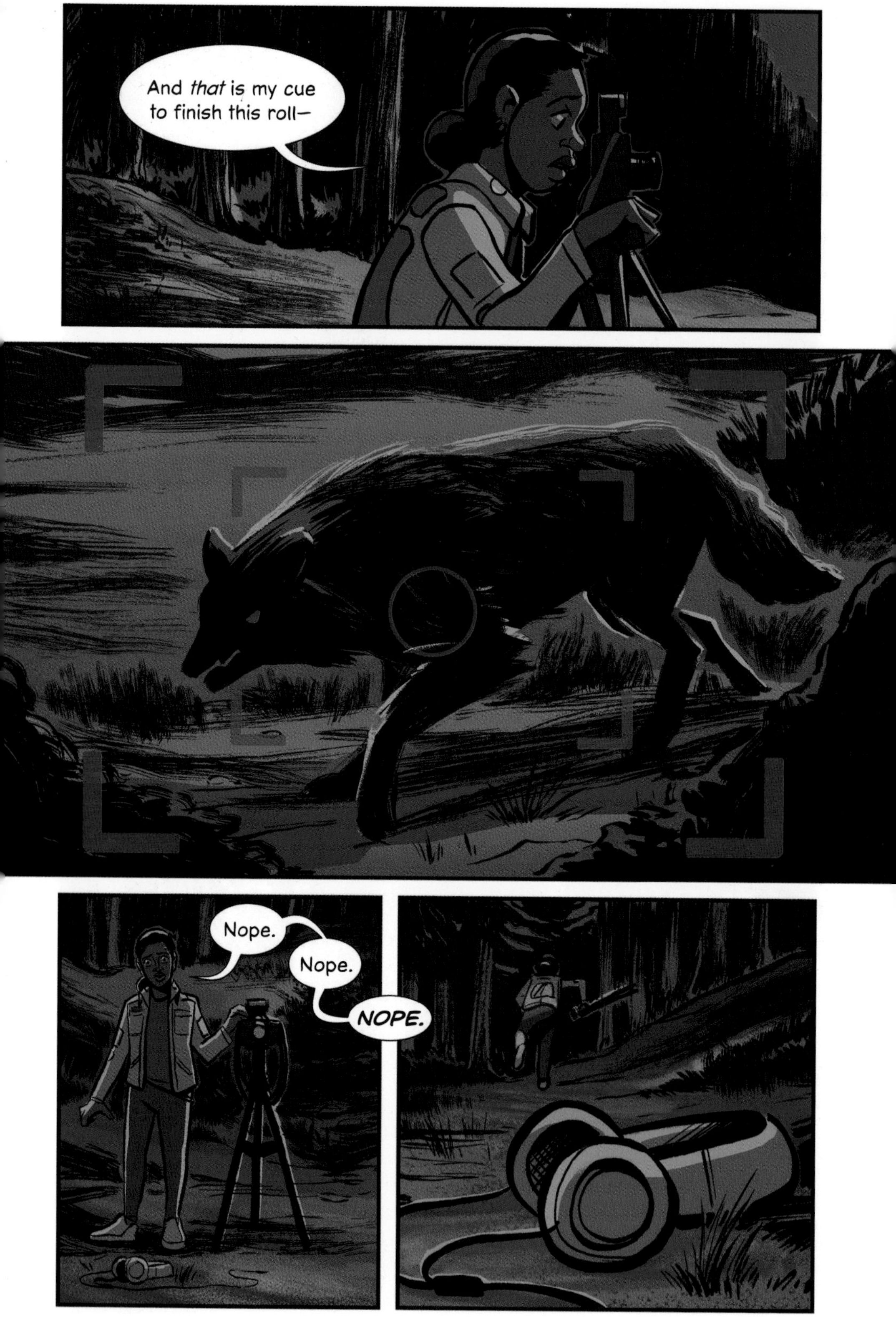
And *that* is my cue to finish this roll—
Nope.
Nope.
NOPE.

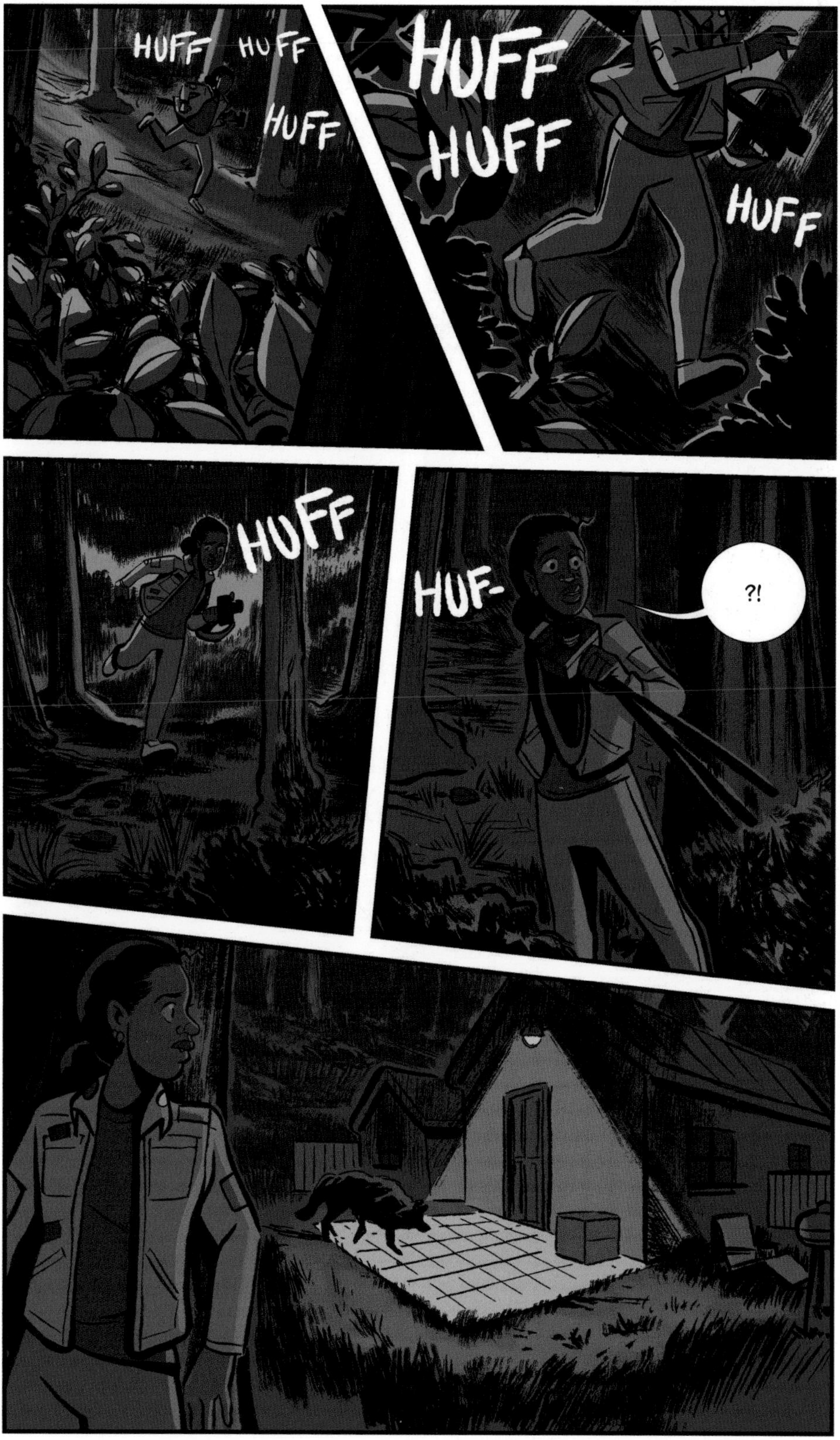
HUFF HUFF
HUFF
HUFF
HUFF
HUFF
HUFF
HUF-
?!

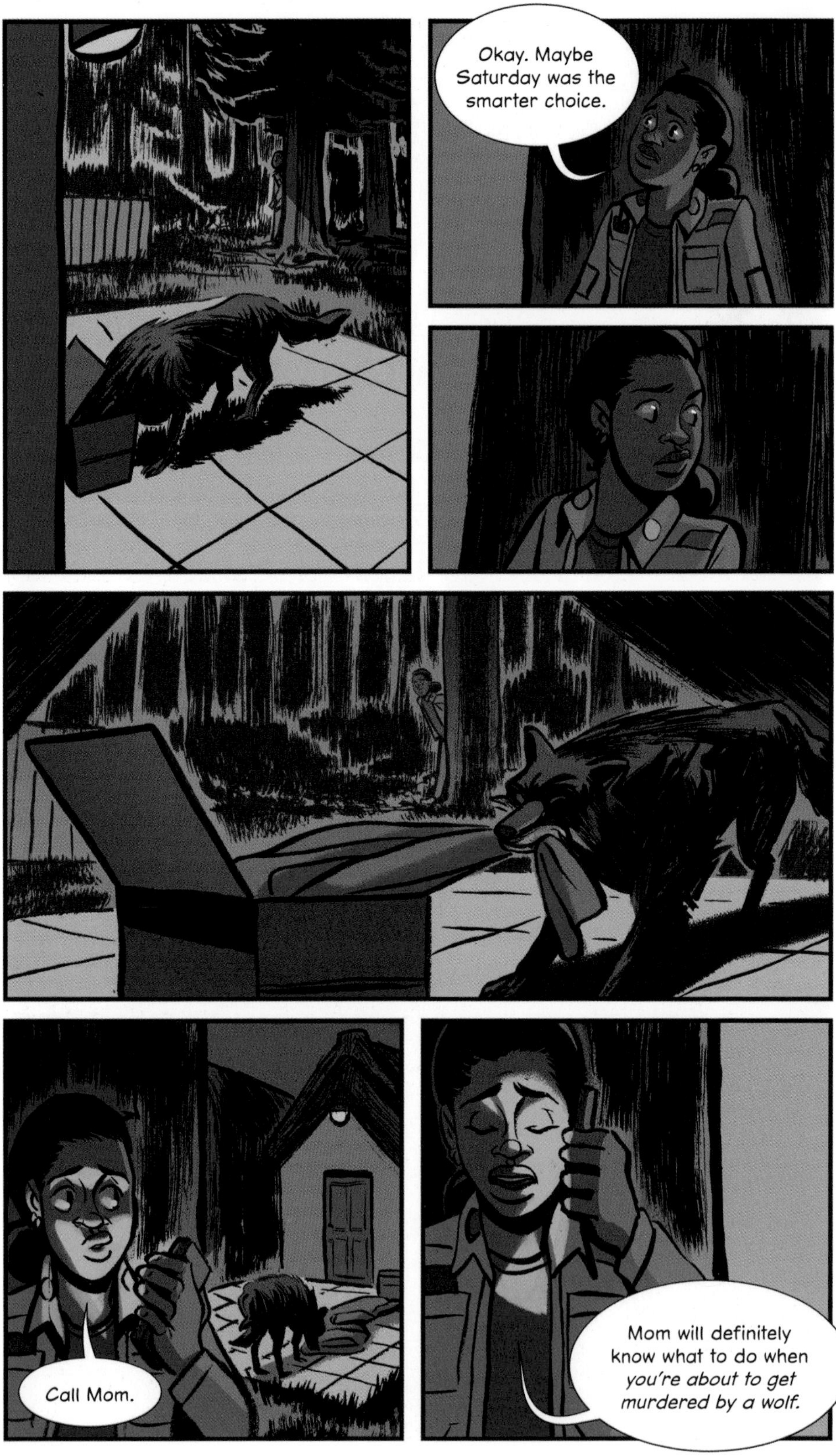
Okay. Maybe Saturday was the smarter choice.
Call Mom.
Mom will definitely know what to do when *you're about to get murdered by a wolf.*

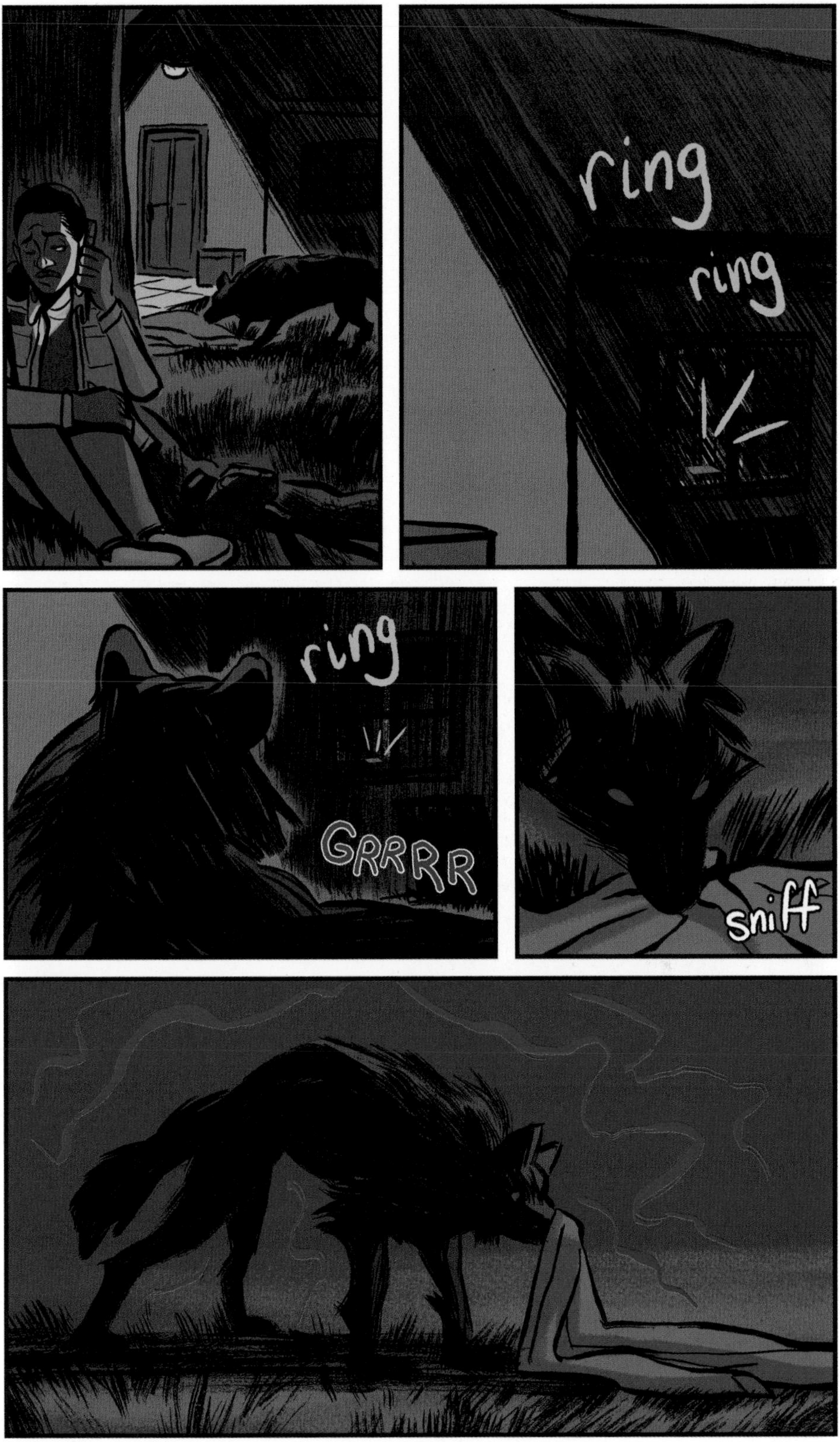
ring
ring
ring
GRRRR
sniff

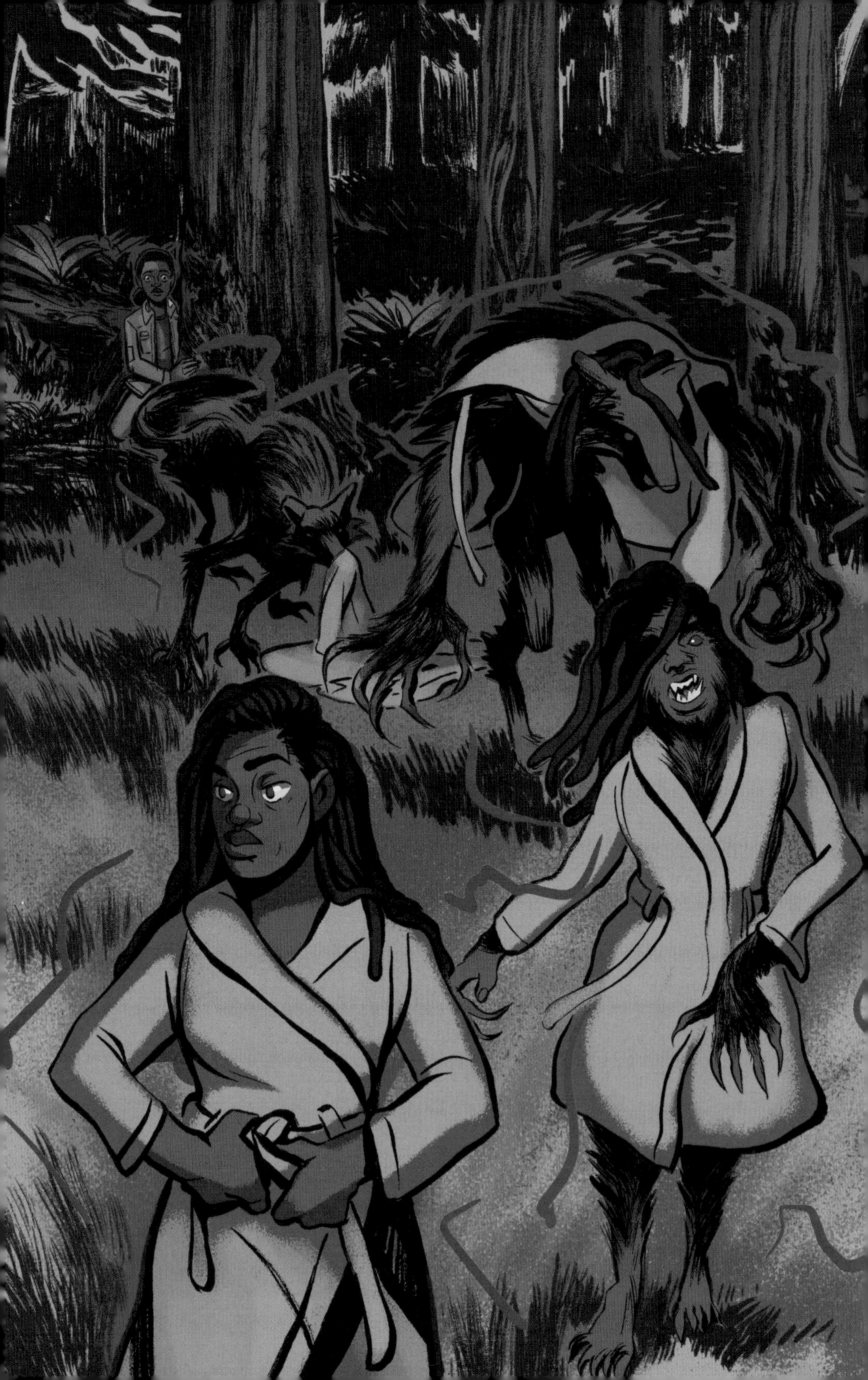

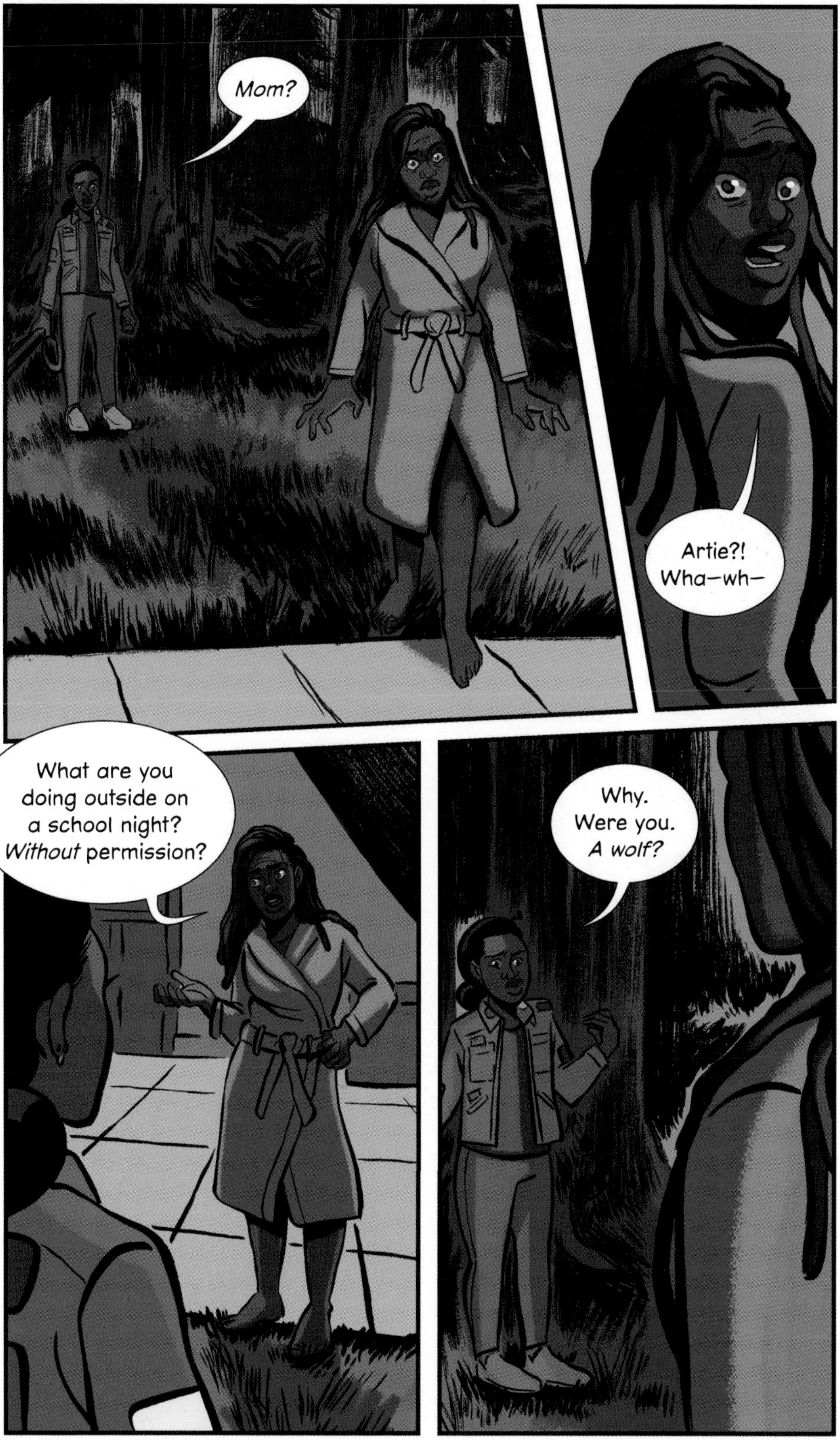

Mom?
Artie?! Wha—wh—
What are you doing outside on a school night? *Without* permission?
Why. Were you. *A wolf?*

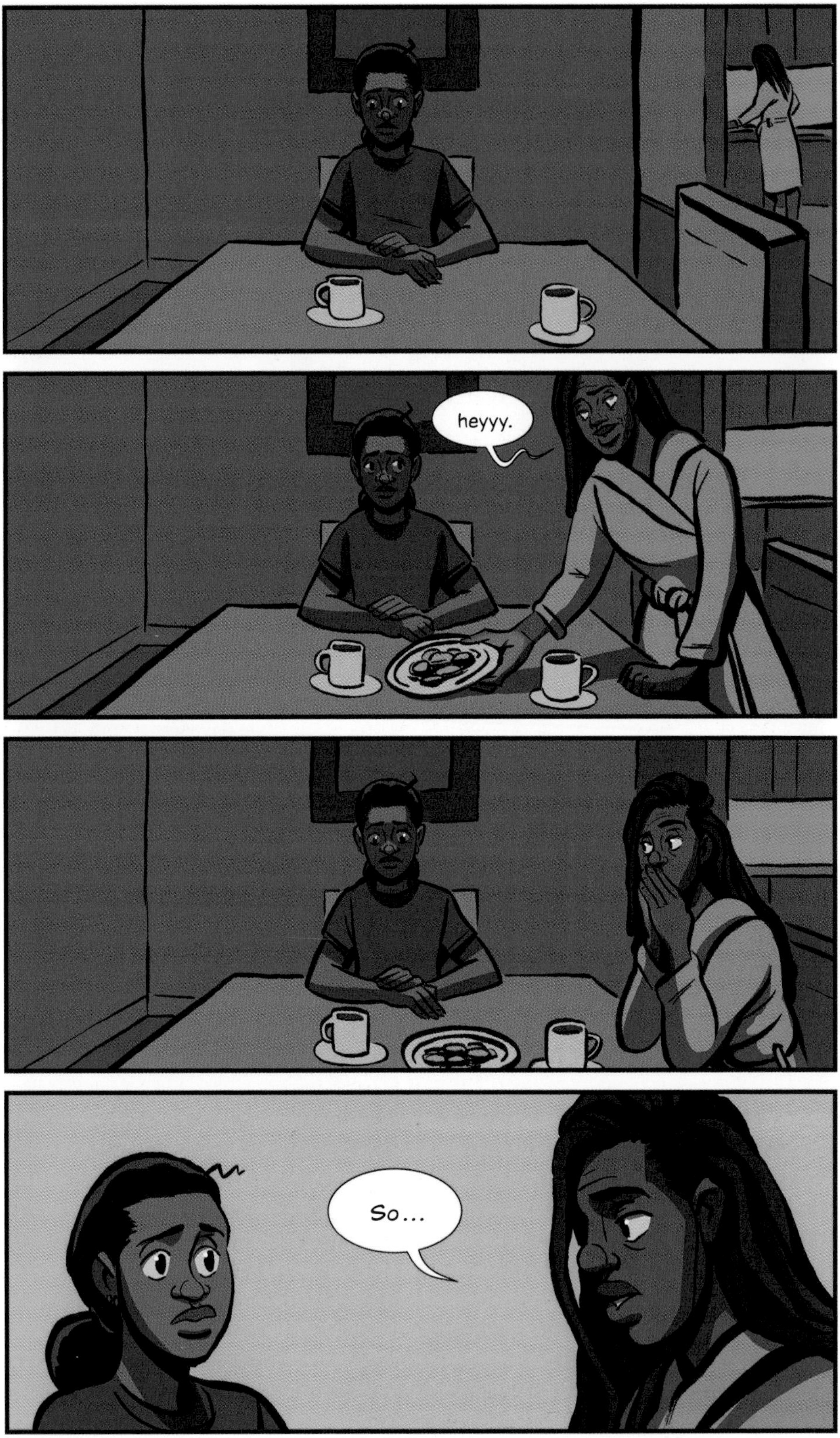
heyyy.
So...

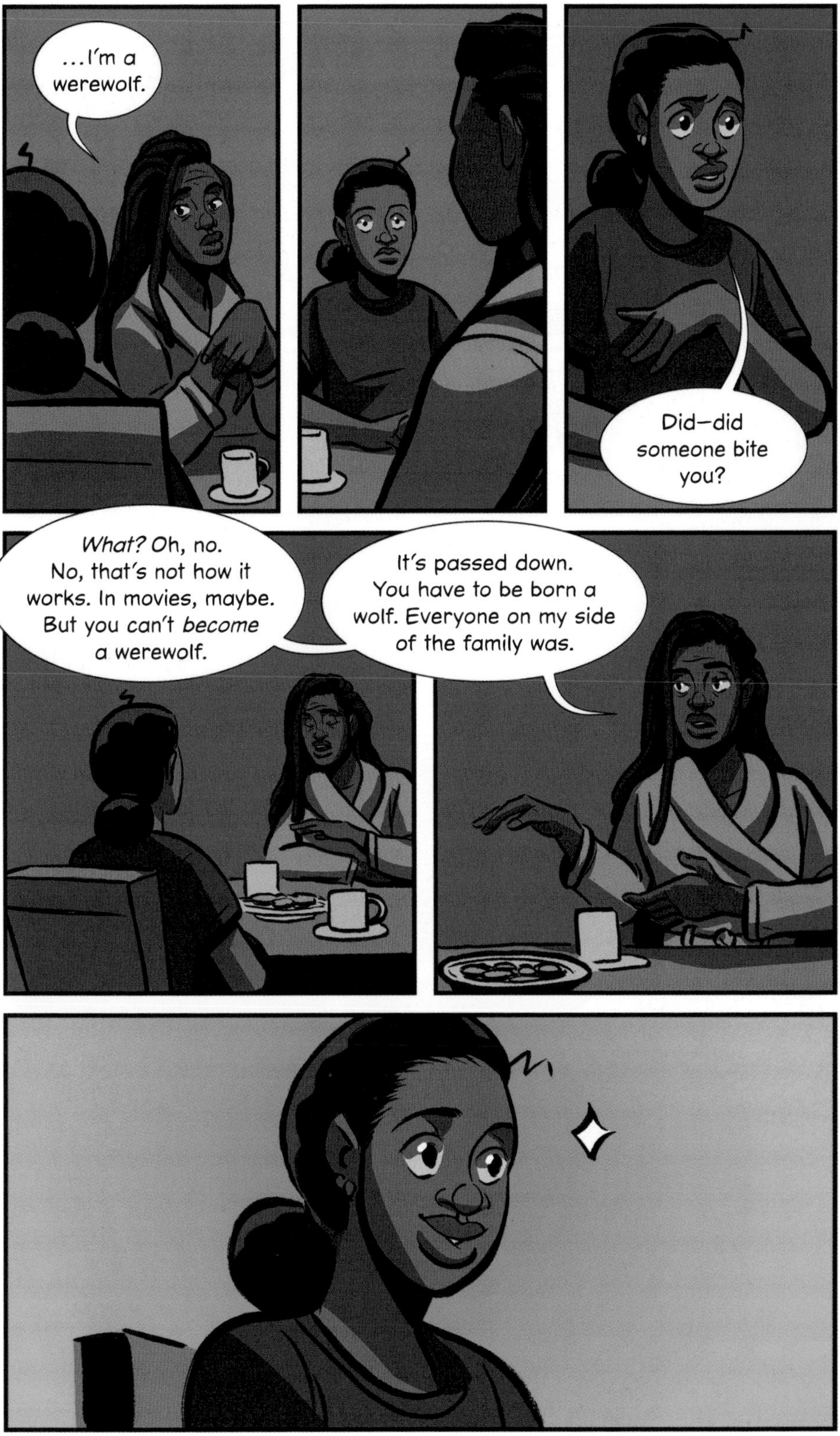
...I'm a werewolf.
Did—did someone bite you?
What? Oh, no. No, that's not how it works. In movies, maybe. But you can't *become* a werewolf.
It's passed down. You have to be born a wolf. Everyone on my side of the family was.

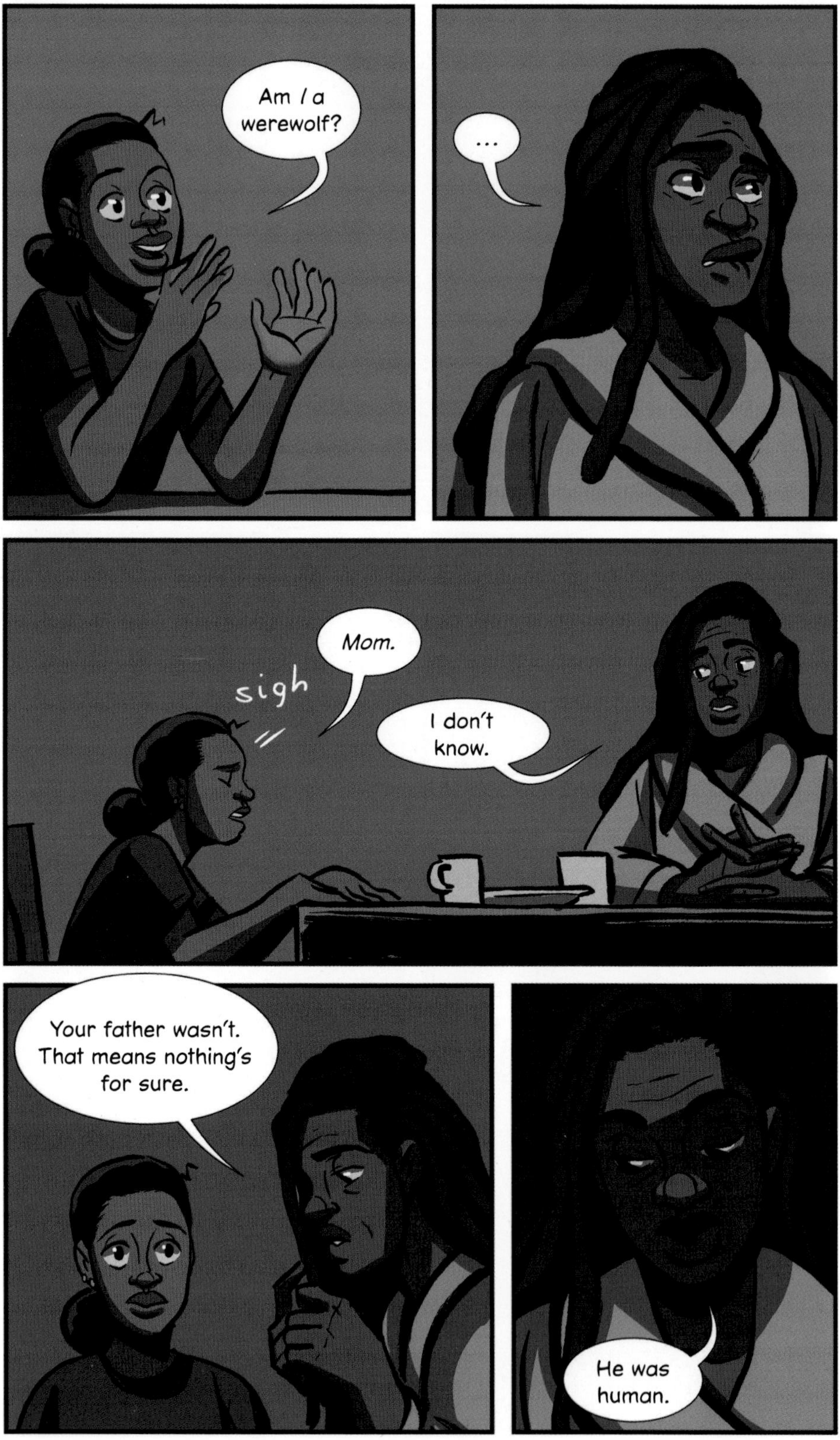
Am I a werewolf?
...
sigh
Mom.
I don't know.
Your father wasn't. That means nothing's for sure.
He was human.

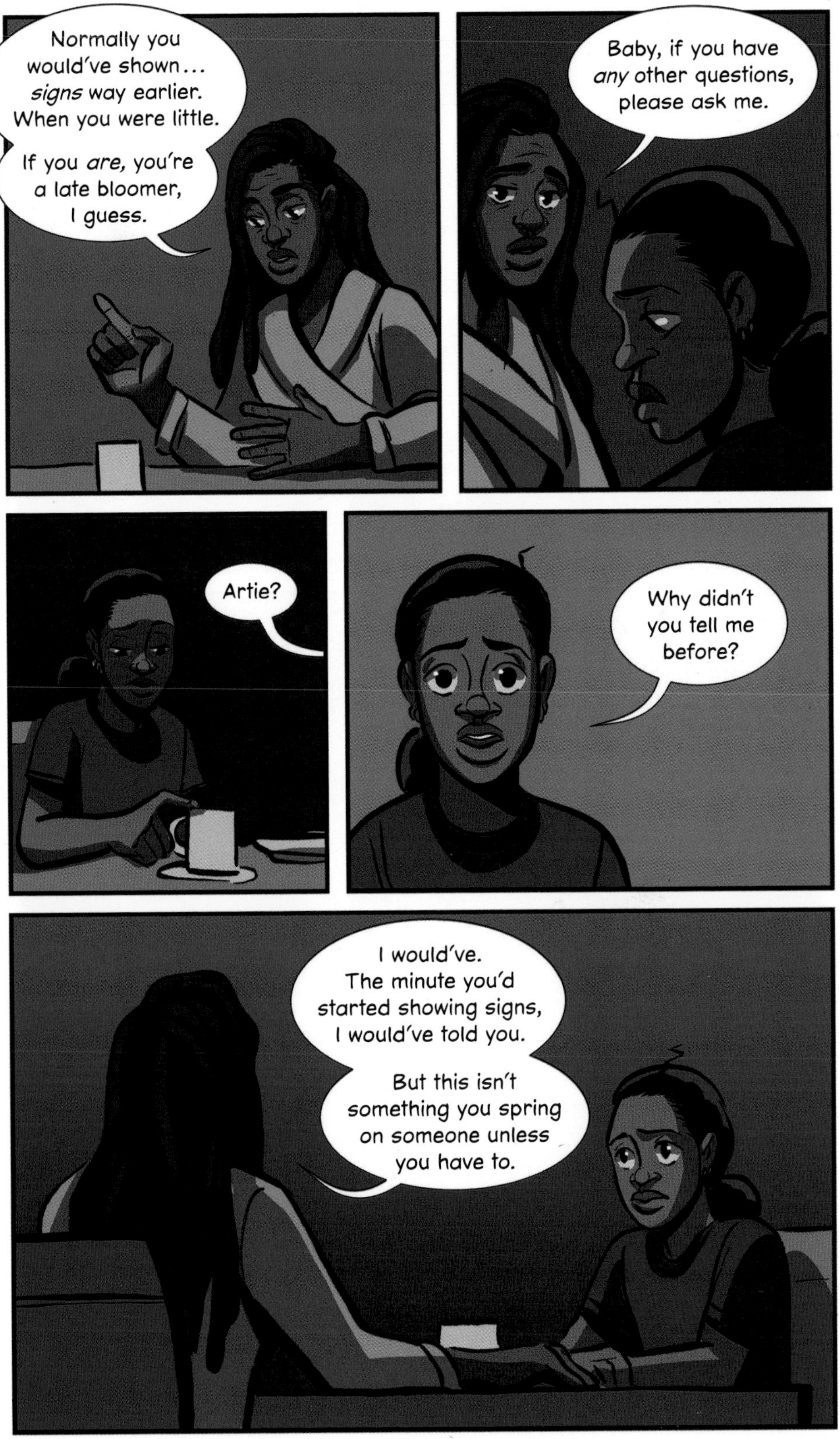
Normally you would've shown... *signs* way earlier. When you were little.
If you *are,* you're a late bloomer, I guess.
Baby, if you have *any* other questions, please ask me.
Artie?
Why didn't you tell me before?
I would've. The minute you'd started showing signs, I would've told you.
But this isn't something you spring on someone unless you have to.

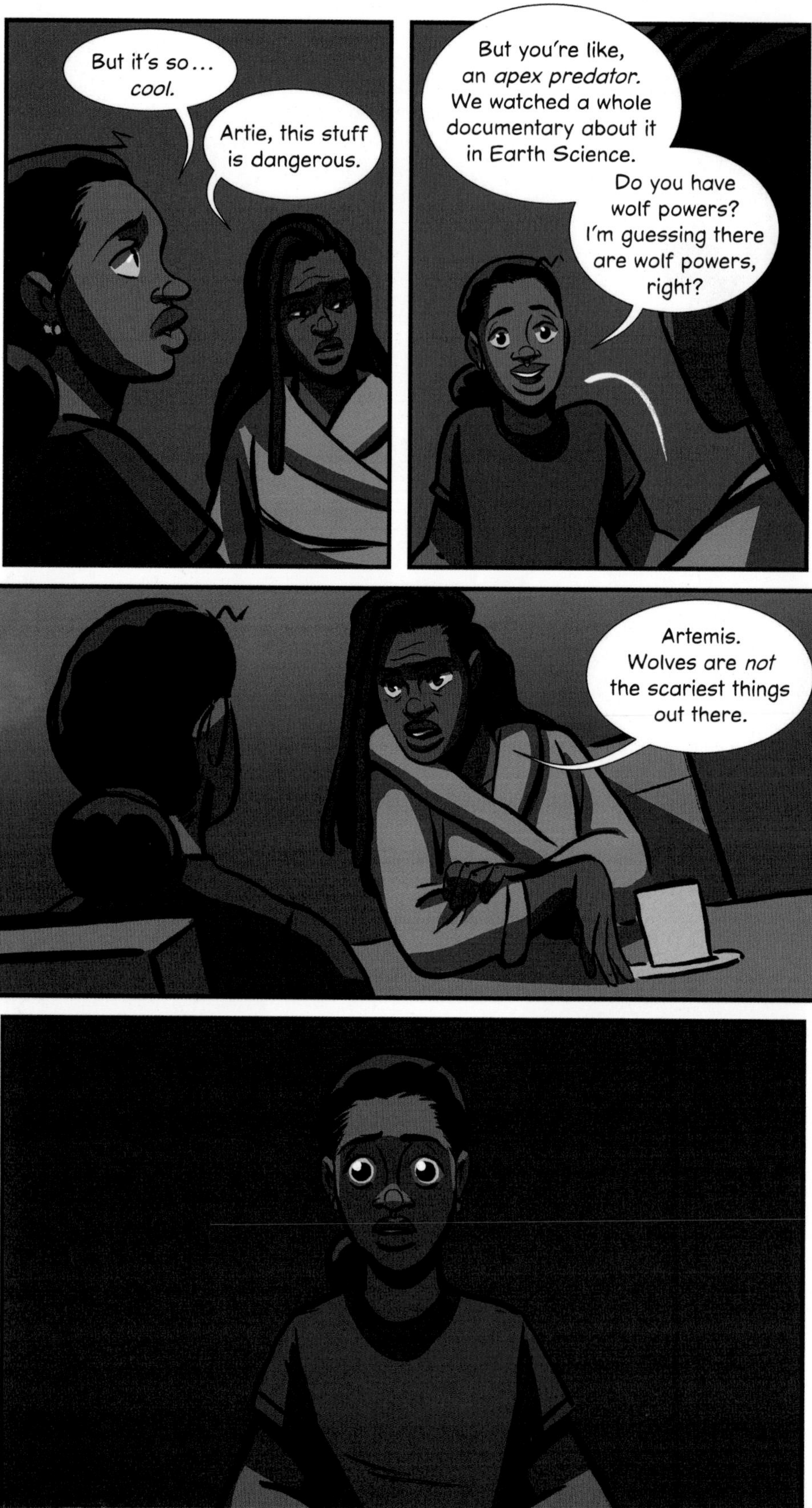

But it's so... *cool.*
Artie, this stuff is dangerous.
But you're like, an *apex predator.* We watched a whole documentary about it in Earth Science.
Do you have wolf powers? I'm guessing there are wolf powers, right?
Artemis. Wolves are *not* the scariest things out there.

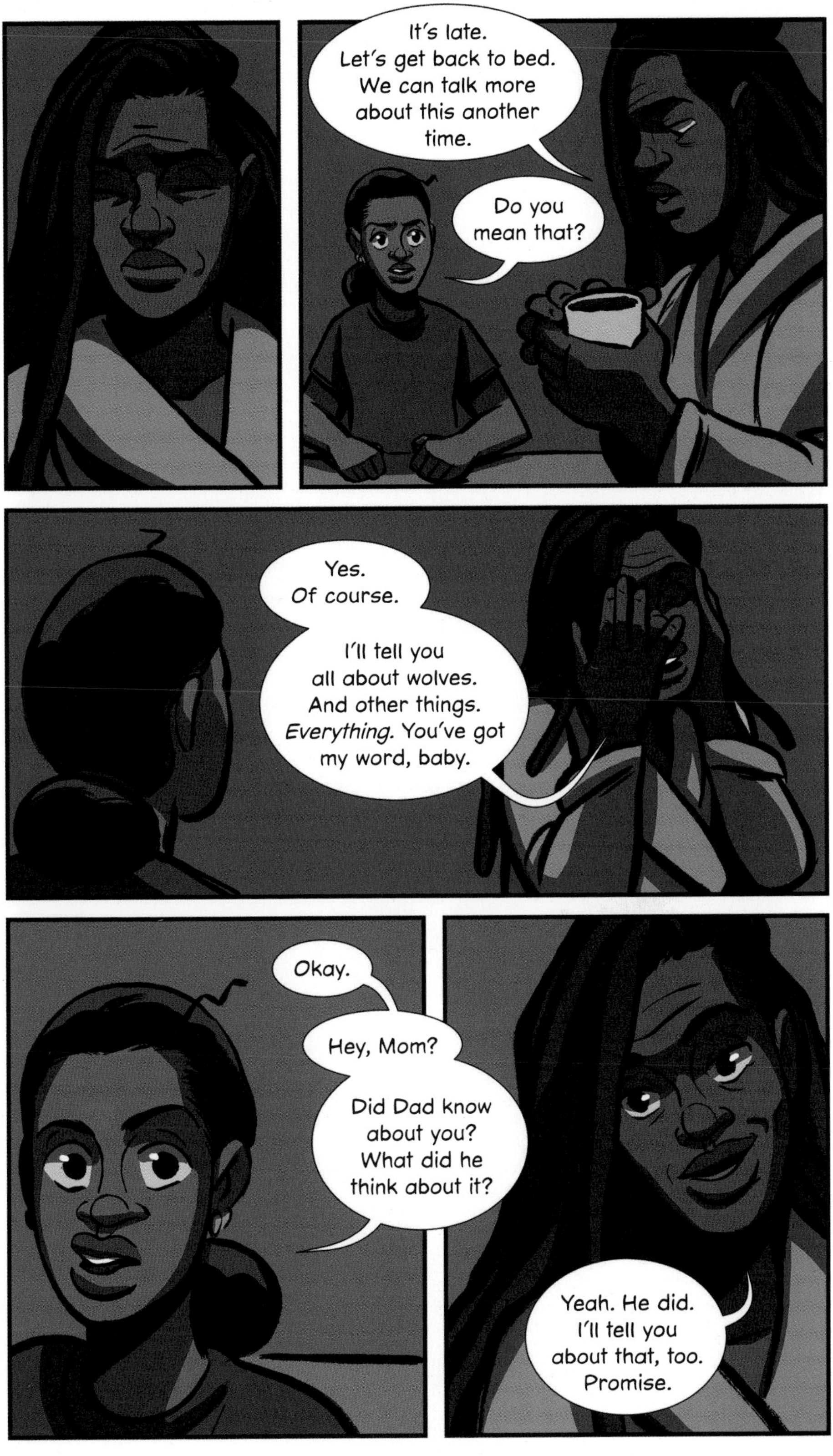
It's late.
Let's get back to bed.
We can talk more
about this another
time.
Do you
mean that?
Yes.
Of course.
I'll tell you
all about wolves.
And other things.
Everything. You've got
my word, baby.
Okay.
Hey, Mom?
Did Dad know
about you?
What did he
think about it?
Yeah. He did.
I'll tell you
about that, too.
Promise.

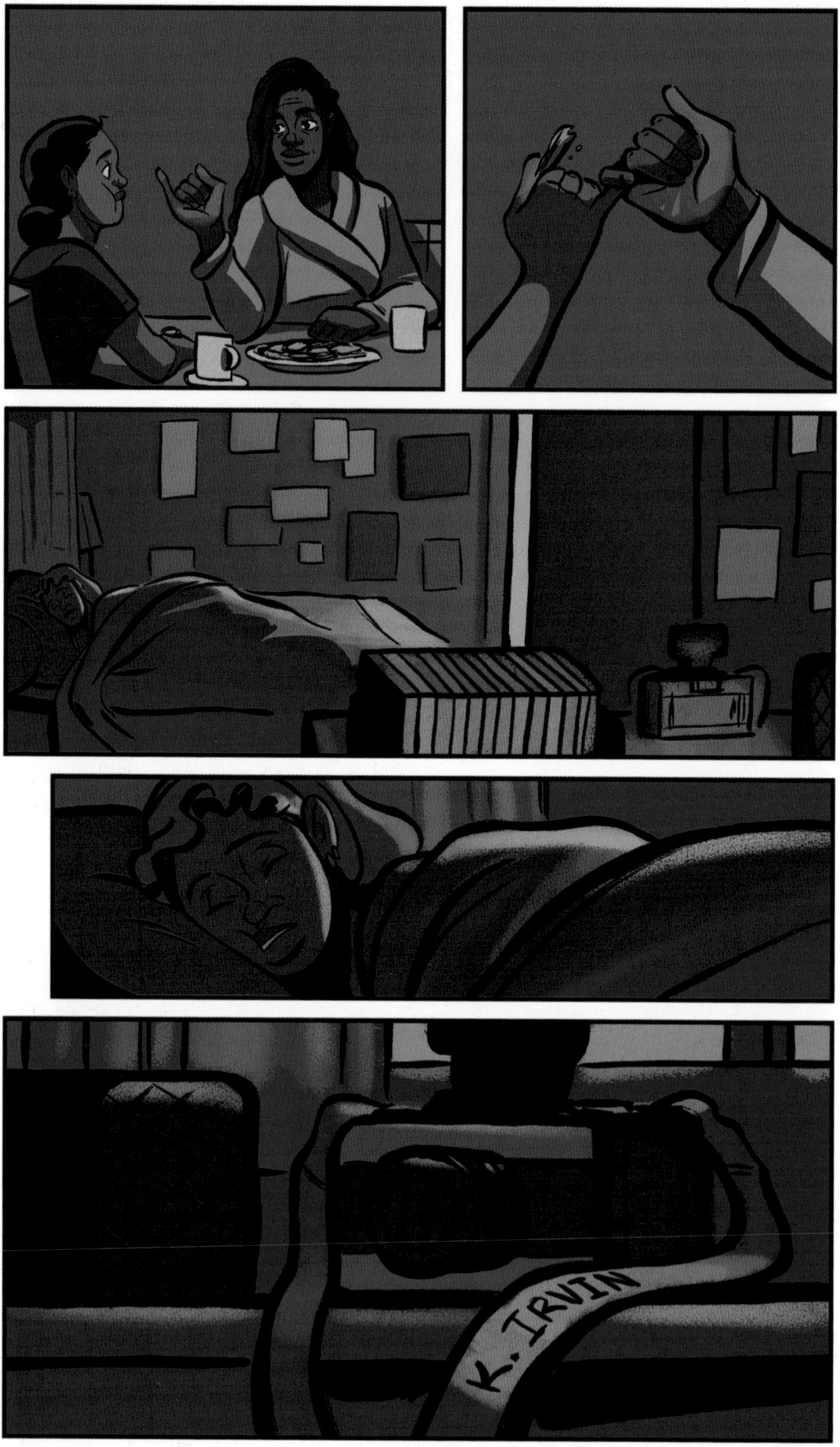
K. IRVIN

CHAPTER TWO

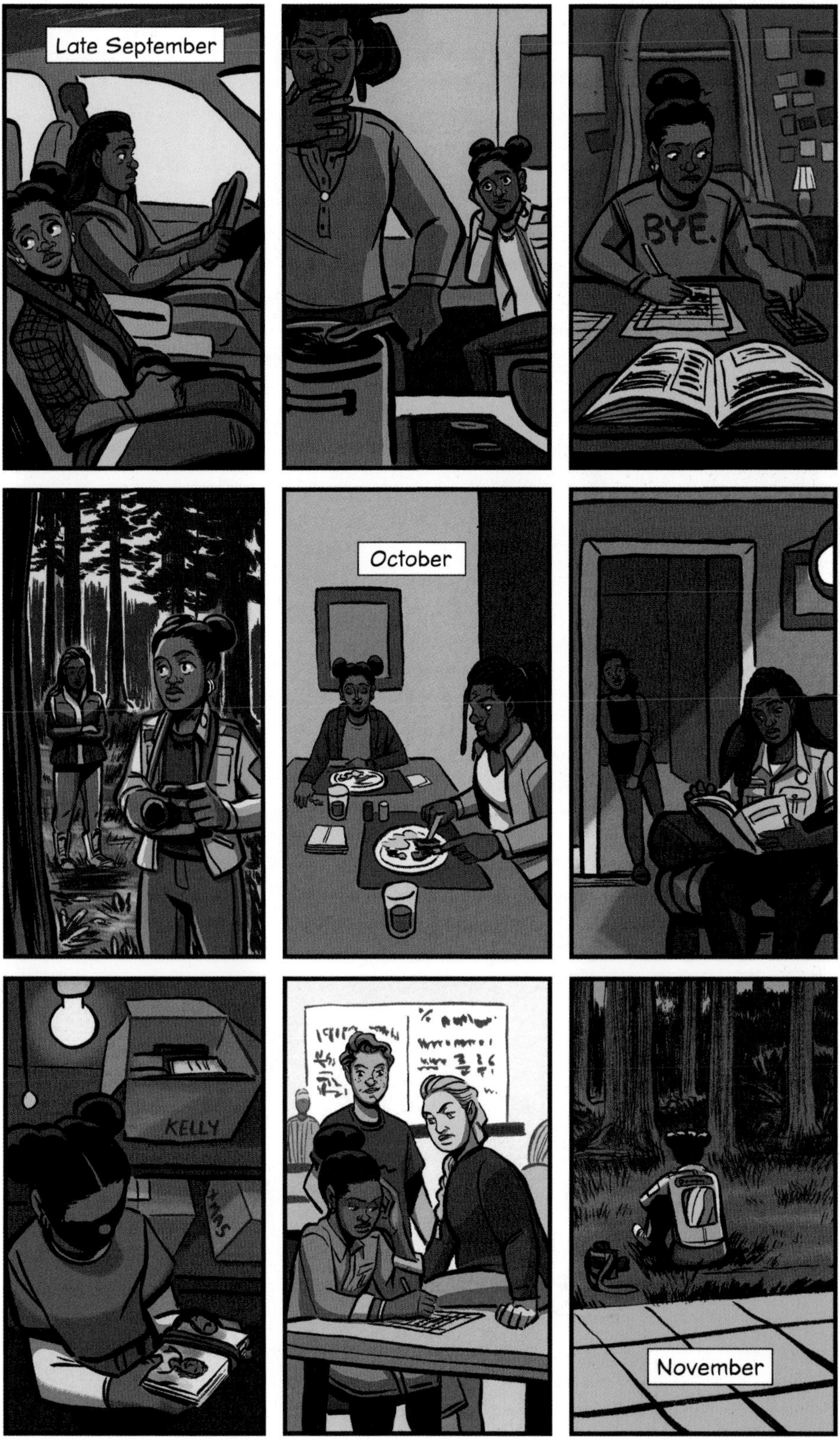
Late September
BYE.
October
KELLY
November

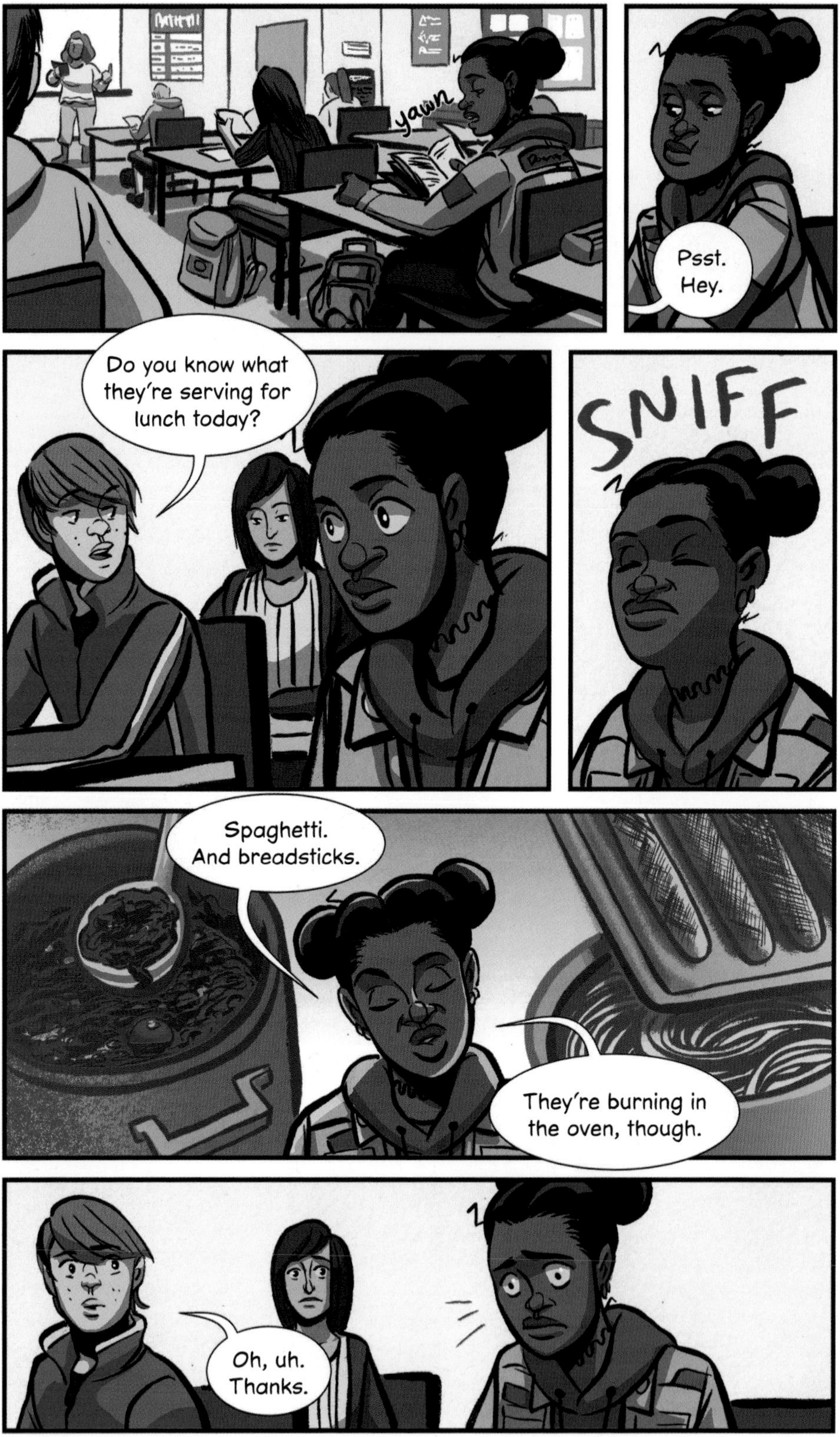
yawn
Psst. Hey.
Do you know what they're serving for lunch today?
SNIFF
Spaghetti. And breadsticks.
They're burning in the oven, though.
Oh, uh. Thanks.

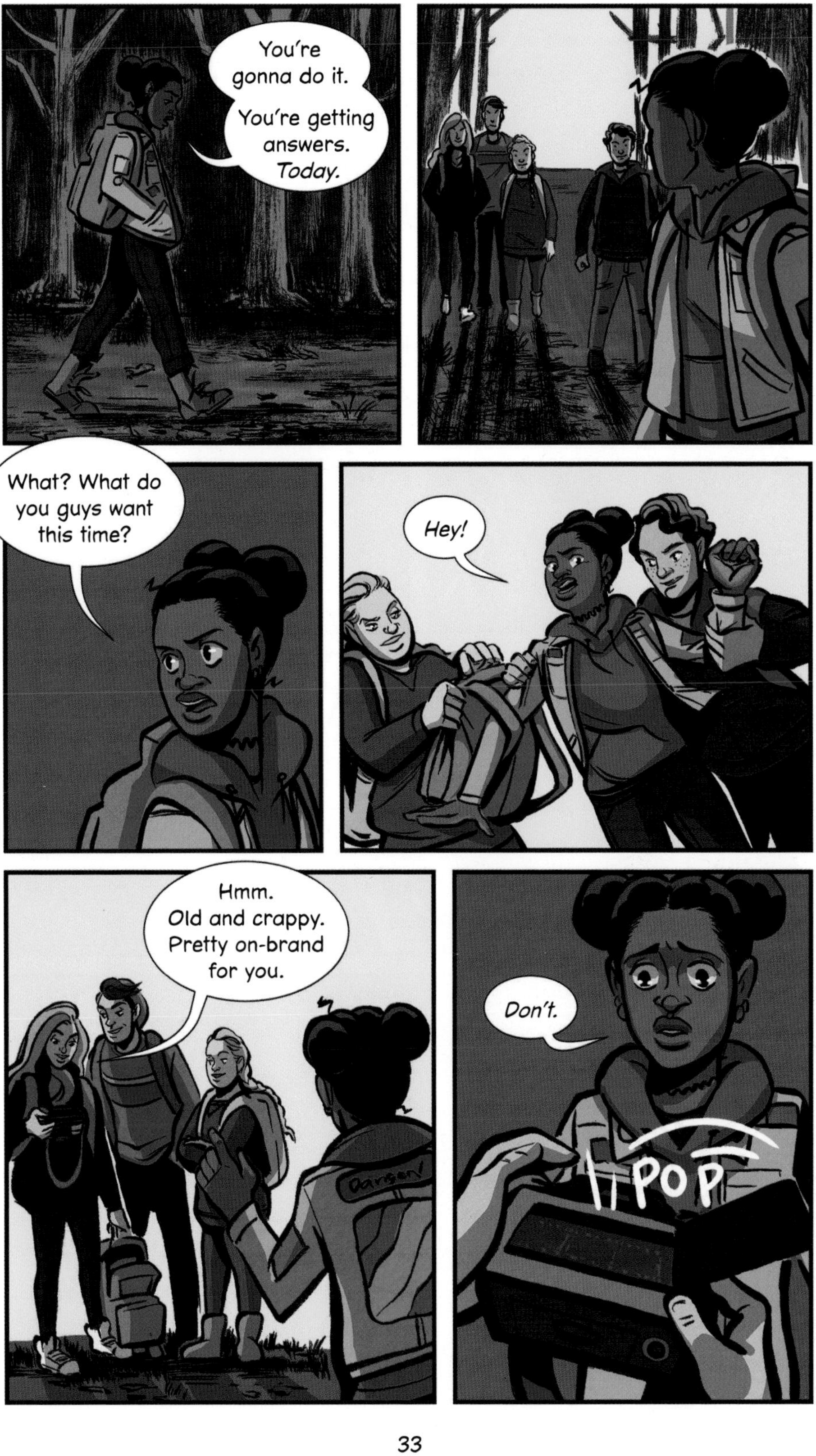
You're gonna do it.
You're getting answers. *Today.*
What? What do you guys want this time?
Hey!
Hmm. Old and crappy. Pretty on-brand for you.
Don't.
POP

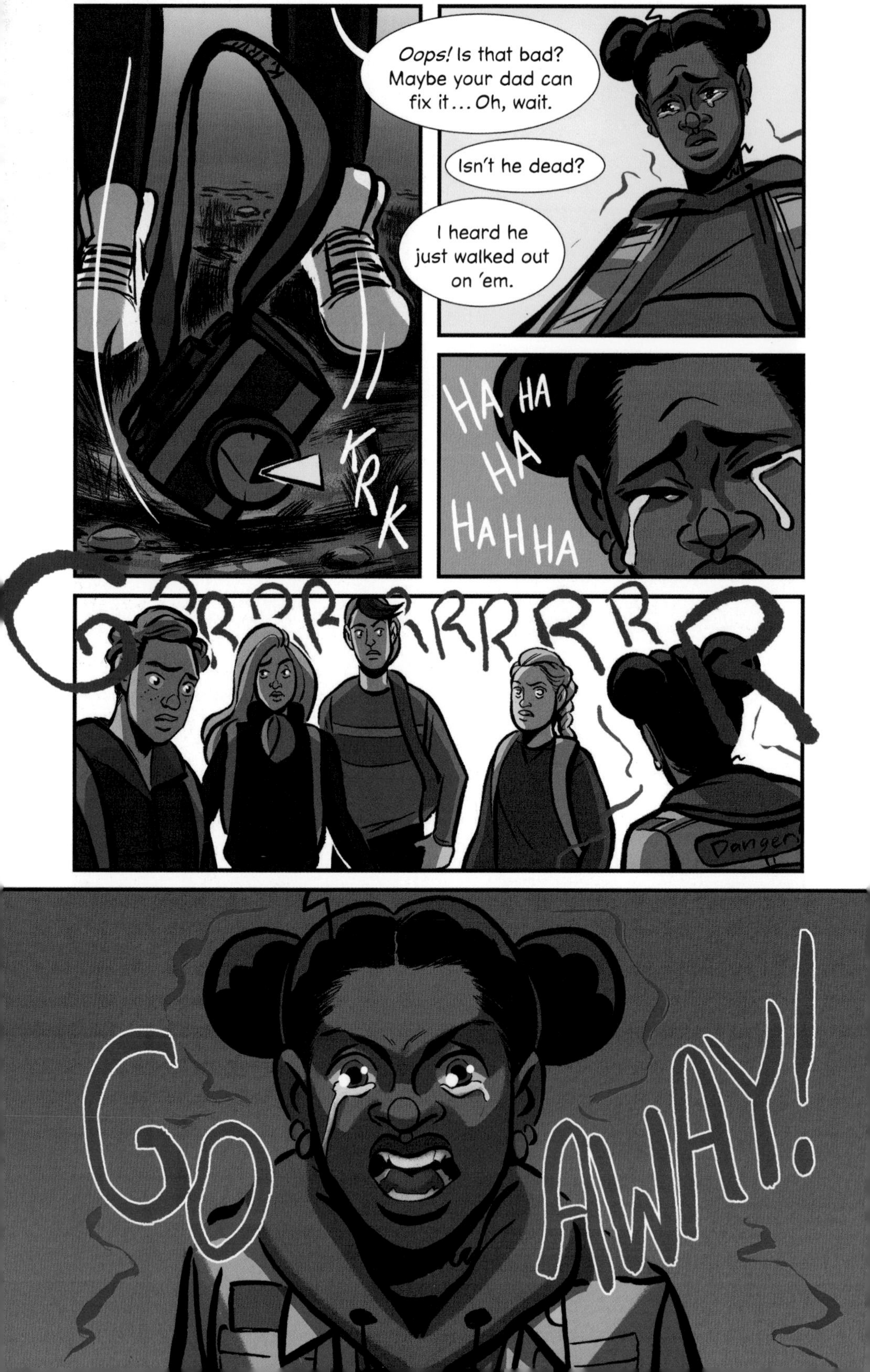

Oops! Is that bad? Maybe your dad can fix it… Oh, wait.
Isn't he dead?
I heard he just walked out on 'em.
KRK
HA HA HA HA HAHHA
GRRRRRRRRRRRR
Danger
GO AWAY!

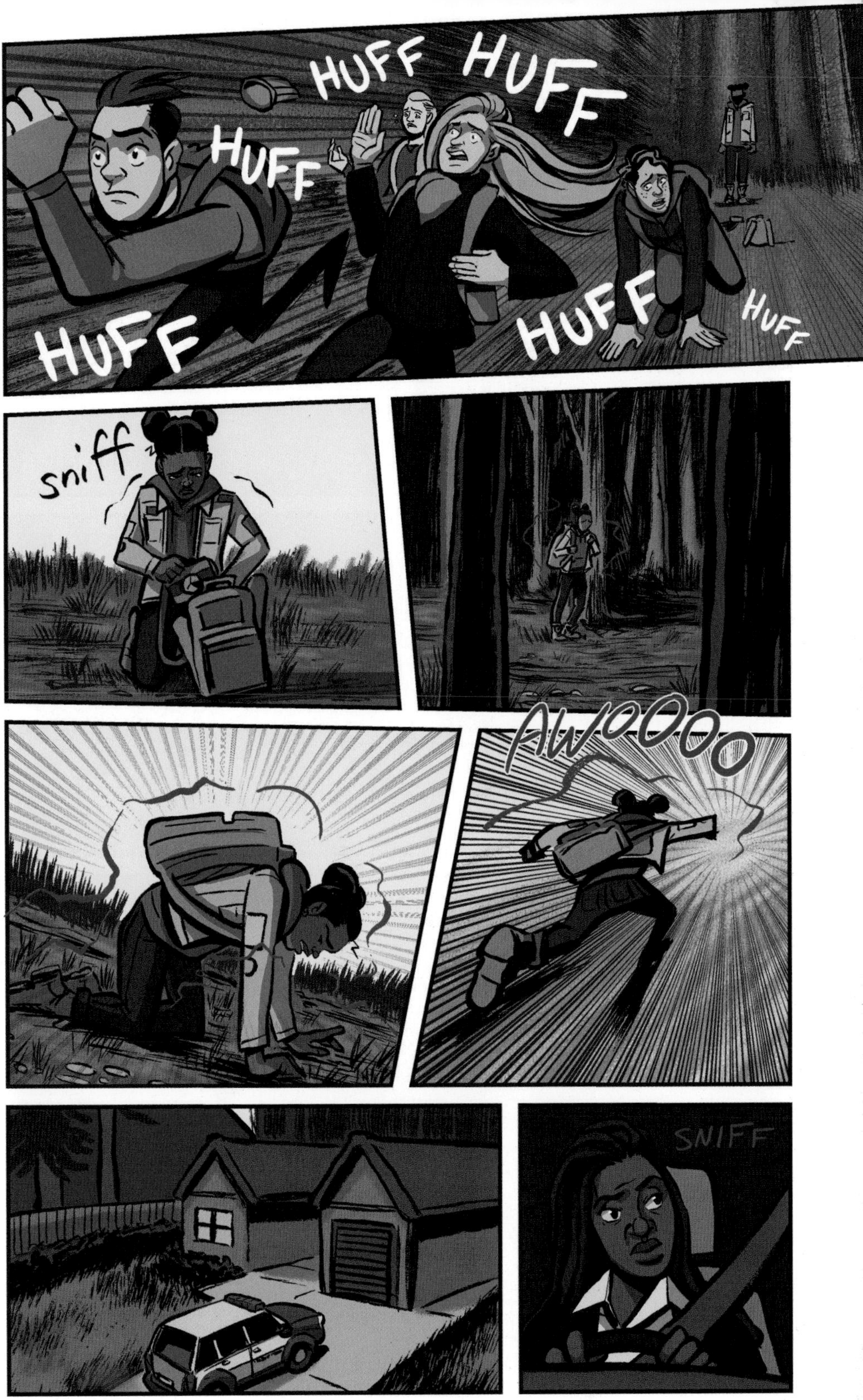
HUFF HUFF
HUFF
HUFF
HUFF
HUFF
sniff
AWOOOO
SNIFF

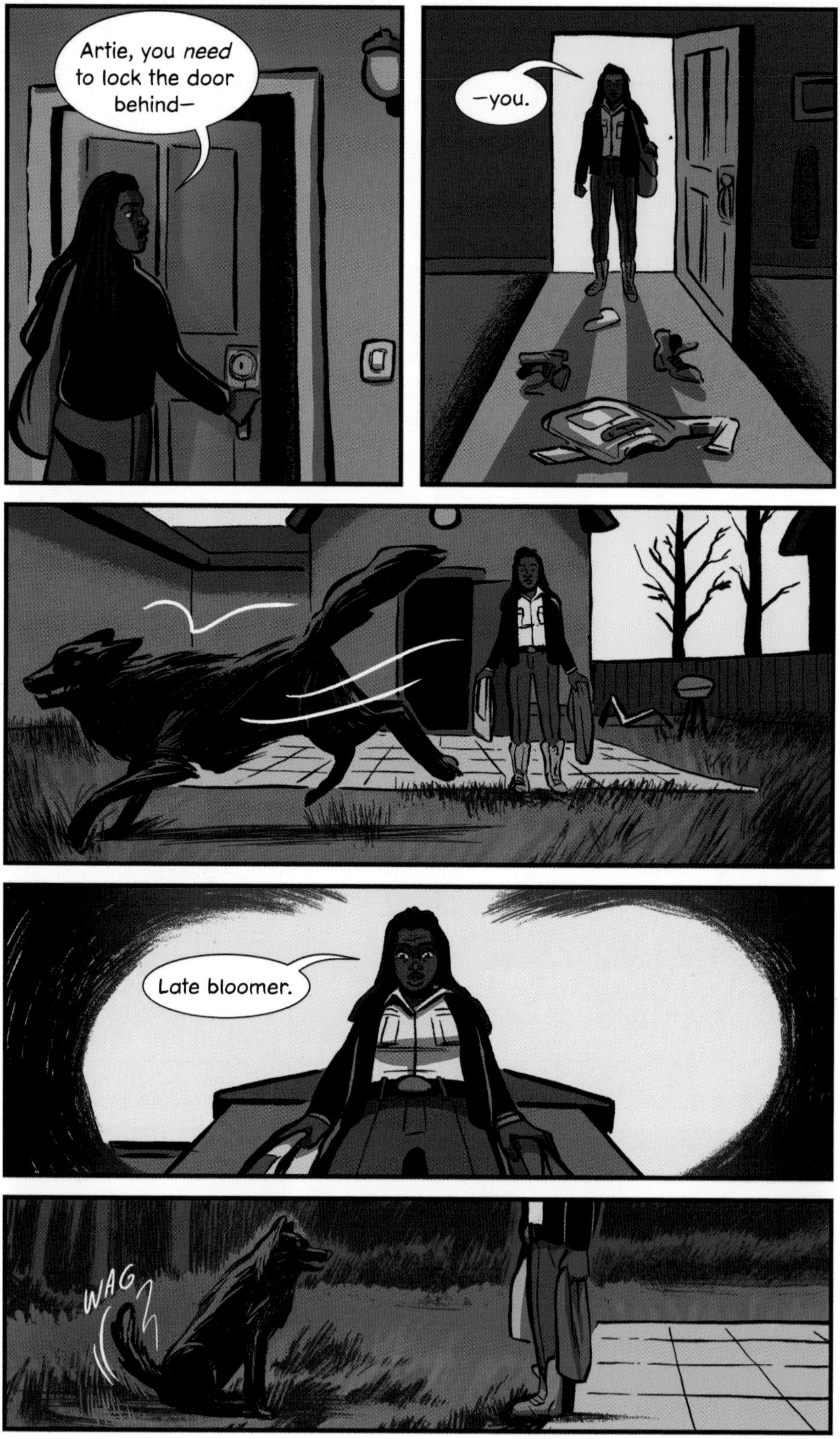
Artie, you *need* to lock the door behind—
—you.
Late bloomer.
WAG

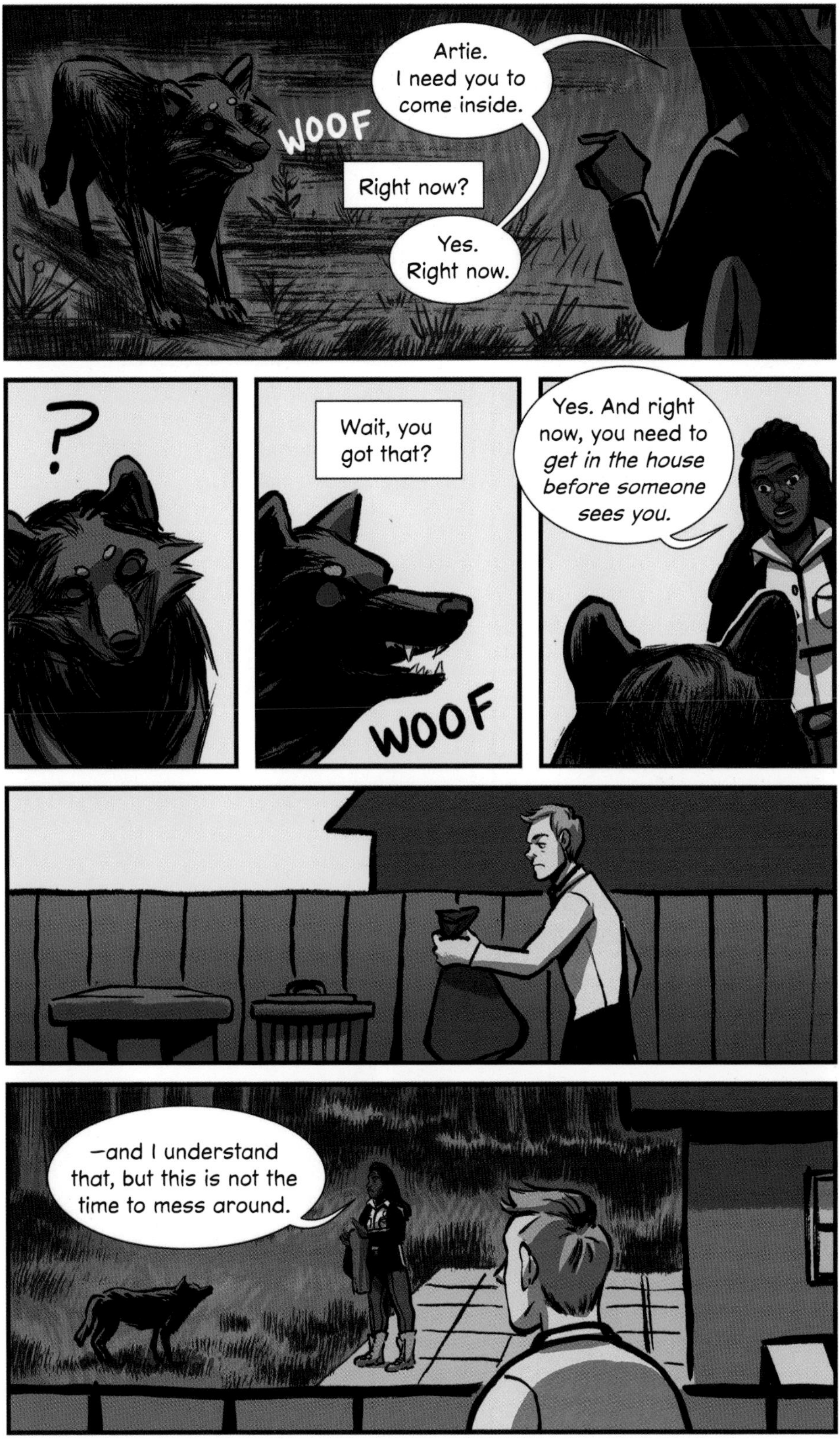
Artie.
I need you to come inside.
WOOF
Right now?
Yes. Right now.
?
Wait, you got that?
WOOF
Yes. And right now, you need to *get in the house before someone sees you.*
—and I understand that, but this is not the time to mess around.

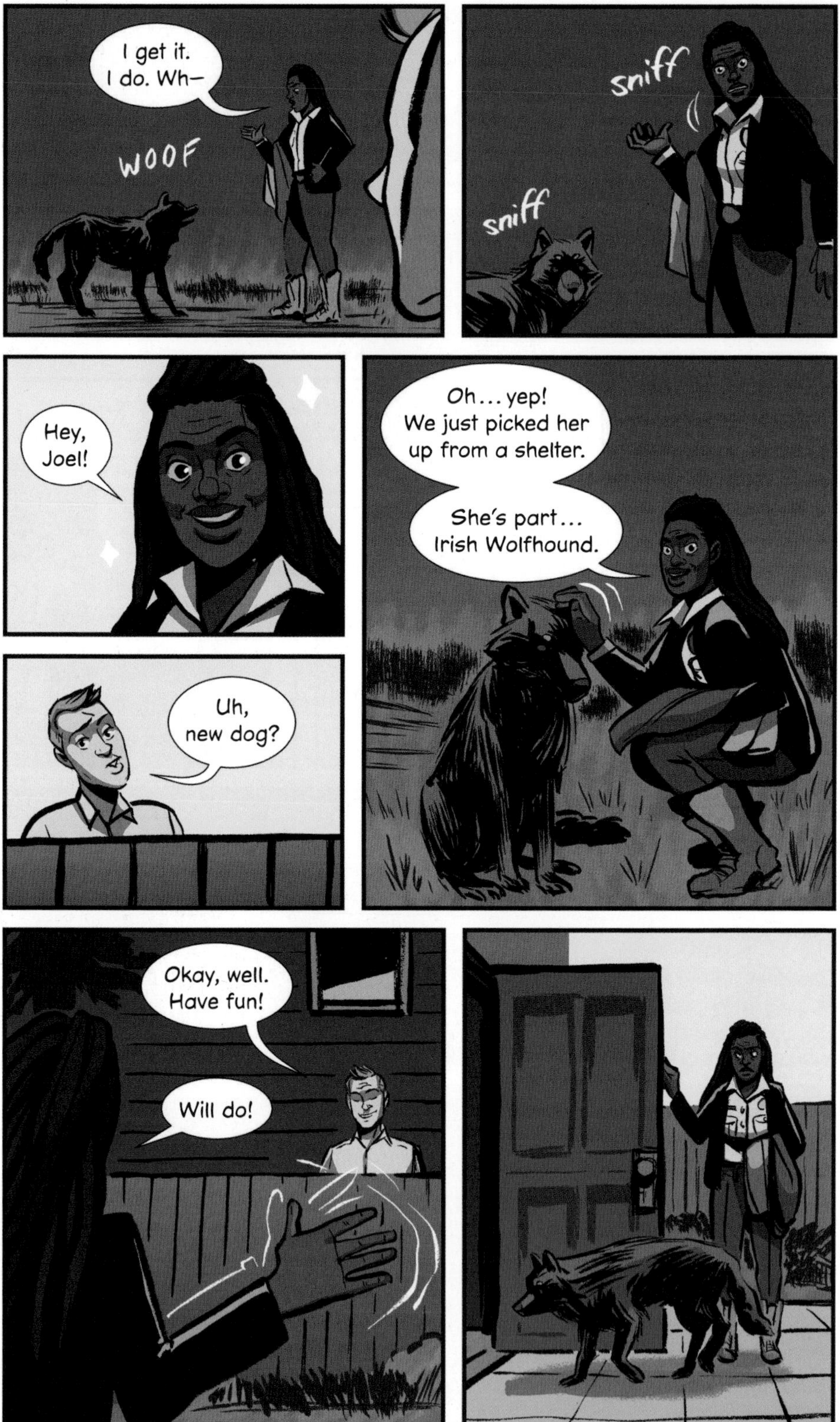
I get it. I do. Wh–
WOOF
sniff
sniff
Hey, Joel!
Uh, new dog?
Oh... yep! We just picked her up from a shelter.
She's part... Irish Wolfhound.
Okay, well. Have fun!
Will do!

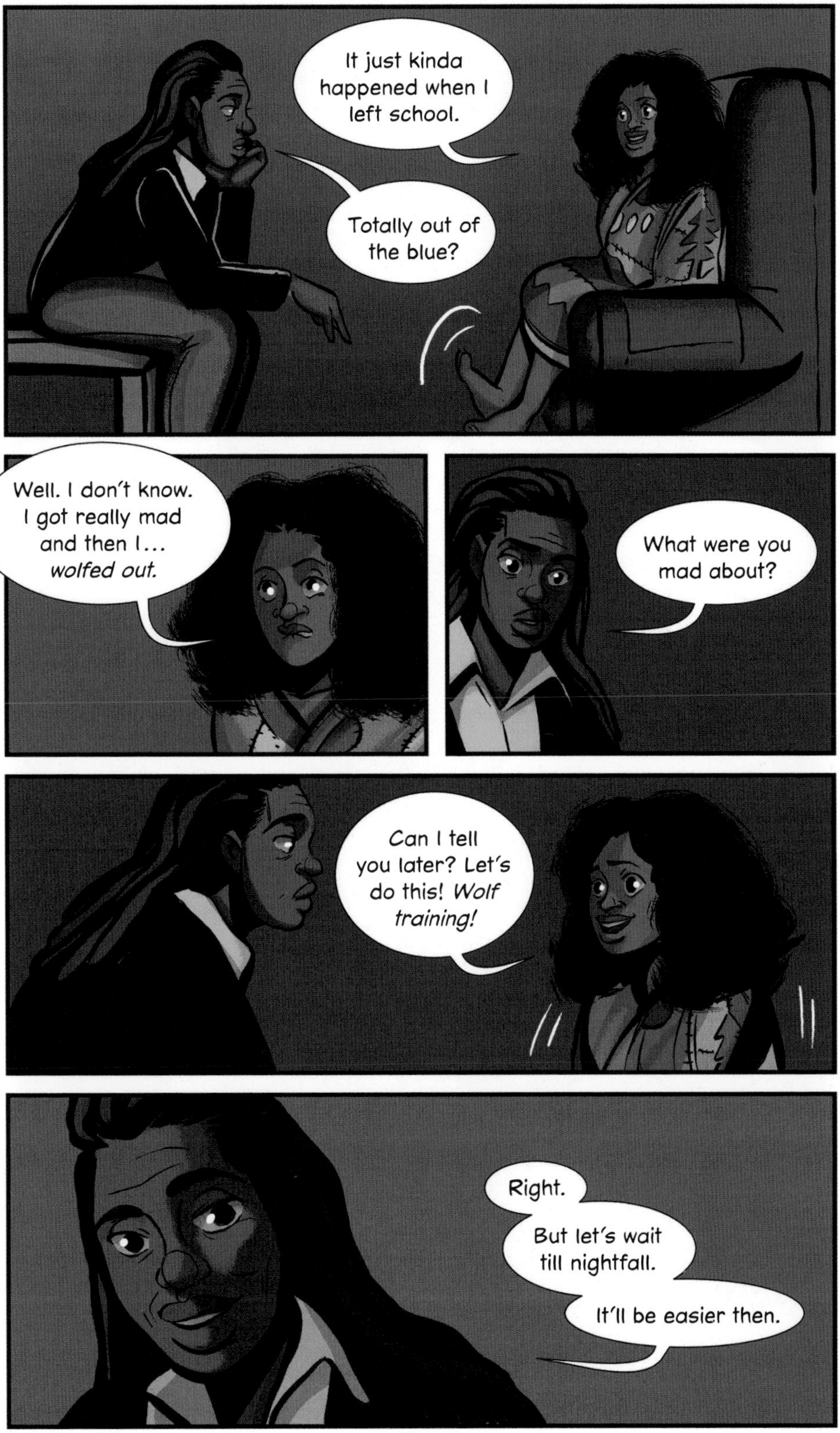
It just kinda happened when I left school.
Totally out of the blue?
Well. I don't know. I got really mad and then I... *wolfed out.*
What were you mad about?
Can I tell you later? Let's do this! *Wolf training!*
Right.
But let's wait till nightfall.
It'll be easier then.

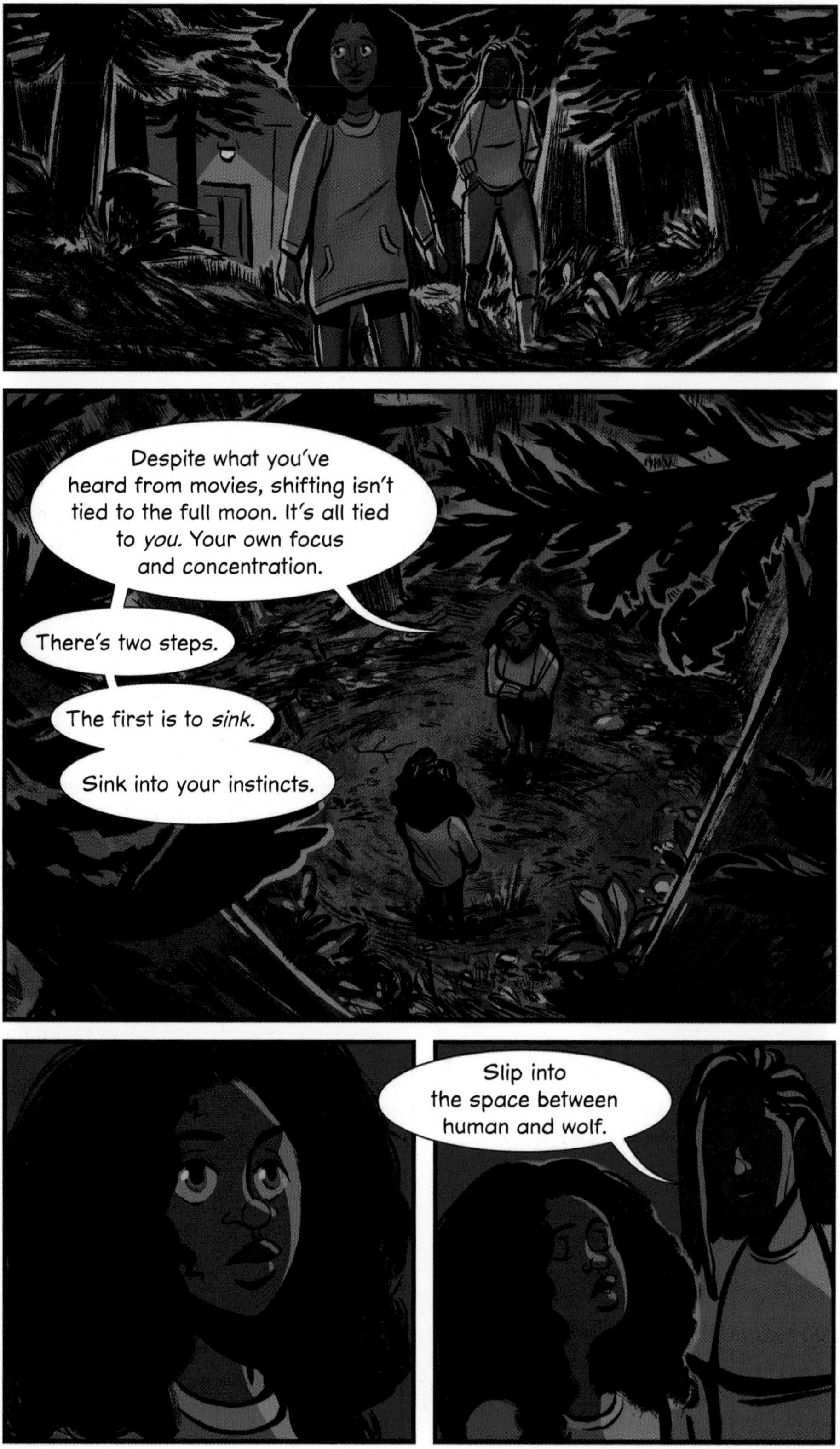
Despite what you've heard from movies, shifting isn't tied to the full moon. It's all tied to *you.* Your own focus and concentration.
There's two steps.
The first is to *sink.*
Sink into your instincts.
Slip into the space between human and wolf.

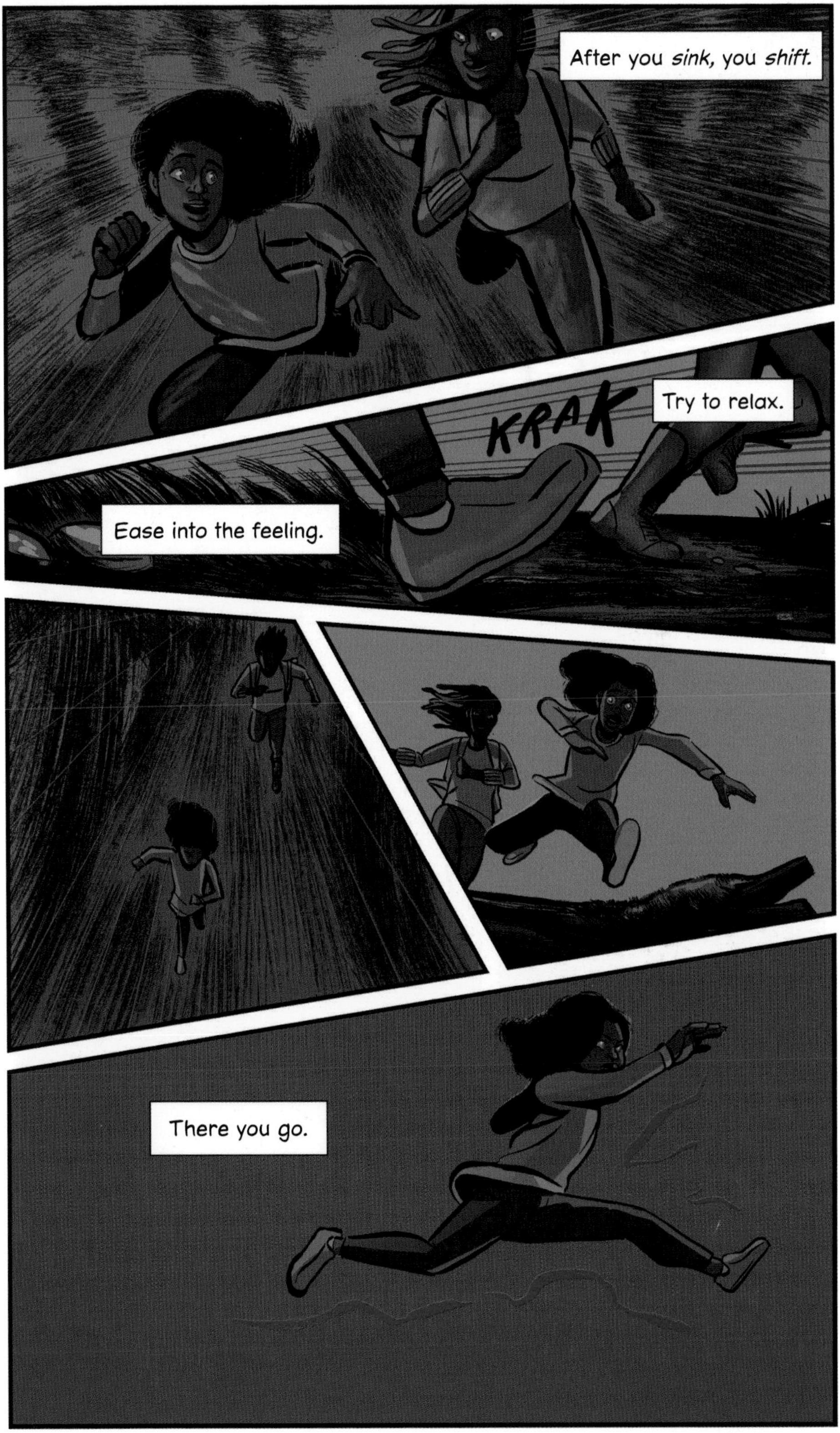
After you *sink*, you *shift*.
Try to relax.
KRAK
Ease into the feeling.
There you go.

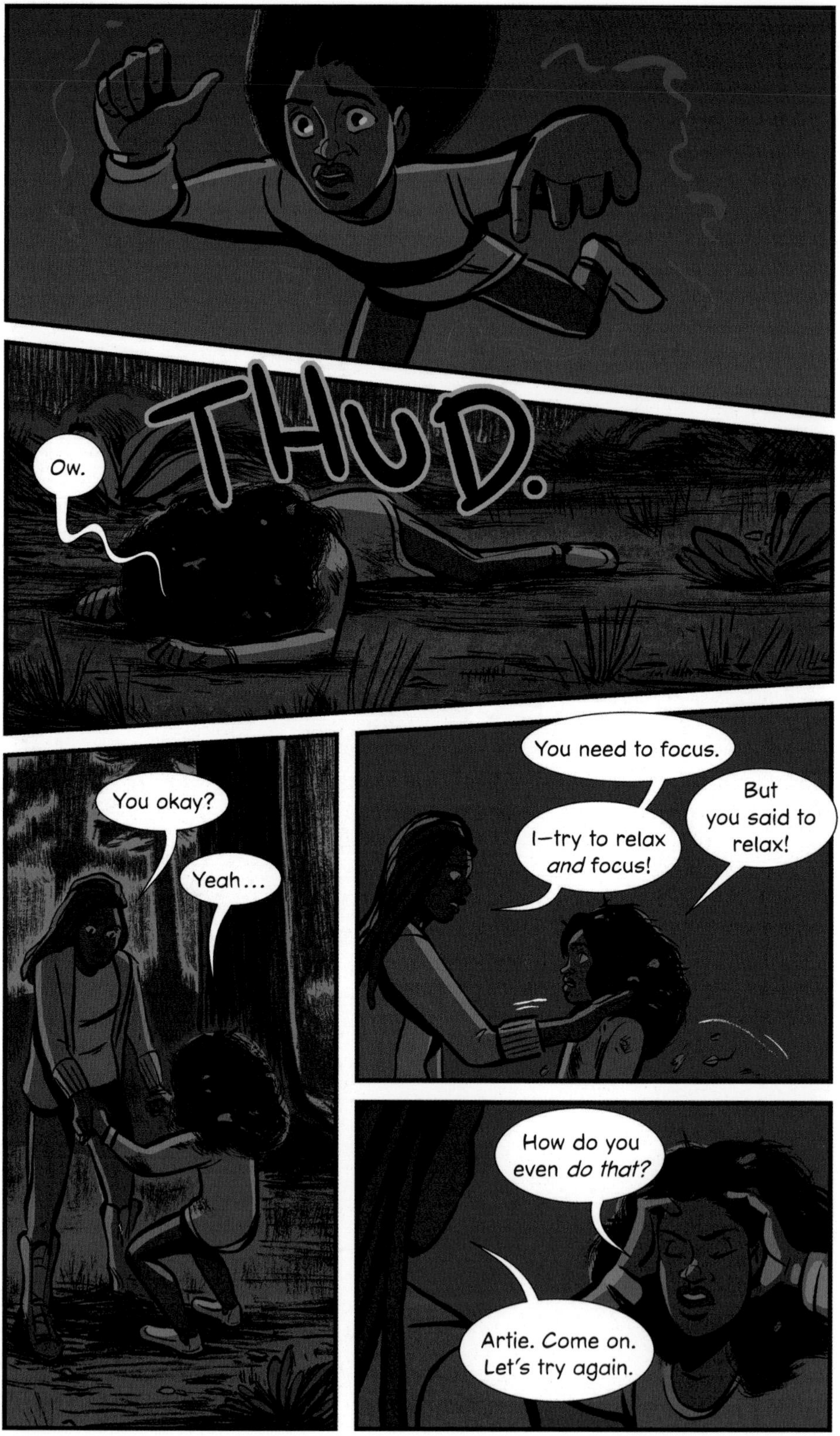
THUD.
Ow.
You okay?
Yeah...
You need to focus.
I—try to relax *and* focus!
But you said to relax!
How do you even *do that?*
Artie. Come on. Let's try again.

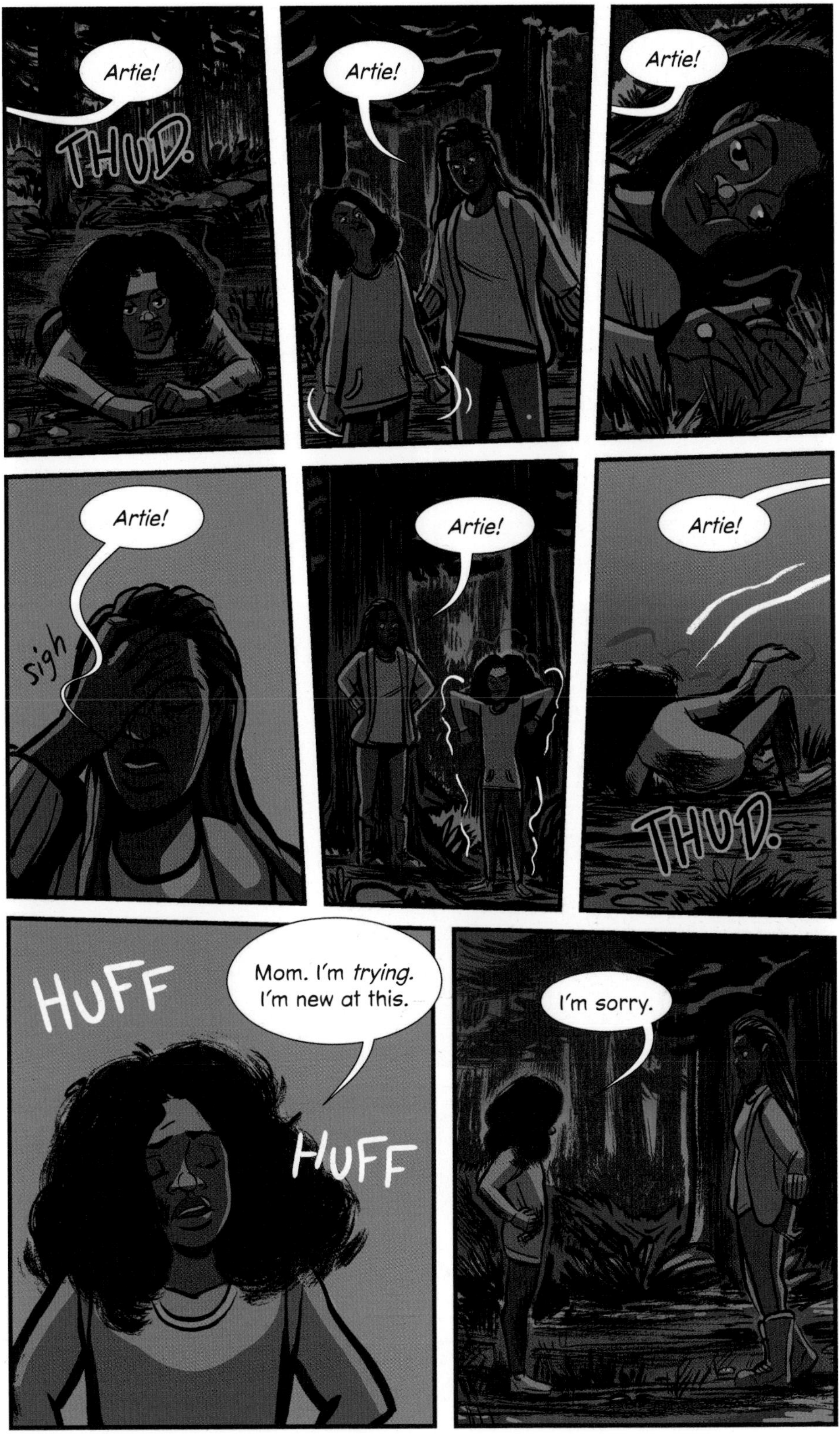
Artie!
THUD.
Artie!
Artie!
Artie!
sigh
Artie!
Artie!
THUD.
HUFF
Mom. I'm *trying.* I'm new at this.
HUFF
I'm sorry.

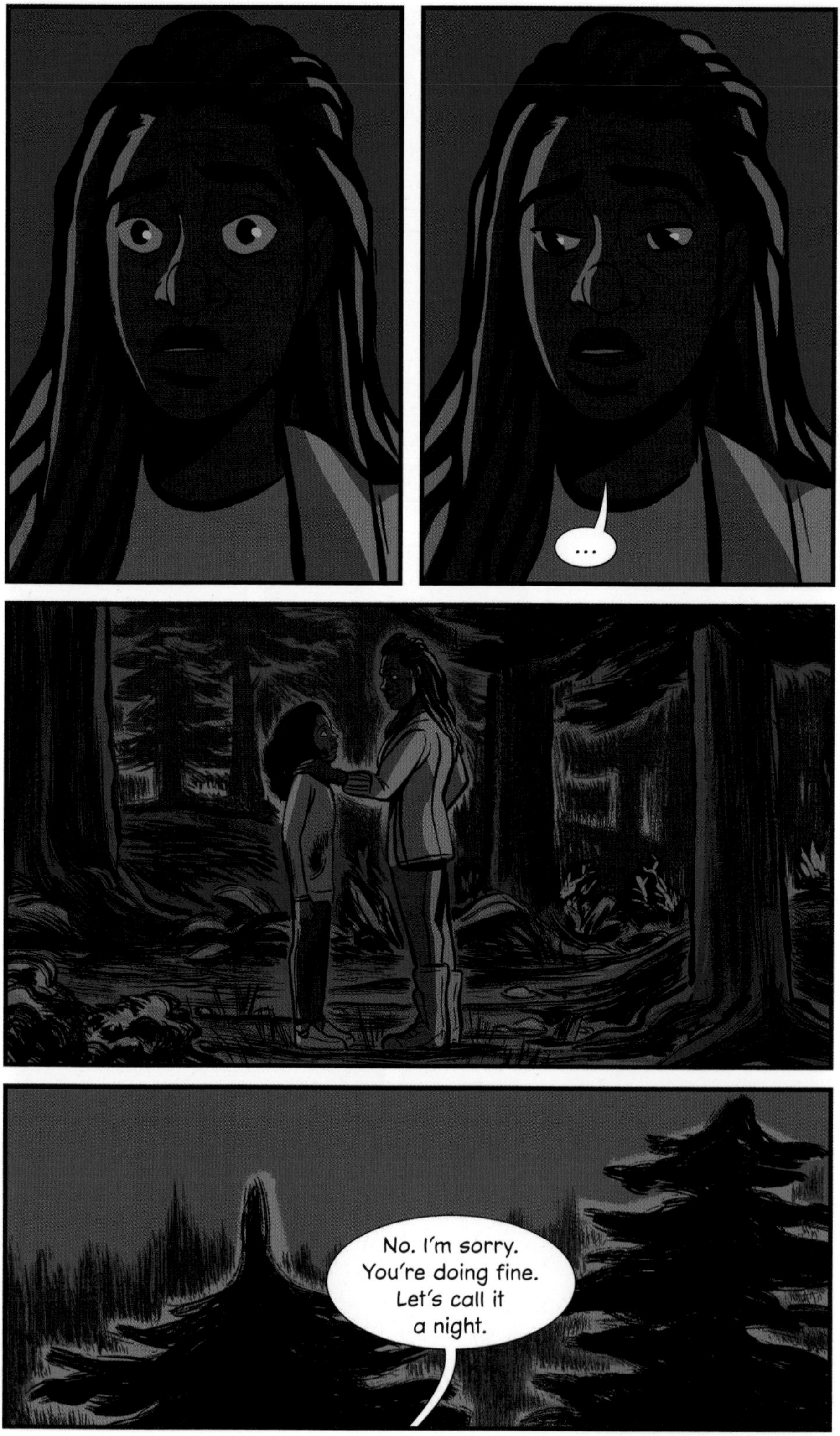
...
No. I'm sorry. You're doing fine. Let's call it a night.

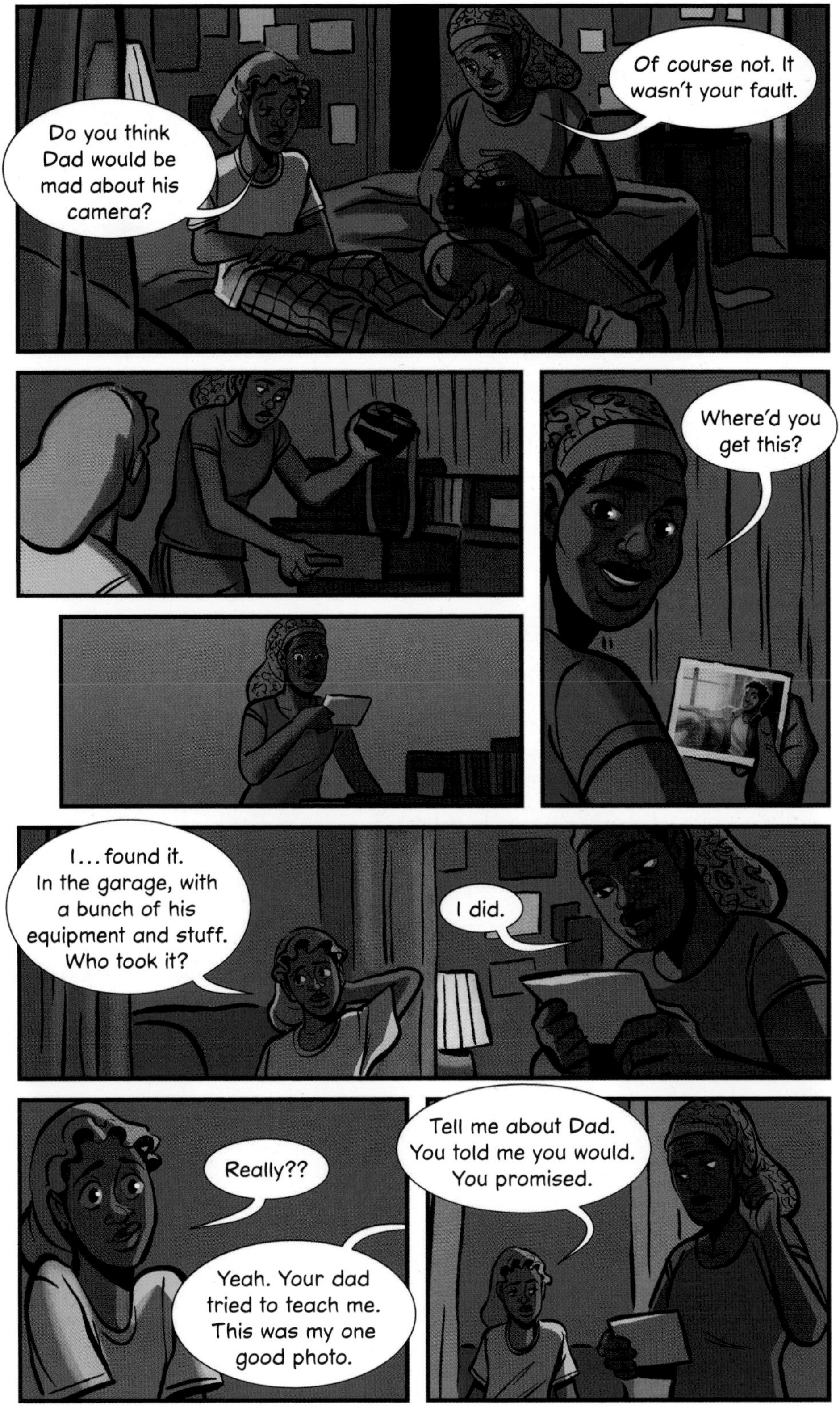
Do you think Dad would be mad about his camera?
Of course not. It wasn't your fault.
Where'd you get this?
I... found it. In the garage, with a bunch of his equipment and stuff. Who took it?
I did.
Really??
Yeah. Your dad tried to teach me. This was my one good photo.
Tell me about Dad. You told me you would. You promised.

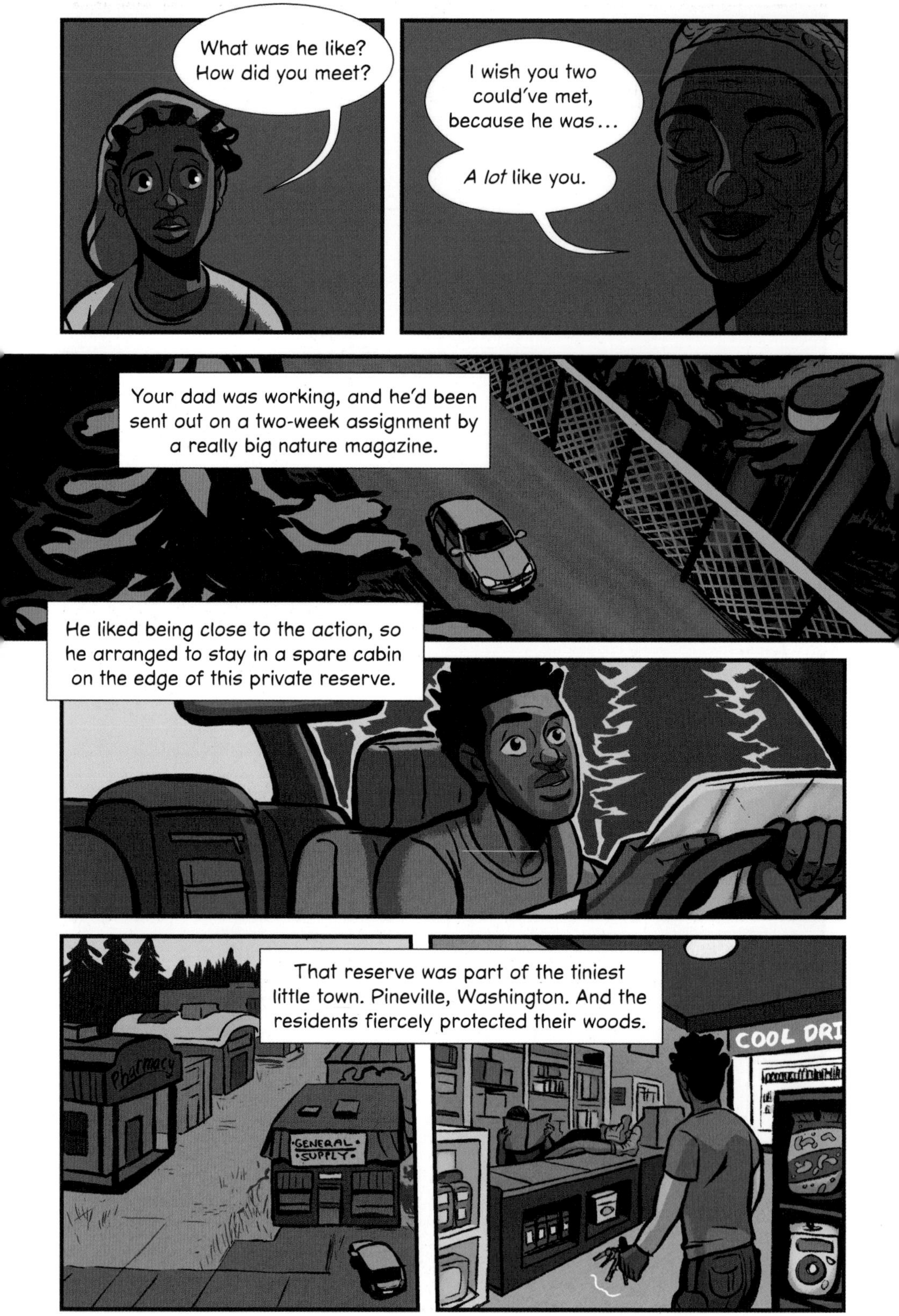
What was he like? How did you meet?
I wish you two could've met, because he was...
A *lot* like you.
Your dad was working, and he'd been sent out on a two-week assignment by a really big nature magazine.
He liked being close to the action, so he arranged to stay in a spare cabin on the edge of this private reserve.
That reserve was part of the tiniest little town. Pineville, Washington. And the residents fiercely protected their woods.
Pharmacy
GENERAL SUPPLY
COOL DRI

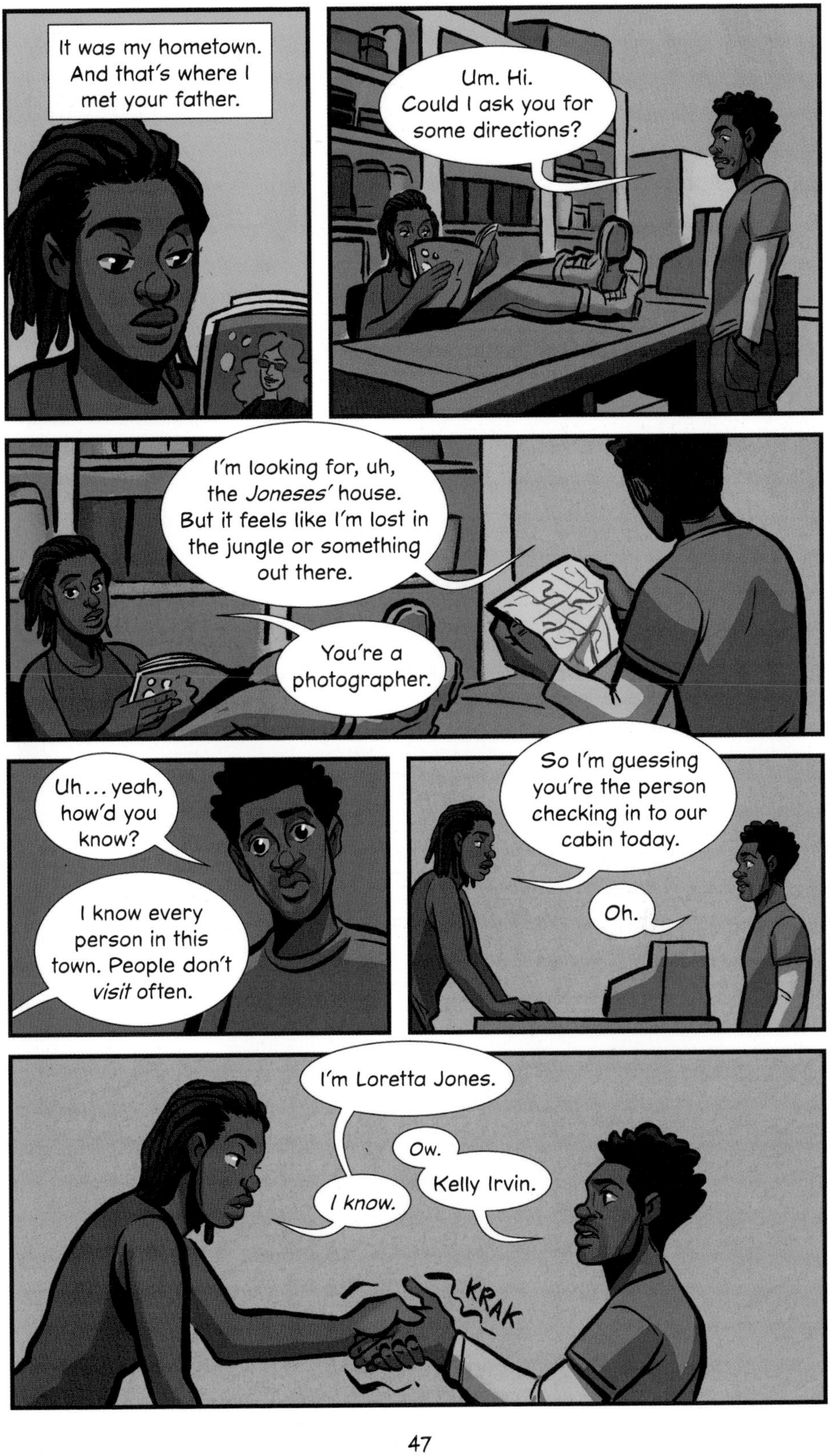
It was my hometown. And that's where I met your father.
Um. Hi. Could I ask you for some directions?
I'm looking for, uh, the *Joneses'* house. But it feels like I'm lost in the jungle or something out there.
You're a photographer.
Uh... yeah, how'd you know?
I know every person in this town. People don't *visit* often.
So I'm guessing you're the person checking in to our cabin today.
Oh.
I'm Loretta Jones.
Ow.
Kelly Irvin.
I know.
KRAK

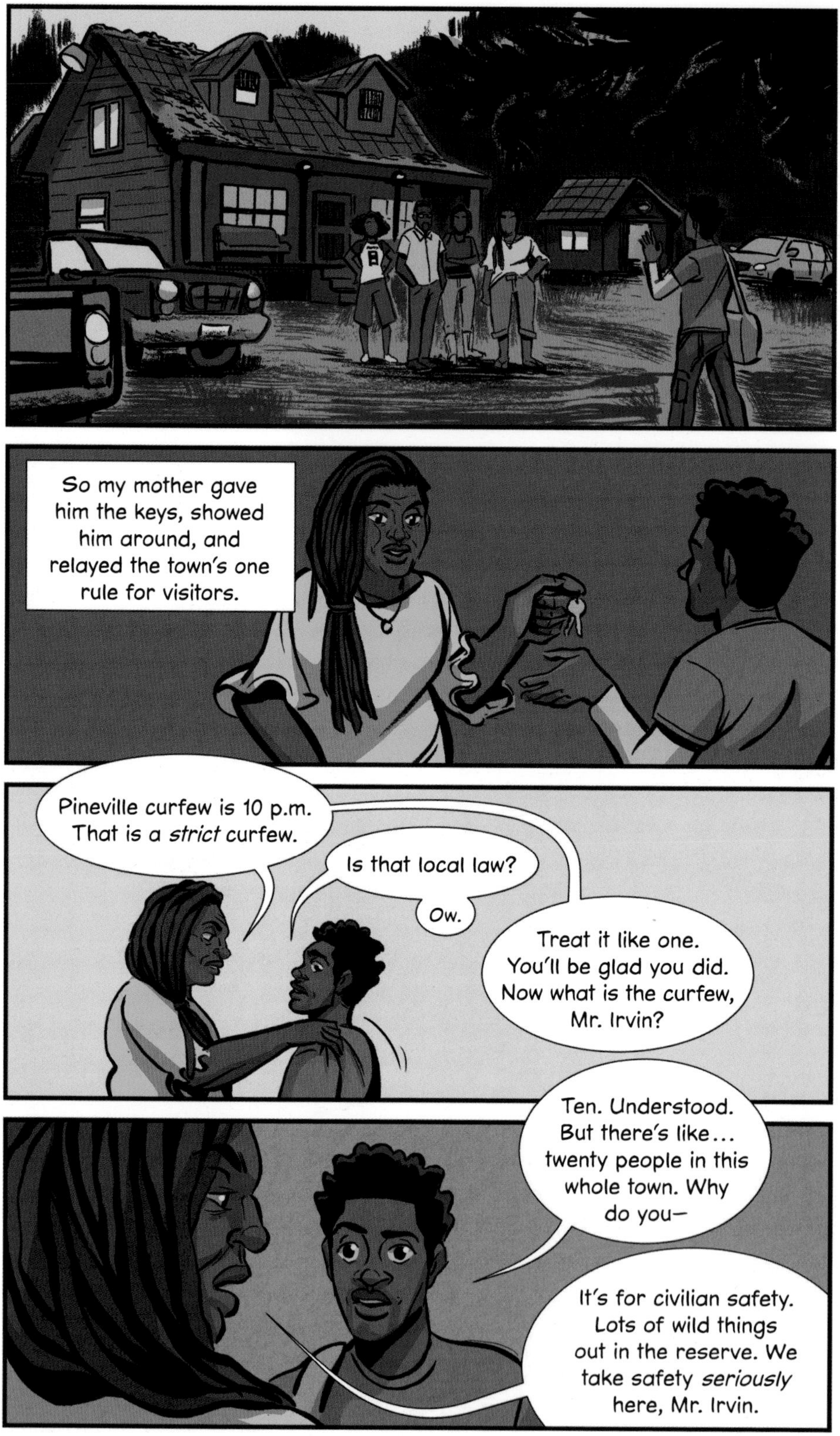
So my mother gave him the keys, showed him around, and relayed the town's one rule for visitors.
Pineville curfew is 10 p.m. That is a *strict* curfew.
Is that local law?
Ow.
Treat it like one. You'll be glad you did. Now what is the curfew, Mr. Irvin?
Ten. Understood. But there's like... twenty people in this whole town. Why do you—
It's for civilian safety. Lots of wild things out in the reserve. We take safety *seriously* here, Mr. Irvin.

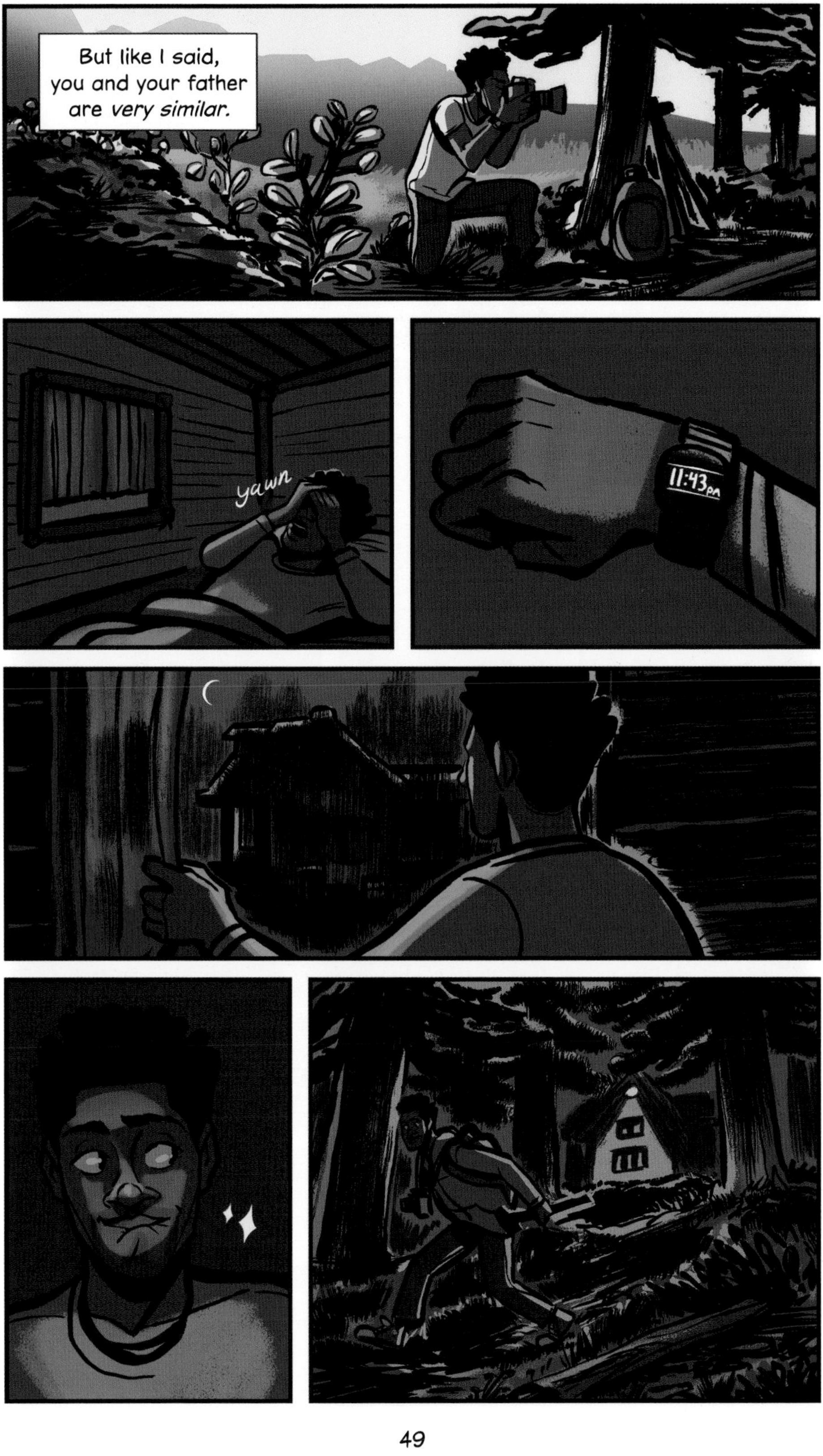
But like I said, you and your father are *very similar.*
yawn
11:43PM

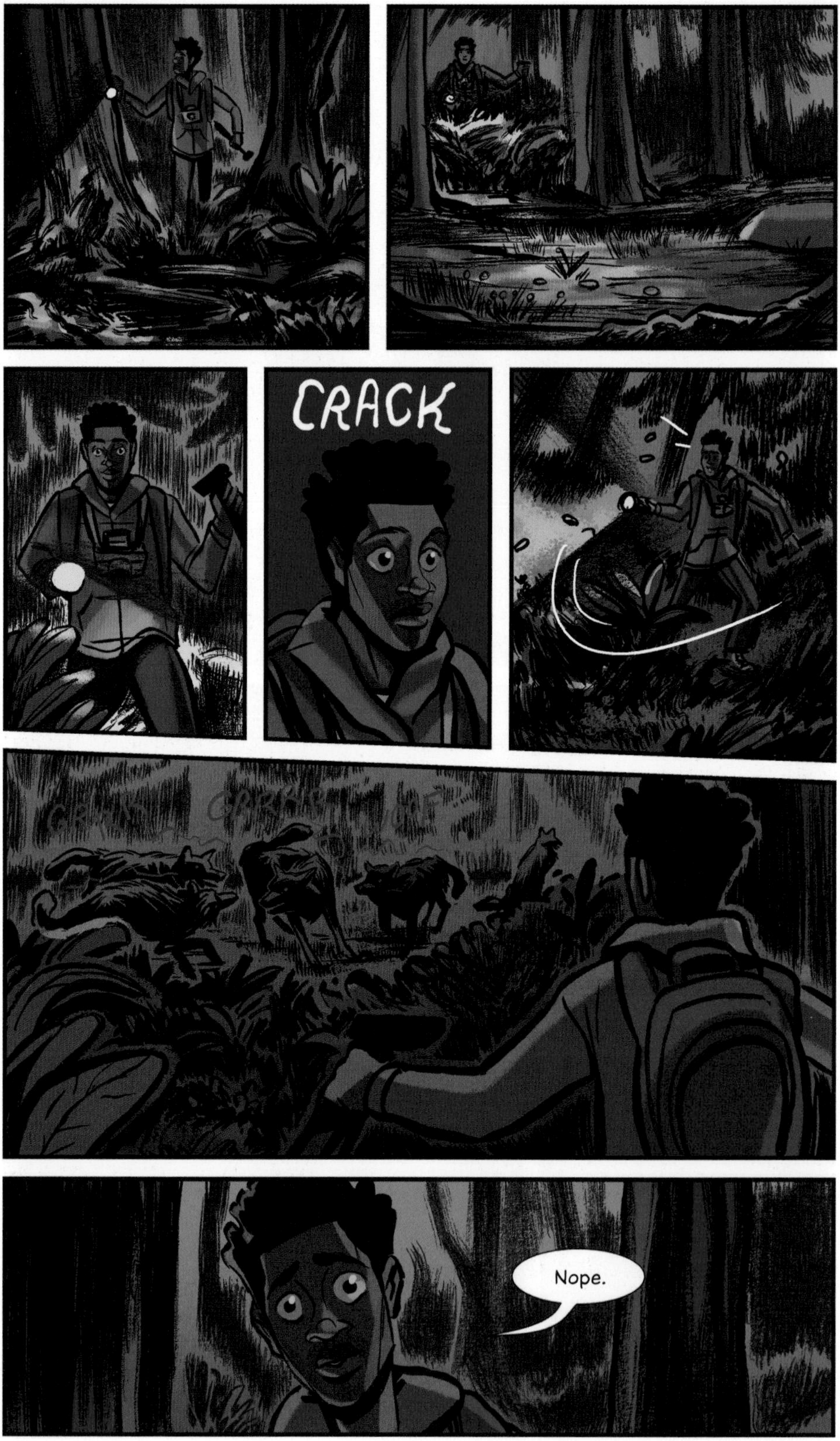
CRACK
Nope.

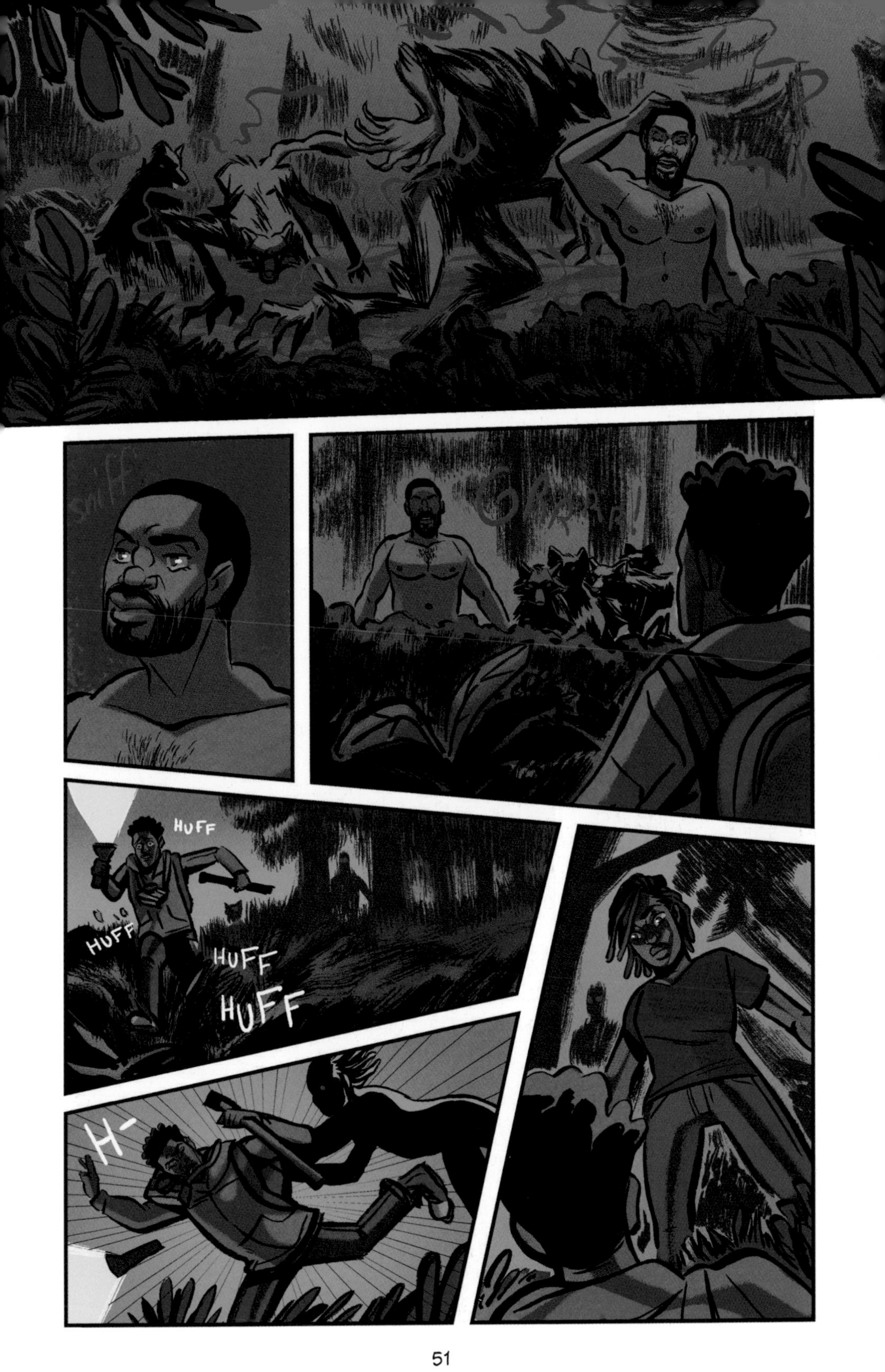
sniff
GRRRR!
HUFF
HUFF
HUFF
HUFF
H-

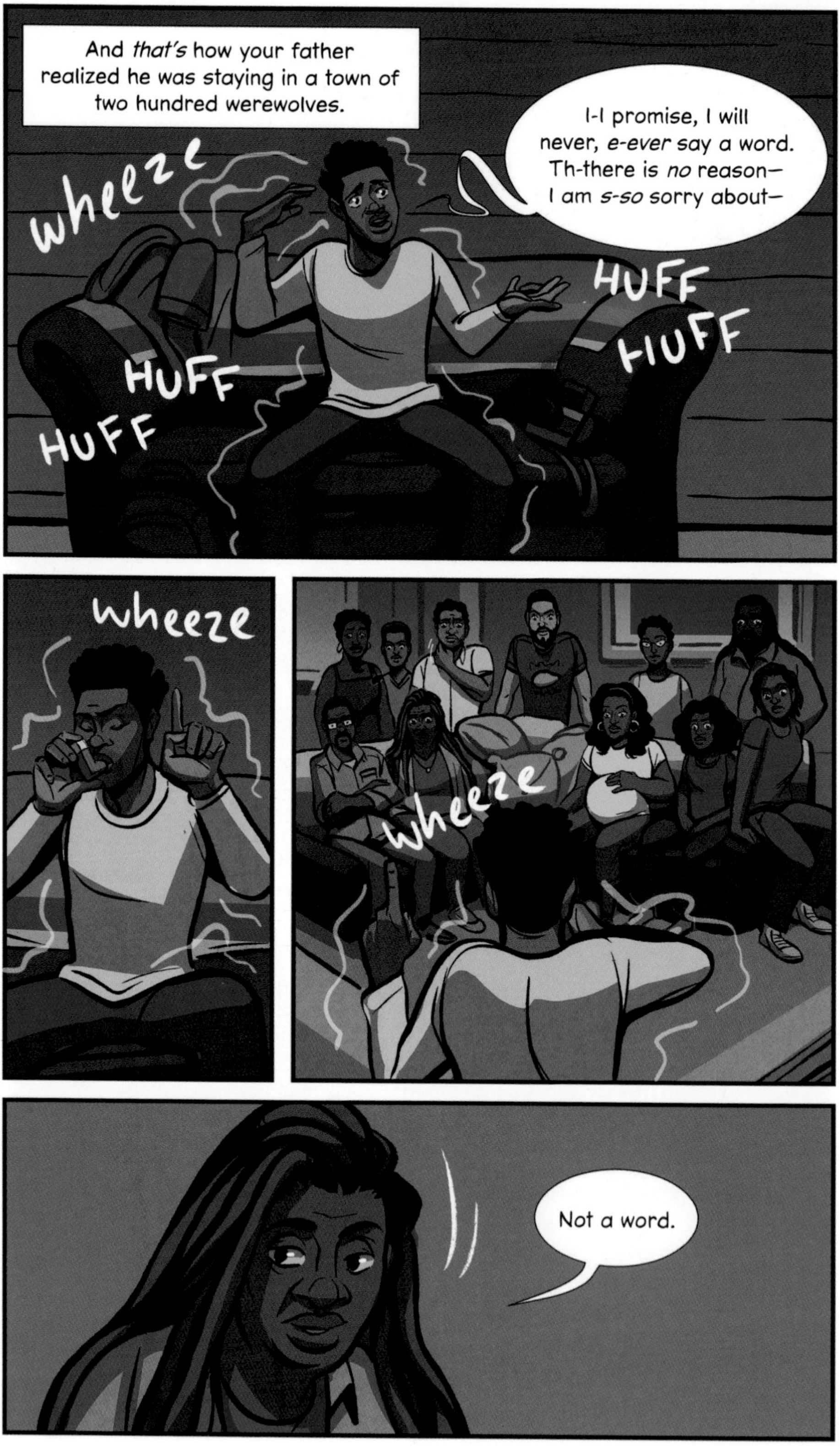
And *that's* how your father realized he was staying in a town of two hundred werewolves.
wheeze
I-I promise, I will never, *e-ever* say a word. Th-there is *no* reason— I am *s-so* sorry about—
HUFF
HUFF
HUFF
HUFF
wheeze
wheeze
Not a word.

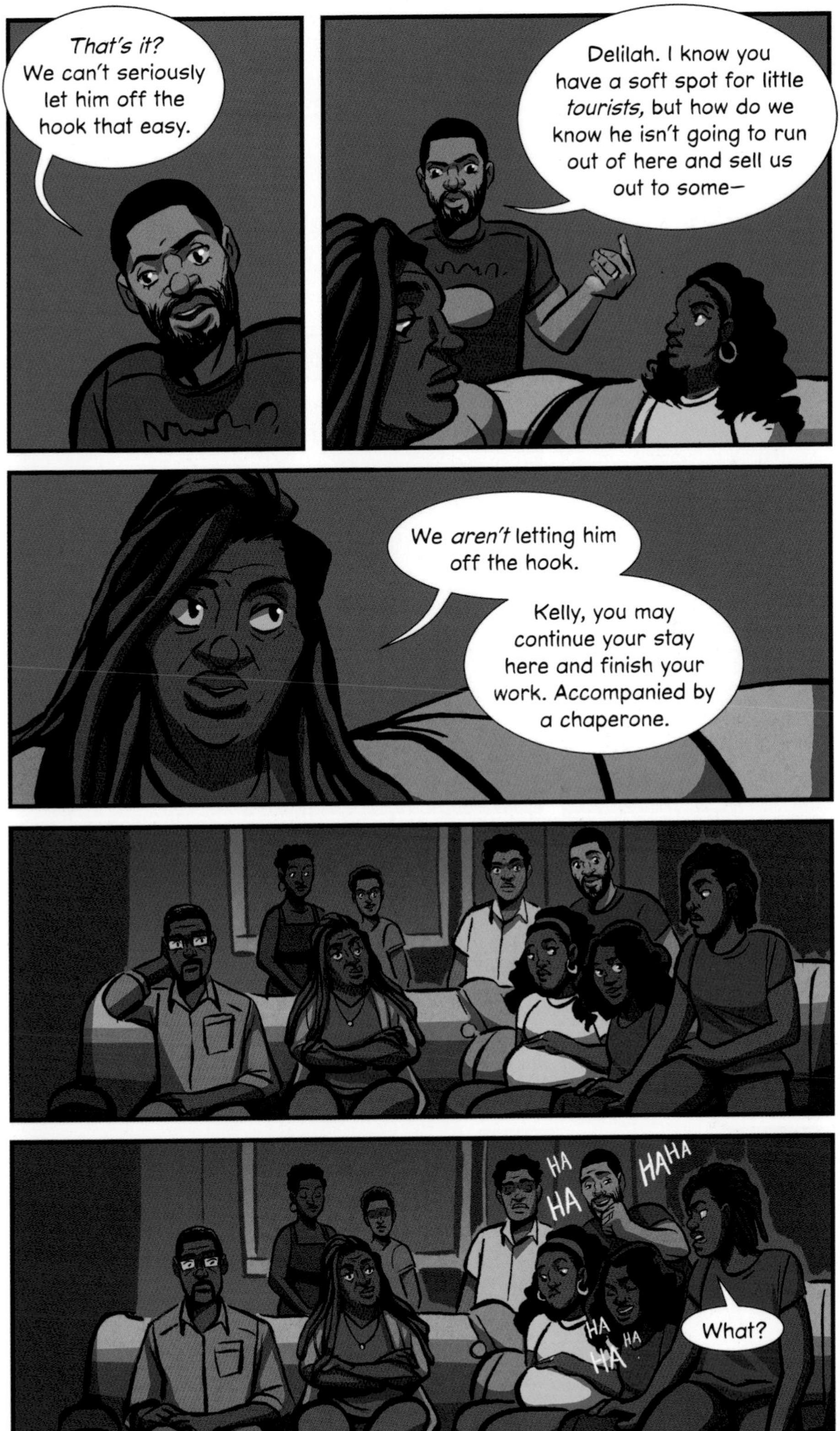
That's it? We can't seriously let him off the hook that easy.
Delilah. I know you have a soft spot for little tourists, but how do we know he isn't going to run out of here and sell us out to some—
We aren't letting him off the hook.
Kelly, you may continue your stay here and finish your work. Accompanied by a chaperone.
HA HA
HAHA
HA HA HA
What?

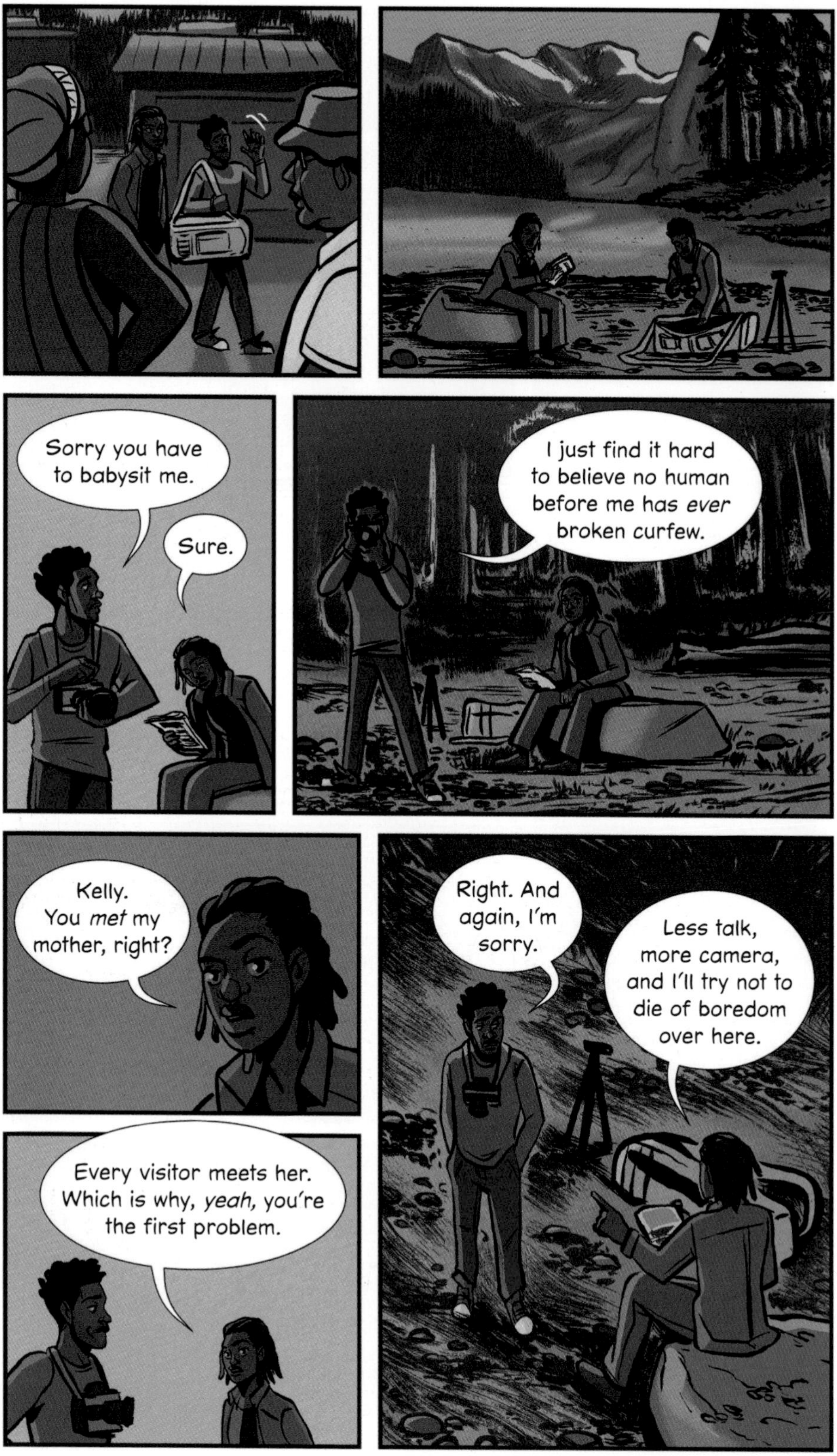
Sorry you have to babysit me.
Sure.
I just find it hard to believe no human before me has *ever* broken curfew.
Kelly. You *met* my mother, right?
Every visitor meets her. Which is why, *yeah,* you're the first problem.
Right. And again, I'm sorry.
Less talk, more camera, and I'll try not to die of boredom over here.

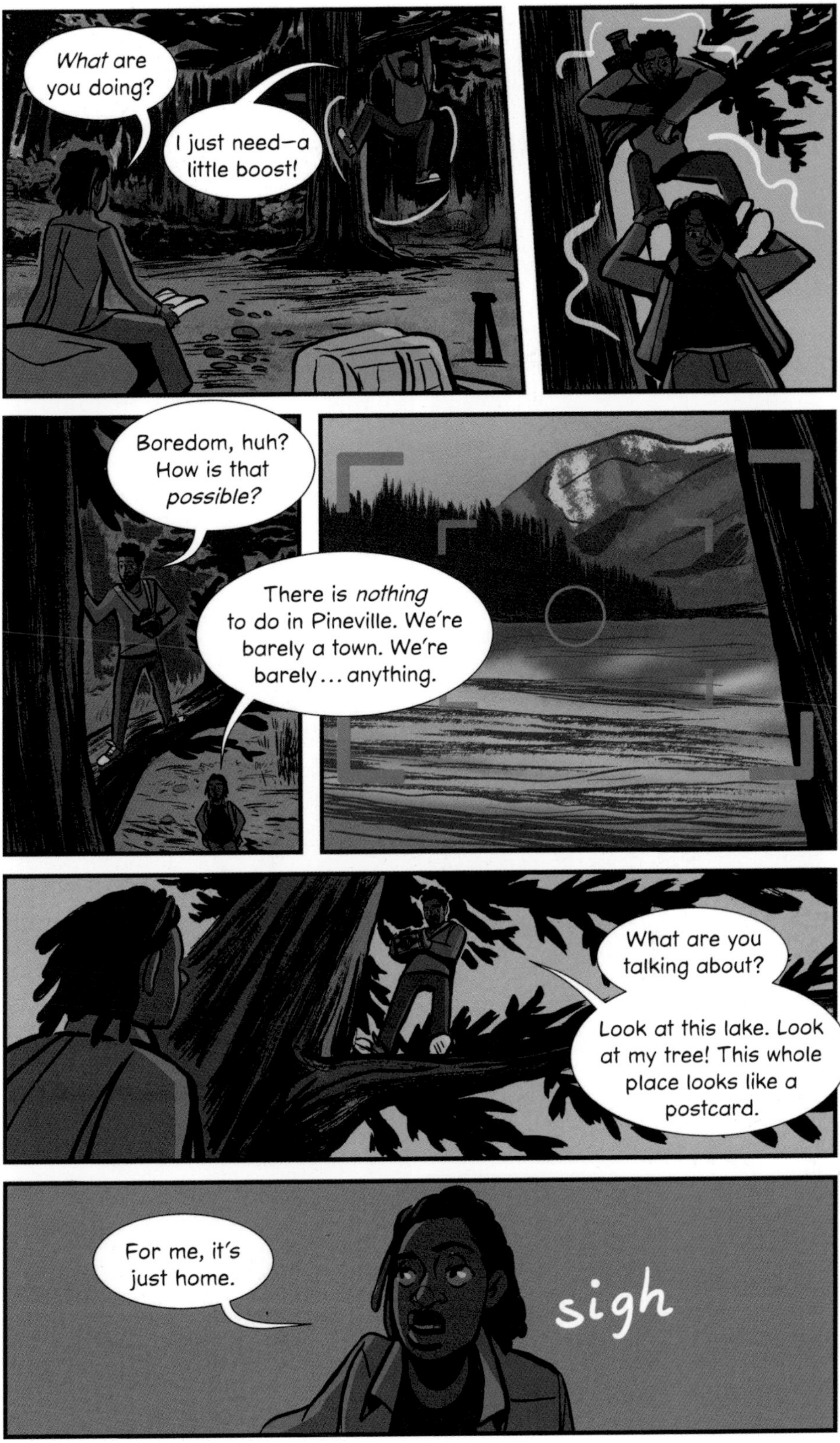
What are you doing?
I just need—a little boost!
Boredom, huh? How is that possible?
There is nothing to do in Pineville. We're barely a town. We're barely... anything.
What are you talking about?
Look at this lake. Look at my tree! This whole place looks like a postcard.
For me, it's just home.
sigh

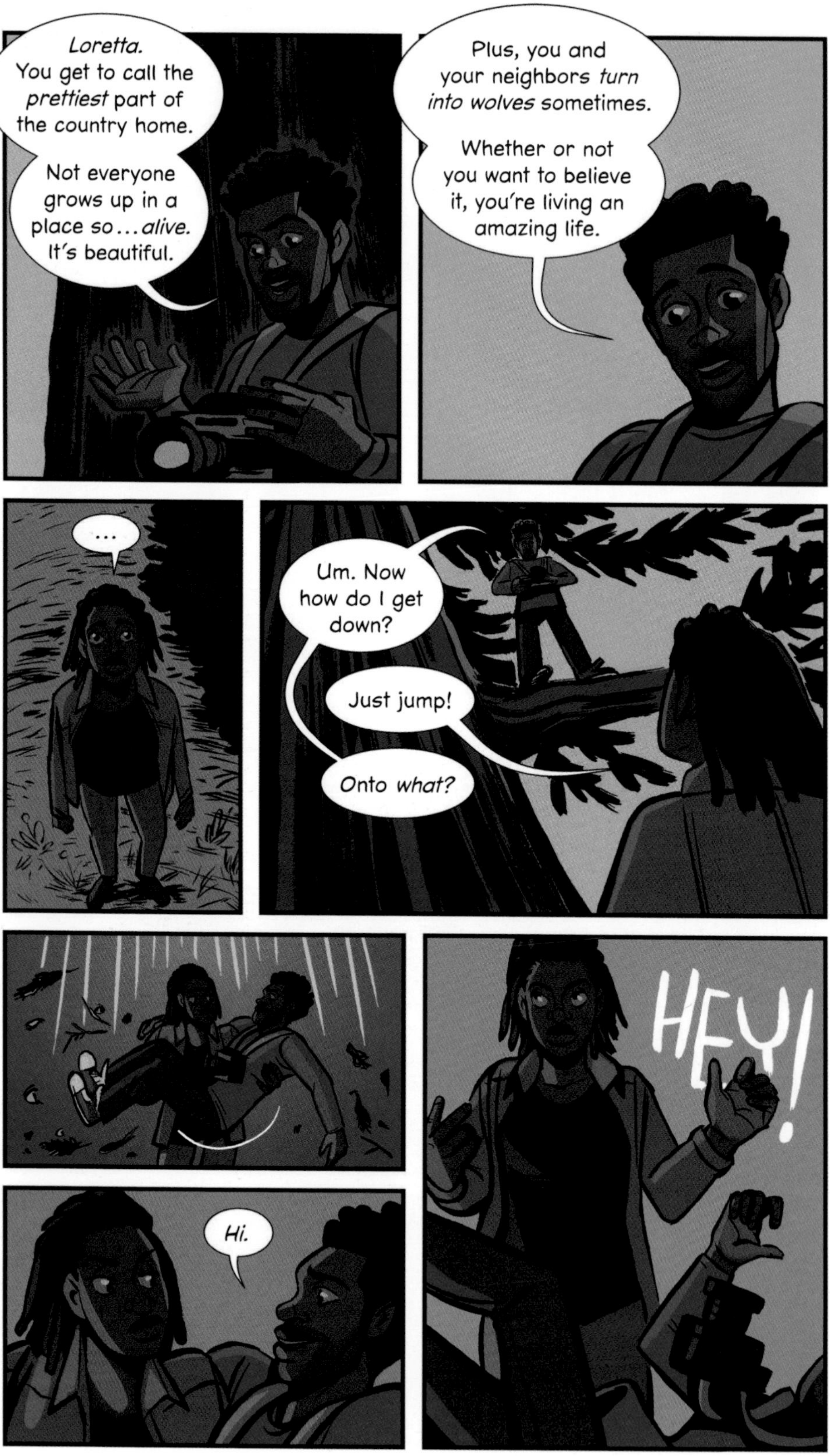
Loretta. You get to call the *prettiest* part of the country home.
Not everyone grows up in a place so... *alive.* It's beautiful.
Plus, you and your neighbors *turn into wolves* sometimes.
Whether or not you want to believe it, you're living an amazing life.
...
Um. Now how do I get down?
Just jump!
Onto *what?*
HEY!
Hi.

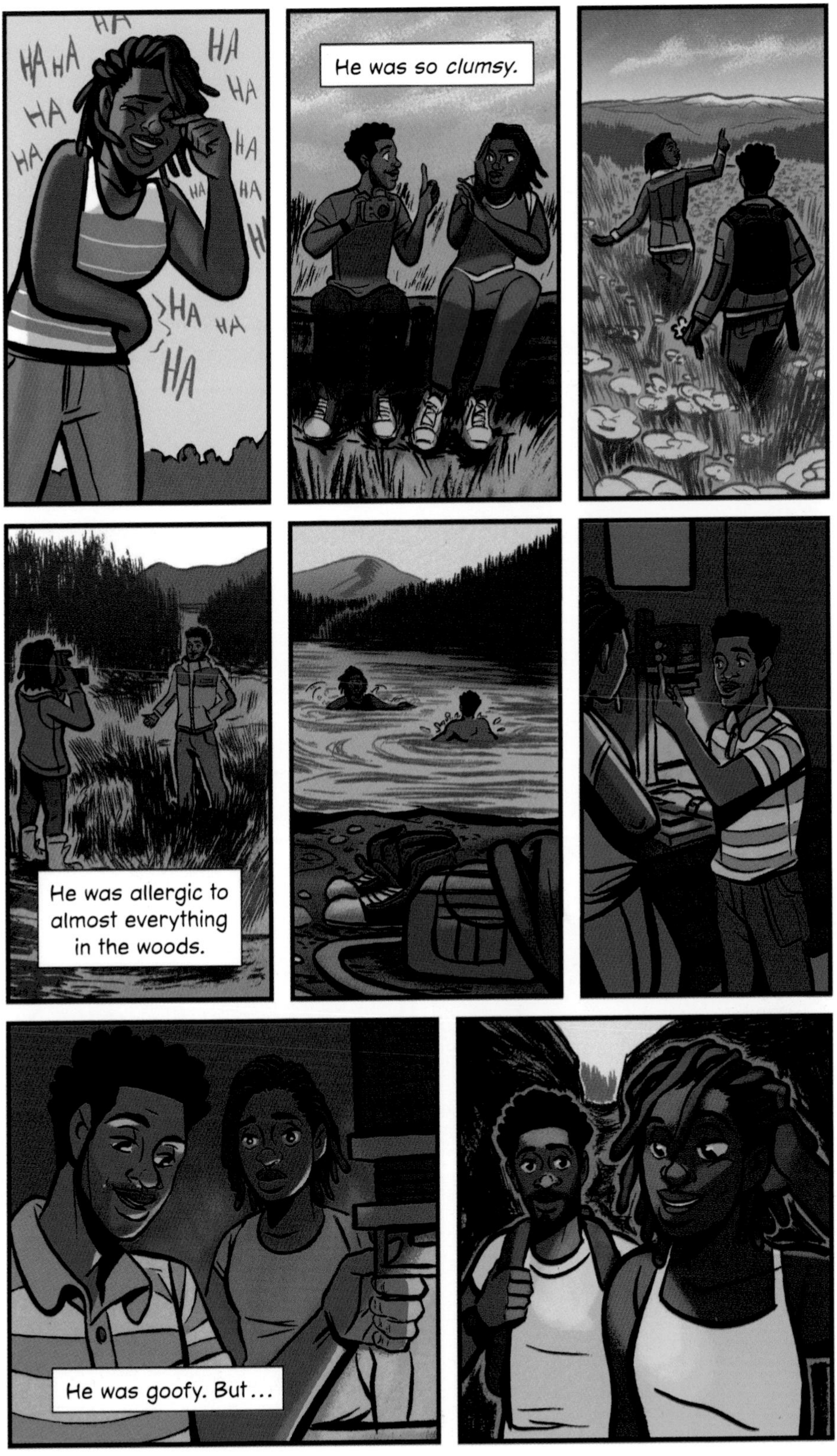
HA HA HA HA HA HA HA HA HA HA HA
HA HA HA
He was so *clumsy.*
He was allergic to almost everything in the woods.
He was goofy. But…

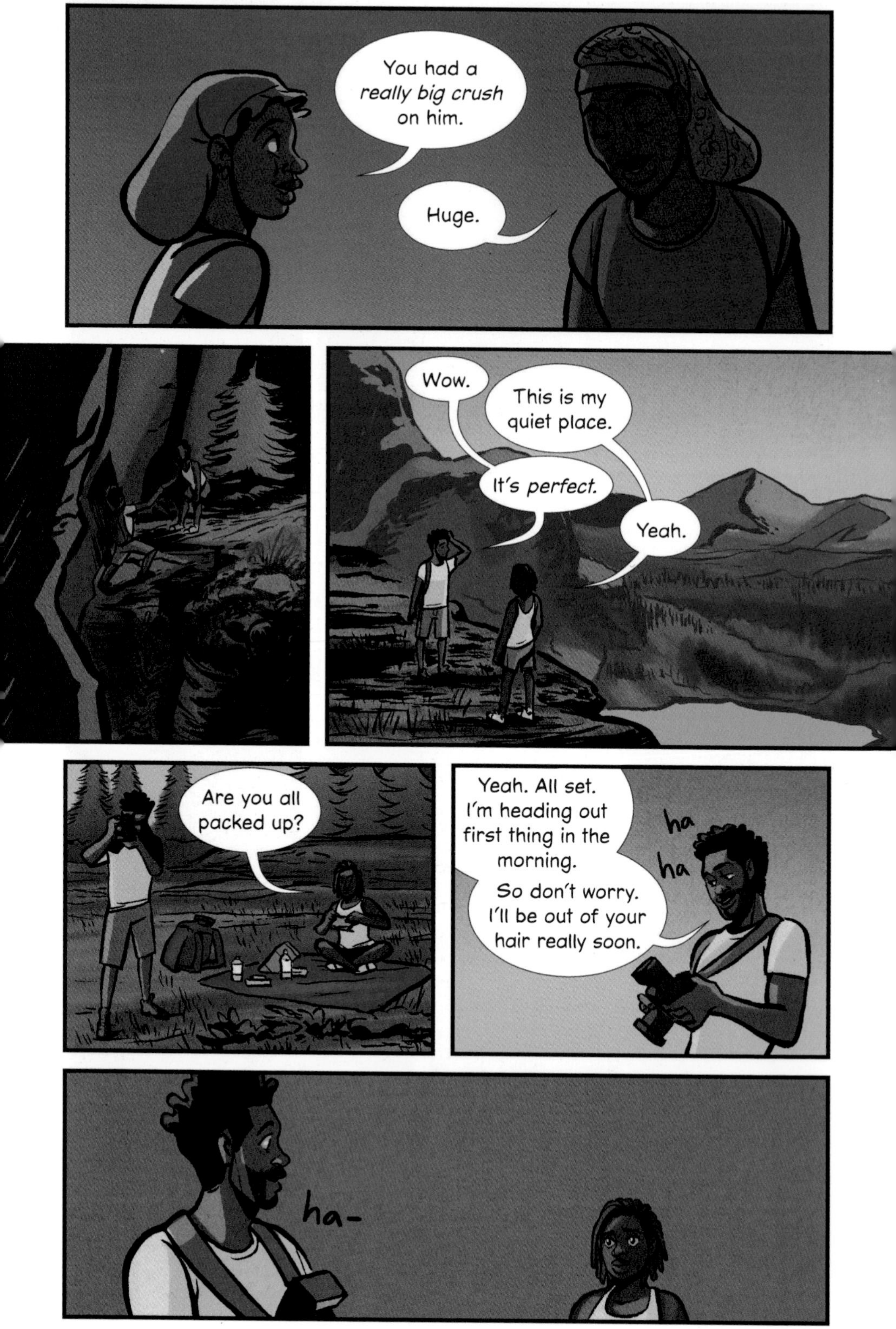
You had a *really big crush* on him.
Huge.
Wow.
This is my quiet place.
It's *perfect.*
Yeah.
Are you all packed up?
Yeah. All set. I'm heading out first thing in the morning.
So don't worry. I'll be out of your hair really soon.
ha
ha
ha-

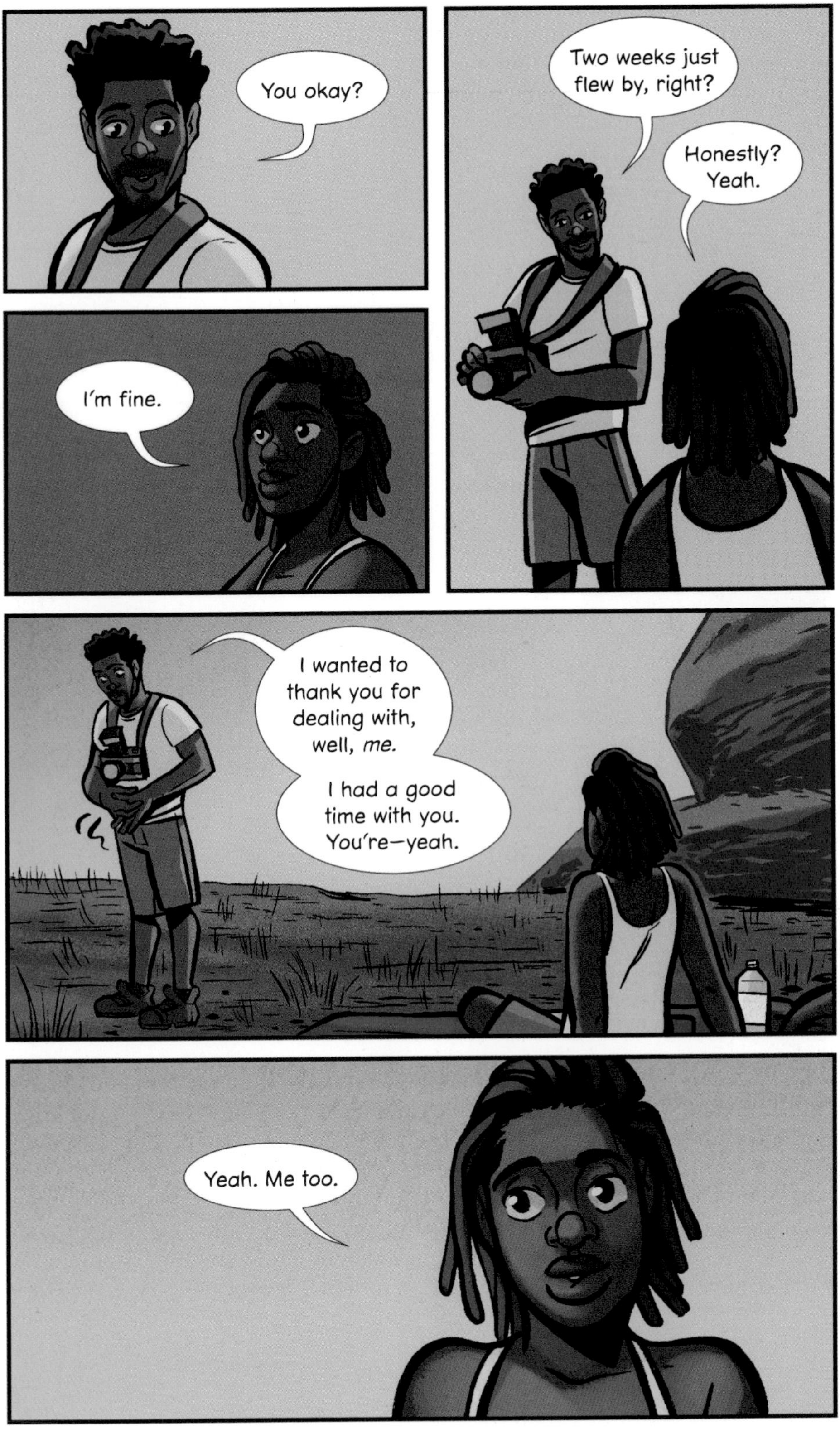
You okay?
Two weeks just flew by, right?
Honestly? Yeah.
I'm fine.
I wanted to thank you for dealing with, well, *me.*
I had a good time with you. You're—yeah.
Yeah. Me too.

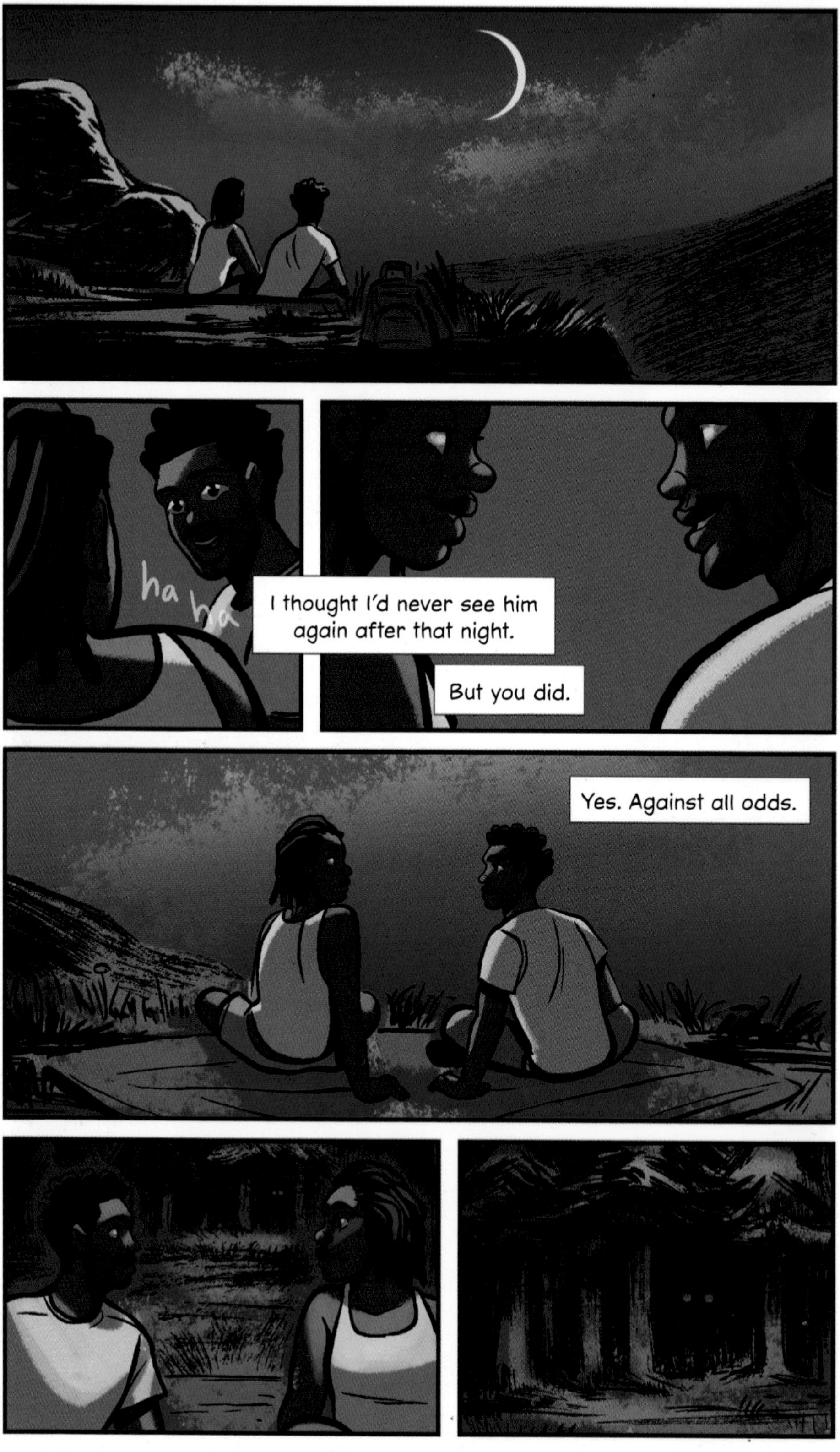
ha ha
I thought I'd never see him again after that night.
But you did.
Yes. Against all odds.

CHAPTER THREE

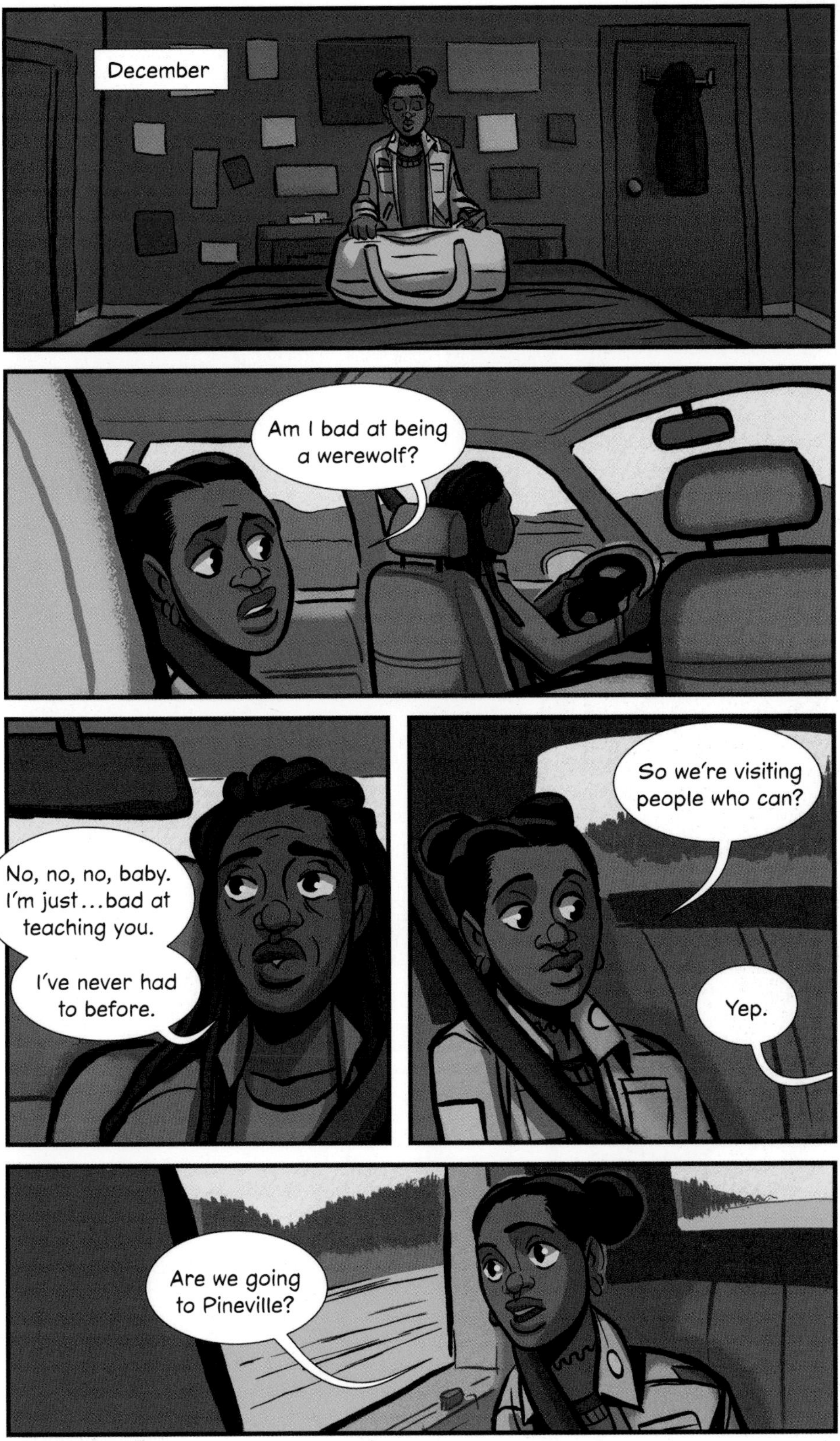
December
Am I bad at being a werewolf?
No, no, no, baby. I'm just...bad at teaching you.
I've never had to before.
So we're visiting people who can?
Yep.
Are we going to Pineville?

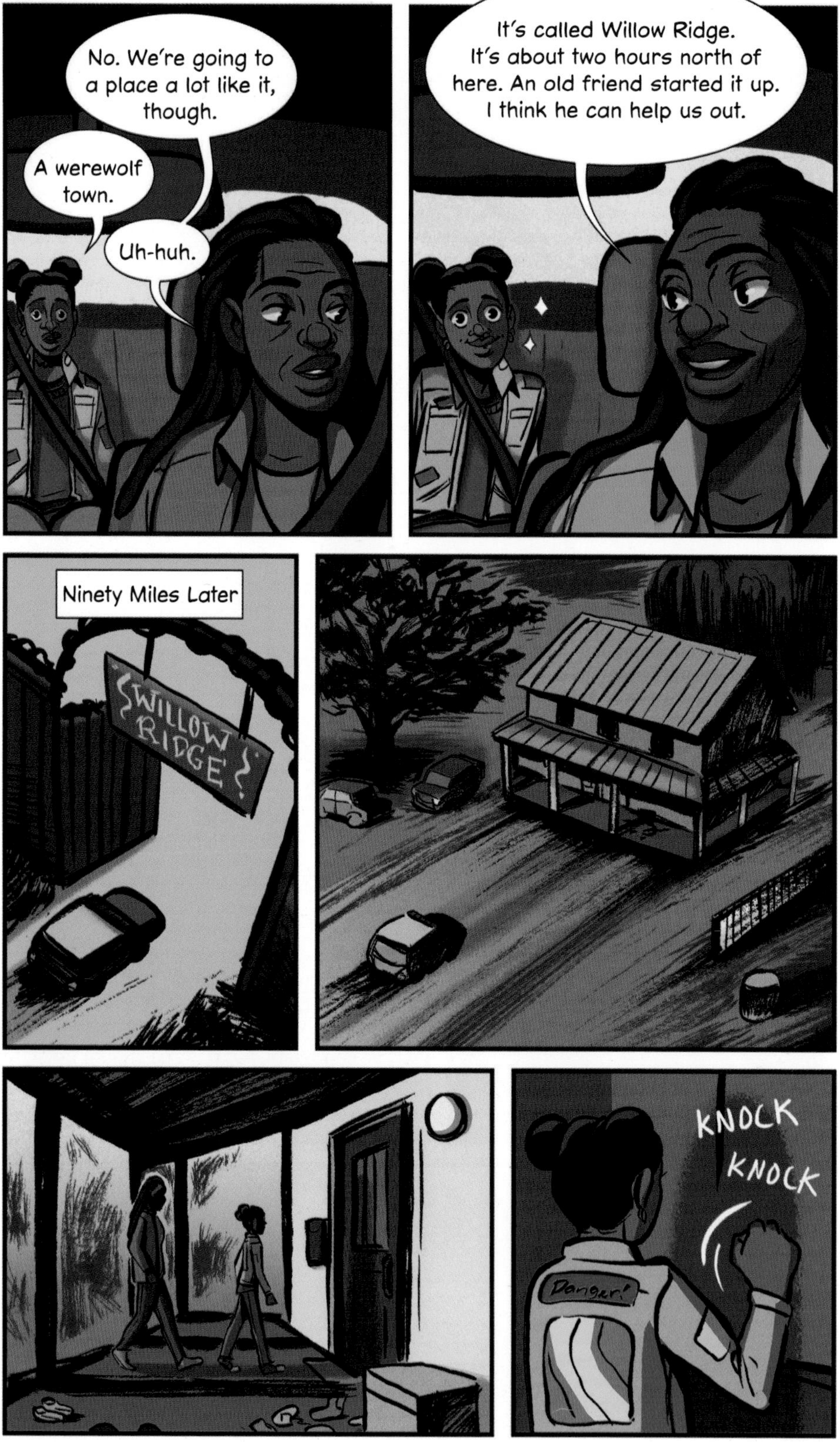

No. We're going to a place a lot like it, though.
A werewolf town.
Uh-huh.
It's called Willow Ridge. It's about two hours north of here. An old friend started it up. I think he can help us out.
Ninety Miles Later
WILLOW RIDGE
Danger!
KNOCK
KNOCK

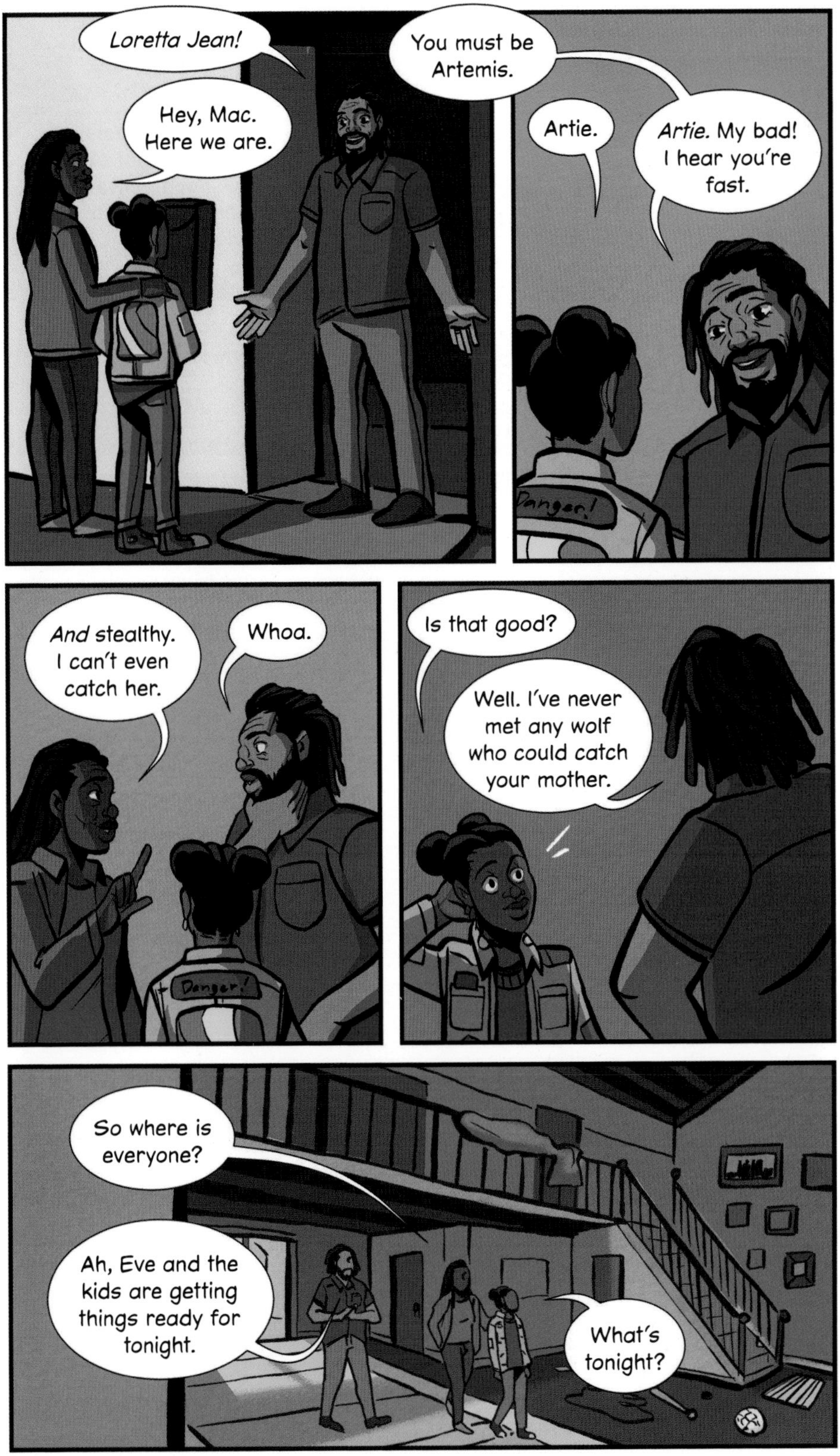
Loretta Jean!
Hey, Mac. Here we are.
You must be Artemis.
Artie.
Artie. My bad! I hear you're fast.
Danger!
And stealthy. I can't even catch her.
Whoa.
Danger!
Is that good?
Well. I've never met any wolf who could catch your mother.
So where is everyone?
Ah, Eve and the kids are getting things ready for tonight.
What's tonight?

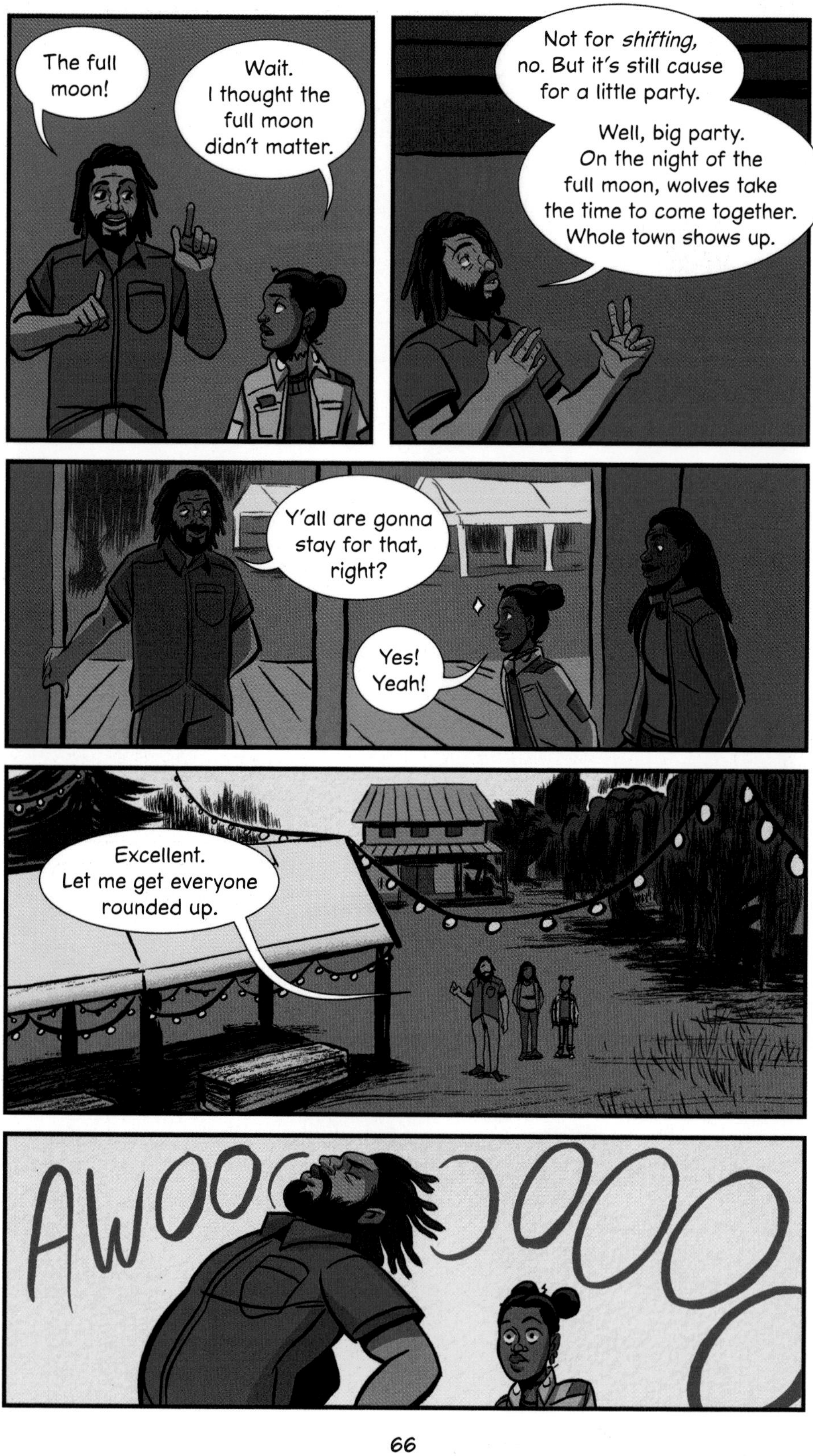

The full moon!
Wait. I thought the full moon didn't matter.
Not for *shifting*, no. But it's still cause for a little party.
Well, big party. On the night of the full moon, wolves take the time to come together. Whole town shows up.
Y'all are gonna stay for that, right?
Yes! Yeah!
Excellent. Let me get everyone rounded up.
AWOOOOOOOOOO

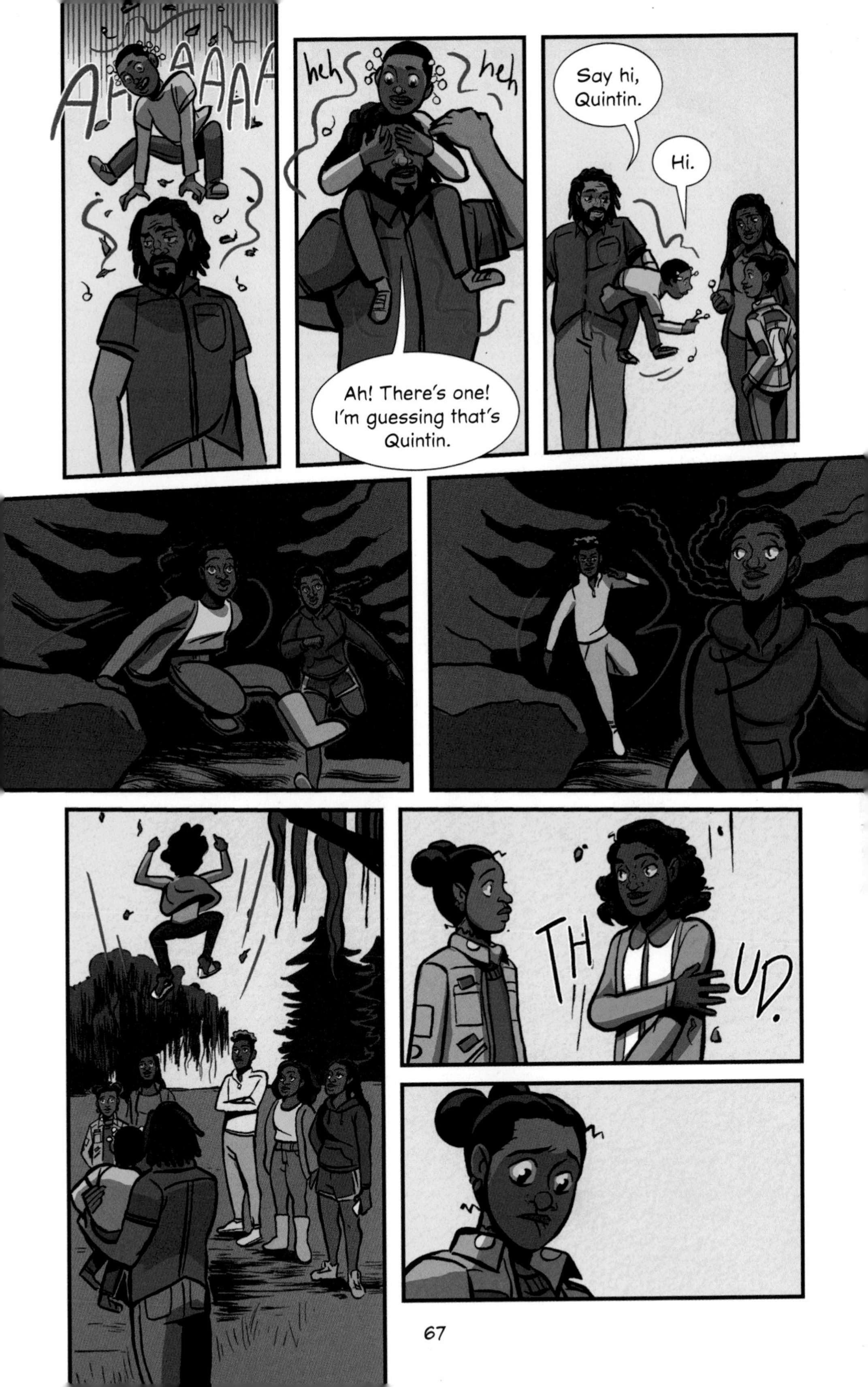
AHHAAAAA
heh heh
Ah! There's one! I'm guessing that's Quintin.
Say hi, Quintin.
Hi.
THUD.

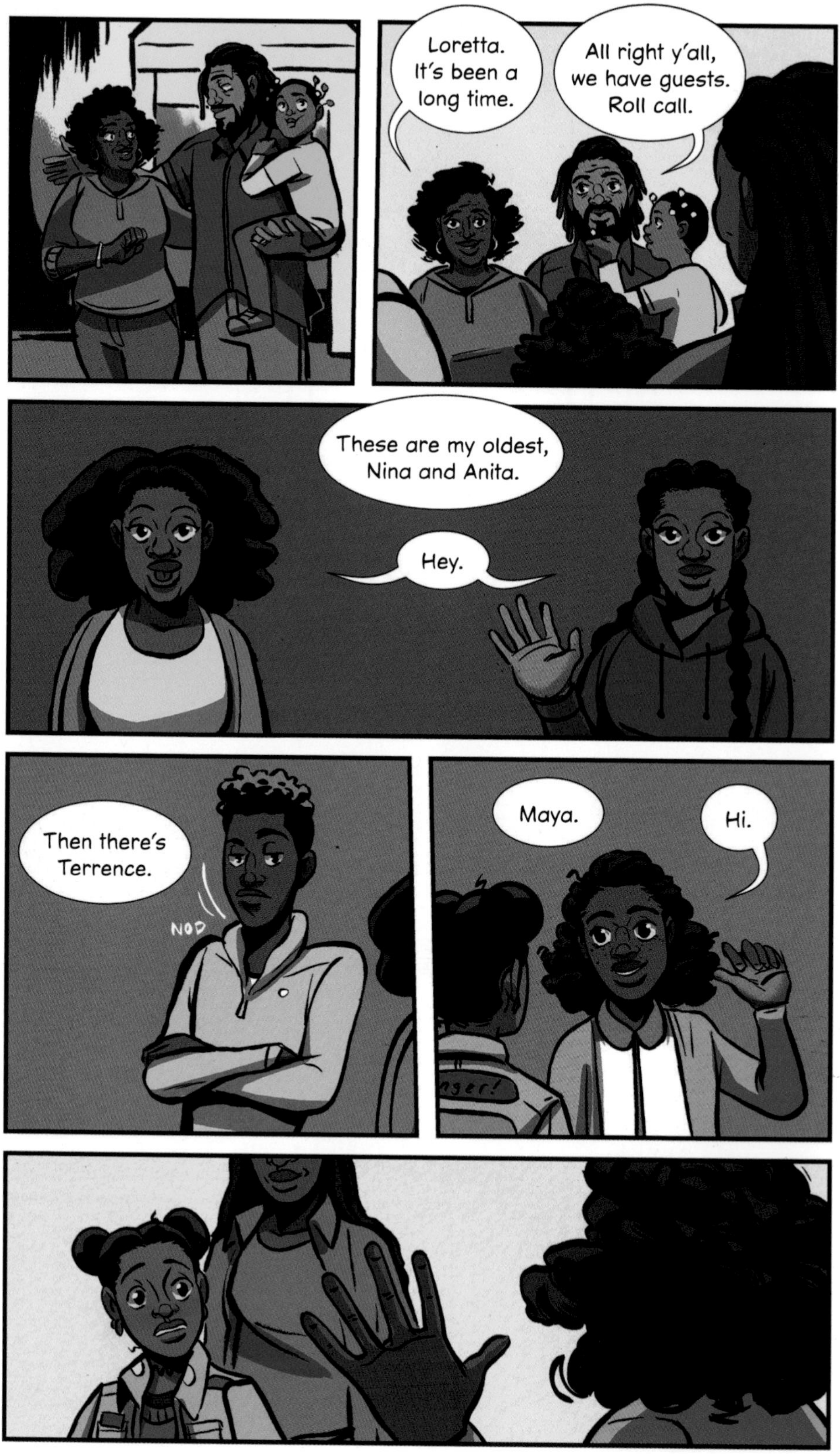
Loretta.
It's been a long time.
All right y'all, we have guests. Roll call.
These are my oldest, Nina and Anita.
Hey.
Then there's Terrence.
NOD
Maya.
Hi.

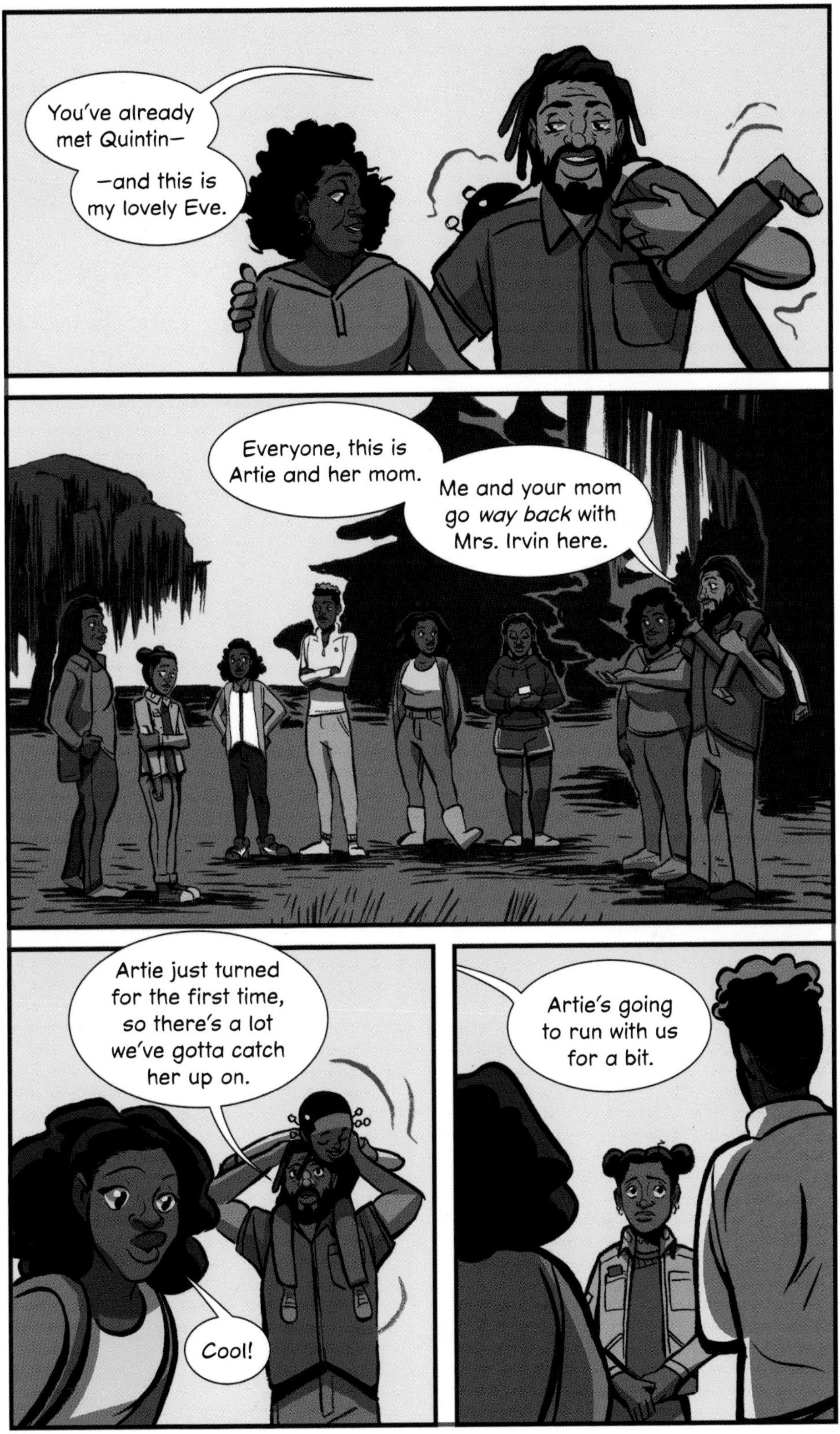
You've already met Quintin—
—and this is my lovely Eve.
Everyone, this is Artie and her mom.
Me and your mom go *way back* with Mrs. Irvin here.
Artie just turned for the first time, so there's a lot we've gotta catch her up on.
Cool!
Artie's going to run with us for a bit.

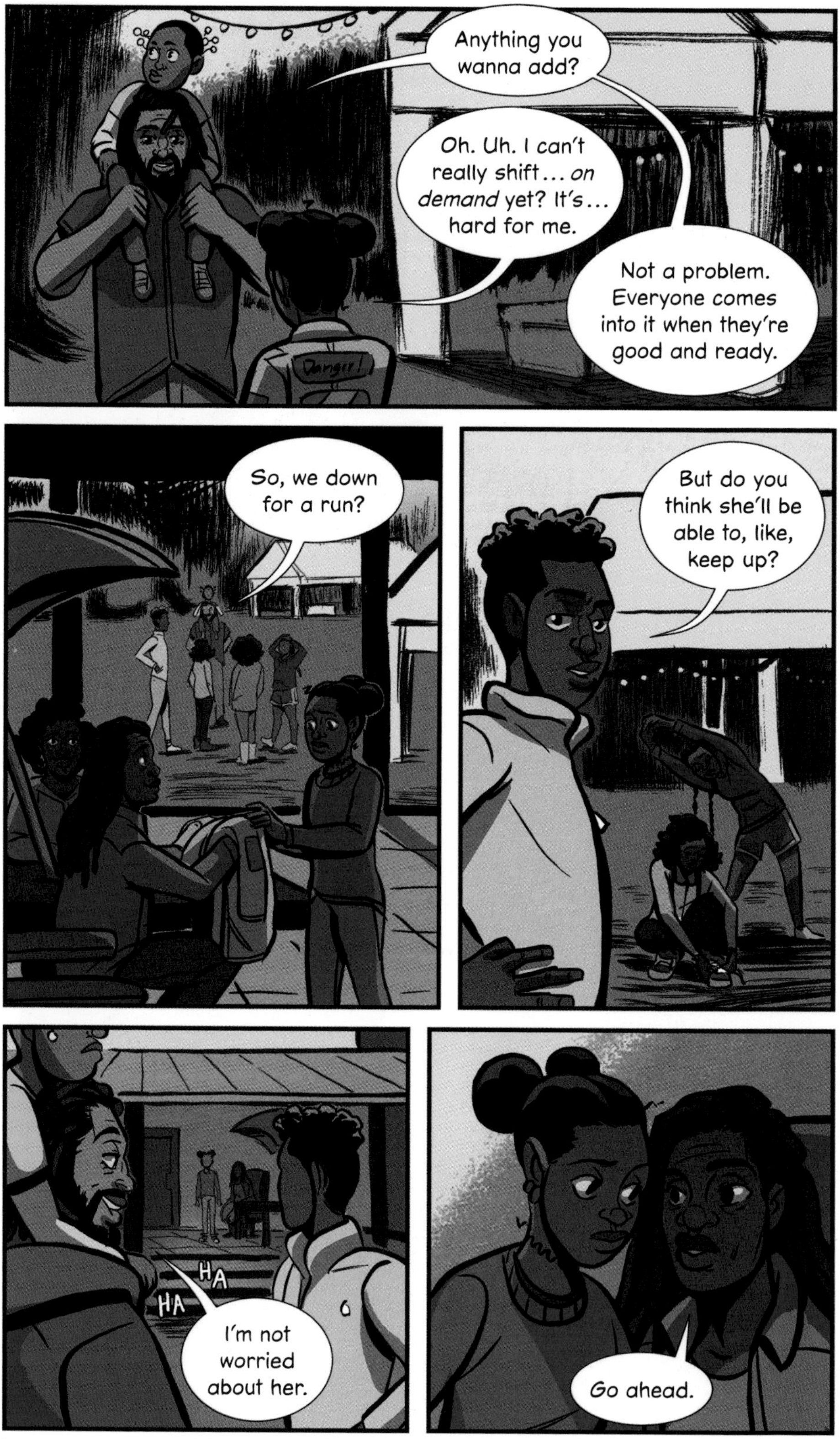
Anything you wanna add?
Oh. Uh. I can't really shift... *on demand* yet? It's... hard for me.
Not a problem. Everyone comes into it when they're good and ready.
Danger!
So, we down for a run?
But do you think she'll be able to, like, keep up?
HA HA
I'm not worried about her.
Go ahead.

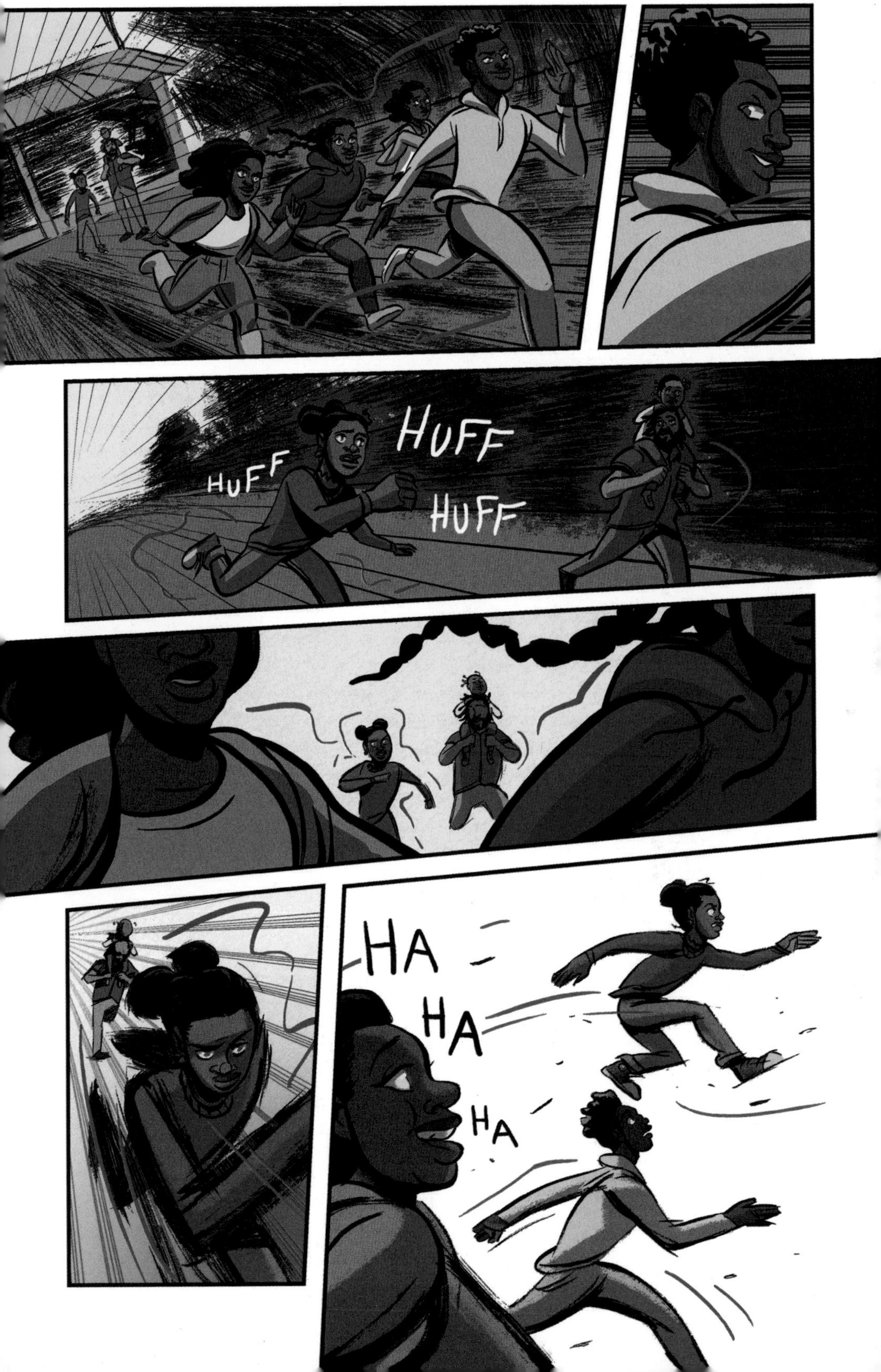
HUFF
HUFF
HUFF
HA
HA
HA

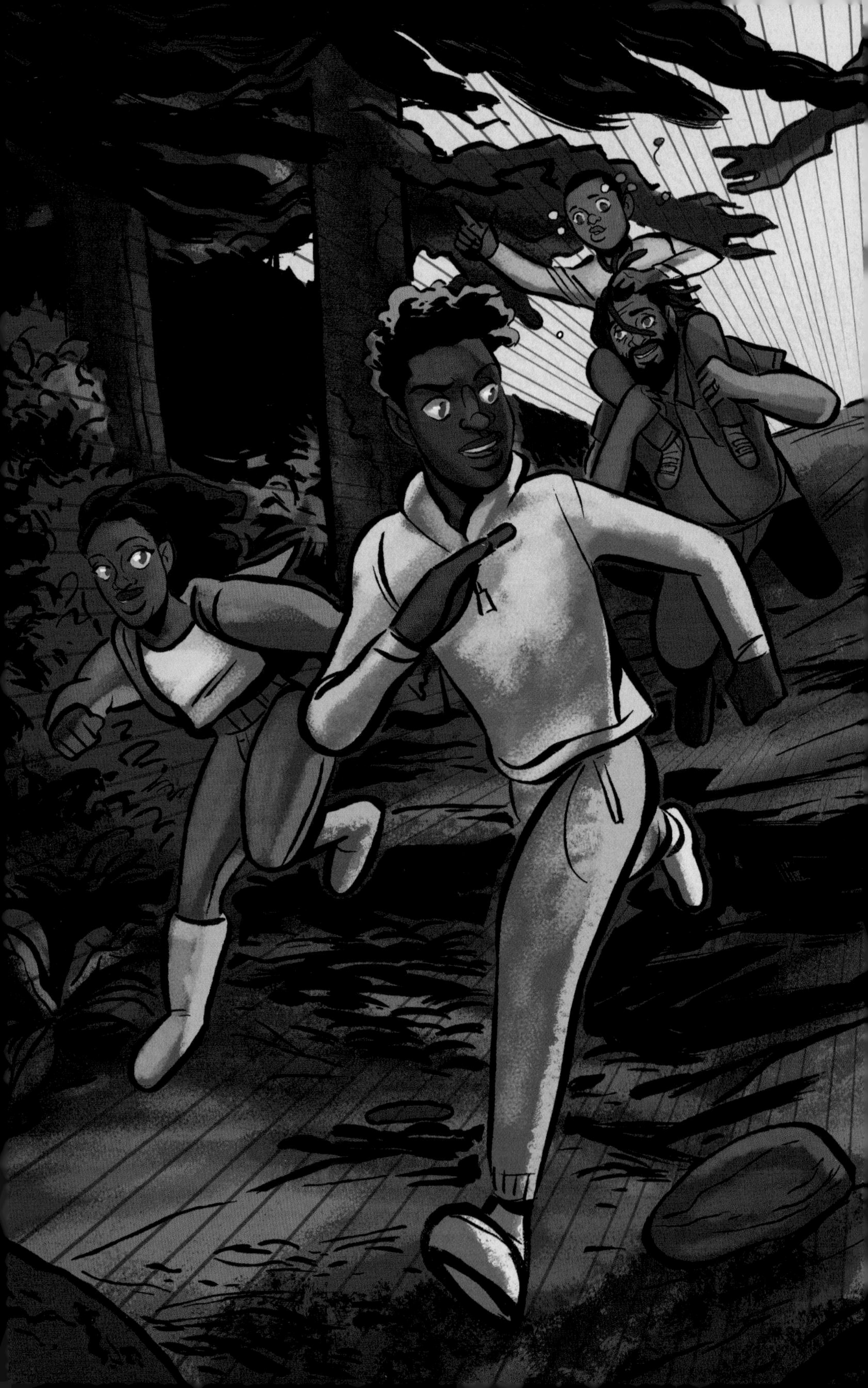

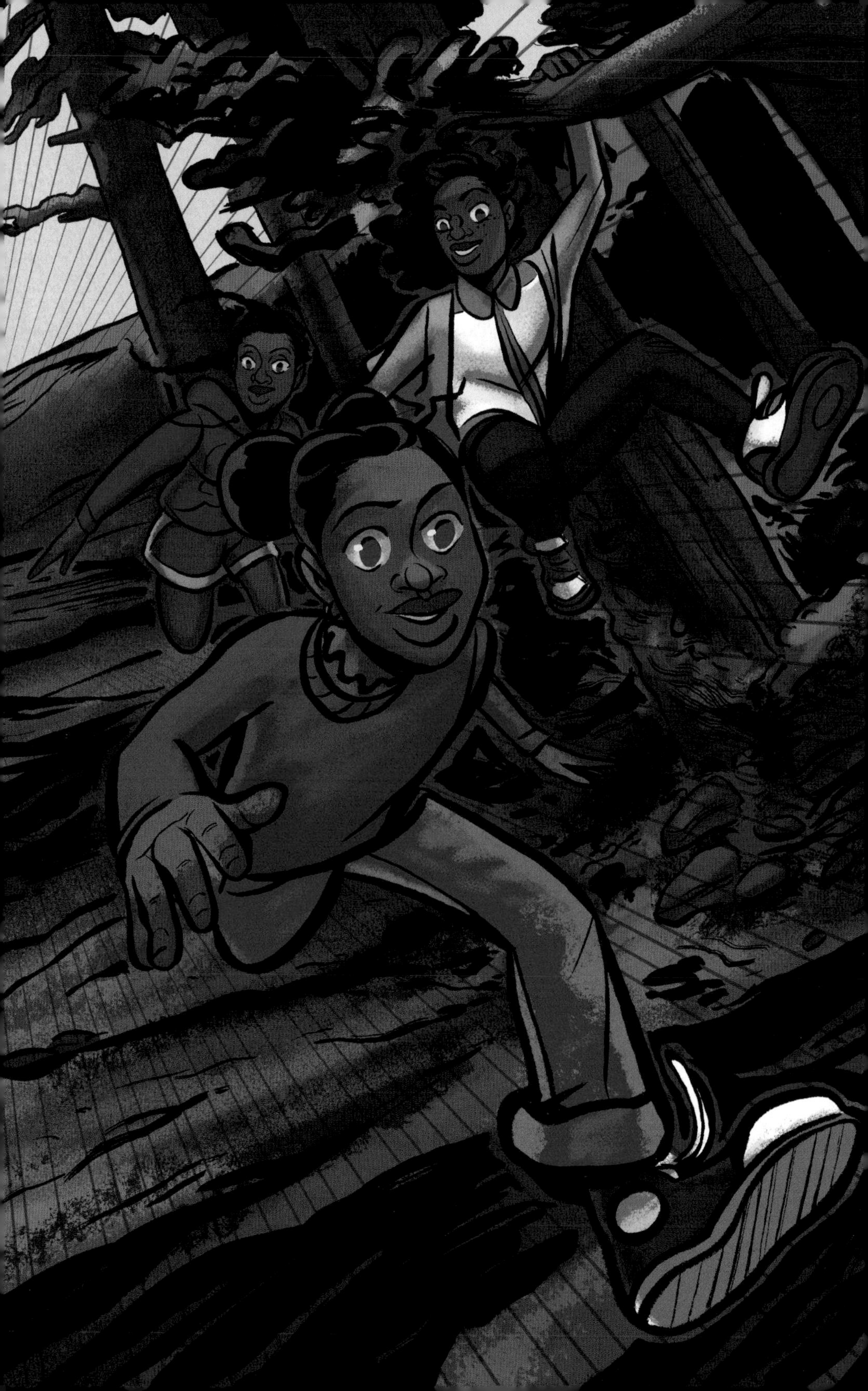

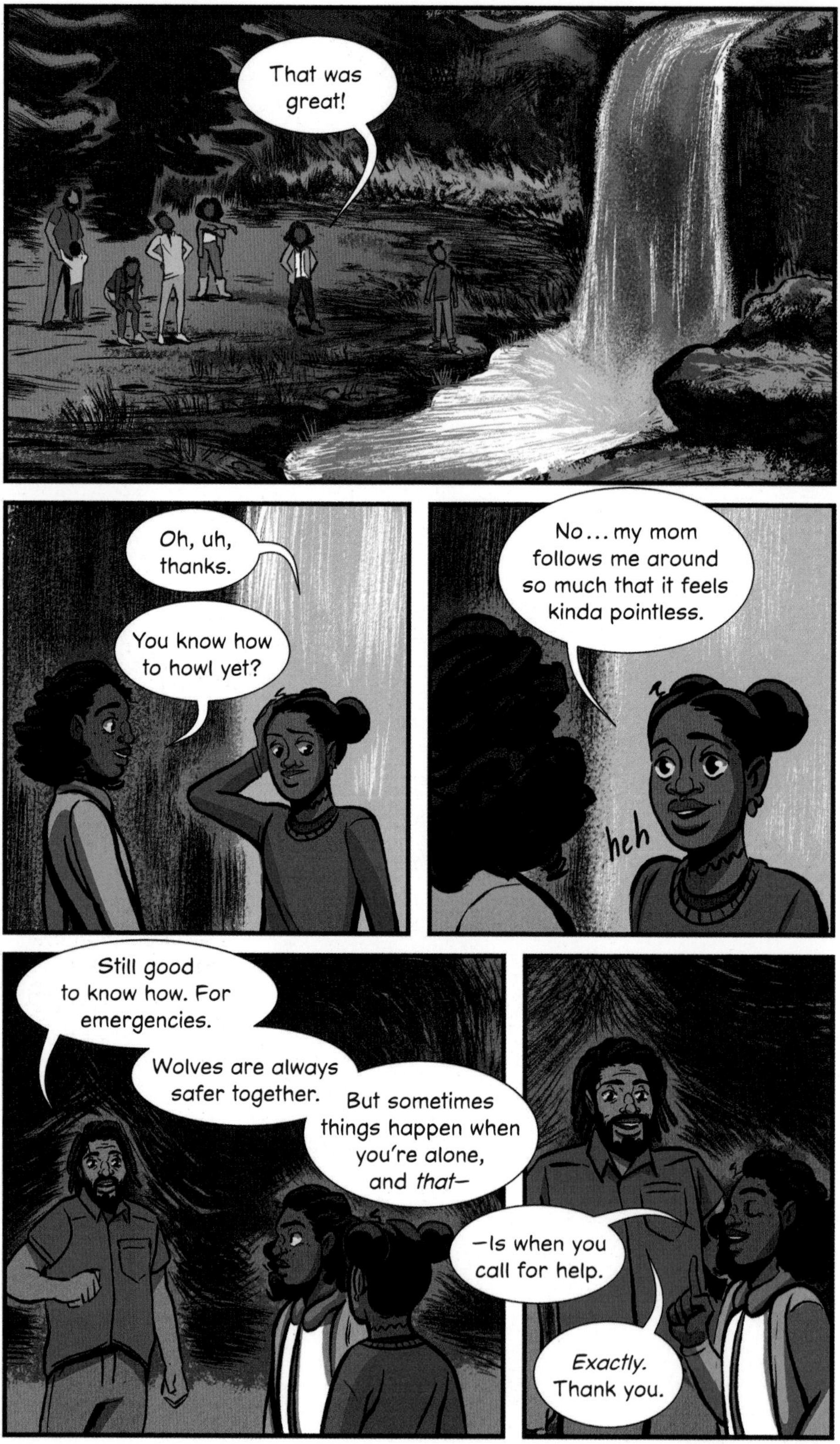
That was great!
Oh, uh, thanks.
You know how to howl yet?
No... my mom follows me around so much that it feels kinda pointless.
heh
Still good to know how. For emergencies.
Wolves are always safer together.
But sometimes things happen when you're alone, and *that*—
—Is when you call for help.
Exactly. Thank you.

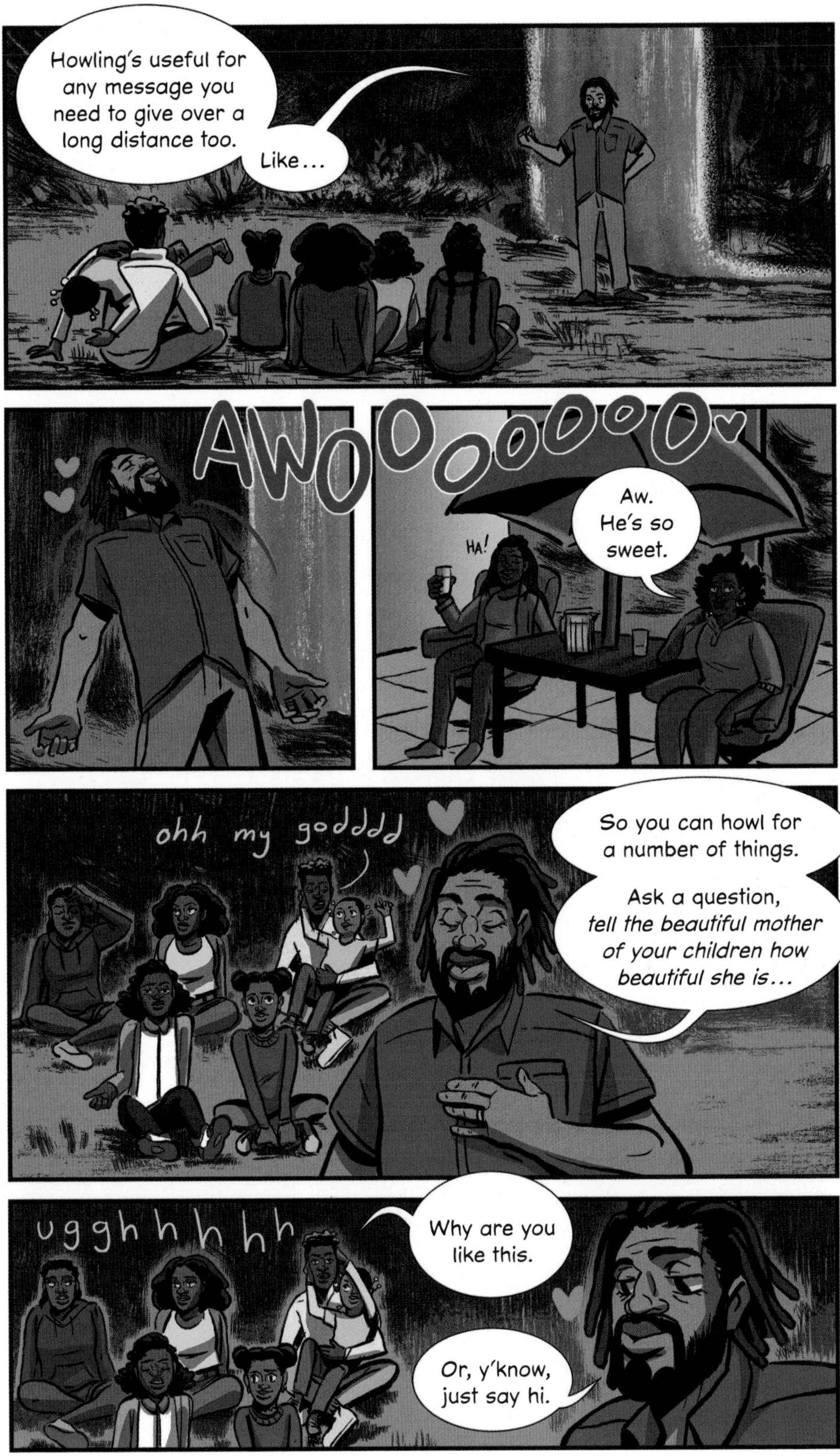
Howling's useful for any message you need to give over a long distance too.
Like...
AWOOOOOOO
HA!
Aw. He's so sweet.
ohh my goddddd
So you can howl for a number of things.
Ask a question, *tell the beautiful mother of your children how beautiful she is...*
ugghhhhh
Why are you like this.
Or, y'know, just say hi.

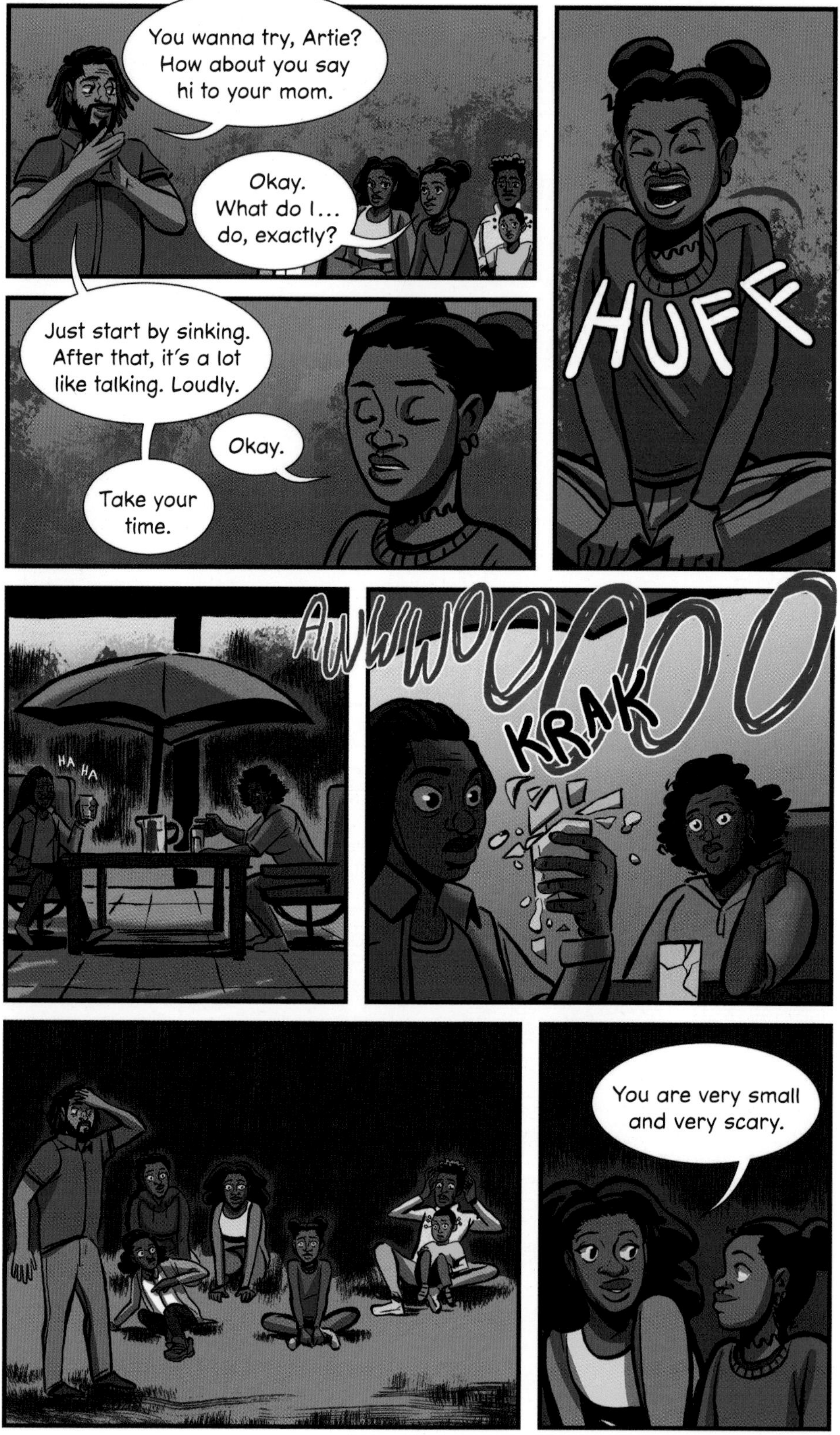
You wanna try, Artie? How about you say hi to your mom.
Okay. What do I... do, exactly?
Just start by sinking. After that, it's a lot like talking. Loudly.
Okay.
Take your time.
HUFF
HA HA
AWWWOOOOOO
KRAK
You are very small and very scary.

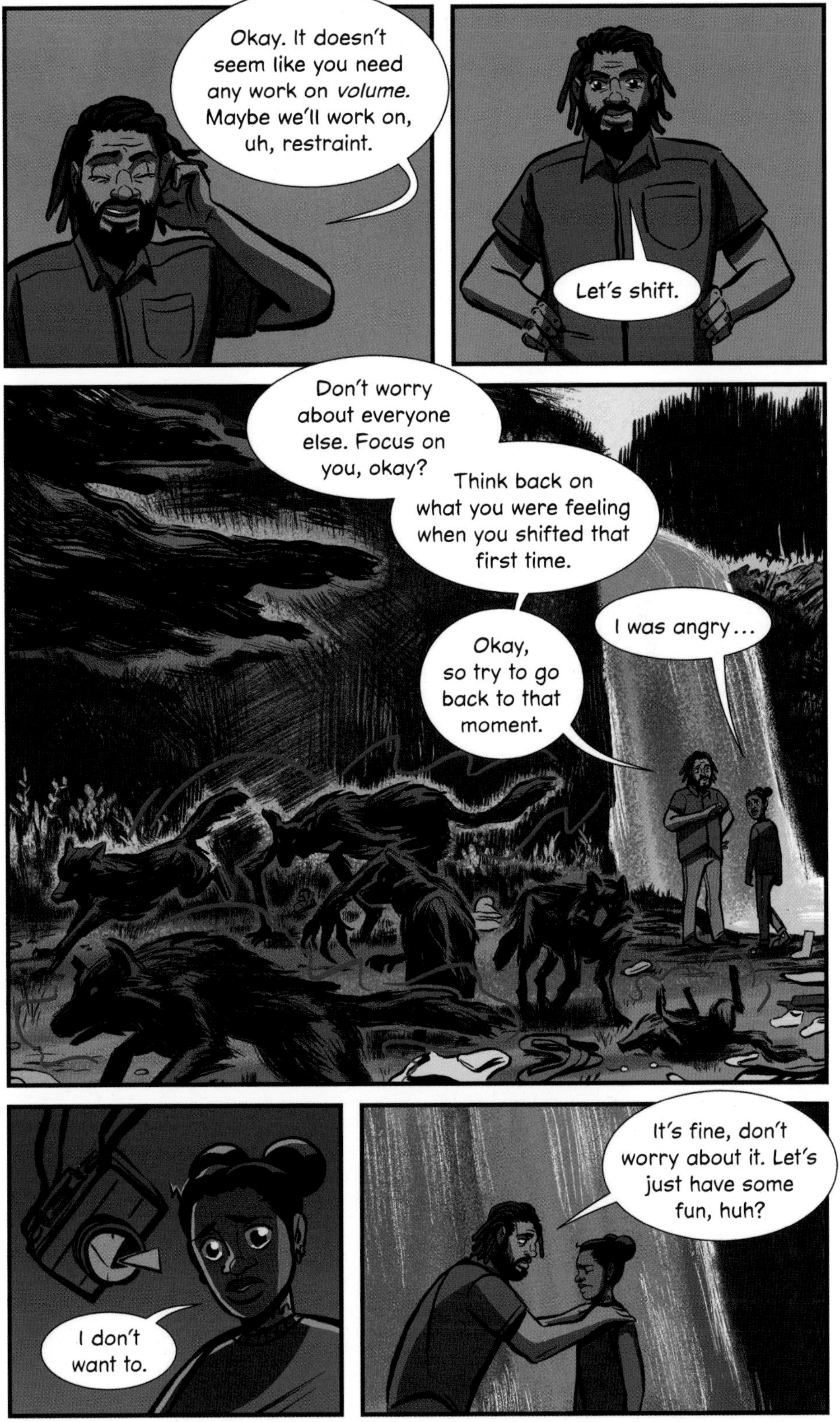
Okay. It doesn't seem like you need any work on *volume.* Maybe we'll work on, uh, restraint.
Let's shift.
Don't worry about everyone else. Focus on you, okay?
Think back on what you were feeling when you shifted that first time.
I was angry...
Okay, so try to go back to that moment.
I don't want to.
It's fine, don't worry about it. Let's just have some fun, huh?

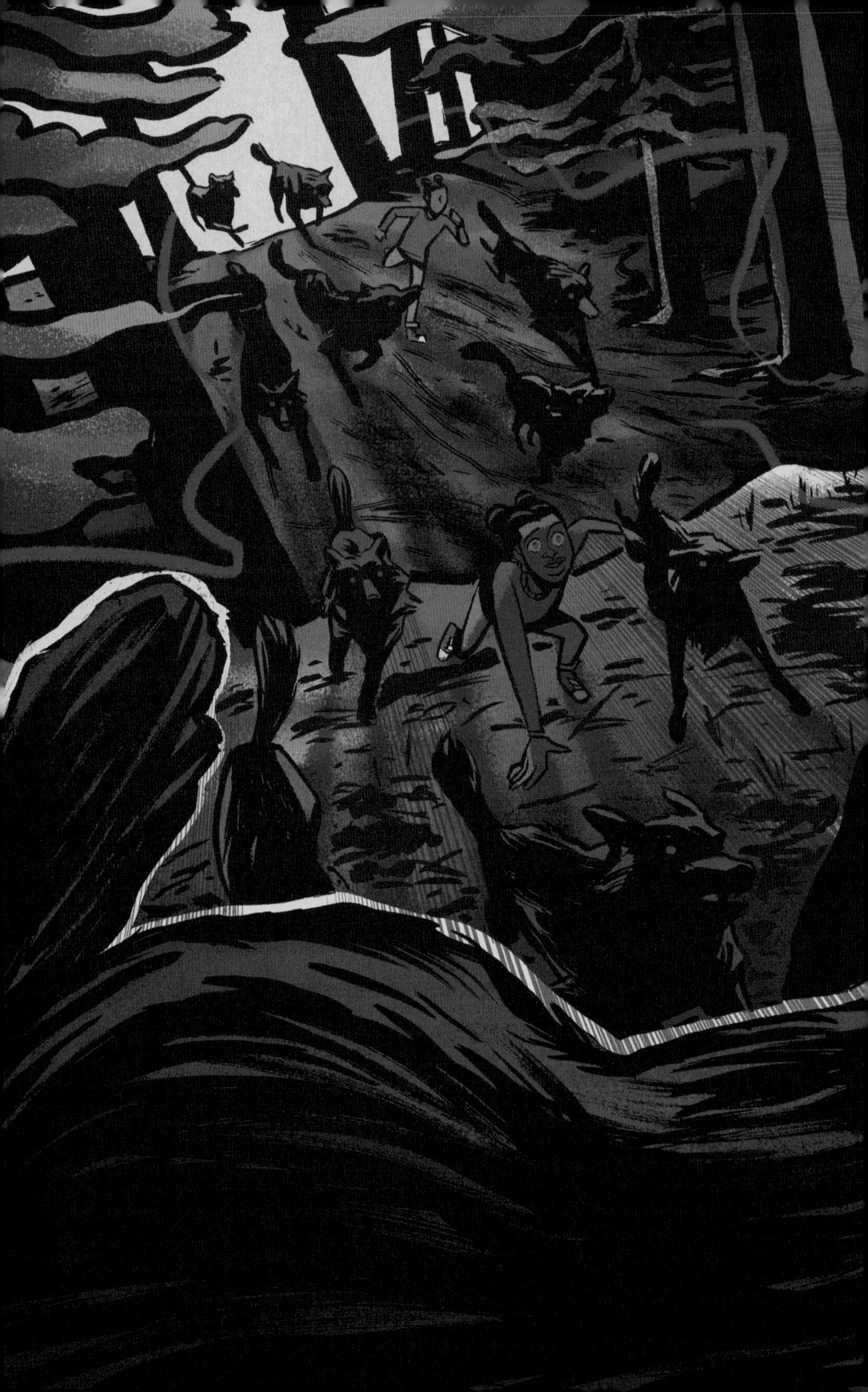

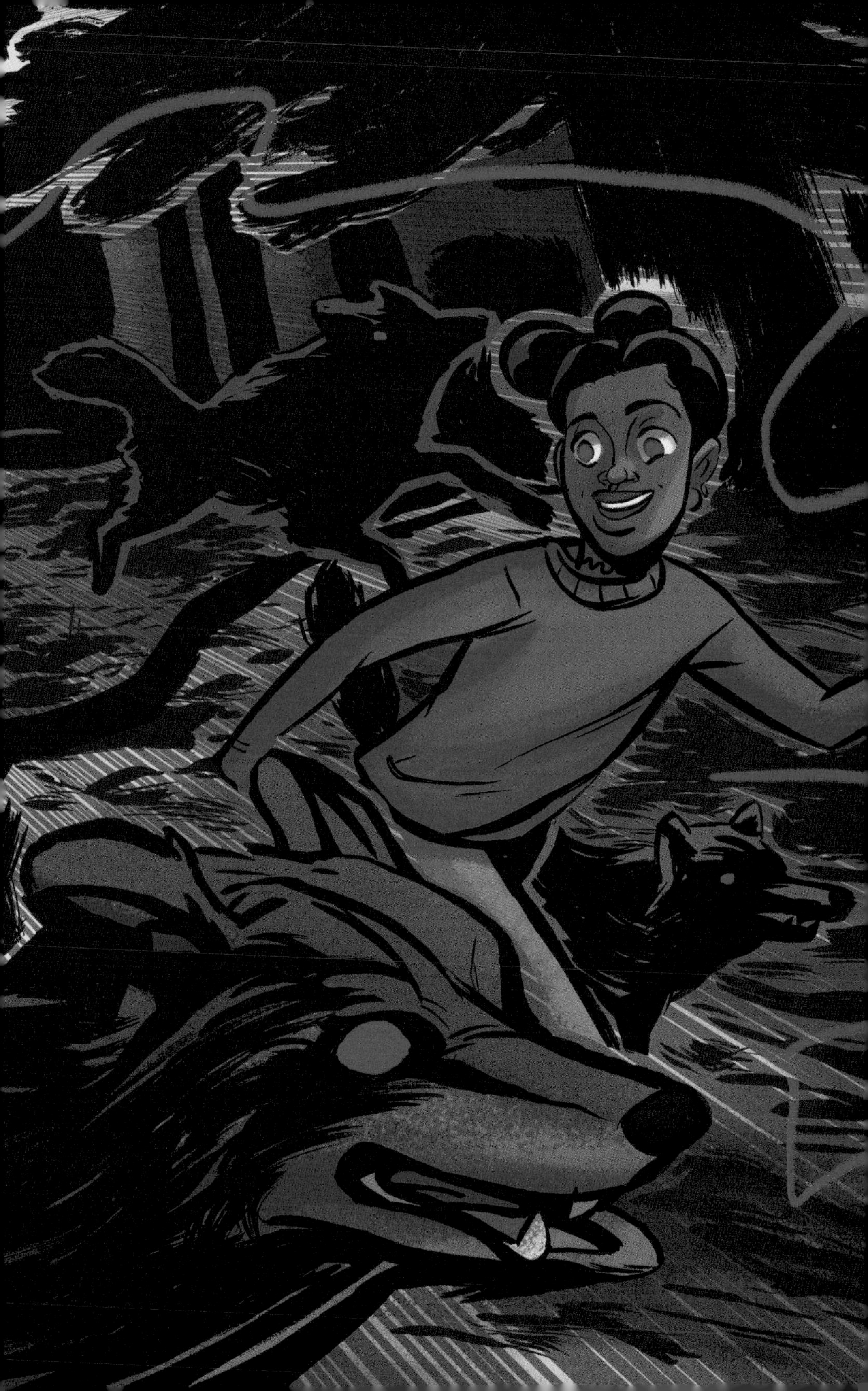

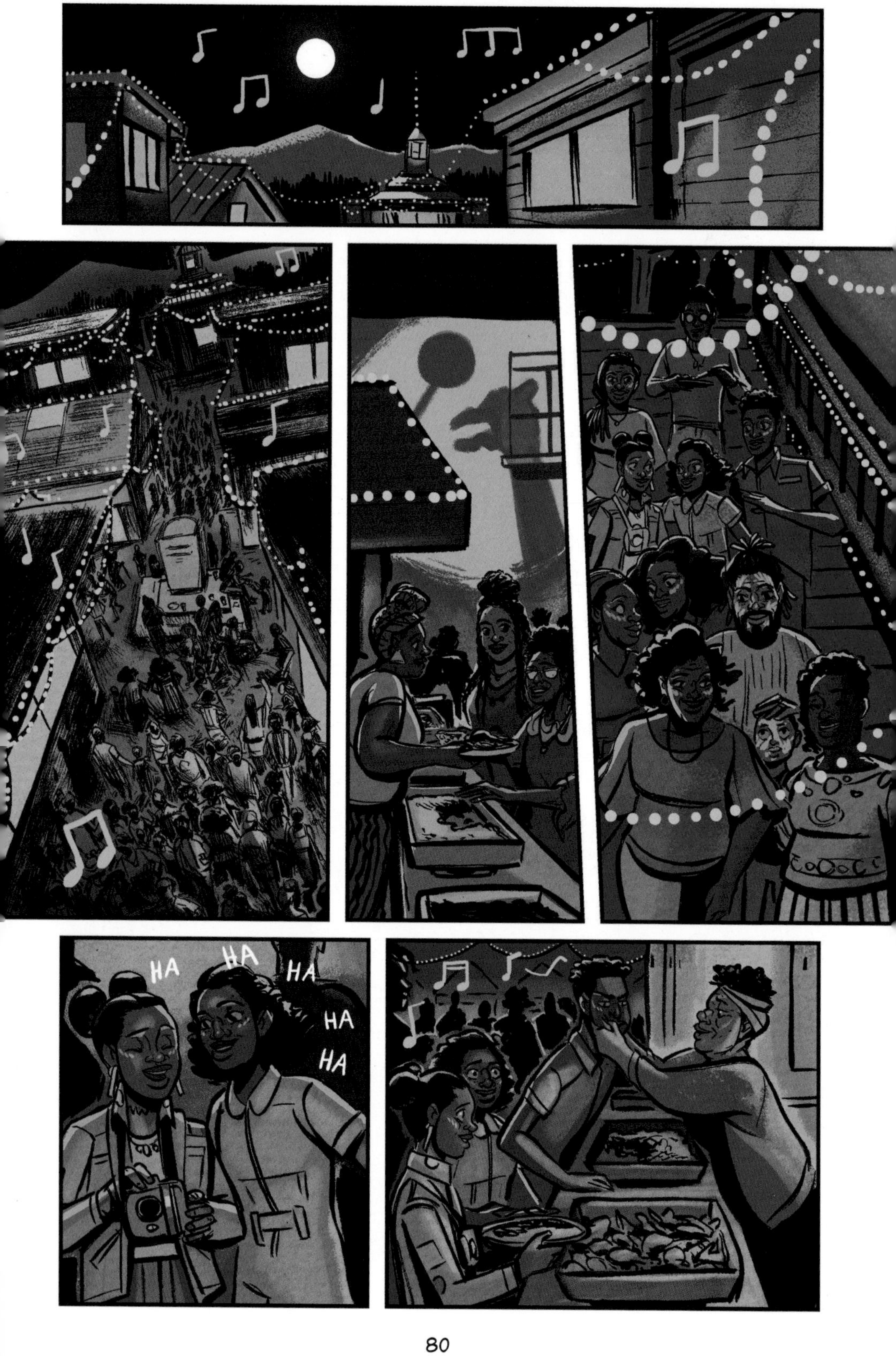
HA
HA
HA
HA
HA

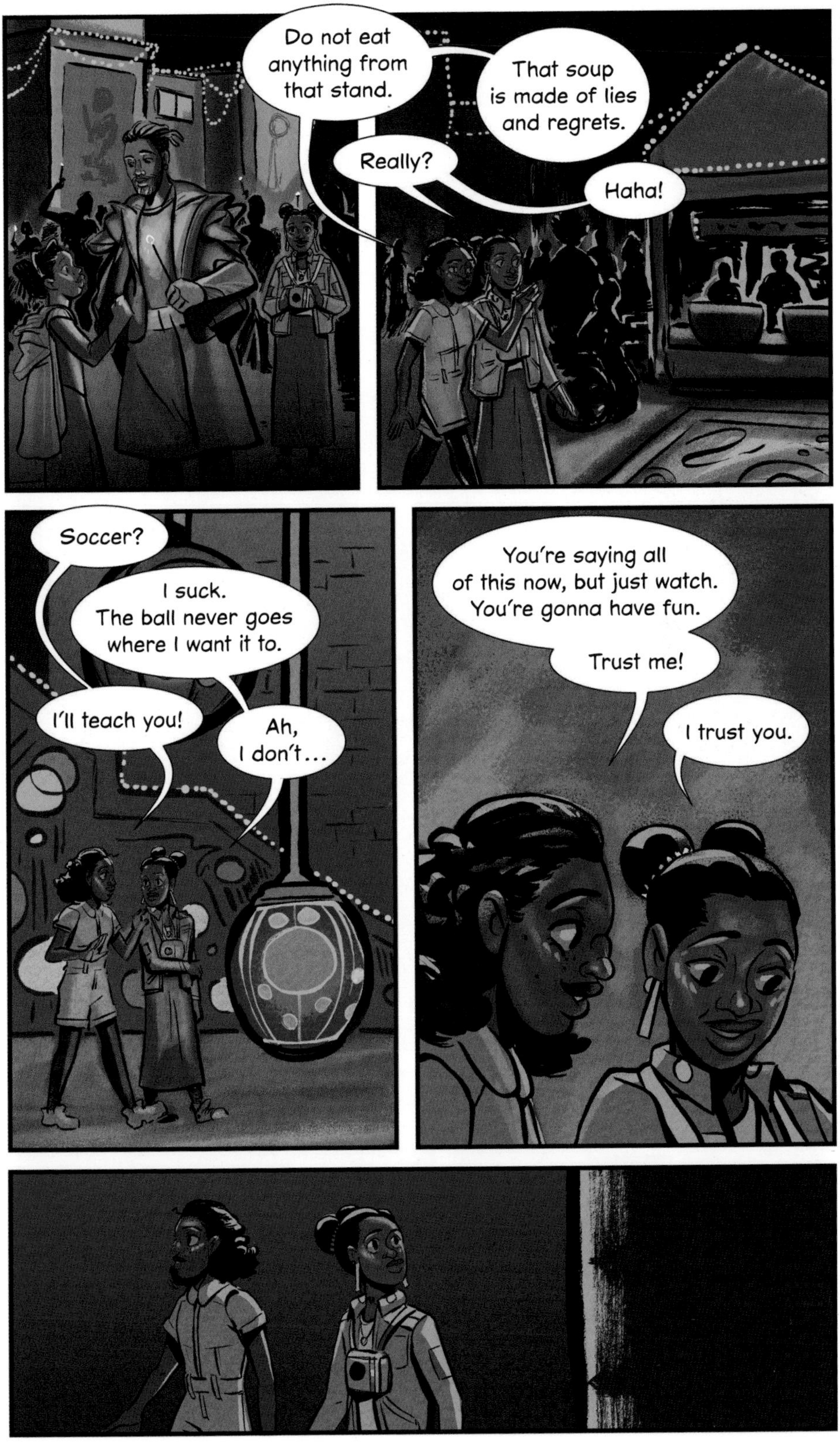
Do not eat anything from that stand.
That soup is made of lies and regrets.
Really?
Haha!
Soccer?
I suck. The ball never goes where I want it to.
I'll teach you!
Ah, I don't...
You're saying all of this now, but just watch. You're gonna have fun.
Trust me!
I trust you.

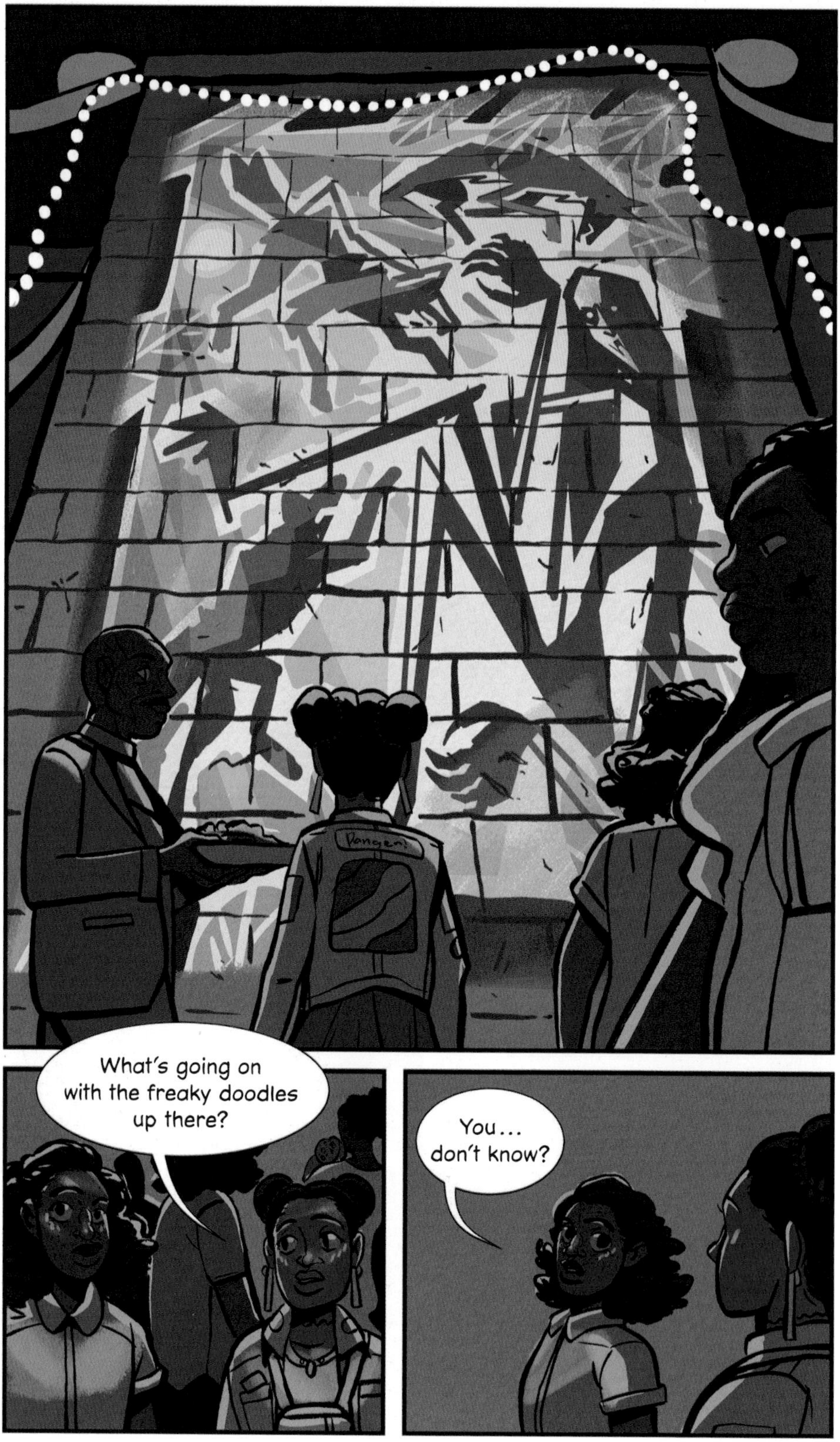
What's going on with the freaky doodles up there?
You... don't know?

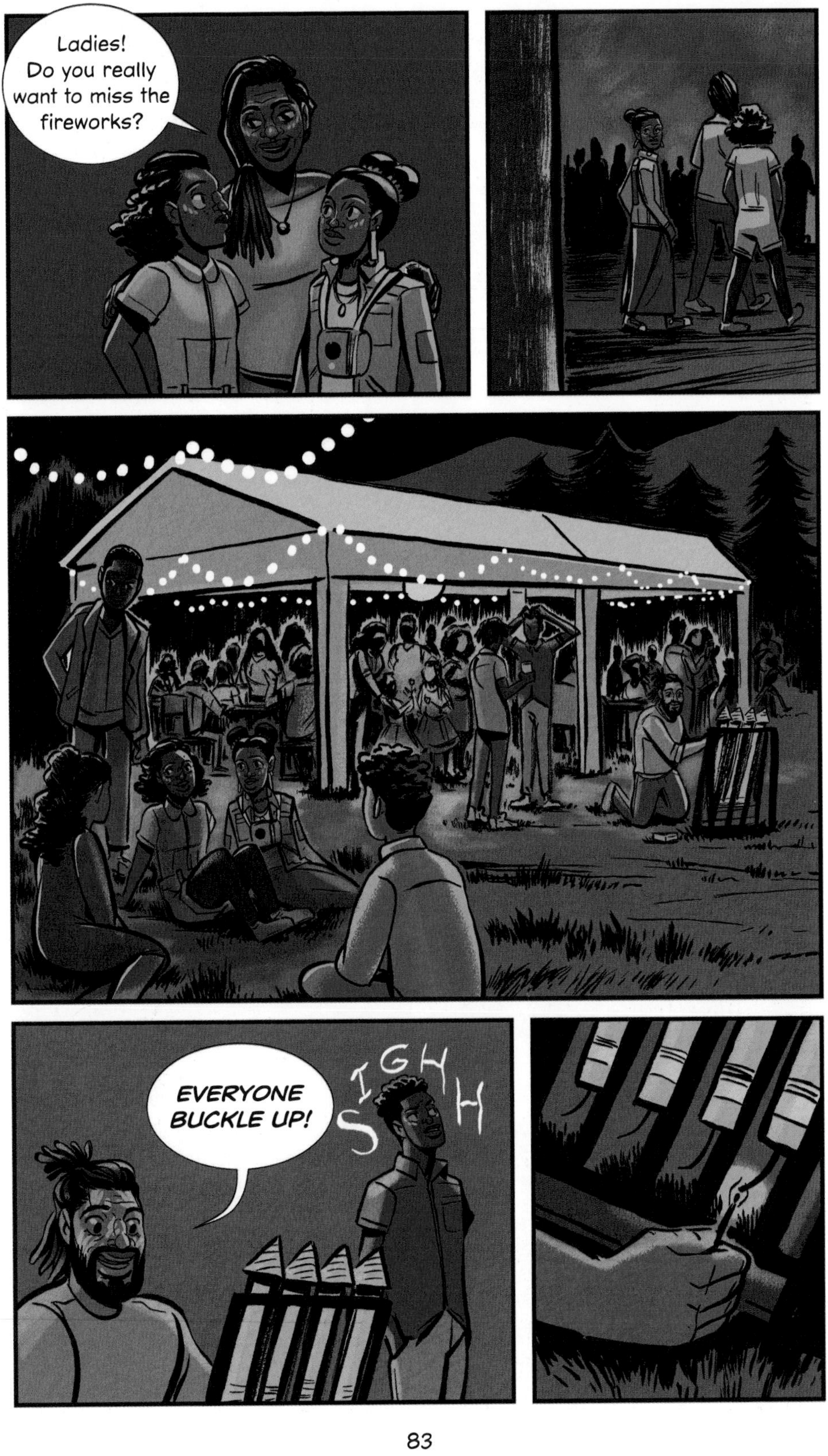
Ladies! Do you really want to miss the fireworks?
EVERYONE BUCKLE UP!
SIGHHH

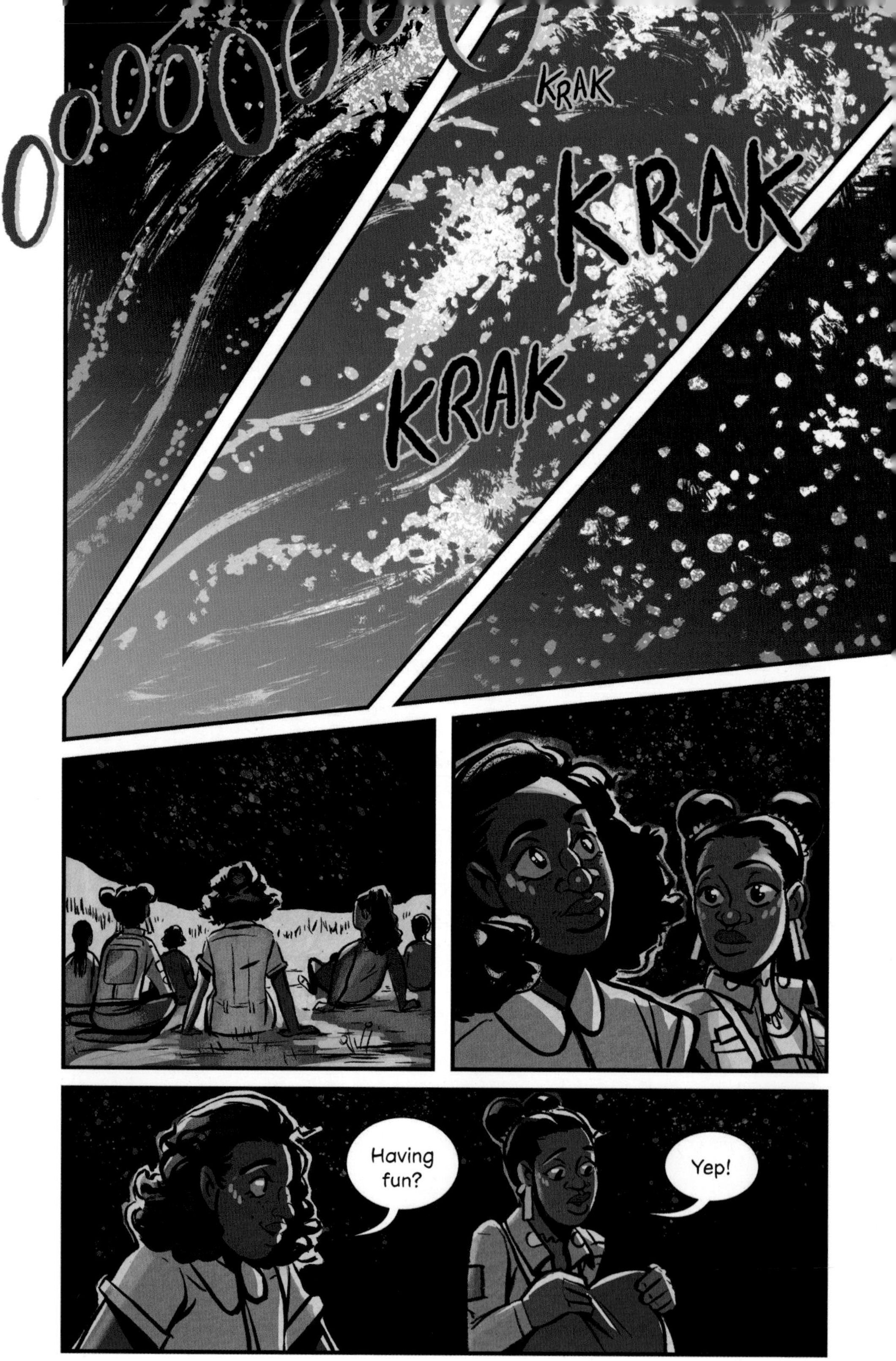
OOOOOOOO
KRAK
KRAK
KRAK
Having fun?
Yep!

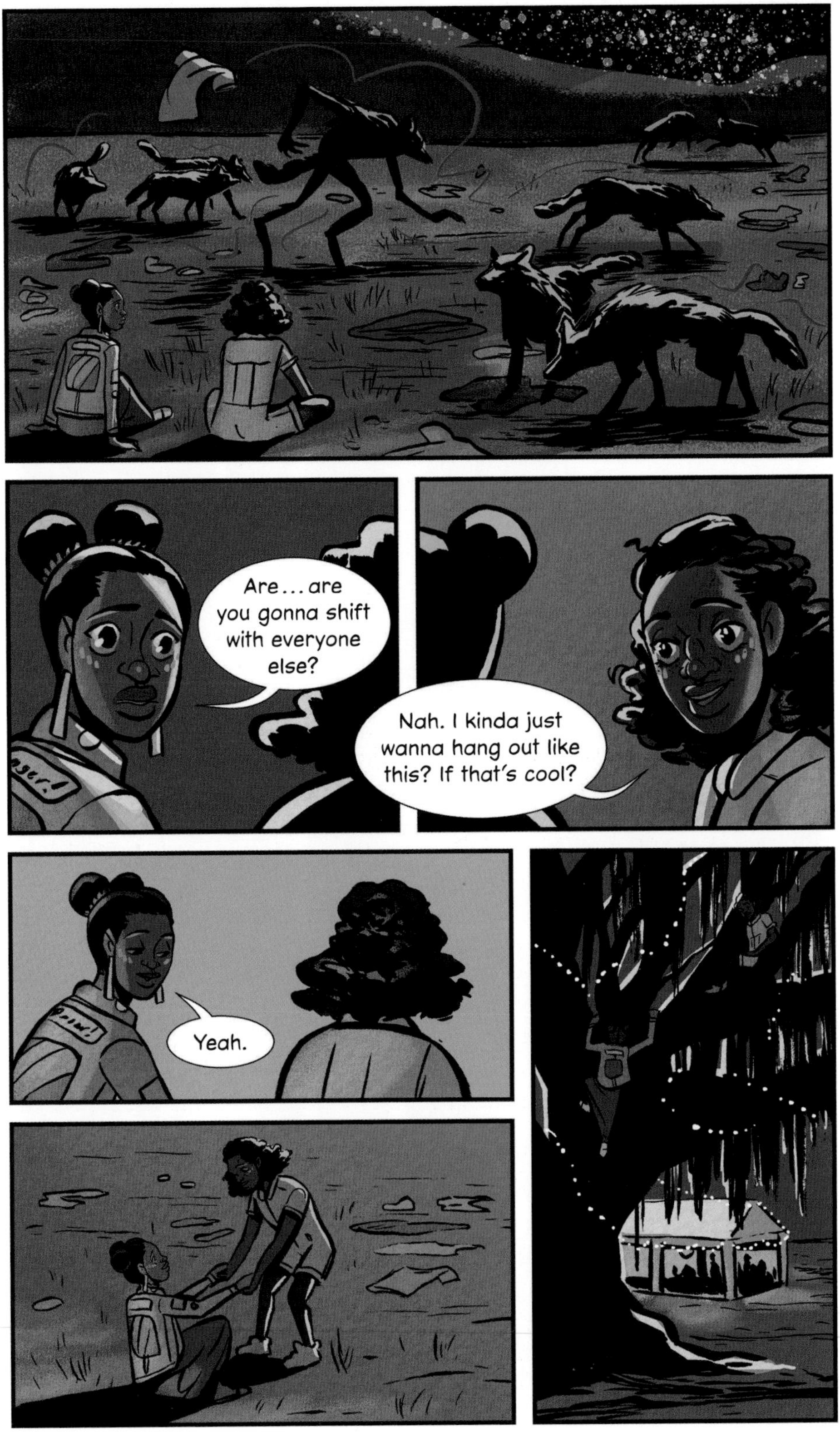

Are...are you gonna shift with everyone else?
Nah. I kinda just wanna hang out like this? If that's cool?
Yeah.

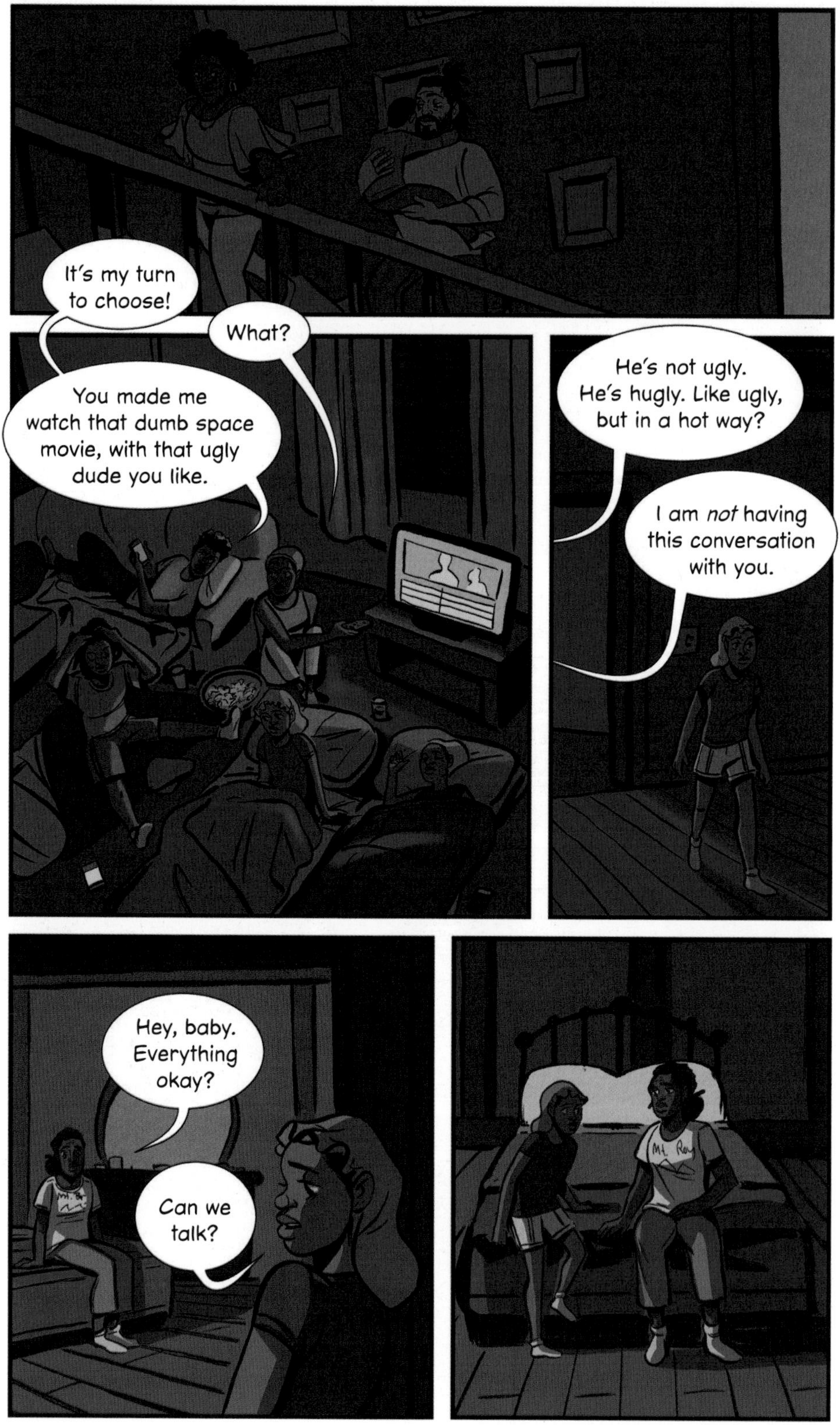
It's my turn to choose!
What?
You made me watch that dumb space movie, with that ugly dude you like.
He's not ugly. He's hugly. Like ugly, but in a hot way?
I am *not* having this conversation with you.
Hey, baby. Everything okay?
Can we talk?
Mt. Ro

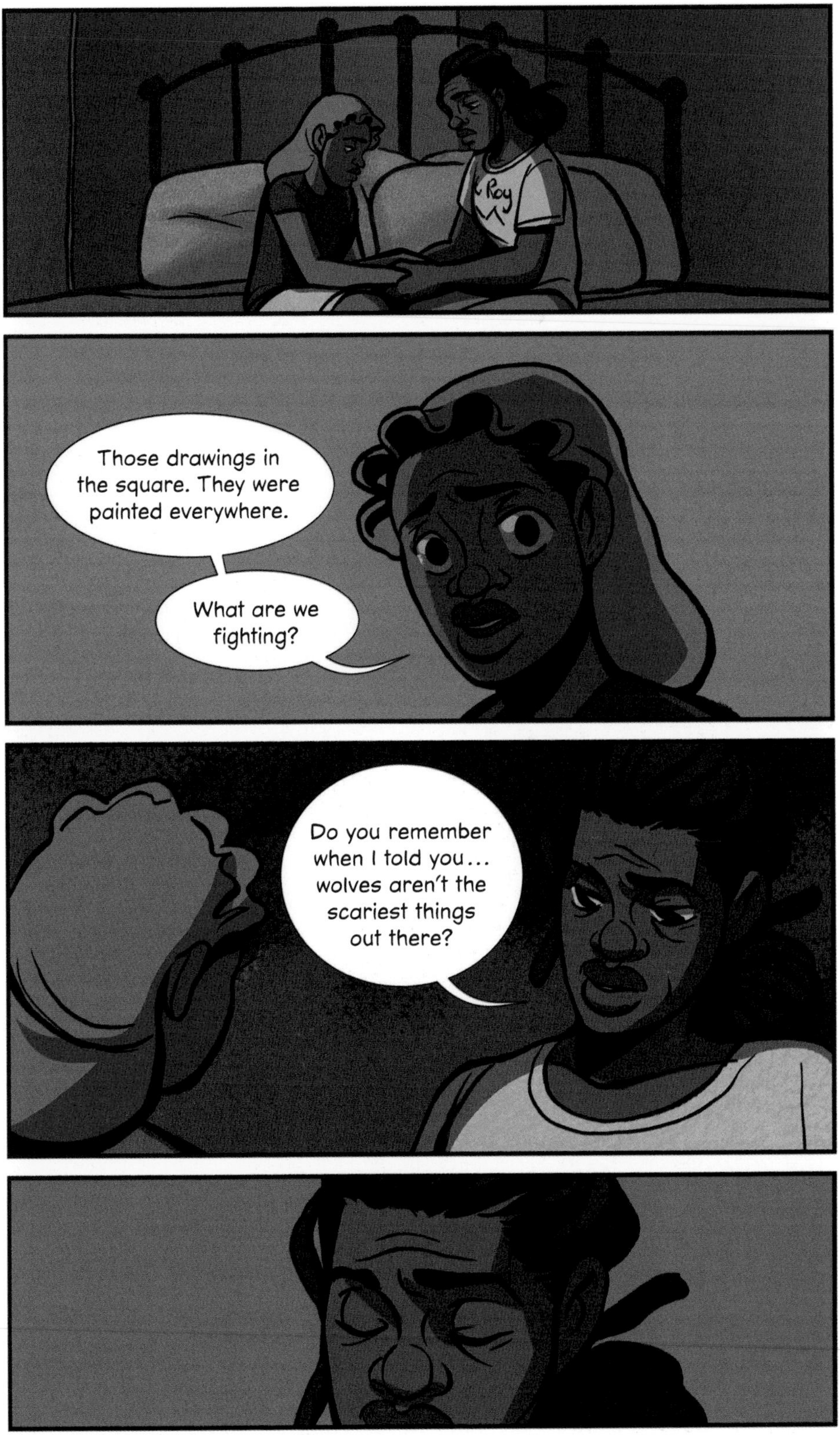
Those drawings in the square. They were painted everywhere.
What are we fighting?
Do you remember when I told you... wolves aren't the scariest things out there?

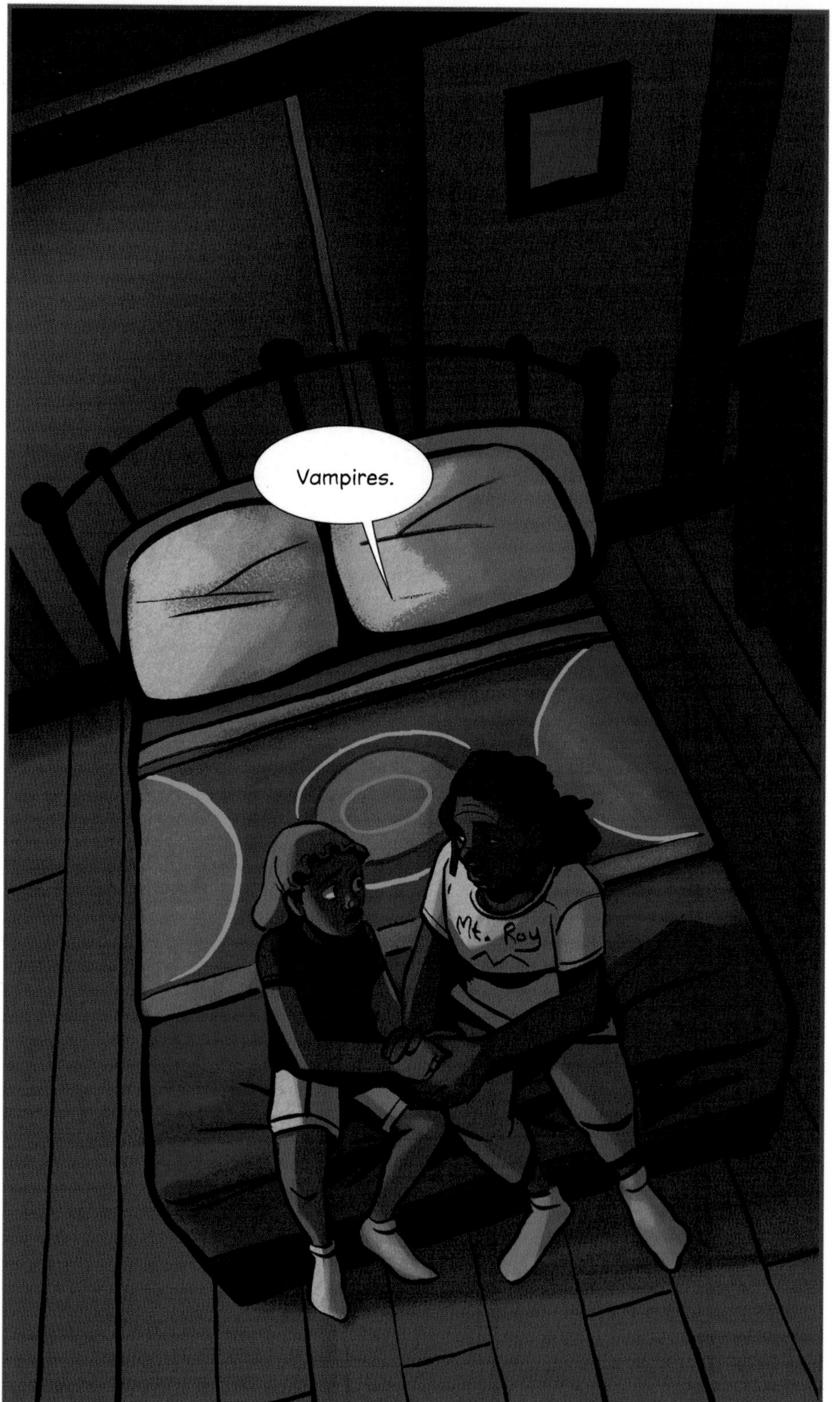
Vampires.
Mt. Roy

CHAPTER FOUR

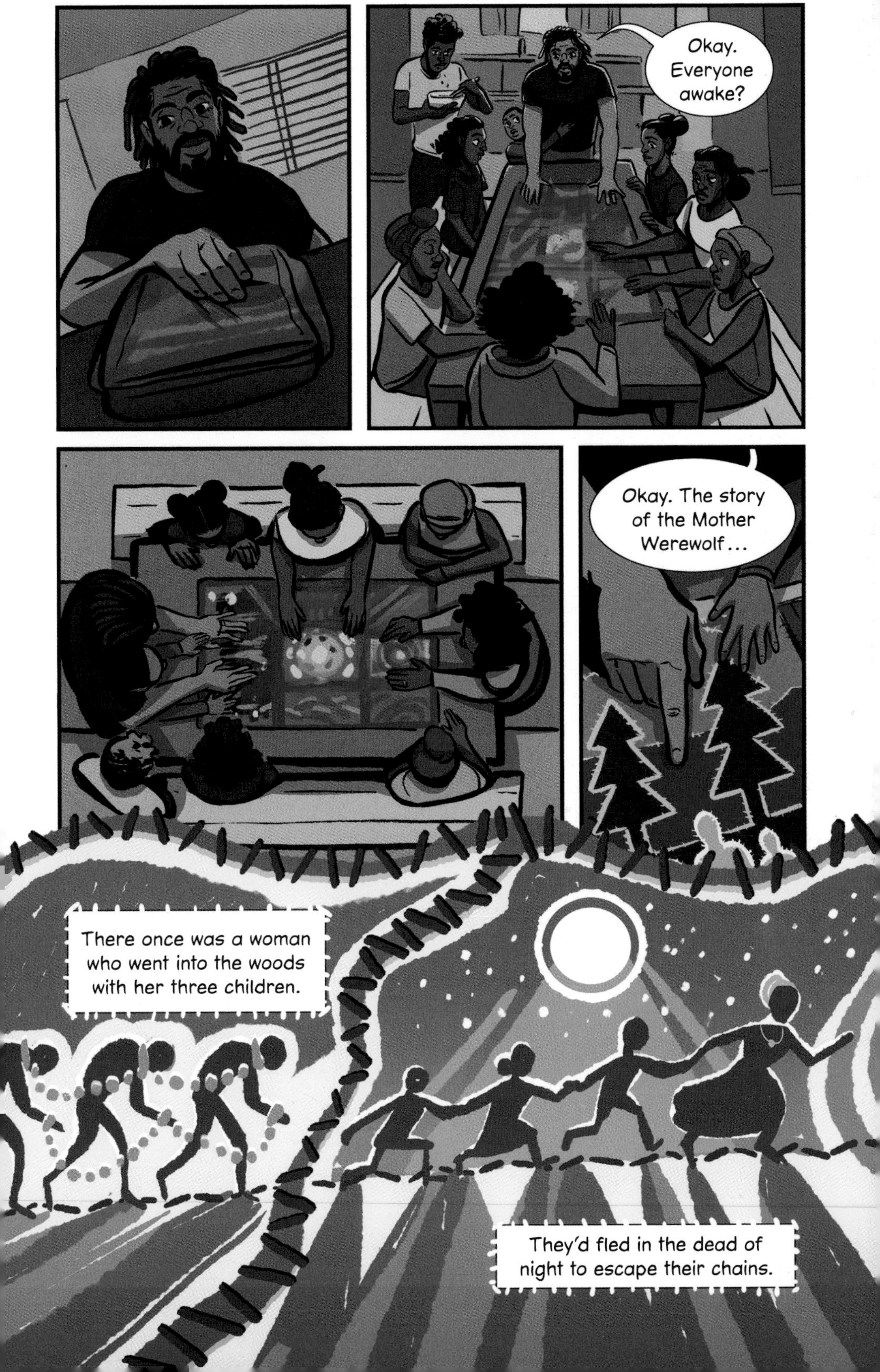
Okay. Everyone awake?
Okay. The story of the Mother Werewolf...
There once was a woman who went into the woods with her three children.
They'd fled in the dead of night to escape their chains.

They ran for days. A storm came. They almost froze. Nearly starved.
And that's when the wolf approached.
But the woman was not afraid. She saw herself in the wolf.
She saw a mother.

The wolf led the woman and her children to food and warmth.
After surviving the storm together, their bond was unspoken but unbreakable.
The wolf gave the woman and her three children the gift of transformation. The gift of freedom.

When the storm cleared, the light of a full moon filled the sky.
And that is why we celebrate— to honor that gift and the strength of family, both real *and* chosen.
There are other clans of werewolves out there, but this woman and her children were some of the first leaders of our kind.

What about vampires?

V-vampires are born from death. No purpose drives them but destruction.

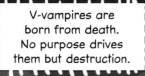

They're travelers and manipulators who feed off our weak and vulnerable.

But when we stay together, we can overcome any enemy. Even vampires. Our bonds are stronger than their bloodlust.

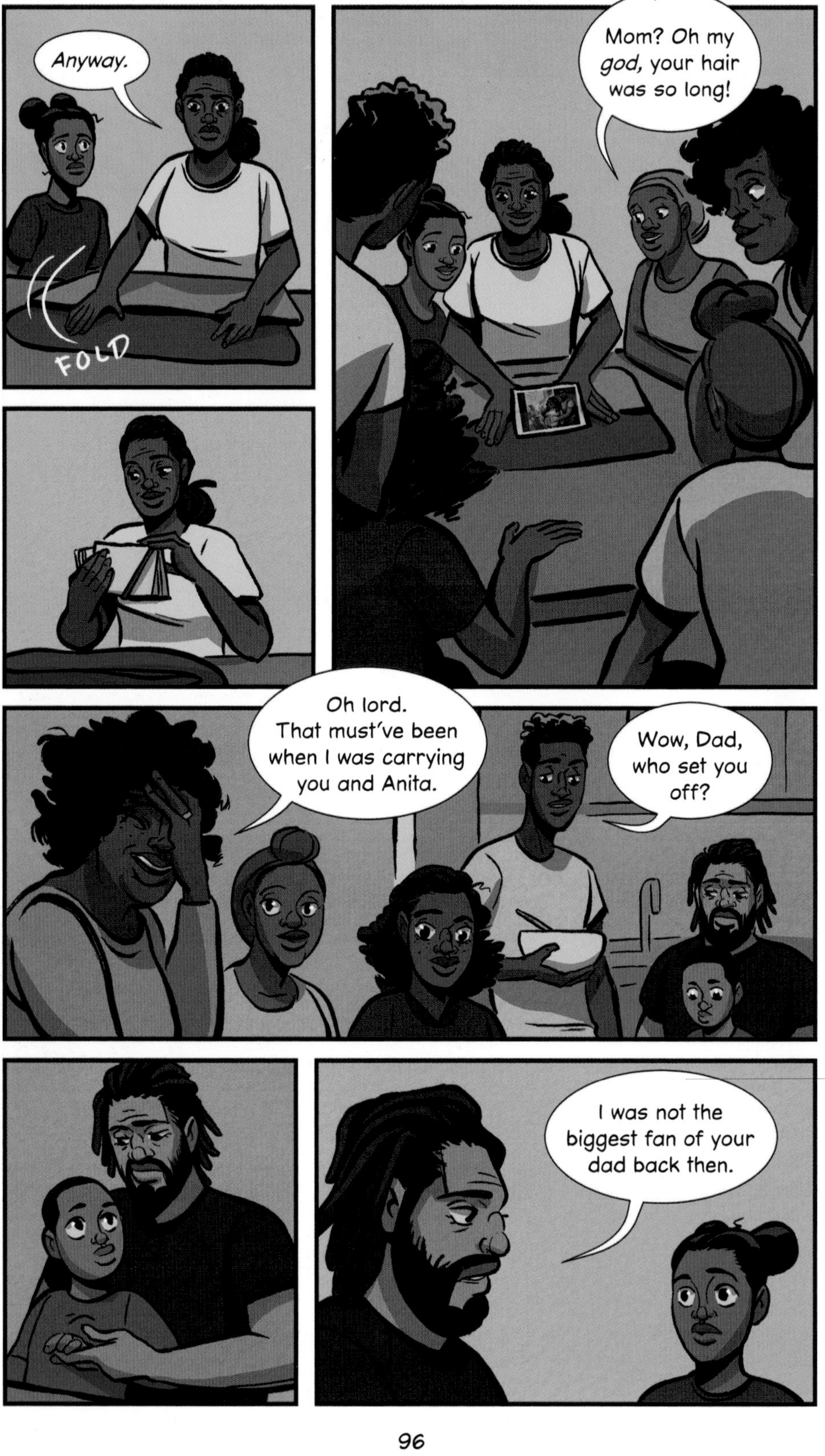
Anyway.
FOLD
Mom? Oh my *god*, your hair was so long!
Oh lord. That must've been when I was carrying you and Anita.
Wow, Dad, who set you off?
I was not the biggest fan of your dad back then.

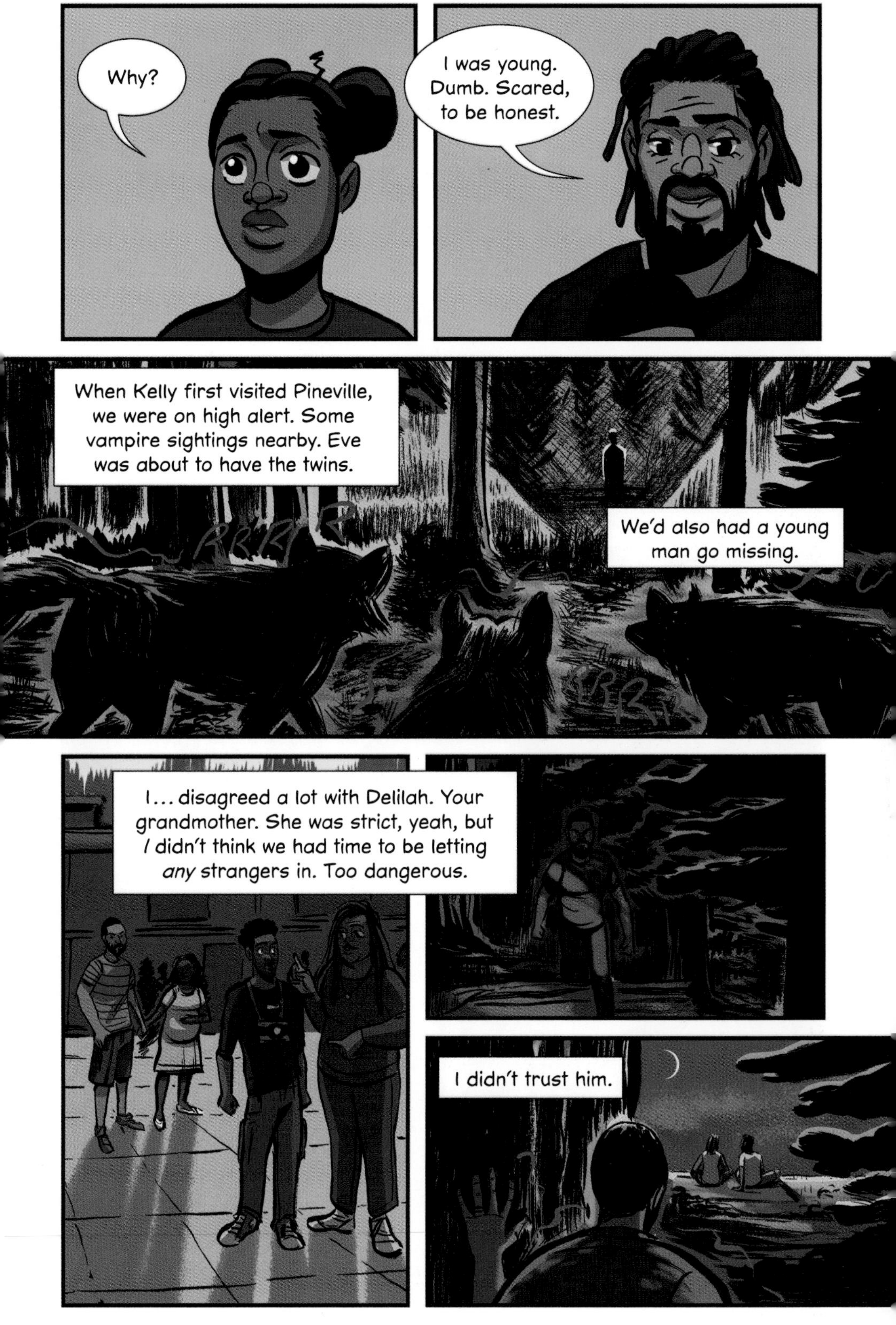
Why?
I was young. Dumb. Scared, to be honest.
When Kelly first visited Pineville, we were on high alert. Some vampire sightings nearby. Eve was about to have the twins.
We'd also had a young man go missing.
I... disagreed a lot with Delilah. Your grandmother. She was strict, yeah, but *I* didn't think we had time to be letting *any* strangers in. Too dangerous.
I didn't trust him.

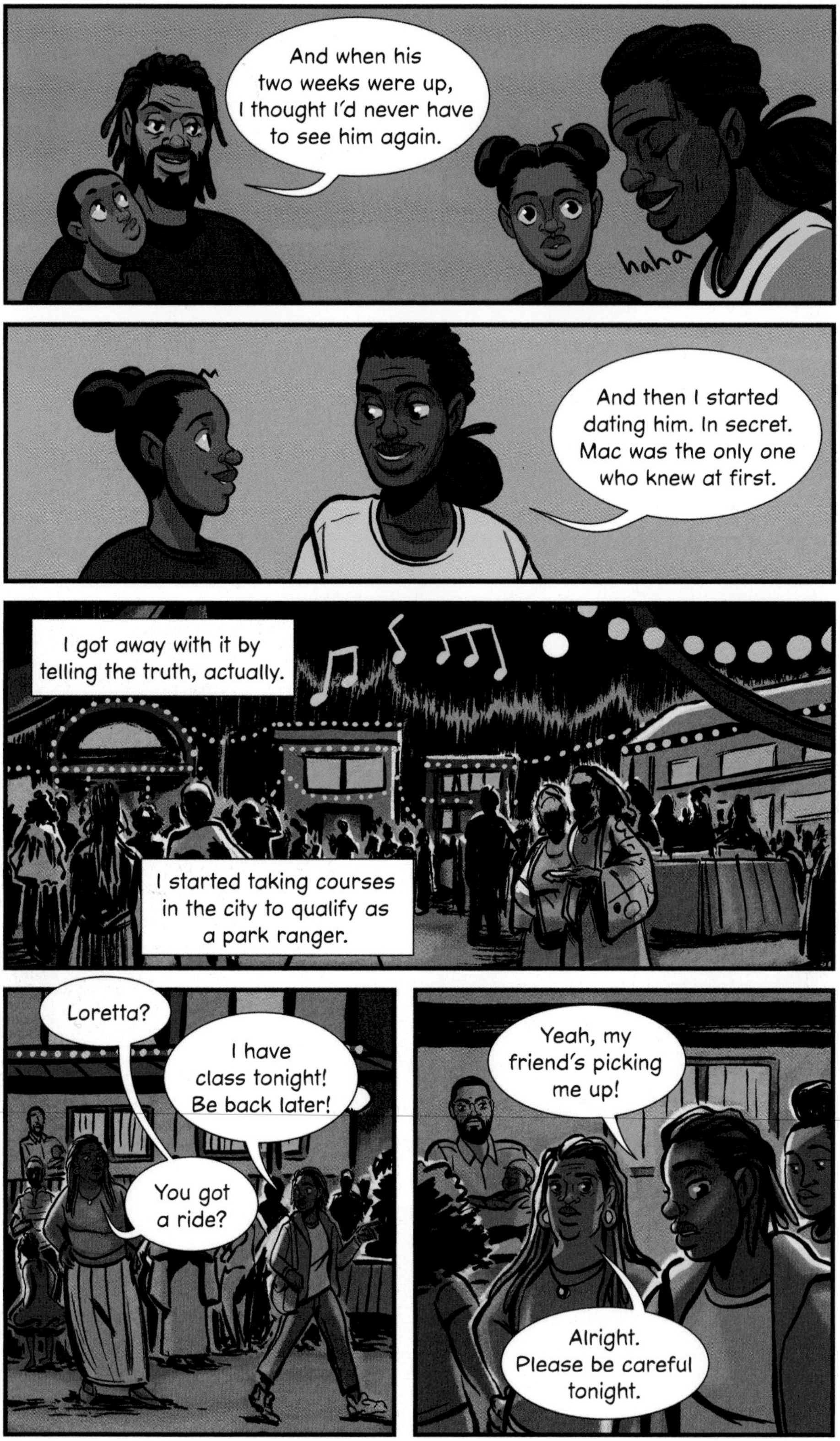
And when his two weeks were up, I thought I'd never have to see him again.
haha
And then I started dating him. In secret. Mac was the only one who knew at first.
I got away with it by telling the truth, actually.
I started taking courses in the city to qualify as a park ranger.
Loretta?
I have class tonight! Be back later!
You got a ride?
Yeah, my friend's picking me up!
Alright. Please be careful tonight.

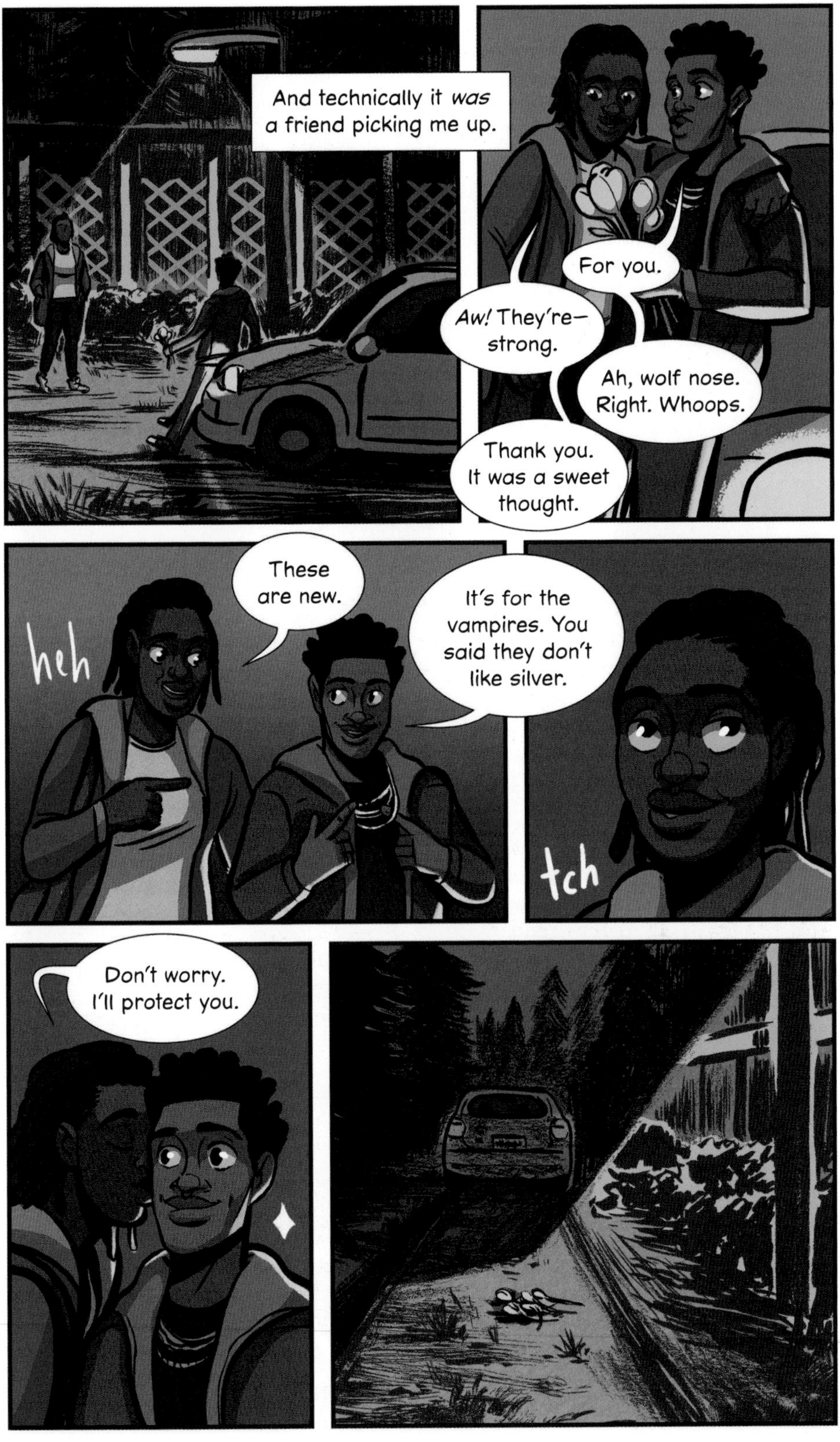
And technically it *was* a friend picking me up.
For you.
Aw! They're—strong.
Ah, wolf nose. Right. Whoops.
Thank you. It was a sweet thought.
heh
These are new.
It's for the vampires. You said they don't like silver.
tch
Don't worry. I'll protect you.

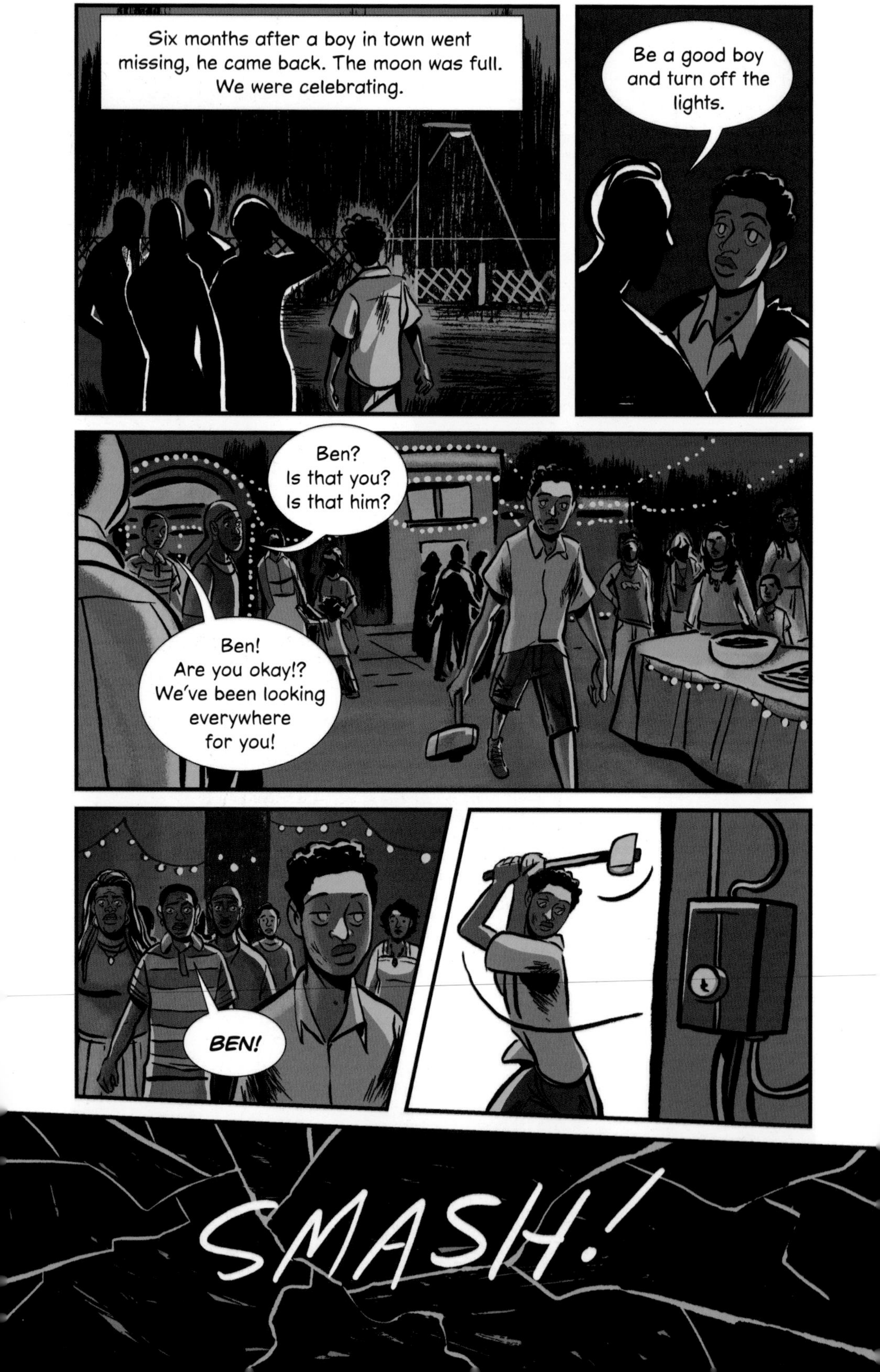

Six months after a boy in town went missing, he came back. The moon was full. We were celebrating.
Be a good boy and turn off the lights.
Ben? Is that you? Is that him?
Ben! Are you okay!? We've been looking everywhere for you!
BEN!
SMASH!

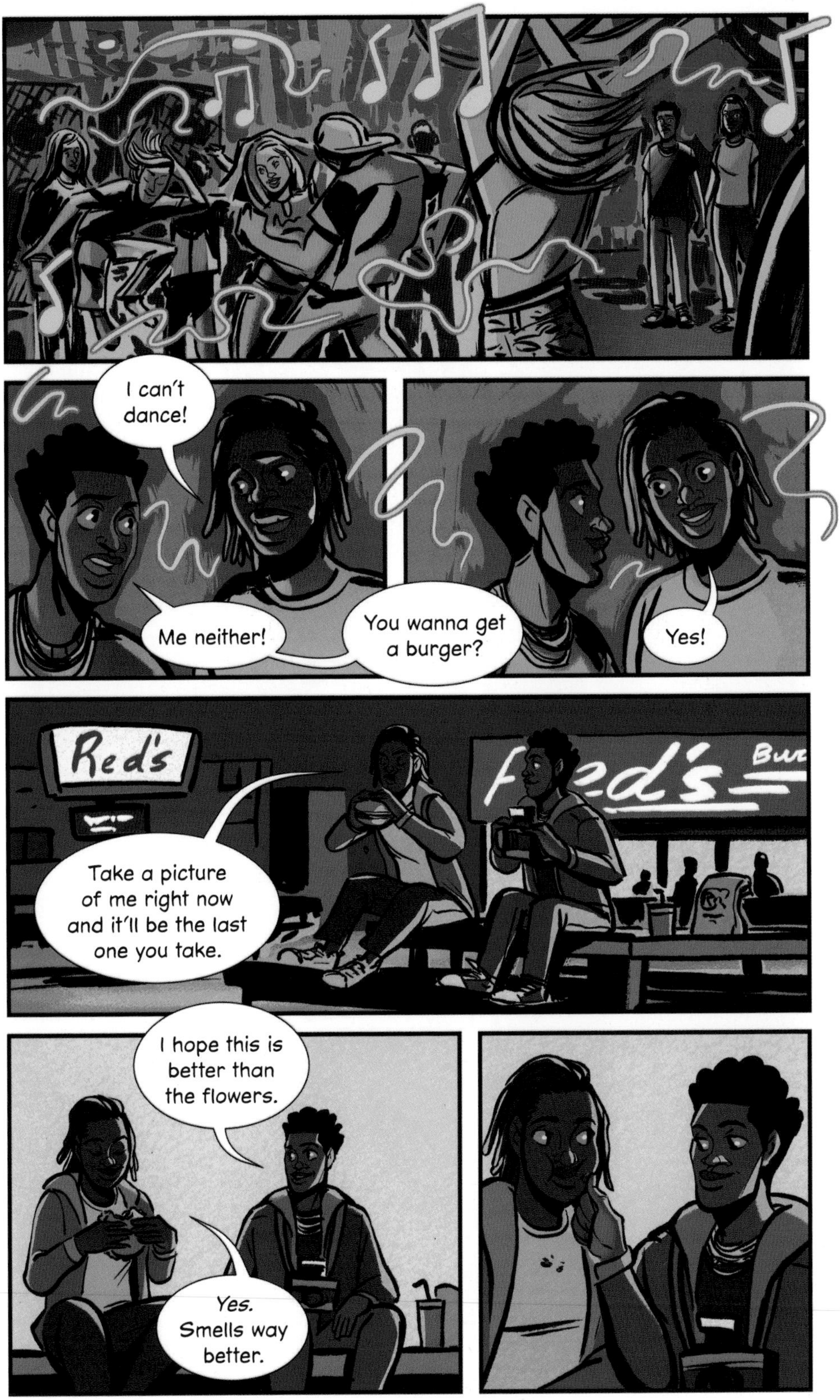
I can't dance!
Me neither!
You wanna get a burger?
Yes!
Red's
Red's Bur
Take a picture of me right now and it'll be the last one you take.
I hope this is better than the flowers.
Yes. Smells way better.

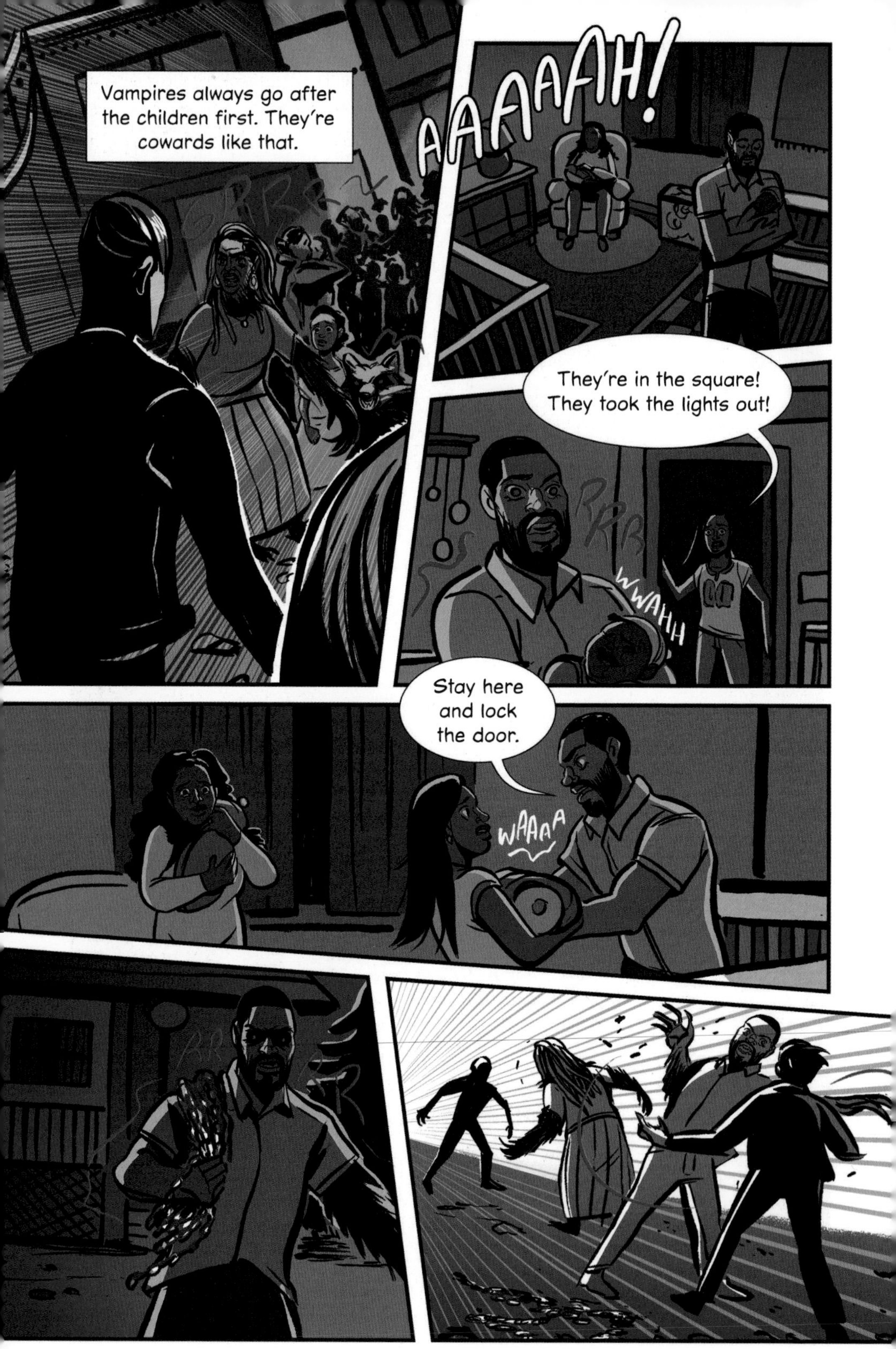

Vampires always go after the children first. They're cowards like that.
GRRR
AAAAAAH!
They're in the square! They took the lights out!
RRR
WWAHH
Stay here and lock the door.
WAAAA
RR

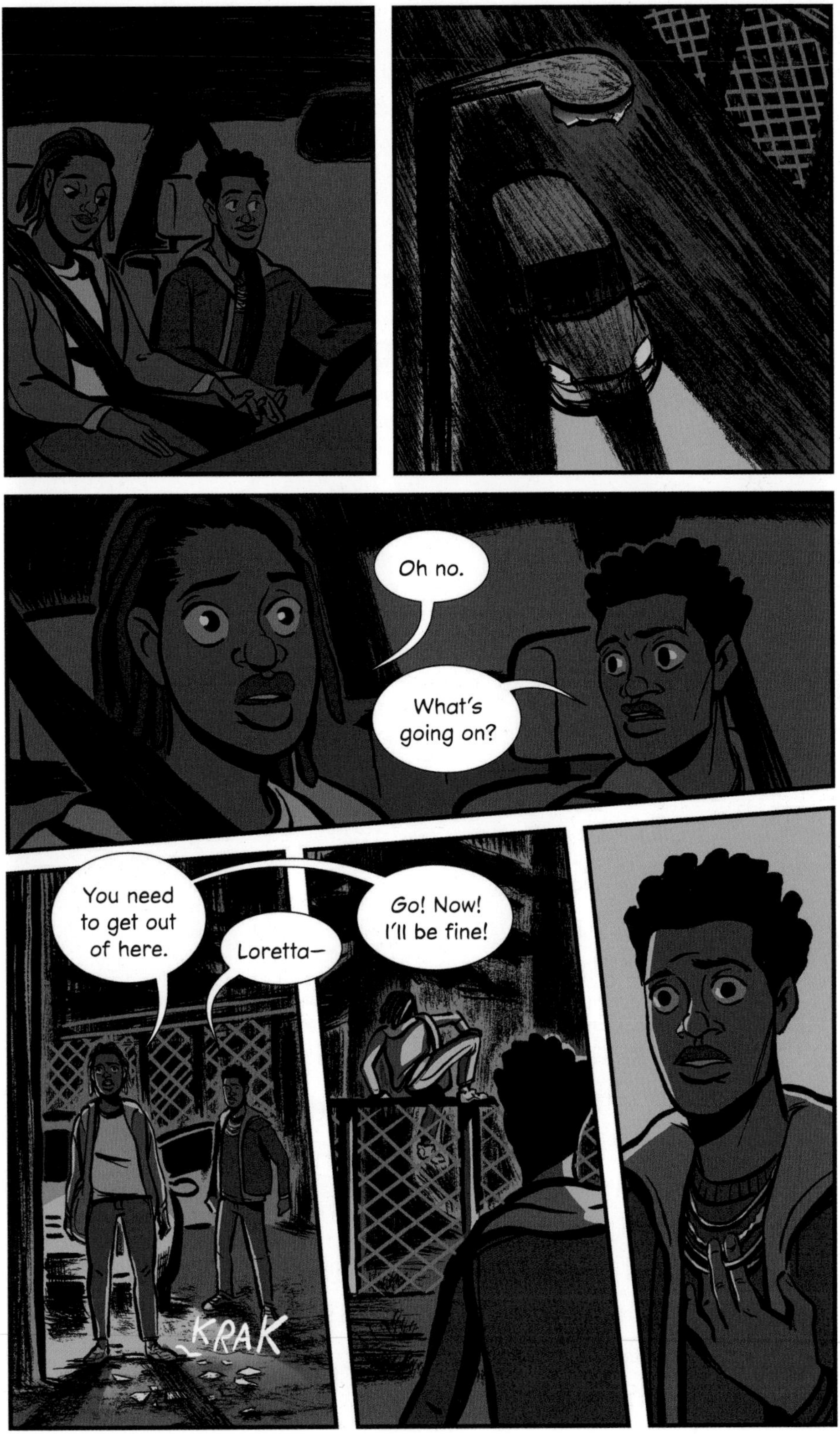
Oh no.
What's going on?
You need to get out of here.
Loretta—
Go! Now! I'll be fine!
KRAK

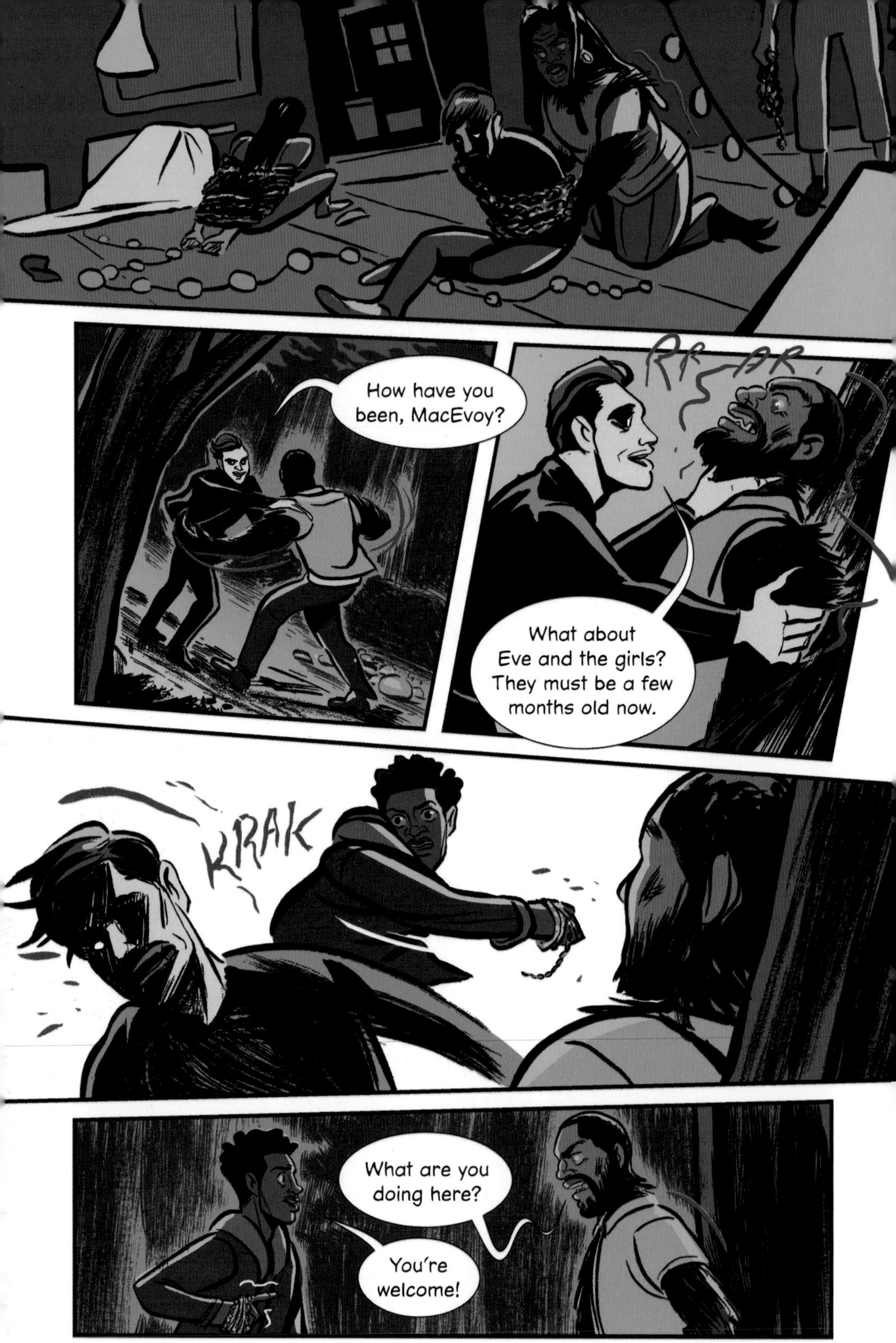
How have you been, MacEvoy?
What about Eve and the girls? They must be a few months old now.
KRAK
What are you doing here?
You're welcome!

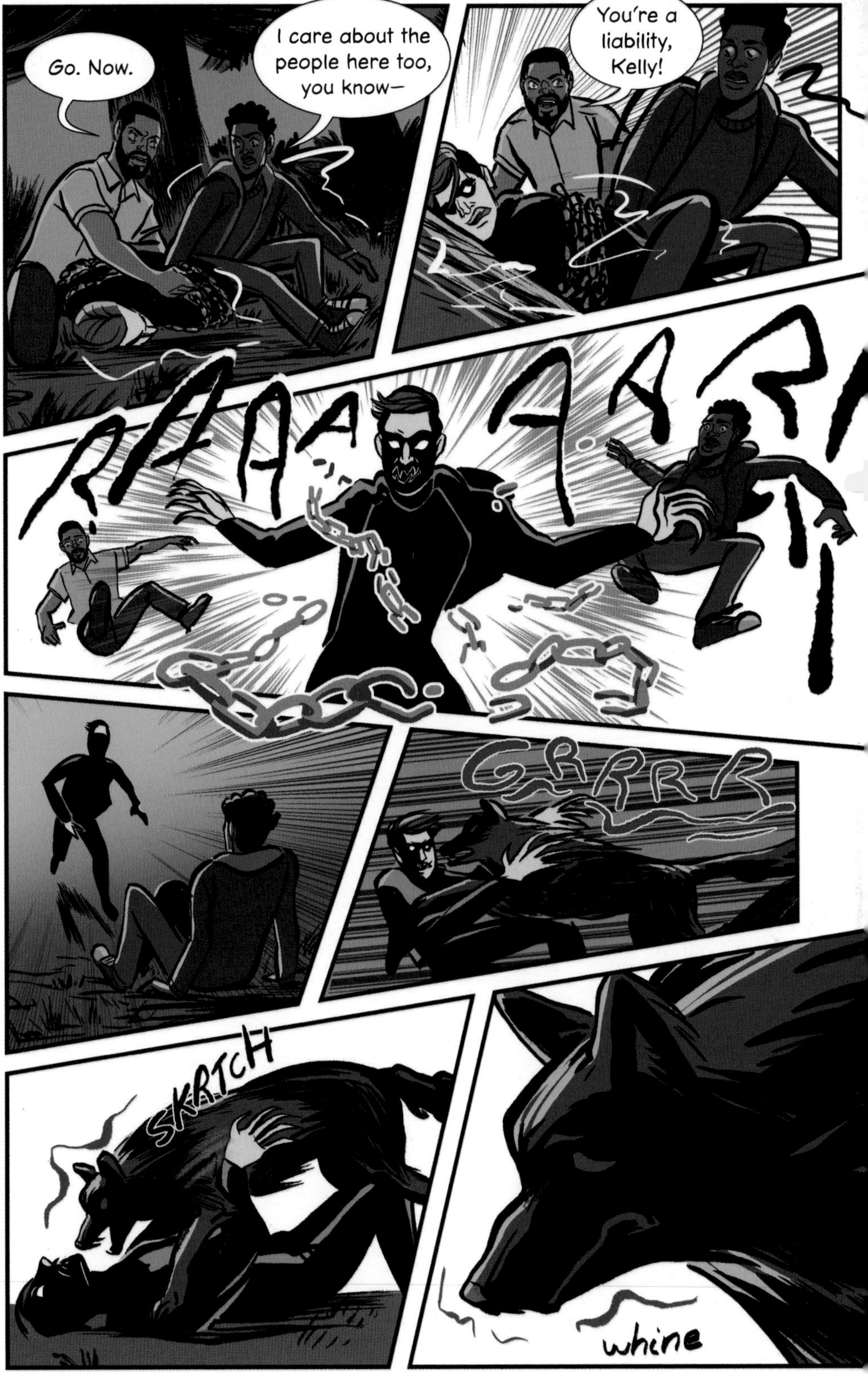
Go. Now.
I care about the people here too, you know—
You're a liability, Kelly!
RAAAAARR
GRRRR
SKRTCH
whine

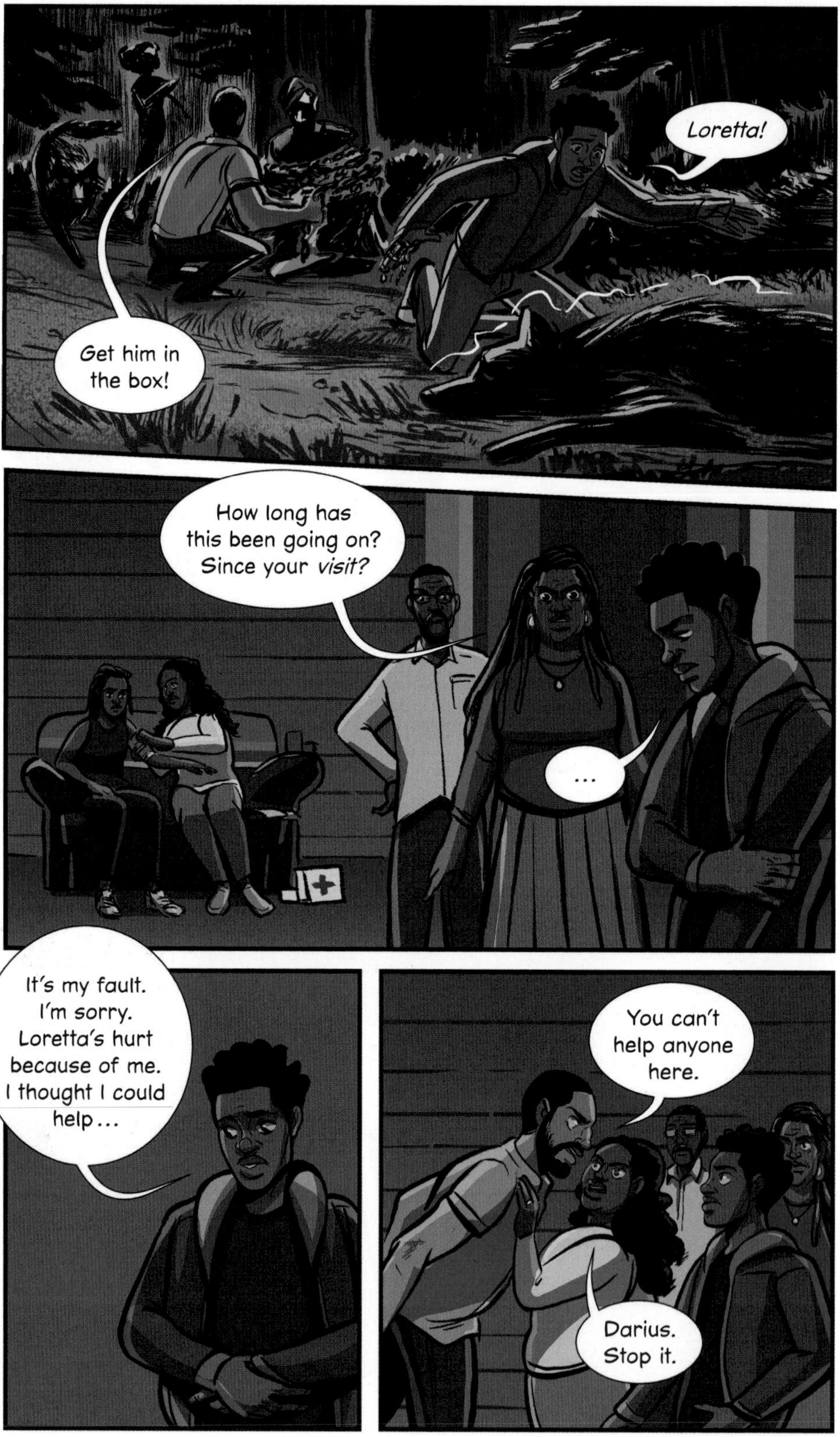
Loretta!
Get him in the box!
How long has this been going on? Since your *visit?*
...
It's my fault. I'm sorry. Loretta's hurt because of me. I thought I could help...
You can't help anyone here.
Darius. Stop it.

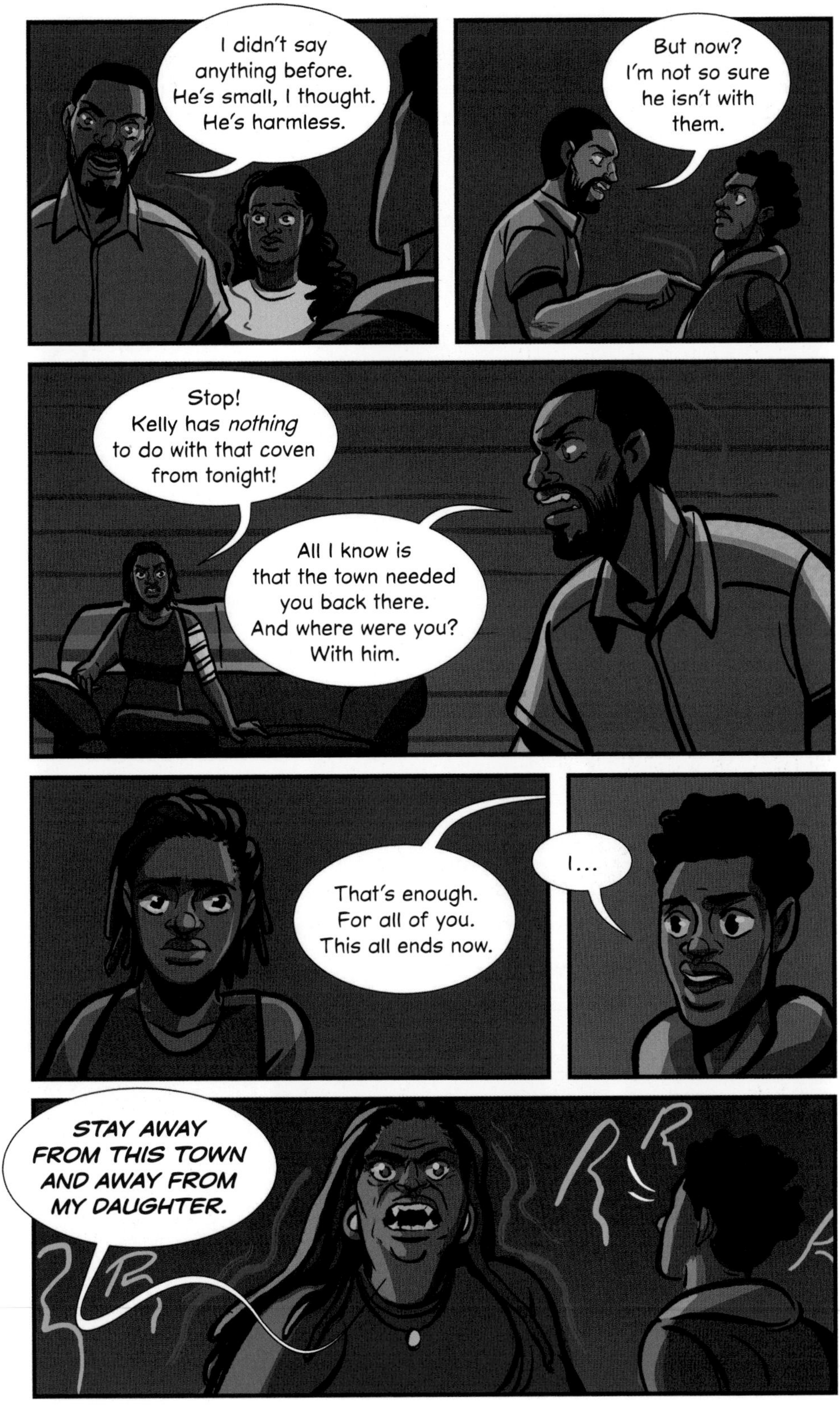
I didn't say anything before. He's small, I thought. He's harmless.
But now? I'm not so sure he isn't with them.
Stop! Kelly has *nothing* to do with that coven from tonight!
All I know is that the town needed you back there. And where were you? With him.
That's enough. For all of you. This all ends now.
I...
STAY AWAY FROM THIS TOWN AND AWAY FROM MY DAUGHTER.

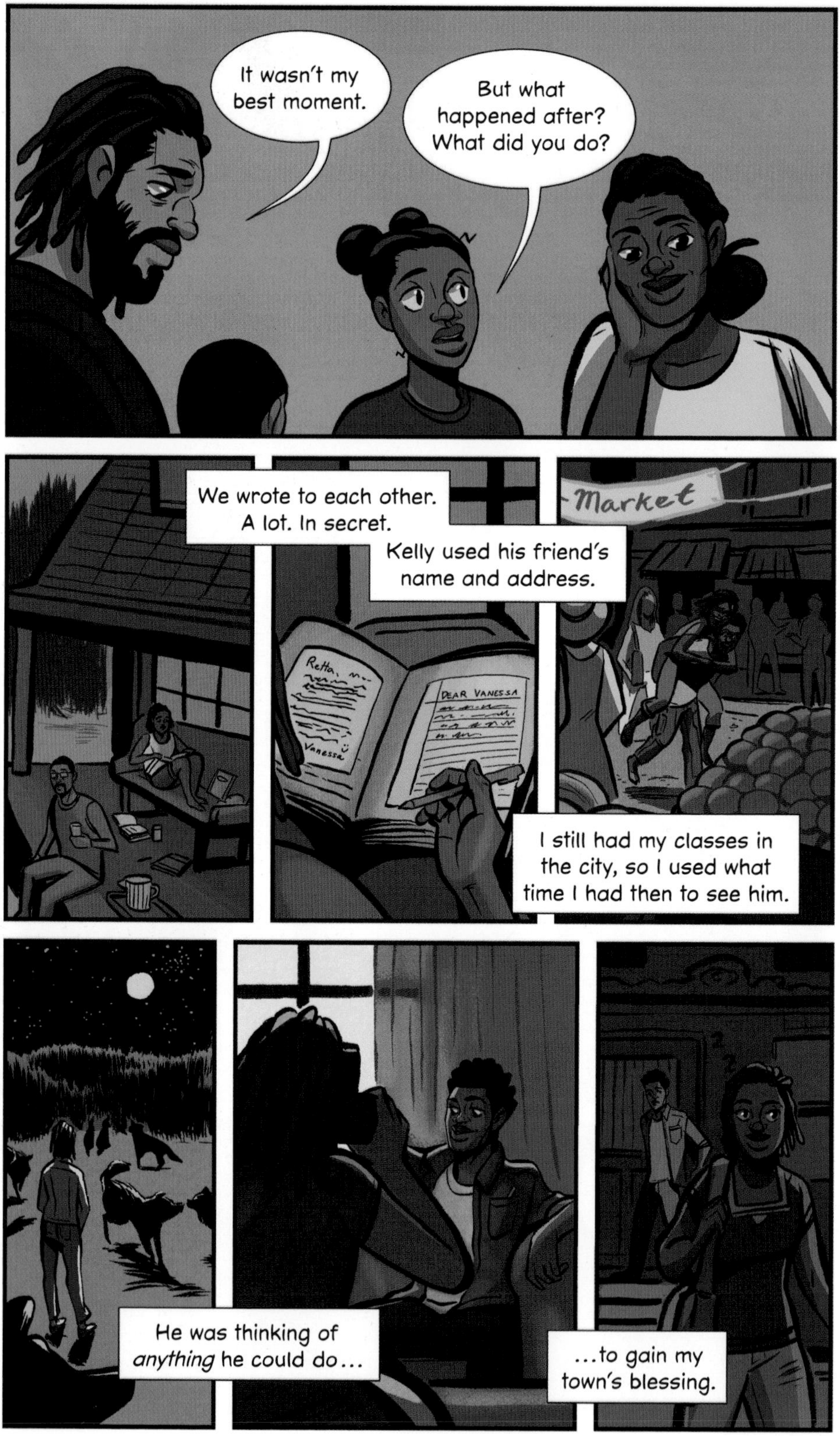
It wasn't my best moment.
But what happened after? What did you do?
We wrote to each other. A lot. In secret.
Retta,
Vanessa
DEAR VANESSA
Kelly used his friend's name and address.
Market
I still had my classes in the city, so I used what time I had then to see him.
He was thinking of *anything* he could do...
...to gain my town's blessing.

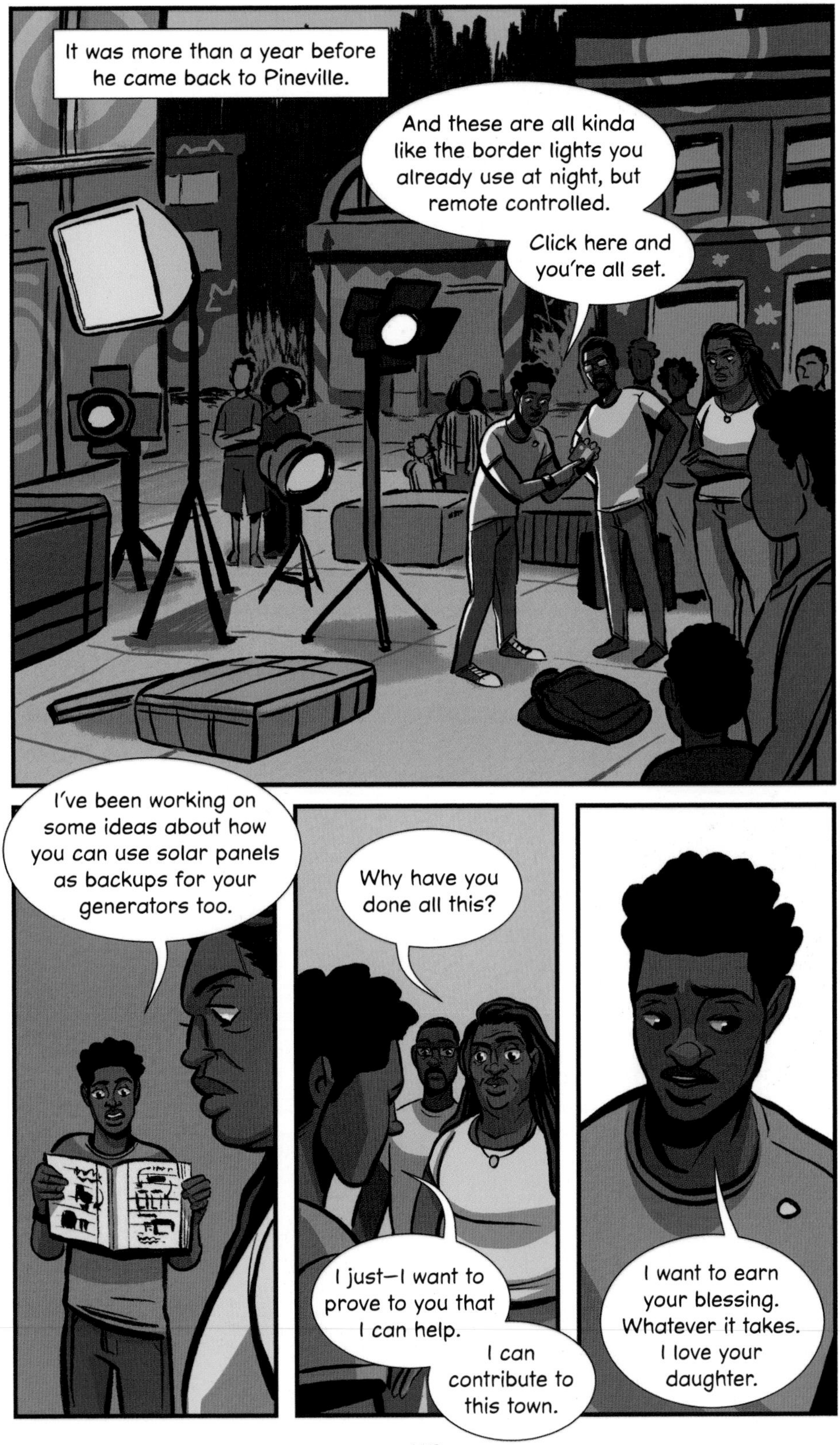
It was more than a year before he came back to Pineville.
And these are all kinda like the border lights you already use at night, but remote controlled.
Click here and you're all set.
I've been working on some ideas about how you can use solar panels as backups for your generators too.
Why have you done all this?
I just—I want to prove to you that I can help.
I can contribute to this town.
I want to earn your blessing. Whatever it takes. I love your daughter.

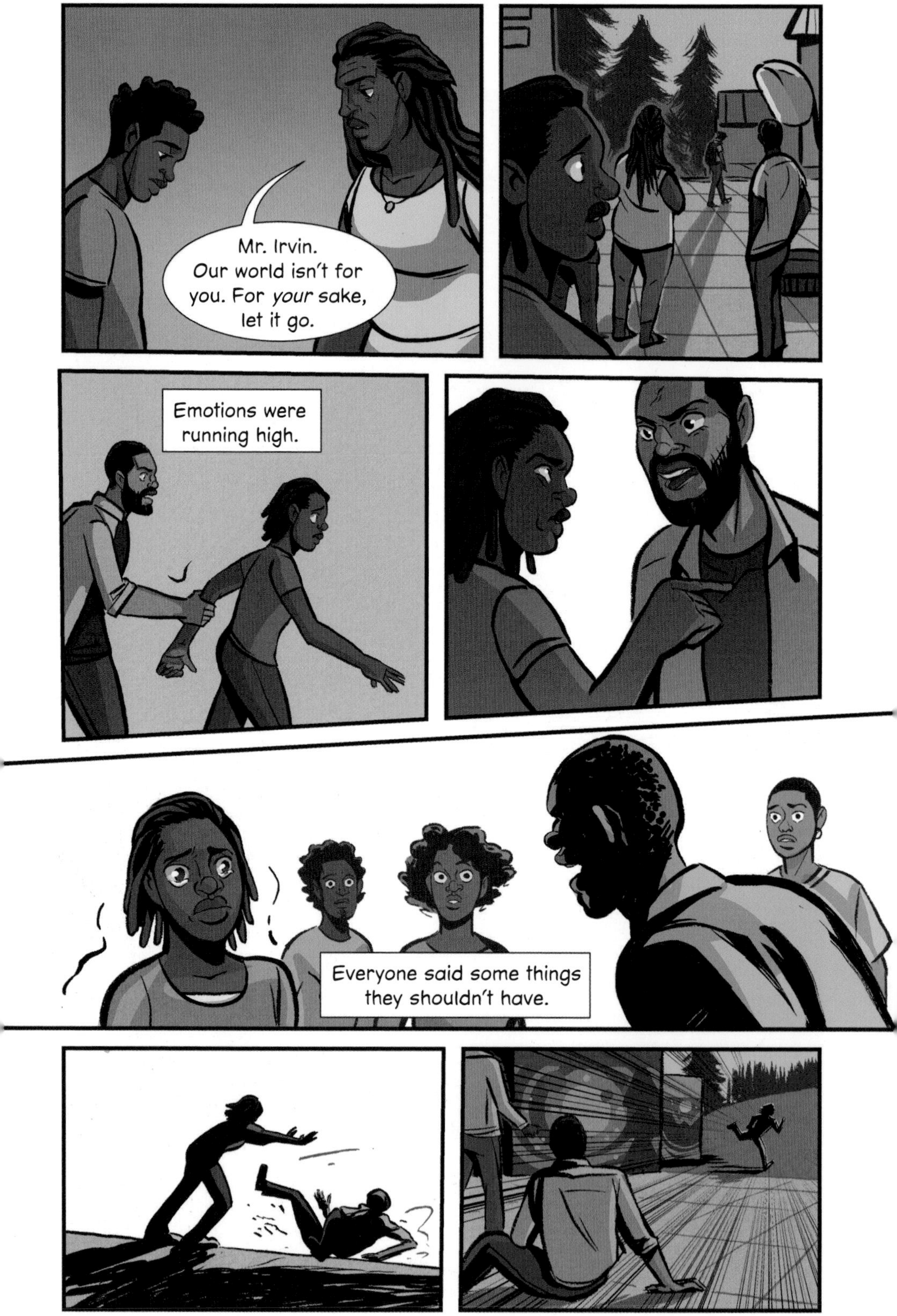
Mr. Irvin. Our world isn't for you. For *your* sake, let it go.
Emotions were running high.
Everyone said some things they shouldn't have.

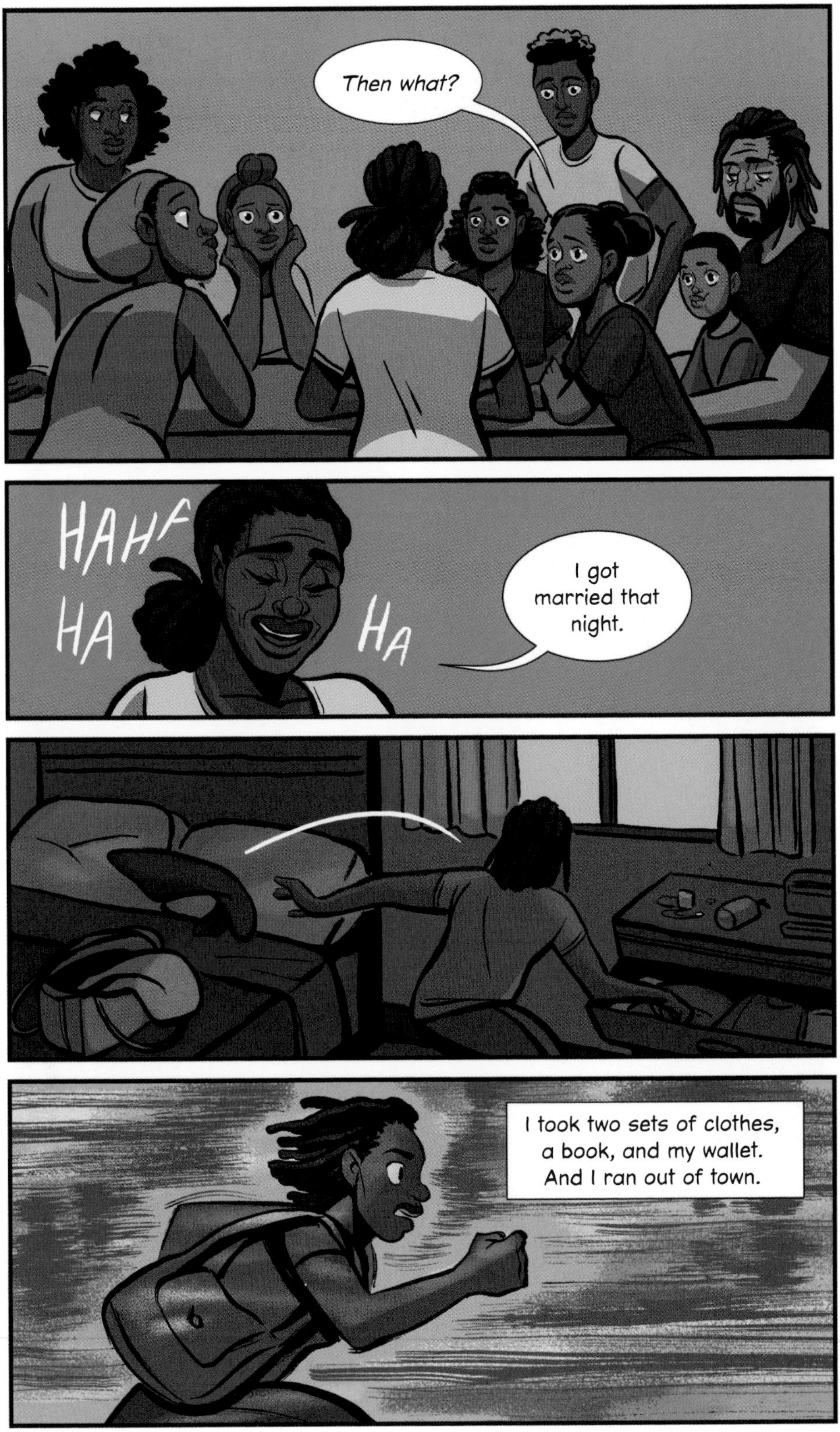
Then what?
HAHA HA
HA
I got married that night.
I took two sets of clothes, a book, and my wallet. And I ran out of town.

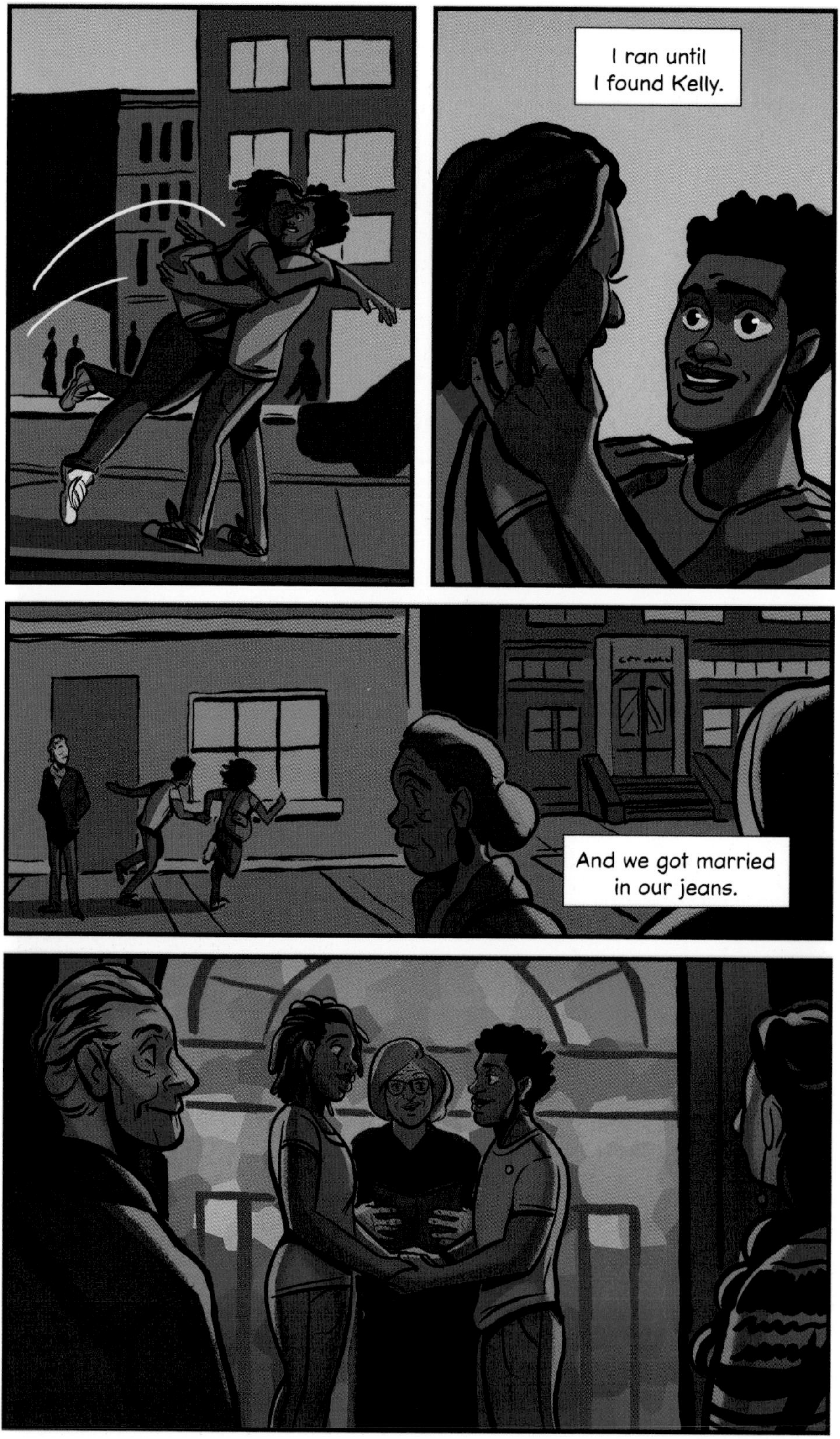
I ran until
I found Kelly.
And we got married
in our jeans.

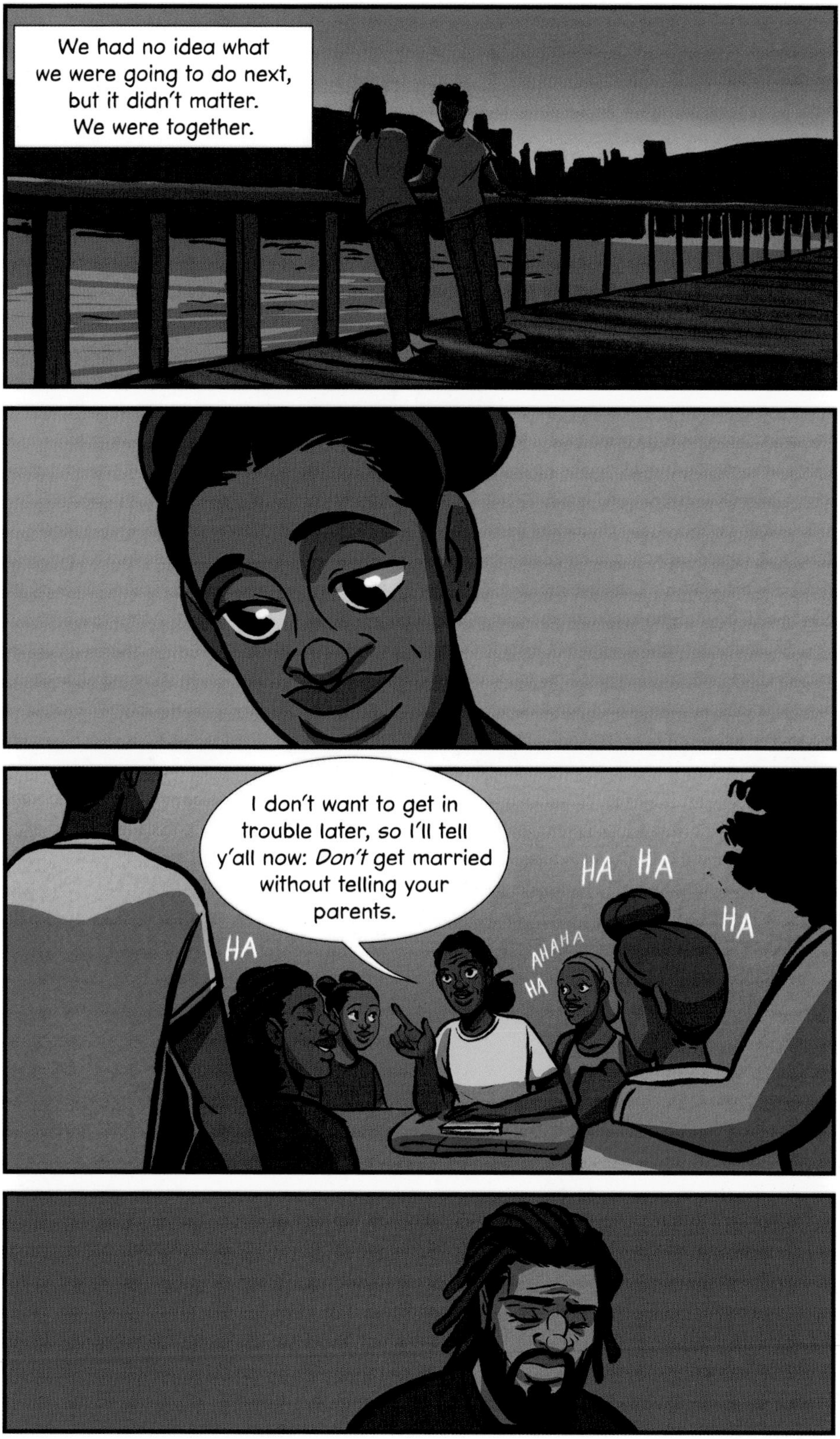
We had no idea what we were going to do next, but it didn't matter. We were together.
I don't want to get in trouble later, so I'll tell y'all now: *Don't* get married without telling your parents.
HA HA
HA
HA
AHAHA
HA

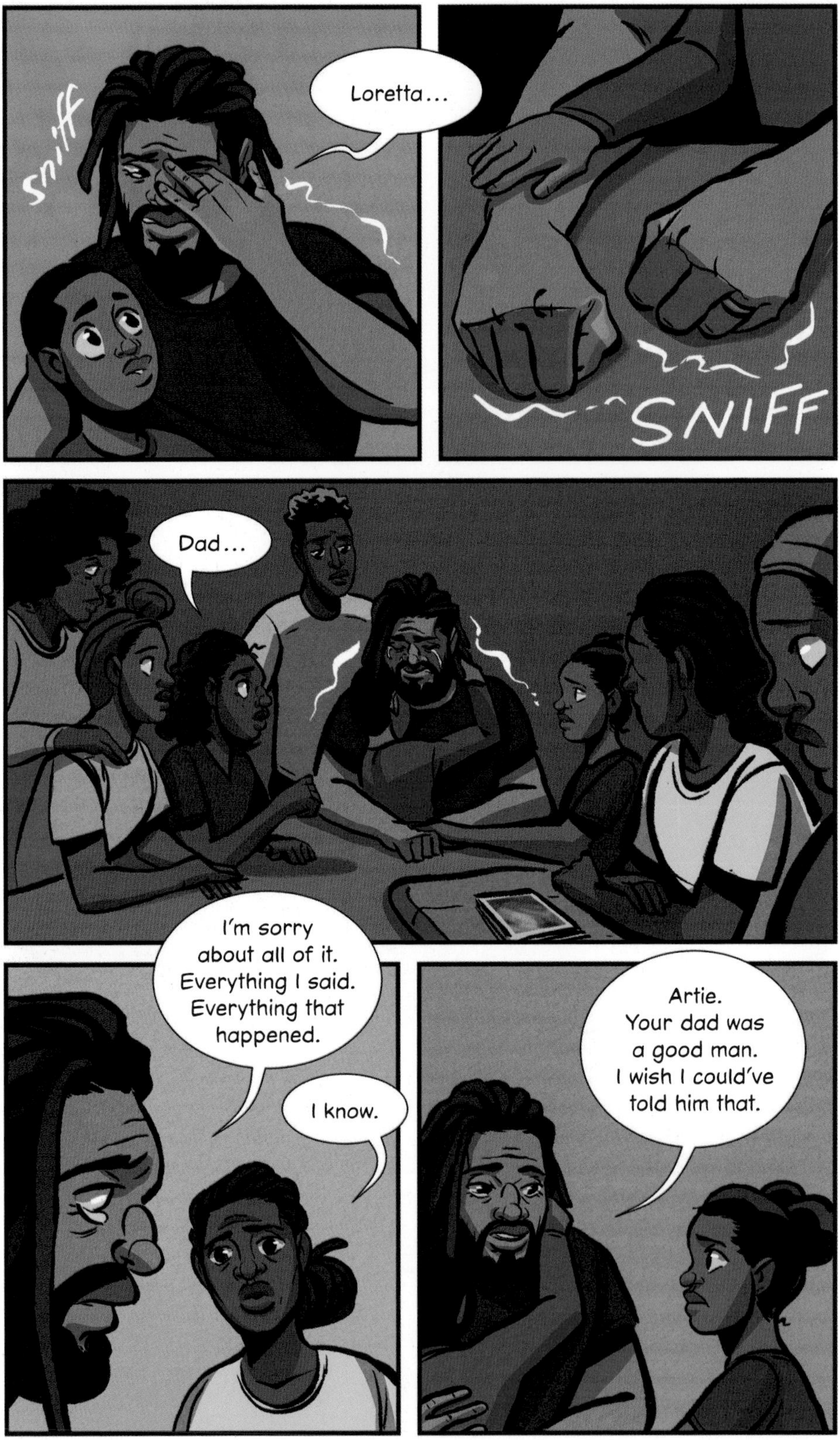
sniff
Loretta...
SNIFF
Dad...
I'm sorry about all of it. Everything I said. Everything that happened.
I know.
Artie. Your dad was a good man. I wish I could've told him that.

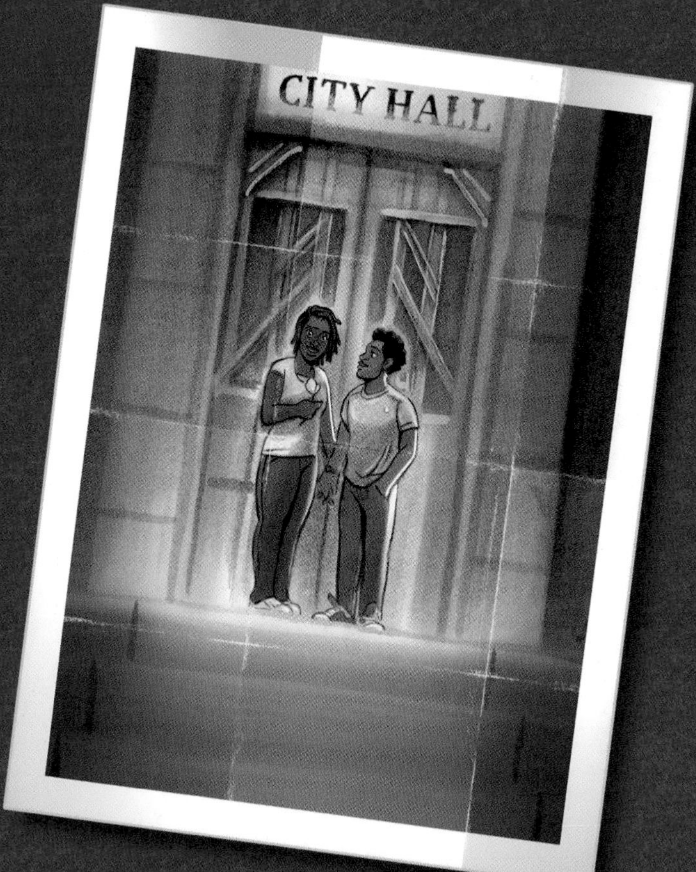
CITY HALL

CHAPTER FIVE

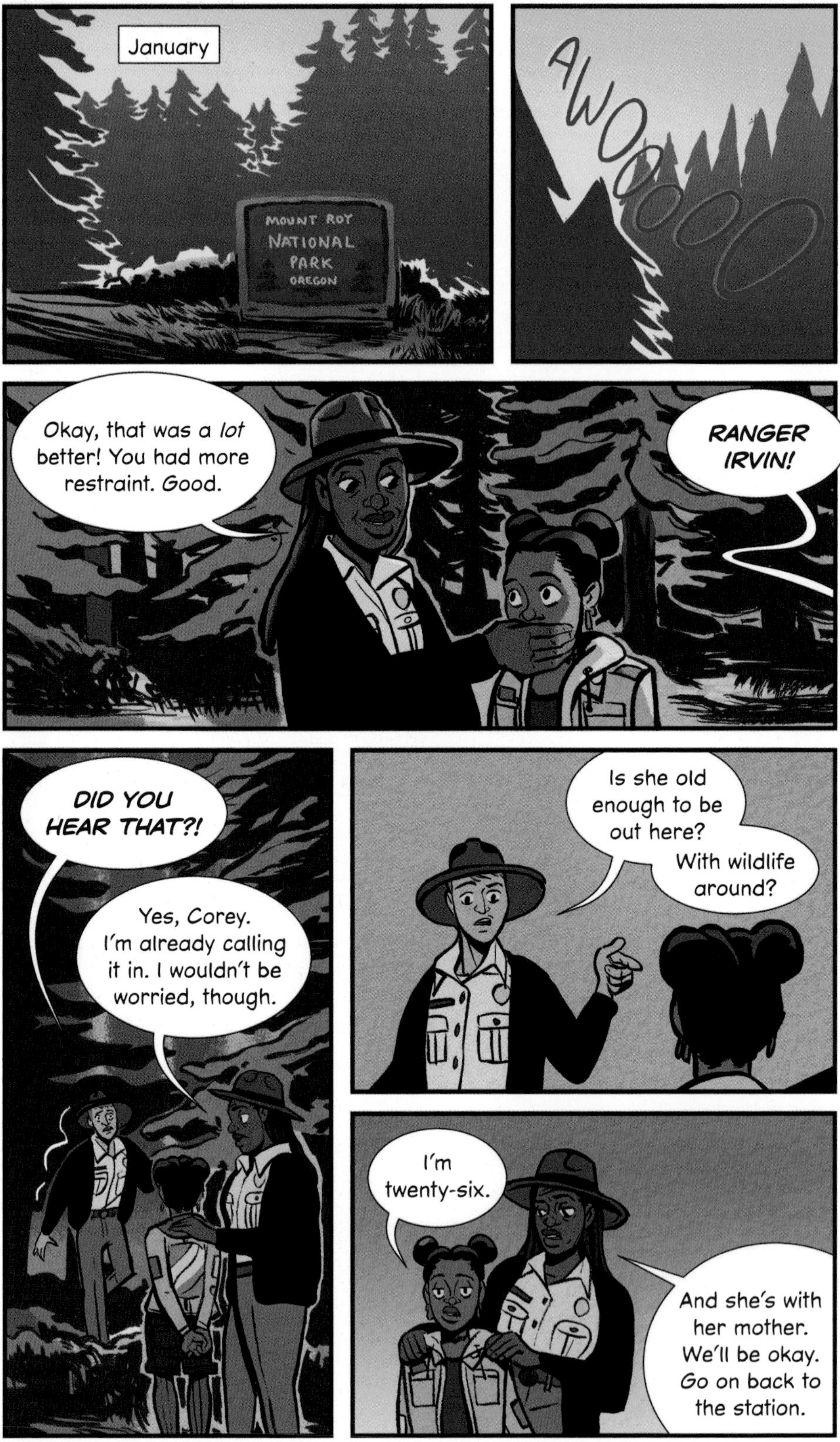

January
MOUNT ROY NATIONAL PARK OREGON
AWOOOOOO
Okay, that was a *lot* better! You had more restraint. *Good.*
RANGER IRVIN!
DID YOU HEAR THAT?!
Yes, Corey. I'm already calling it in. I wouldn't be worried, though.
Is she old enough to be out here?
With wildlife around?
I'm twenty-six.
And she's with her mother. We'll be okay. *Go* on back to the station.

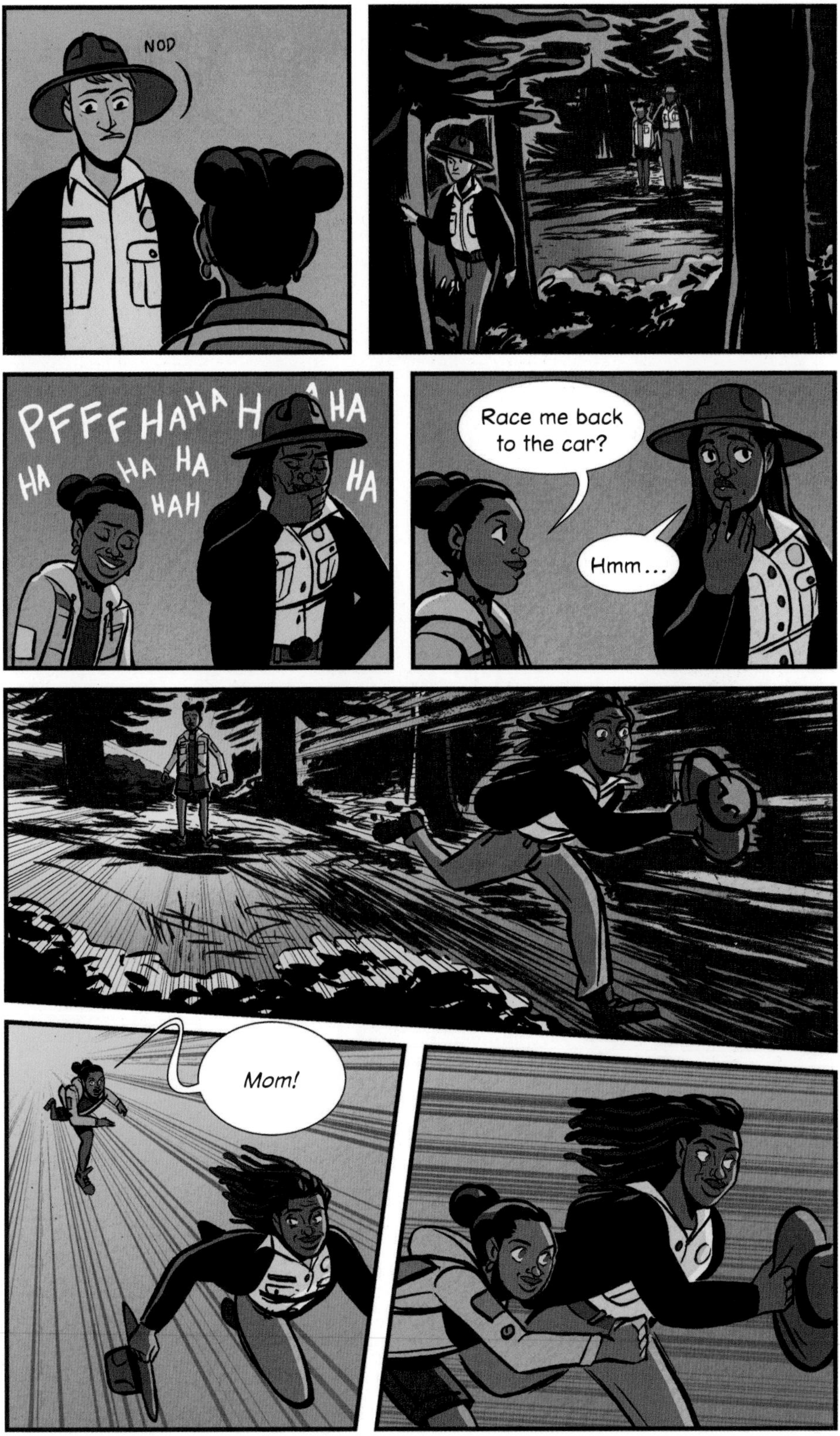
NOD
PFFFHAHAH HAHA
HA HA HA HAH HA
Race me back to the car?
Hmm...
Mom!

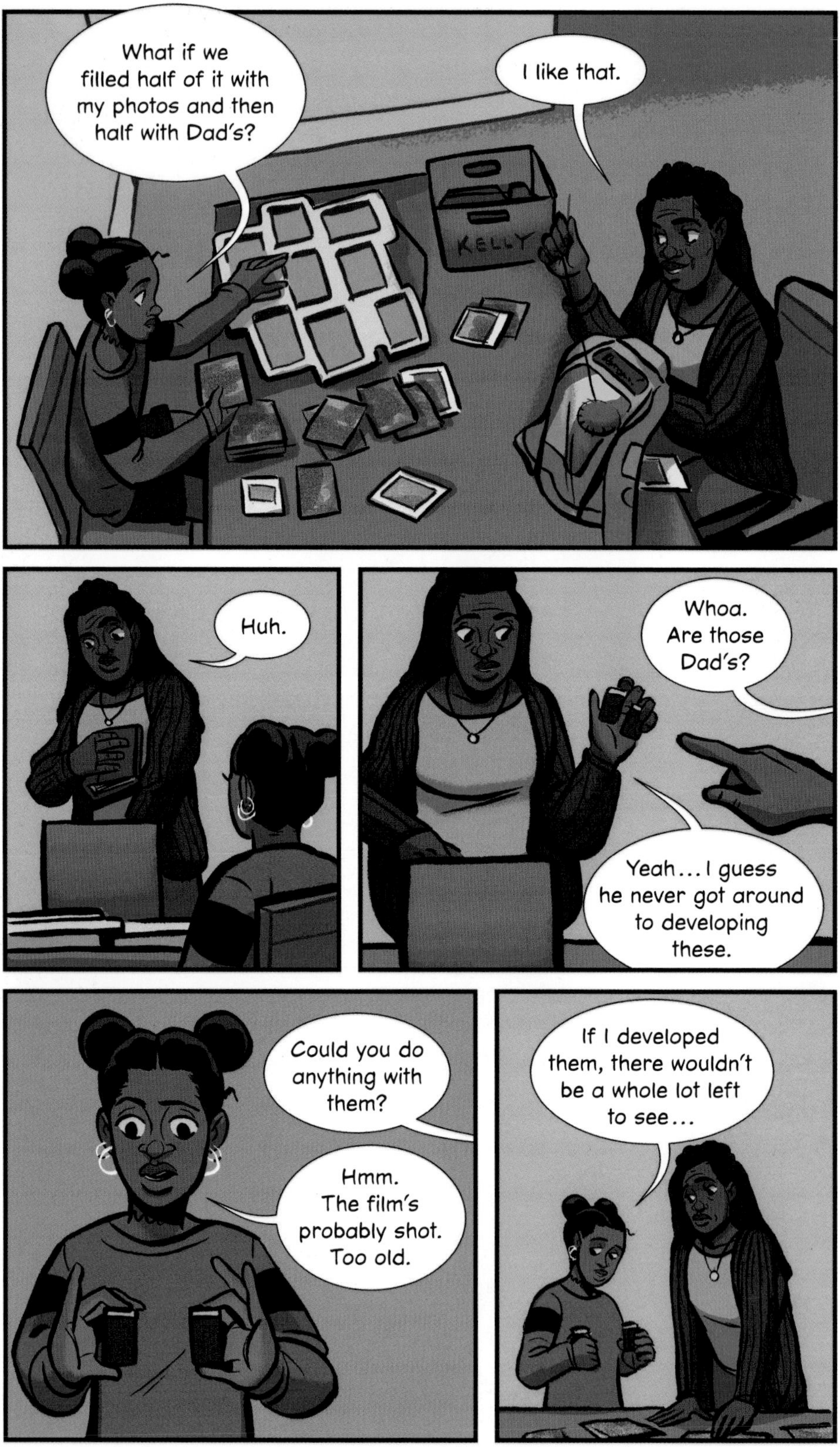
What if we filled half of it with my photos and then half with Dad's?
I like that.
KELLY
Huh.
Whoa. Are those Dad's?
Yeah... I guess he never got around to developing these.
Could you do anything with them?
Hmm. The film's probably shot. Too old.
If I developed them, there wouldn't be a whole lot left to see...

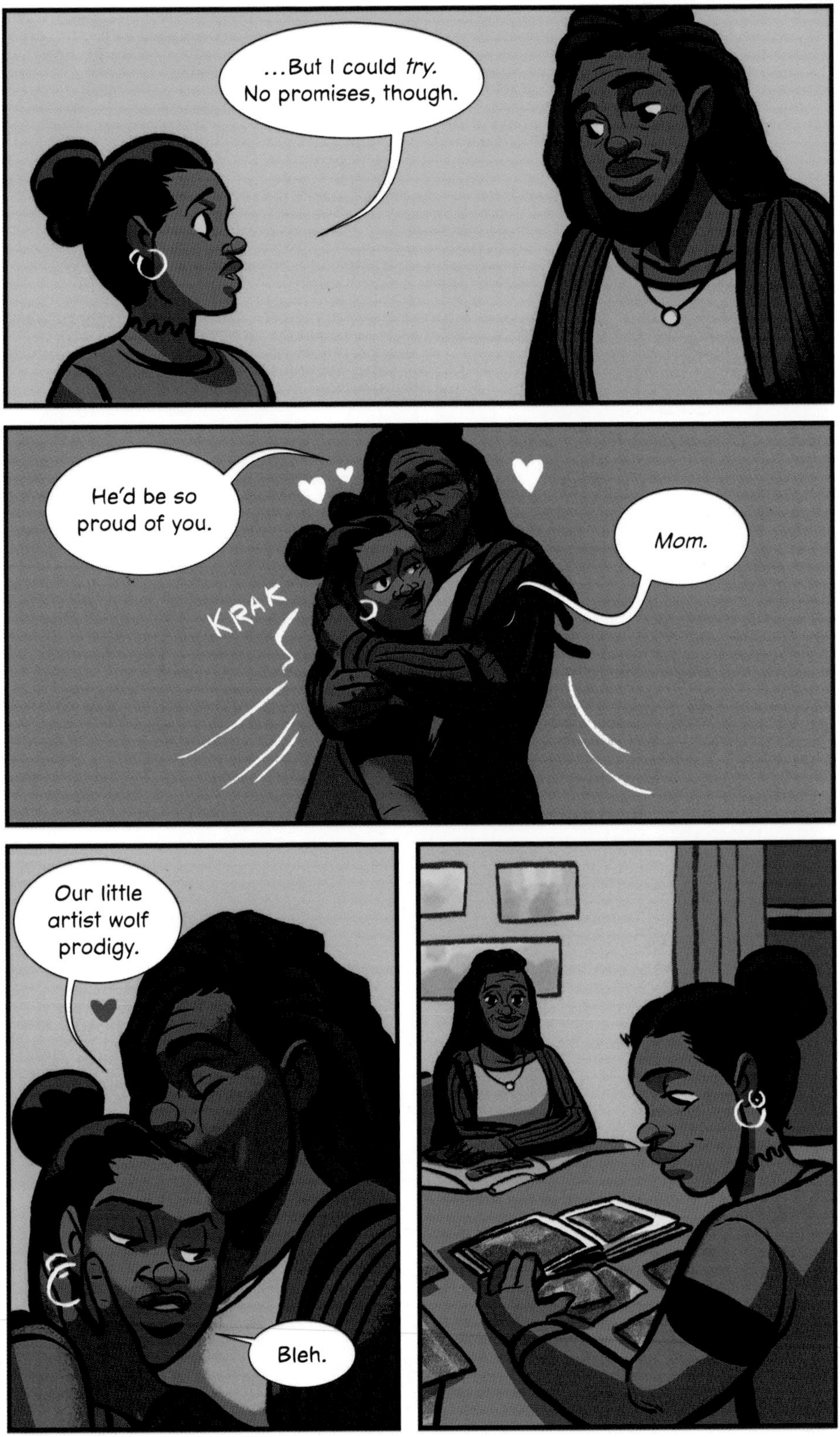
...But I could *try*. No promises, though.
He'd be so proud of you.
KRAK
Mom.
Our little artist wolf prodigy.
Bleh.

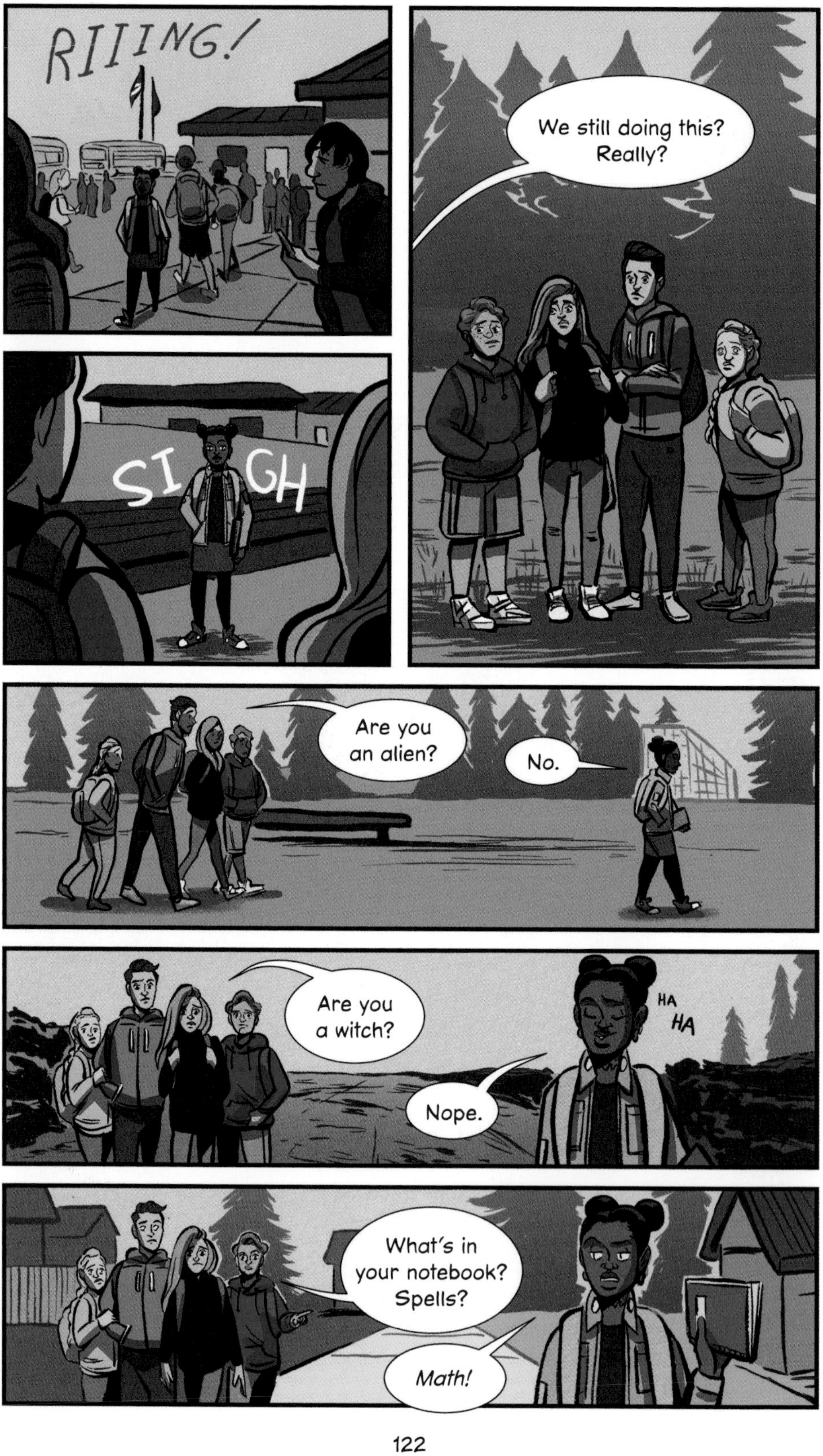
RIIING!
SIGH
We still doing this? Really?
Are you an alien?
No.
Are you a witch?
HA HA
Nope.
What's in your notebook? Spells?
Math!

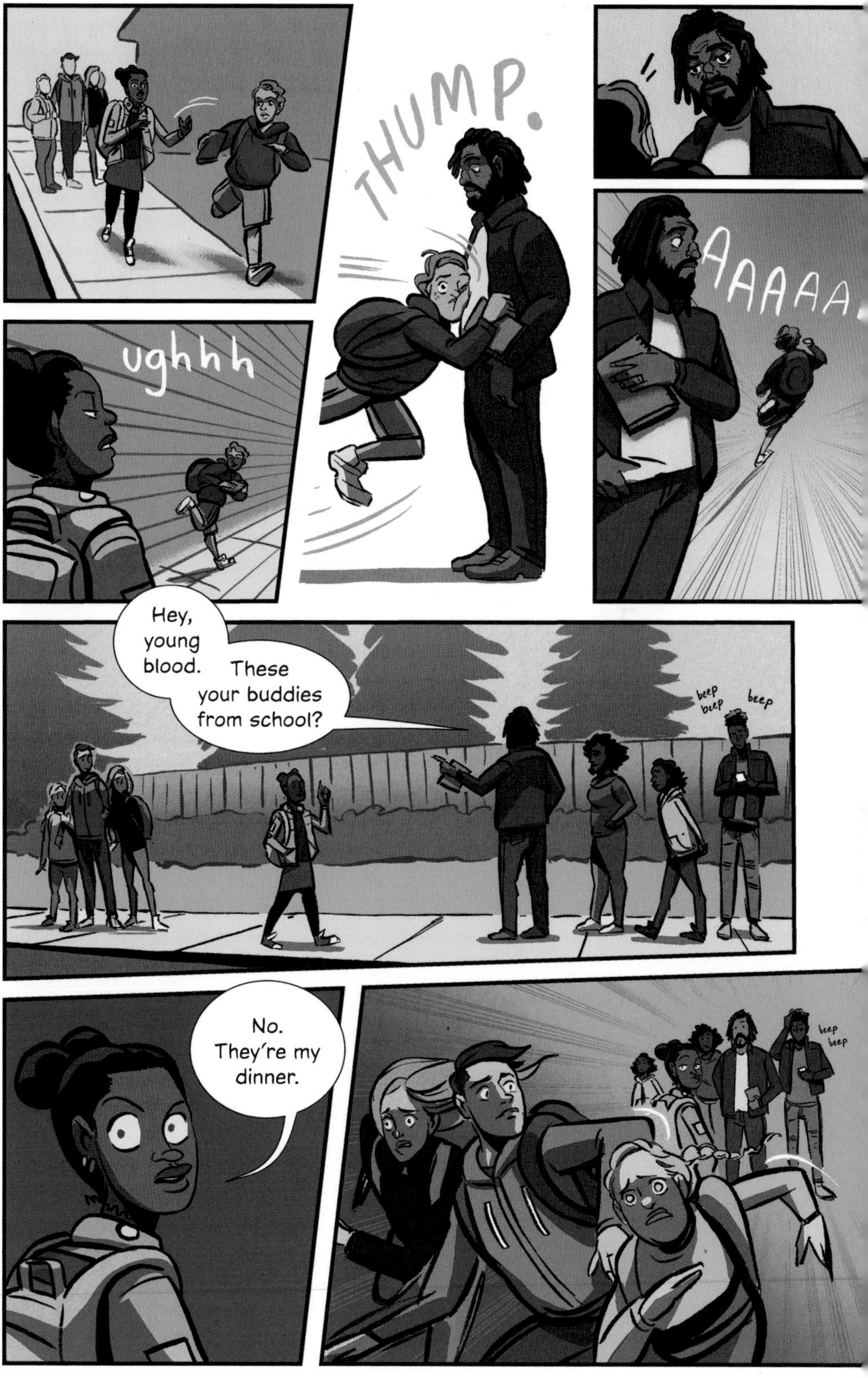
THUMP.
ughhh
AAAAA
Hey, young blood.
These your buddies from school?
beep beep
beep
No. They're my dinner.
beep beep

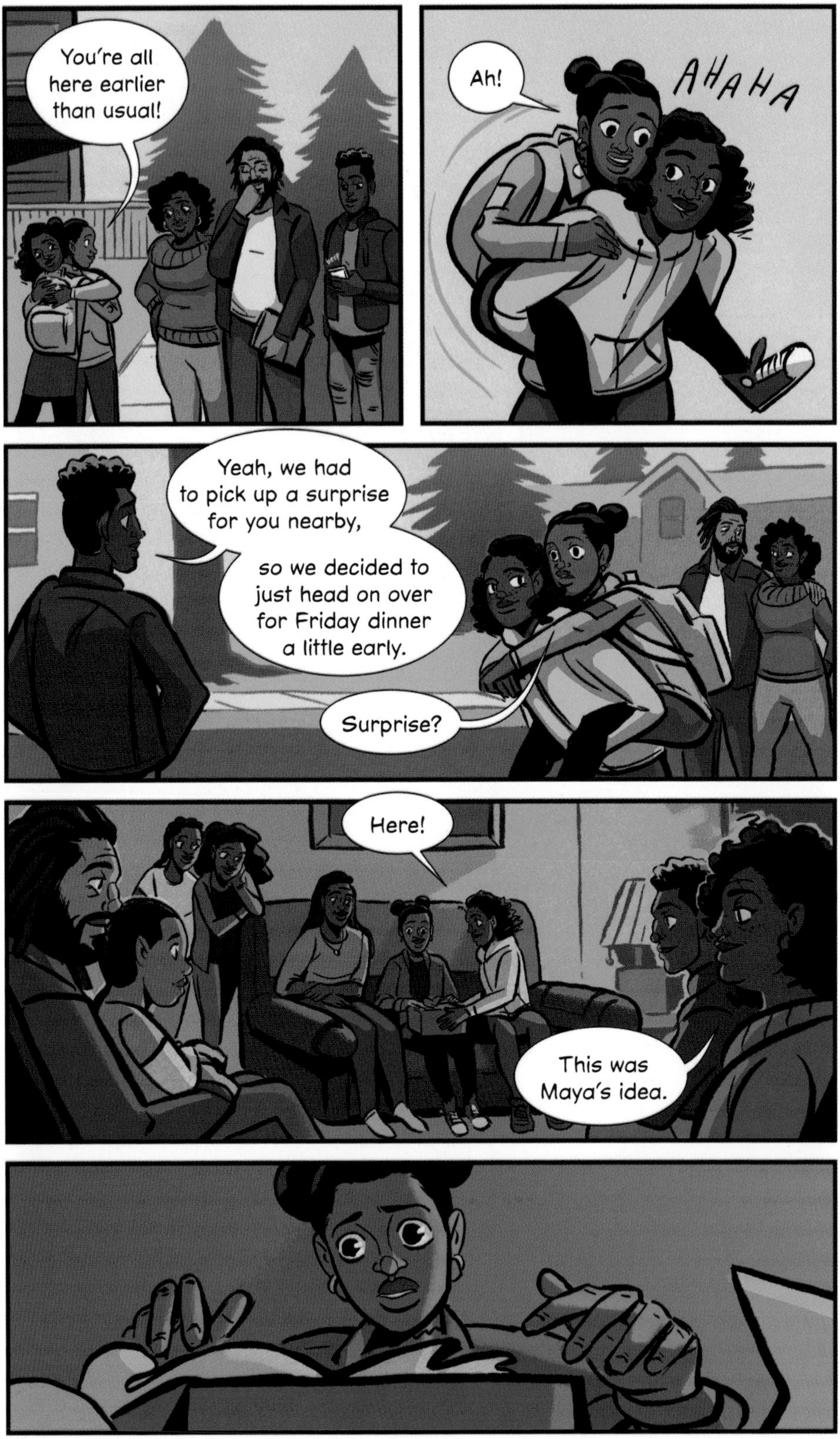
You're all here earlier than usual!
Ah!
AHAHA
Yeah, we had to pick up a surprise for you nearby,
so we decided to just head on over for Friday dinner a little early.
Surprise?
Here!
This was Maya's idea.

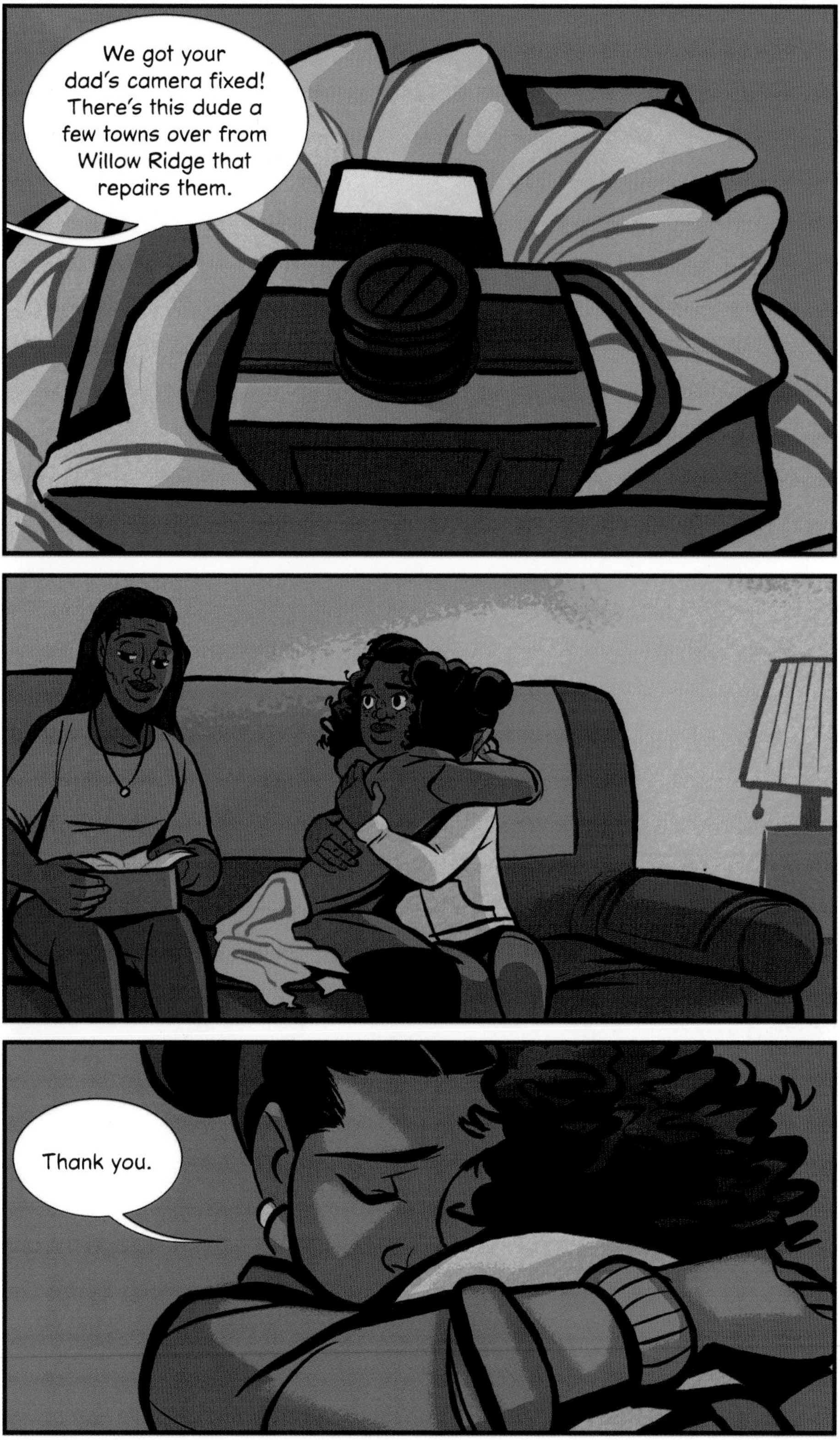
We got your dad's camera fixed! There's this dude a few towns over from Willow Ridge that repairs them.
Thank you.

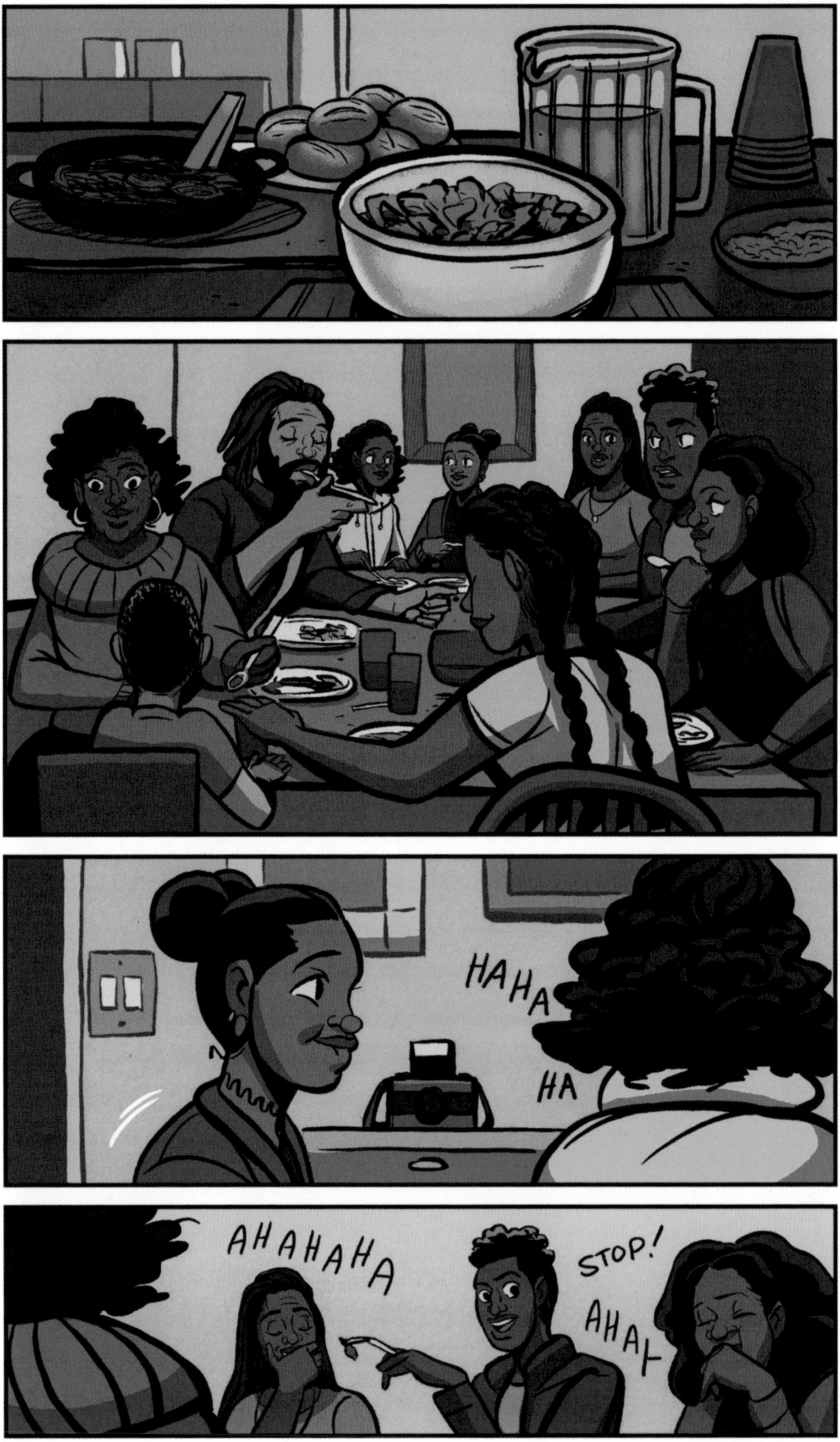
HAHA
HA
AHAHAHA
STOP!
AHAH

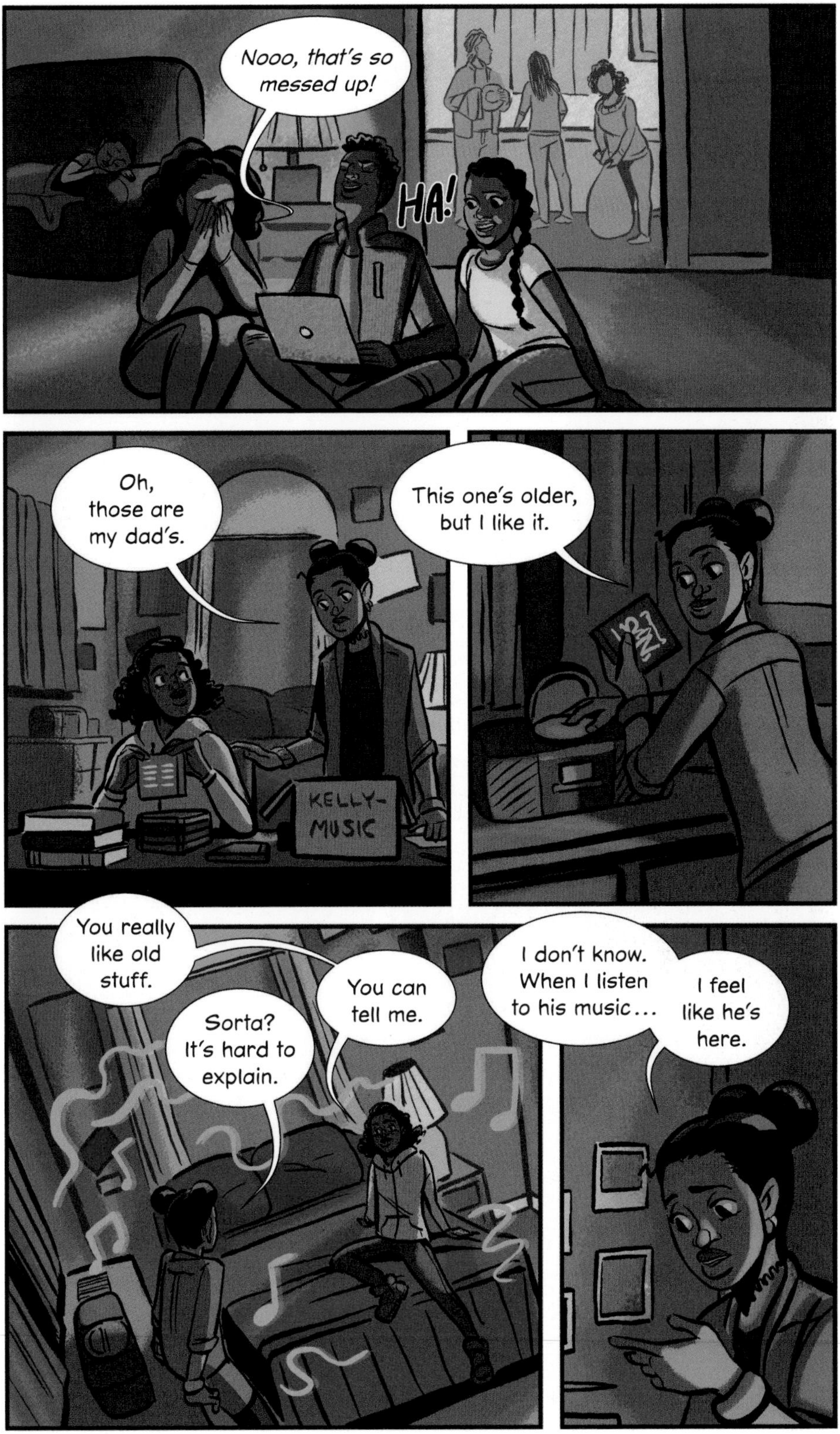
Nooo, that's so messed up!
HA!
Oh, those are my dad's.
KELLY- MUSIC
This one's older, but I like it.
You really like old stuff.
Sorta? It's hard to explain.
You can tell me.
I don't know. When I listen to his music...
I feel like he's here.

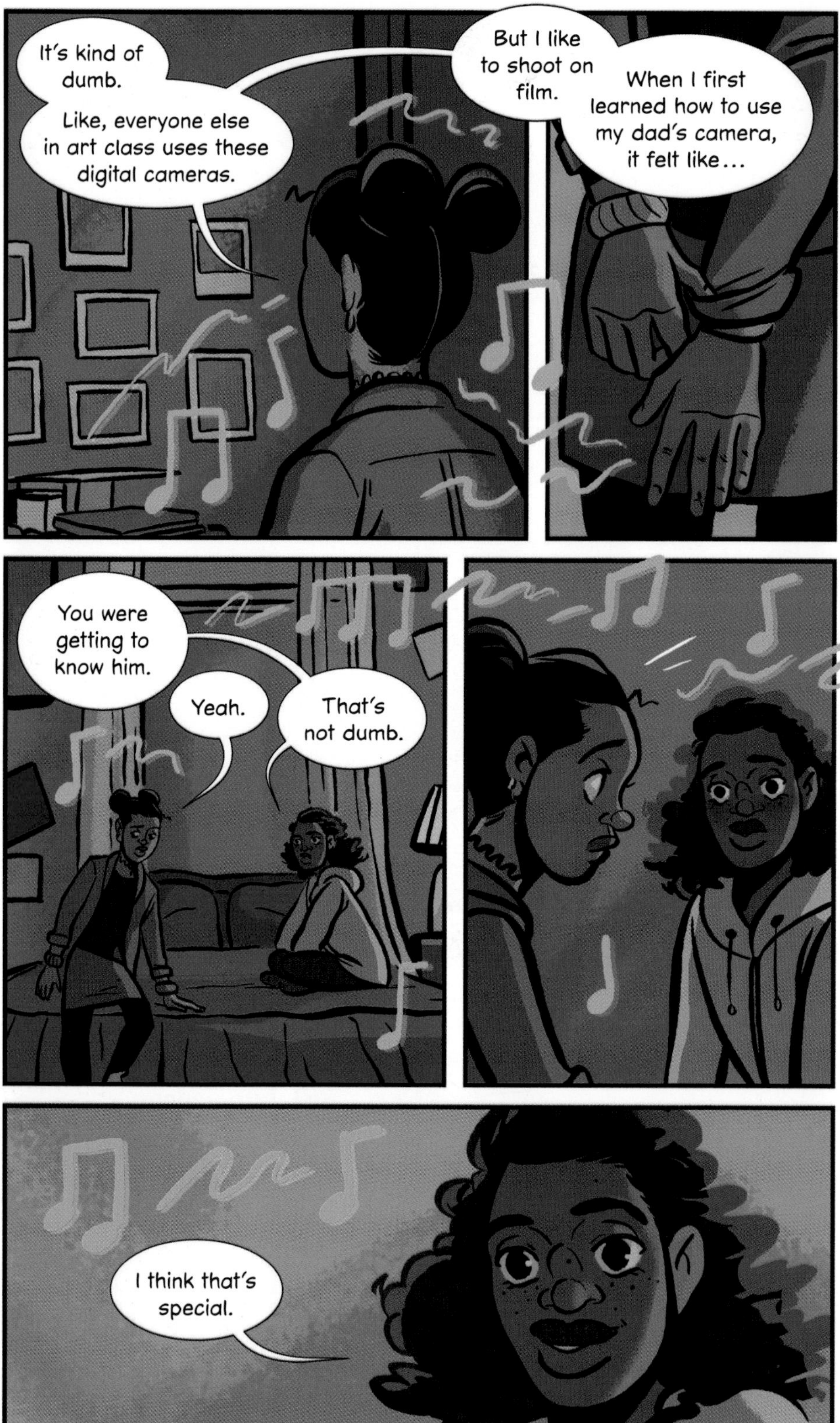
It's kind of dumb.
Like, everyone else in art class uses these digital cameras.
But I like to shoot on film.
When I first learned how to use my dad's camera, it felt like...
You were getting to know him.
Yeah.
That's not dumb.
I think that's special.

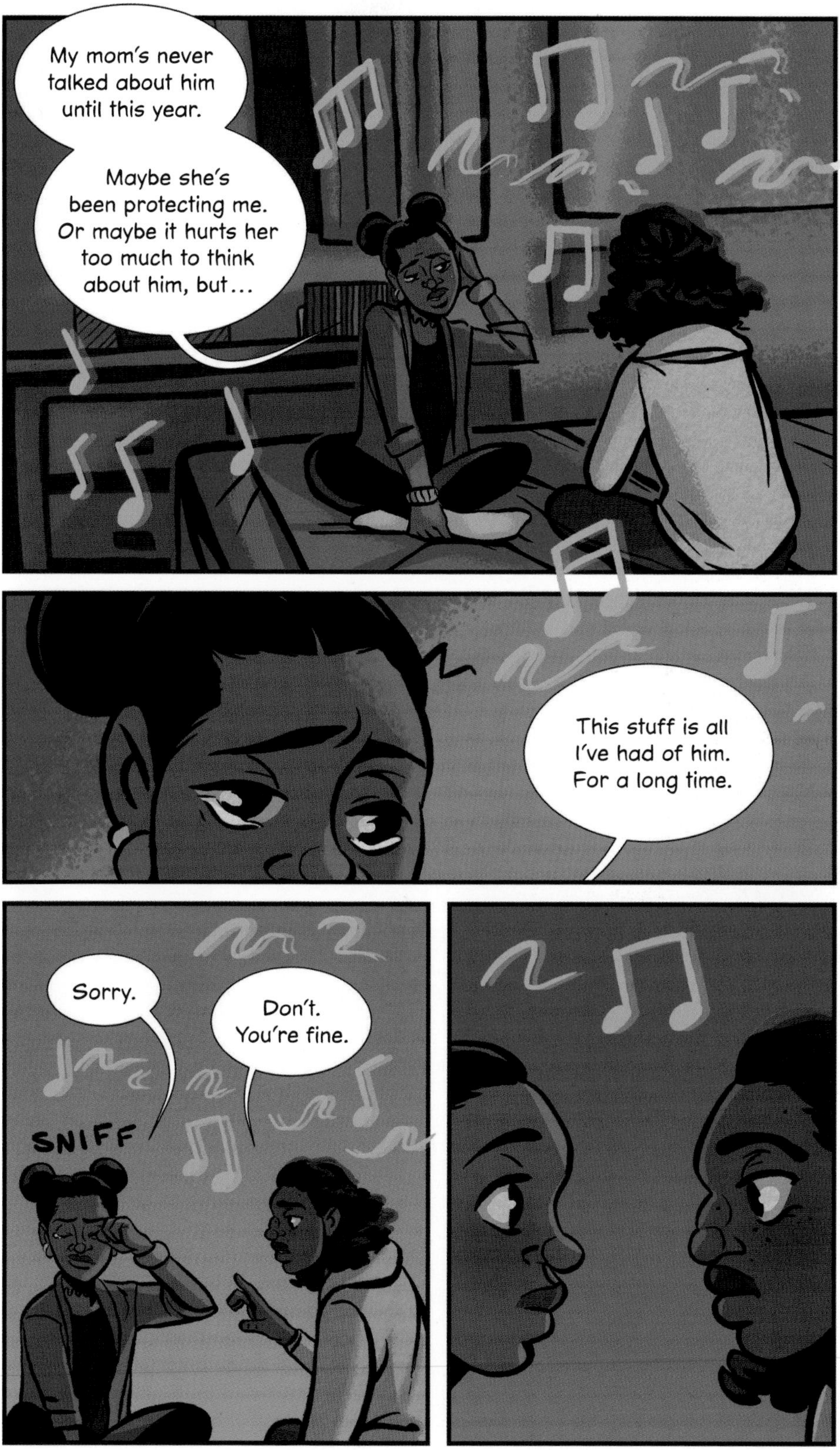
My mom's never talked about him until this year.
Maybe she's been protecting me. Or maybe it hurts her too much to think about him, but...
This stuff is all I've had of him. For a long time.
Sorry.
Don't. You're fine.
SNIFF

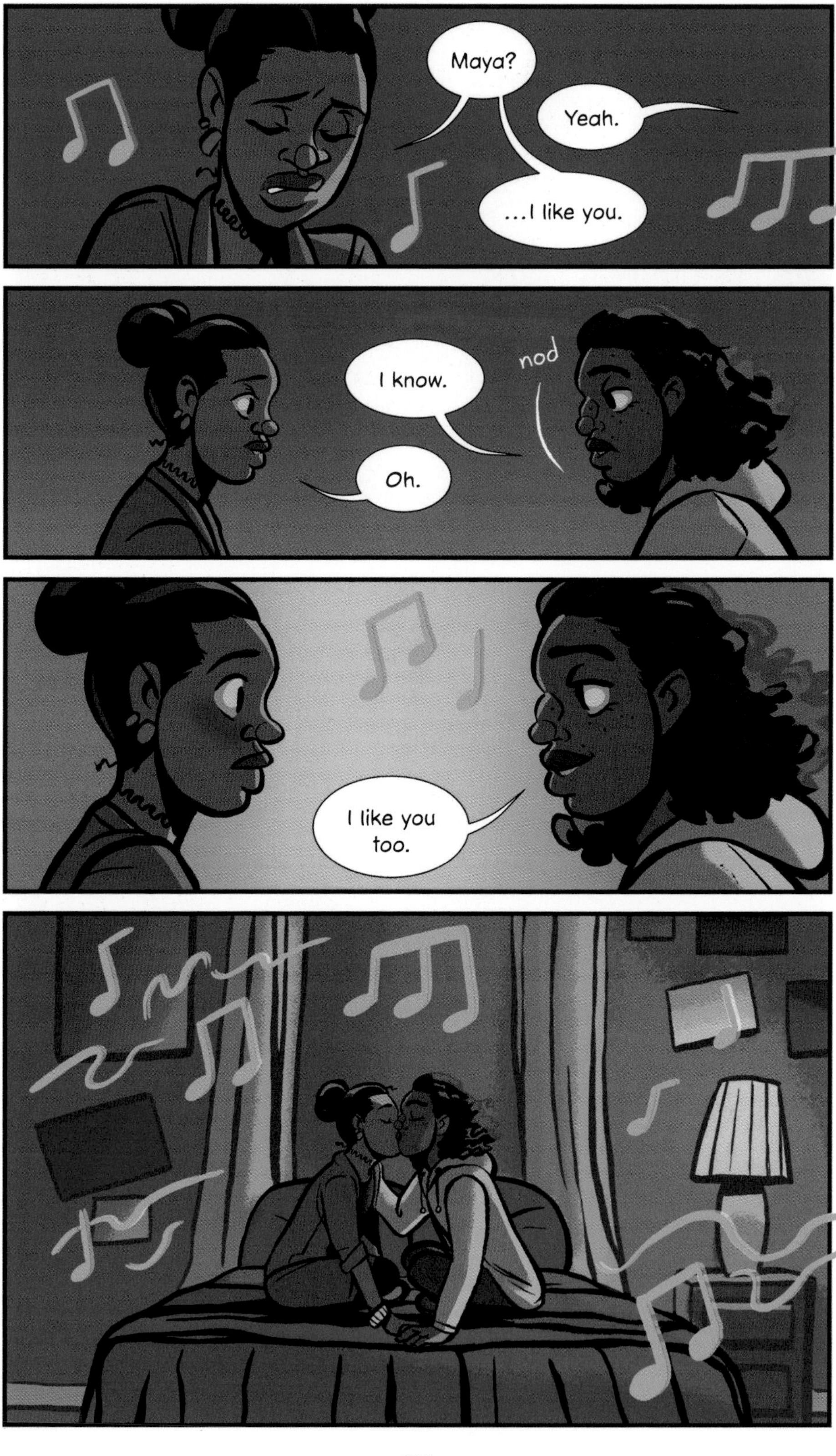
Maya?
Yeah.
...I like you.
I know.
nod
Oh.
I like you too.

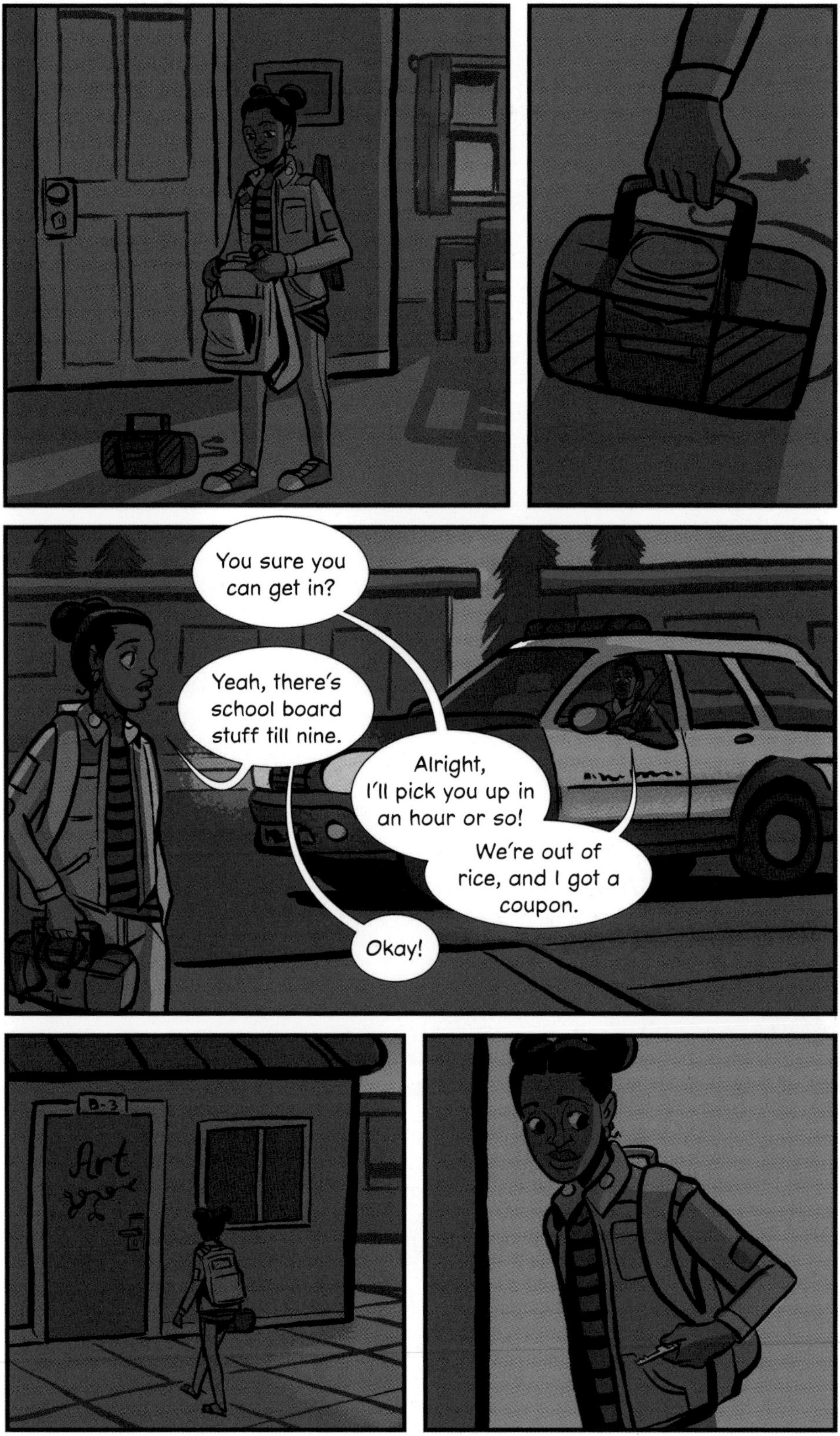
You sure you can get in?
Yeah, there's school board stuff till nine.
Alright, I'll pick you up in an hour or so!
We're out of rice, and I got a coupon.
Okay!
B-3
Art

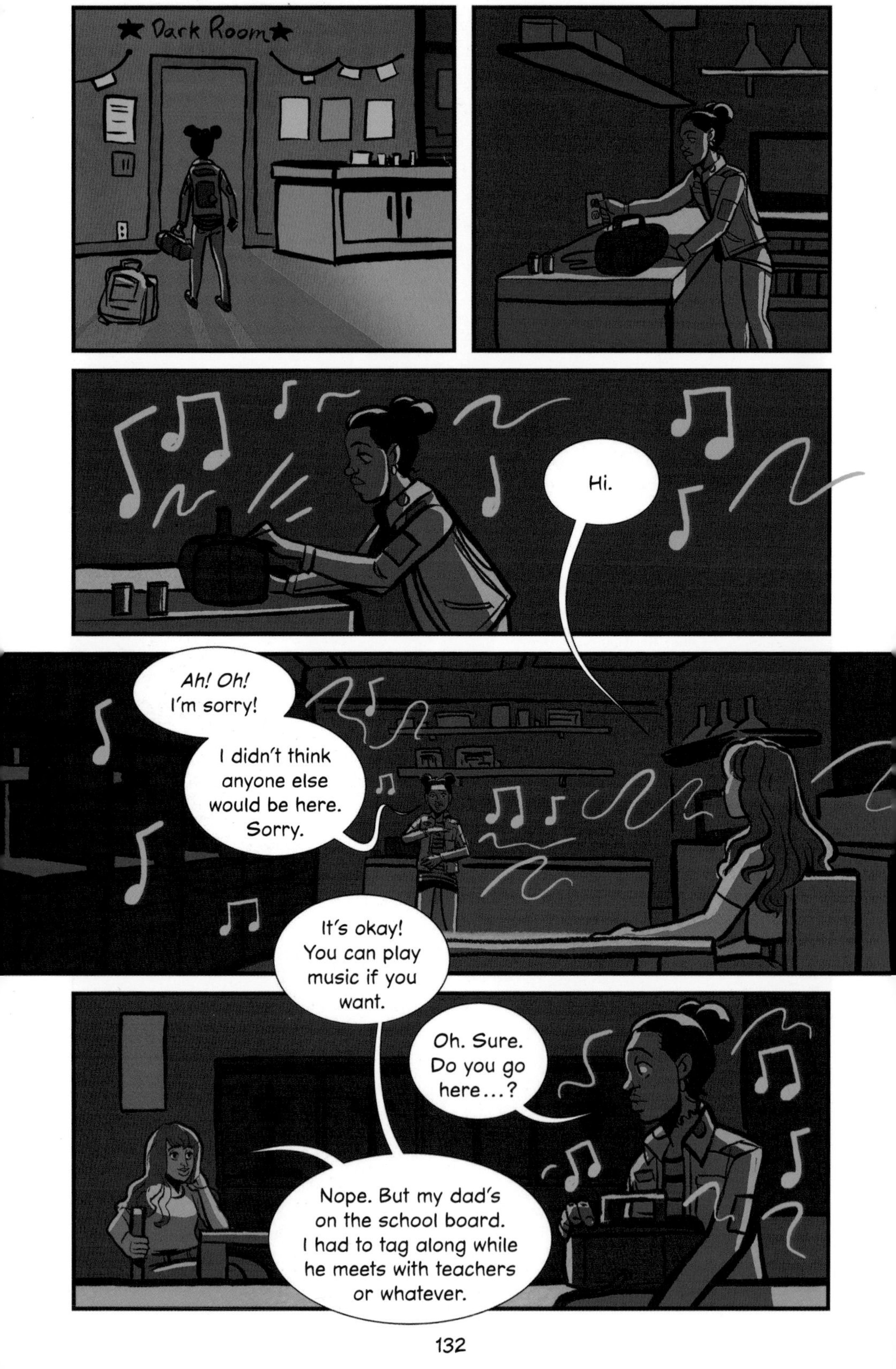
★Dark Room★
Hi.
Ah! Oh! I'm sorry!
I didn't think anyone else would be here. Sorry.
It's okay! You can play music if you want.
Oh. Sure. Do you go here...?
Nope. But my dad's on the school board. I had to tag along while he meets with teachers or whatever.

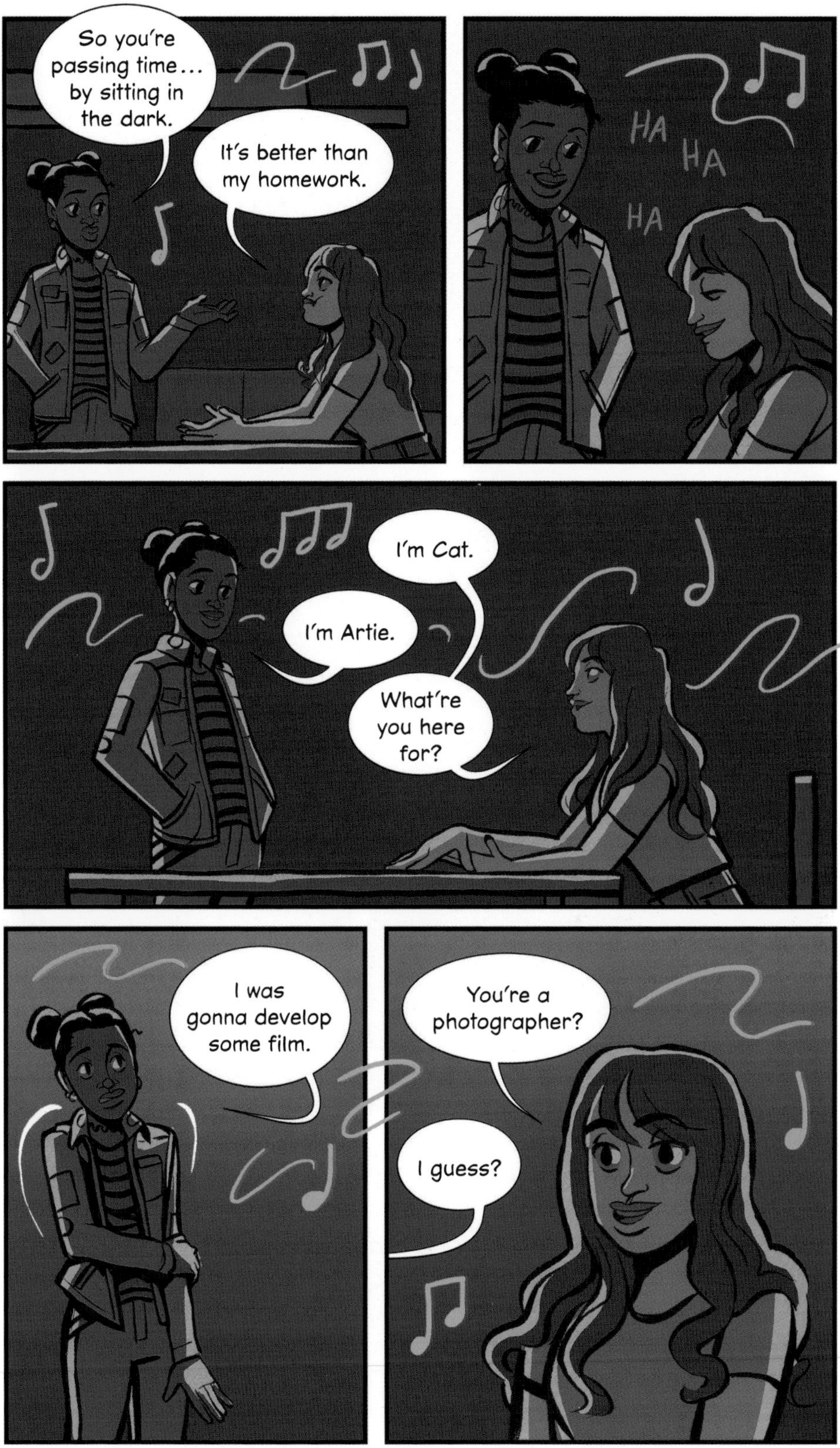
So you're passing time... by sitting in the dark.
It's better than my homework.
HA HA HA
I'm Cat.
I'm Artie.
What're you here for?
I was gonna develop some film.
You're a photographer?
I guess?

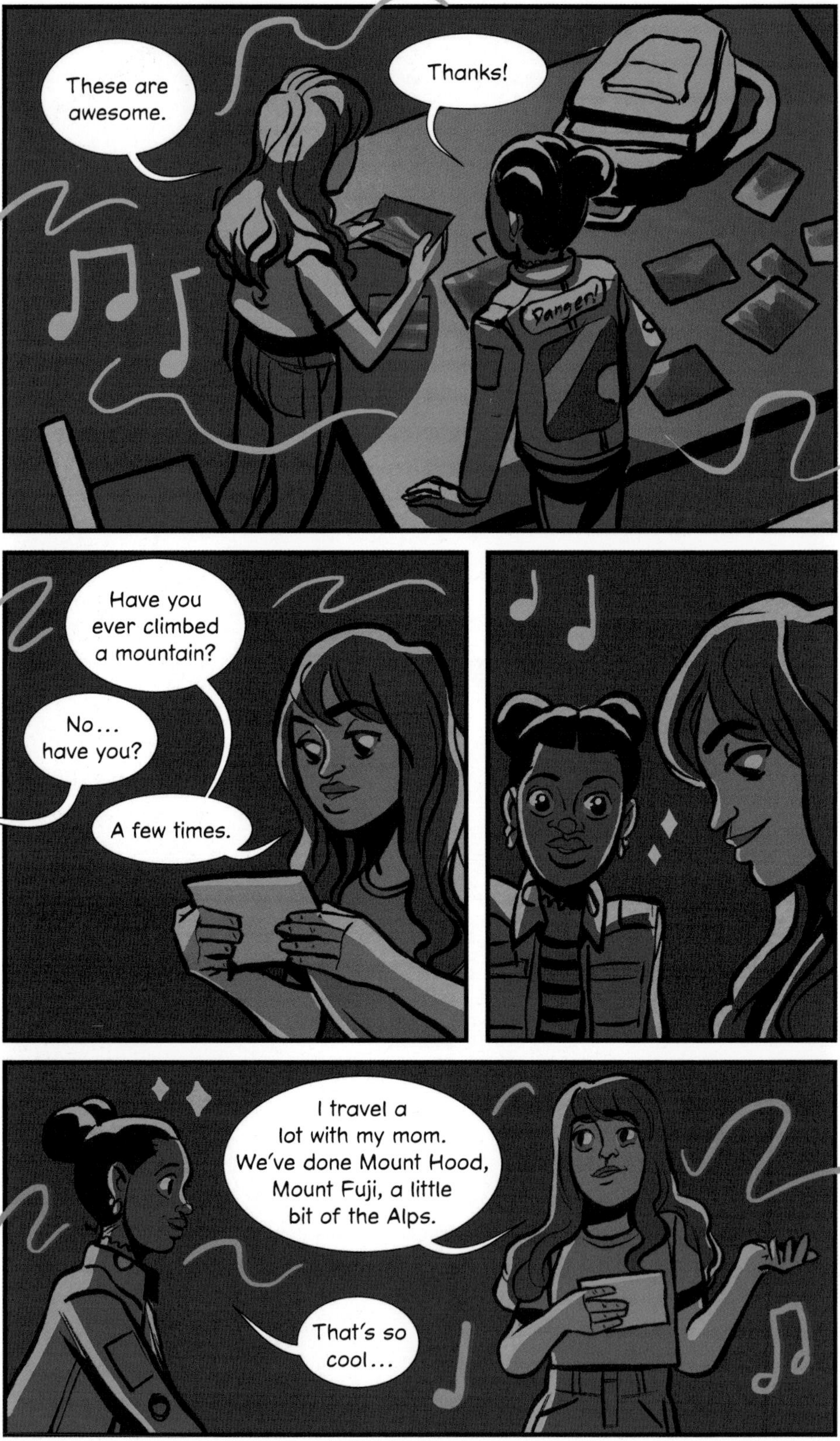
These are awesome.
Thanks!
Have you ever climbed a mountain?
No... have you?
A few times.
I travel a lot with my mom. We've done Mount Hood, Mount Fuji, a little bit of the Alps.
That's so cool...

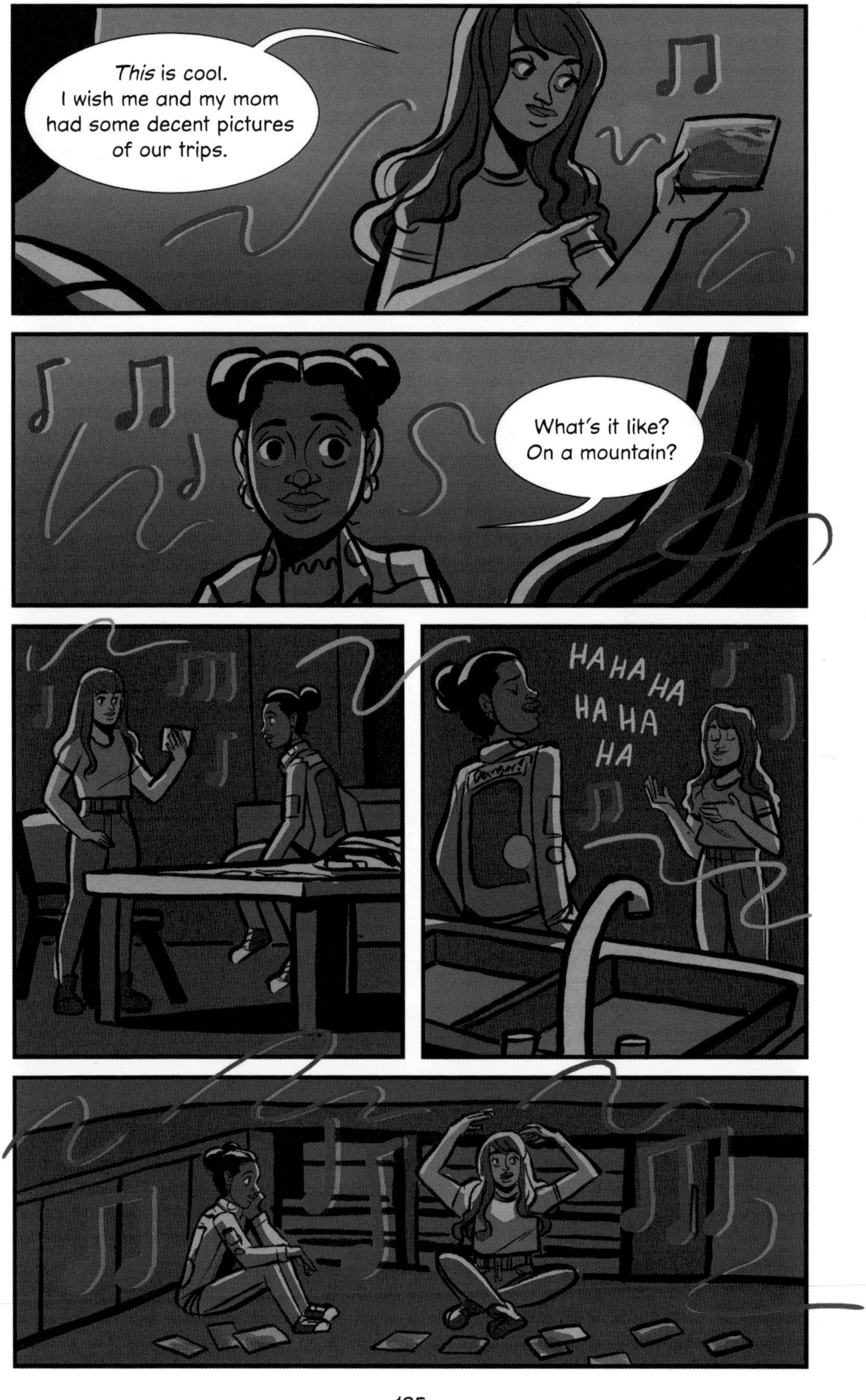
This is cool. I wish me and my mom had some decent pictures of our trips.
What's it like? On a mountain?
HA HA HA HA HA HA HA

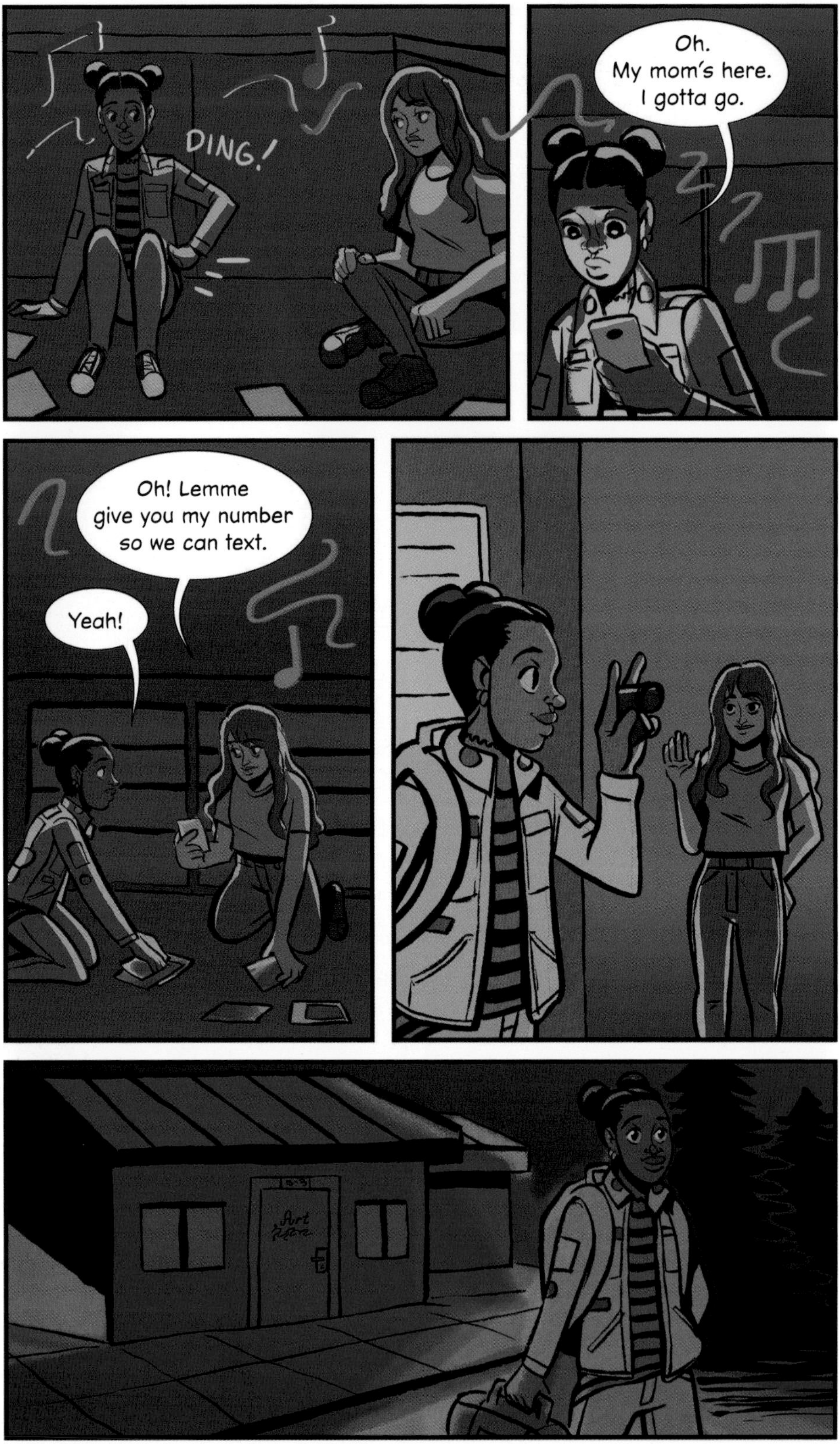
DING!
Oh. My mom's here. I gotta go.
Oh! Lemme give you my number so we can text.
Yeah!
Art

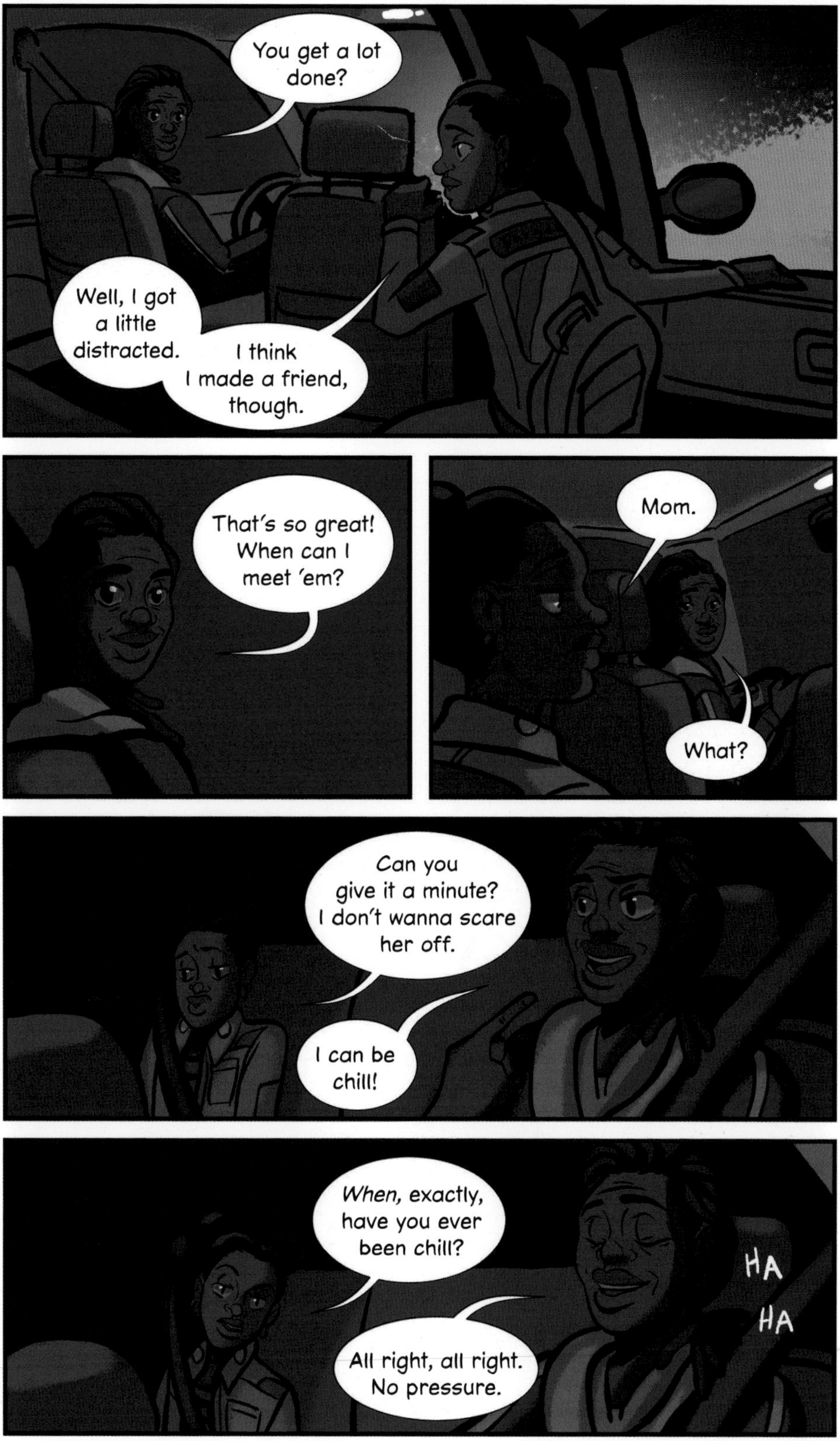
You get a lot done?
Well, I got a little distracted.
I think I made a friend, though.
That's so great! When can I meet 'em?
Mom.
What?
Can you give it a minute? I don't wanna scare her off.
I can be chill!
When, exactly, have you ever been chill?
HA HA
All right, all right. No pressure.

CHAPTER SIX

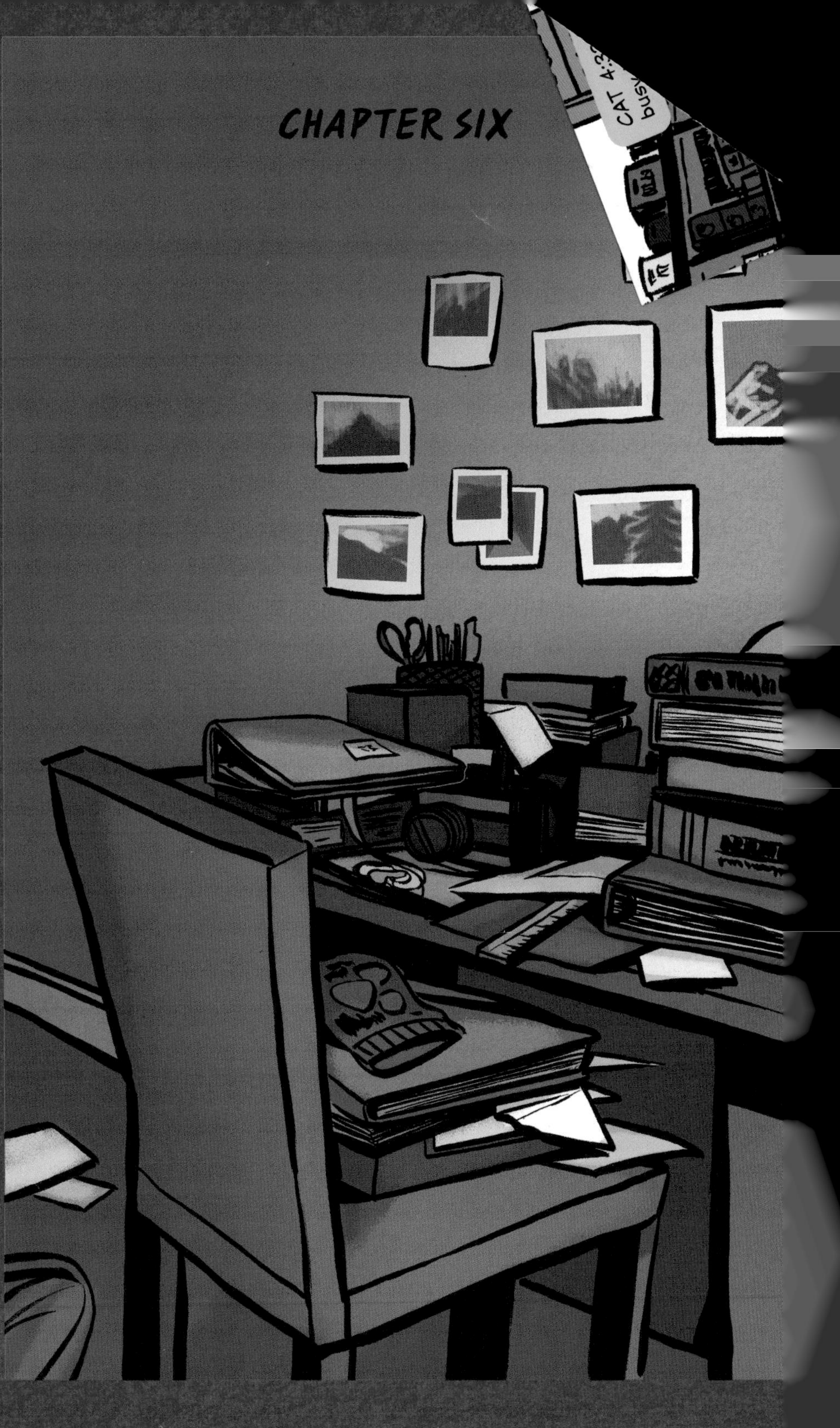

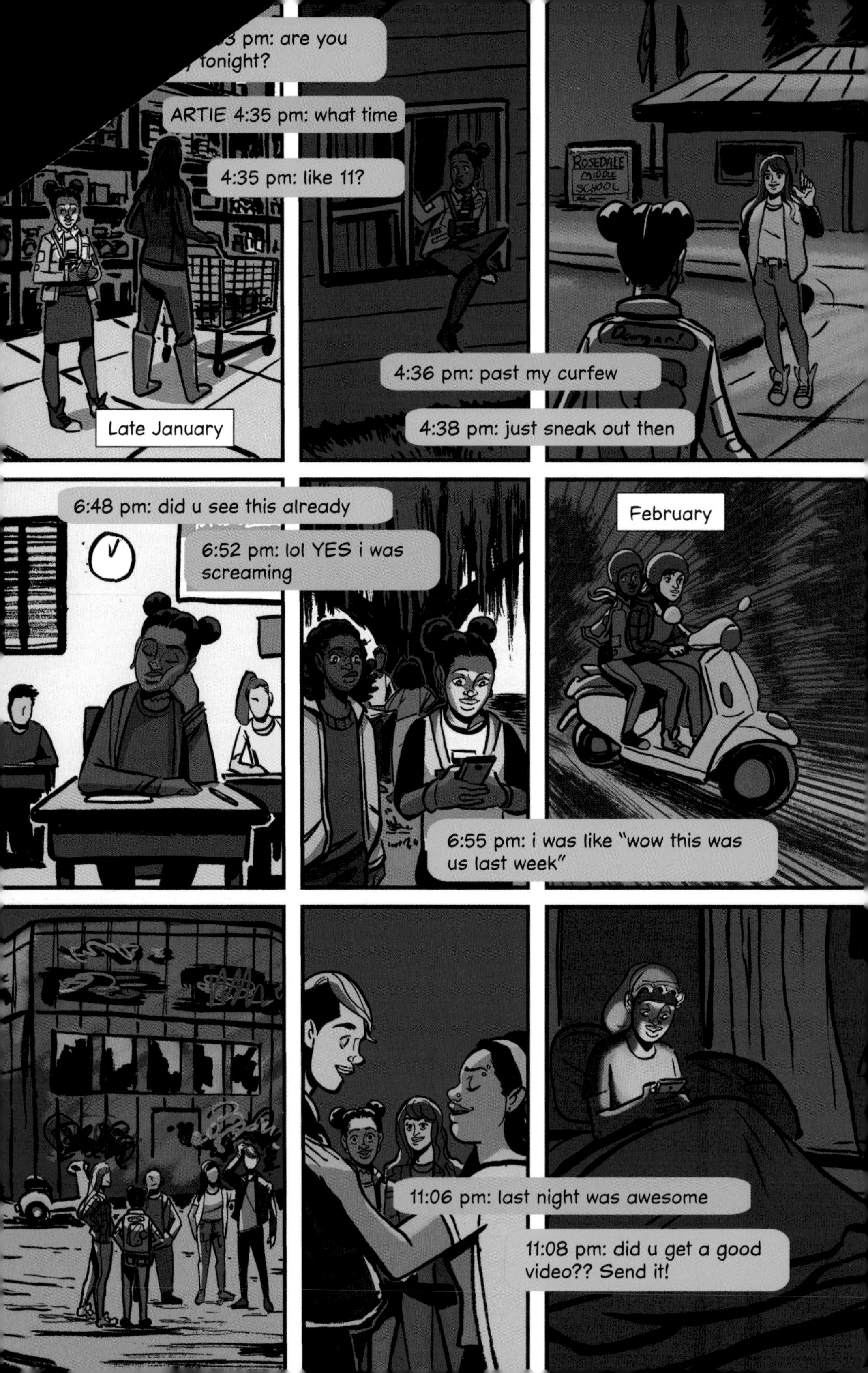
3 pm: are you
tonight?
ARTIE 4:35 pm: what time
4:35 pm: like 11?
Late January
ROSEDALE MIDDLE SCHOOL
4:36 pm: past my curfew
4:38 pm: just sneak out then
6:48 pm: did u see this already
6:52 pm: lol YES i was screaming
February
6:55 pm: i was like "wow this was us last week"
11:06 pm: last night was awesome
11:08 pm: did u get a good video?? Send it!

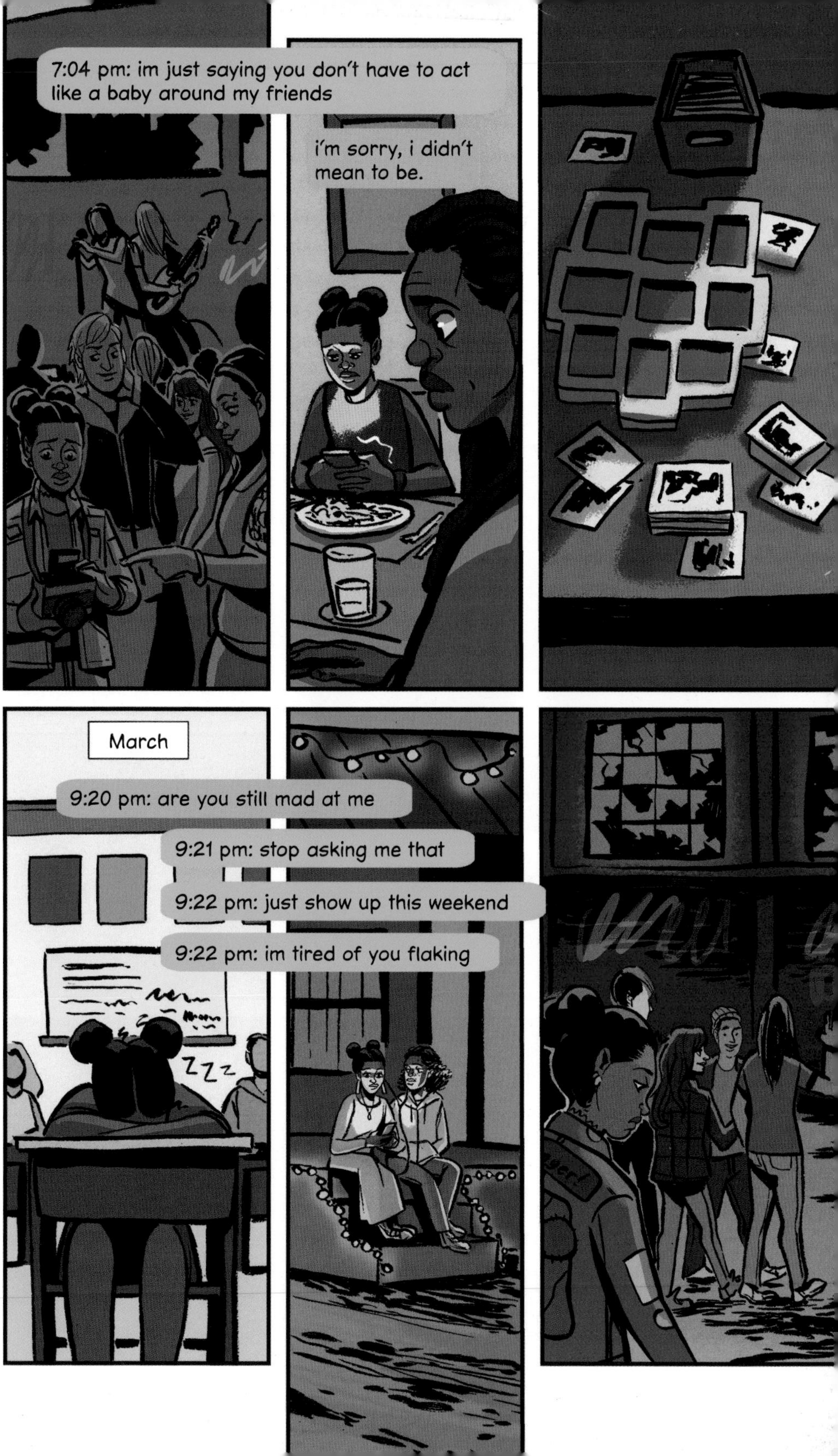
7:04 pm: im just saying you don't have to act like a baby around my friends
i'm sorry, i didn't mean to be.
March
9:20 pm: are you still mad at me
9:21 pm: stop asking me that
9:22 pm: just show up this weekend
9:22 pm: im tired of you flaking
ZZz

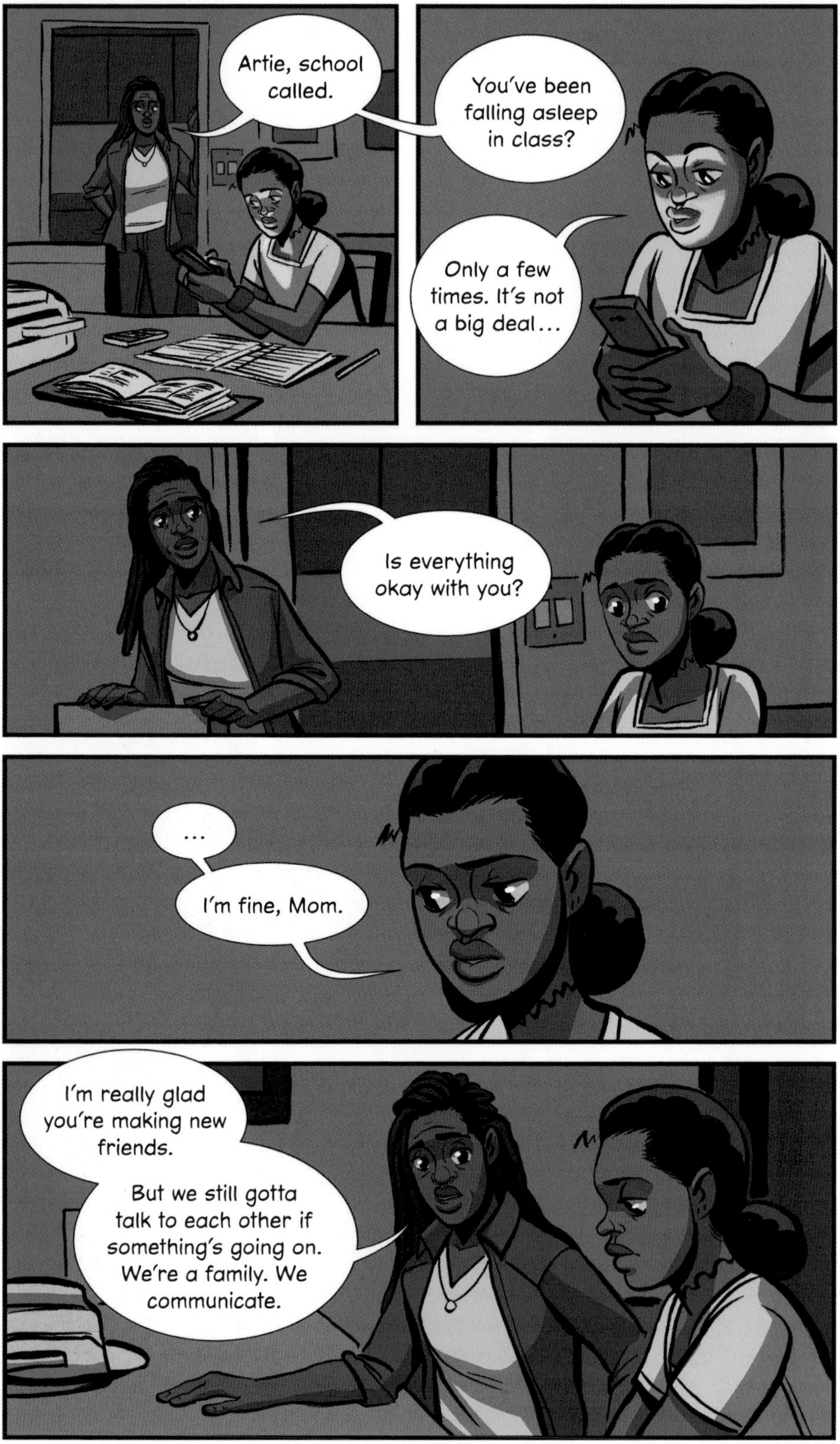
Artie, school called.
You've been falling asleep in class?
Only a few times. It's not a big deal...
Is everything okay with you?
...
I'm fine, Mom.
I'm really glad you're making new friends.
But we still gotta talk to each other if something's going on. We're a family. We communicate.

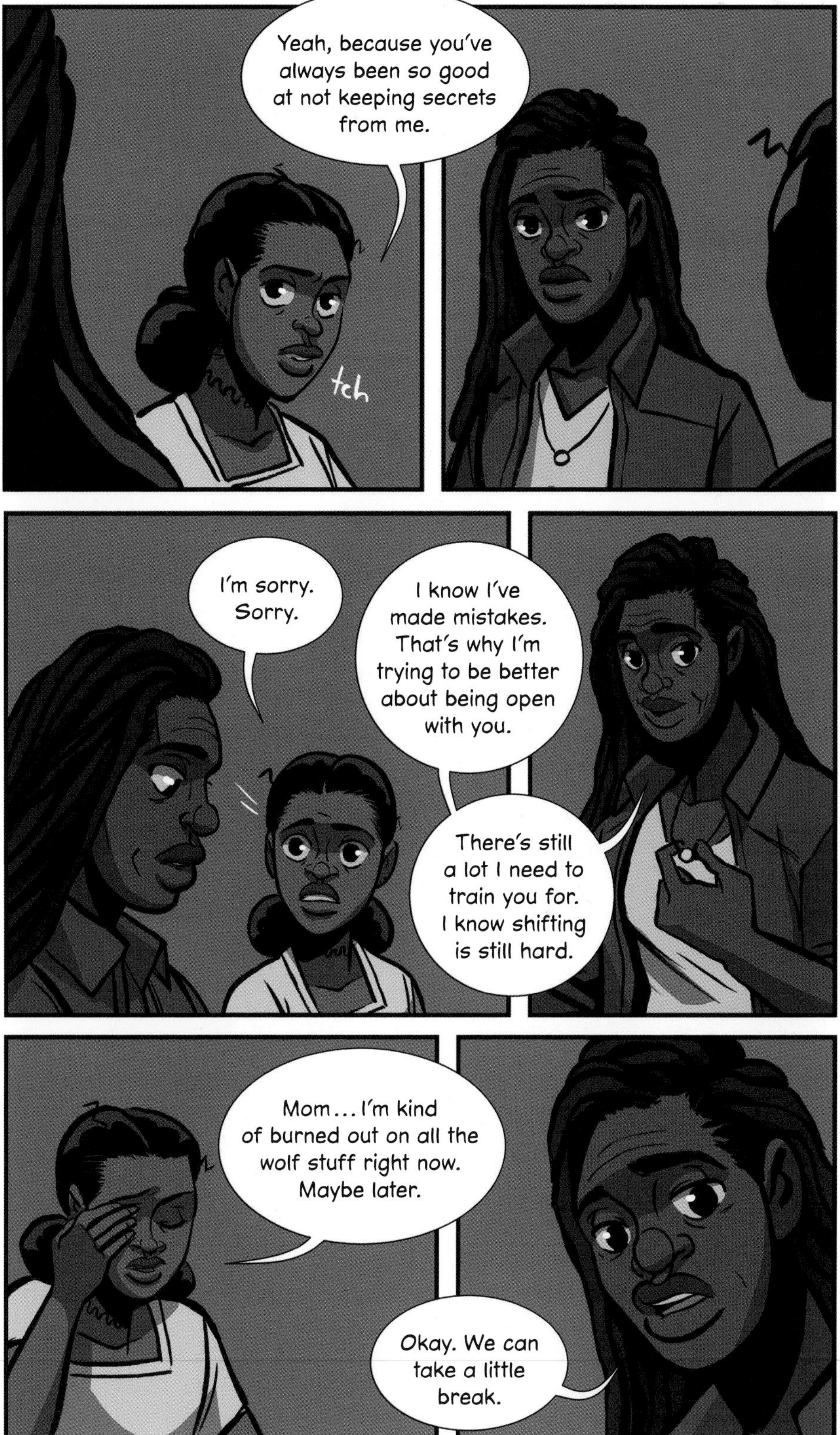
Yeah, because you've always been so good at not keeping secrets from me.
tch
I'm sorry. Sorry.
I know I've made mistakes. That's why I'm trying to be better about being open with you.
There's still a lot I need to train you for. I know shifting is still hard.
Mom... I'm kind of burned out on all the wolf stuff right now. Maybe later.
Okay. We can take a little break.

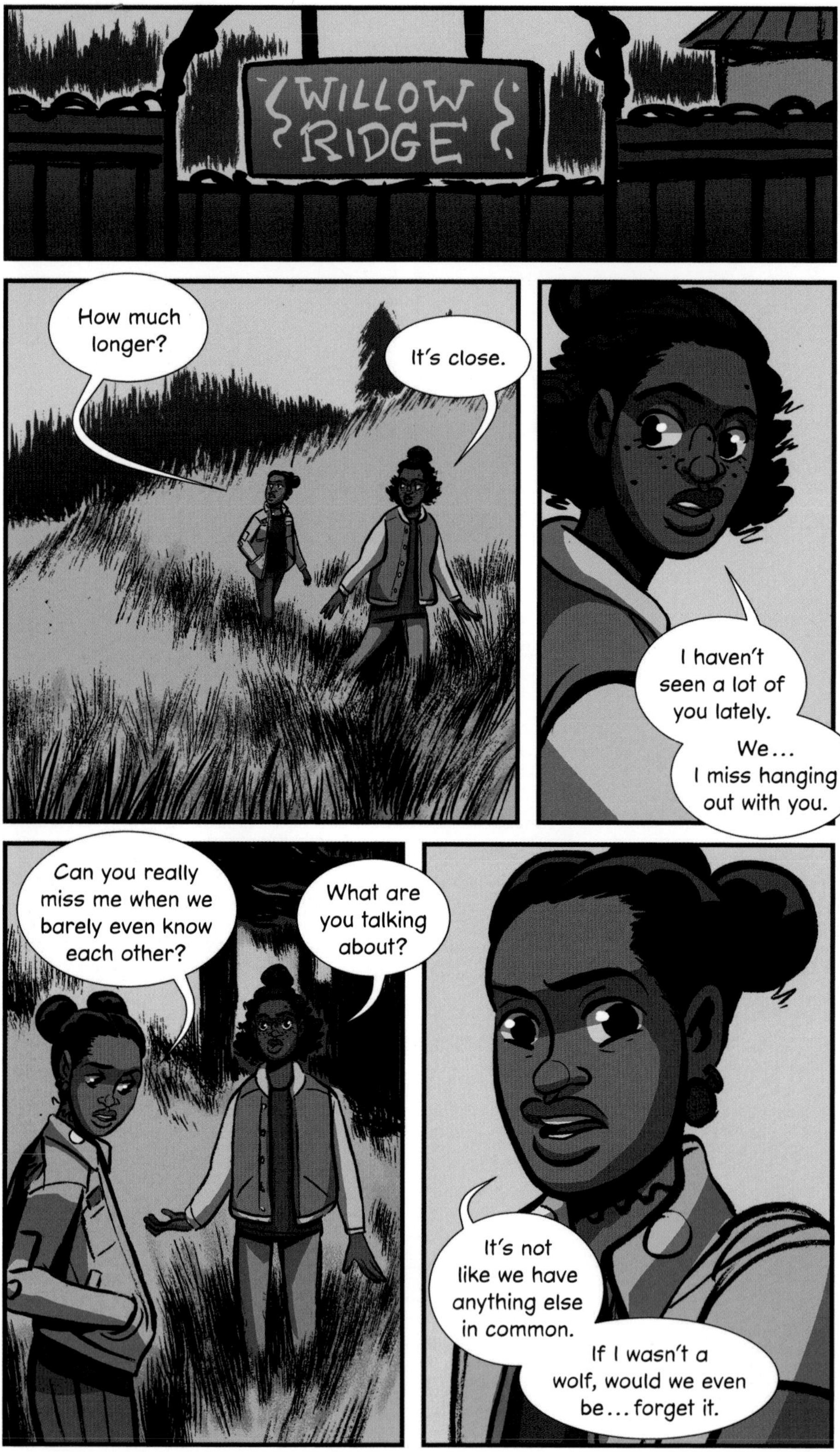
WILLOW RIDGE
How much longer?
It's close.
I haven't seen a lot of you lately.
We... I miss hanging out with you.
Can you really miss me when we barely even know each other?
What are you talking about?
It's not like we have anything else in common.
If I wasn't a wolf, would we even be... forget it.

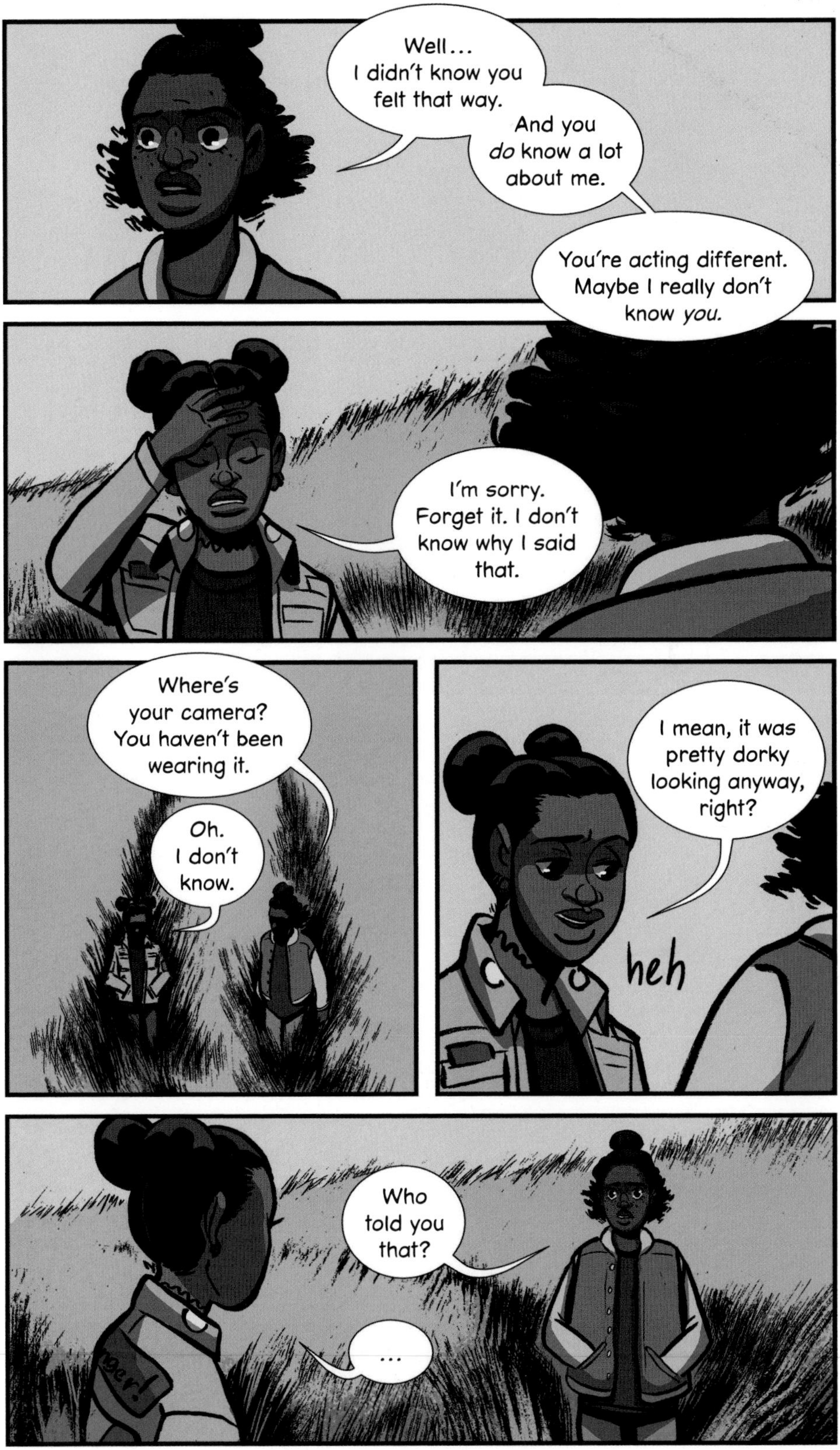
Well... I didn't know you felt that way.
And you *do* know a lot about me.
You're acting different. Maybe I really don't know *you.*
I'm sorry. Forget it. I don't know why I said that.
Where's your camera? You haven't been wearing it.
Oh. I don't know.
I mean, it was pretty dorky looking anyway, right?
heh
Who told you that?
...

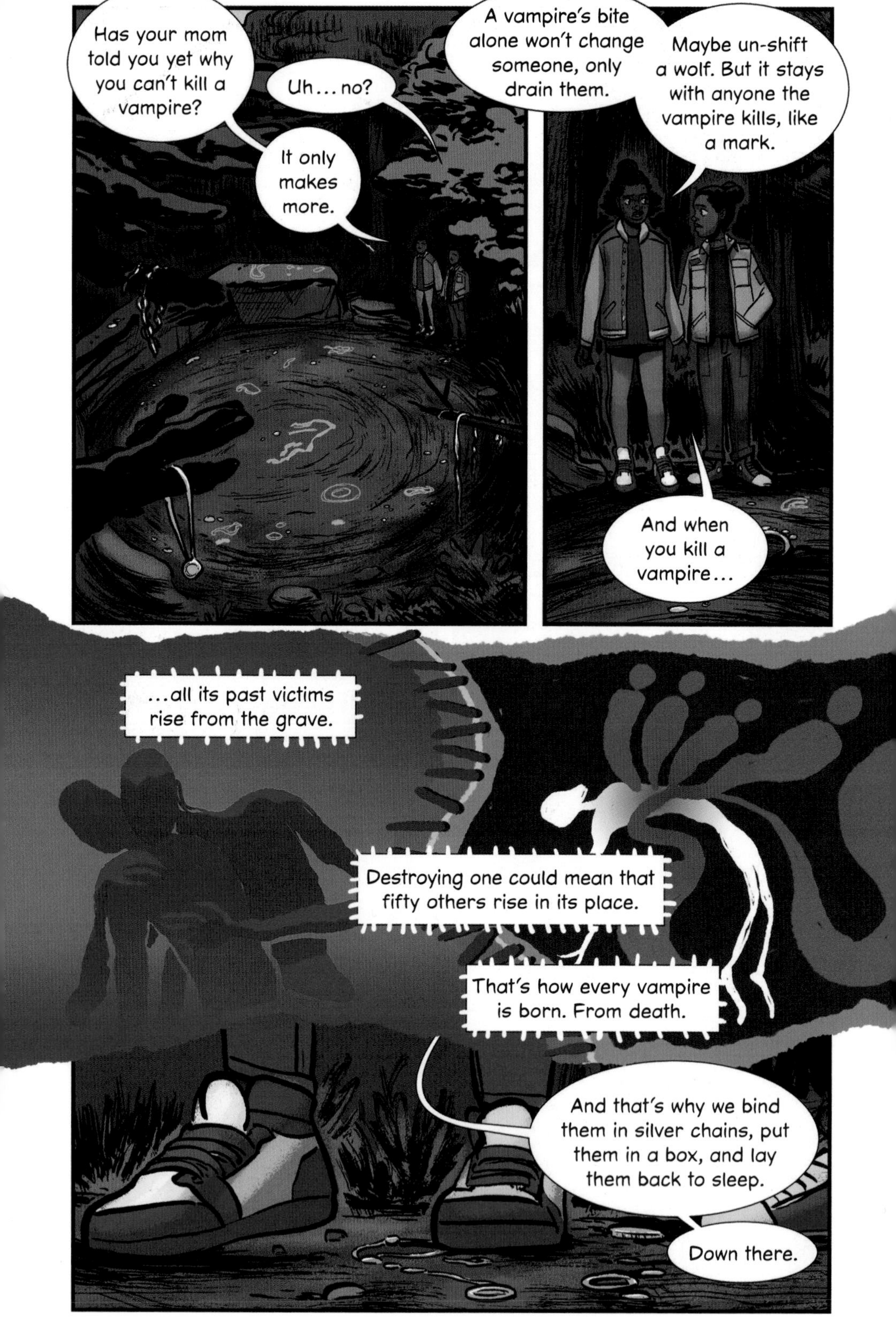
Has your mom told you yet why you can't kill a vampire?
Uh... no?
It only makes more.
A vampire's bite alone won't change someone, only drain them.
Maybe un-shift a wolf. But it stays with anyone the vampire kills, like a mark.
And when you kill a vampire...
...all its past victims rise from the grave.
Destroying one could mean that fifty others rise in its place.
That's how every vampire is born. From death.
And that's why we bind them in silver chains, put them in a box, and lay them back to sleep.
Down there.

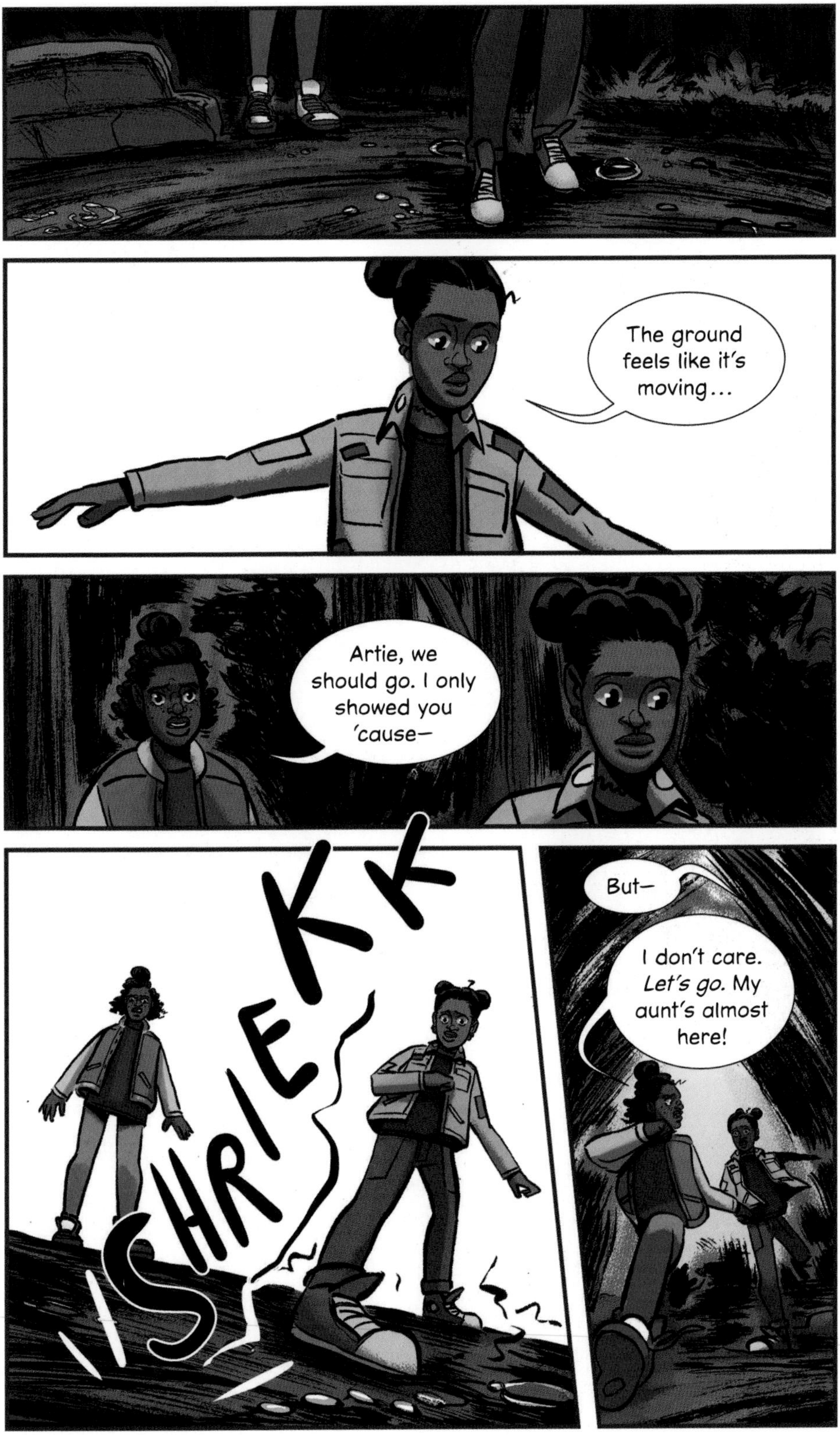
The ground feels like it's moving...
Artie, we should go. I only showed you 'cause—
SHRIEKK
But—
I don't care. *Let's go.* My aunt's almost here!

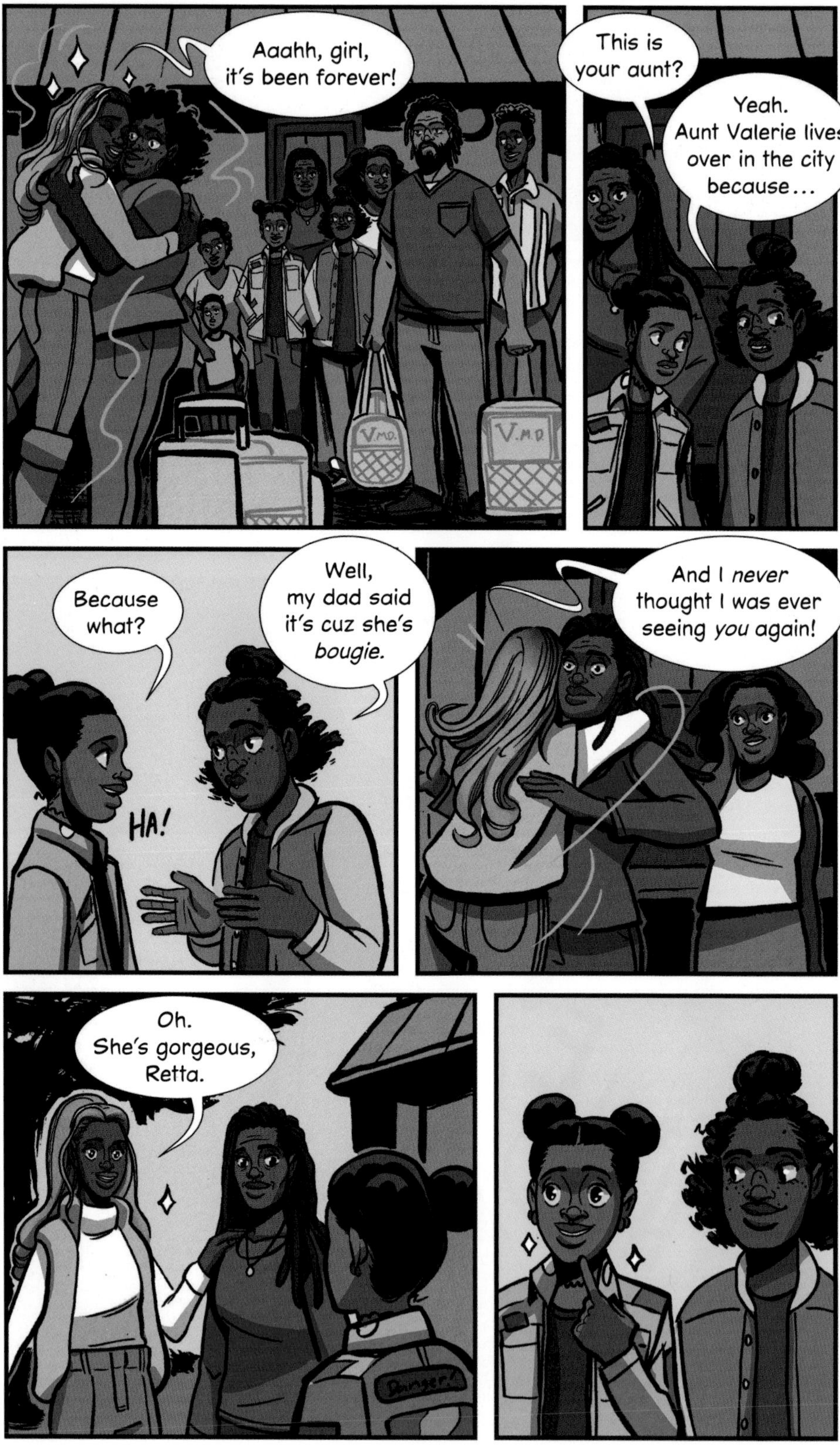
Aaahh, girl, it's been forever!
This is your aunt?
Yeah. Aunt Valerie lives over in the city because...
Because what?
Well, my dad said it's cuz she's *bougie.*
HA!
And I *never* thought I was ever seeing *you* again!
Oh. She's gorgeous, Retta.

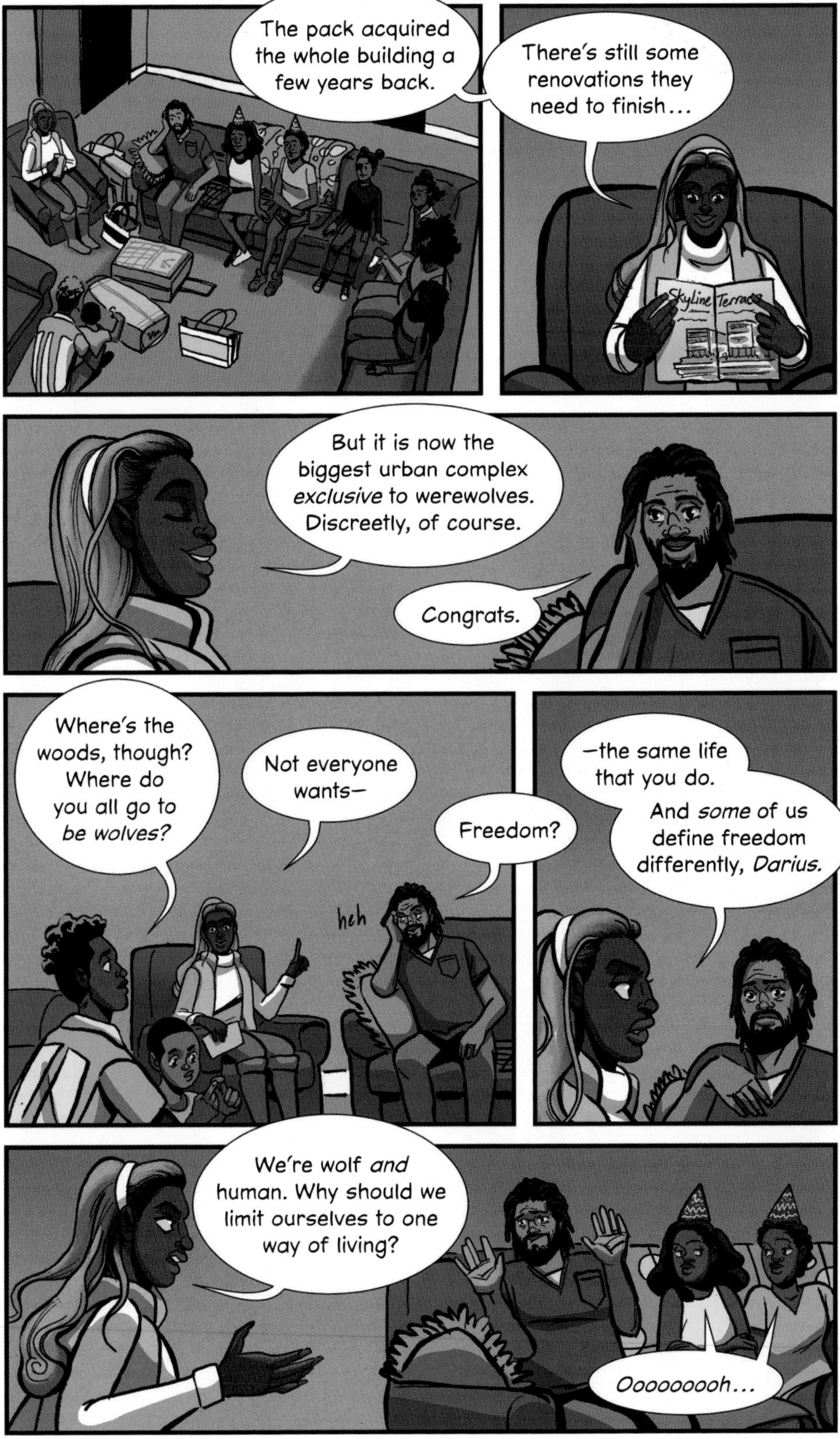
The pack acquired the whole building a few years back.
There's still some renovations they need to finish...
But it is now the biggest urban complex *exclusive* to werewolves. Discreetly, of course.
Congrats.
Where's the woods, though? Where do you all go to *be wolves?*
Not everyone wants—
heh
Freedom?
—the same life that you do.
And *some* of us define freedom differently, *Darius.*
We're wolf *and* human. Why should we limit ourselves to one way of living?
Oooooooh...

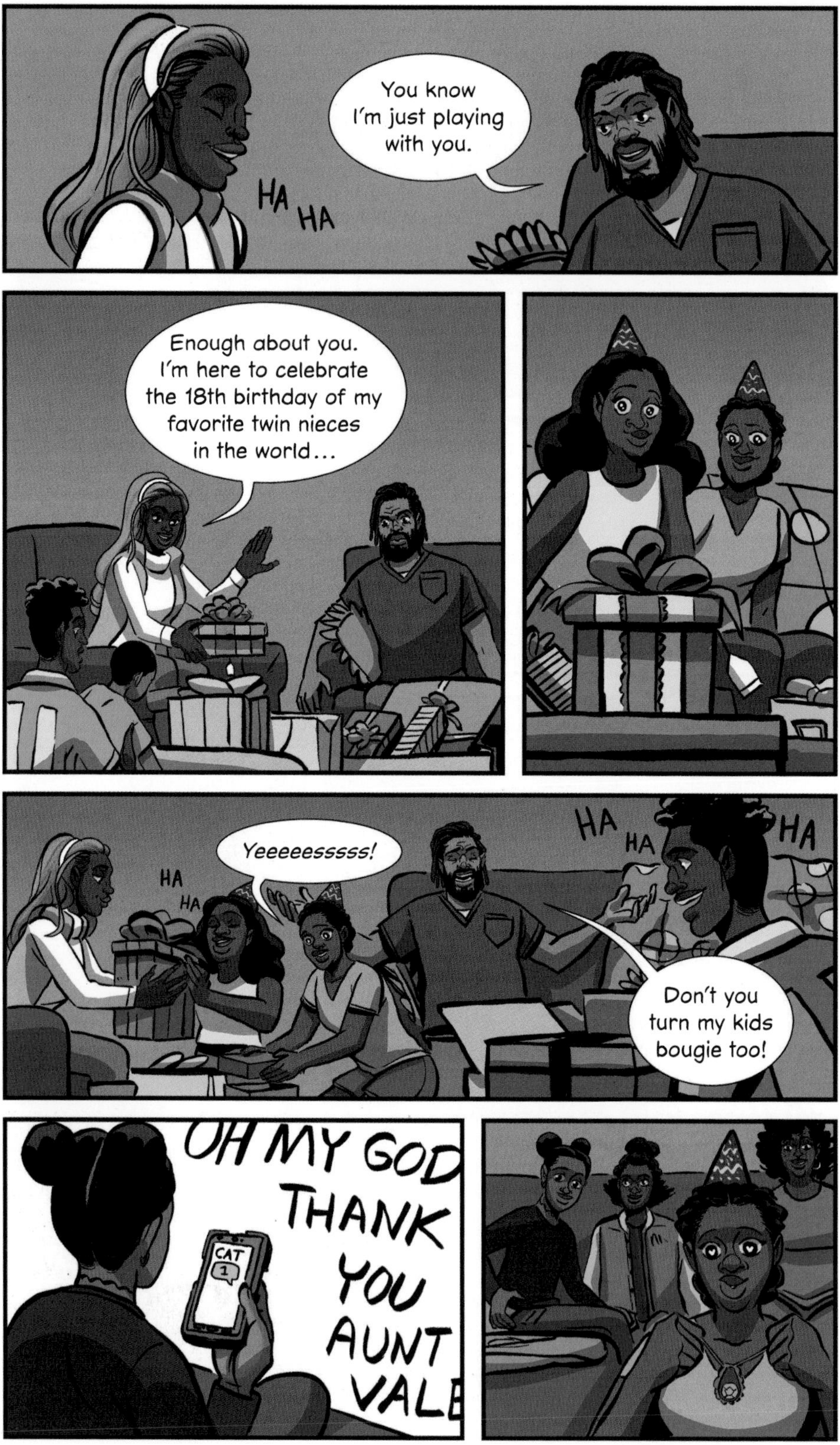
You know I'm just playing with you.
HA HA
Enough about you. I'm here to celebrate the 18th birthday of my favorite twin nieces in the world...
Yeeeeesssss!
HA HA
HA HA HA
Don't you turn my kids bougie too!
CAT 1
OH MY GOD THANK YOU AUNT VALE

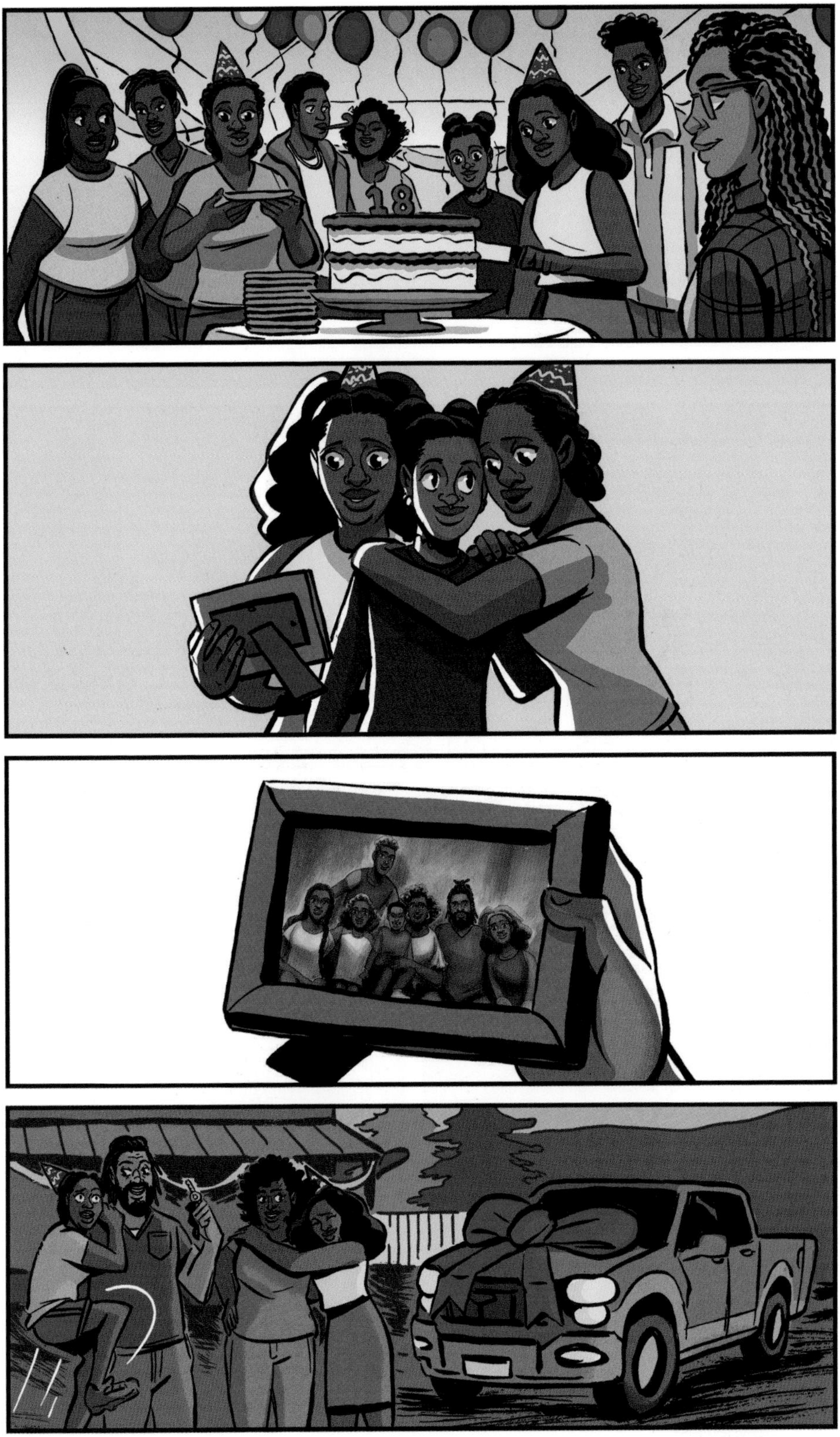
18

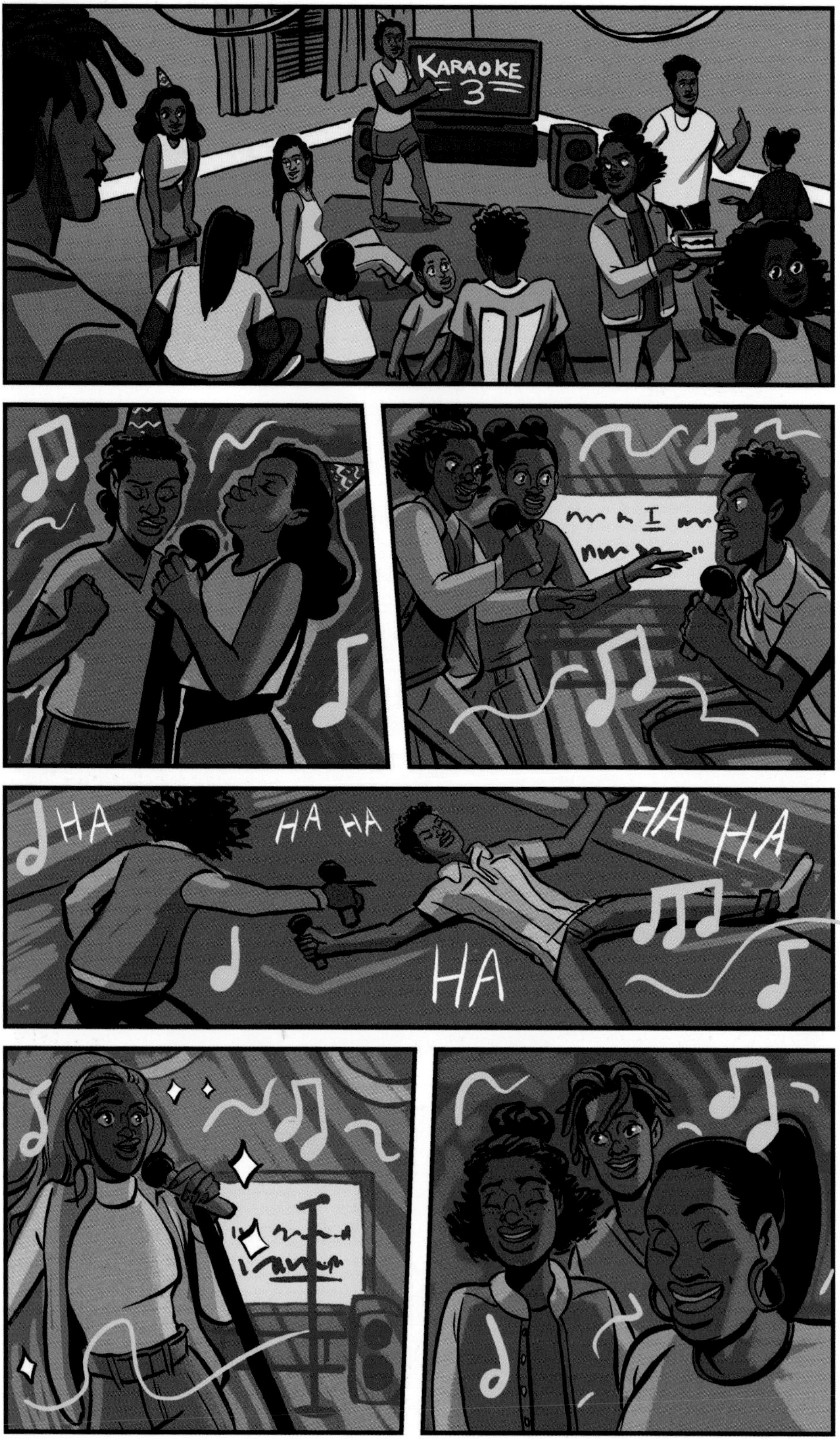
KARAOKE
3
HA
HA HA
HA HA
HA

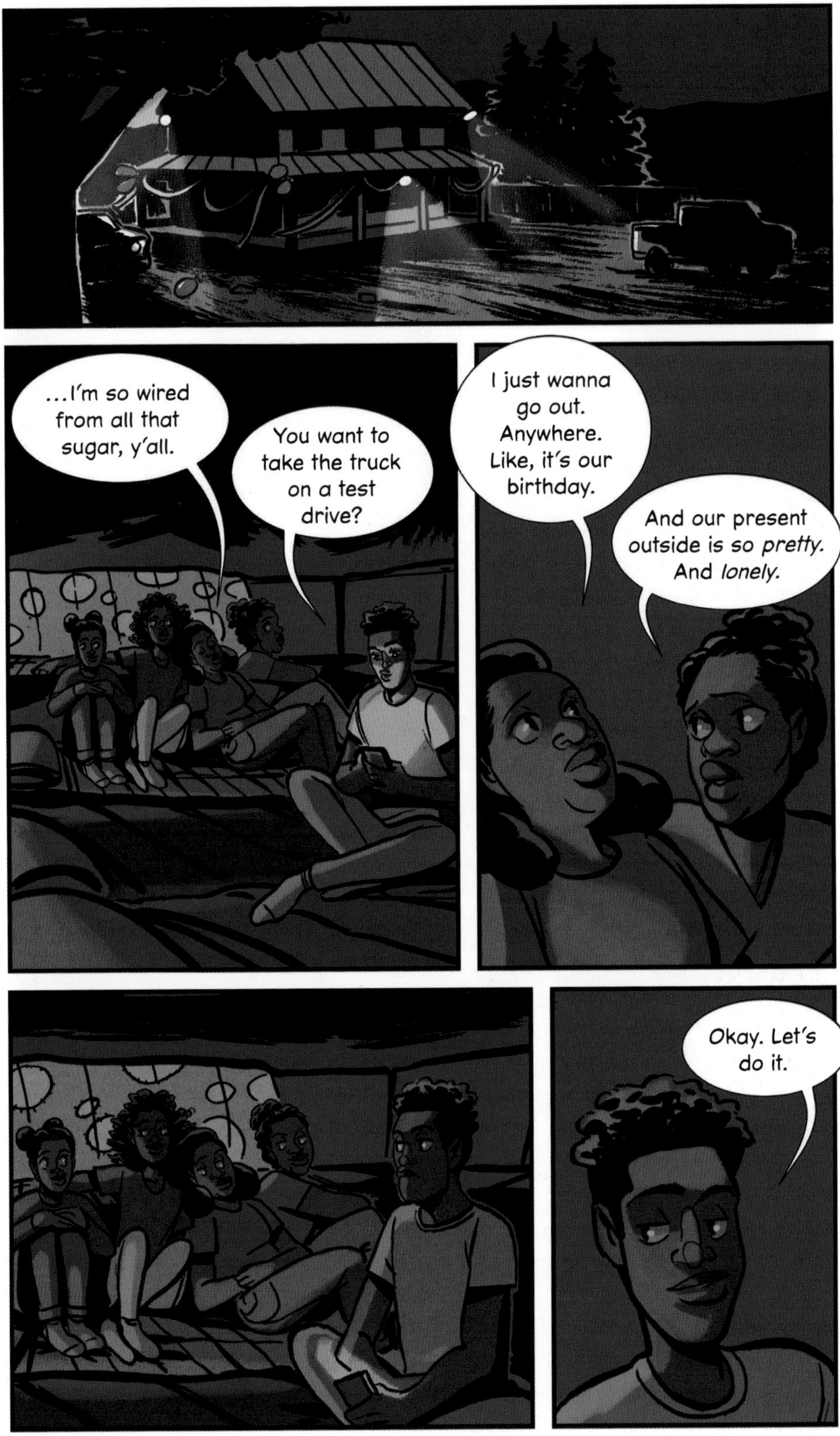
...I'm so wired from all that sugar, y'all.
You want to take the truck on a test drive?
I just wanna go out. Anywhere. Like, it's our birthday.
And our present outside is so *pretty.* And *lonely.*
Okay. Let's do it.

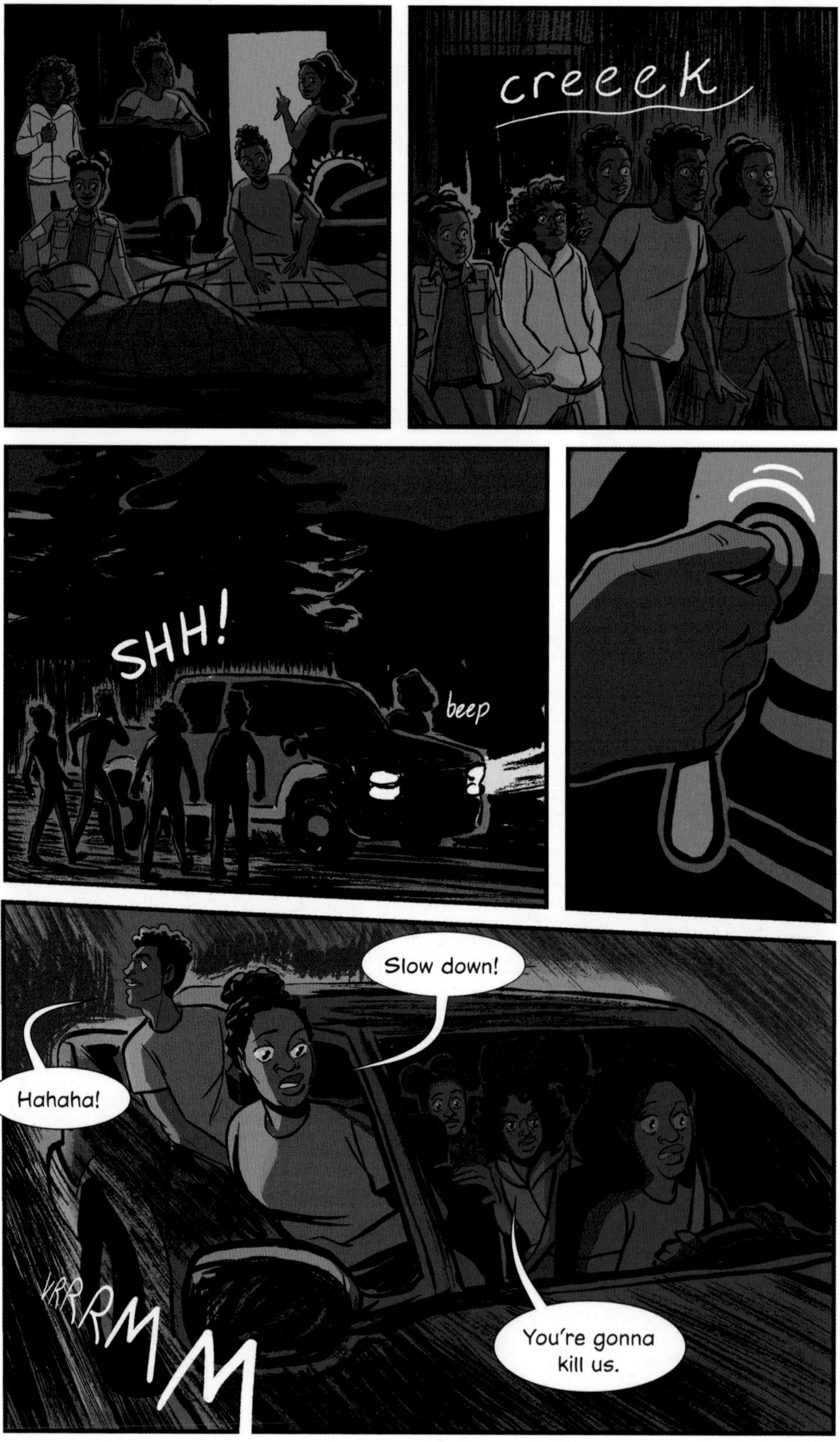
creeek
SHH!
beep
Slow down!
Hahaha!
VRRRMM
You're gonna kill us.

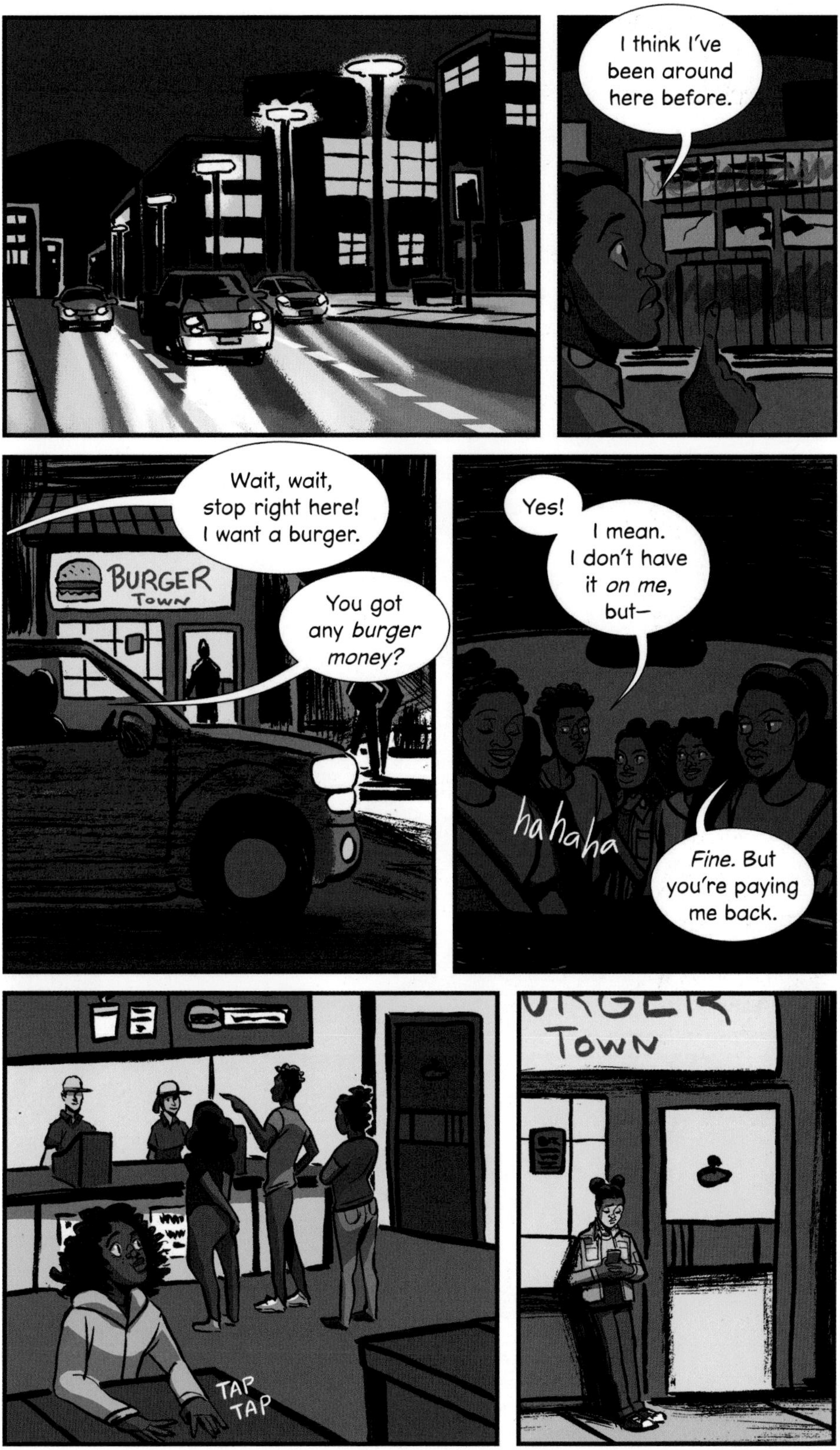
I think I've been around here before.
Wait, wait, stop right here! I want a burger.
BURGER TOWN
You got any *burger money?*
Yes!
I mean. I don't have it *on me,* but—
hahaha
Fine. But you're paying me back.
TAP TAP
URGER TOWN

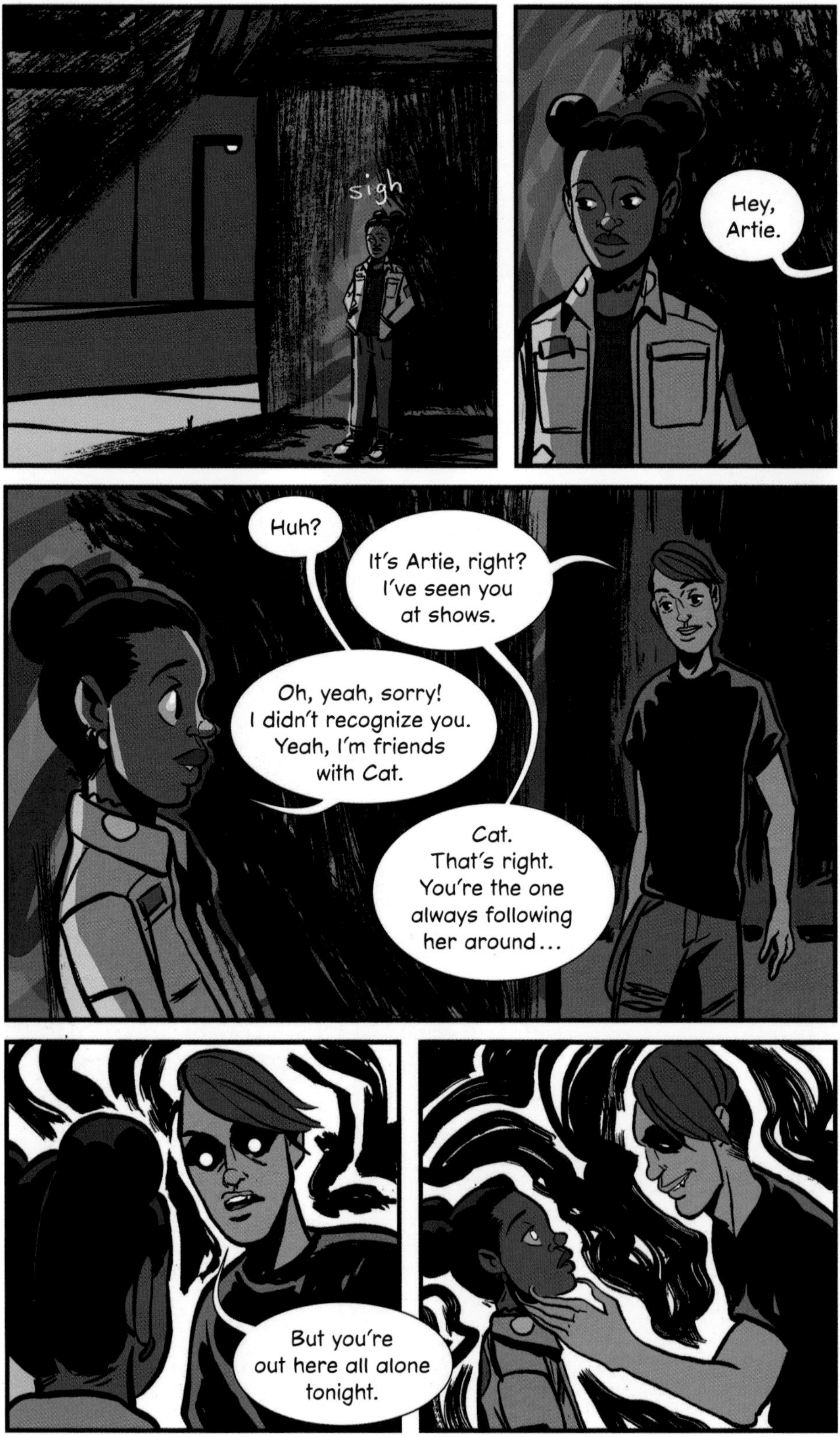
sigh
Hey, Artie.
Huh?
It's Artie, right? I've seen you at shows.
Oh, yeah, sorry! I didn't recognize you. Yeah, I'm friends with Cat.
Cat. That's right. You're the one always following her around...
But you're out here all alone tonight.

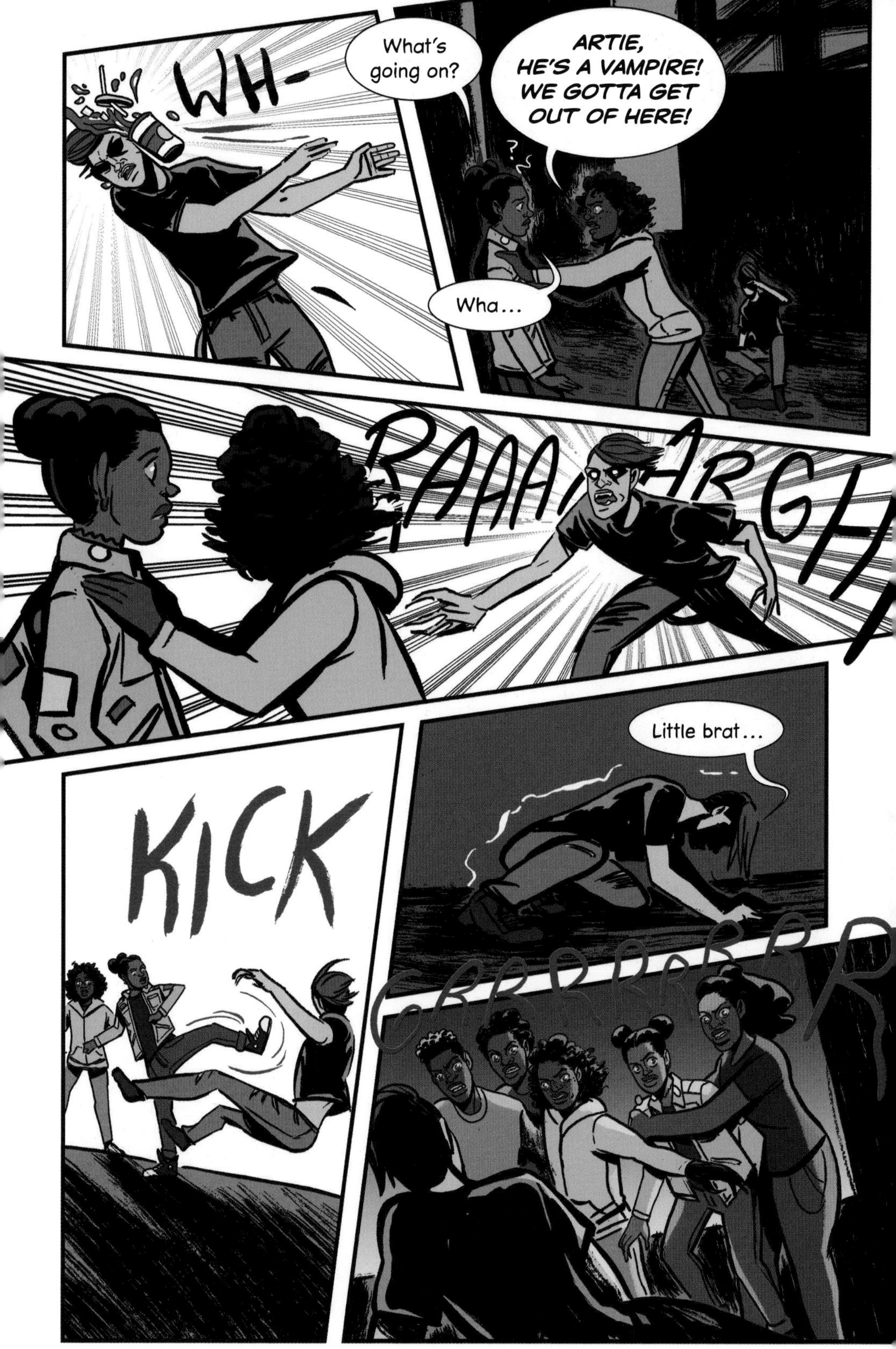
WH-
What's going on?
ARTIE, HE'S A VAMPIRE! WE GOTTA GET OUT OF HERE!
Wha...
RAAAARGH
KICK
Little brat...
GRRRRRRRRR

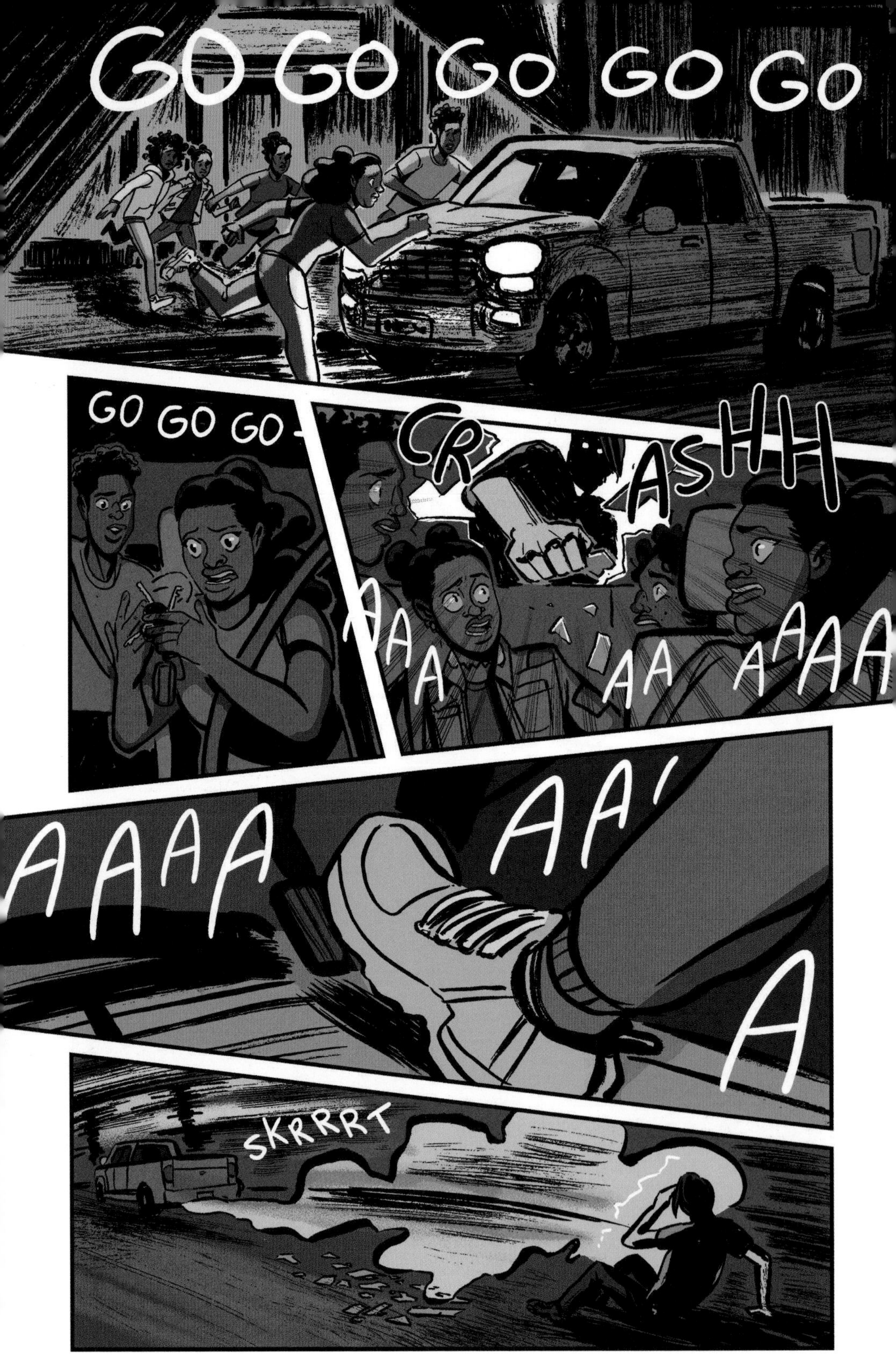
GO GO GO GO GO GO
GO GO GO-
CRASHH
AAAA
AA
AAAAA
AAAA
AA
A
SKRRRT

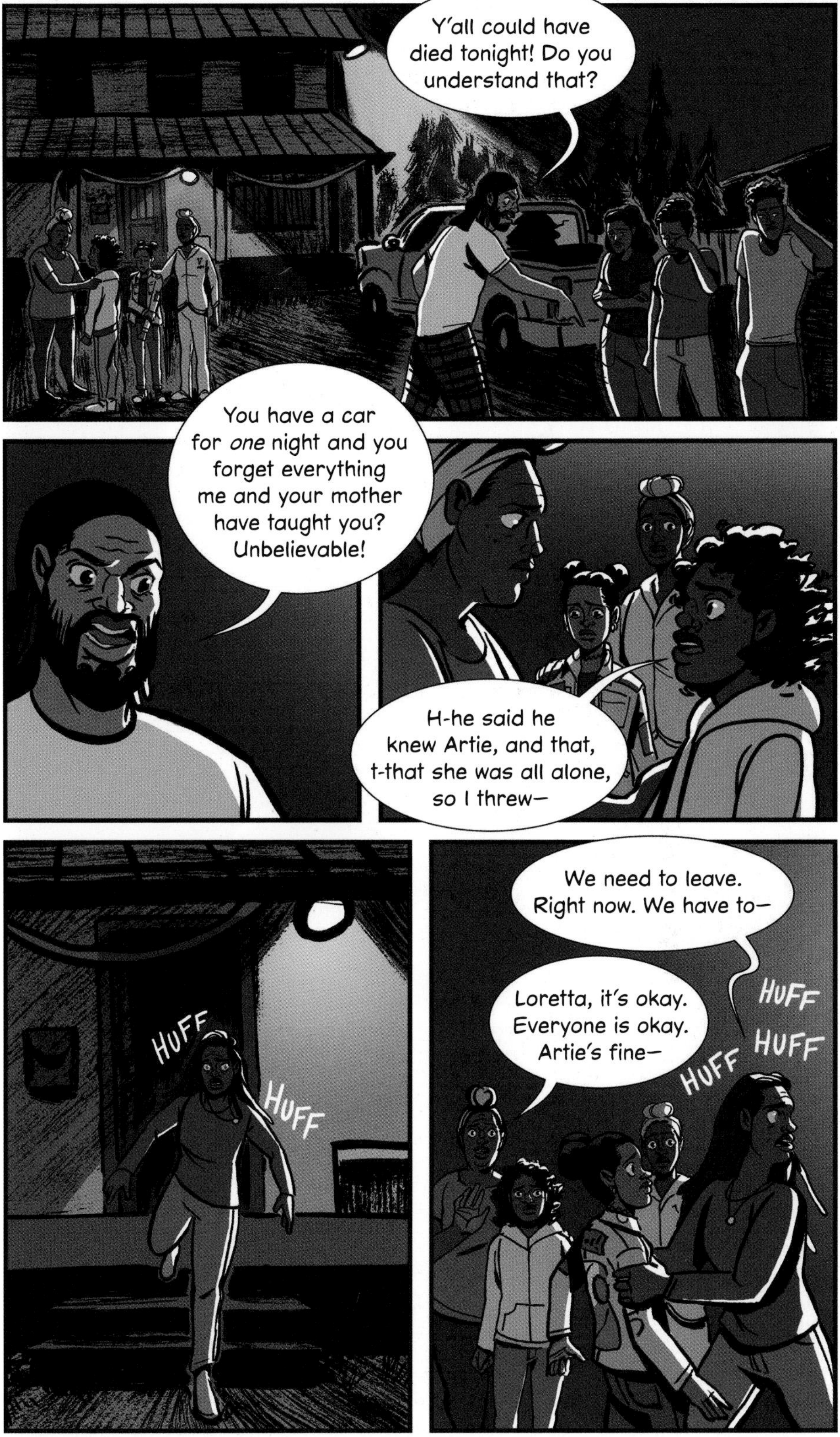
Y'all could have died tonight! Do you understand that?
You have a car for *one* night and you forget everything me and your mother have taught you? Unbelievable!
H-he said he knew Artie, and that, t-that she was all alone, so I threw—
HUFF
HUFF
We need to leave. Right now. We have to—
HUFF
HUFF
HUFF
Loretta, it's okay. Everyone is okay. Artie's fine—

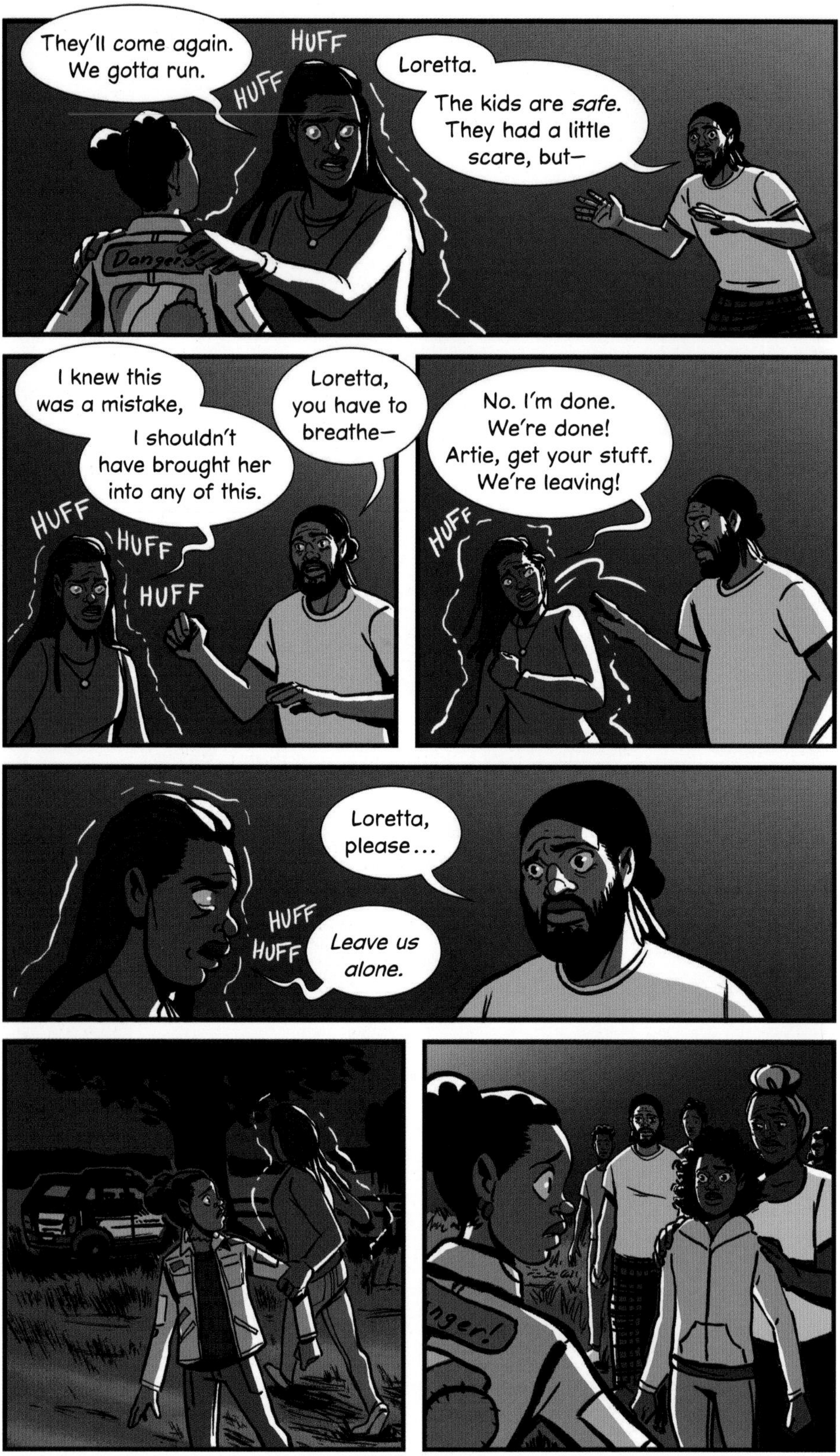
They'll come again. We gotta run.
HUFF
HUFF
Loretta.
The kids are *safe*. They had a little scare, but—
Danger!
I knew this was a mistake,
I shouldn't have brought her into any of this.
Loretta, you have to breathe—
HUFF
HUFF
HUFF
No. I'm done. We're done! Artie, get your stuff. We're leaving!
HUFF
Loretta, please...
HUFF
HUFF
Leave us alone.
nger!

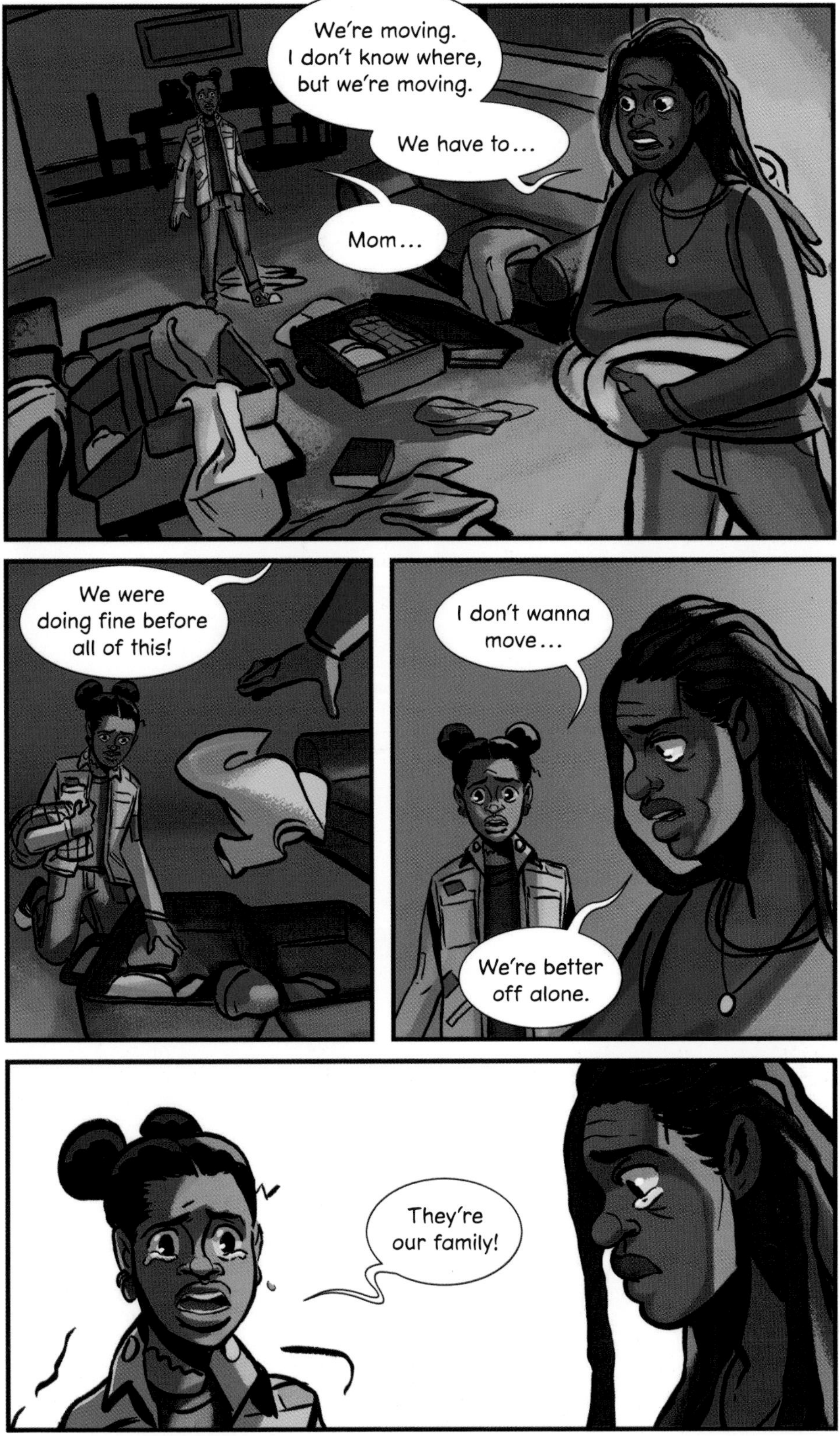
We're moving. I don't know where, but we're moving.
We have to...
Mom...
We were doing fine before all of this!
I don't wanna move...
We're better off alone.
They're our family!

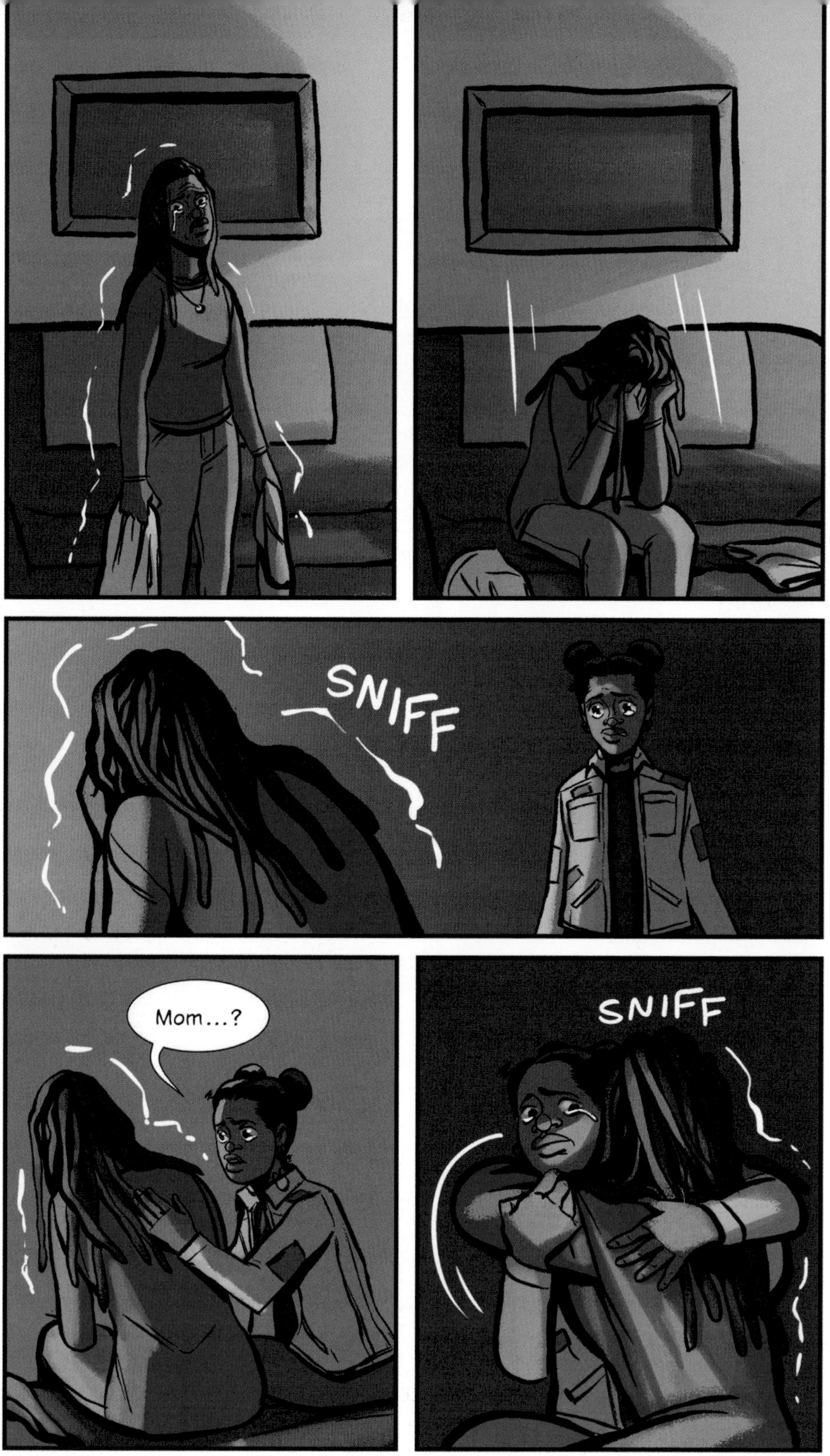
SNIFF
Mom...?
SNIFF

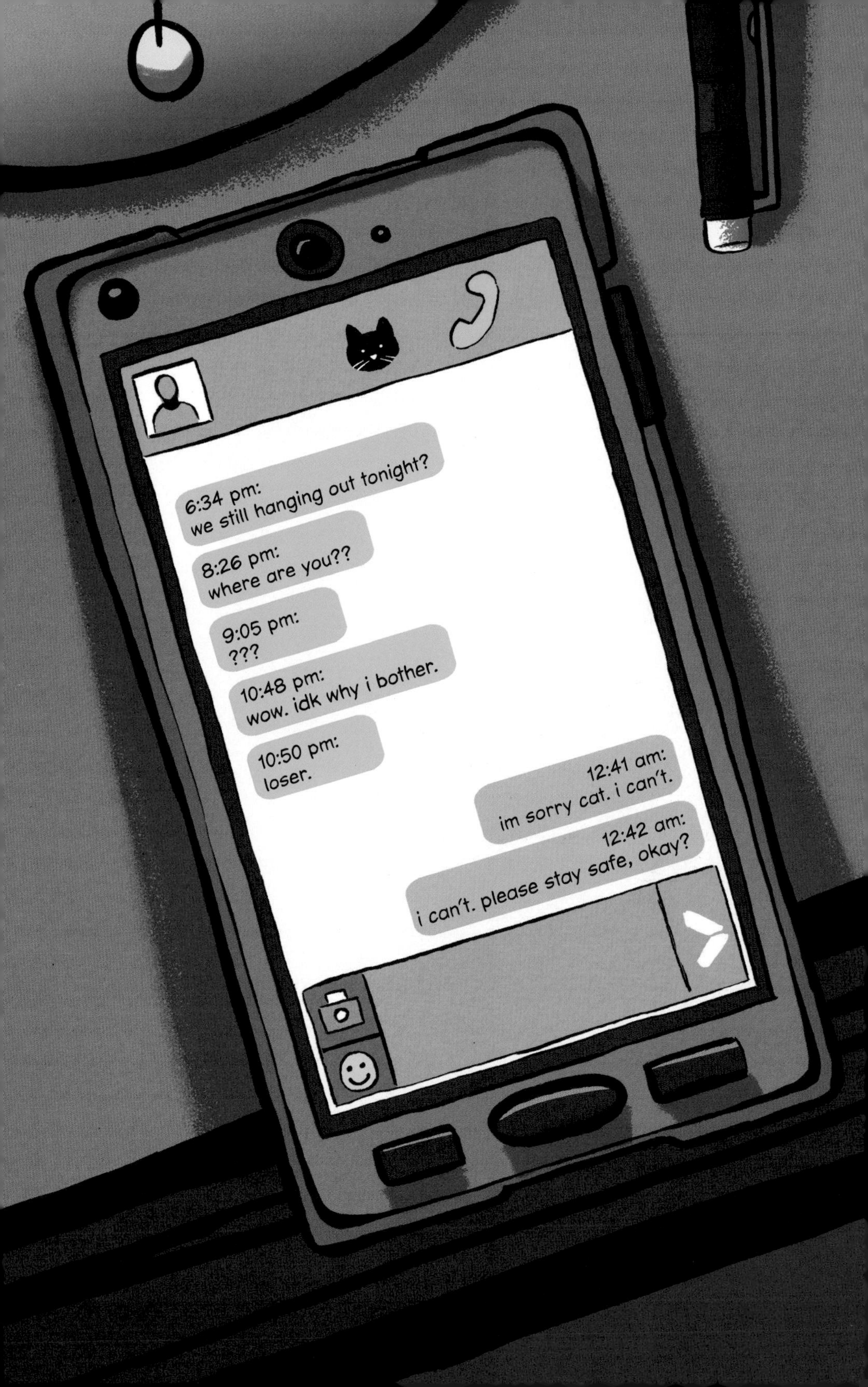

6:34 pm:
we still hanging out tonight?
8:26 pm:
where are you??
9:05 pm:
???
10:48 pm:
wow. idk why i bother.
10:50 pm:
loser.
12:41 am:
im sorry cat. i can't.
12:42 am:
i can't. please stay safe, okay?

CHAPTER SEVEN

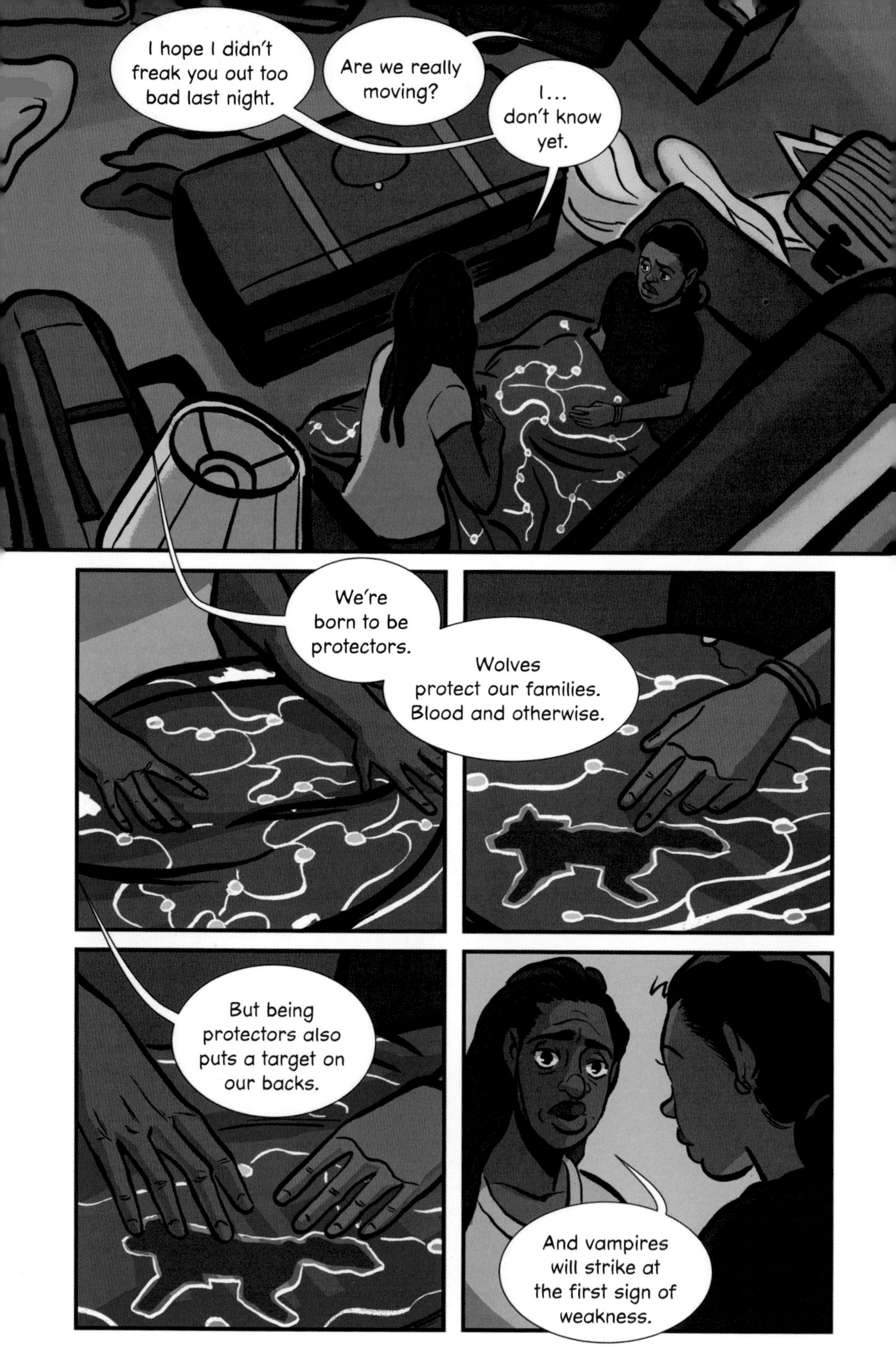
I hope I didn't freak you out too bad last night.
Are we really moving?
I... don't know yet.
We're born to be protectors.
Wolves protect our families. Blood and otherwise.
But being protectors also puts a target on our backs.
And vampires will strike at the first sign of weakness.

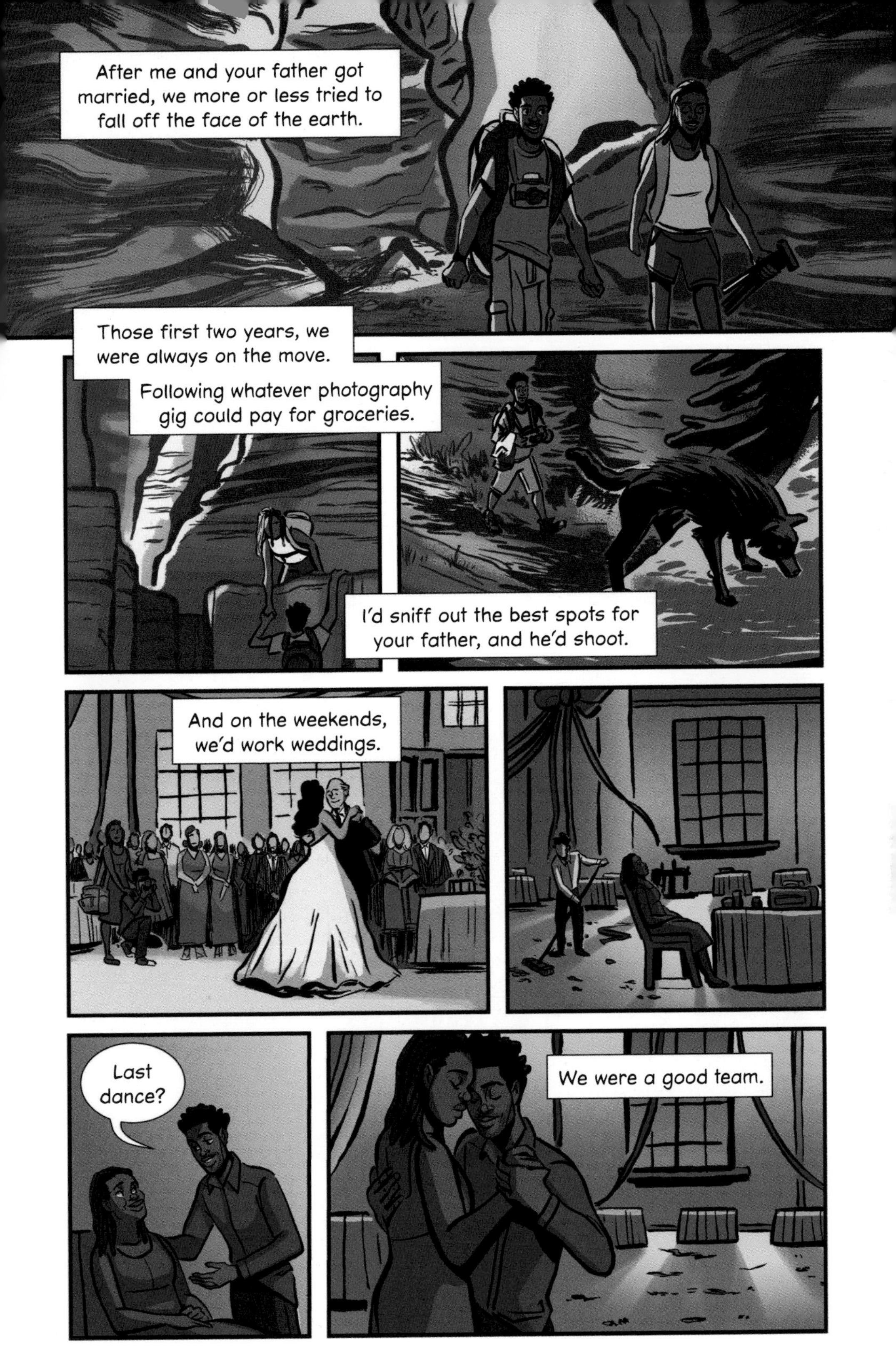
After me and your father got married, we more or less tried to fall off the face of the earth.
Those first two years, we were always on the move.
Following whatever photography gig could pay for groceries.
I'd sniff out the best spots for your father, and he'd shoot.
And on the weekends, we'd work weddings.
Last dance?
We were a good team.

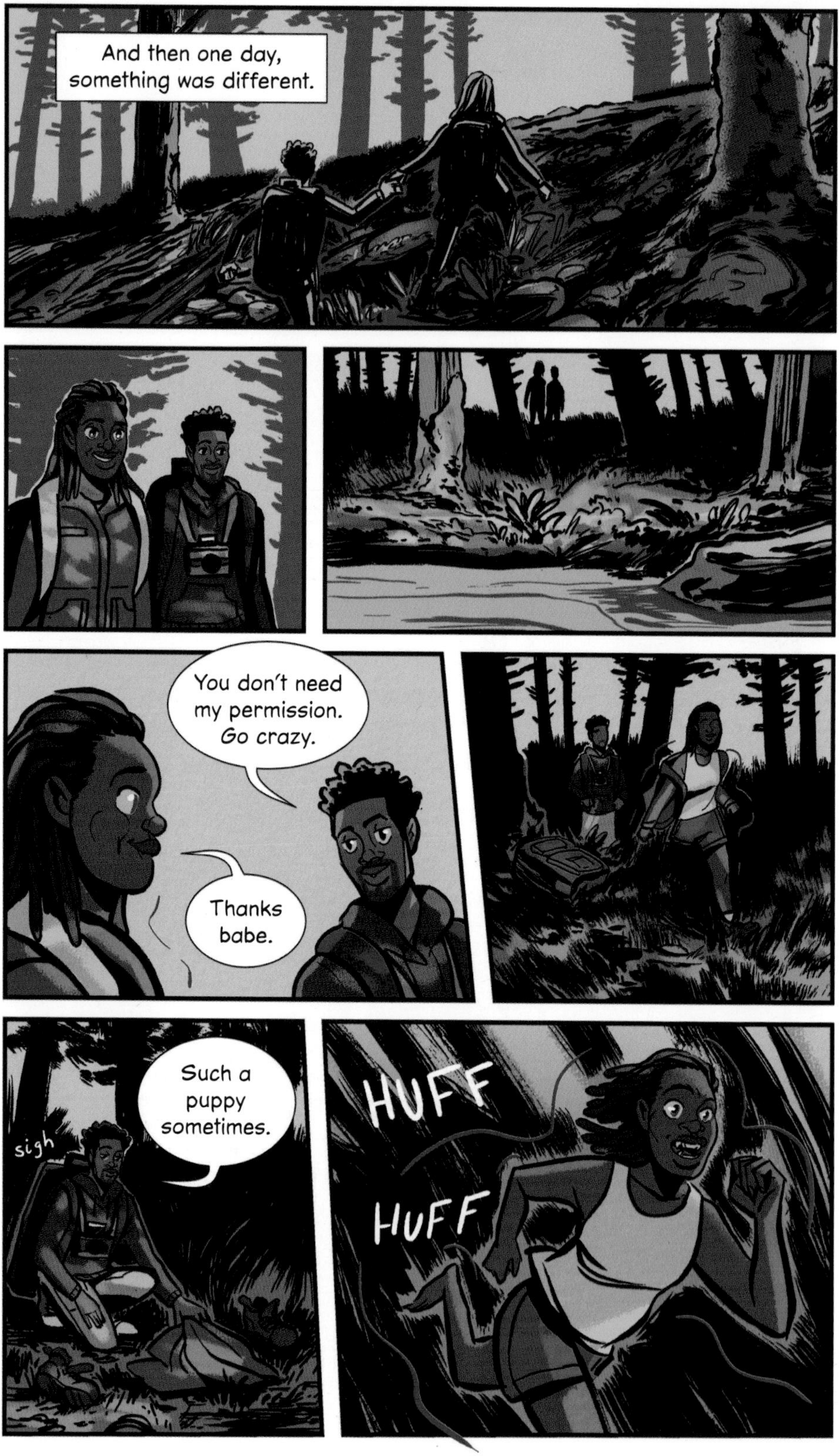
And then one day, something was different.
You don't need my permission. Go crazy.
Thanks babe.
sigh
Such a puppy sometimes.
HUFF
HUFF

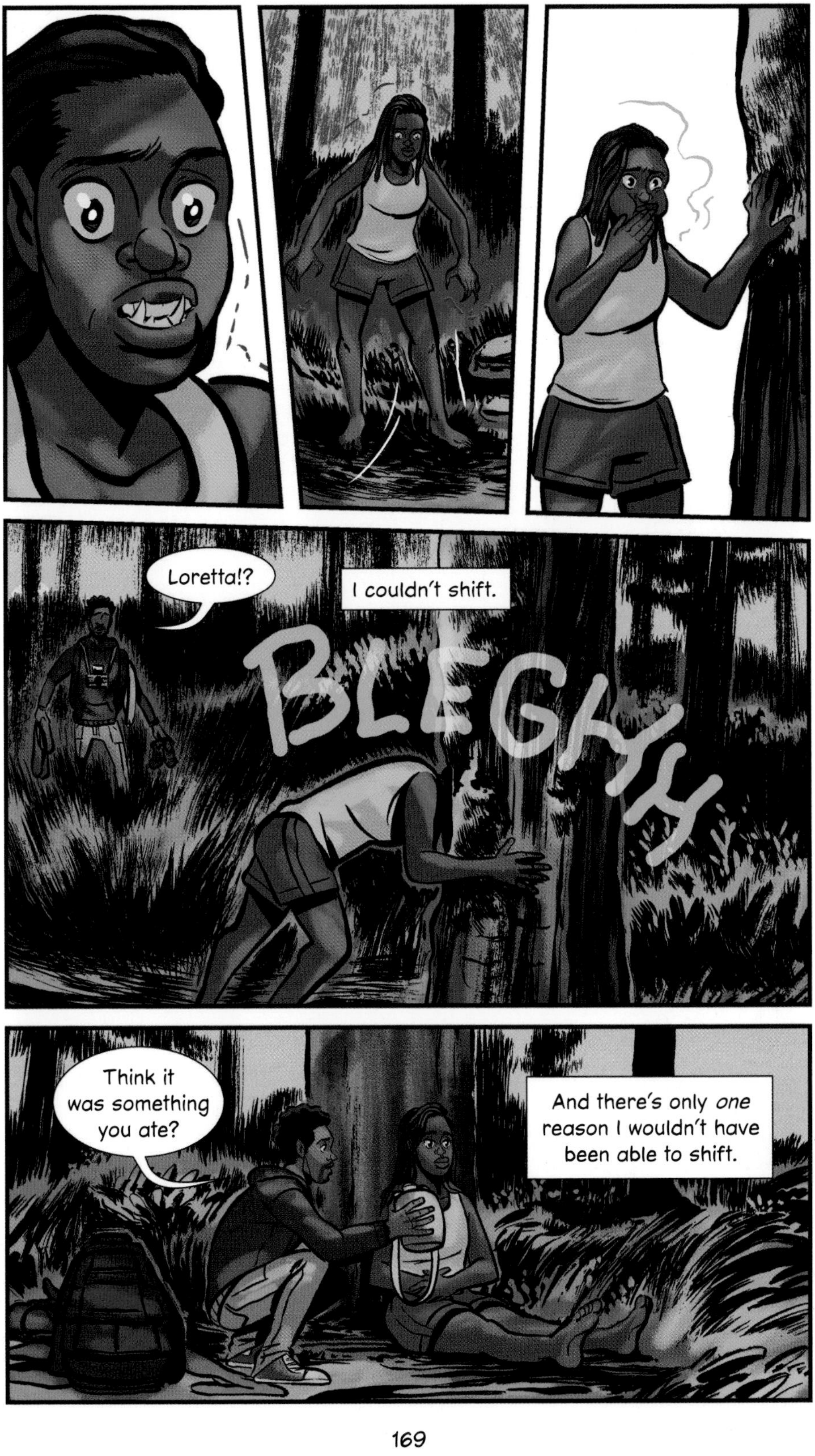
Loretta!?
I couldn't shift.
BLEGHH
Think it was something you ate?
And there's only *one* reason I wouldn't have been able to shift.

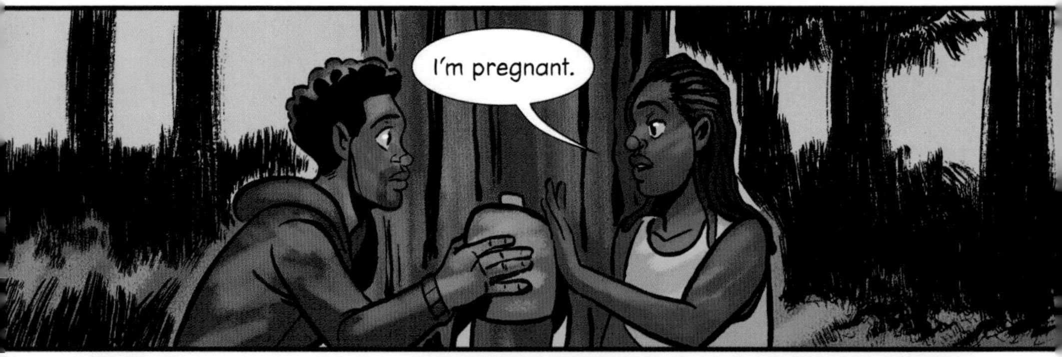
I'm pregnant.

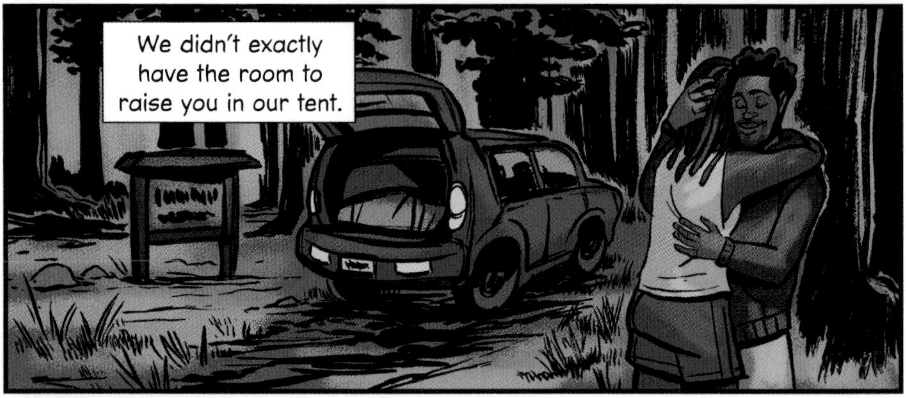
We didn't exactly have the room to raise you in our tent.

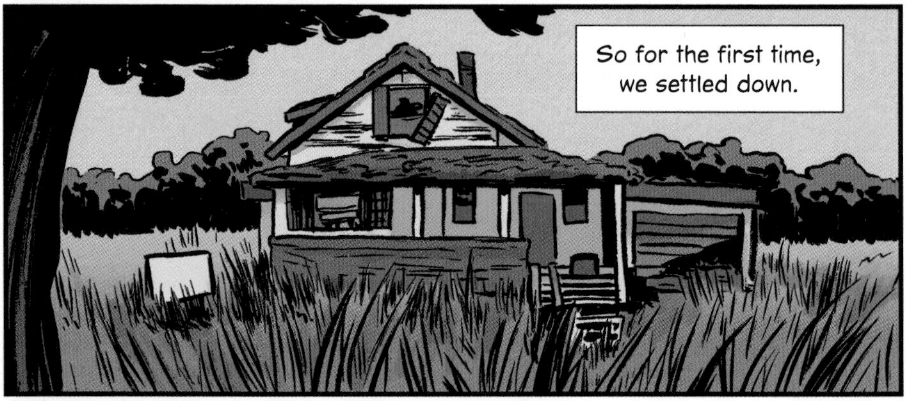
So for the first time, we settled down.

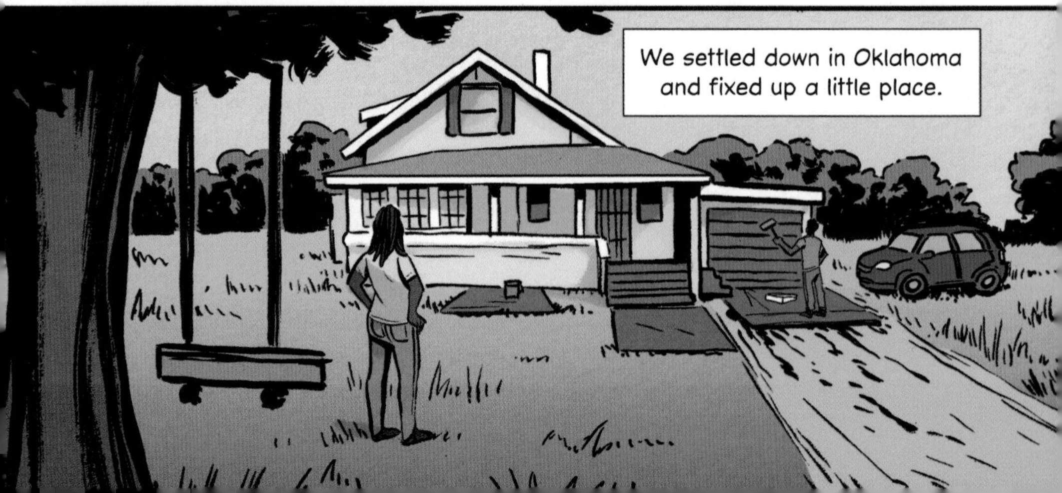
We settled down in Oklahoma and fixed up a little place.

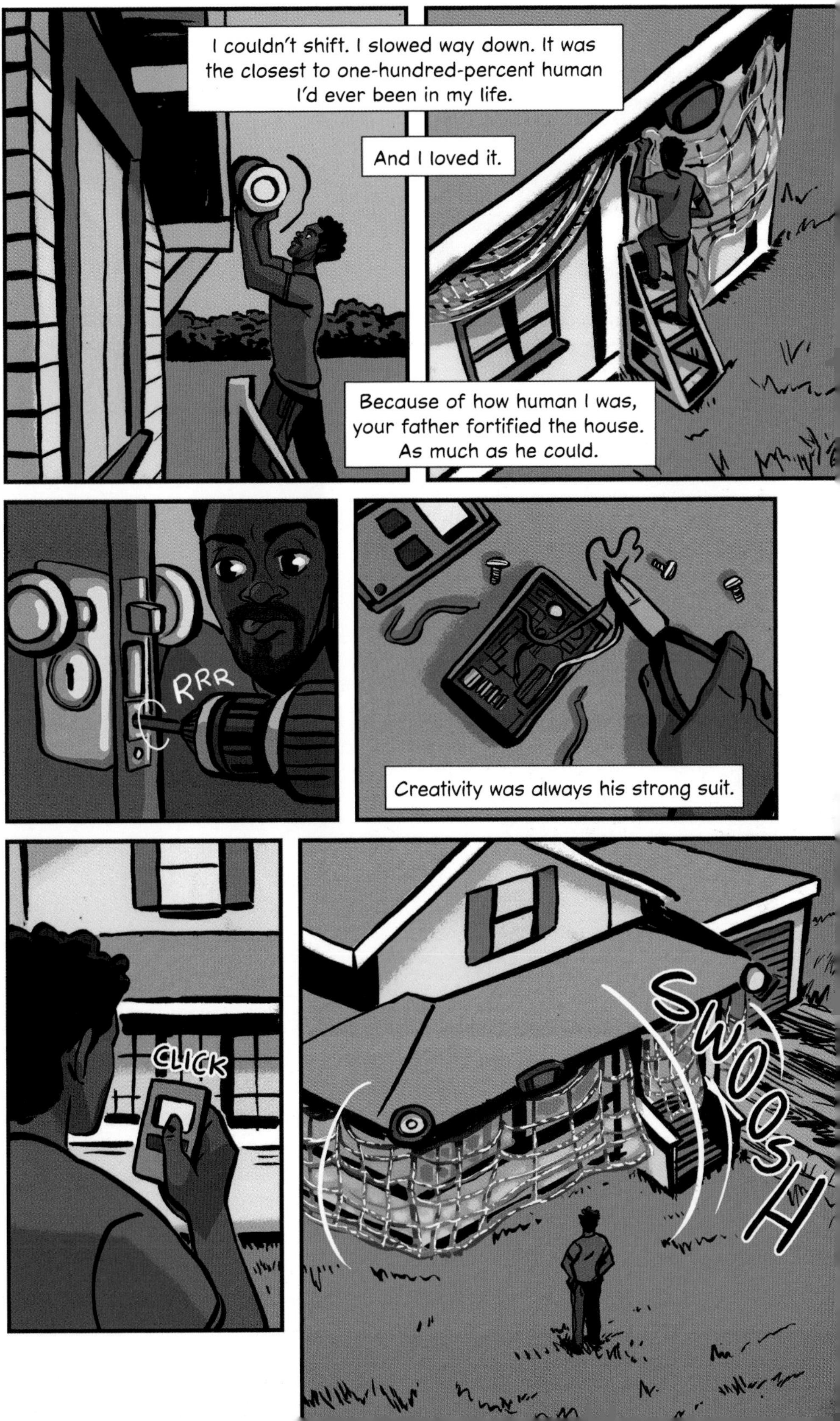
I couldn't shift. I slowed way down. It was the closest to one-hundred-percent human I'd ever been in my life.
And I loved it.
Because of how human I was, your father fortified the house. As much as he could.
RRR
Creativity was always his strong suit.
CLICK
SWOOSH

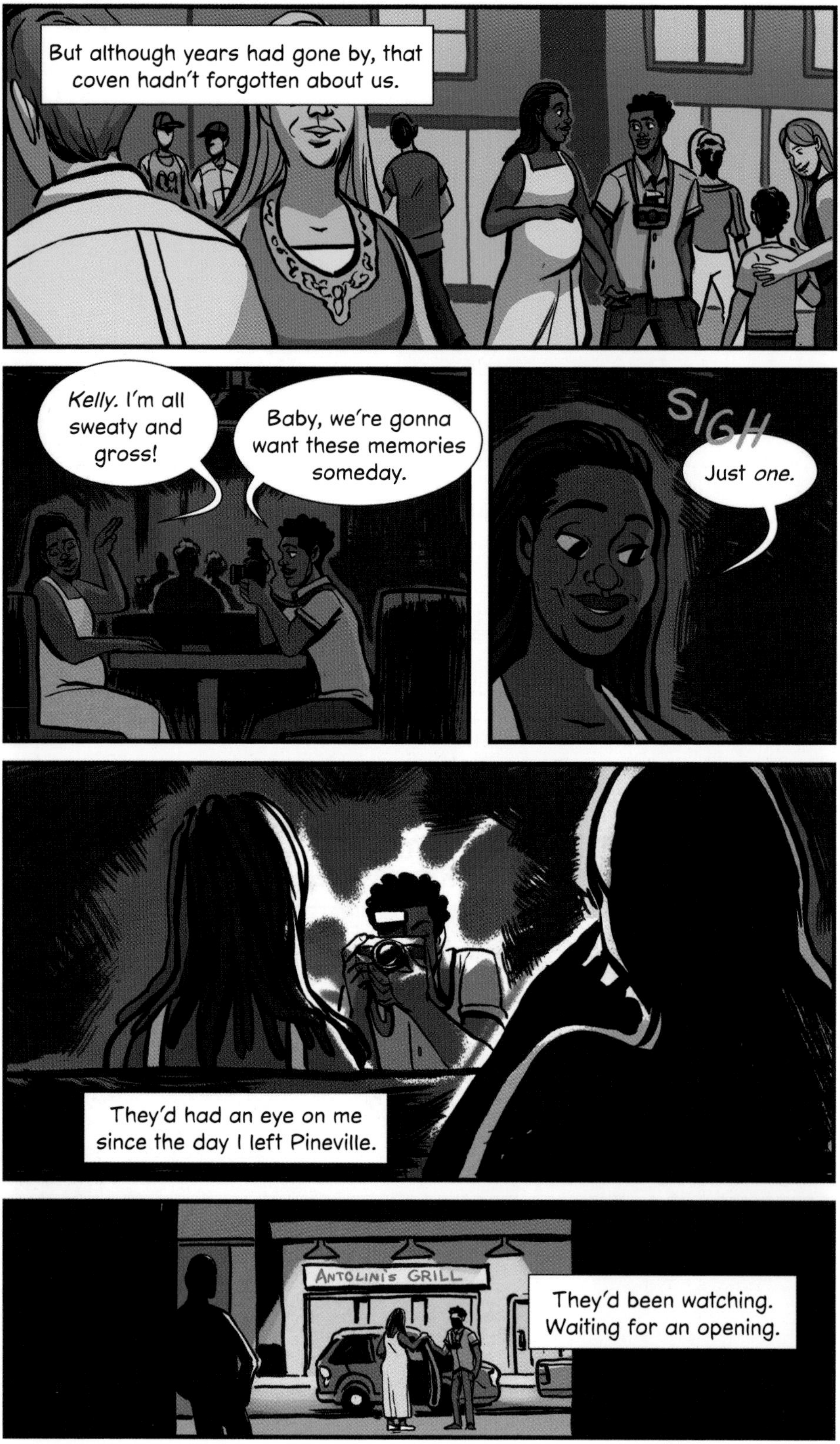
But although years had gone by, that coven hadn't forgotten about us.
Kelly. I'm all sweaty and gross!
Baby, we're gonna want these memories someday.
SIGH
Just *one.*
They'd had an eye on me since the day I left Pineville.
ANTOLINI'S GRILL
They'd been watching. Waiting for an opening.

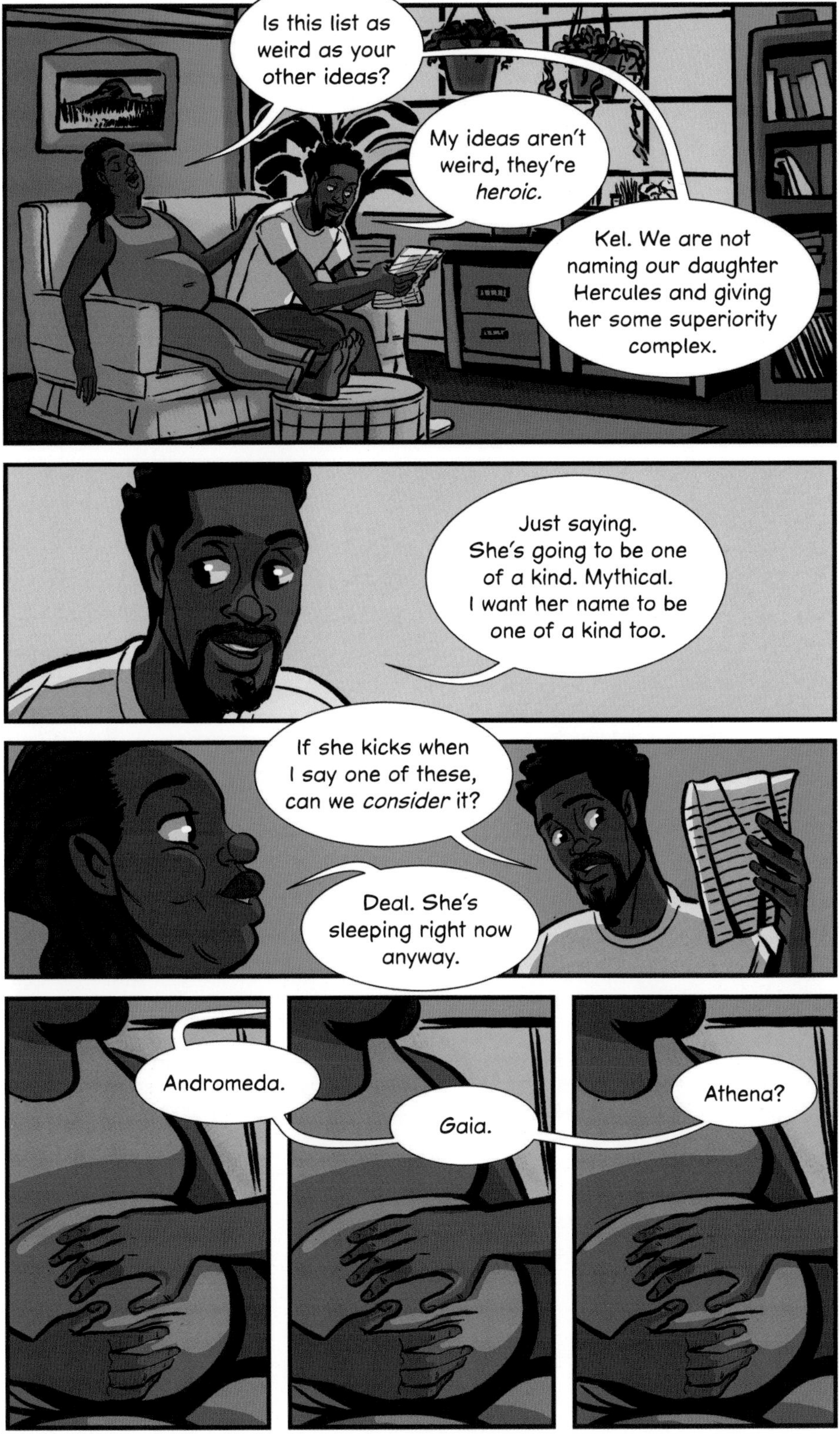
Is this list as weird as your other ideas?
My ideas aren't weird, they're *heroic.*
Kel. We are not naming our daughter Hercules and giving her some superiority complex.
Just saying. She's going to be one of a kind. Mythical. I want her name to be one of a kind too.
If she kicks when I say one of these, can we *consider* it?
Deal. She's sleeping right now anyway.
Andromeda.
Gaia.
Athena?

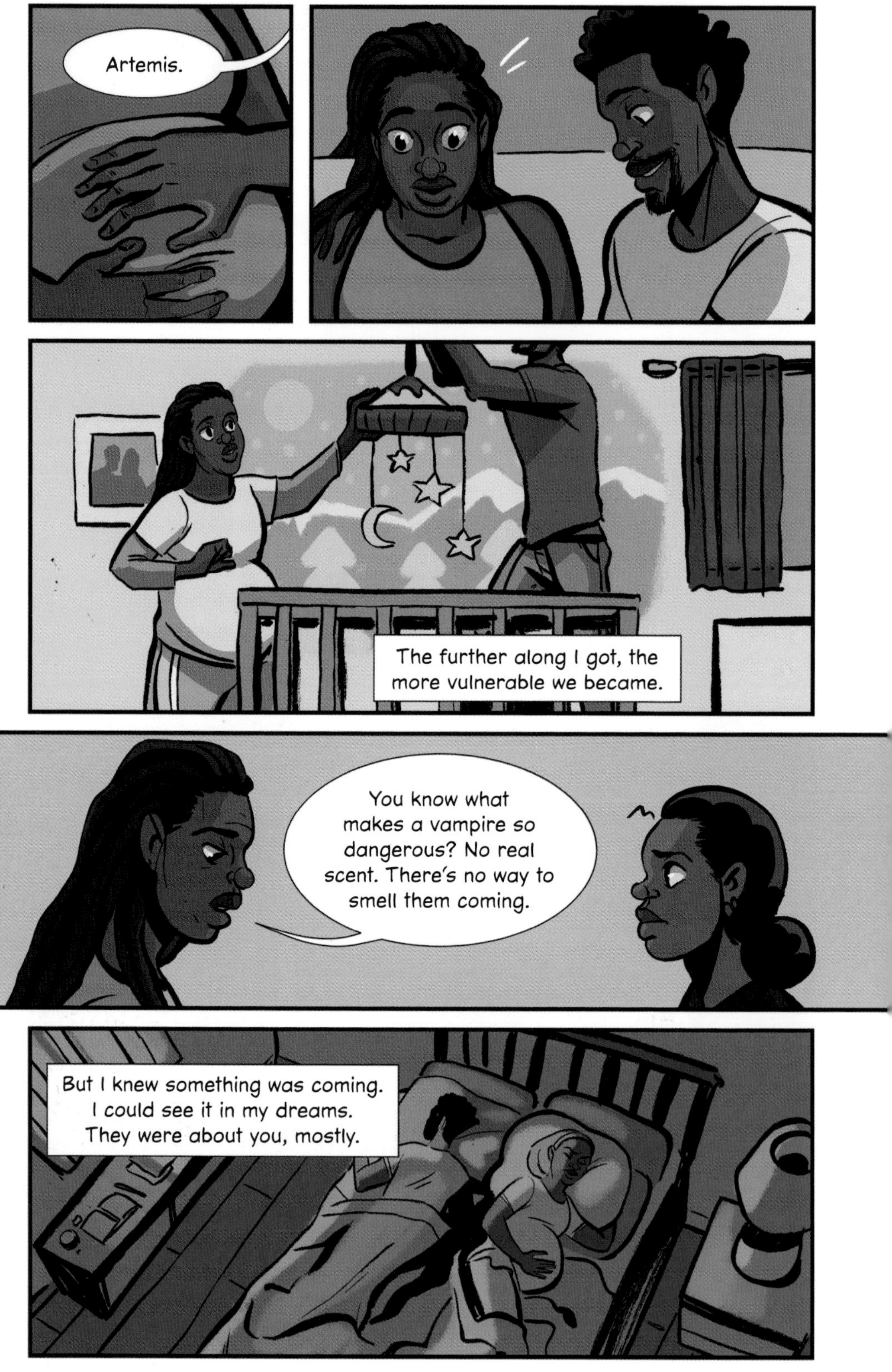
Artemis.
The further along I got, the more vulnerable we became.
You know what makes a vampire so dangerous? No real scent. There's no way to smell them coming.
But I knew something was coming. I could see it in my dreams. They were about you, mostly.

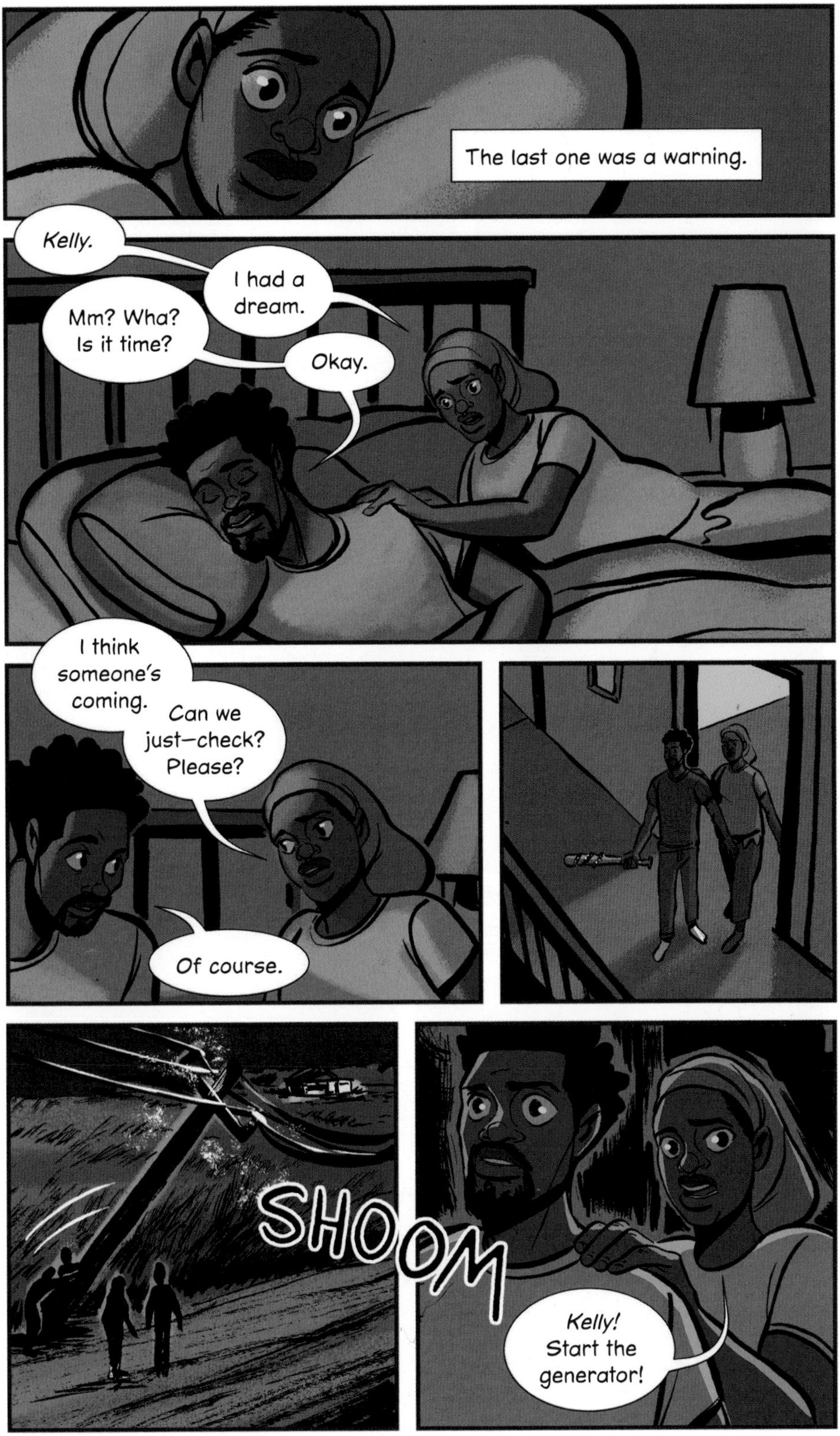
The last one was a warning.
Kelly.
I had a dream.
Mm? Wha? Is it time?
Okay.
I think someone's coming.
Can we just—check? Please?
Of course.
SHOOM
Kelly! Start the generator!

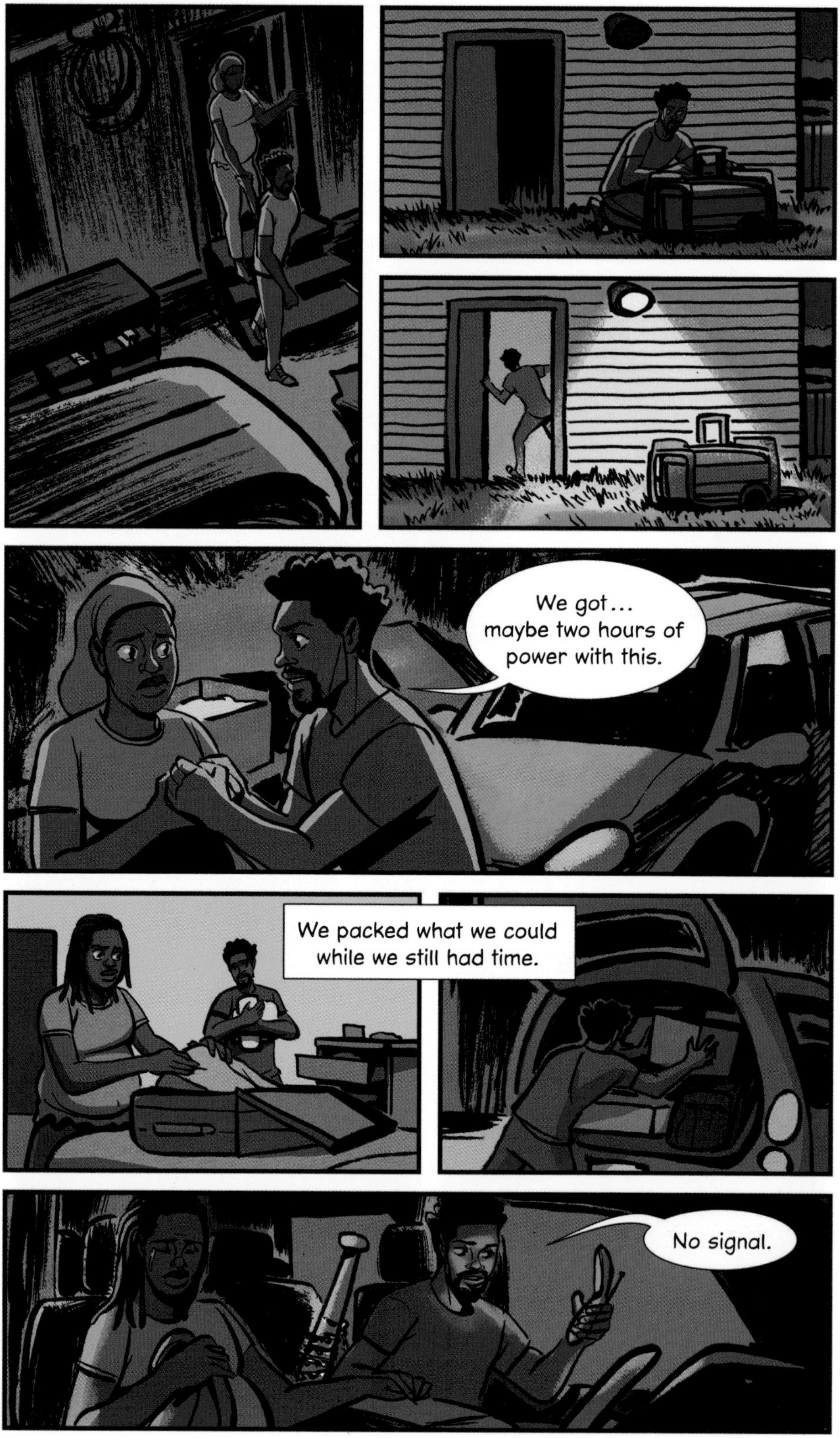
We got...
maybe two hours of
power with this.
We packed what we could
while we still had time.
No signal.

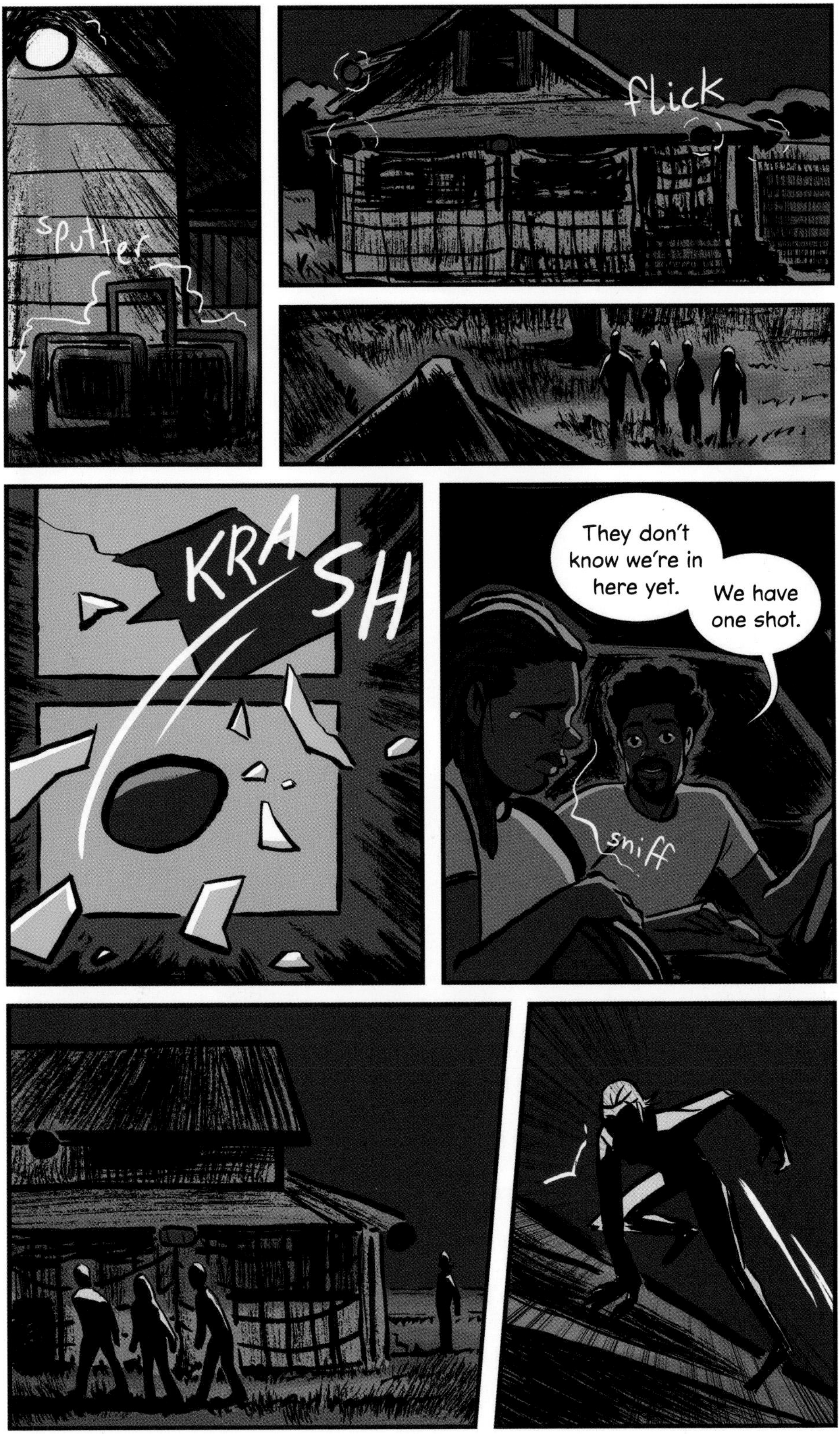
sputter
flick
KRASH
They don't know we're in here yet.
We have one shot.
sniff

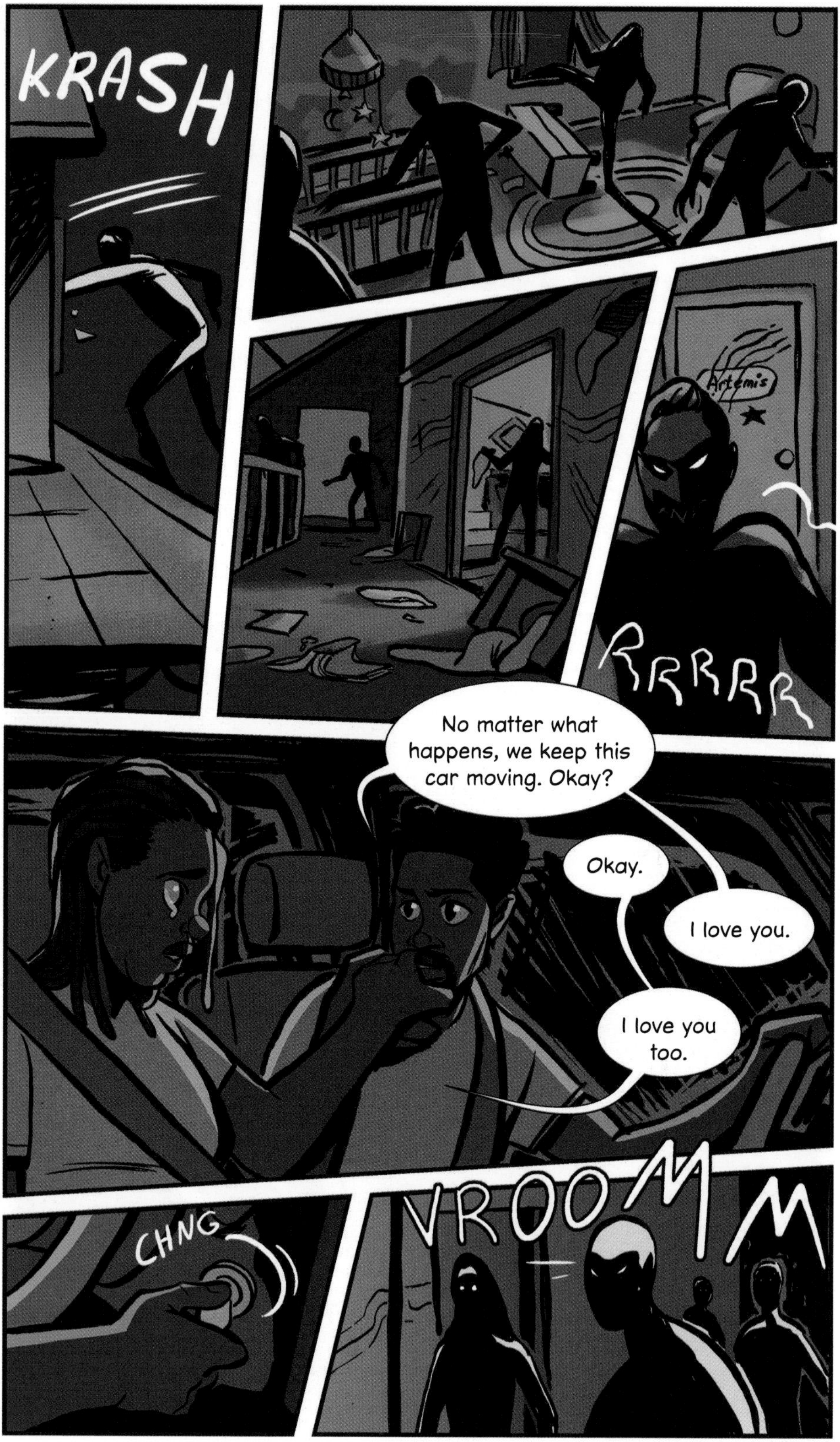
KRASH
Artemis
RRRRR
No matter what happens, we keep this car moving. Okay?
Okay.
I love you.
I love you too.
CHNG
VROOMM

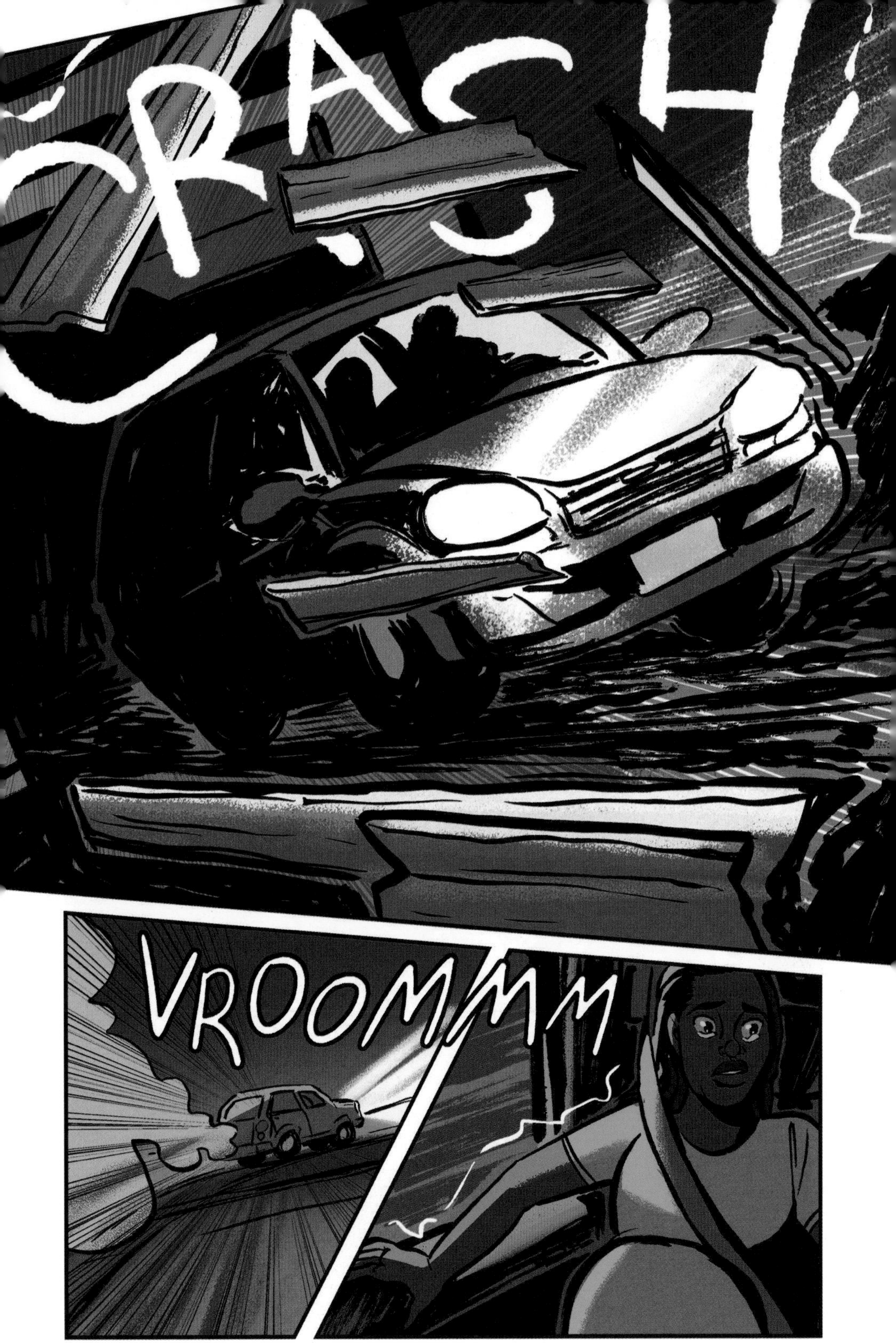
CRASH
VROOMMM

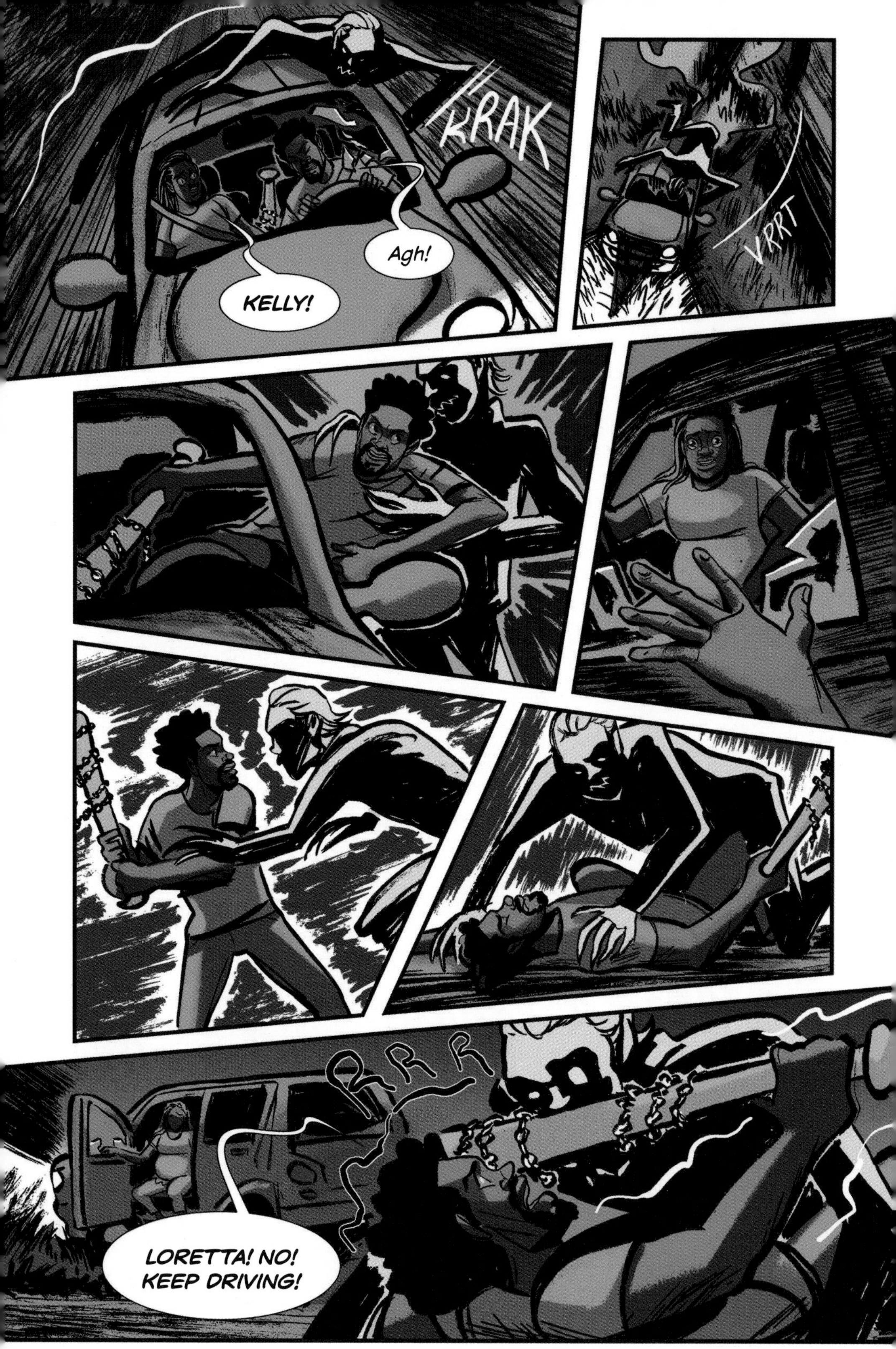
KRAK
KELLY!
Agh!
VRRT
RRR
LORETTA! NO!
KEEP DRIVING!

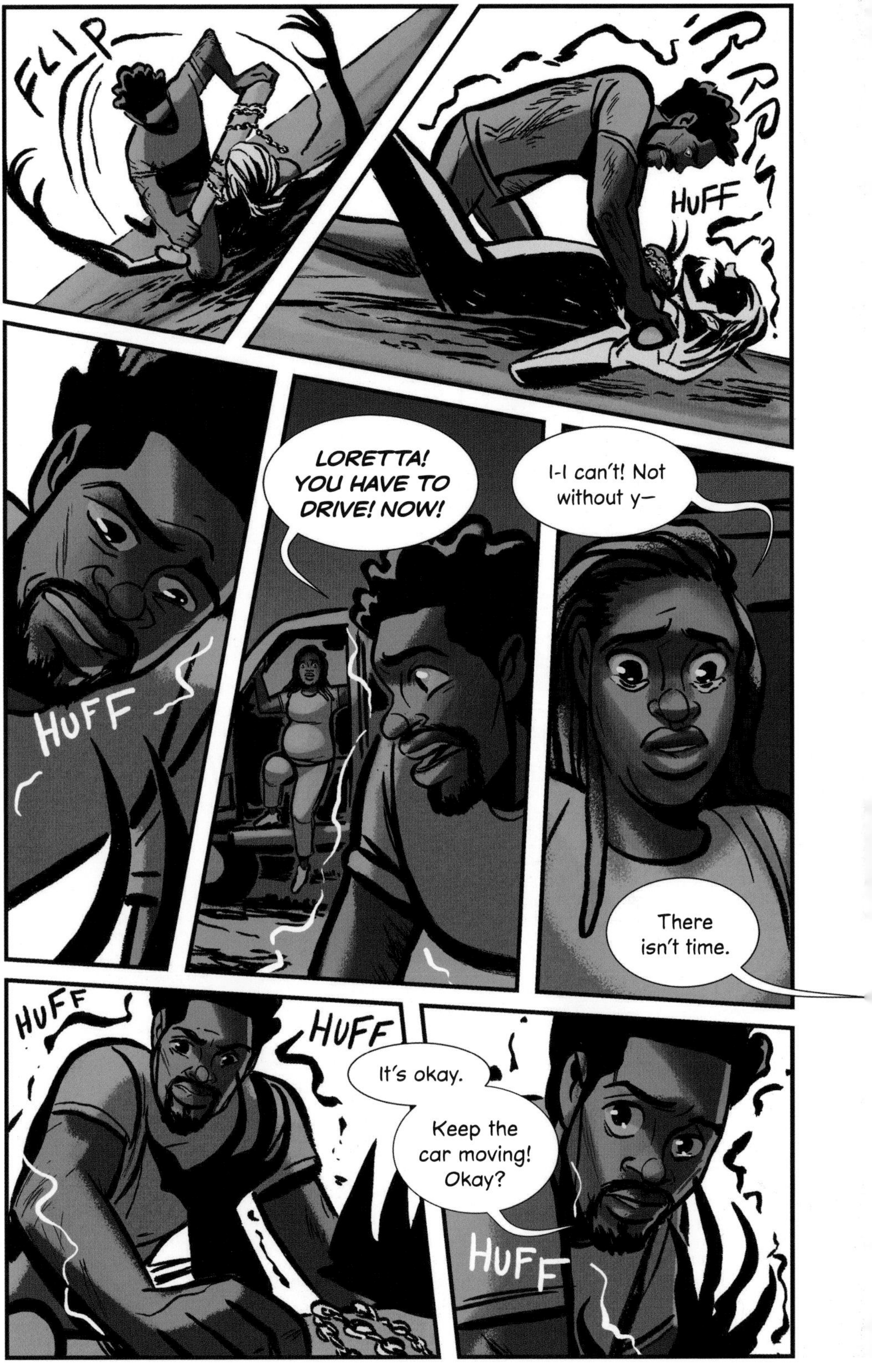
FLIP
RRR
HUFF
HUFF
LORETTA! YOU HAVE TO DRIVE! NOW!
I-I can't! Not without y—
There isn't time.
HUFF
HUFF
It's okay.
Keep the car moving! Okay?
HUFF

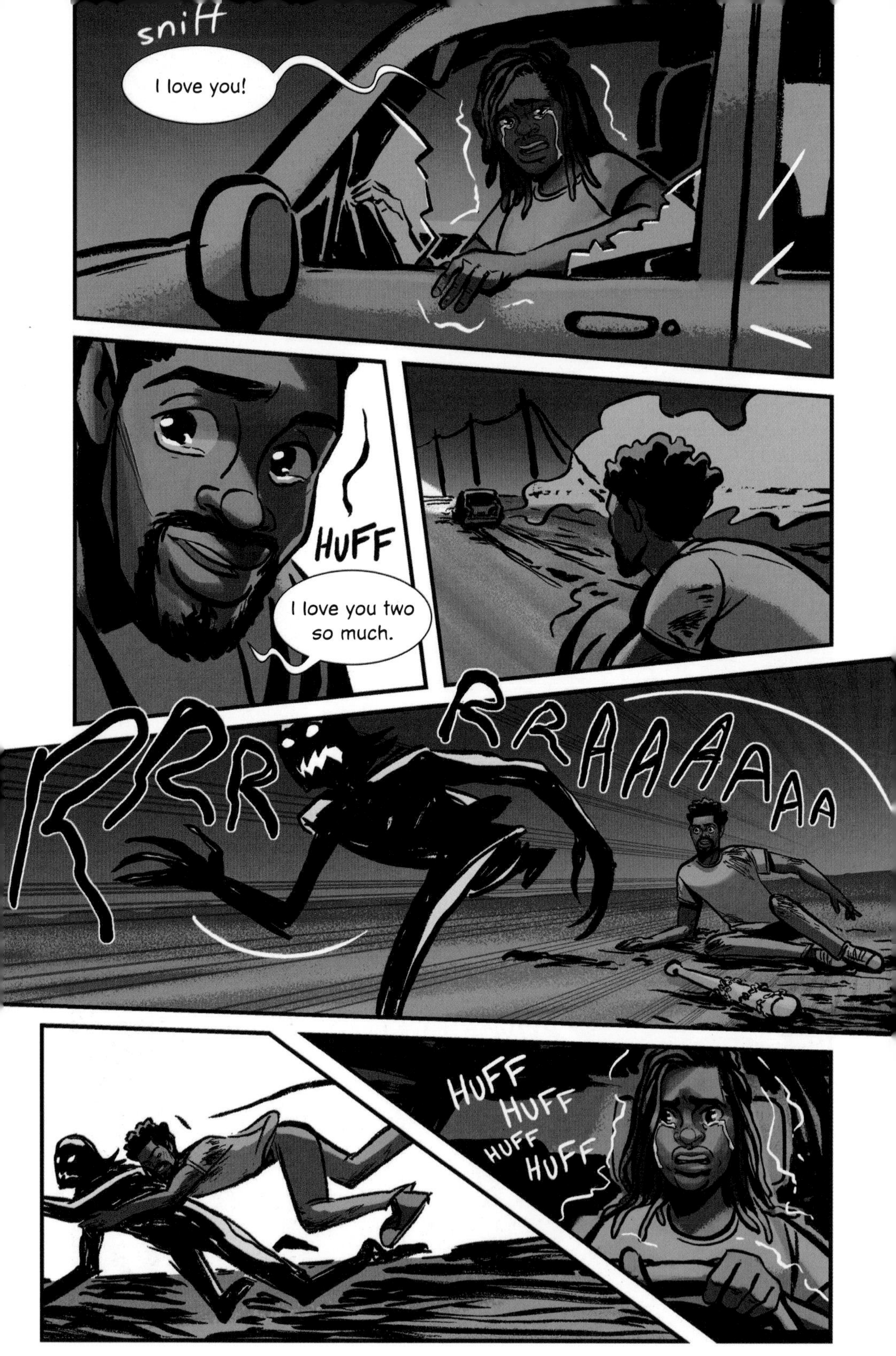

sniff
I love you!
HUFF
I love you two so much.
RRRRRAAAAAAAA
HUFF
HUFF
HUFF
HUFF

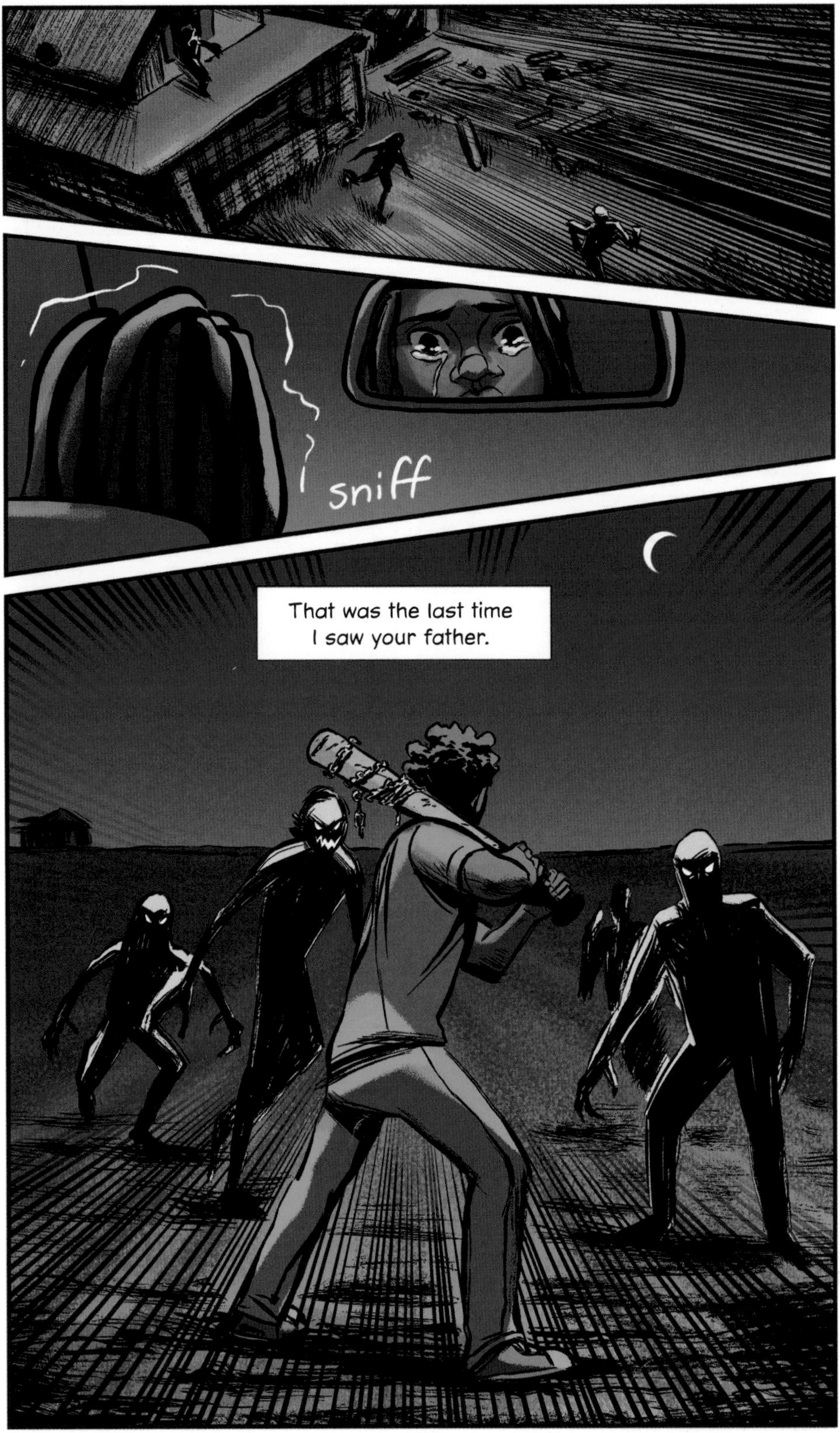
sniff
That was the last time I saw your father.

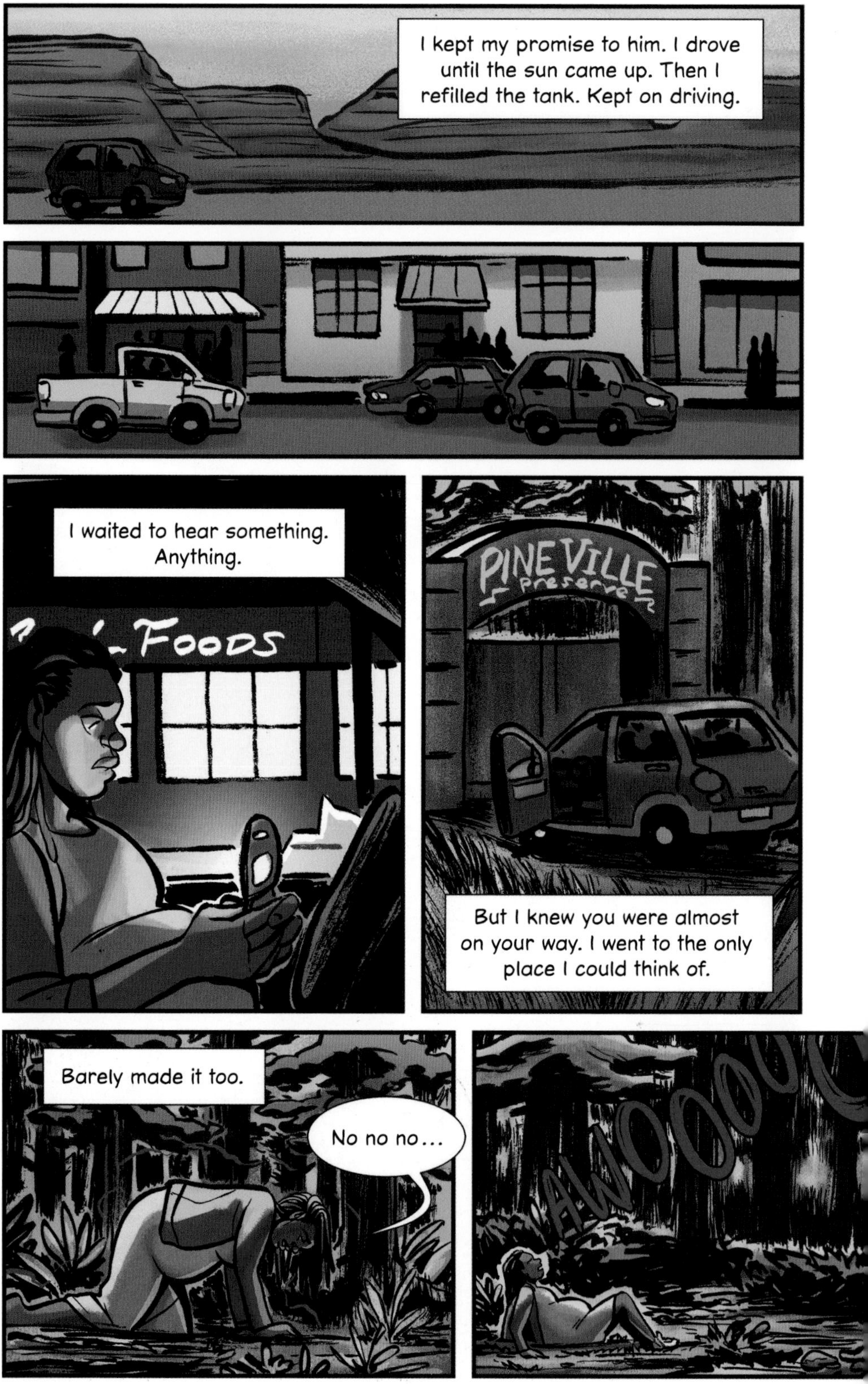
I kept my promise to him. I drove until the sun came up. Then I refilled the tank. Kept on driving.
I waited to hear something. Anything.
FOODS
PINEVILLE preserve
But I knew you were almost on your way. I went to the only place I could think of.
Barely made it too.
No no no...
AWOOOO

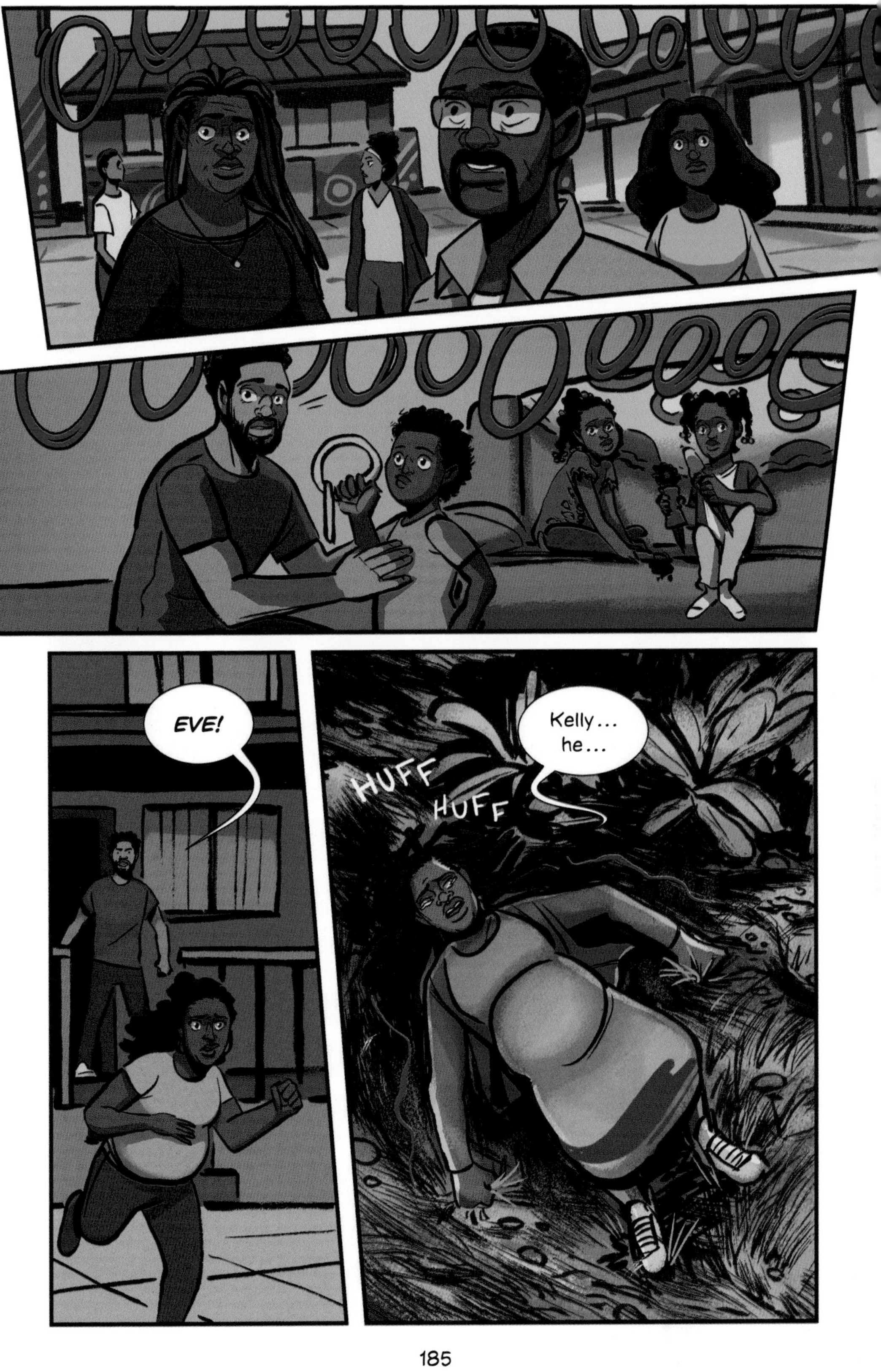
EVE!
HUFF
HUFF
Kelly... he...

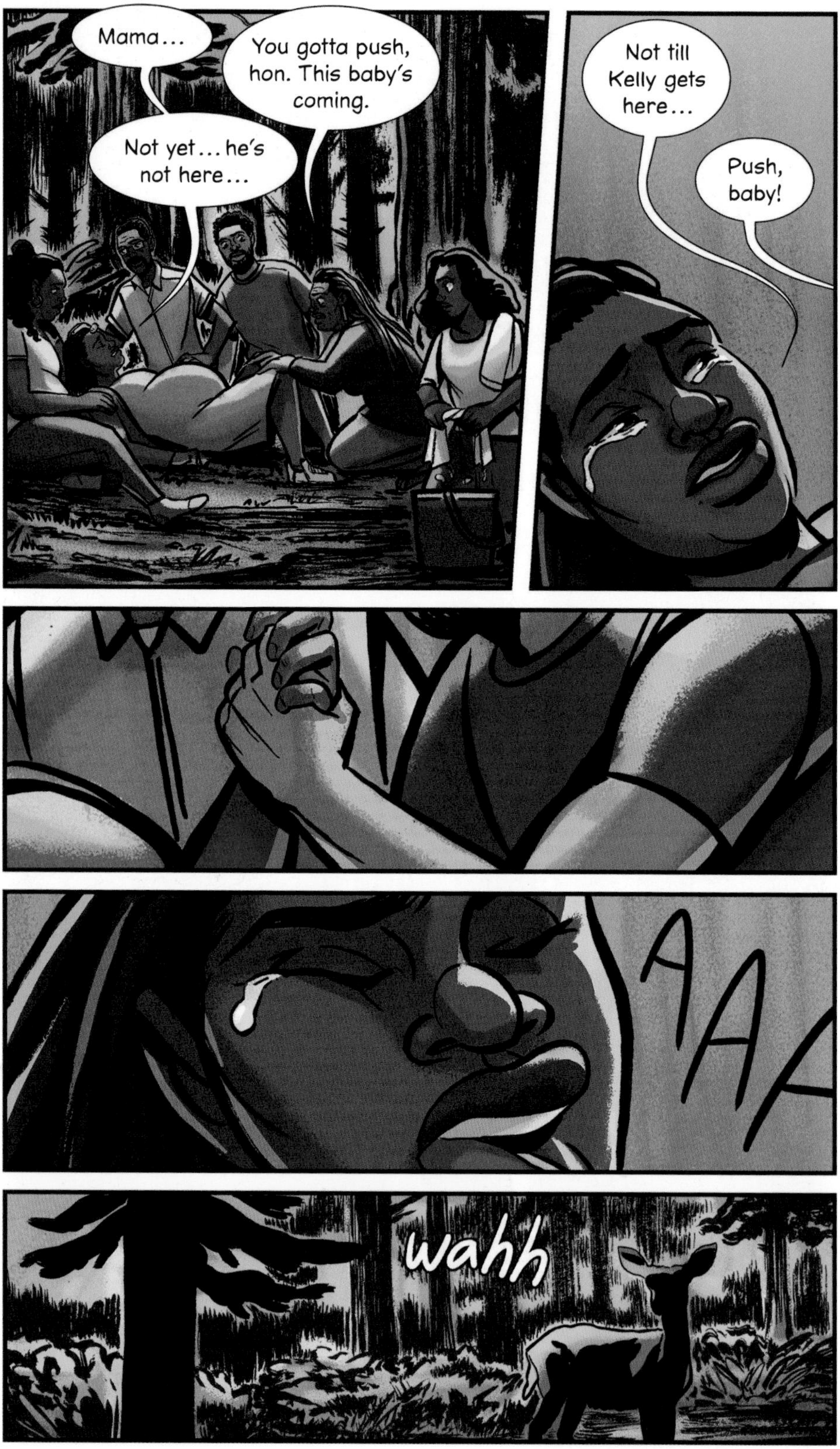
Mama...
You gotta push, hon. This baby's coming.
Not yet... he's not here...
Not till Kelly gets here...
Push, baby!
AAAA
wahh

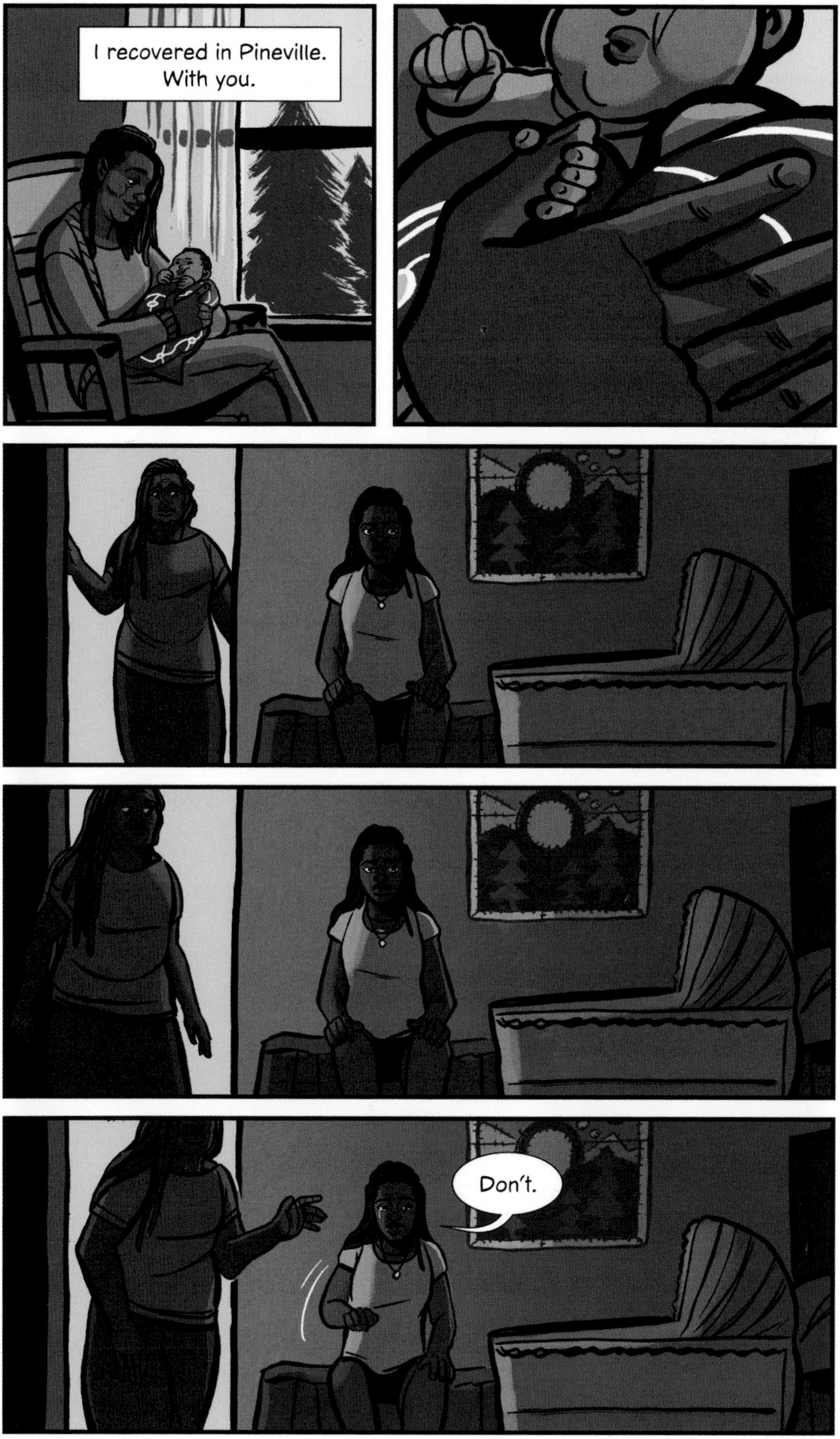
I recovered in Pineville. With you.
Don't.

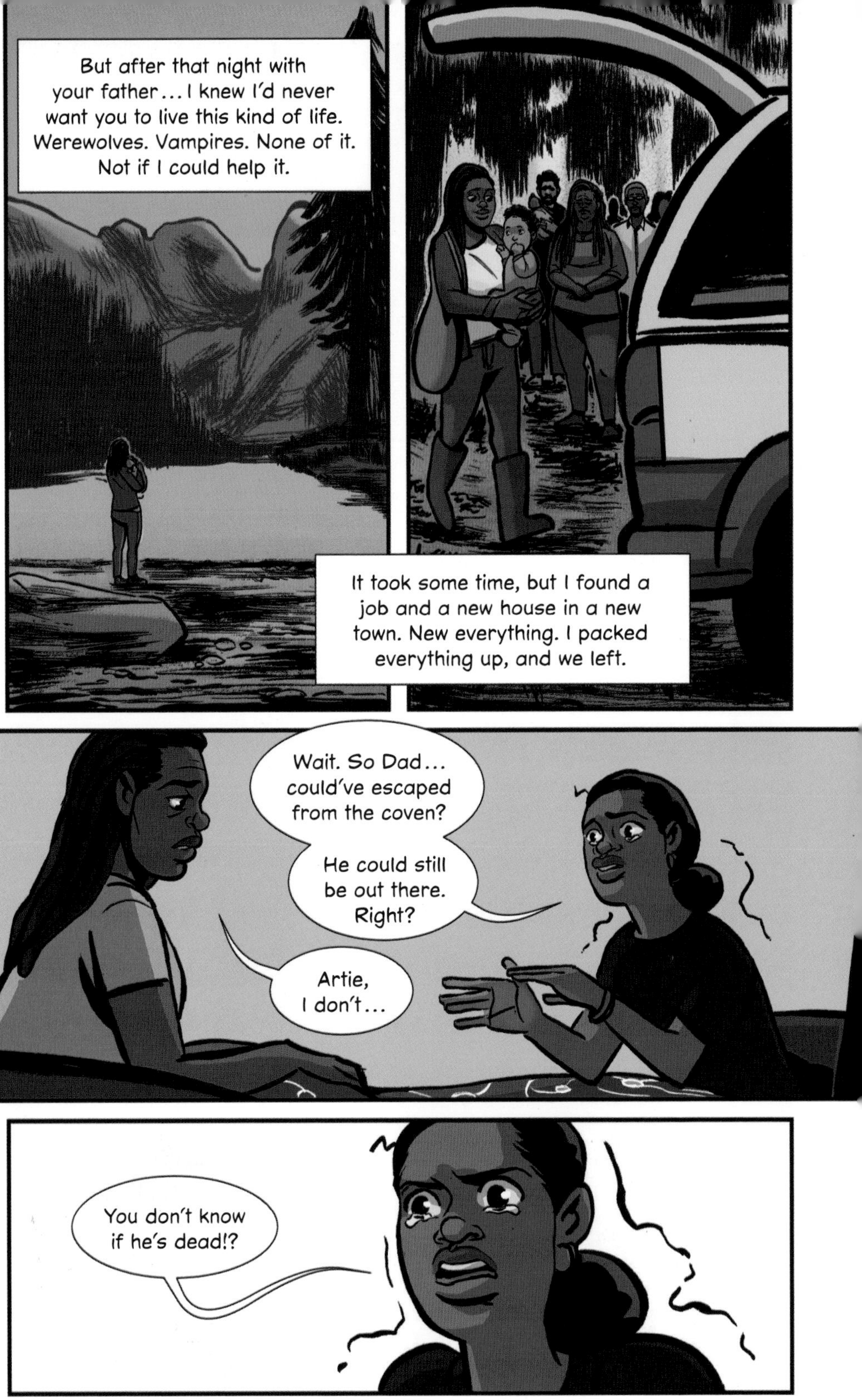
But after that night with your father... I knew I'd never want you to live this kind of life. Werewolves. Vampires. None of it. Not if I could help it.
It took some time, but I found a job and a new house in a new town. New everything. I packed everything up, and we left.
Wait. So Dad... could've escaped from the coven?
He could still be out there. Right?
Artie, I don't...
You don't know if he's dead!?

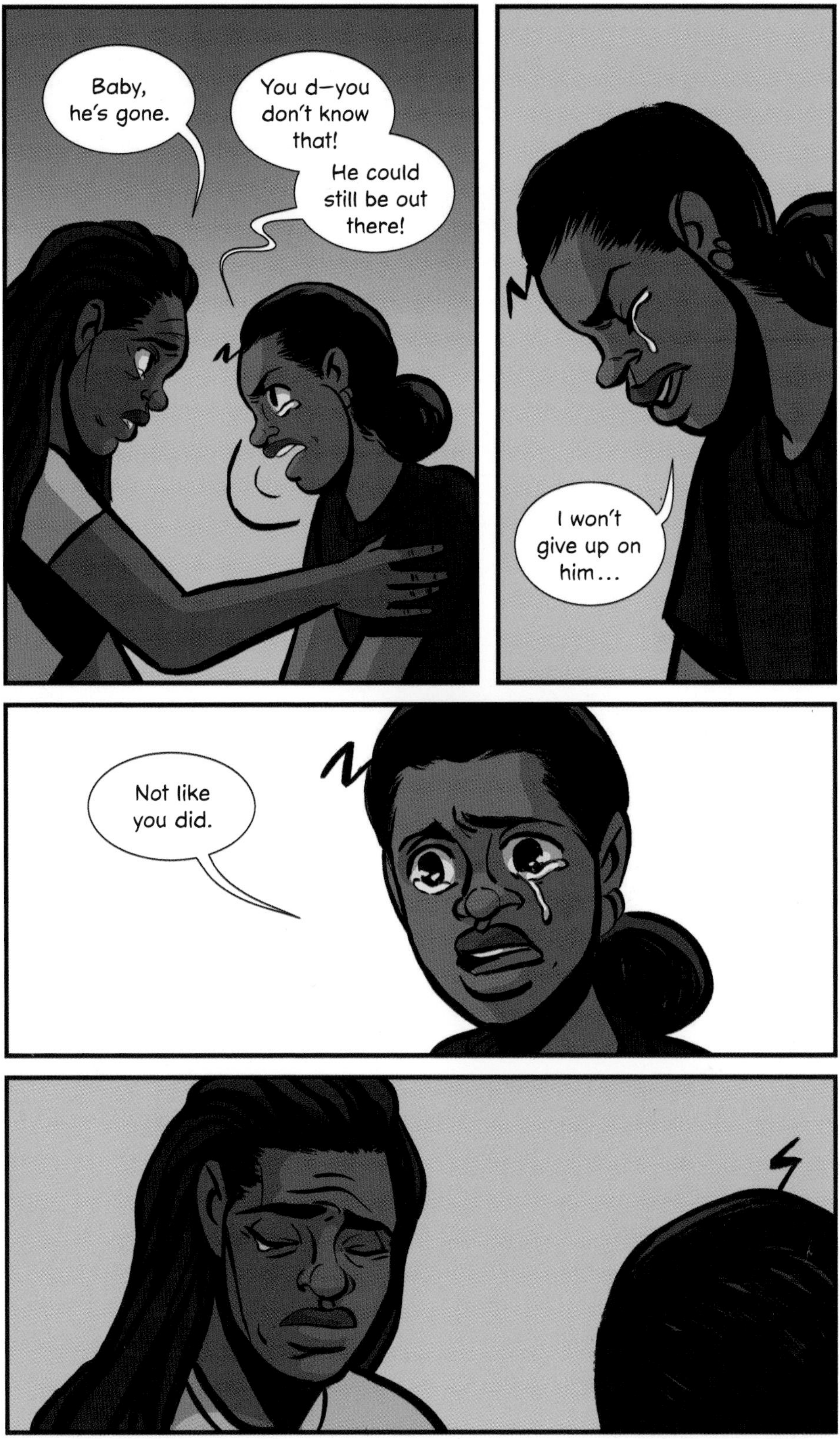
Baby, he's gone.
You d—you don't know that!
He could still be out there!
I won't give up on him...
Not like you did.

CHAPTER EIGHT

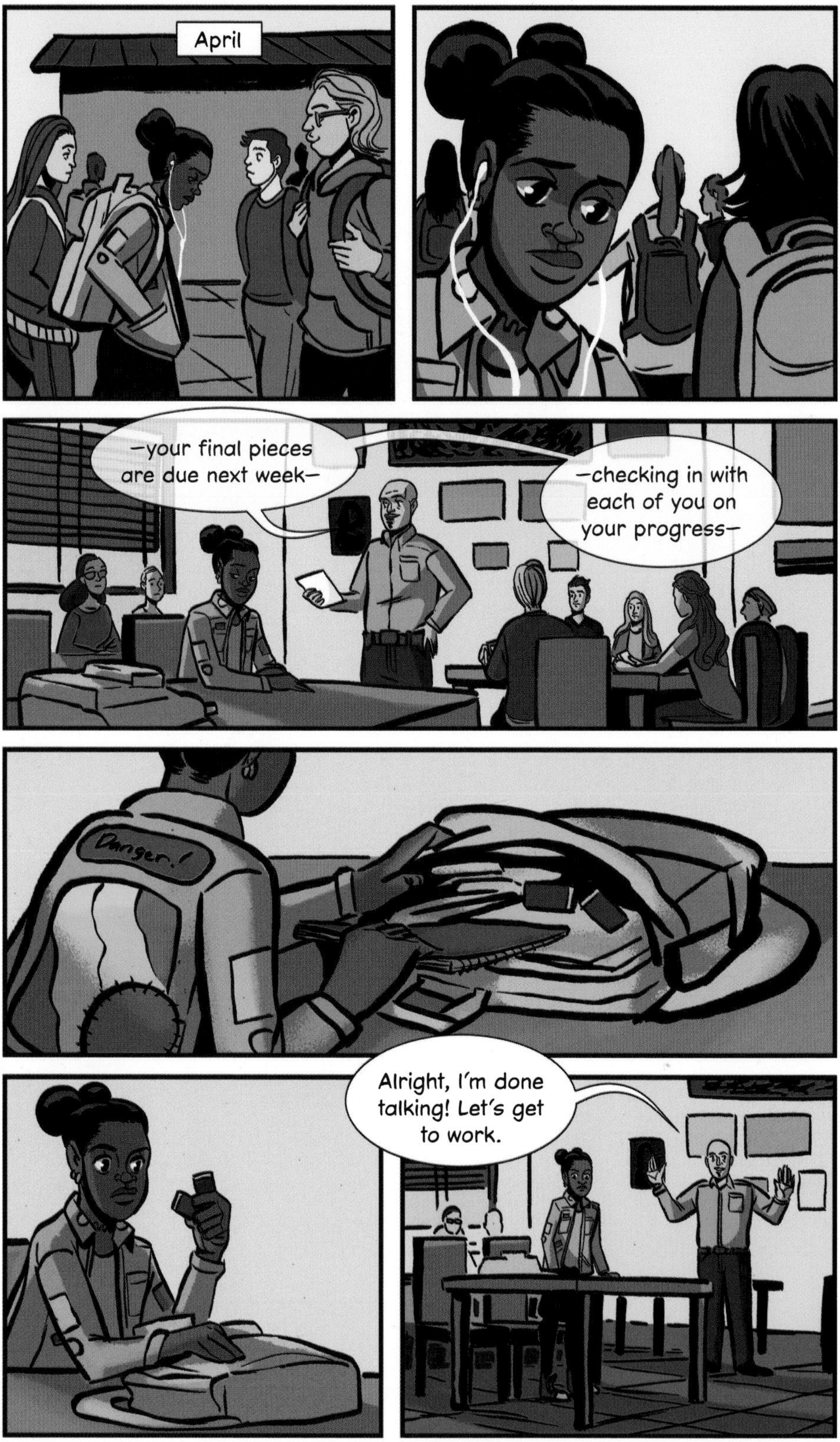
April
—your final pieces are due next week—
—checking in with each of you on your progress—
Danger.!
Alright, I'm done talking! Let's get to work.

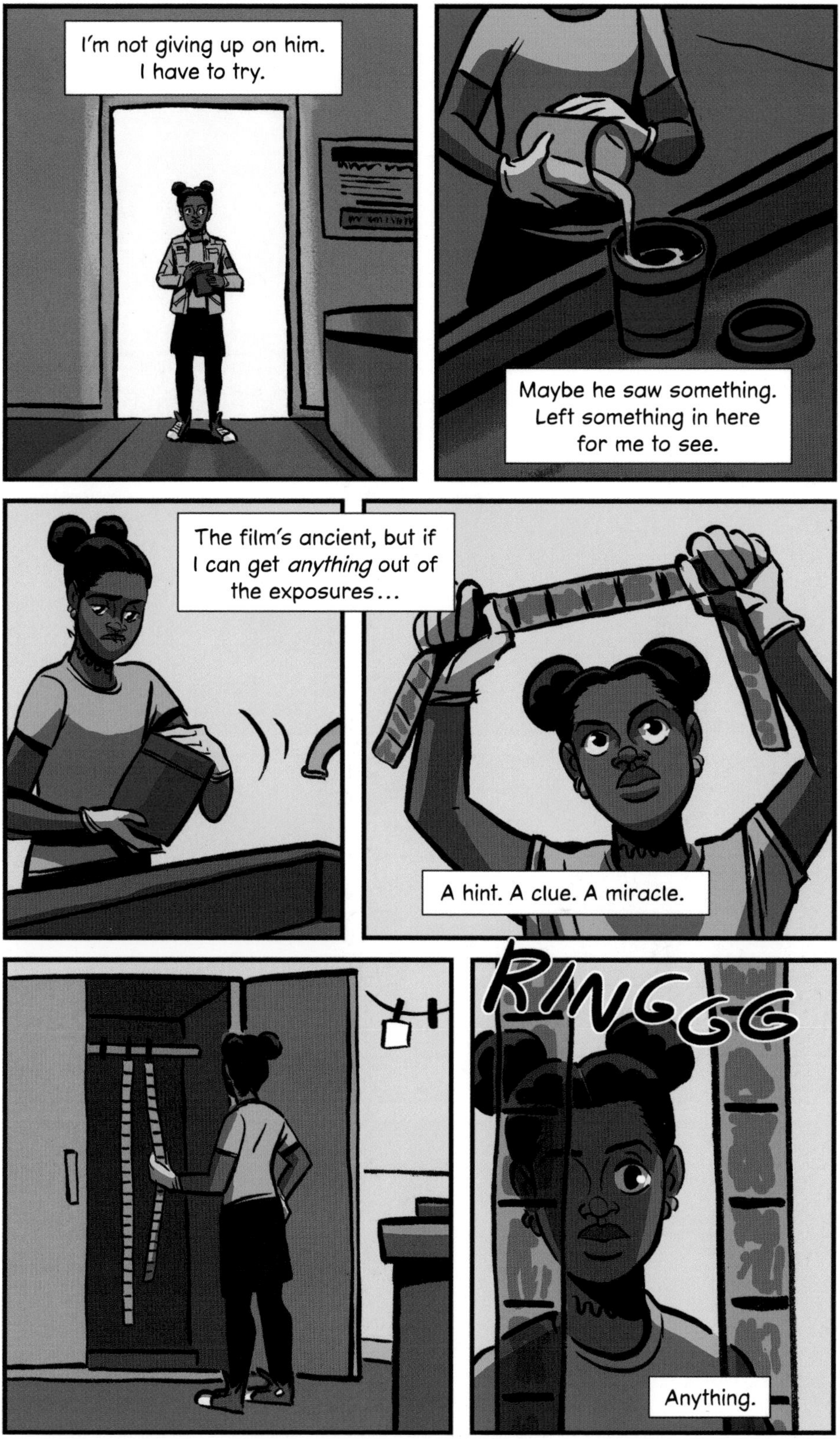
I'm not giving up on him.
I have to try.
Maybe he saw something.
Left something in here
for me to see.
The film's ancient, but if
I can get *anything* out of
the exposures...
A hint. A clue. A miracle.
RINGGG
Anything.

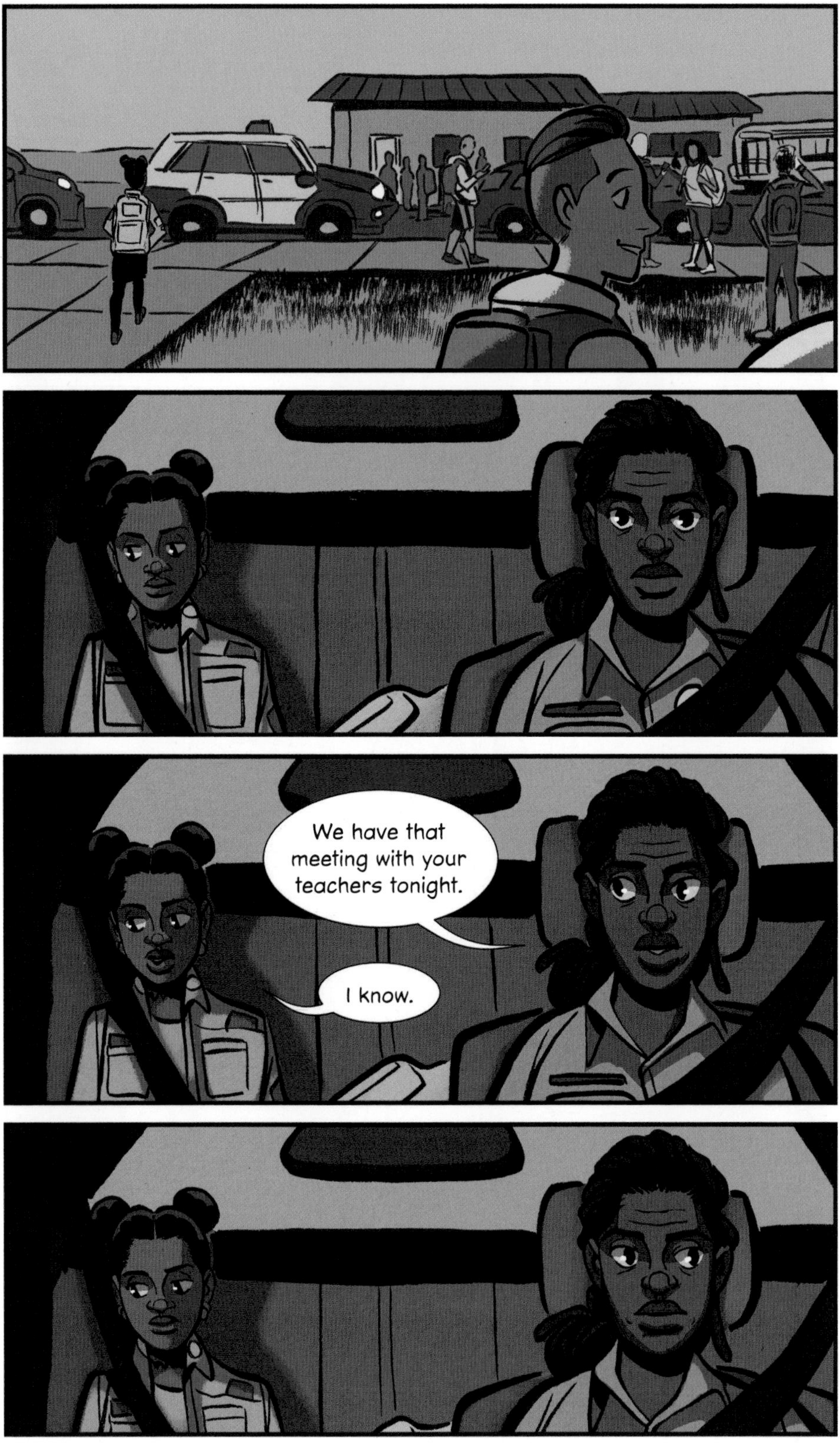
We have that meeting with your teachers tonight.
I know.

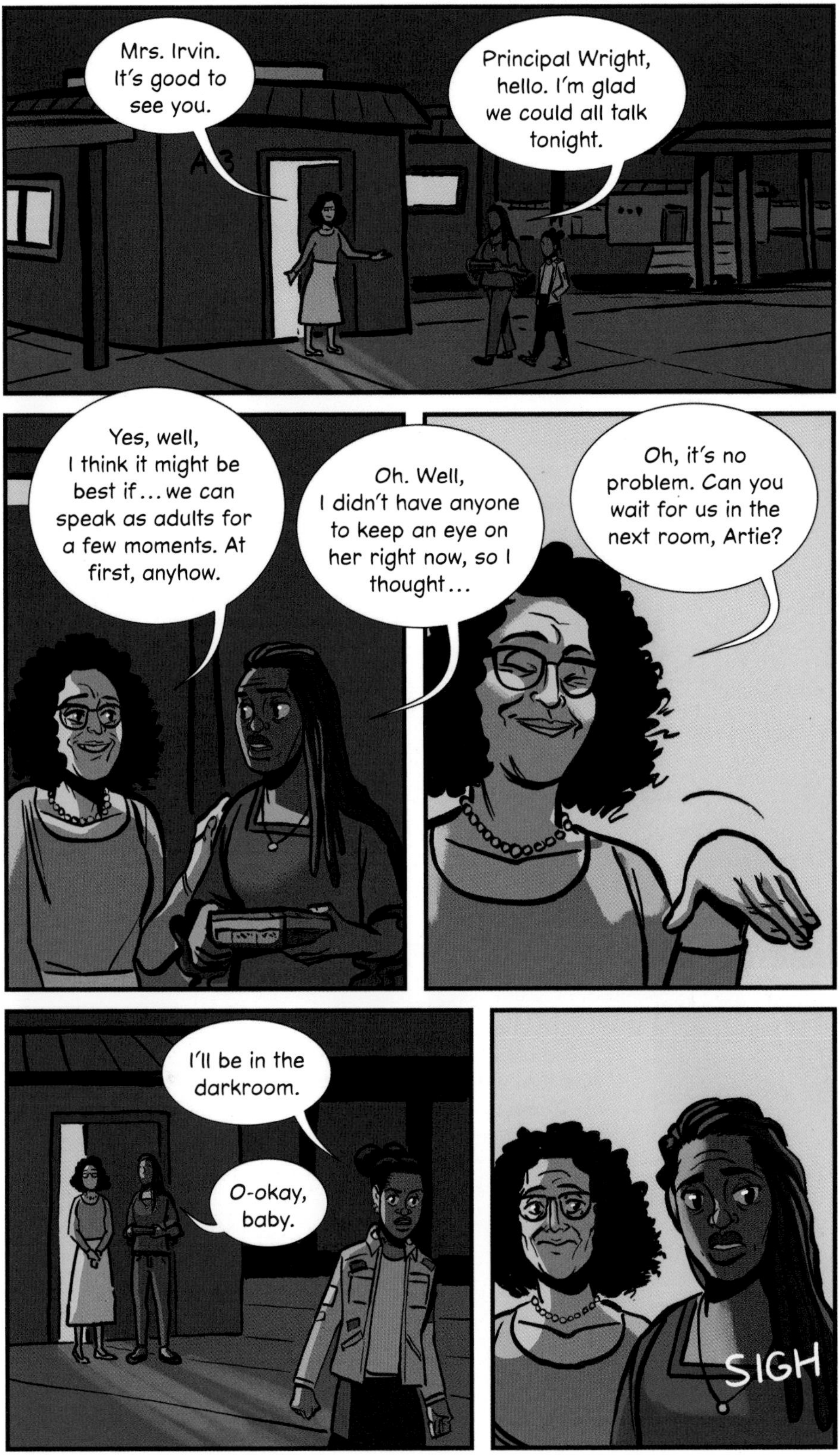
Mrs. Irvin. It's good to see you.
Principal Wright, hello. I'm glad we could all talk tonight.
Yes, well, I think it might be best if...we can speak as adults for a few moments. At first, anyhow.
Oh. Well, I didn't have anyone to keep an eye on her right now, so I thought...
Oh, it's no problem. Can you wait for us in the next room, Artie?
I'll be in the darkroom.
O-okay, baby.
SIGH

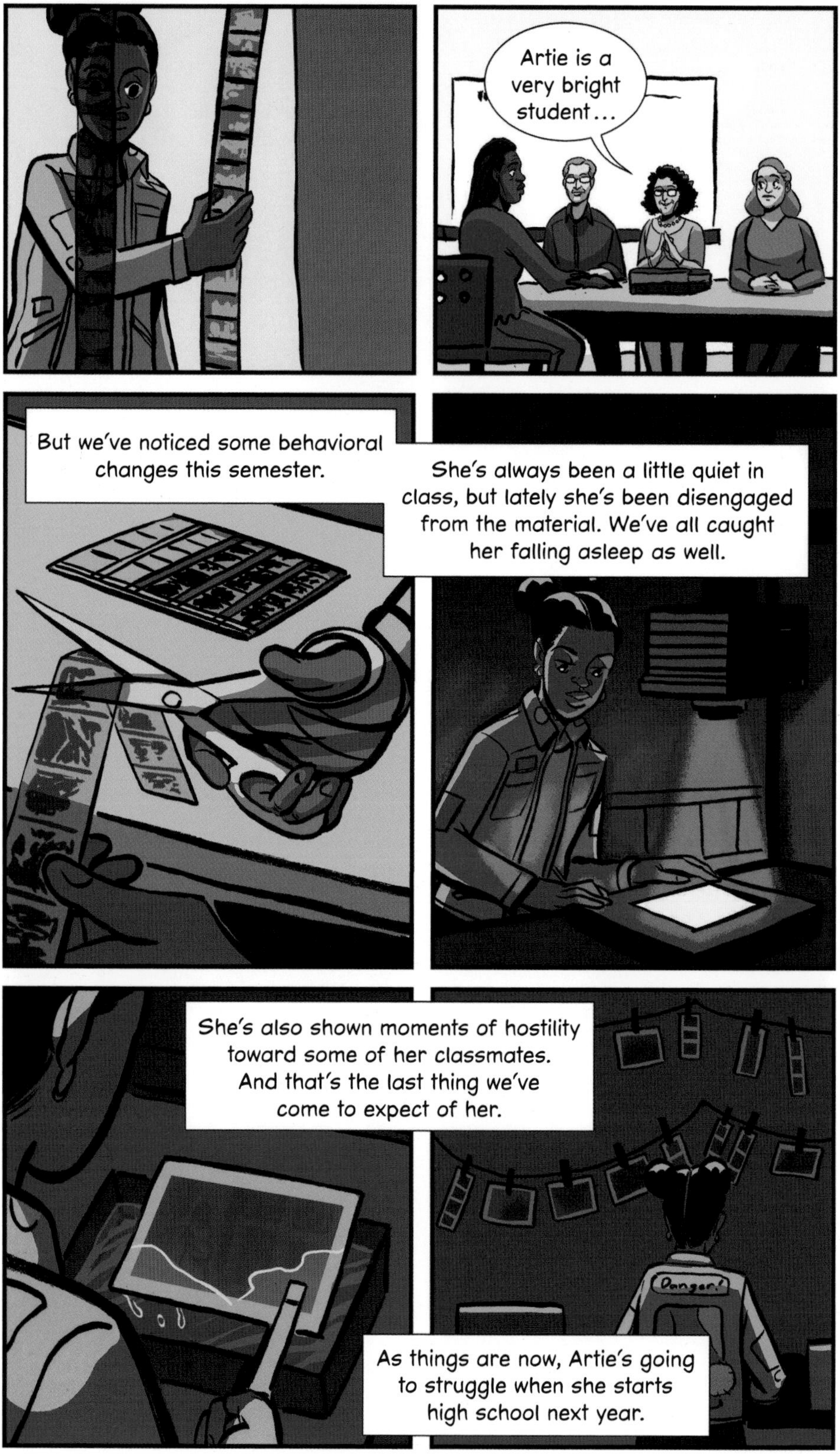
Artie is a very bright student...
But we've noticed some behavioral changes this semester.
She's always been a little quiet in class, but lately she's been disengaged from the material. We've all caught her falling asleep as well.
She's also shown moments of hostility toward some of her classmates. And that's the last thing we've come to expect of her.
Danger!
As things are now, Artie's going to struggle when she starts high school next year.

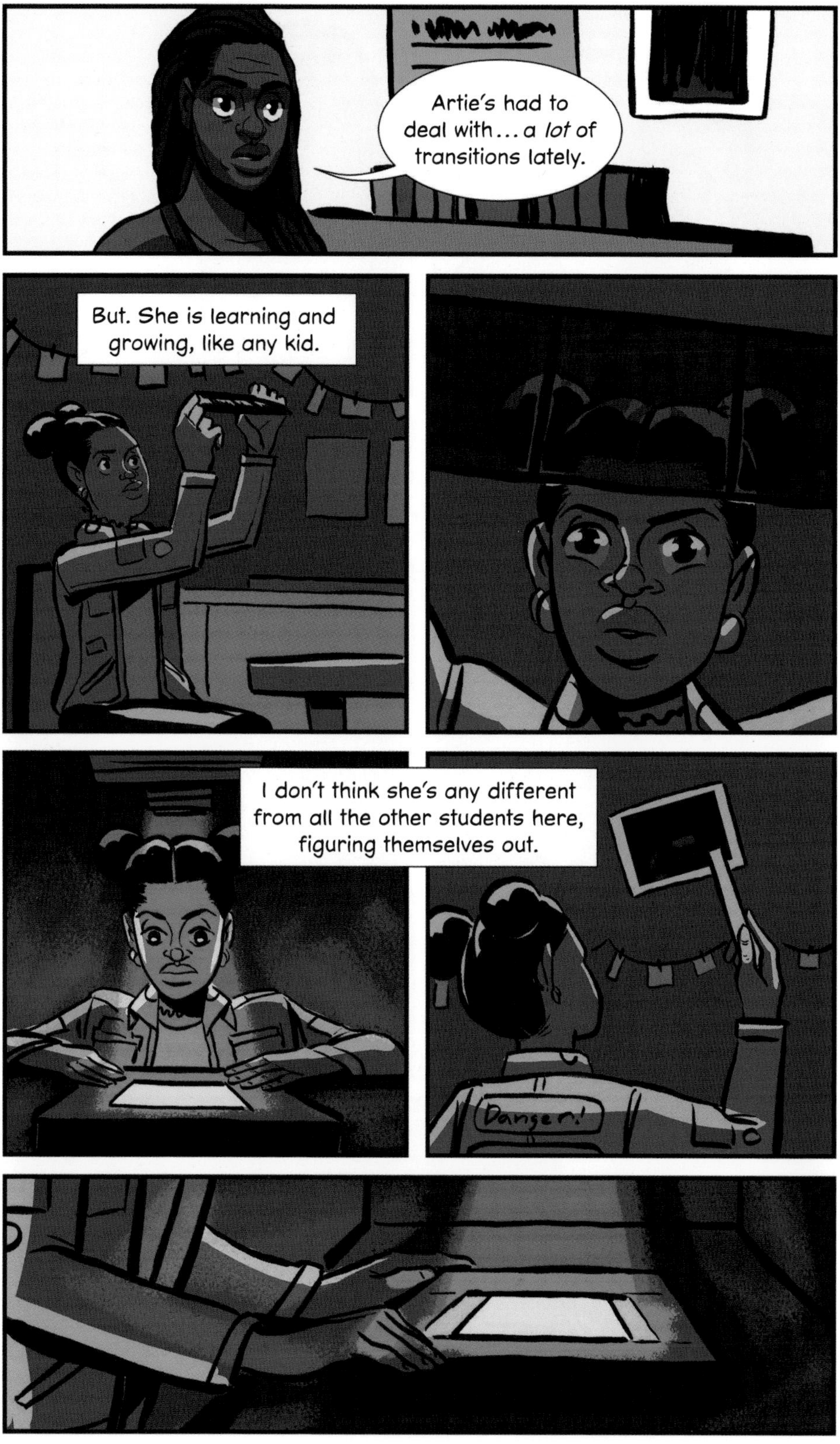
Artie's had to deal with... a *lot* of transitions lately.
But. She is learning and growing, like any kid.
I don't think she's any different from all the other students here, figuring themselves out.
Danger!

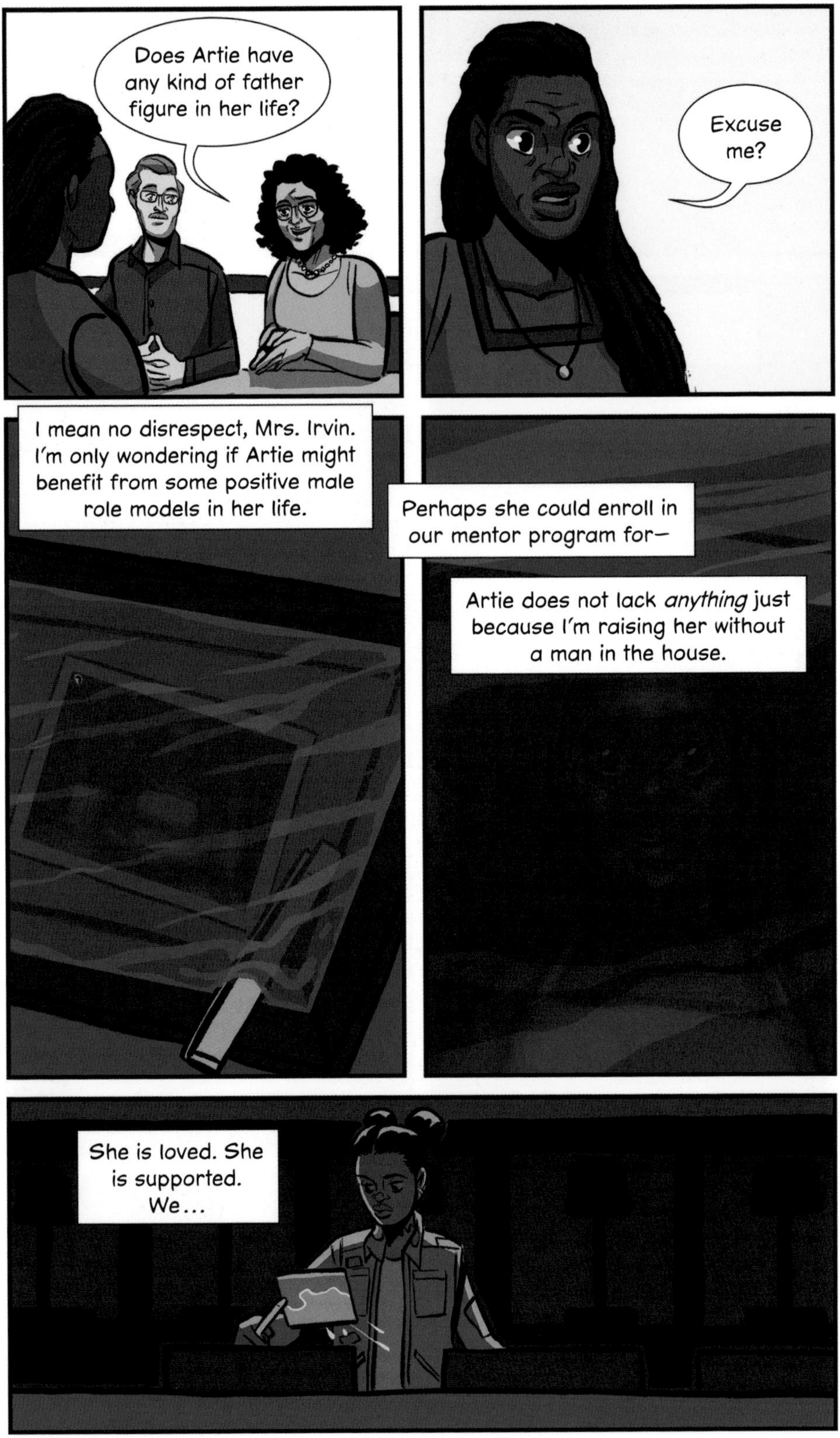
Does Artie have any kind of father figure in her life?
Excuse me?
I mean no disrespect, Mrs. Irvin. I'm only wondering if Artie might benefit from some positive male role models in her life.
Perhaps she could enroll in our mentor program for—
Artie does not lack *anything* just because I'm raising her without a man in the house.
She is loved. She is supported. We...

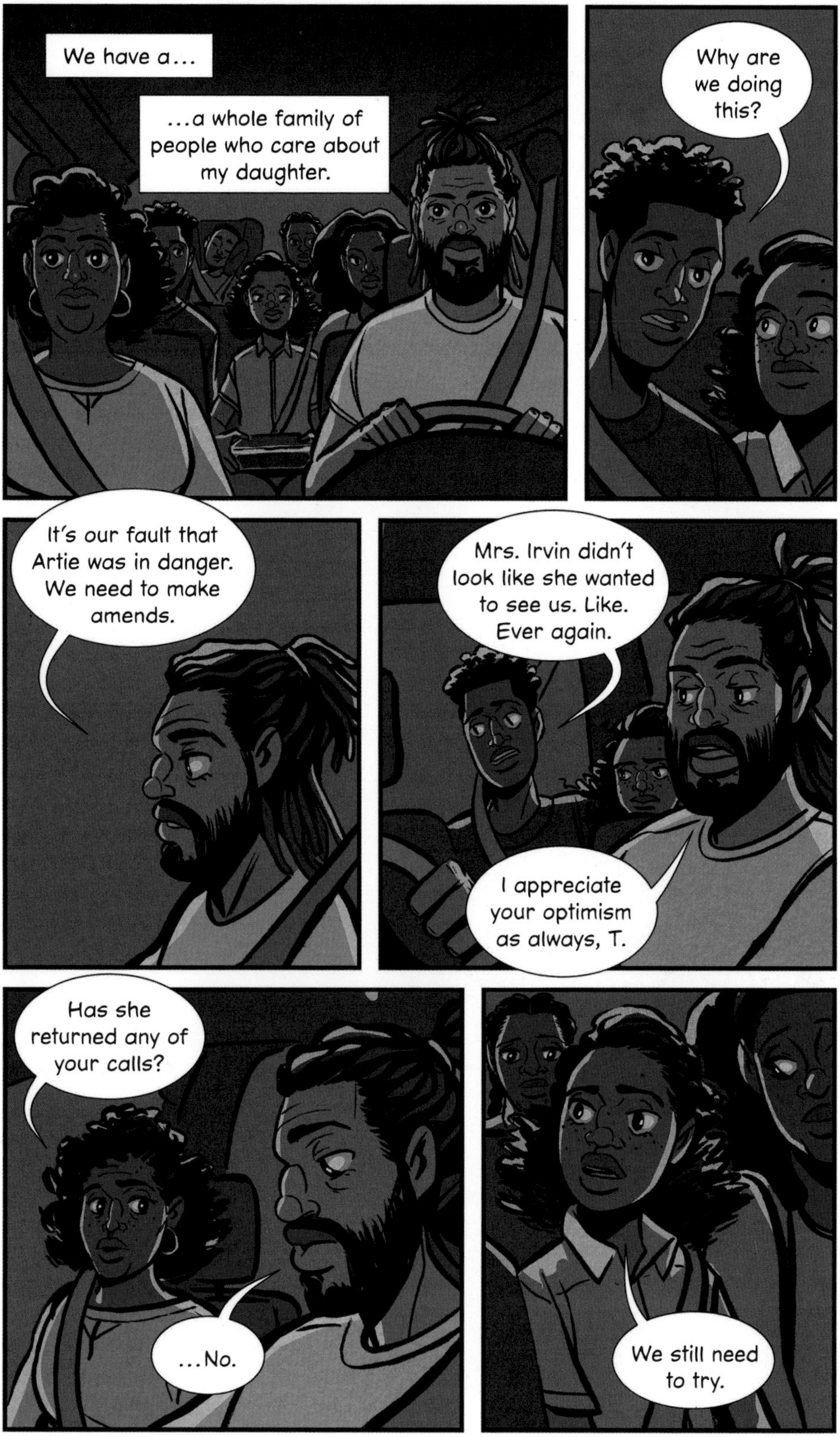
We have a...
...a whole family of people who care about my daughter.
Why are we doing this?
It's our fault that Artie was in danger. We need to make amends.
Mrs. Irvin didn't look like she wanted to see us. Like. Ever again.
I appreciate your optimism as always, T.
Has she returned any of your calls?
...No.
We still need to try.

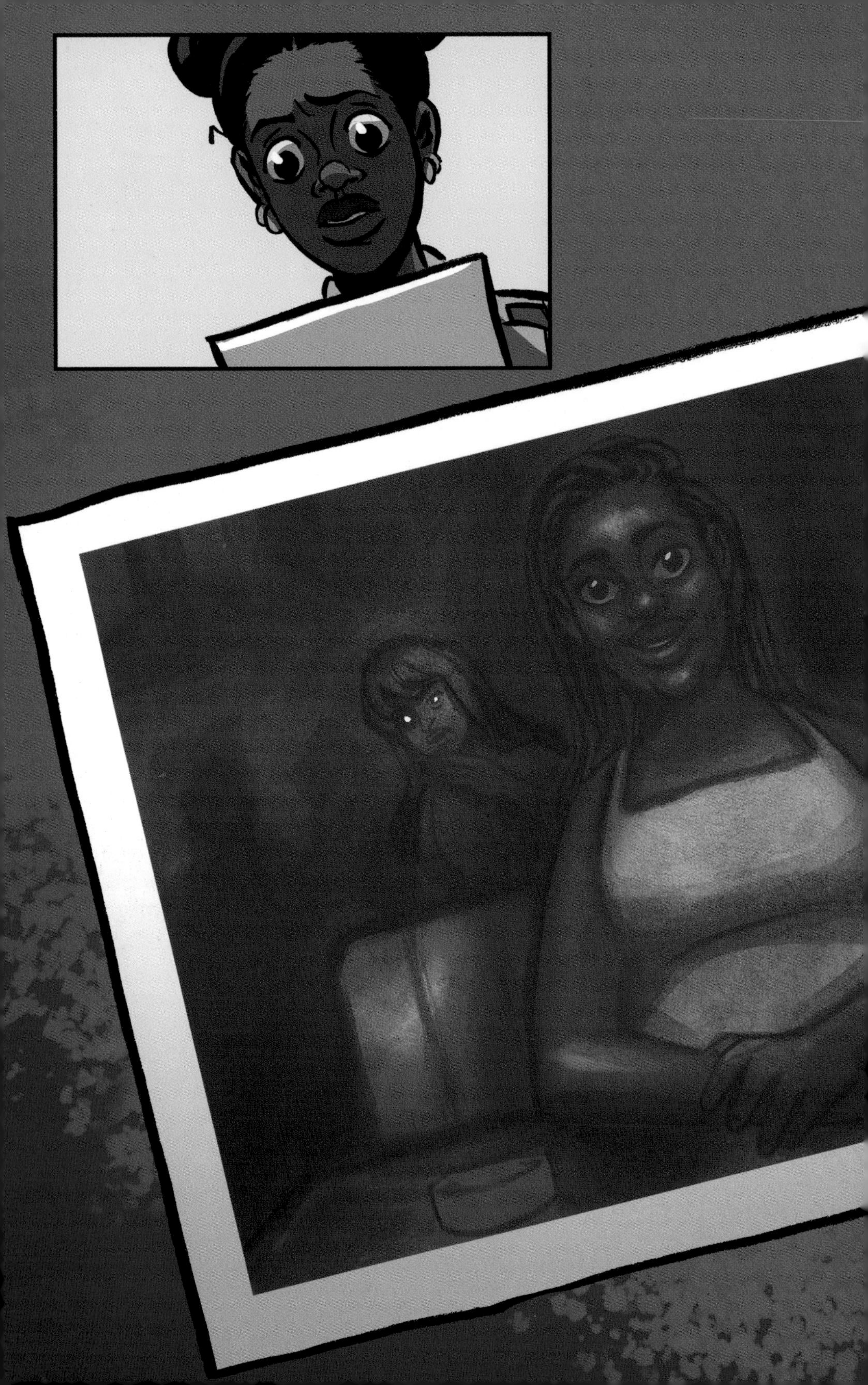

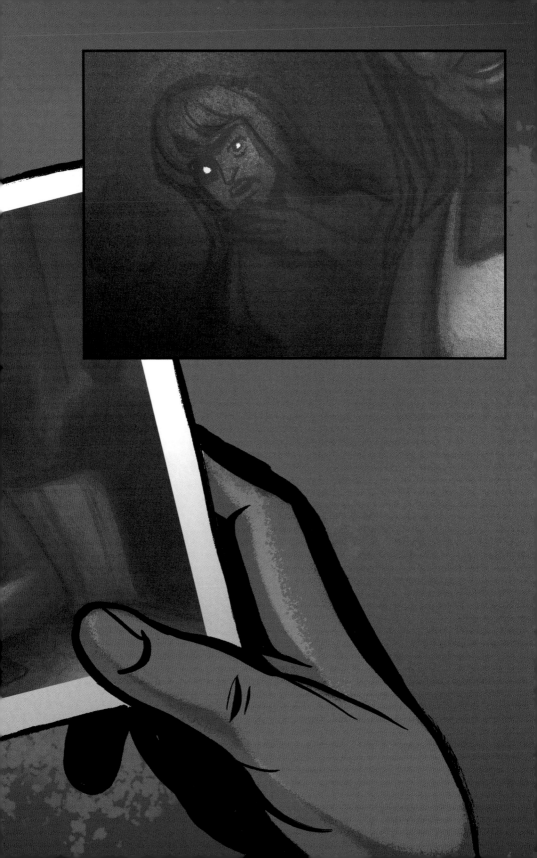

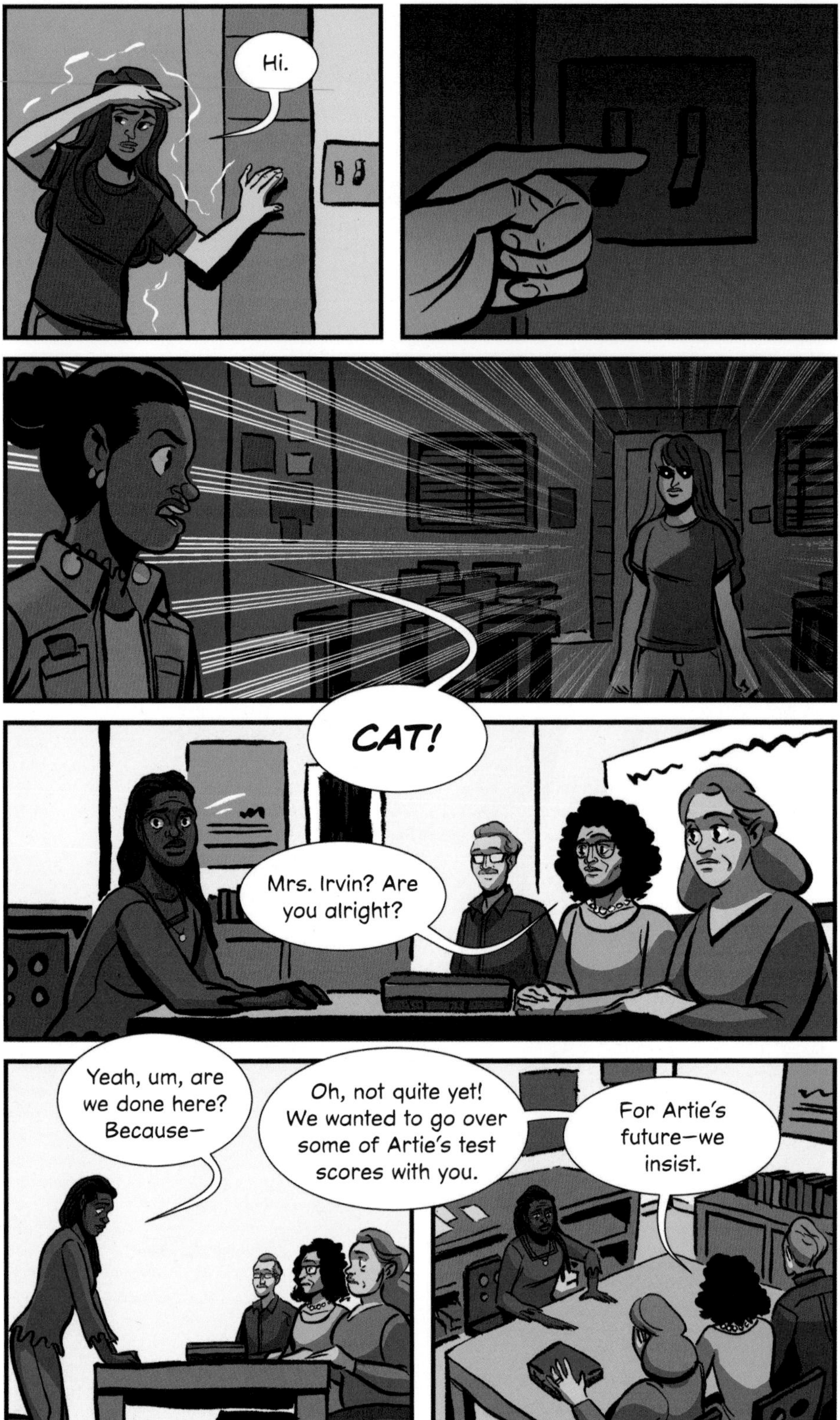
Hi.
CAT!
Mrs. Irvin? Are you alright?
Yeah, um, are we done here? Because—
Oh, not quite yet! We wanted to go over some of Artie's test scores with you.
For Artie's future—we insist.

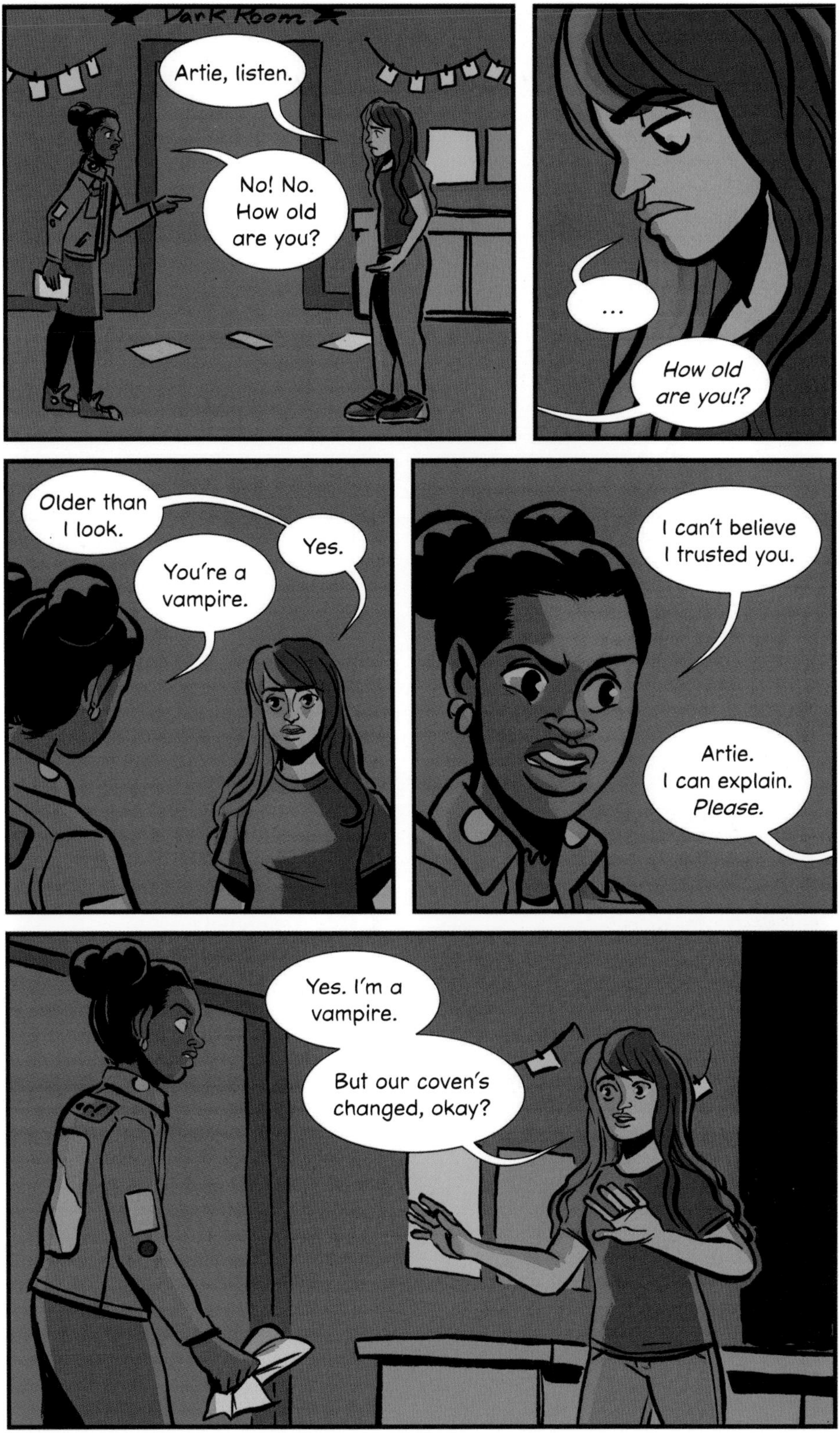
Dark Room
Artie, listen.
No! No. How old are you?
...
How old are you!?
Older than I look.
You're a vampire.
Yes.
I can't believe I trusted you.
Artie. I can explain. *Please.*
Yes. I'm a vampire.
But our coven's changed, okay?

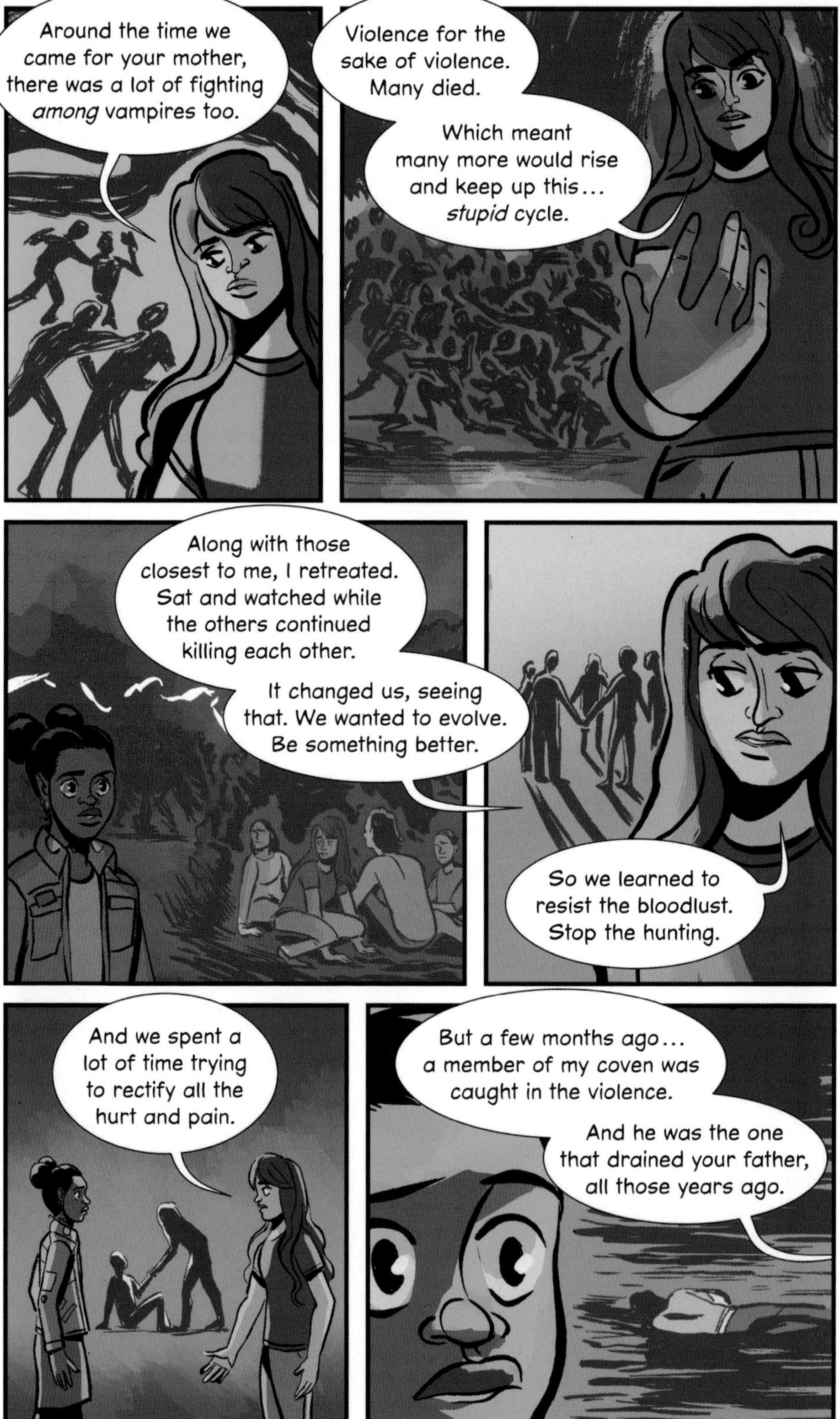

Around the time we came for your mother, there was a lot of fighting *among* vampires too.
Violence for the sake of violence. Many died.
Which meant many more would rise and keep up this... *stupid* cycle.
Along with those closest to me, I retreated. Sat and watched while the others continued killing each other.
It changed us, seeing that. We wanted to evolve. Be something better.
So we learned to resist the bloodlust. Stop the hunting.
And we spent a lot of time trying to rectify all the hurt and pain.
But a few months ago... a member of my coven was caught in the violence.
And he was the one that drained your father, all those years ago.

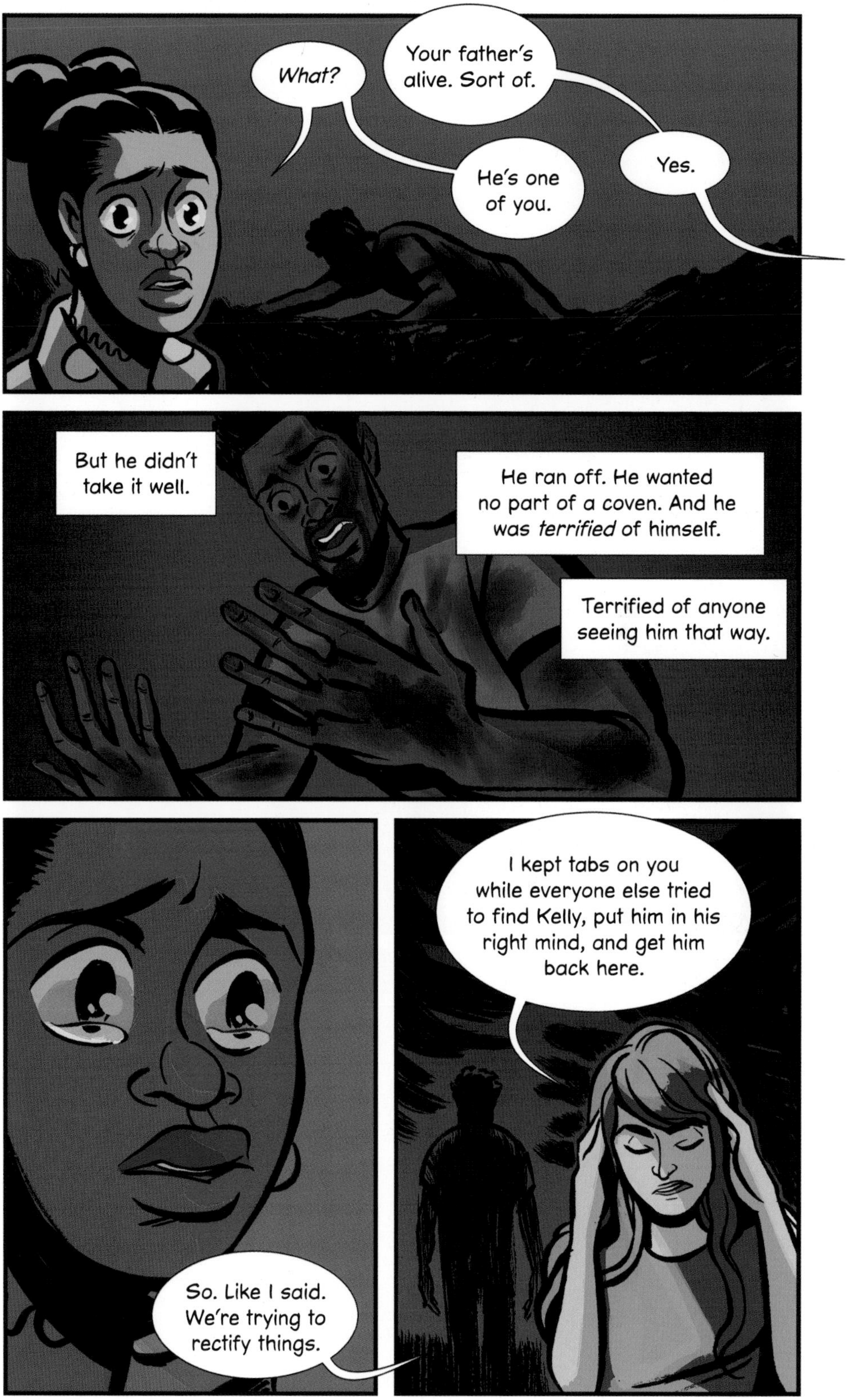
What?
Your father's alive. Sort of.
He's one of you.
Yes.
But he didn't take it well.
He ran off. He wanted no part of a coven. And he was *terrified* of himself.
Terrified of anyone seeing him that way.
I kept tabs on you while everyone else tried to find Kelly, put him in his right mind, and get him back here.
So. Like I said. We're trying to rectify things.

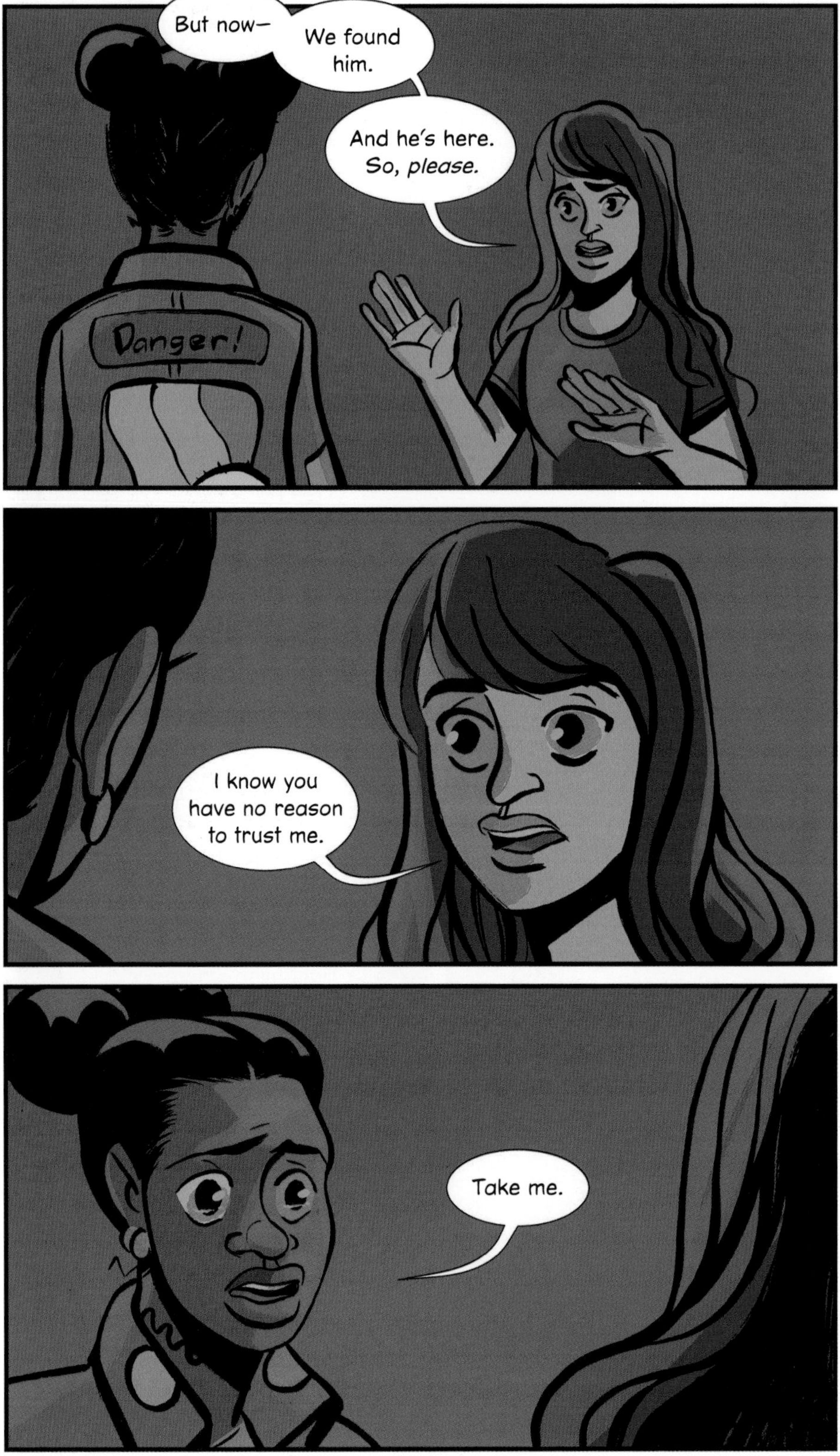
But now—
We found him.
And he's here. So, *please.*
Danger!
I know you have no reason to trust me.
Take me.

CHAPTER NINE

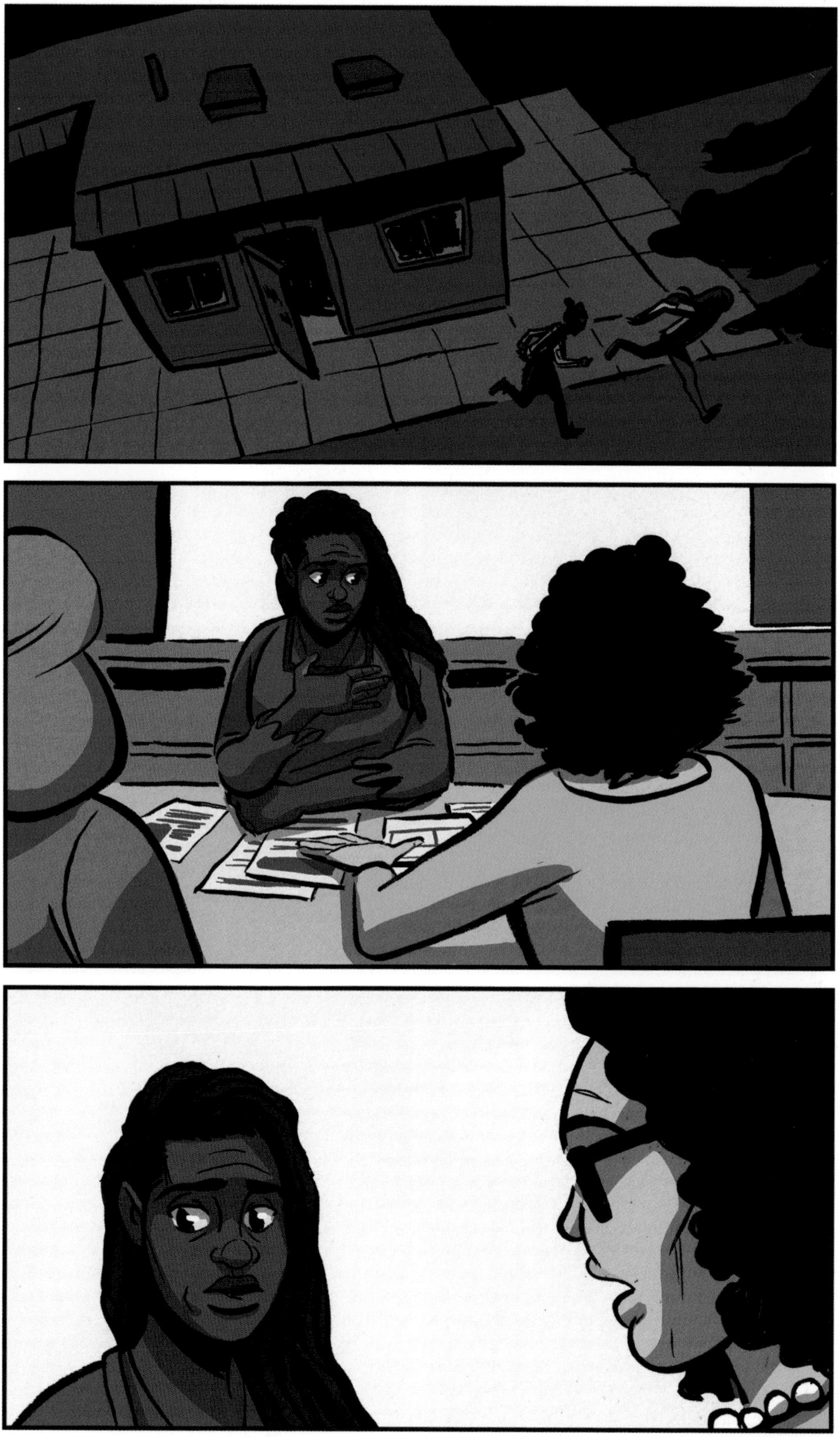

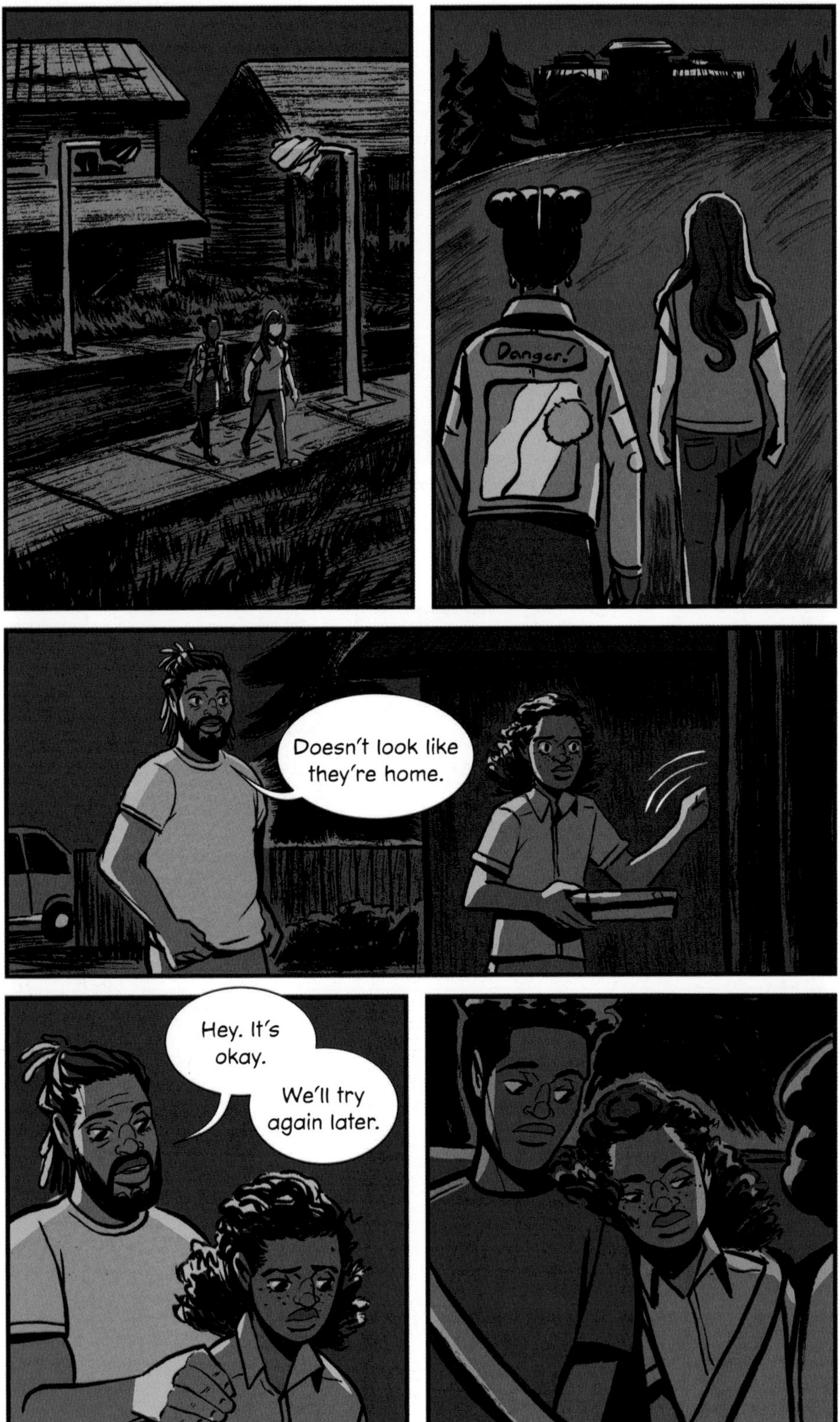
Danger!
Doesn't look like they're home.
Hey. It's okay.
We'll try again later.

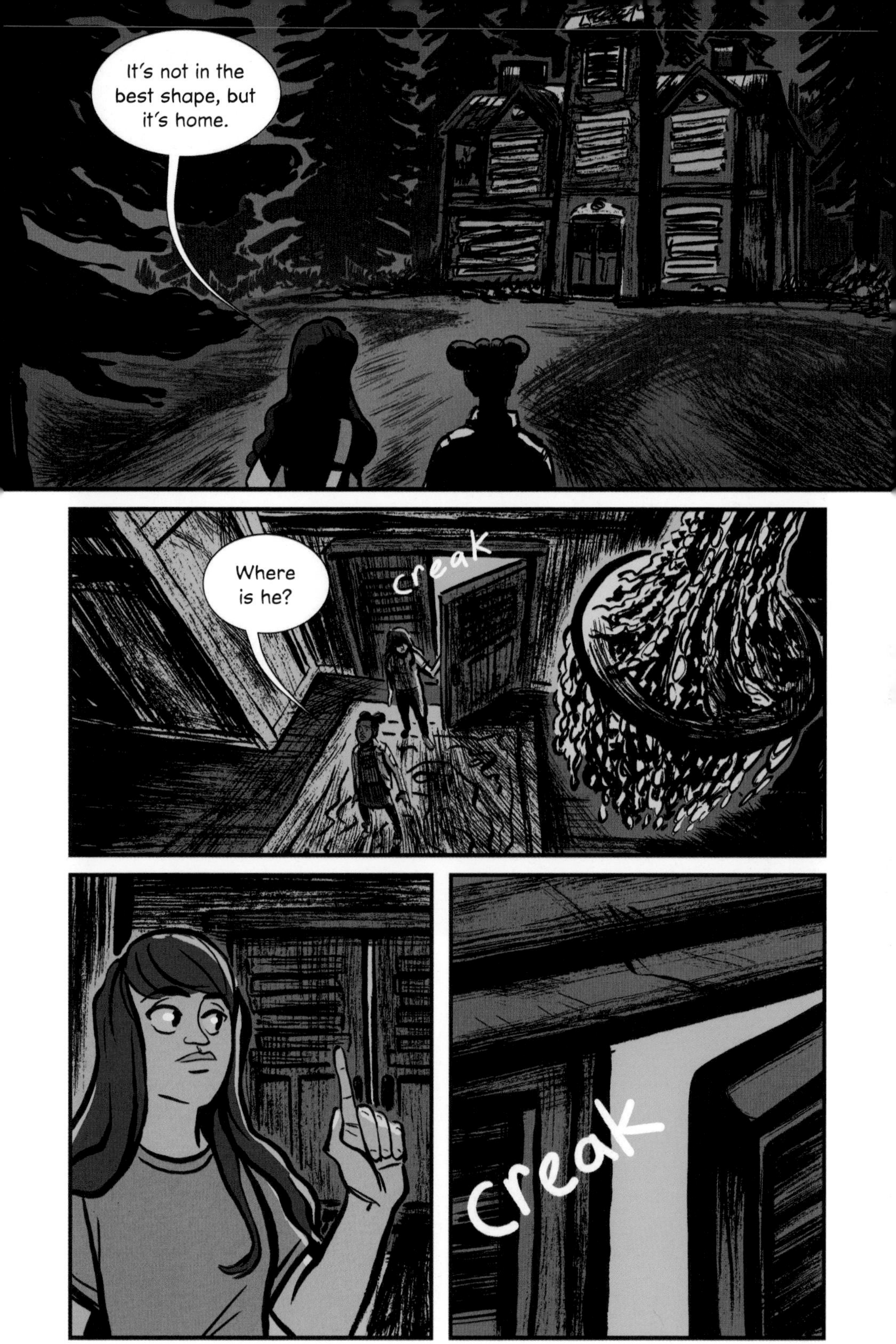
It's not in the best shape, but it's home.
Where is he?
creak
creak

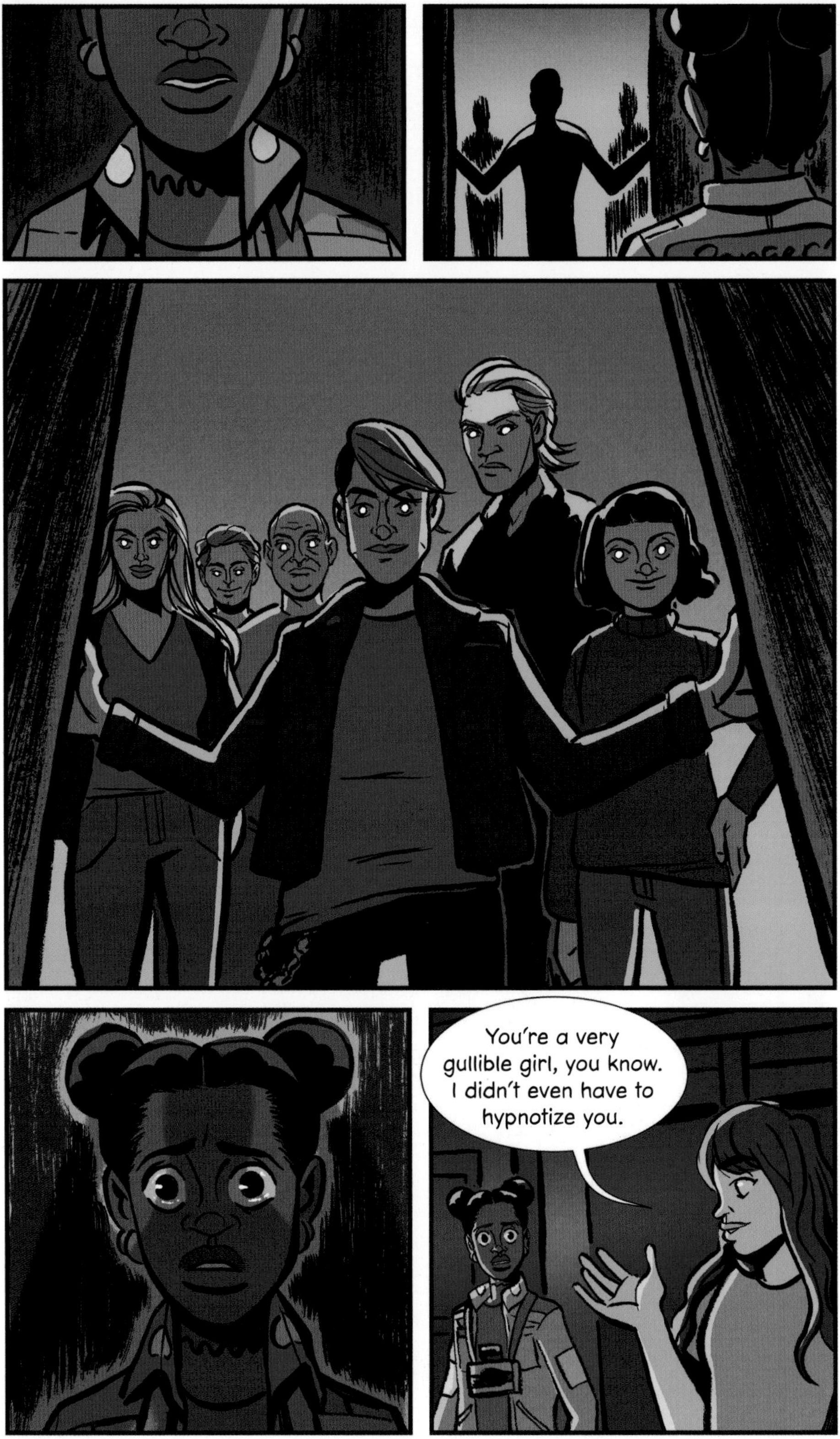
You're a very gullible girl, you know. I didn't even have to hypnotize you.

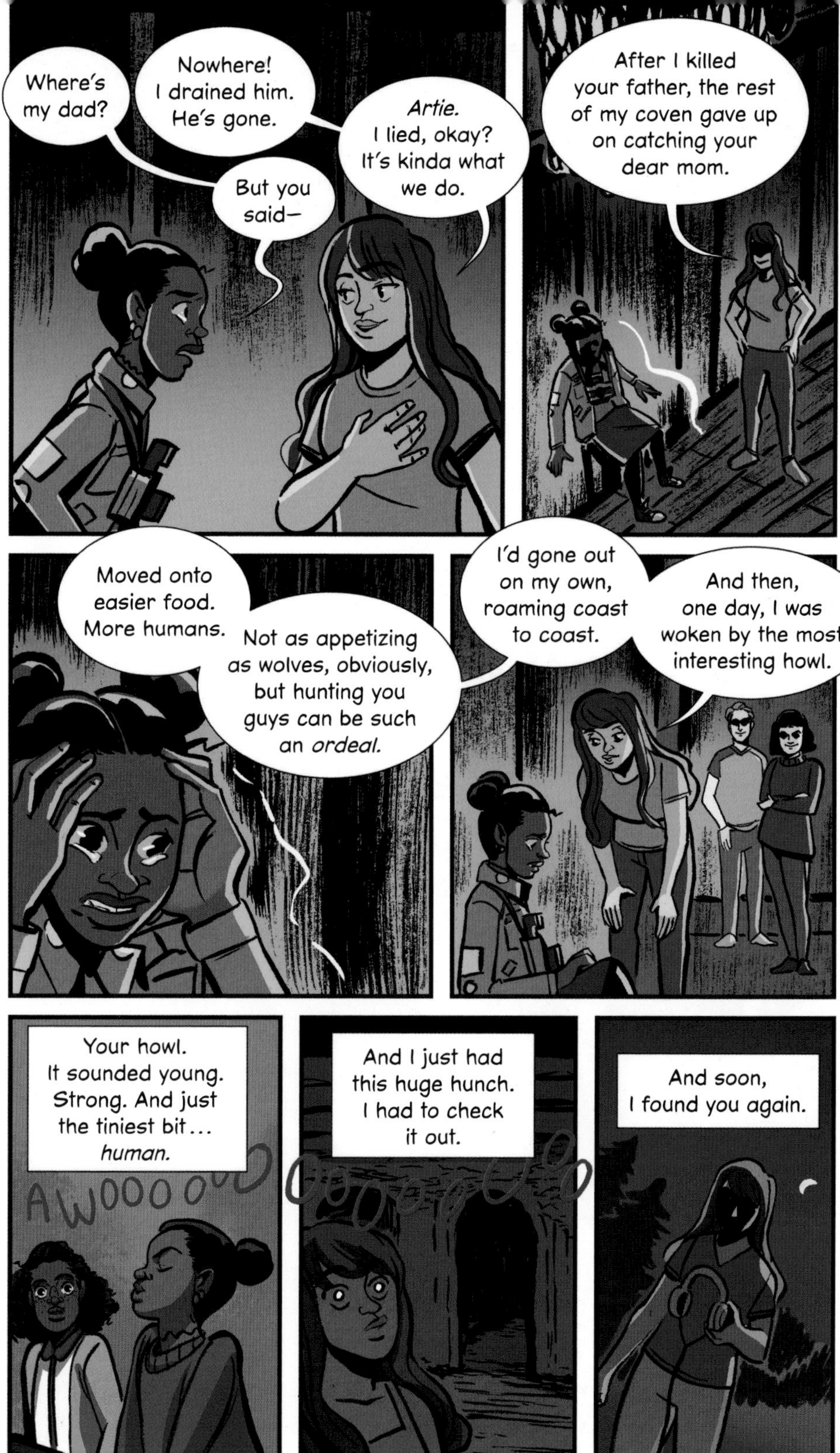
Where's my dad?
Nowhere! I drained him. He's gone.
But you said—
Artie. I lied, okay? It's kinda what we do.
After I killed your father, the rest of my coven gave up on catching your dear mom.
Moved onto easier food. More humans.
Not as appetizing as wolves, obviously, but hunting you guys can be such an *ordeal.*
I'd gone out on my own, roaming coast to coast.
And then, one day, I was woken by the most interesting howl.
Your howl. It sounded young. Strong. And just the tiniest bit... *human.*
AWOOOOOOOOOOOOOOO
And I just had this huge hunch. I had to check it out.
And soon, I found you again.

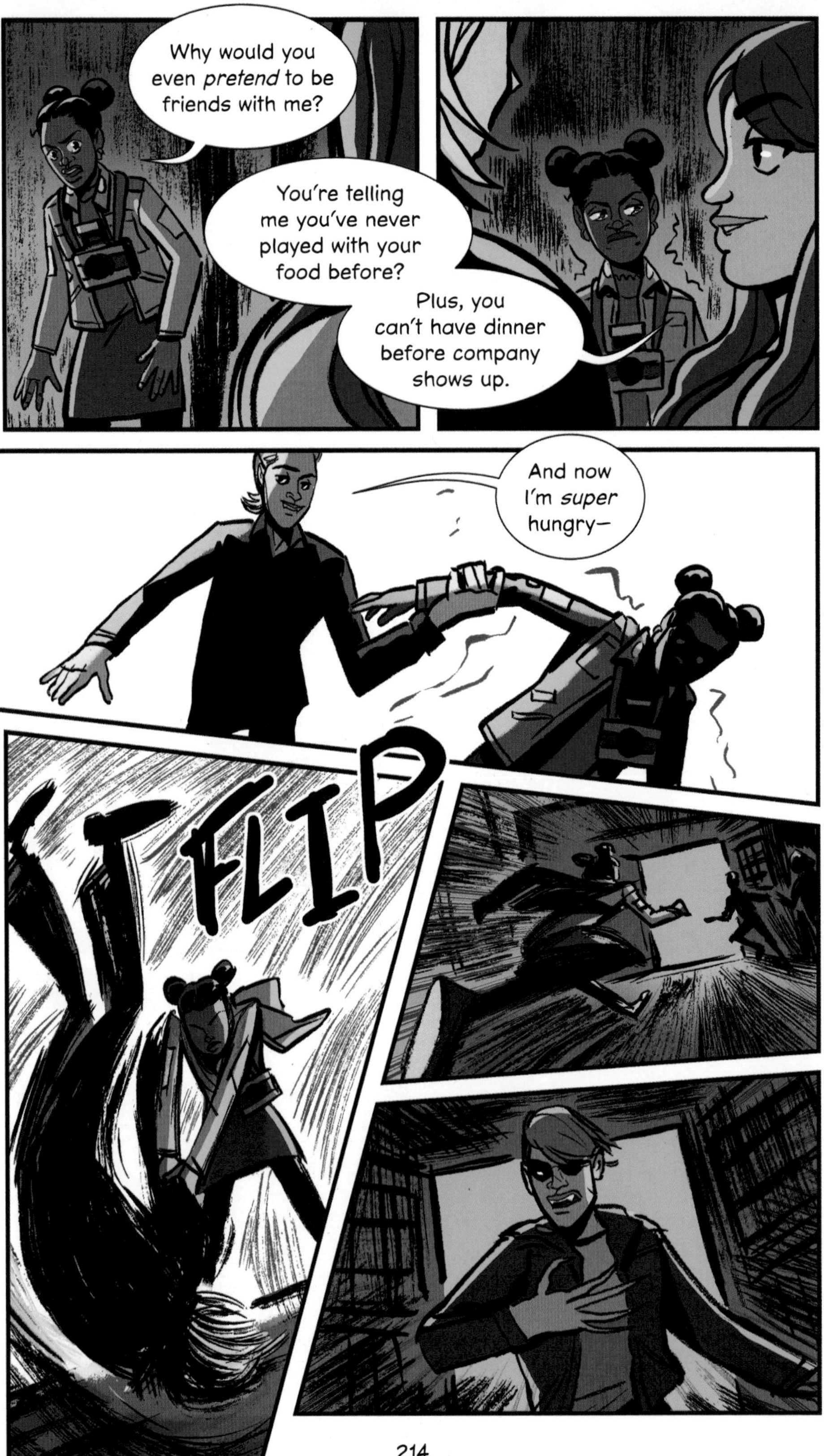
Why would you even *pretend* to be friends with me?
You're telling me you've never played with your food before?
Plus, you can't have dinner before company shows up.
And now I'm *super* hungry—
FLIP

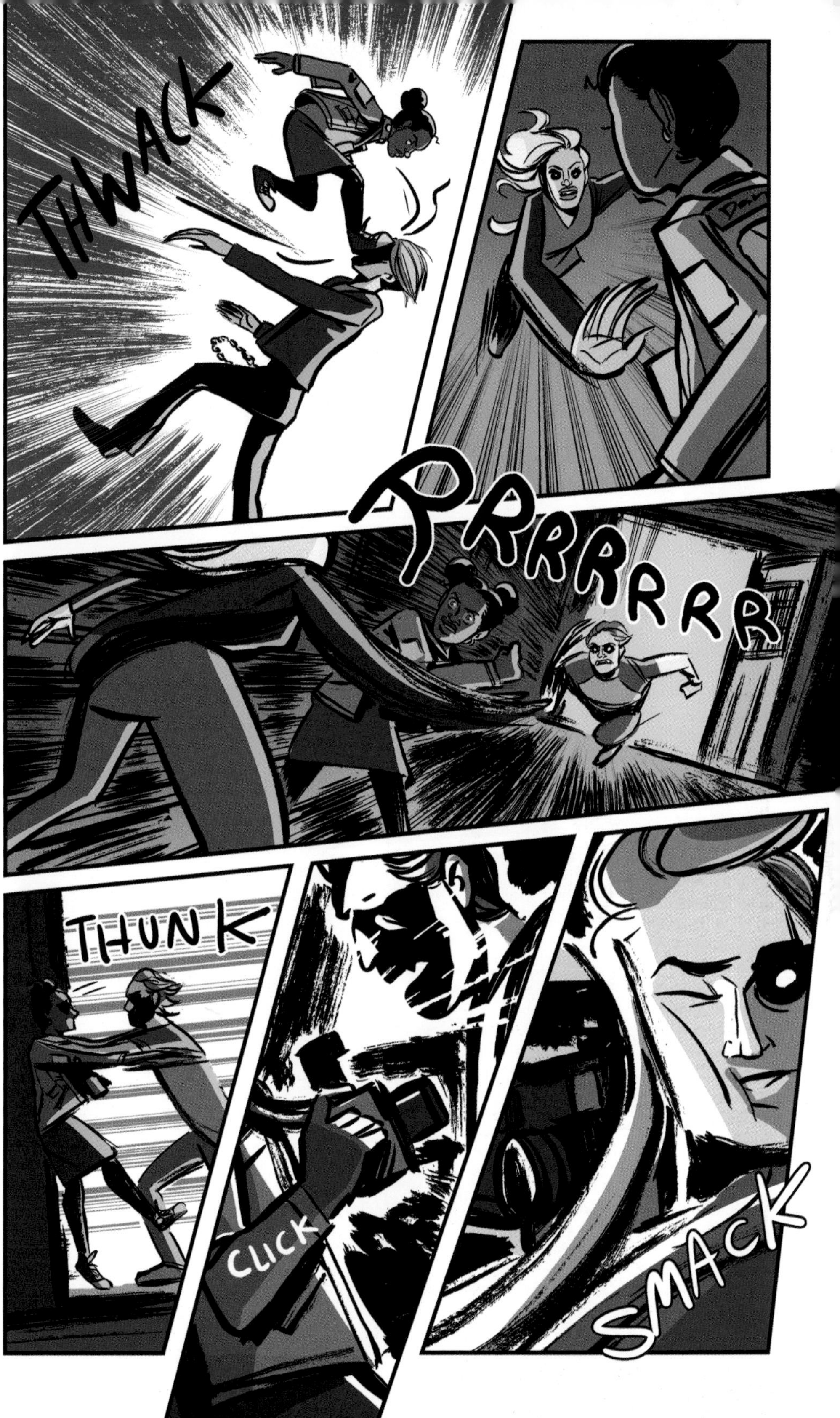
THWACK
RRRRRRR
THUNK
CLICK
SMACK

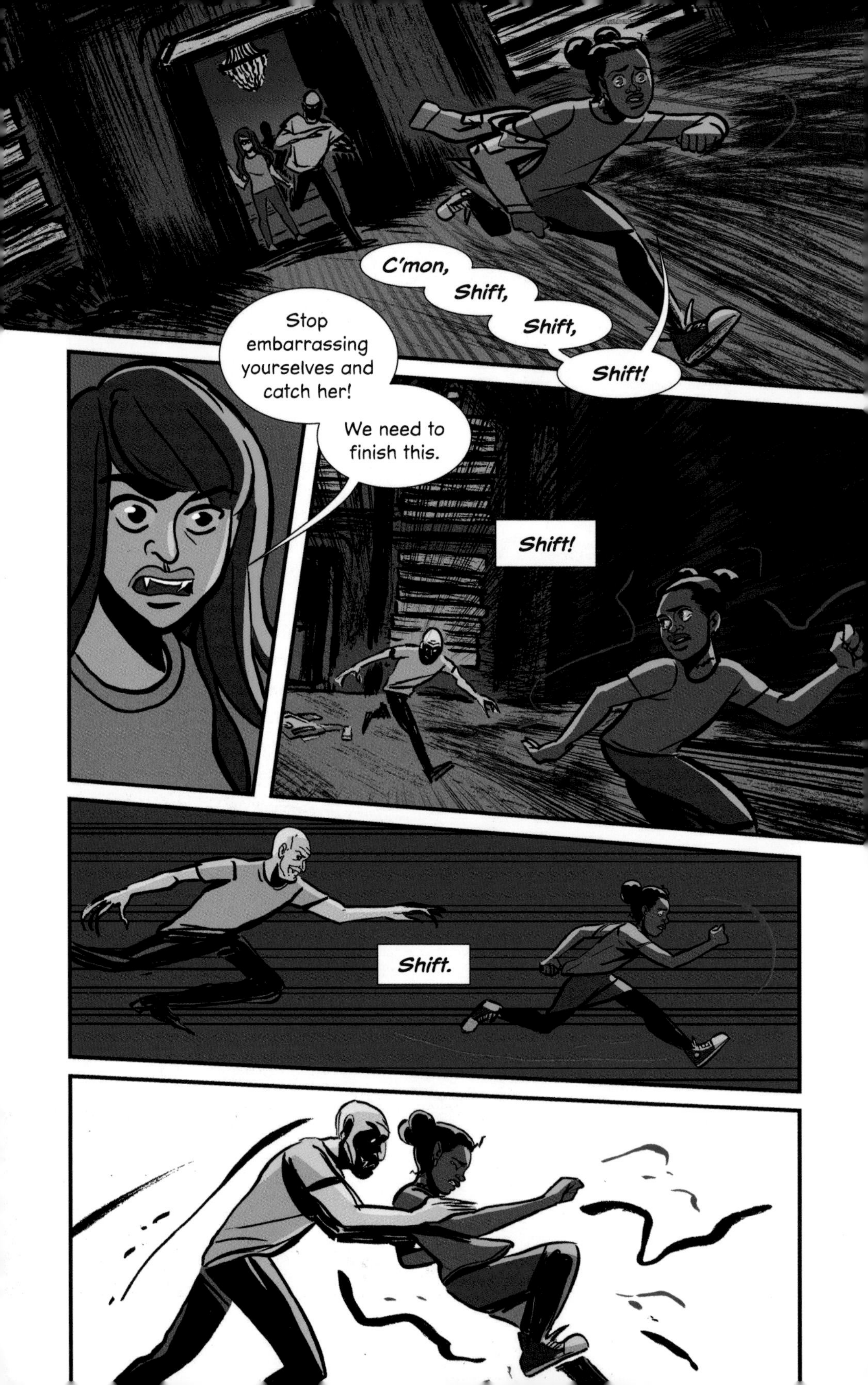
C'mon,
Shift,
Shift,
Shift!
Stop embarrassing yourselves and catch her!
We need to finish this.
Shift!
Shift.

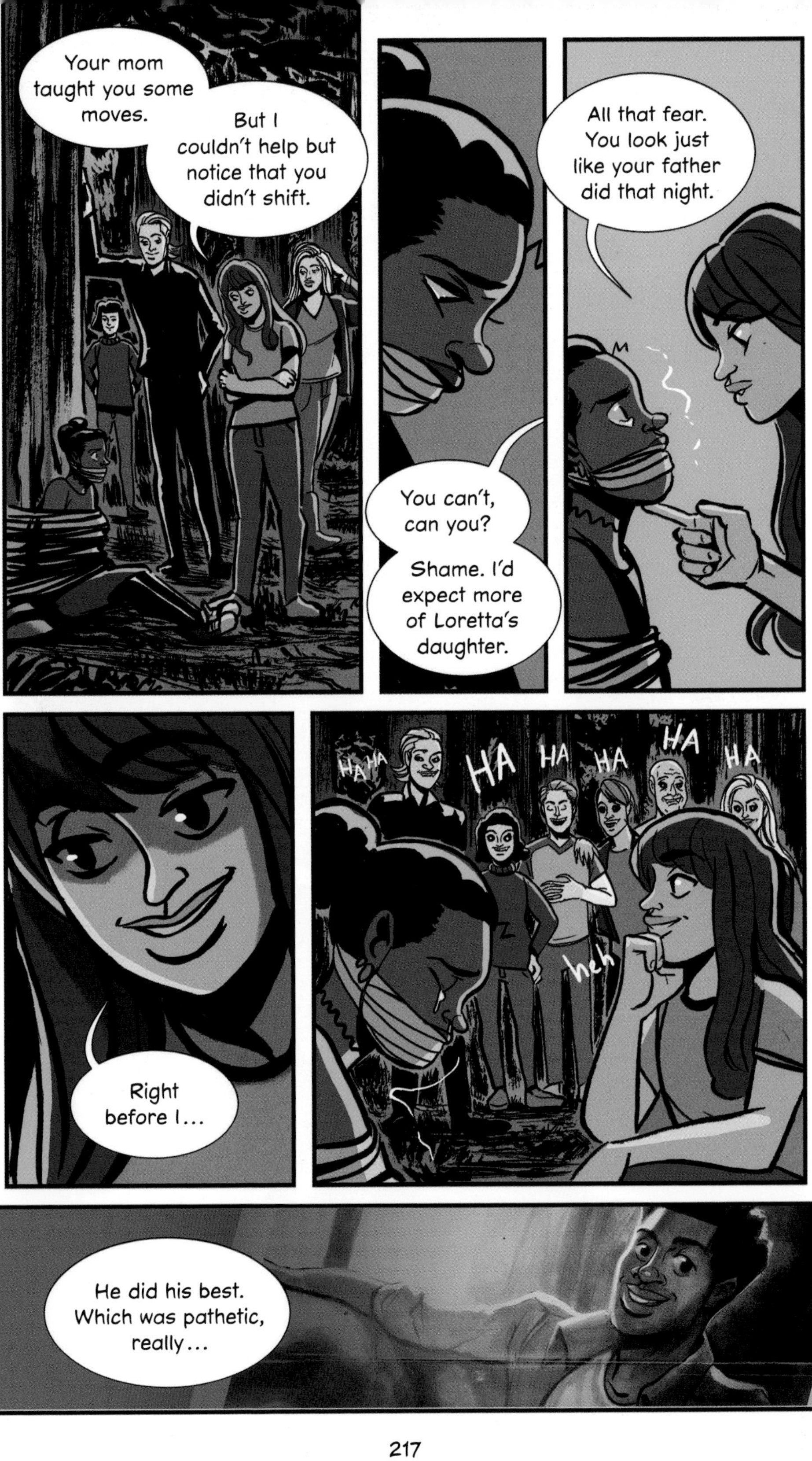
Your mom taught you some moves.
But I couldn't help but notice that you didn't shift.
You can't, can you?
Shame. I'd expect more of Loretta's daughter.
All that fear. You look just like your father did that night.
Right before I...
HA HA
HA
HA
HA
HA
HA
heh
He did his best. Which was pathetic, really...

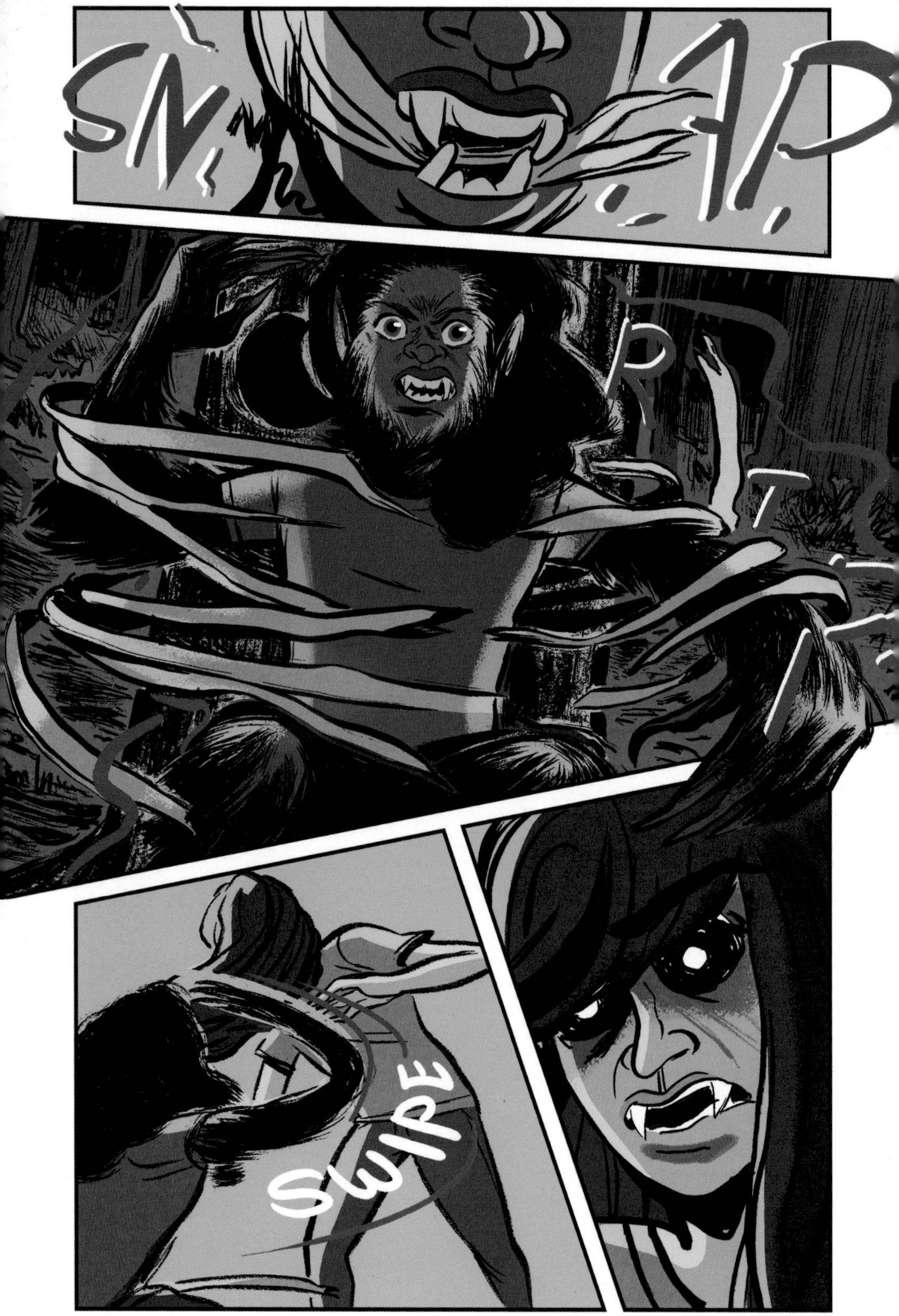
SNAP
SWIPE

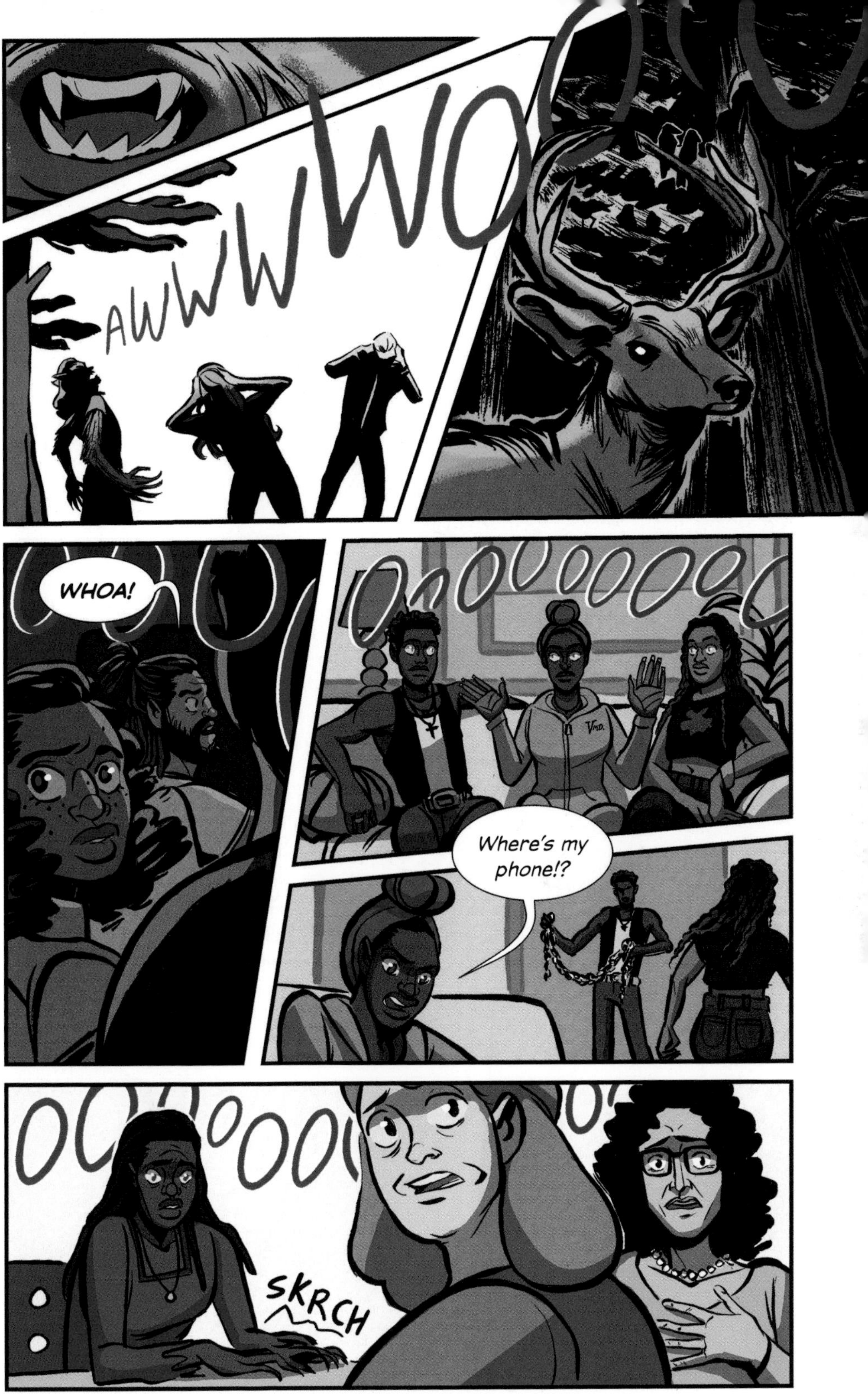
AWWWWOOOOO
WHOA!
OOOOOOOOOOO
Where's my phone!?
OOOOOOOOO
SKRCH

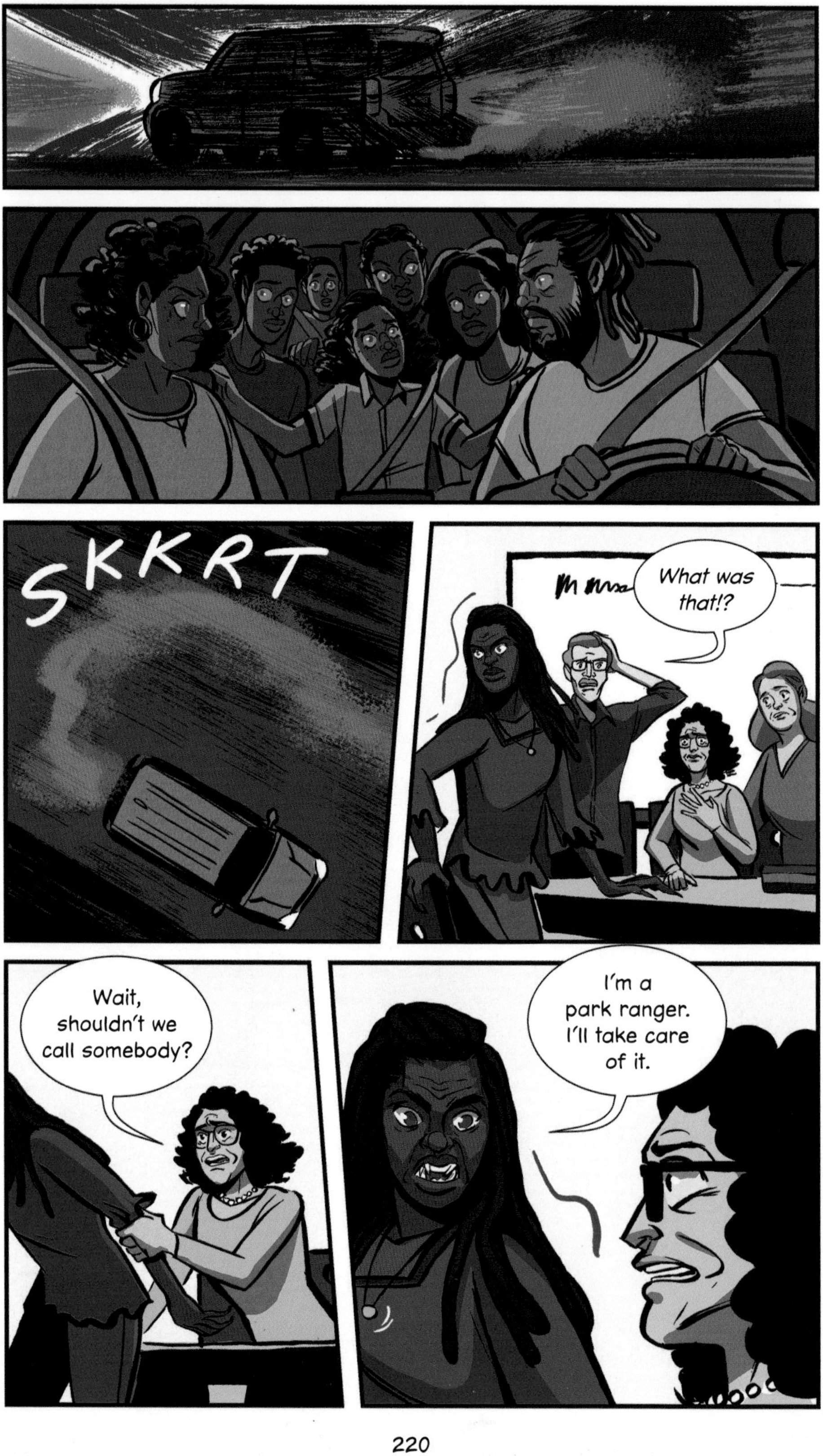
SKKRT
What was that!?
Wait, shouldn't we call somebody?
I'm a park ranger. I'll take care of it.

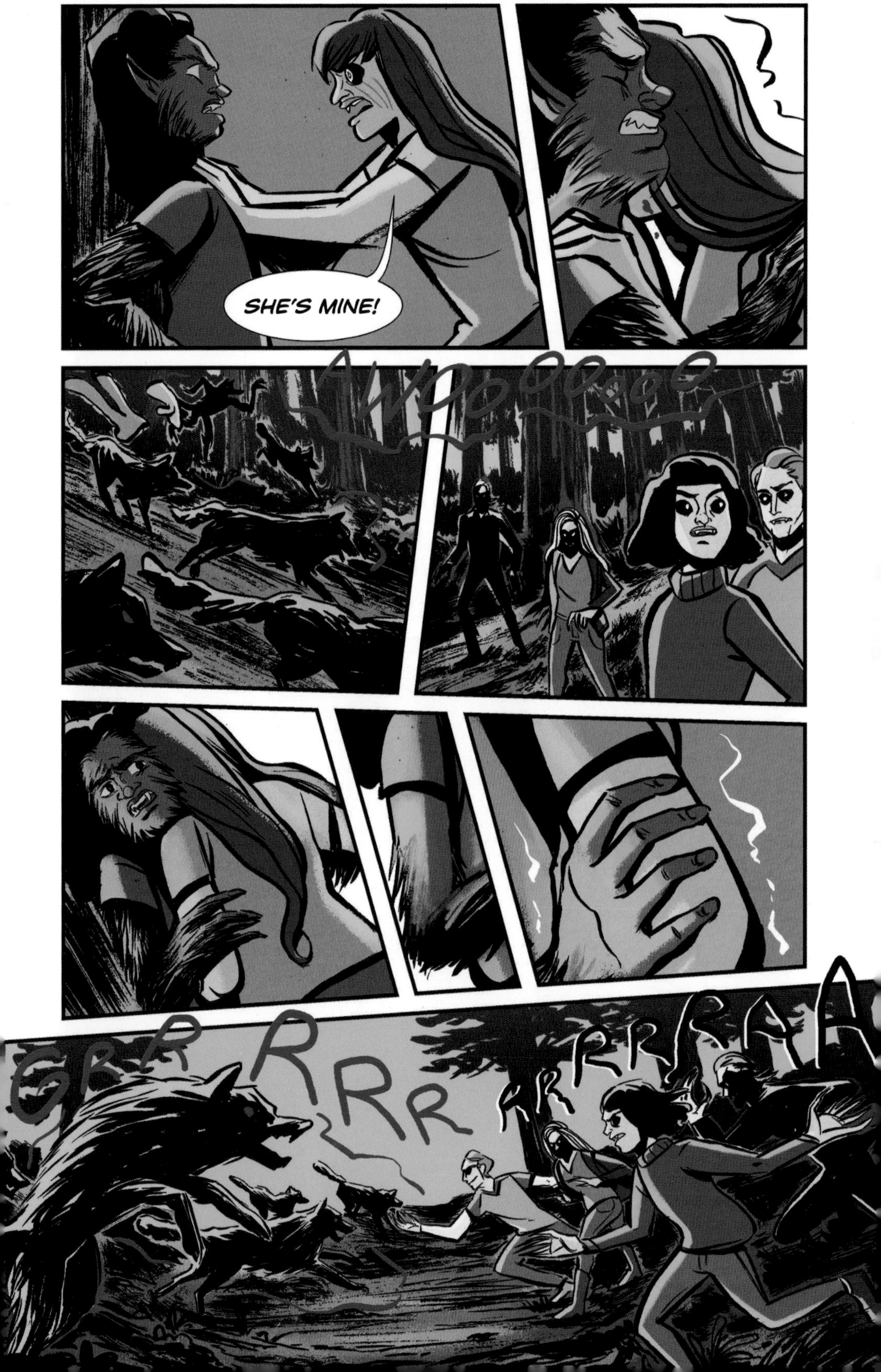
SHE'S MINE!
AWOOOOOOOO
GRRRRRRRRRRRAA

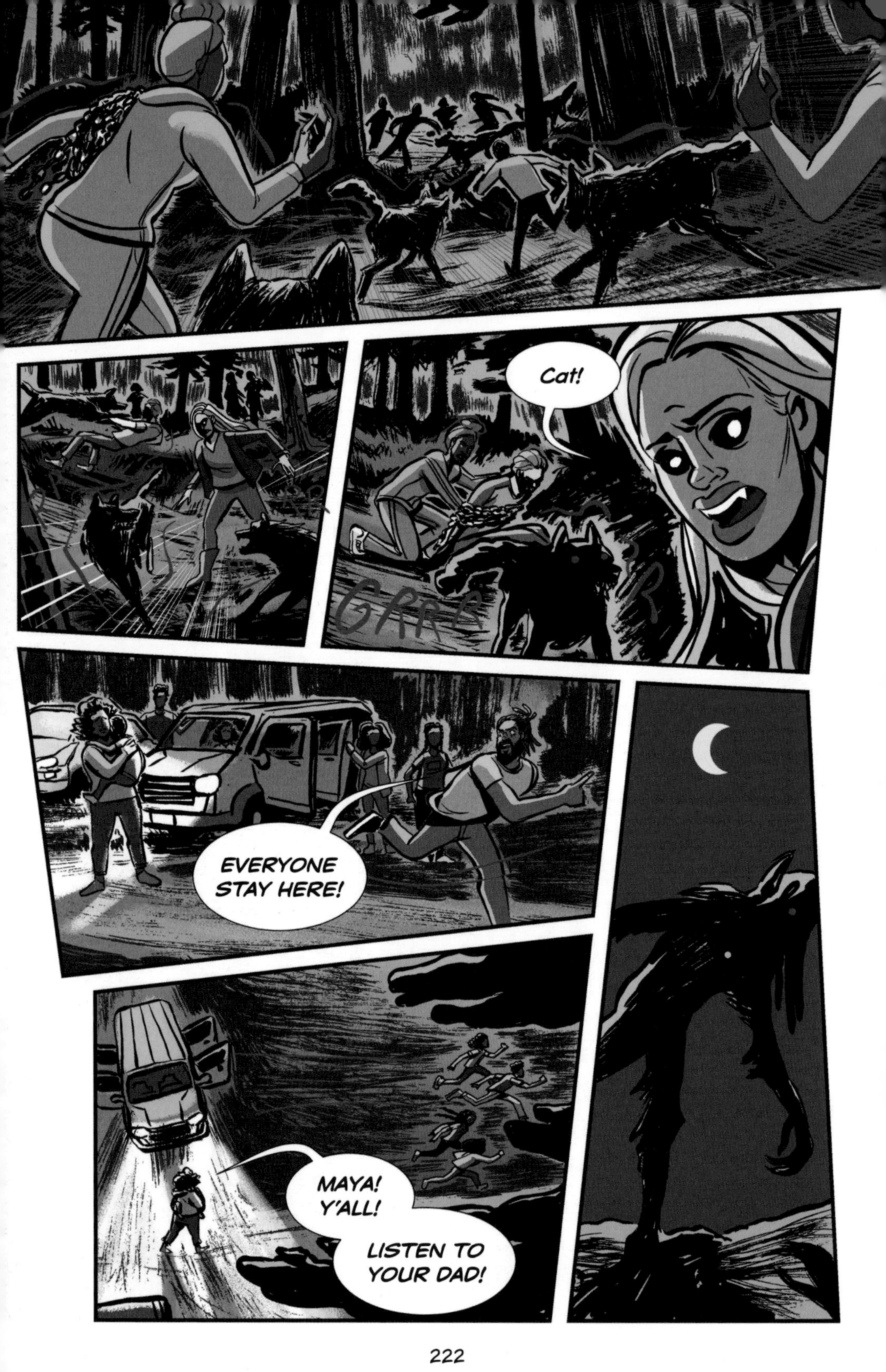
Cat!
GRRR
EVERYONE STAY HERE!
MAYA! Y'ALL!
LISTEN TO YOUR DAD!

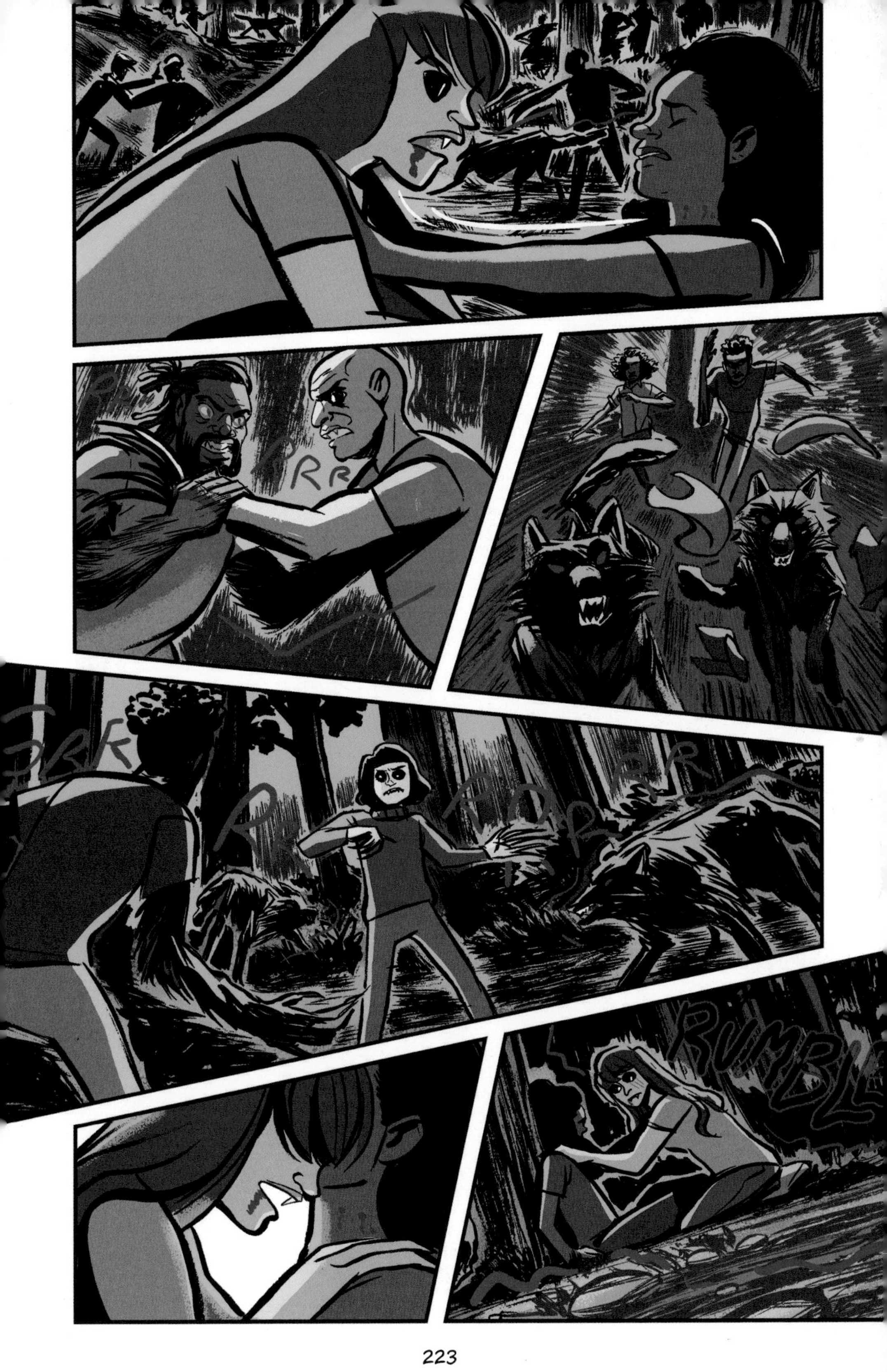
RRR

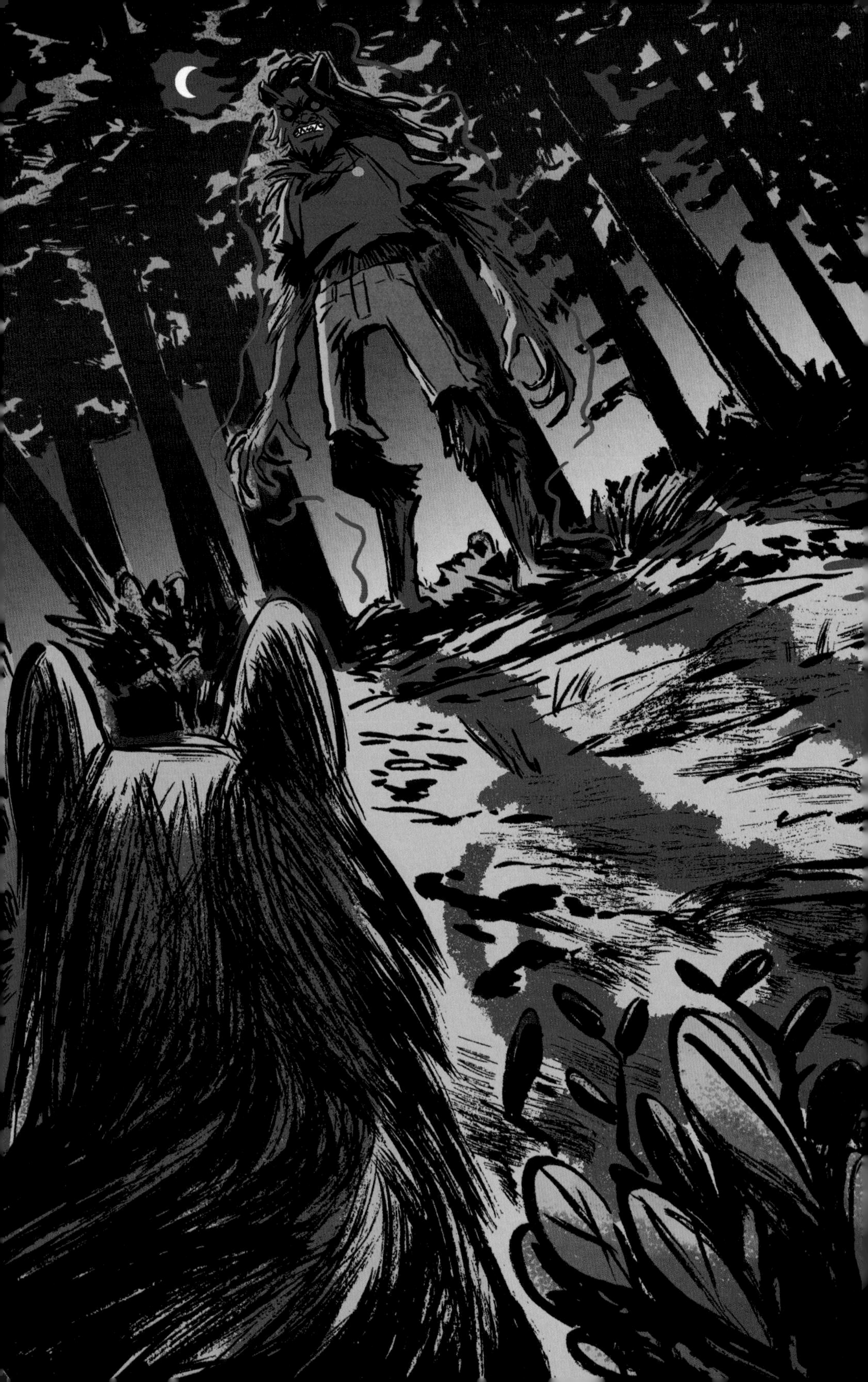

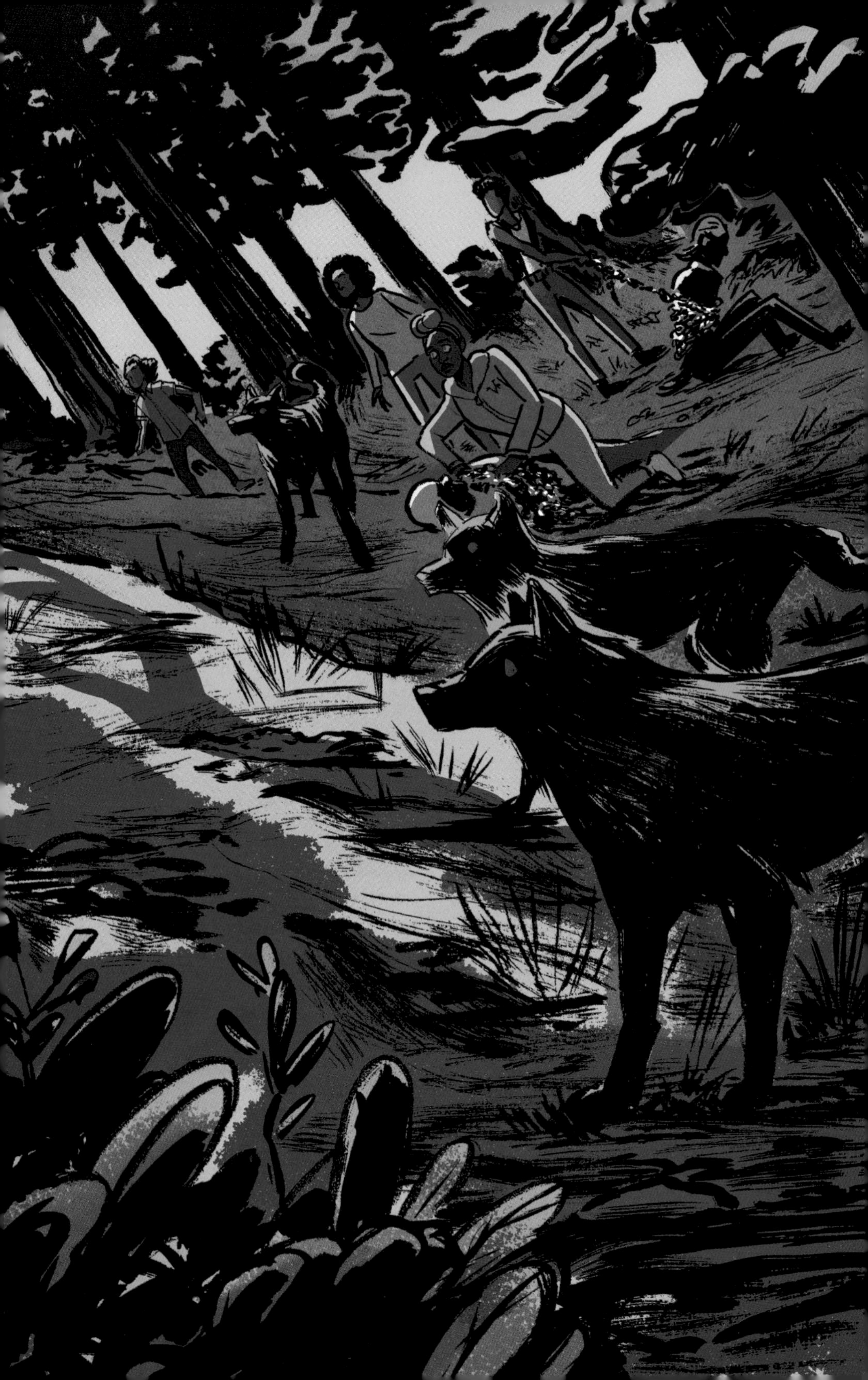

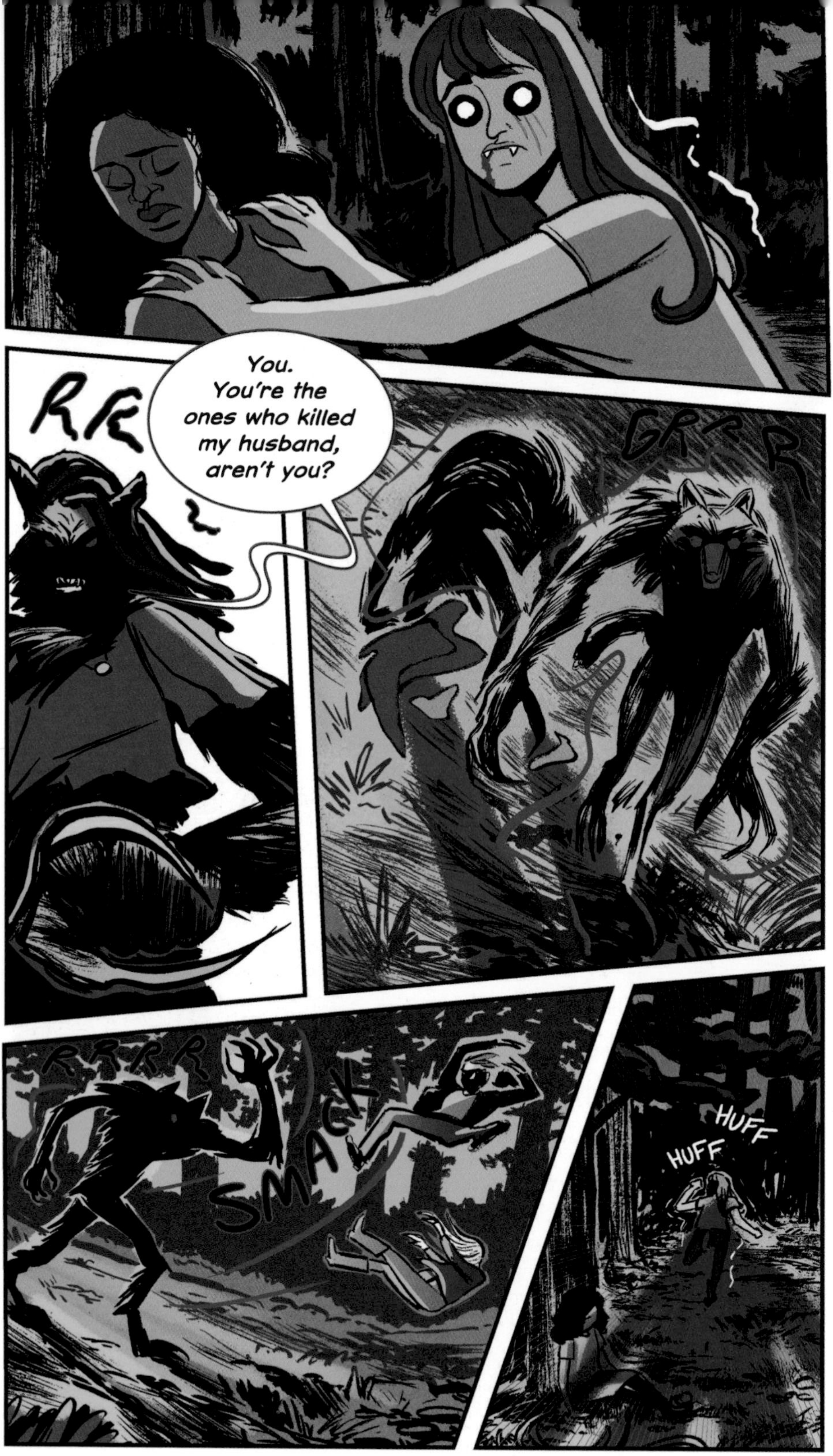
RR
You. You're the ones who killed my husband, aren't you?
GRRR
RRRR
SMACK
HUFF
HUFF

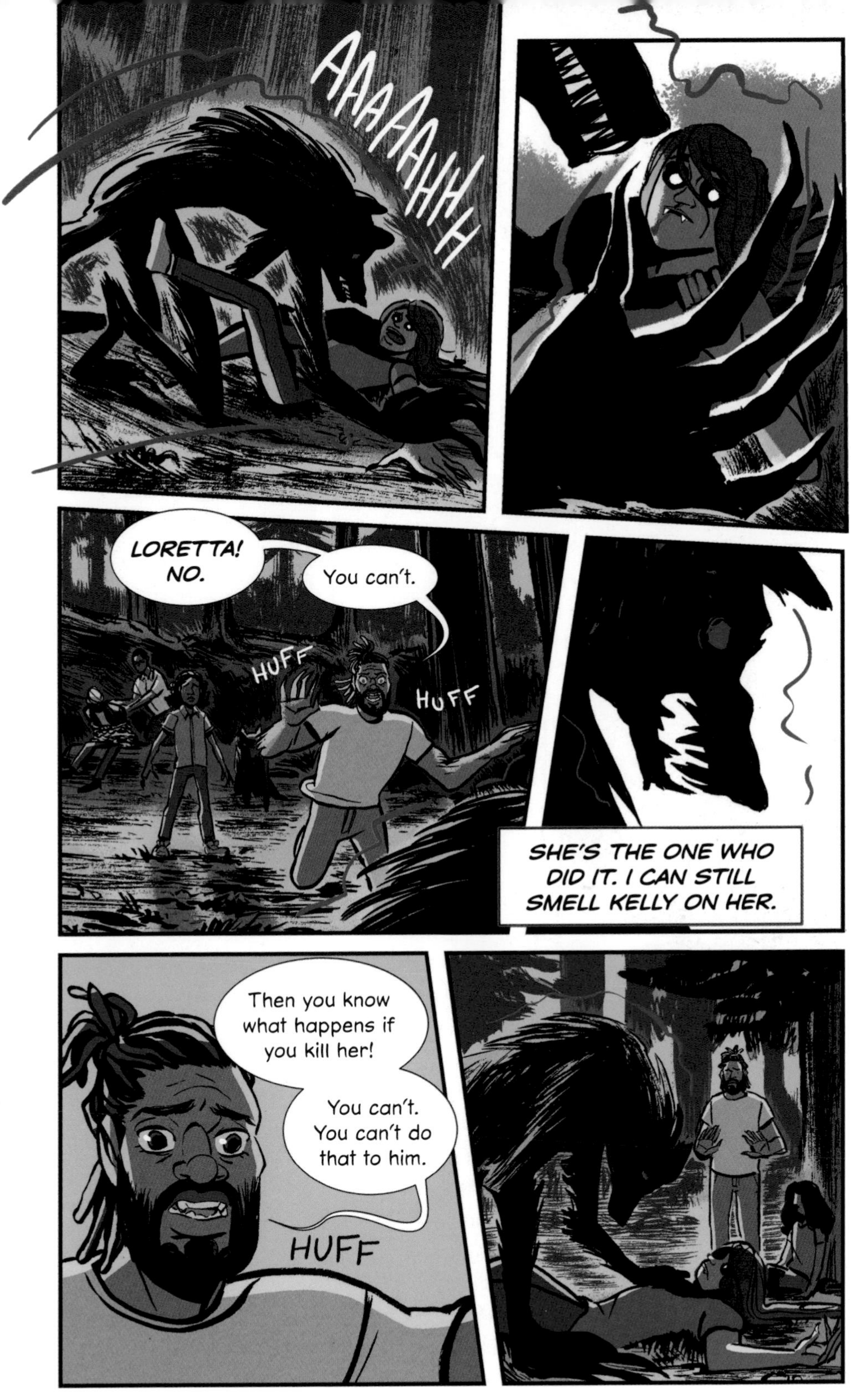
AAAAAAHHH
LORETTA! NO.
You can't.
HUFF
HUFF
SHE'S THE ONE WHO DID IT. I CAN STILL SMELL KELLY ON HER.
Then you know what happens if you kill her!
You can't. You can't do that to him.
HUFF

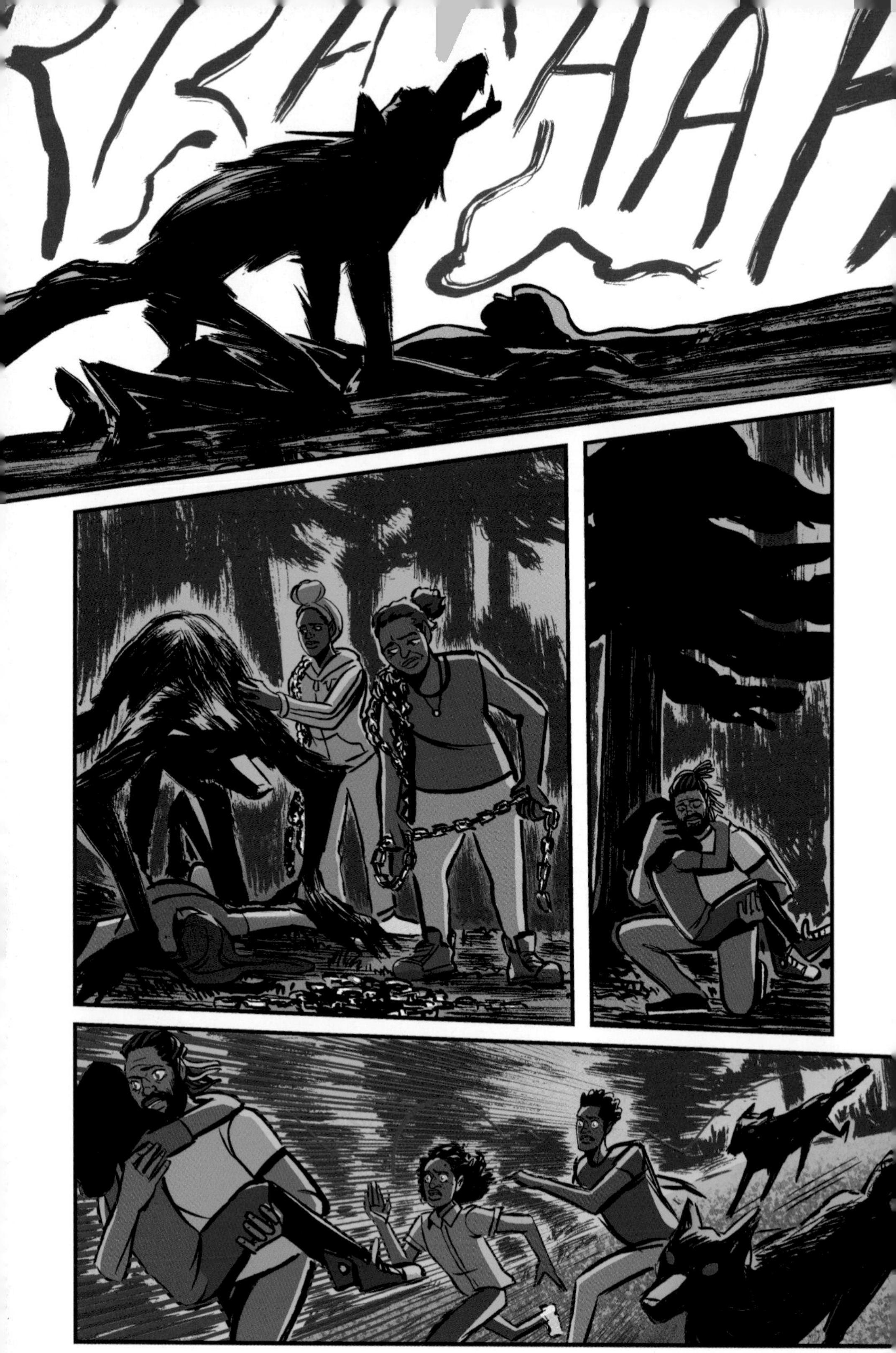

CHAPTER TEN

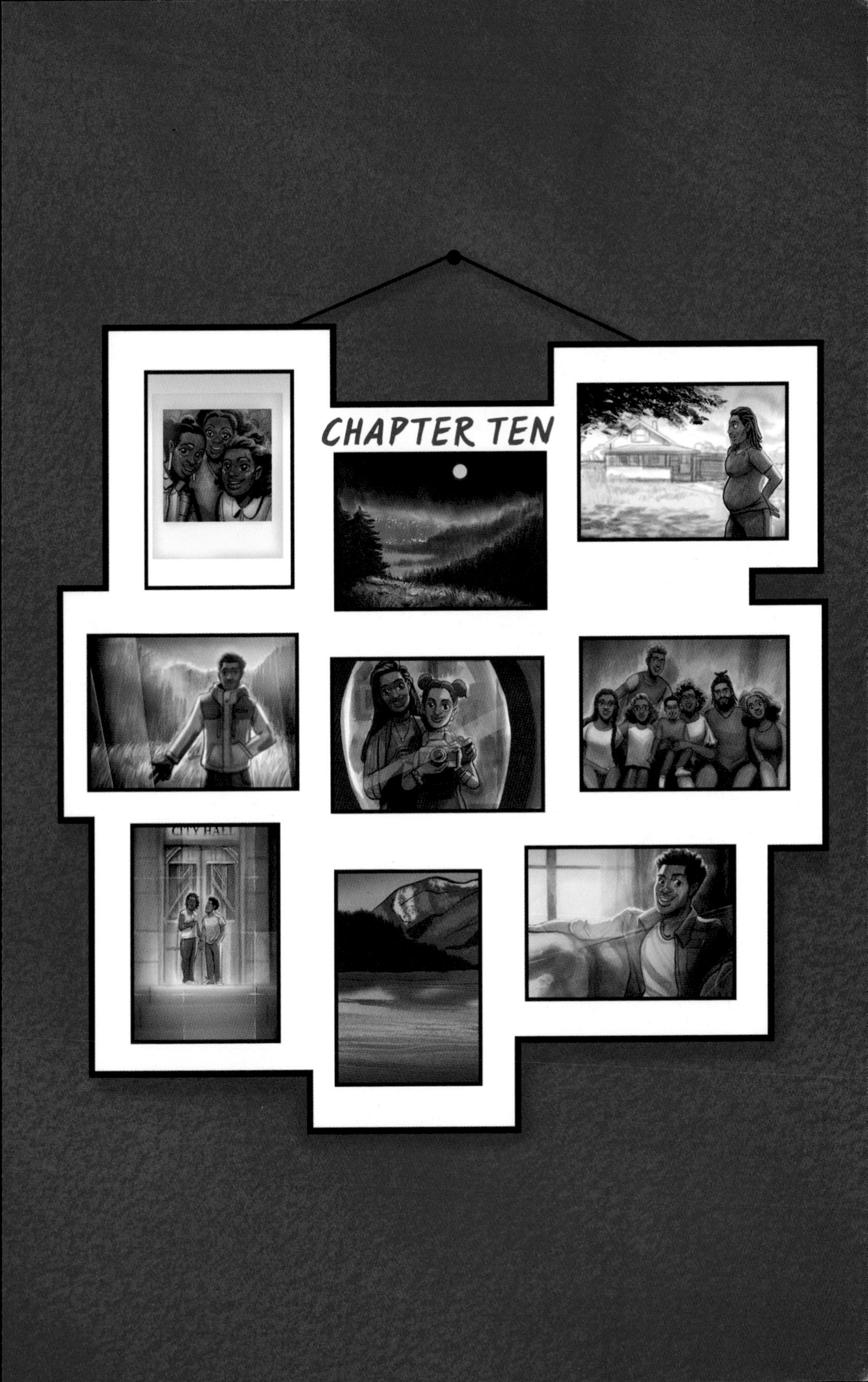

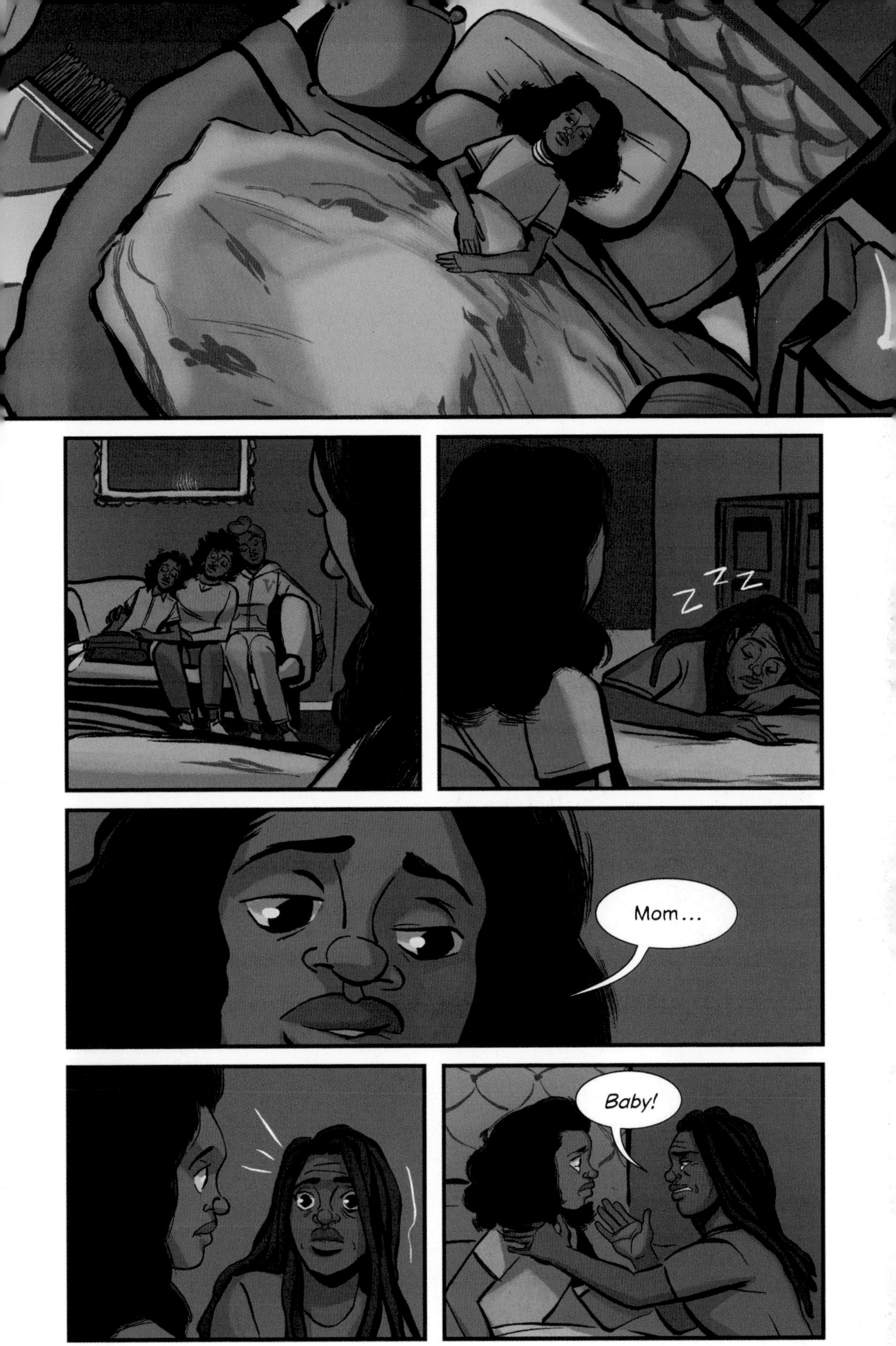
Z Z Z
Mom...
Baby!

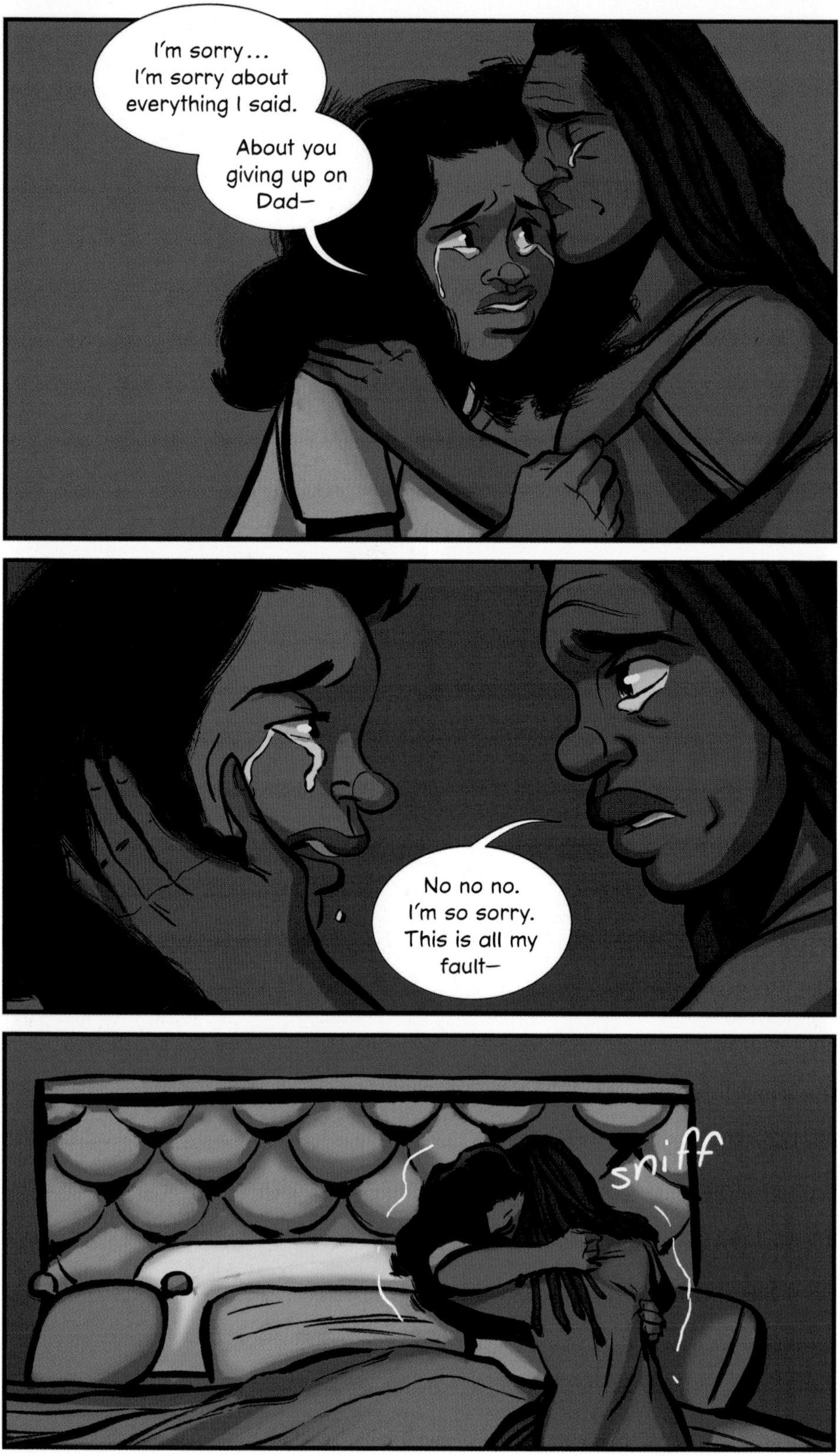
I'm sorry... I'm sorry about everything I said.
About you giving up on Dad—
No no no. I'm so sorry. This is all my fault—
sniff

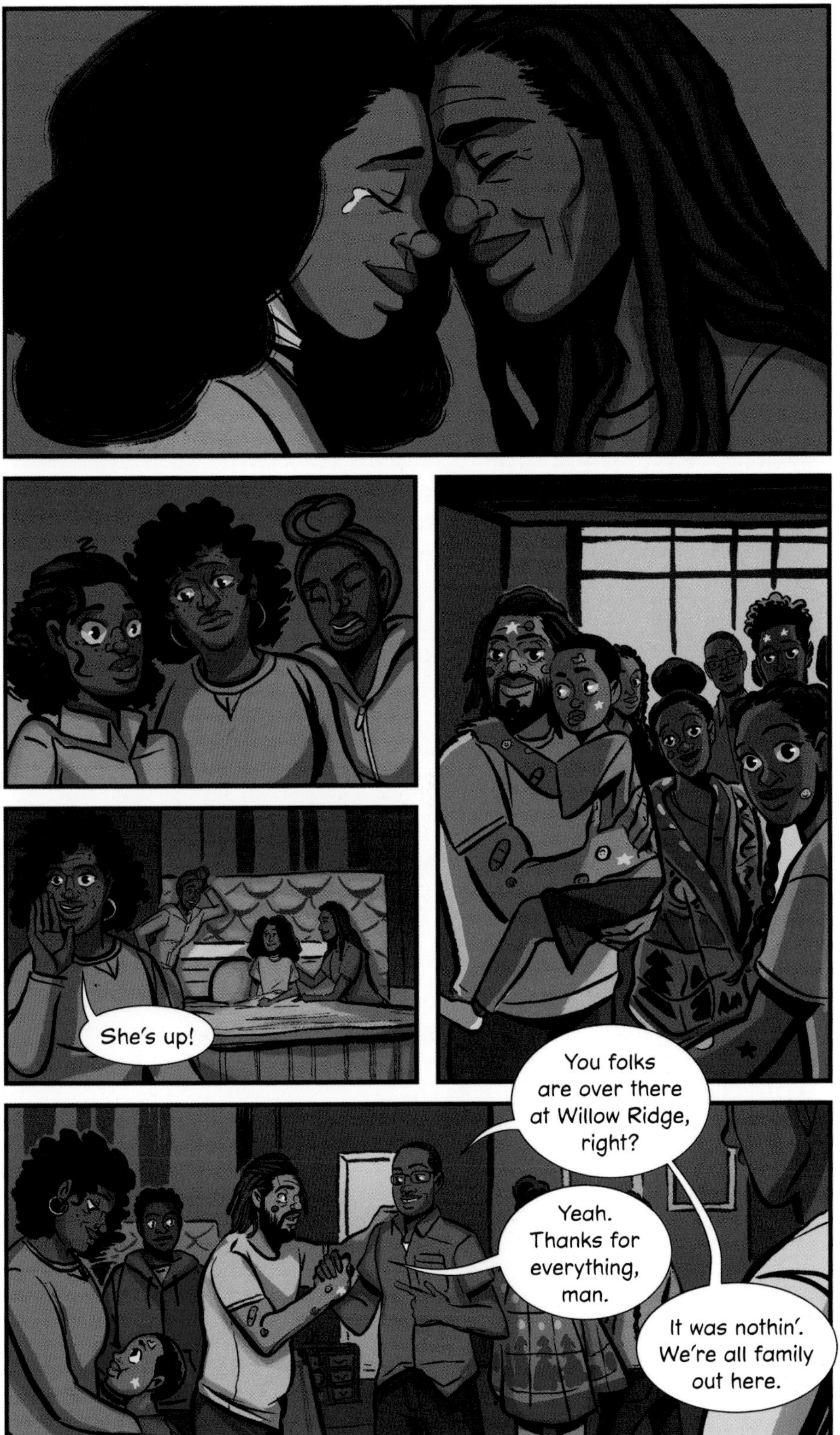
She's up!
You folks are over there at Willow Ridge, right?
Yeah. Thanks for everything, man.
It was nothin'. We're all family out here.

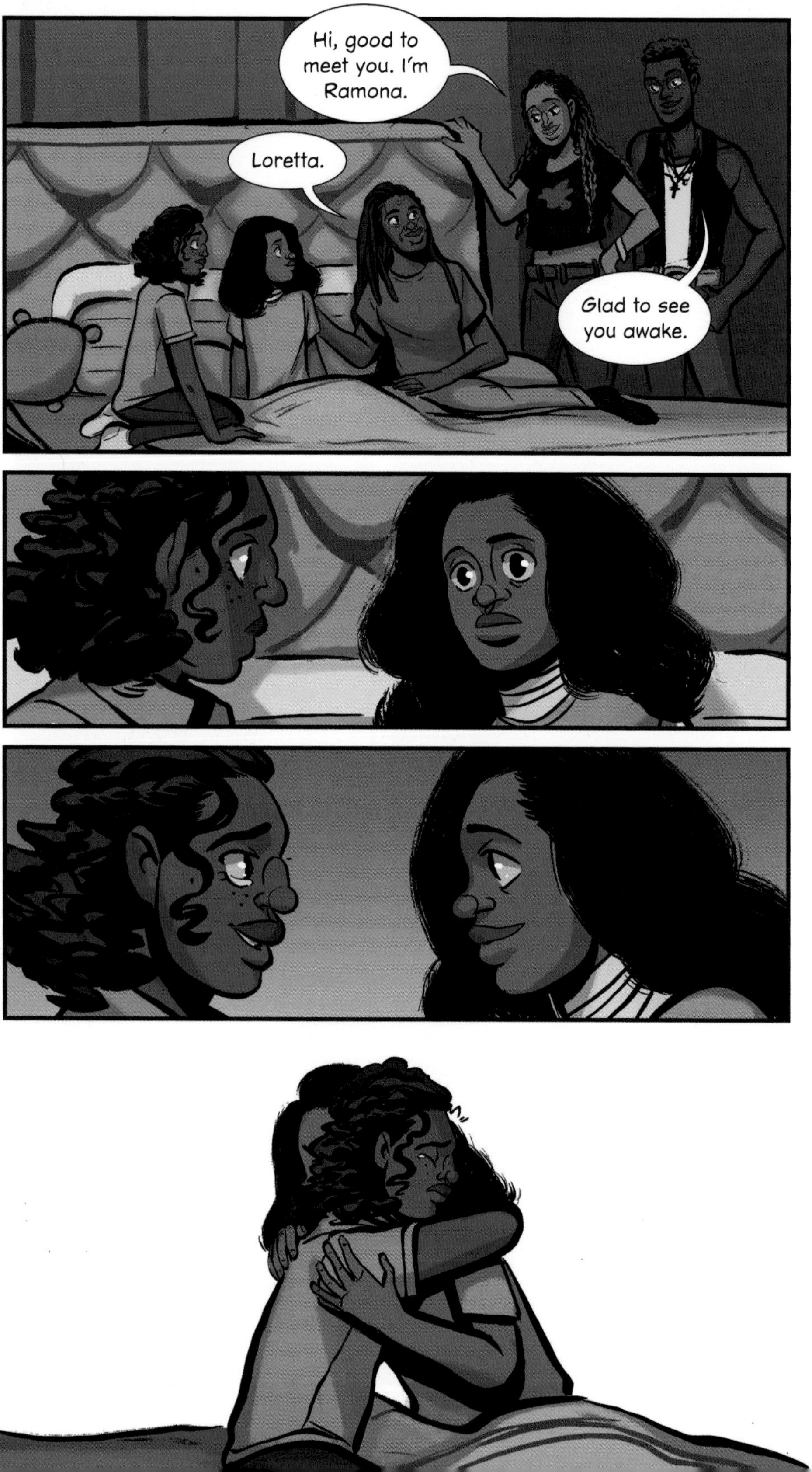
Hi, good to meet you. I'm Ramona.
Loretta.
Glad to see you awake.

June

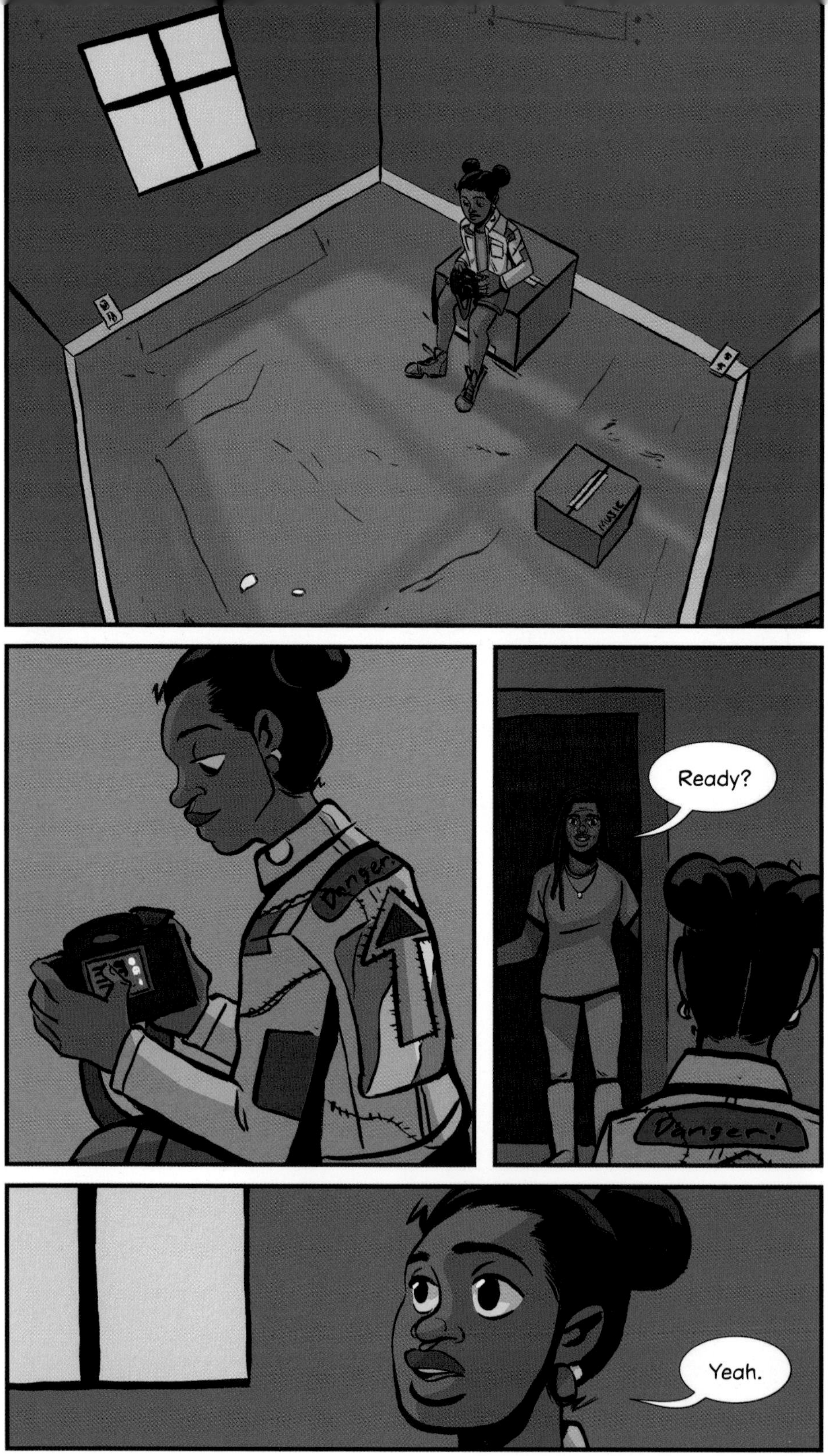
Music
Danger
Ready?
Danger!
Yeah.

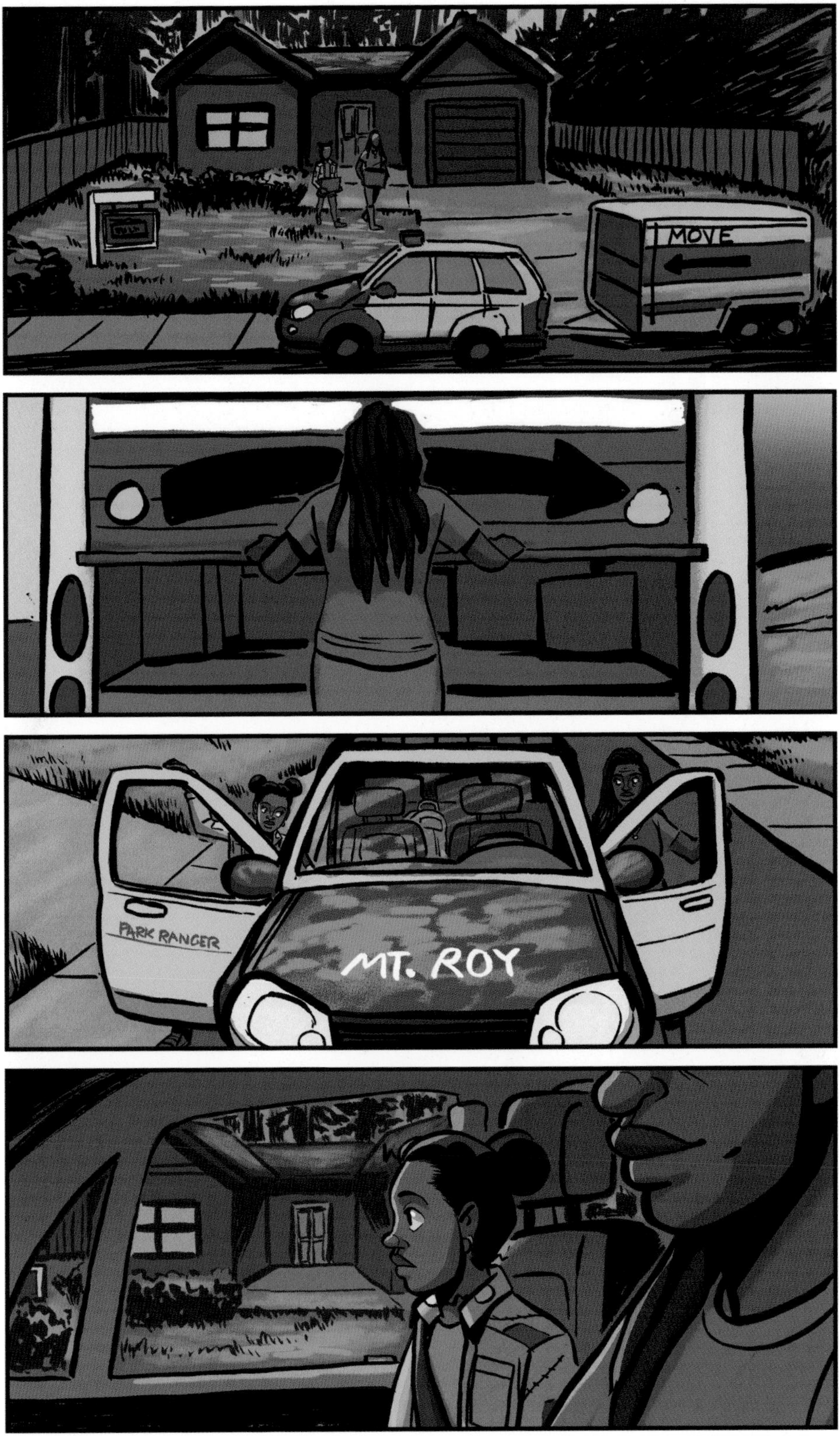
MOVE
PARK RANGER
MT. ROY

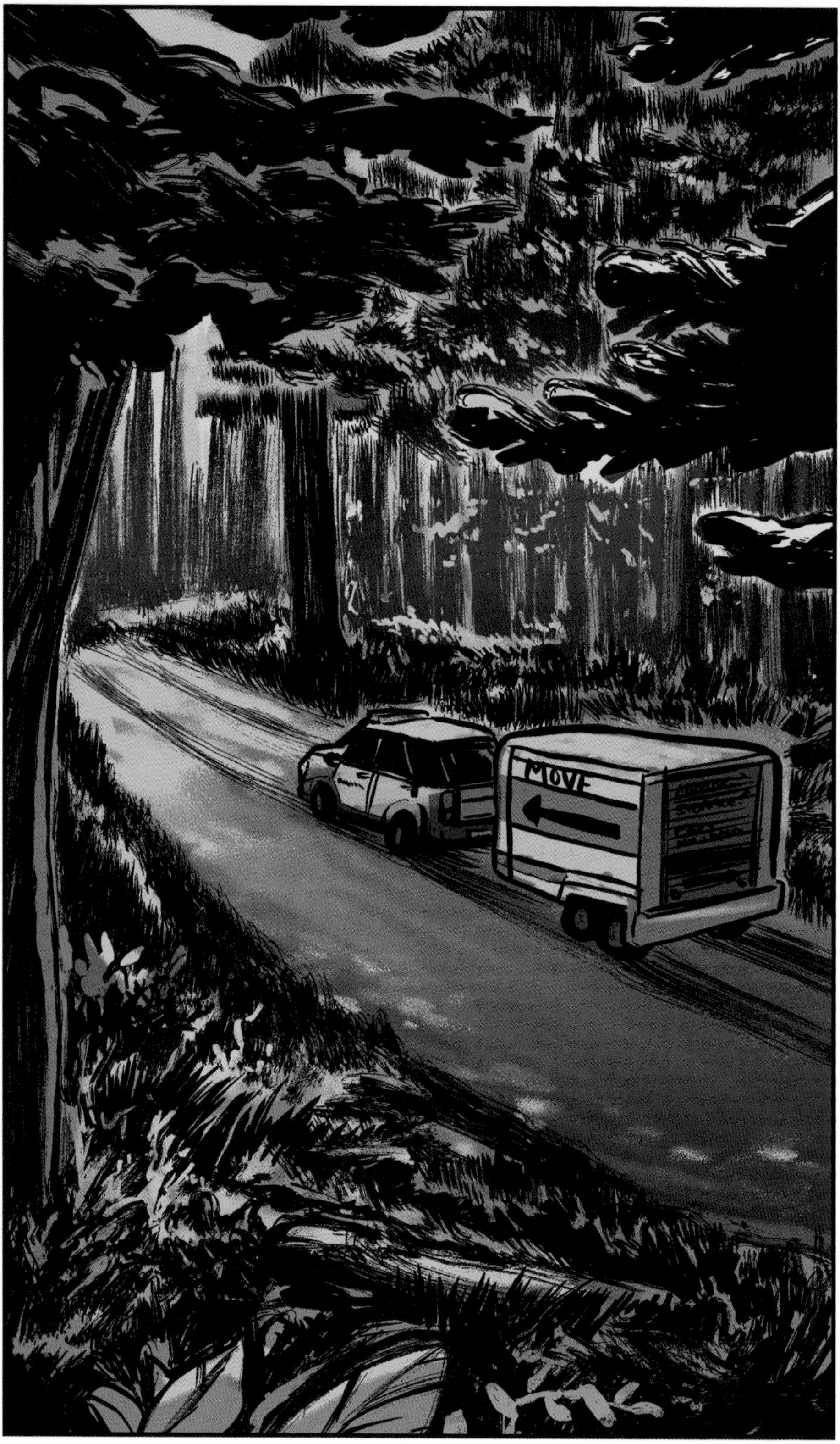
MOVE

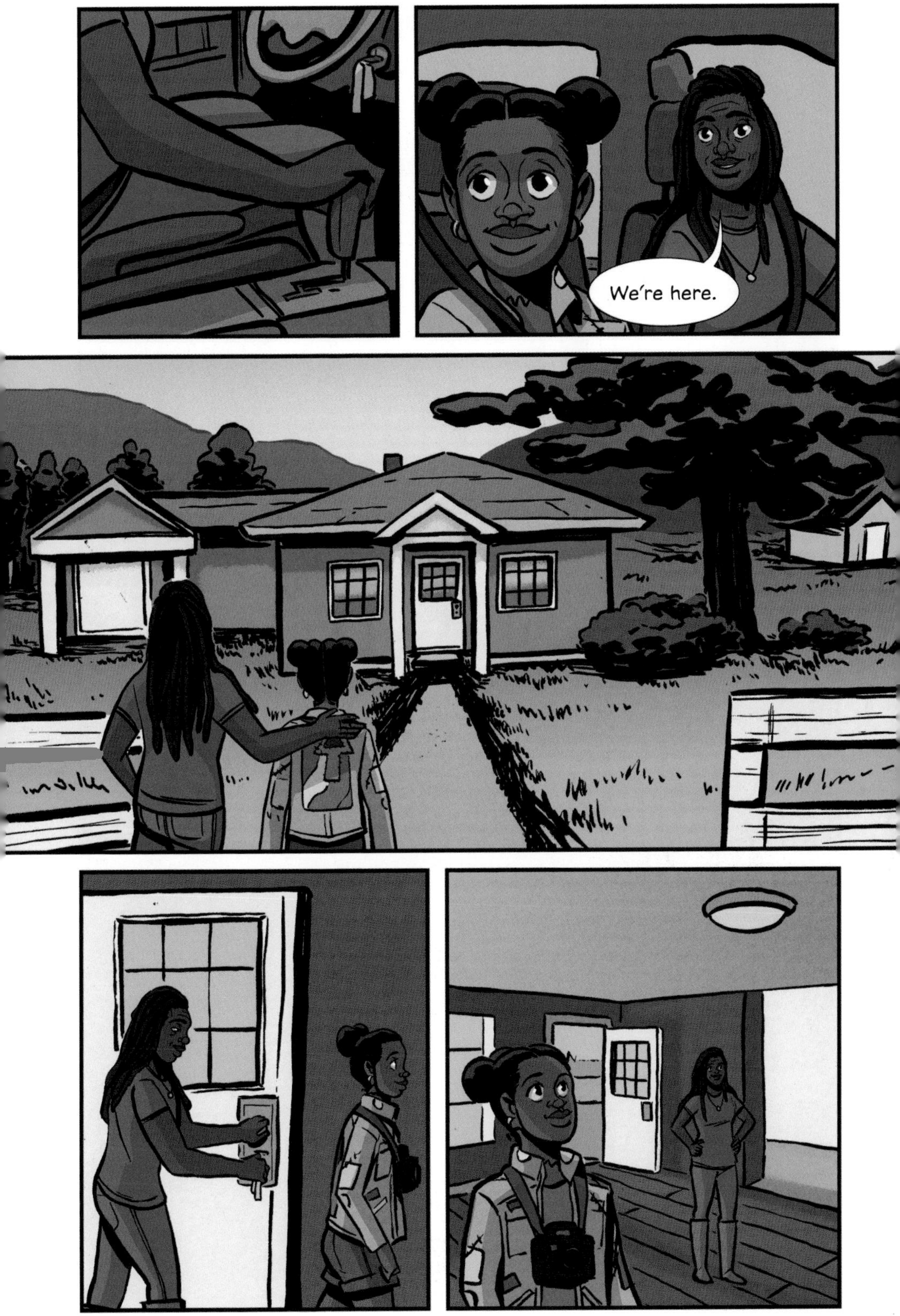
We're here.

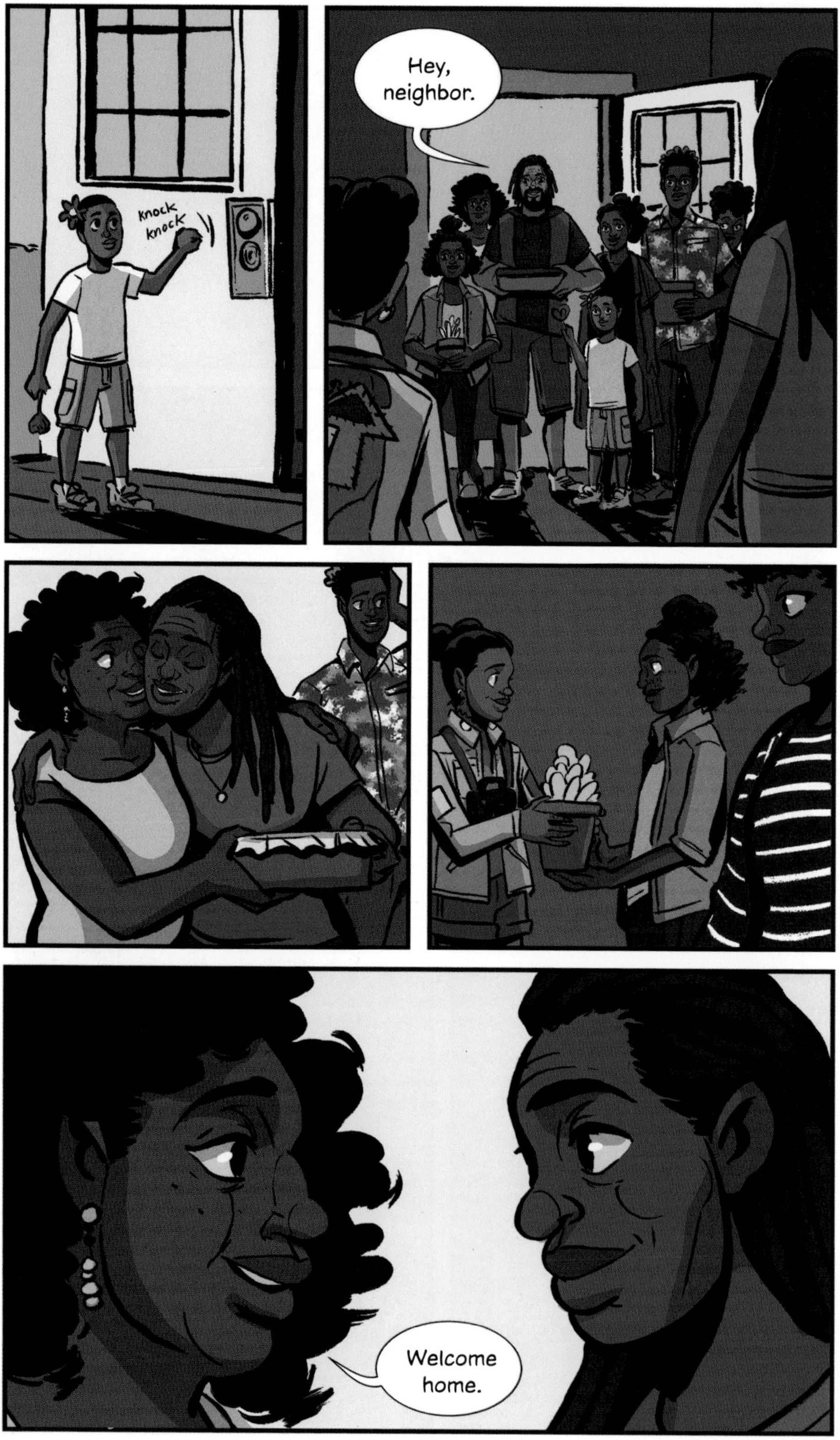
knock knock
Hey, neighbor.
Welcome home.

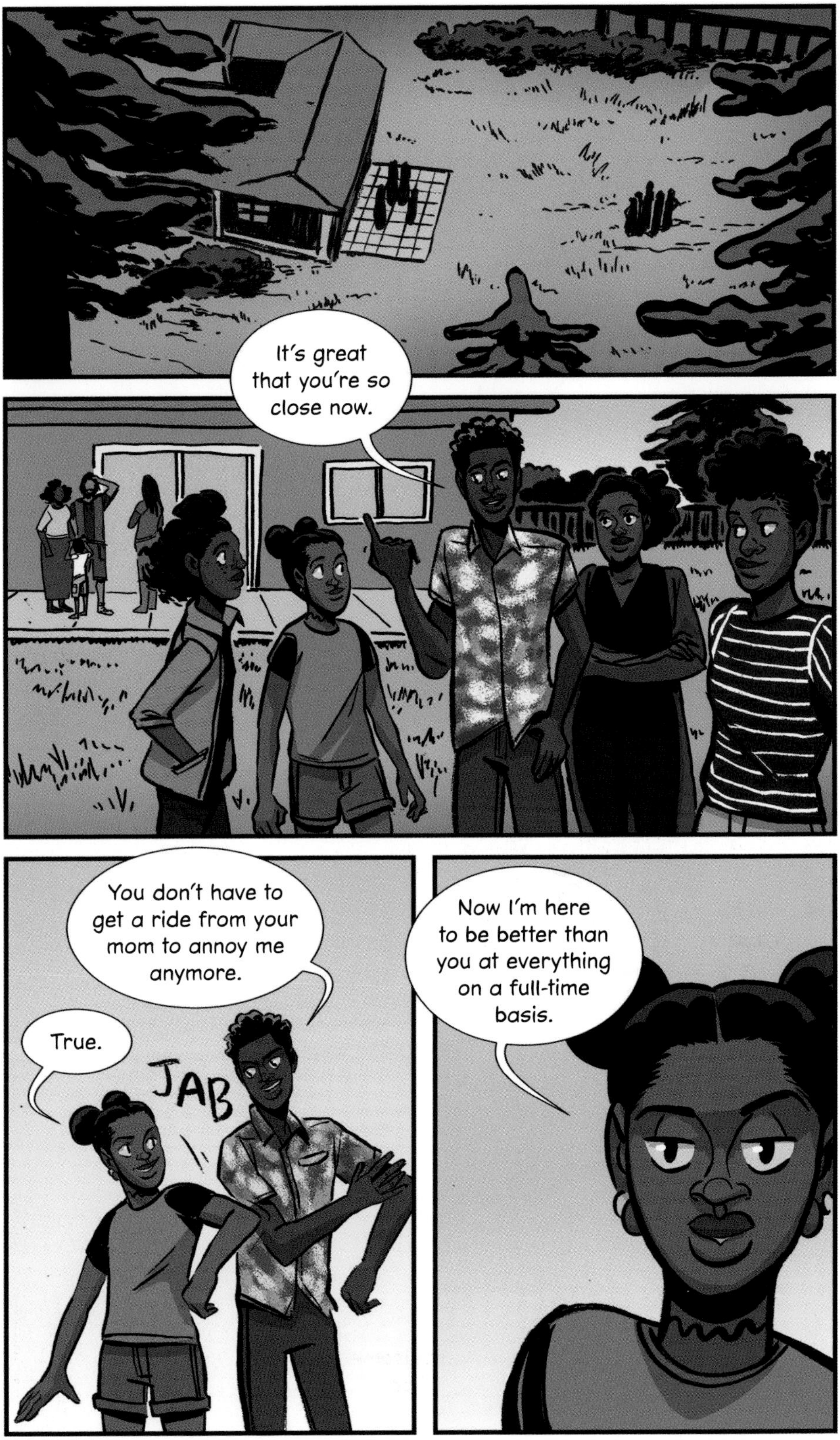
It's great that you're so close now.
You don't have to get a ride from your mom to annoy me anymore.
True.
JAB
Now I'm here to be better than you at everything on a full-time basis.

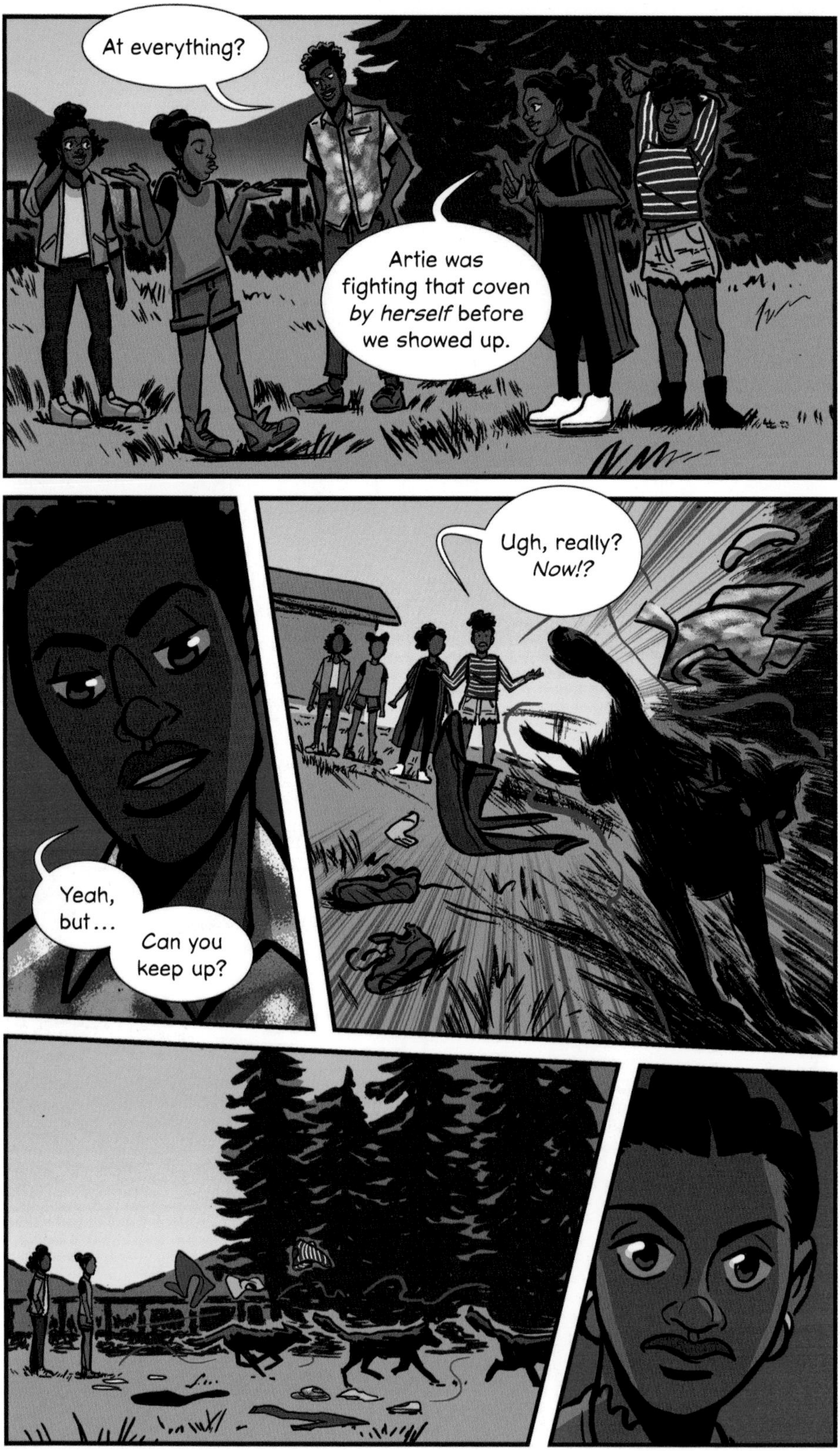
At everything?
Artie was fighting that coven *by herself* before we showed up.
Yeah, but...
Can you keep up?
Ugh, really? *Now!?*

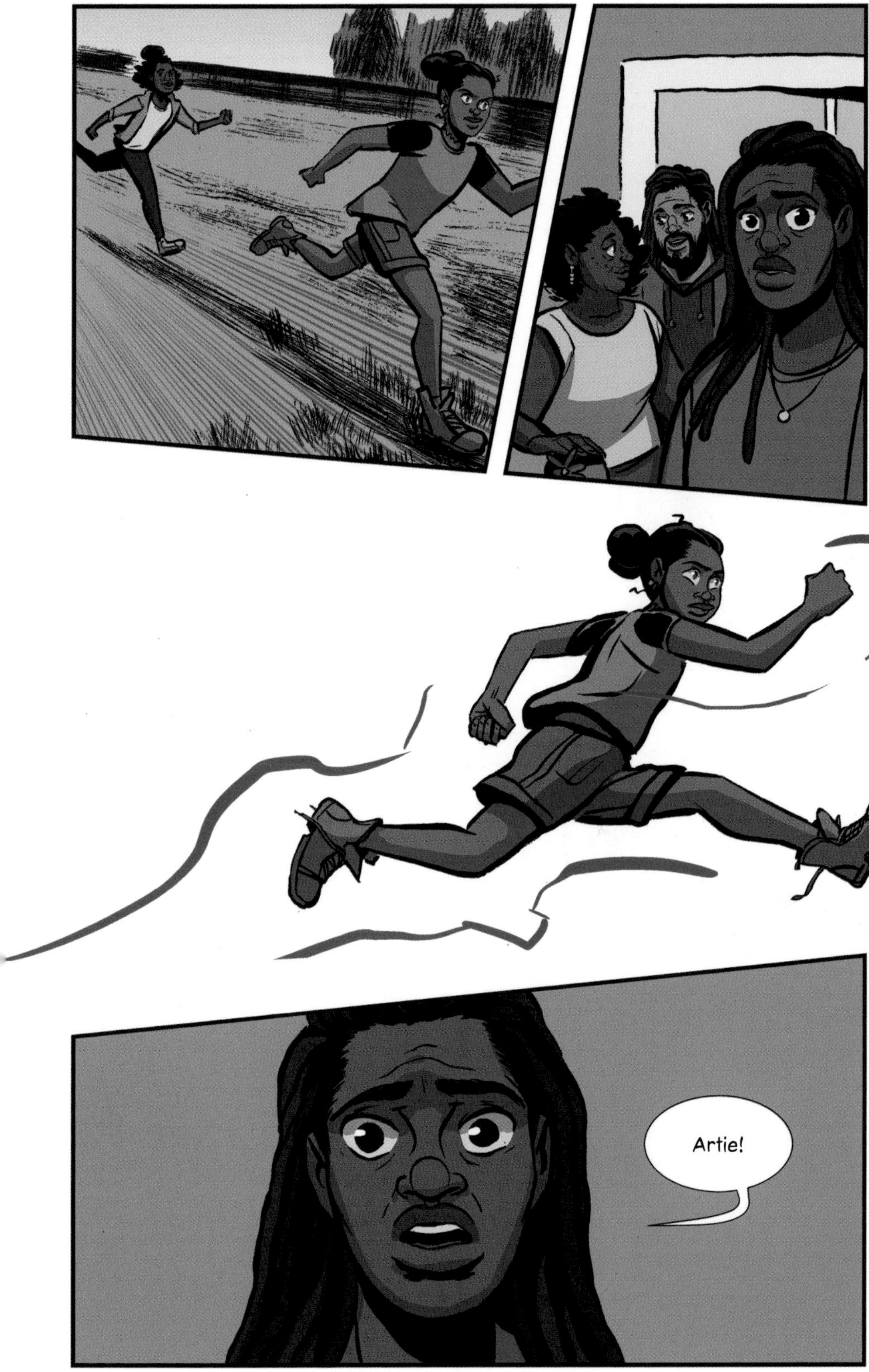
Artie!

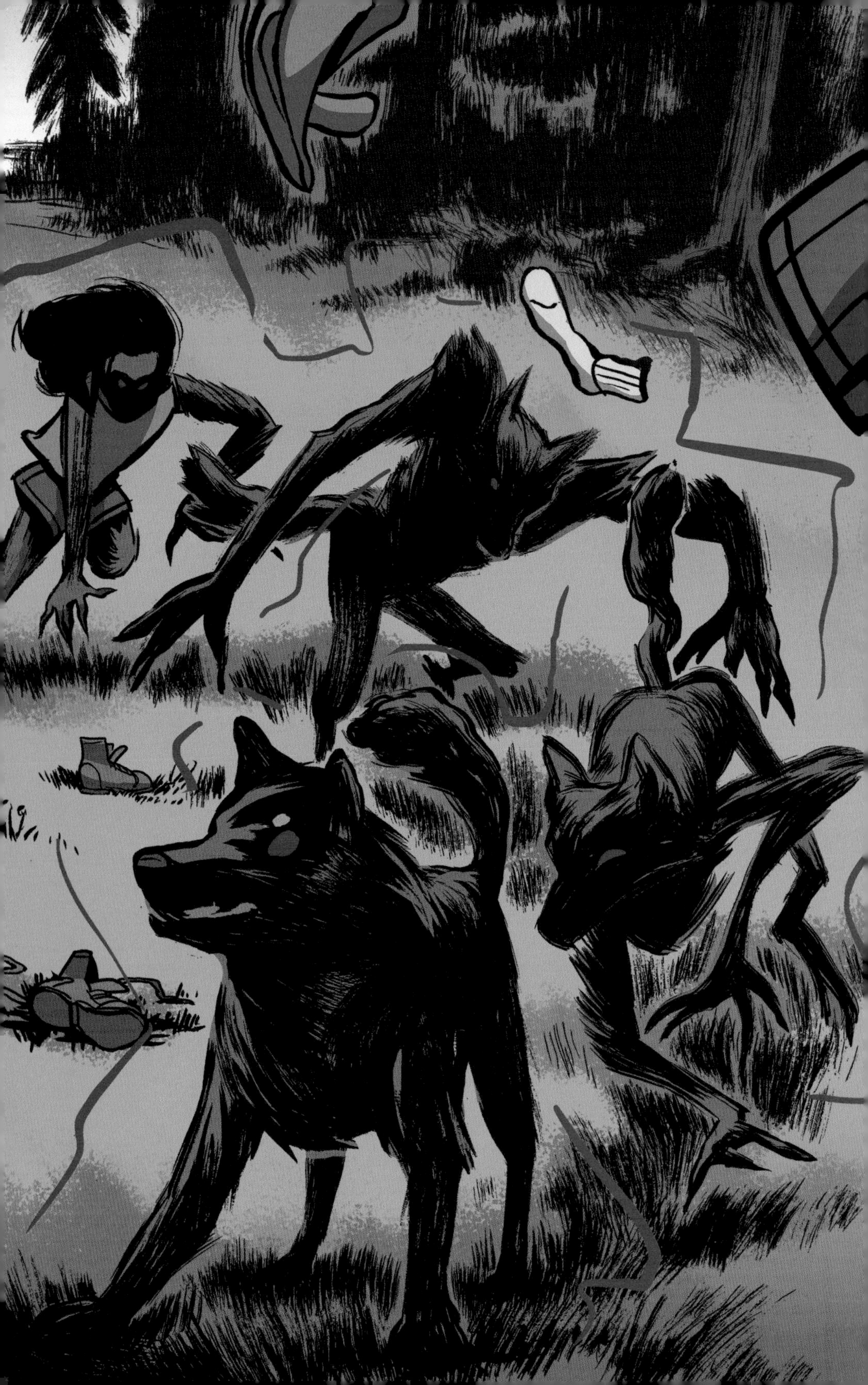

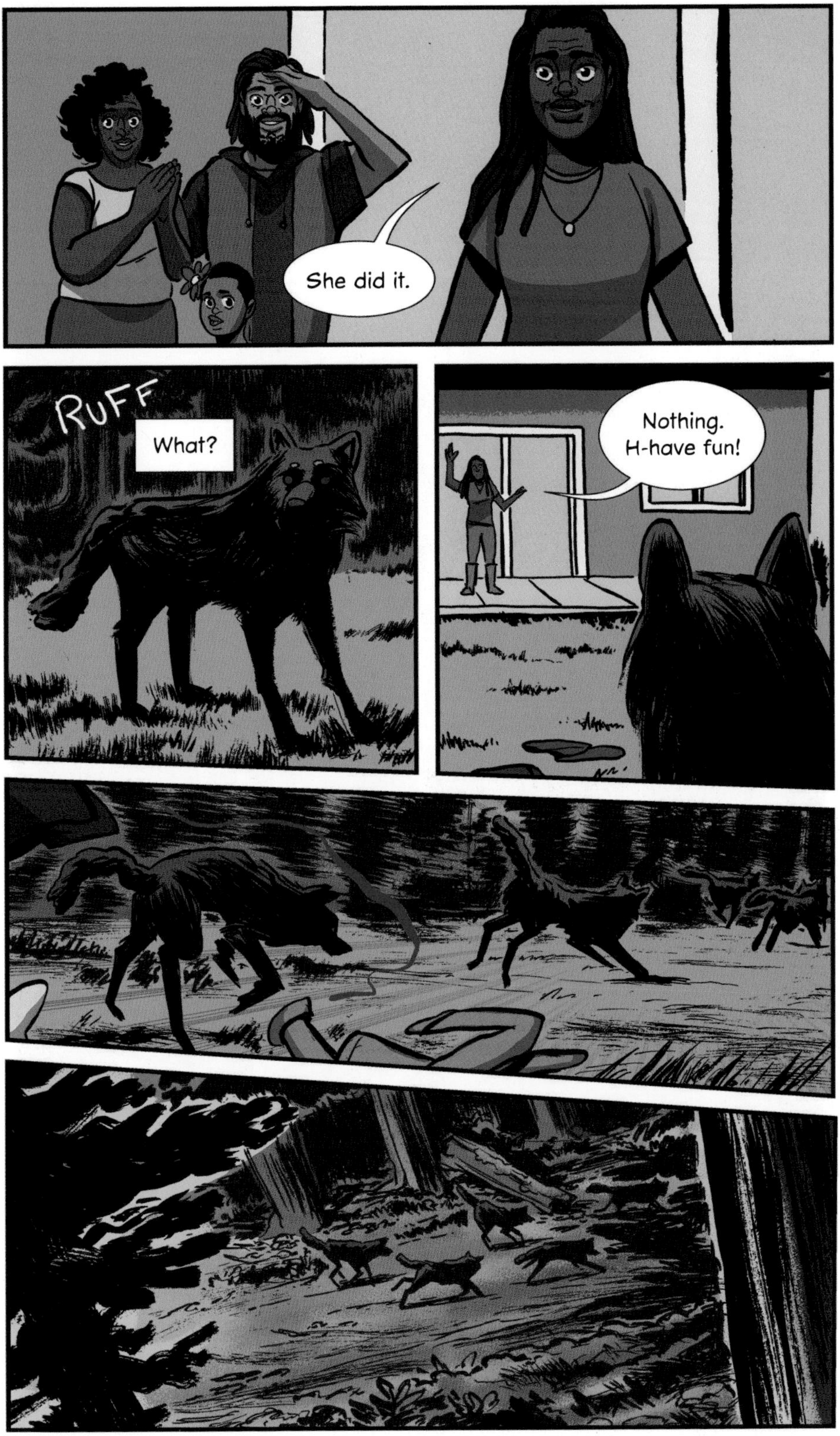
She did it.
RUFF
What?
Nothing.
H-have fun!

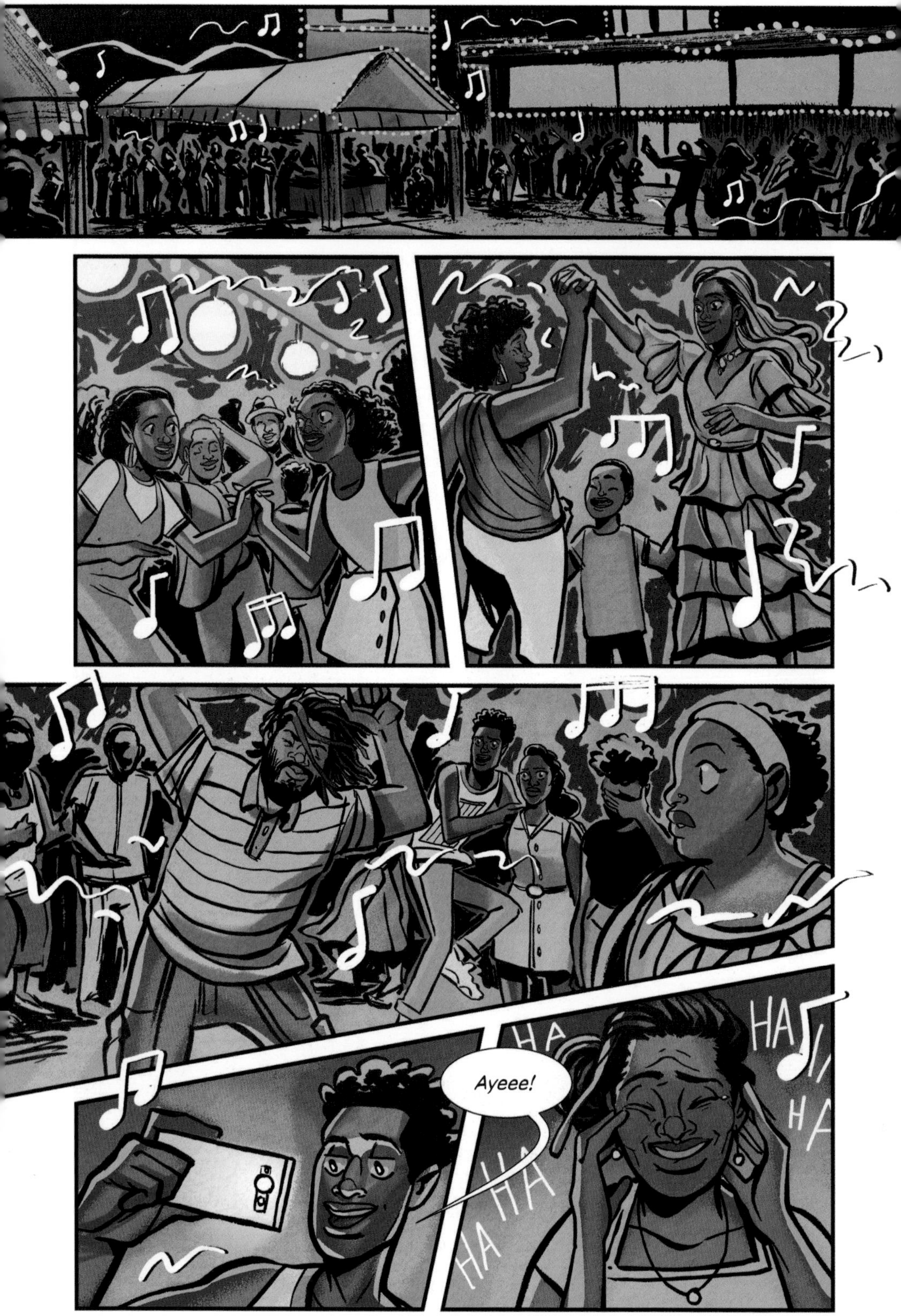
HA
HA
HA
Ayeee!
HA
HA
HA
HA
HA

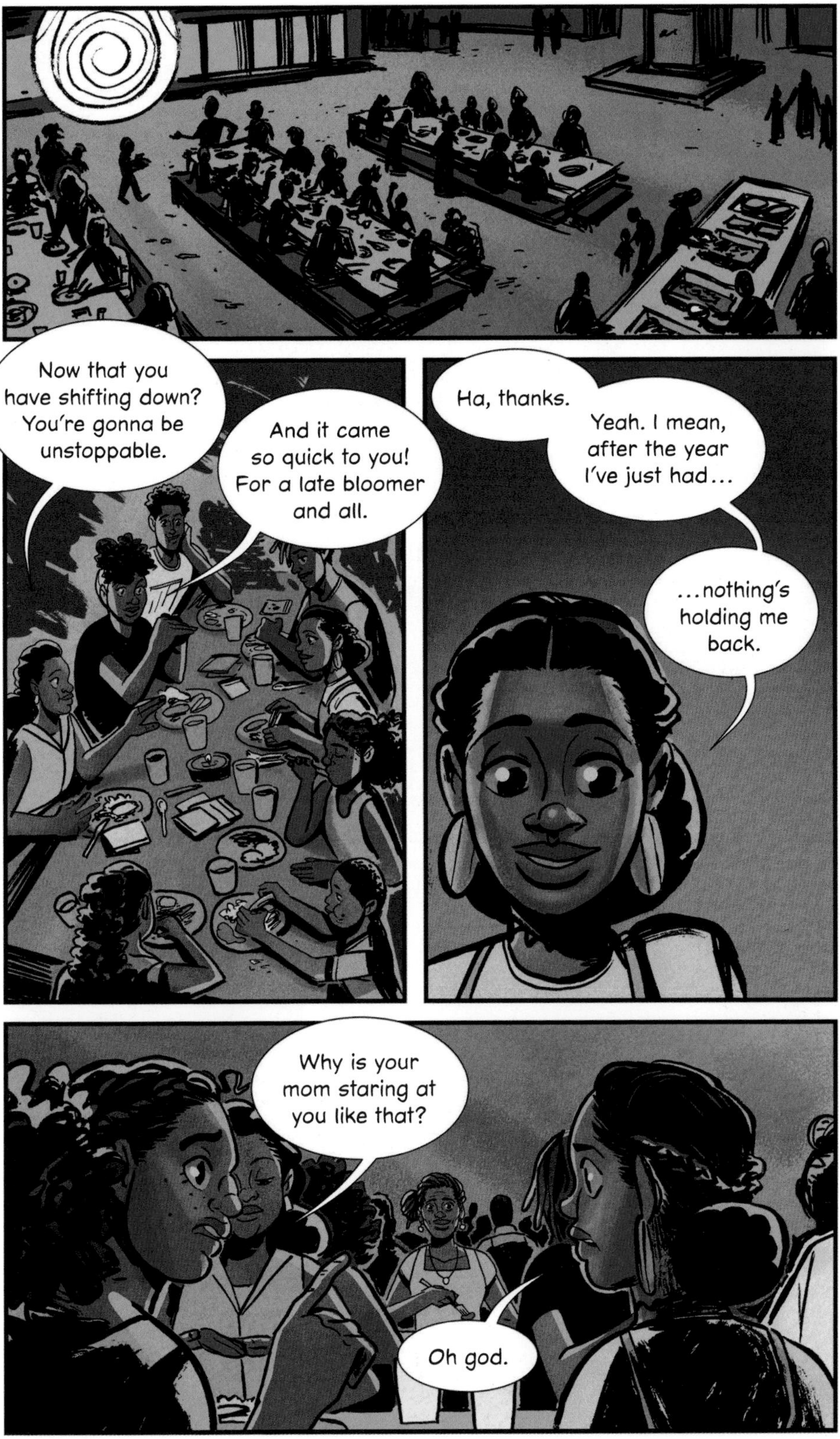
Now that you have shifting down? You're gonna be unstoppable.
And it came so quick to you! For a late bloomer and all.
Ha, thanks.
Yeah. I mean, after the year I've just had...
...nothing's holding me back.
Why is your mom staring at you like that?
Oh god.

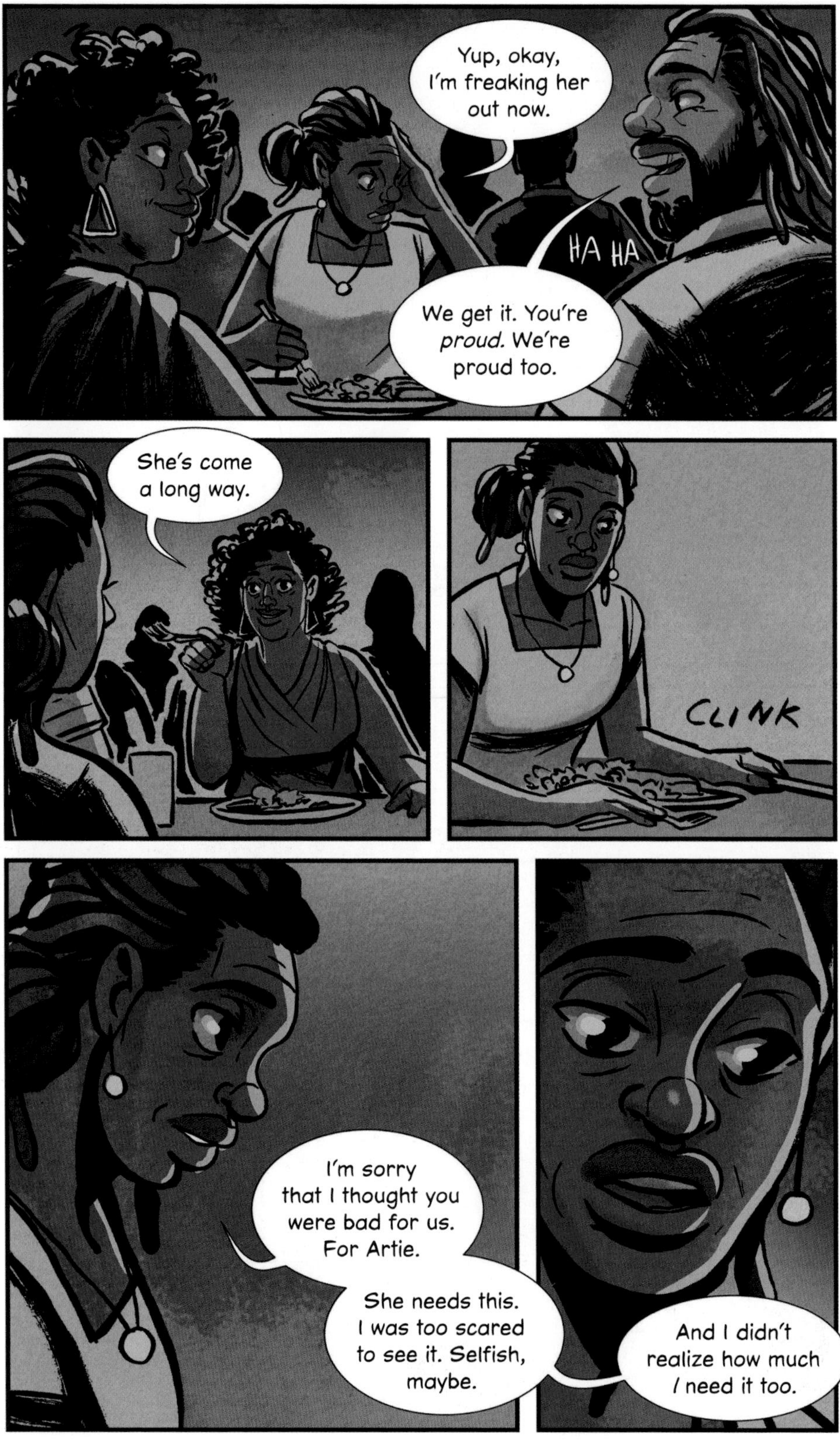
Yup, okay, I'm freaking her out now.
HA HA
We get it. You're *proud.* We're proud too.
She's come a long way.
CLINK
I'm sorry that I thought you were bad for us. For Artie.
She needs this. I was too scared to see it. Selfish, maybe.
And I didn't realize how much *I* need it too.

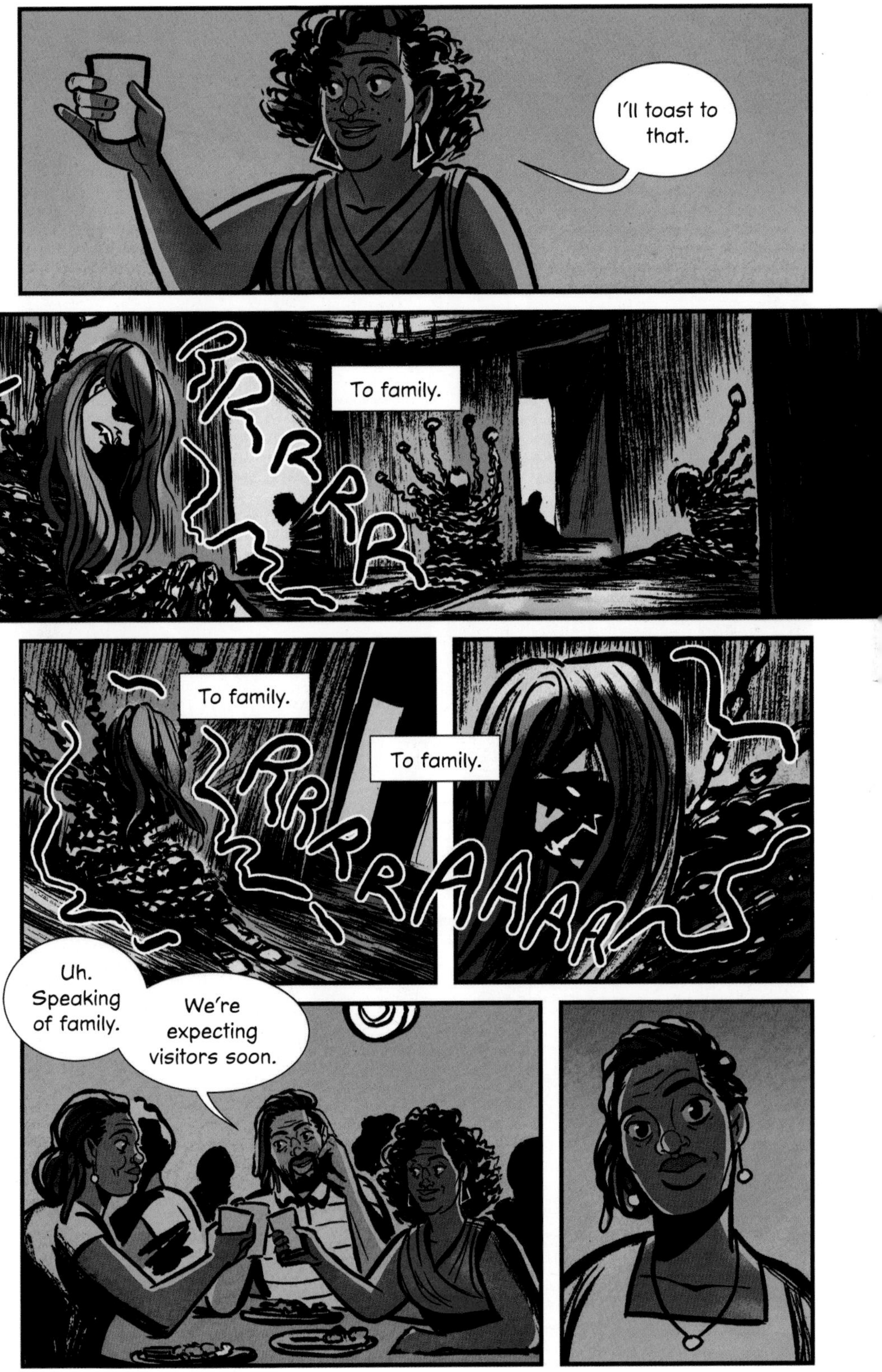
I'll toast to that.
To family.
RRRRR
To family.
To family.
RRRRRAAAAA
Uh. Speaking of family.
We're expecting visitors soon.

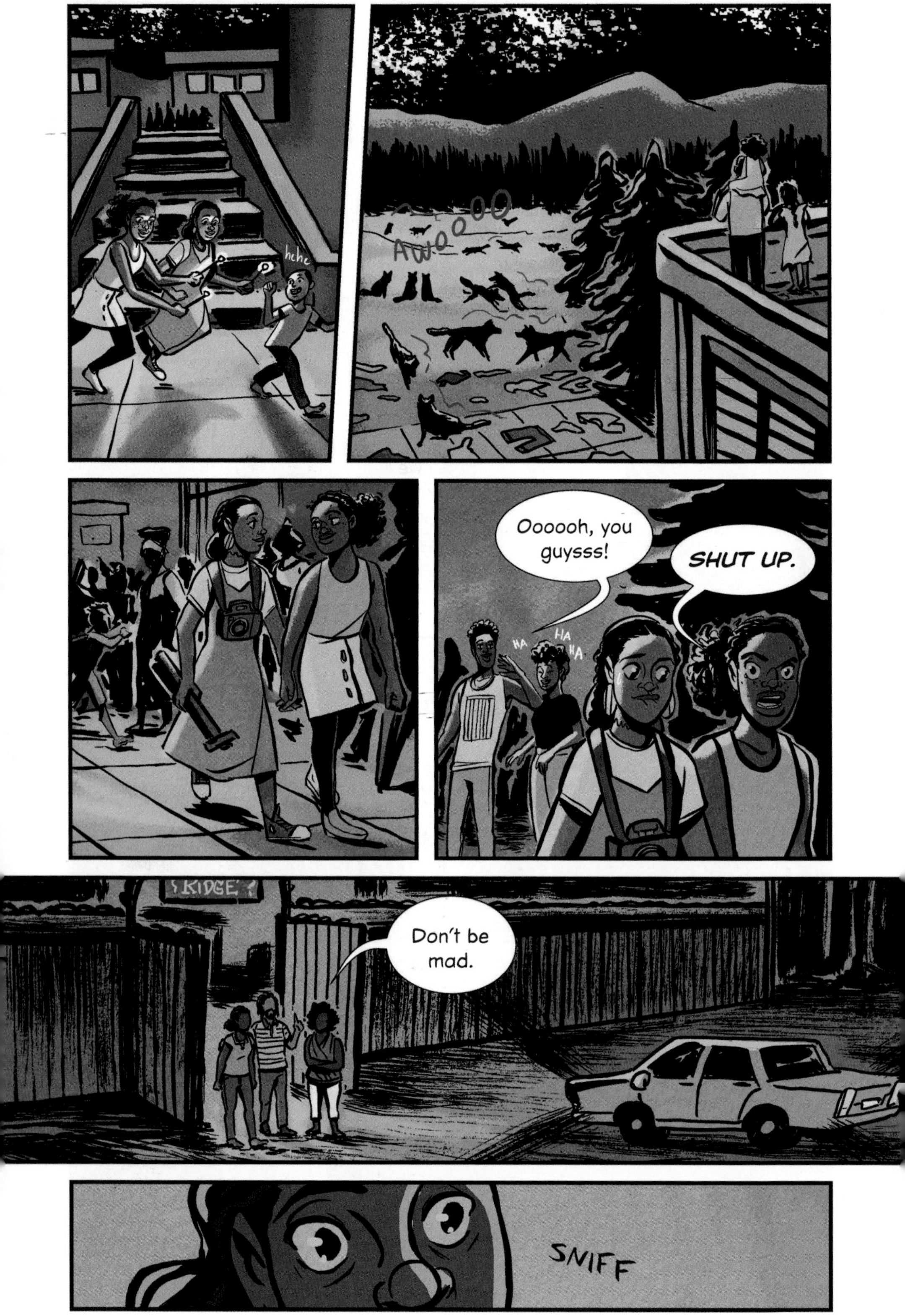
hehe
AWOOOOO
Oooooh, you guysss!
HA
HA
HA
SHUT UP.
Don't be mad.
SNIFF

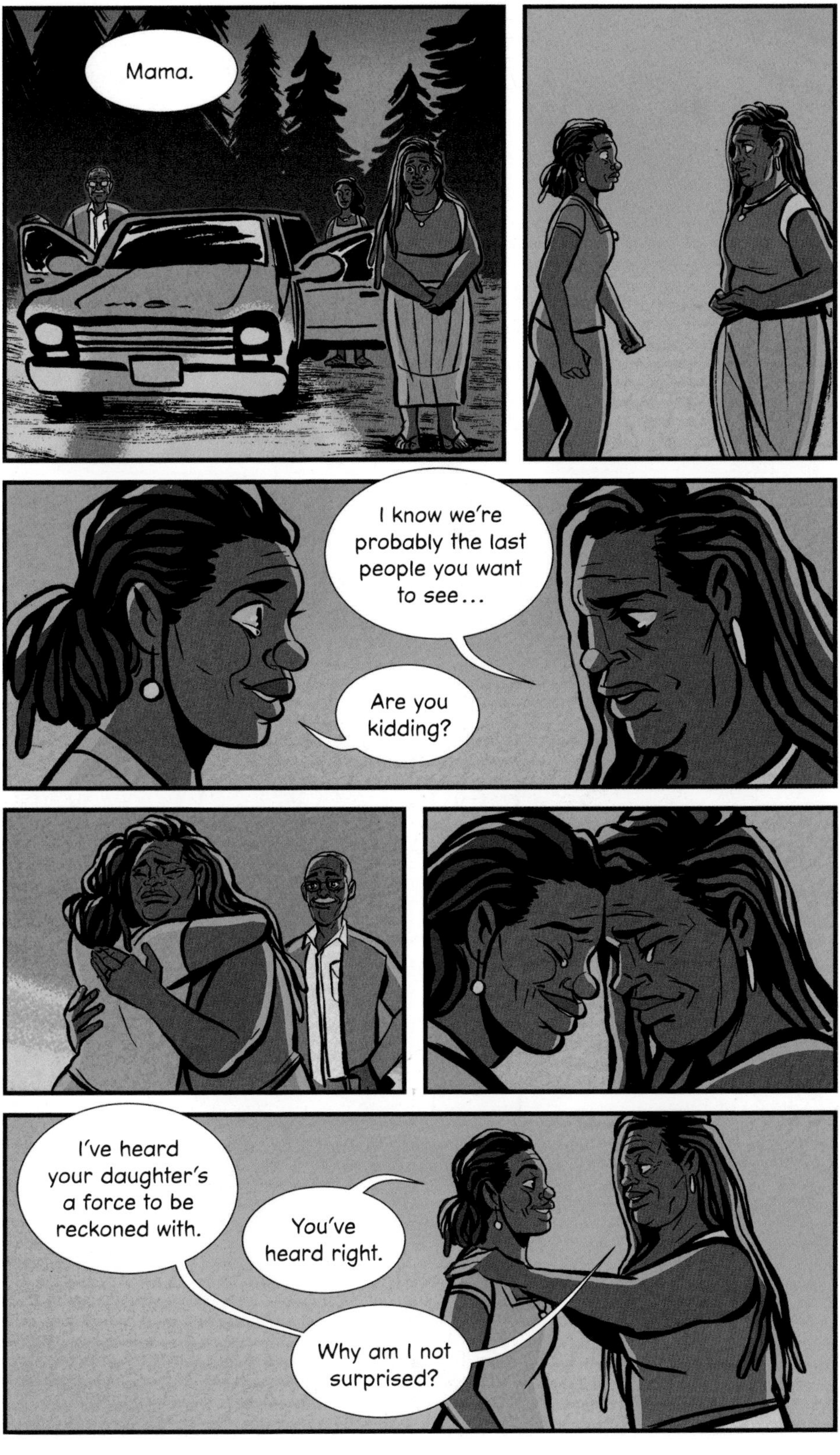
Mama.
I know we're probably the last people you want to see...
Are you kidding?
I've heard your daughter's a force to be reckoned with.
You've heard right.
Why am I not surprised?

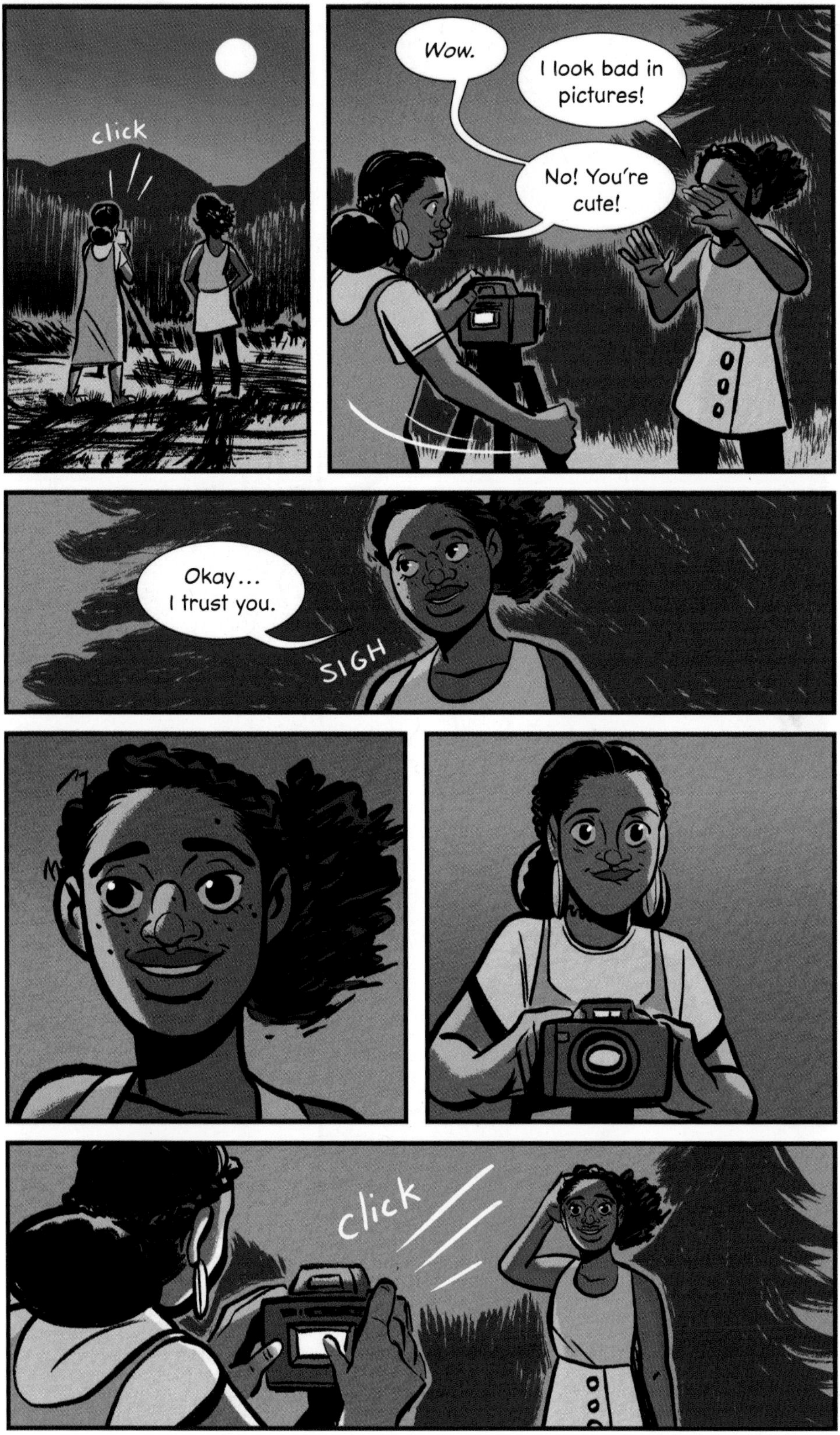
click
Wow.
I look bad in pictures!
No! You're cute!
Okay... I trust you.
SIGH
click

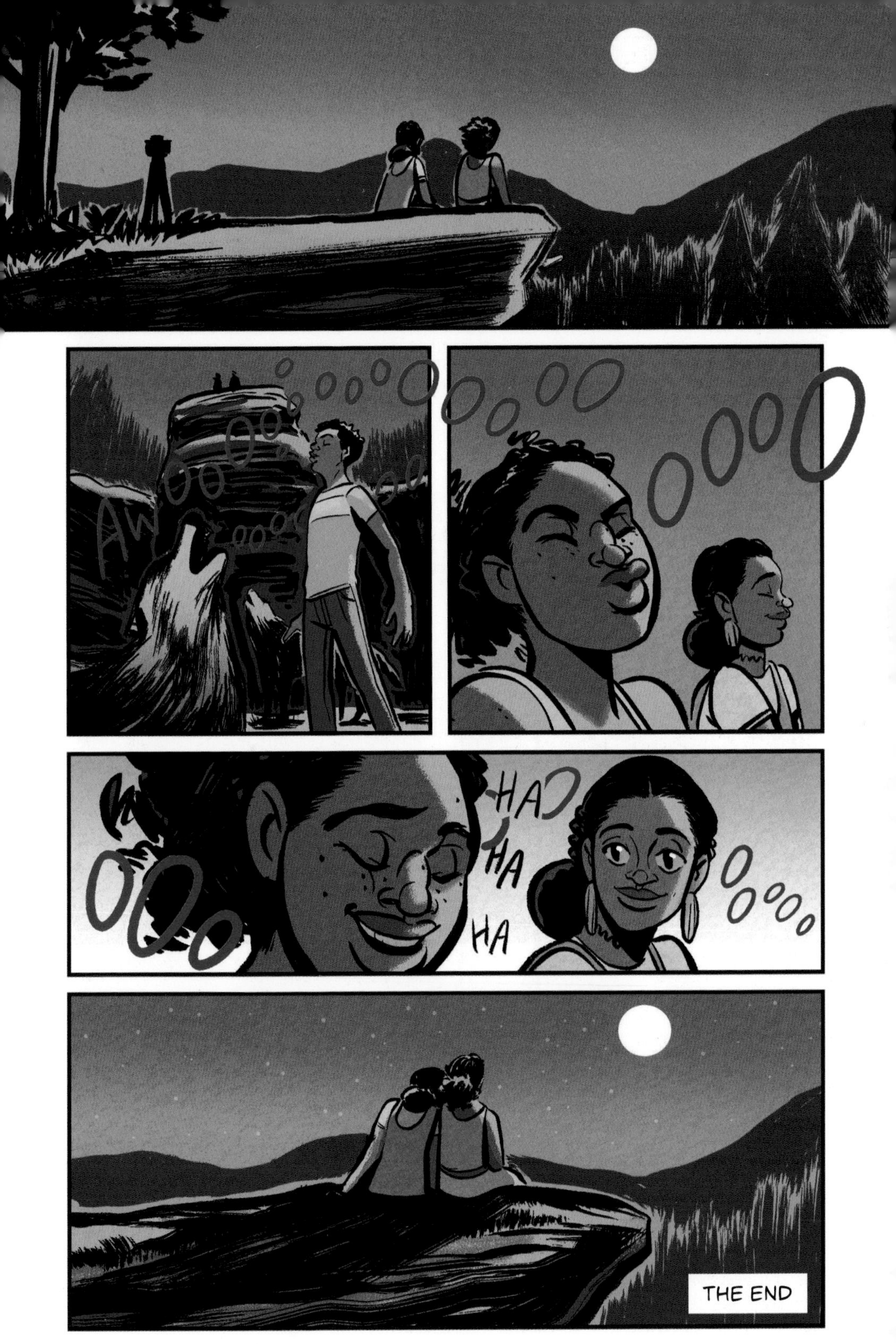
AWOOOOOOOOOOOOOOOOO
OOOOO
HA HA
HA
HA
OOOO
OOOOO
THE END

ACKNOWLEDGMENTS

This book would not exist without the efforts of countless people. Thank you to Mary Jane Begin, for her mentorship and enthusiastic support of my weird little story at its earliest stages. To Jennifer Linnan, for believing in Artie and becoming her champion. To my editor Greg Hunter, for his copious amounts of patience and expertise, and for making this book even better than I ever thought possible. A huge thanks to Kimberly Morales and everyone at Lerner who worked tirelessly to bring this book into the world in its best form.

An immense thank you to my incredible army of flatters and assistants: Mercedes Catarina Acosta, Laura Arce, Cynthia Yuan Cheng, Umaimah Damakka, Desolina Fletcher, Beniam C. Hollman, Ryan LeCount, Mikhaila Leid, Monica Nguyen-Vo, Emry Peterson, Amara Sherm, Kimberly Wang, Jasmine Walls, S. Allise Wilson, Shannon Wright, and Juliana M. Xavier.

Thank you to my family, both biological and chosen, for always having my back. To my parents, for their endless pep talks (and to my mother, for eagerly reading every bit of script that I shoved at her along the way). There are far too many friends to name here, but to everyone who has offered a kind word to me over the course of making this book: Thank you, from the bottom of my heart.

Thank you to the trees, and all that lies within them.

ABOUT THE AUTHOR

Olivia Stephens is a graphic novelist, illustrator, and writer from the Pacific Northwest. *Artie and the Wolf Moon* is her debut graphic novel. She has illustrated for a number of publications, including the *New York Times*, the *Guardian*, and *FIYAH Literary Magazine of Black Speculative Fiction*. Olivia graduated with a BFA in Illustration from the Rhode Island School of Design. When not drawing, she enjoys eating spicy foods and losing her voice at rock concerts.